I0763453

The Music Mystery Series

DANIELLE PALLI

The Music Mystery Series:

If I Didn't Care

Pennies from Heaven

It Had to Be You

ISBN: 978-1-7367982-7-0 (Print)

Contents

IF I DIDN'T CARE

PENNIES FROM HEAVEN

IT HAD TO BE YOU

If I Didn't Care

It is with enormous gratitude that I thank the following people for their support in not just this book, but for all the books, projects, and creative works I've produced over the years. It's rare to find someone willing to go down the rabbit hole with you during your sometimes-crazy schemes and cheer you on the whole way down. And, it seems I have an entire team.

Thank you to Cindy Readnower, who has been a true friend and colleague providing publishing, promotional and editorial support for all of my books, workshops, and other professional endeavors. To Jane Parker for her keen insight into human nature and beta-reading skills that helped me give more depth to my characters. To Elizabeth Von Hohen Brosha for hand-painting the cover of this book. To Graham Mack for co-producing the audio version of all my books, helping bring my characters to life. And a special thank you to my husband, John Palli, for providing technical guidance, beta reading, and loving support for this book and everything I do. I'm a lucky gal.

Prologue

~

The year is 1997 and at the height of the Tech Boom. Startups are all the rage, and a select few have access to inventions that won't be readily available to the public for another decade or more. The Internet is still considered a passing fad, and only a small percentage of people carry cell phones. For those of us who were there to bear witness to how quickly technology has evolved over the past few decades, we might laugh. What we once considered in 1997 the "Tech Boom" might now be referred to as the "Stone Age."

CHAPTER 1
But He Didn't

A Thursday Evening in 1997: Rue's Apartment

Rue Brennan was used to him forgetting. In some ways, she blamed herself. Or at least, she blamed her parents...that was easier. You see, "Rue" meant "regret" and "Brennan" meant "sorrow." So, her parents had, by choice, given her a name that meant "regret" and "sorrow" and, by golly, she was determined to live up to it.

Rue lived in a one-bedroom walk-up apartment in the Lower East Side of Manhattan. It was one of those "open" designs where there was no door separating the bedroom from the kitchen and dining area, just a cut-out space where a door and a kitchen hatch should be, giving the illusion that the place was larger than it truly was. The bathroom was, unfortunately, just beyond the kitchen. It had a large built-in bookshelf. Rue never understood why you would want to keep books on the shelf in a room that got humid when you ran the shower.

Of course, if it were Spencer, it would be one non-fiction book at a time that he'd conveniently leave on the top of the toilet bowl so it was there the next time he needed it. He'd often disappear into her bathroom with a book, most likely about the French Revolution or some time in history that wasn't the present, and she wouldn't hear from him for a good half hour.

It should be noted here that no one else thought this was a bookshelf at all, but a place to hold towels and linens and such. But since Rue only had two towels and as many washcloths to her name, but hundreds of books that she refused to part with, she had to settle on the bathroom to house her collection—for now.

She caught a glimpse of herself in the bathroom mirror just as she'd settled on pulling her slightly worn copy of *The Alchemist* from the shelf. From what she could tell, she didn't look all that much different from yesterday. Her hair was still a murky dark brown, framing her round face in a bob. The bags under her hazel eyes didn't seem any baggier, though the crow's feet that extended from the edges did look just a little deeper and more pronounced. Rue was underweight and waif-like, not that you'd know it from her face. *No matter how much weight I lose, I still look like a chipmunk with cheeks full of nuts.* She decided to blame this on her parents as well as her unfortunate name.

There was a knock on the window. The only actual windows in her little hovel were in the bedroom. She set the book back on the shelf and made her way, barefoot, across the hardwood floor.

Peering through the window, with hair as curly and red as a Raggedy Ann doll, was her neighbor, Midge. She was standing on the fire escape, holding up a bottle of wine and what looked like a semi-wrapped block of cheese. Rue struggled to open the rather stubborn window. Finally...success.

"Happy birthday, Rue!" Midge thrust the bottle of wine through the window by way of presentation. "It's not super fancy, but eco-friendly and organic, so at least we won't be drinking pesticides and additives."

Midge remembered my birthday, Rue thought. *But Spencer didn't.*

"Aww, thanks Mensa. You are the sweetest," Rue smiled sadly in spite of herself. "Why don't I join you on the ledge? Give me a second to throw something on other than pajamas. I have a red dress that I had planned to wear this evening for a date I no longer appear to be going on. Let me put that on."

Midge set the bottle down on the windowsill.

"And don't worry," Rue wrenched the knit dress free from the tiny closet where hangers weren't really needed to hold the clothes up. They all supported each other as if they feared sudden abandonment. "I'll wear leggings, so I don't accidentally flash any pedestrians on the ground level." Rue darted behind the wall separating the kitchen from the bedroom to change.

"Don't forget the wine glasses," Midge called. "And a blanket if you have one. I still have ass prints from sitting on the metal rails last time." Midge hailed from the Tri-State area, having lived in New York, New Jersey and Philadelphia. Her blended accent reflected that.

Rue pulled on her thick black leggings that came down to her ankles, pulled the dress over her head, and then dutifully grabbed two stemless red wine glasses from the kitchen and a single towel from the bathroom. "Here," she handed Midge the towel, "the other one is drying over the shower bar. But don't worry, I don't mind ass prints." She laughed. "You can use this one, and I can sit on the rails."

"Want me to go back upstairs and grab one of mine?" Midge offered.

"Nah, don't bother," After offering Midge the glasses, she climbed through the window and onto the fire escape. Midge had set the cloth-wrapped cheese on a checkered red kitchen towel with the bottle of wine and glasses next to it. Rue shimmied to one corner of the fire escape, sitting carefully with her feet dangling over the ladder. Midge did the same, on the opposite side, facing her friend. "This was awfully nice of you, Mensa."

"Mensa" was Rue's pet-name for Midge, even though Midge pretended to hate it. They became friends a year ago when they both learned they had a penchant for people-watching from the fire escape, Rue on the third floor, Midge on the fifth. They didn't know who lived on the fourth. Drapes covered the windows, and no one ever seemed to go in or come out of the place.

Rue had just moved to the Big Apple from a little town in Pennsylvania. Manhattan seemed like the best place to go if you wanted to escape from your past and get swallowed up and lost in a big city. No one would think to look for her here, would they? For the first month, she didn't know anyone.

Then, one night, when Midge had gone through a nasty breakup, Rue invited her neighbor down to her apartment, and consoled her with margaritas and nachos. This is the time when they both learned that tequila was not their friend. In a semi-drunken state, Midge proclaimed, “The problem is that I’m just too smart for them.” She had waved her plastic margarita cup in the air, threatening to spill it from the fifth floor of the fire escape. Her words were ever-so-slightly...slushy. “I told Darius that he was as big a troglodyte as the lot of ‘em. He couldn’t appreciate the fact that I have a 146 IQ and am very smart. That’s why men don’t like me for very long. I’m too much of a challenge. They don’t like to be challenged.” She blinked and swayed slowly in the breeze.

Rue had felt the need to gently call Midge out on her bullshit. “Well, Mensa, are you sure it’s not that they’re put off by you calling them troglodytes?”

Midge eyed her slowly, before laughing so hard she spit a little. “Maybe,” she acknowledged. “And don’t call me ‘Mensa’ when I have a perfectly good name...Midge. I’m named after a blood-sucking fly.” She laughed again. The “Philly” in her accent getting stronger the more she drank.

“Here, open the bottle. It’s a twist-top.” Midge brought Rue out of her daydream. Today’s Midge was not drunk and after sending Darius packing, followed by Ben, and then Dave, she decided she had sworn off men for a while.

Rue dutifully opened the bottle. Midge leaned forward and carefully held the glasses out in front of her for Rue to pour them each some wine. She handed one to Rue.

A fresh breeze blew through the street and Rue shivered a little. Perhaps, this was the last official day where she could get away with wearing only a dress and leggings as the Fall weather was becoming progressively colder.

“A toast.” Midge raised her glass, the sun shining on her face, making her complexion look even paler in contrast to her crayon-red wavy hair. "To the birthday gal! May the next year be full of adventure and fun surprises!”

“I’ll drink to that,” Rue smiled, clinking her glass against Midge’s. The wine was earthier than she expected.

“It’s a Rioja,” Midge offered. “I figured it would go with the

Manchego I bought." She broke off a chunk of the cheese with her fingers and handed it, open-palmed, to Rue. Rue took it without complaining. *What's a few germs between friends?"* she thought. "*I'm probably dying of something right now and don't even know it."*

Midge watched as Rue took a nibble of the cheese. "Take another sip of wine, quick," Midge commanded. "They go well together, right?"

Rue nodded. She wasn't really sure how to tell, but she was all about free food and beverage, and she sure as hell wouldn't be spending *her* meager savings on fancy wine and cheeses anytime soon.

"So, where's Spencer taking you this evening?" Midge wanted to know.

"Not sure he's taking me anywhere," Rue confessed. "I don't think he even remembered it was my birthday."

Midge let out a huff. "And *how* long have you been together?"

"Midge, don't start. I'm already bummed."

"Sorry," Midge offered, taking a sip of her wine and sheepishly averting her eyes.

In truth, Spencer and Rue had only been dating a little over a year. Therefore, she reasoned, he'd only been through one birthday previously. And she's pretty sure he missed that one, too.

It never used to be like this, Rue thought to herself. In the beginning, Spencer seemed sweet and kind and understanding. After all, she had led a rather sheltered life before moving to New York. He didn't mind her naivete and seemed excited to introduce the world to her. But lately, the more hobnobbing he did with the upper echelon of society, the less patient he became with her, as if she suddenly didn't fit in with the new world he was creating for himself.

As if he were somewhere, hearing her thoughts, Midge's cell phone rang. She set down the wine and cheese and fished it out of her back pocket.

"Hullo?" She raised her eyebrow and waved her hand in confusion. "Spencer? Why are you callin' me? Oh, yeah, she's right here." Midge thrust the phone toward Rue. "He says he's been trying to call you on the phone all afternoon."

"Hello?" Rue answered. "We're out on the fire escape," she yelled over the roar of an ambulance that went barreling down the street.

She covered her left ear and leaned into the phone as if that would make a difference. "Where are you?"

"Down here." From the street, Spencer waved his arm wildly, phone still against his ear. Rue saw him and waved back.

There, stood Spencer. Good old practical Spencer, dressed in a suit and tie with overpriced cuff links and shoes that he had professionally shined.

"C'mon up. I'll let you in," Rue answered. She could see him nod before hanging up.

"Well, that's my cue." Midge stood.

"No, you don't have to go so soon. Come inside and chat for a bit."

"No thanks. Spencer is..." she paused to find the right words, "so perfectly coiffed, I'm afraid his head might explode just being in the same room with me."

"Suit yourself, Mensa. But hey," she called as her friend started her climb back up to her apartment, "thanks for the wine and cheese. Much appreciated."

"No prob, friend," Midge saluted her. "Yuz guys enjoy." With that, a fire of red hair and bell bottoms that went out of style more than two decades ago ascended to her flat above Rue's.

Simultaneously, there was a knock at the door. Rue grabbed the left-over food and wine and struggled through the window. "Hang on!" she called. "Almost there!"

She plopped the leftovers on the kitchen counter and sprang to the door, flinging it open with all the enthusiasm of someone who was secretly hoping her boyfriend held a wonderful birthday present in his arms for her. He didn't.

"Hi, Rue, sorry I'm later than planned," he apologized, giving her a quick peck on the lips. "Work was beastly today. You have no idea. But that's all over now and I have a surprise for you." He took her by the shoulders and smiled. Midge was right, his wavy brown hair was quite perfectly placed. His skin equally radiant. Rue suspected it was an experimental age-remedy called "Botox," but Spencer never offered that info, so she never asked since she wasn't sure it was even legally on the market yet. She just noticed over in the past year that one day he had worry lines and the next, they seemed to magically disappear.

Rue's eyes grew wide with hope. "What's the surprise?"

With that, Spenser reached into his pocket and pulled out a business card, handing it to her as if it were the key to the city.

"What's this?" She wrinkled her nose at it, confused.

"A business card," he answered, eyeing the wine on the table. He tilted the bottle back with one hand, eyeing it distastefully.

"Darwin Fennec," she read. "Contract Cyber Forensic Consultant and Private Investigator." She lowered the card. "What's this about?"

"Well, you were complaining last week that you were, and I quote, 'on the fast track to middle age with nothing to show for it' and wanted a career beyond fluff journalism and posing nude."

"That last part was not at all what I said," she corrected. "And being a figure model for one of the most prestigious art universities in the country is a bit different from the way you describe it. There is some skill to it, and yet, you make me sound like a prostitute posing for a trash magazine on weekends."

Spencer cleared his throat, uncomfortably. "You know that I support all of your endeavors, darling. But you have to admit, it is a little embarrassing for the founder and CEO of an up-and-coming tech company to have to explain your particular...skill set...to investors."

"Sorry my career is so embarrassing for you, Spencer." Rue flopped into a kitchen chair.

"Oh, come on. Be reasonable." He ran his hand over the top of her head. "That's not a career, that's something you do to work your way through college. Not something an older woman does as a—" He stopped when he saw her face and took a moment to glance between his girlfriend and the wine and cheese on the table.

"What am I missing?" he finally asked.

"My birthday, Spencer," Rue answered flatly. "You're missing my birthday."

"Oh, my darling," He stroked her head again. "I'm so sorry. How unthoughtful of me." He paused a moment. "So, who left the wine?" He cringed at the label.

"My upstairs neighbor, Midge."

"Oh, is that the small unpleasant gal with the bright red hair."

"Yes, but I don't find her unpleasant at all. She's my friend and I like her...and," Rue added, "*she* remembered my birthday."

"I said I was sorry, and from the looks of the wine she bought, she's not that good of a friend. I don't know what that is, but I wouldn't qualify that dime-store swill as wine."

"Snob," Rue wrinkled her nose at him and attempted a smile. Rue rarely got to celebrate birthdays in the past, which made his forgetting sting all the more. Maybe she was making too much of it?

"Tell you what," he finally said, "get dressed, and I'll take you someplace really nice for your birthday to celebrate."

Rue looked down at her dress. "I kinda thought I already was dressed."

Spencer paused, awkwardly. "Oh, right."

"You know what, Spencer? Turns out, I'm really tired after a long day. Maybe we can take a raincheck on my birthday dinner?"

"Of course, my darling. Whatever you say." Spencer seemed somewhat relieved. "Just do me one favor?"

"What's that?"

Spencer pointed toward the business card still clenched tightly between Rue's fingers. "Call Darwin in the morning."

"Who is he?"

"He's a guy I hired to do a little contract investigative work for my company. Remember how I told you I suspect B. A. Ellis industries, SpencerTech's competitor...my competitor...is stealing proprietary info from us?"

Rue's blank expression indicated that she did not.

Spencer dismissed it. "Anyway, I got into a conversation with him waiting in line at the coffee shop and learned he's looking for an administrative assistant." He fanned his hands open in the air as if placing something in the lights over Broadway. "Administrative assistant...doesn't that sound nice? There's real potential there."

Rue bit back several expletives. "Thanks for looking out for me, Spencer." She clenched her jaw.

"Don't look at me like that," Spencer chastised. "I told him all about you and he's eager to interview you."

"I'm a figure model and journalist. Not sure if there are transferable skills there that lend themselves to administrative work."

"Come on, now," Spencer reasoned, "how hard can it be? Answer a few phone calls, schedule a few meetings..."

"While I'm sure there's more to it than that, how is this better for me than being a journalist?" Rue wanted to know.

"Because you wouldn't be scrounging for freelance work, day in and day out. It's a steady, respectable job with growth potential. You would get to work with a detective, which has to be more exciting than...what was your last gig? Covering Drag Queen Bingo at a local diner in Tribeca."

"I had no idea you thought so highly of my work," Rue pursed her lips.

Spencer took her shoulders. "Sweetheart, I just see more potential in you. And think of your career move as an investment in...us."

"How is this an investment in 'us'?" Rue wanted to know. "This sounds more like an investment in 'you,' meaning you require a girlfriend whose work and friends don't embarrass you."

"You're being overly emotional...is it that time of the month again?" Rue's face turned crimson and it appeared as if she were ready to, literally, let off steam through her nostrils and ears. "I'm sorry. I know you're still cross with me because I forgot your birthday. I promise I'll make it up to you. Just do me one teensy favor and call him in the morning? I've got a good feeling about him." Spencer pulled Rue into his chest for a hug. After a minute of her arms awkwardly hanging by her side, she relented, hugging him back and settling into his embrace for a moment.

"Fine," she conceded, breaking from his hug. "I'll be certain to reach out to this..." she read the card again, "Darwin Fennec in the morning."

CHAPTER 2
Darwin Fennec

Saturday Morning at Pier 17

"This seems a little odd to me." Midge took two small steps to each of Rue's long strides. "Why would he have you meet him by a park bench at the pier instead of his office? Doesn't he work in the financial district?"

"I don't know," Rue answered, her long ruffled skirt making swishing noises in the breeze as she walked briskly toward their destination. She tugged at the fitted black cotton blouse that was bunching up under her arms and kept moving. "But Spencer seems to trust this guy."

"Yeah, well I don't trust nobody," Midge answered, looking over her shoulder as they passed under a bridge near the East River, heading toward the South Street Seaport. "What's this joker look like, anyways?"

"He said he would wearing a white polo shirt and a blue baseball cap."

"What team?" Midge asked.

"What are you talking about?"

"The cap...New York Yankees or somebody else?"

"He didn't specify." Rue and Midge reached Pier 17 and started walking along the edge of the water. Rue shielded her eyes from the sun with her hand.

"Excuse me," a male voice from behind her asked quietly. "Are you Rue Brennan?" Rue turned to see a tall man, his features obscured until her eyes adjusted to the light. White polo shirt, blue cap with no distinguishing marks on it. A few pieces of brown hair stuck out from the edges of the cap.

"Who wants to know?" Midge nudged Rue aside, placing herself between Rue and the man as if a shield.

"Oh, I beg your pardon," he apologized. "I'm Darwin Fennec and I have an interview today with a woman named Rue Brennan."

"No, you're not," Midge retorted.

"Sorry," the man furrowed his brow, confused. "I'm not...what?"

"You're not Darwin Fennec."

"I'm afraid I am."

Midge was persistent.

"There is no way your name can be Darwin Fennec. That's a made-up name. Who's named after two different types of foxes?"

Darwin found this amusing and reached into his back pocket to retrieve his wallet. From it, he flashed his driver's license at Midge, who eyeballed it closely as if it were a fake.

"I am," he answered simply. To Rue, he offered his hand. "I'm assuming I was correct the first time...you are Rue Brennan?"

"Yes," Rue shook his hand in return. "But how is it that you picked me out of a crowd so easily?"

"I am an investigator, after all," he answered, removing his cap and running his hands through his disheveled hair in an attempt to reset it from wearing the ball cap all morning. "Kinda my thing." The side of his mouth curled up on one side in an unbalanced grin.

The sun passed behind a cloud, enabling Rue to observe his features a little more closely. His hair was parted to one side with medium-length brown locks fringing the sides of his long face. From what she could tell, his eyes were a pale gray.

He then offered a hand to Midge who took it and leaned in to get a closer look; then her demeanor changed entirely. "Well, aren't you a tall drink of water?" (Except when she says it, it comes out "whuh-tr.)

Her head tilted to look up at him. If Midge cleared five feet tall, Rue would have been surprised. "Mr. Darwin Fennec, would you mind sitting down? I'm getting a crick in my neck just trying to look into those beautiful eyes of yours."

"That's okay," Rue intervened. "Midge isn't staying." Rue glared at her friend as she started to protest. "It was nice running into you, Midge. Perhaps when you're done with your errands, we can meet up here for lunch? Say, in an hour?" There was nothing subtle about Rue's expressive facial features. And yet, Darwin Fennec didn't seem to notice, even when Midge abruptly dropped his hand.

"Okay," Midge relented, "be back here in an hour." But she leaned over, tilting her body between Rue and Darwin, both of whom had already taken a seat on the bench. "Here if you need me," she placed a reassuring hand on Rue's arm.

"Uh, thanks, Midge." Rue didn't really see the need for Midge, but did notice that her friend was, for the second time in a row, aware of the happenings in her life, unlike some people. Case in point, Spencer had both forgotten her birthday and was absent this weekend...working on a project with a tight deadline and seemingly having no qualms about her meeting a strange man about a job on a bench at the South Street Seaport.

Once Midge had made her exit, Darwin turned to Rue and asked, "Do you often bring friends to job interviews?"

Rue bristled a little, leaning forward on the bench. "I don't know," she answered curtly, peering up at him. "Do you always conduct job interviews on a park bench?"

"Touché," he replied, pausing a moment as if considering his next move. Rue's small frame fit neatly on the bench, which sat low to the ground. But Darwin was noticeably oversized in height and his knees seemed to fold almost up into his chest as he sat. Noticing her gaze, he quickly stretched his legs casually out in front of him, crossing one ankle over the other. "Sorry about that," he answered. It was only then that she noticed he was carrying a faux leather attaché case that was strikingly out of place for a man wearing jeans and a polo shirt (now, sans blue cap). He set it on his lap and reached inside, pulling out a simple yellow legal pad, clipboard and pen. "My office is being renovated today and since I am need of a new assistant sooner, rather than later, I thought this was the best option."

"What happened to your old assistant?" Rue was curious. It should be noted that Rue had been a freelance journalist for more than a decade and she therefore had lost her ability to present well on interviews. She was, however, completely comfortable asking the questions.

"She moved on to other interests," he answered cryptically, sucking in his breath. "Now about your qualifications..."

"I have none," Rue blurted out.

"I see," Darwin tapped the edge of his pen against his yellow notepad. After an unbearably long silence, he asked, "Rue, do you even want to be here?"

Rue let out a sigh. "Honestly, no." She shook her head.

"Darwin!"

Darwin cleared his throat, uncomfortably, as two young women descended on them. "It's so nice to see you!" A tall woman with black hair, a red scarf and bright plum lips leaned over the bench and gave him a kiss on the cheek before he could protest, leaving a lipstick stain in its wake. The other, a curly blonde-haired, twenty-something-year-old tousled his hair before eyeing Rue, distastefully.

"Who's she?"

"My new assistant," Darwin answered without hesitation.

"Oh," the blonde woman bit a long, lacquered nail. "What happened to Ashley?"

Darwin let out a sigh. "She moved on."

For the briefest of moments, the black-haired woman's eyes lit up. By Rue's estimation, they were nearly two decades younger than the brown-haired Darwin who had tiny wisps of gray hair creeping in. *Guess he likes 'em young,* she thought to herself.

"Aww," the woman pouted her lips, pinching Darwin's cheek while he tucked his chin as if embarrassed. "That's too bad. Who would up and leave our Darwin?"

Darwin adopted that sheepish grin again, the one that Midge seemed taken by, but to which Rue was unaffected. He even seemed to be blushing a little.

"It's all right, I suppose," he answered with a quiver in his voice. At that moment, with his head hanging down, his eyes floated up briefly to meet Rue's gaze. And that's when she saw it. The tiniest of glimmers. He was messing with her.

"Well, Darwin," the blonde answered, peering over her shoulder at Rue. "You have my number. Be sure to give me a call if this...new arrangement doesn't work out. I may not be as polished as Ashley, but I'm sure I can handle answerin' phones and such."

"Actually, I have a bit of contract work for both of you. I'll be in touch soon with your next assignment."

"We'll be waiting with bated breath." The black-haired woman blew Darwin a kiss, clenching the red scarf against her neck.

Rue bit back a few choice words. From her estimation, Darwin Fennec, cyber forensic whatever-the-hell-that-was, was also Darwin Fennec...cad.

After they left, Darwin turned to Rue. "So, where were we?"

"I was just leaving." Rue stood. "Sorry to waste your time, but this meeting was a mistake."

"Hang on," Darwin stood, putting his hands out in front of him as if to stop her from leaving. Unfortunately, as he held them in the air, they seemed to line up perfectly with Rue's breasts. She backed away. He realized how his gesture may have been perceived and lowered his arms.

Rue let out a huff. "What?"

"It is clear to me that you don't like me very much—" he began.

"You are a very observant detective," Rue countered. Darwin was taken aback by her brutal honestly and lack of impulse control.

"Investigator," he corrected. "However, I suspect that it means a lot to you to make your boyfriend Spencer happy—"

"What do you know about it?" she challenged.

"Not much," he admitted. "But let's just say that I am in desperate need of an assistant...or at least someone to *pose* as my assistant, at least for the time being."

"What the hell does that mean?"

"I really can't say," he answered.

In truth, he *could* say. He just *didn't*.

"Then I really have to go." Rue started to leave.

"No, wait...please," Darwin requested. "What salary would your Spencer deem acceptable?"

"Excuse me?"

"C'mon, we both know you wouldn't be here if it weren't for him. I'm asking what would get your boyfriend off your back? Enough where you could give up whatever it is you're doing that he so disapproves of and come work for me for twenty-five hours or so a week with potential for full time if it all works out."

"Why are you doing this, Mr. Fennec?" Rue demanded. "You have no idea as to my qualifications, and, as you've pointed out, we are not exactly compatible on a personality level."

"No," Darwin agreed. "But I suspect we need each other."

"Do we?"

Darwin's expression grew somber. "You have no idea what's at stake," he said.

He searched her eyes for some level of compassion.

Rue's eyes peered back, expressionless.

Finally, Darwin's face crumbled as he covered it with his palm as if covering up some level of desperation.

"Cut the bullshit, Mr. Fennec."

Darwin dropped his hand and the act, confused. "Why are you so mean?"

"I don't like fake," Rue answered. Unfortunately, as she did so, images of Spencer in his Bergdorf suits and Ivy League haircut wafted through her mind. "And you, Mr. Darwin Fennec, are as fake as they come."

"Perhaps," he smiled, knowingly. "But you have my card, yes?"

"Yes," she answered. "But I won't be calling."

"Well, if you change your mind and decide to work for me—"

"I won't."

"Very well," Darwin answered. "Thanks for meeting me, anyway." With that, Darwin pulled on the blue cap that he had tucked into his back pocket, placed it on his head and tipped it, as if sauntering off into the sunset.

Rue also stood, taking a moment to stretch out her legs before heading home. As if on cue, Midge sidled up beside Rue, hunched over as if she were going to steal Rue's purse. She grabbed Rue's arm with such force that Rue turned and nearly walloped her friend with her free fist.

"Whoa!" Midge called. "Hold the phone, sista. Just seeing if yuz was okay."

Rue let out a sigh. "Midge, don't scare the crap out of me like that." She turned and kept walking. "But yeah. I'm fine."

"So, what happened with Gumbie?"

"What? Oh, nothing."

"What do you mean, 'nothing'? Didn't the interview go well?"

"It was less of an interview and more me deciding that this was a horrible mistake."

"Wait! Why?" Midge stepped in front of Rue, nearly tripping her friend. Rue stopped abruptly.

"I get the impression that he's a womanizing lech."

"So, what does that have to do with working for him?" Midge was confused. "Do you think he'd put the moves on you, or something?"

"No, but I have standards."

"I'm failing to see the connection between his personal life and his work life. With that said, I have an important question for you."

"What's that?" Rue let out a huff.

"Since it seems you are not interested in him, personally *or* professionally, mind if I have a go?"

"A go at what? Personal was never an option. I have a boyfriend."

"Yeah," Midge twirled her finger in the air in mock awe. "Spencer."

"What's wrong with Spencer?" Rue demanded.

"I don't think we have that kind of time," Midge retorted as they resumed their brisk walk toward Delancey Street.

Spencer may have been a little overbearing lately, but Rue was certain that he was simply struggling to fit in with the big wigs in the tech world, to be swimming with the sharks.

"Yeah, I get it. You two don't exactly like each other. But he's my boyfriend, and I like him just fine." Rue kept walking. "But what, exactly, did you want to have a go at? Did you want to apply as Darwin's assistant or something?"

Midge contorted her face in a "don't be ridiculous" way. "I'm a senior level Information Security Expert. While his detective agency could benefit from my skills tremendously, I'm pretty sure he can't afford me."

"Snob," Rue stuck her tongue out at Midge. "You and Spencer may be more alike than you think."

"I resent that," Midge countered. "But no, not professionally. I mean, personally."

"Really? I'm not sure that's wise. He seems to be sort of a player." Rue replayed the encounter with the two women who surfaced during their interview.

"Just my type," Midge concluded.

"Really?" Rue was surprised.

"What? Don't judge me. I like a challenge. He'll be eating out of my hand in no time."

Well, Rue thought to herself. *Then perhaps Midge is in luck. Because Mr. Darwin Fennec certainly appears to be quite the challenge.*

Back in the Office of Darwin Fennec

Darwin returned from his meeting with Rue to an office in disarray. The front door was wide open with papers scattered all over the floor, some of which had already blown into the street. One filing cabinet was overturned with a couple of chairs knocked over, in what Darwin could have sworn was "on principle." His minimalist oak desk had been ransacked, the drawers dumped on the floor with a variety of files, pens, rubber bands, paper clips, notepads, and the odd hole punch strewn everywhere.

Darwin took a moment to sift his hand through the mess...and smiled. Things were going exactly according to plan.

"Okay to come in?" a voice asked. Darwin looked up to observe a woman of medium height with mahogany hair tied back with a red ribbon. She wore a form-fitting navy top and white linen pants, appearing as if she'd stepped off the cover of a Macy's catalog. The single oddity was her plastic black gloves...and the fact that she was obviously very pregnant.

"Of course," Darwin flashed a grin. "So, what happened?"

The woman set a pair of binoculars on Darwin's desk and removed the gloves. "Took the bait just as you expected," she reported. "Oh, and the gals left thank you messages for you today, you scoundrel!" She wiggled her eyes suggestively, slapping him on the arm. The woman handed him the phone messages that she had carefully scribbled on post-it notes. "I left them on the answering machine if you wanted to listen for yourself, 'Darwin honey.'" She rolled her shoulder and pursed her lips, imitating the baby-doll sounding voice messages she'd retrieved.

"Excellent," he smiled, ignoring her gestures. "Thank you, Ashley."

"No problem. Oh," she remembered, dropping her shoulder, "how did it go with the girl today? The one Spencer is dating?"

Darwin thought a moment. "Honestly, I'm not sure."

"Really?" Ashley was surprised. "The famous Darwin Fennec unsure?"

Darwin blushed a little, but unlike the presentation he made to the women at the pier, this one was quite a bit more genuine.

"Unfortunately, yes."

"Hmm," she thought a moment before planting a kiss on his cheek. "That's okay, you'll figure it out."

"I hope so," Darwin answered, a hint of skepticism in his voice.

"Do you need help cleaning up the mess all over the street? Hope those particular papers were not terribly important."

"Not terribly, no. And I can manage, thanks." He glanced at her large belly and thought better of asking her to do any of the cleanup.

"Well," Ashley wrinkled her nose at him, "you know where I'll be if you need me. Otherwise, see you in a few months."

Darwin wrapped his arms around her in as tight a hug as he could give a very pregnant woman as she turned her belly to the side. "Thanks, Ashley," he answered. "I can always count on you. I love you, you know."

CHAPTER 3
The Gambler

Sunday Morning at Rue's Apartment

~

Rue awakened to a tapping at her window. She rolled over and groaned, forcing her eyes open to gaze at the clock beside her bed. It was only 7:23 am. She sat up and made her way toward the tapping and pulled back the pillowcase curtain to reveal an overly energetic Midge smiling at her. She held up a bottle of champagne and a carton of orange juice.

Rue lifted the window. "Mensa, it's Sunday. Why are you at my window so early? And furthermore, how come you never use the front door anymore?"

Midge thrust the orange juice through the window for Rue to take, which she did, walking it to the kitchen table while Midge clumsily stepped over the sill, carrying the champagne.

"For one thing," Midge smiled, "I wanted to share the news." She waited for Rue to ask 'what news' but she didn't. Instead, Rue leaned in on the table with her hand and let out a yawn. She hadn't even changed out of her nightgown yet, a fact that made Midge's visit that much more annoying.

"Anyways," Midge continued, "it's a shorter distance to climb down the escape versus using the stairs. If you were as smart as me, you'd have realized that." She glanced back at the pillowcases over the window. "Ever think of blinds?"

Rue gazed at the makeshift drapes above the windows of her bedroom. They were, essentially, two pillowcases nailed above each window, each one tied together with a yellow ribbon that wrapped around yet another nail situated on the far ends of the windows. At night, she unraveled the ribbons for privacy. Juvenile, perhaps, but at the time, she hadn't really seen herself living there for more than a year, so practical things such as drapes and frames around pictures hanging on the wall seemed like an impractical waste of effort.

A long pause ensued. "Aren't you going to invite me to sit down?" Midge complained. "After all, I brought us mimosas. At the very least, you could offer me toast or something."

"Please," Rue clenched her jaw. "Sit down." Moving over to the counter, Rue procured one flute glass and one small juice glass. "I think we need to have a talk about boundaries, Mensa. You can't keep showing up at my window unannounced. Maybe call first to see if I'm even up for company...or even better, to see if I already *have* company?"

"Oh please, when has Spencer ever stayed over at your place? He's too pretty to hang out for more than ten minutes in a hovel like this."

"Lots of times," Rue protested, handing the flute glass to Midge.

"I counted twice over the past year."

"How would you even know that, Mensa?"

"Let's just say that the walls in this building are thin," Midge answered, followed by a well-timed pop from the champagne cork.

Rue turned red. Midge went to add champagne to Rue's glass, but she covered it with her palm. "No thanks. It's not even 8 a.m. yet. I'll just stick with juice." She poured a little orange juice into her glass.

Midge shrugged and added a healthy dose of champagne to her own glass. "Mimosas are a perfectly acceptable breakfast drink," she protested. "Sunday Fun Day and all." She held up the bottle again, in case Rue changed her mind, but Rue shook her head.

“Did you actually want some toast?” Rue asked.

“Nah,” Midge answered. “It’ll just ruin the flavor of the mimosa.” Midge took a seat at the table. Rue sat in the other. “Come to think of it, so will the juice.” With that, she topped off her glass with more champagne.

“I’m surprised you drink so much, Mensa, given how smart you are. Doesn’t alcohol kill brain cells?”

“Only the weak ones,” she reasoned. “The good ones will survive.”

“I don’t think it works that way,” Rue argued. “So, what’s your news?”

“I have a date with Darwin Fennec Wednesday night.”

“Really?” Rue’s eyebrows shot up. “That was...fast.”

“If you see something you want in this world, you just gotta go after it!” Midge pounded her fists on the table, nearly spilling her drink.

“Well, if a womanizing charlatan is your thing, then congratulations.”

Midge pointed a finger at Rue. “You don’t know that. You just assume that based on very little information.” Midge took a sip of her drink. “And besides, I really don’t care.”

“Just be careful.”

“And while we’re on the subject of Darwin, I really think you should take the job working for him...and this I say despite the fact that it was Spencer’s idea.”

“I’m not taking the job. Why would I?”

“Working for a cyber forensic analyst and detective...”

“Investigator,” Rue corrected.

“What?” Midge lost her train of thought. “Anyways,” she waved a hand in the air, “sounds intriguing to me. Maybe he’ll train you. Not a bad career move, if you ask me. And Darwin is not exactly awful to look at.”

“Why would you want me looking at your future boyfriend?”

“Whoa, let’s not jump the gun!” Midge held her hands up. “Besides, I’m not selfish. I don’t mind sharing.”

“That’s disgusting, Mensa.”

“To yous, maybe,” she defended. “What-chew got goin’ on today?”

“Oh, I have an advertorial to write for a new boutique pet store and have to create an online events calendar for a holistic center.”

"Sounds riveting," Midge answered flatly.

"It's bad enough I have to work on a Sunday; I don't need you and Spencer dissing my work."

"I'm sorry. You know I only have your best interest at heart. Anyhoo..." Midge stood. "I was going to invite you to take a road trip down to the shore with me, but since you're busy..."

"You know, we have closer beaches, right?" Rue asked, eyeing the now nearly empty bottle of champagne.

"Well, duh," Midge rolled her eyes. "But you can't gamble there. I wanna try my luck with the one-armed bandit in Atlantic City, and there's a bus leaving from the Port Authority in less than an hour...so, I gotta scoot." She paused, with one leg stretched over the sill in an amazing display of flexibility. "And don't think I didn't notice you eyeing the bottle. I'm not driving, nosey-pants." She climbed onto the escape before remembering something. "Oh, and can you be a dear and recycle that for me? Thanks!"

Rue let out a sigh as she picked up the bottle and set it by the door as a reminder to take it down the hall to the recycle bin later that day—which also meant that she'd probably actually have to change out of her nightgown at some point and put some clothes on.

Just then, Rue's phone rang. "Hey Rue, it's Donna over at Garnet Media. Sorry for calling early on a Sunday morning."

"Oh, hey, Donna," Rue replied, stretching the phone cord and tucking the receiver between her ear and shoulder. "No problem at all. In fact, I'm slated to work on the calendar and pet store advertorials today and the entertainment section tomorrow. I'm making good progress." Rue placed the leftover orange juice in the frig and closed the door.

"Oh," Donna sounded disappointed. "Listen, Rue, I really hate to do this to you because you're my favorite journalist but..."

The pit in Rue's stomach dropped.

Donna continued, "But my boss just called after reviewing the budget. Somehow, his team missed a huge discrepancy, and the Early Edition doesn't actually have the funding it thought it did, so..."

"What are you saying, Donna?"

"We're shutting down the print and new electronic site immediately and all journalists, editors, and graphic designers on the contract are being temporarily put on hold. I'm really sorry, Rue; I don't know how this happened, but I promise to cover you for the pieces you are currently writing—no need to finish them though. Just invoice me and I'll take care of it."

Rue's entire face felt hot. The Early Edition was, by far, her largest contract. Without it, she was left with modeling, which Spencer disapproved of, an as-needed gig writing press releases and blogs for a local optometrist, and...she hated that this had even entered the equation—becoming the administrative assistant to Cyber Forensic Analyst and Private Investigator Darwin Fennec.

~

Ten Minutes Later...

"HELLO MS. BRENNAN," Darwin greeted, picking up the phone on the second ring.

"How did you know it was me?" Rue asked, suspiciously.

"It's my job to know, Rue," he answered smugly.

Rue bit her lip. Her rent was due in two weeks and short of asking Spencer for help (which she vowed never to do), this was the quickest way to an income. "Then you know why I'm calling," she answered, not without a hint of sarcasm.

"I suspect I do, yes. You've re-thought my offer?"

"Of working for you, yes. But you didn't actually tell me what I'd be doing or how I'd be paid."

"Tell you what, meet me at my office tomorrow morning. Eight a.m. would be ideal. You know the skyscraper on the river, 200 West Street?"

"Wow," Rue was impressed. "That's your office?"

"Not even close," he continued. "But if you follow that street to the end, you'll find the only one-story triangular building on the corner with a blue door. You'll see a Cyber Security and Investigations sign on the window. That's my office."

"Oh," Rue seemed disappointed. "Well, I'm sure I can find it. But about everything else?"

"I can give you more details tomorrow, and we can talk numbers, sound good?"

"Are the renovations finished already?"

"The what?" Darwin thought a moment. "Oh, yes. Just finished this afternoon."

"Convenient," Rue muttered. "Okay," she finally answered reluctantly, "see you tomorrow morning."

"Don't sound so thrilled," Darwin teased. "Oh, gotta run. Talk tomorrow."

With that, he abruptly hung up the phone.

CHAPTER 4
Gretchen

Monday Morning in Battery Park

A tall woman, dressed in an overabundance of beige, slunk her way into Darwin Fennec's office at precisely 7:13 a.m., exactly three minutes after Darwin, himself, had arrived. He hadn't even had a chance to lock the door behind him and was still brewing a morning cup of coffee in the kitchenette area when she arrived. She wore a matching scarf, hat and dark sunglasses, shielding her face. She closed the door quietly behind her, fighting as it caught clumsily on the door frame. Eyeing the small window to the outside world, she quickly drew the blinds.

"Good morning, Mrs. Ellis," Darwin greeted, without turning around.

"Good morning, Darwin," Gretchen Ellis answered with a level of sophistication that was matched only by her love of beige. She unwrapped her scarf and removed her hat, revealing a short, cropped bleached-blonde hairdo that never once moved when she removed her hat (probably out of fear). "You are a clever boy, aren't you?"

Darwin turned around, holding a cup of freshly brewed black coffee in his hand. "Coffee?"

"No, thank you," she answered. "I shan't be long. I just wanted to talk with you for a moment, if I may." Gretchen Ellis removed her glasses, revealing somewhat striking pale blue eyes and slight crow's feet around her otherwise stretched-looking face.

Darwin offered her a chair, but she declined. Instead, she stood by the doorway, already preparing to make her exit.

"I know you've been investigating my family," she revealed.

"Yes," Darwin answered flatly. "That was made evident when you had your security guards ransack my office the other day."

"Sorry about that," she sniffed unpleasantly. "It would have been easier if you'd just told me what dirt you'd dug up for Spencer Hargrove."

"You know I can't do that, client confidentiality and all. It would be unethical."

"Hmmm," Gretchen eyed him curiously. "I didn't realize that ethics were a concern of yours." She turned dramatically toward the window, suddenly remembering that there was nothing to see as she'd closed the blinds. She pressed on, "Since Spencer sees fit to trust you, I'd like to employ your services."

"Really?" Darwin was cautious. "In what capacity?"

Gretchen turned to face him. "I want you to investigate my son."

"Astor? But why?" He suspected he already knew.

"Oh, come now, Darwin. Don't pretend to be stupid. You know as well as I do that Astor has an eye for the ladies. He's soon to be taking over as CEO for his father's company, and that's not the kind of press we need, particularly when he's about to be married."

Ah, yes. Darwin thought. *Portia LaMonte, socialite, yuppie, and heir to her family's line of pet products. Who knew there was so much money to be had in squeaky dog toys and ferret hammocks?*

Gretchen reached into her purse, which had up until now, blended in with the rest of her. "Here," she handed him a folded piece of paper. "The latest of my son's trysts."

Darwin accepted the note. In it, was a handwritten message, signed with a name and a physical address.

"Clarissa Sauer?" Darwin read the name.

"Let's drop the charade, Darwin. Shall we?" She waved her hands in the air. "You know who she is as you've already been investigating Astor and my husband to find evidence suggesting we're stealing company secrets from SpencerTech."

SpencerTech was Spencer Hargrove's baby, a start-up company he founded last year and a soon-to-be direct competitor for her husband, Byron Ellis's, well-established company, B. A. Ellis Industries. Spencer was on the verge of developing a new animation product that would bring computer animation into the forefront of movie making. What's more, there was not the need for pesky plug-ins to allow his graphic design program to talk seamlessly with others, no matter the operating system or version.

Spencer bragged about this regularly to both Rue, and apparently, Darwin. By his estimation, his integration would enhance cinematography and animation while cutting production time for artists and designers by a good 35%. And that, he reasoned, was very good for business.

Distracted at this moment, Darwin had only one thought. *Why are all of these men so obsessed with naming their companies after themselves?*

Darwin re-directed his attention toward the current conversation. "What is it you'd like to have me do, Mrs. Ellis?"

"Clarissa Sauer is pregnant," Gretchen Ellis answered flatly. "She's been not-so-subtly requesting money so that we could 'make the problem go away.'"

"I see," Darwin answered, folding the note.

"No, I don't think you do, Darwin," Gretchen retorted. "While my son is a playboy, he's definitely *not* the father."

"There are tests for that."

"My son is sterile, Darwin." She held up her hand. "Please don't ask me how I know."

"Don't worry," Darwin reassured her. "I won't."

"Then, just yesterday, this arrived." Back into the purse she went, digging around until she'd found what she was after. She pulled out a second piece of paper. This one was a printout from her personal email.

"Emma Post," Gretchen read the name. "I don't know how she even got my email address. I've only just recently begun using email and barely remember my own address. Look at the message."

Darwin read the text. *Dear Ms. Ellis, or should I call you Mom? Astor and I are expecting. Just thought you should know. Perhaps we can schedule a time to meet to discuss it?"*

"So not one, but two women are coming forward claiming that Astor Ellis is the father of their babies?"

"Quite," Gretchen pursed her lips, bitterly. "All happily coinciding with Astor's impending marriage, his rise in the ranks at B. A. Ellis Industries, and with Byron on the verge of launching a new invention that will put him within the top 2% of the richest men alive. Which, I might add, has nothing to do with Spencer Hargrove's meager start-up."

"How very inconvenient," Darwin acknowledged.

"I don't want Portia LaMonte to get wind of my son's infidelity. The marriage will be very good for our families."

"So, what would you have me do?"

"Find out exactly who Astor has been running around with and any dirt you can about them. It will make getting rid of them that much easier."

"Getting rid of them?" Darwin was skeptical.

"Paying them off, Darwin," Gretchen was exasperated. "Obviously, it's a scheme cooked up by these gold diggers to get money out of the Ellis family. But I don't intend to make ongoing payments for babies that don't exist...or at least aren't ours. I'm willing to offer each of these whores a one-time payout to keep their mouths shut if they did have romantic liaisons with my son. But first, I need you to confirm who they are because I'd be willing to bet that Astor has never laid eyes on either of these girls, let alone anything else."

"My rate is $300 an hour, Mrs. Ellis," Darwin explained.

"Preposterous," she answered. "I happen to know you're only charging Spencer $200 an hour and much of the investigative work overlaps." Mrs. Ellis then realized her mistake. She smiled. "You certainly are crafty, Darwin Fennec. I'll agree to your $300 per hour on one condition."

"And what's that, Mrs. Ellis?"

"That you share any information you give to Spencer Hargrove about my family with me."

"You know I can't do that, Mrs. Ellis," Darwin explained.

"Right," she nodded. "Code of ethics."

"Exactly."

"But taking a case that's a clear conflict of interest with the one you're currently on is perfectly acceptable?" Gretchen eyed him suspiciously.

"Perfectly," Darwin nodded. "My code. My rules."

"I see. Does your *code* include how much you charge your clients?" Gretchen demanded.

"Completely unrelated," he admitted.

"Then why, may I ask, are you charging me more than what you're charging Spencer Hargrove? Tell me you're not taking advantage of the fact that I have money?"

"Not at all," Darwin answered.

"Then, why?"

"It's very simple, Mrs. Ellis." He paused for a moment. "I don't like you."

"Oh, I see," Gretchen Ellis's eyes grew wide in surprise, a small smirk forming at the corner of her lips. "So, you base your fees on how much you like a client. Am I to assume you like Spencer Hargrove?"

"No," Darwin shook his head. "As it turns out, I don't like him very much either." A sad fact that he'd learned too late.

"And yet you haven't raised his rates. Why?"

At that moment the door handle fumbled. Rue had arrived early for her first day on the job. Darwin glanced up, surprised, before remembering.

"Mrs. Ellis, I'm afraid I will have to cut this meeting a bit short. I have an appointment to keep."

Rue finally managed to jar the door open, and when it finally gave, she almost smacked Gretchen Ellis, who now had her sunglasses and hat back on and was in the process of wrapping the scarf to cover her chin.

"Oh," Rue's eyes opened wide. "I'm so sorry."

Darwin stifled back a laugh.

"It's okay, Ms. Brennan," Gretchen answered, "I was just leaving." She brushed past Rue, almost knocking the much smaller young woman over in the process. Before she'd crossed the threshold, she glanced over at Darwin. "Oh, and I agree to your fees. I'll see to it that a deposit is wired to you by the end of the day. Nice working with you, Darwin."

"Oh, and Mrs. Ellis?" Darwin stopped her.

"Yes? What is it?"

Darwin walked over to the door and handed Gretchen Ellis his business card. "My email is on here. Would you please forward Emma Post's message so we can look into it?"

After one final glance at Rue, Gretchen answered, "Of course." With that, she forcefully shut the door behind her.

Rue gestured in Gretchen's direction. "Who was that and how'd she know who I was?"

"Good morning, Ms. Brennan," Darwin greeted, ignoring her question.

Rue hadn't realized they were being so formal. "Uh, morning, Mr. Fennec." Without thinking, she plopped her duffel bag filled with a wrapped peanut butter and jelly sandwich and a bottle of water on the chair in front of Darwin's desk—one of the two meant for clients—and proceeded to remove a tattered rain jacket from her shoulders (even though it was sunny that day).

"And that was?" she reminded him.

"Yes, of course," he walked over and motioned to her belongings. "Might want to throw these under the counter in the kitchen," he said, pointing. "We should leave these seats open for clients."

"Oh, right." Rue realized her mistake and moved her belongings.

"That was one of our new clients, Mrs. Gretchen Ellis," Darwin called after her.

Rue started for a moment. Why was that name familiar? She tossed her belongings under the counter, but only after she'd retrieved her lunch. Eyeing the kitchen, she spotted a mini-refrigerator located just underneath where the coffeemaker sat on the counter. "Okay if I store my sandwich in the frig?" she asked.

"Sure," he answered. "Might need to move stuff around to find room."

Rue fumbled with the door and, getting it open, spotted a jar of green powder, a half-drunk smoothie in a glass, and a deli-bought salad. She threw her sandwich on top of the salad container.

Darwin waited for Rue to finish organizing her things before continuing. "Which brings me to our first item on the agenda for today."

"Oh, what's that, Mr. Fennec?"

"Client confidentiality is our most important code. I only stay in business because my clients trust me. Therefore, while I know that Spencer Hargrove is your boyfriend, he's just one of several clients we currently have."

"Which means?"

"That anything unrelated to his case, no matter what it is, is strictly confidential and can't be shared with anyone—not even him. In fact, it might be best if all the information about the investigation comes from me, not you, just in case."

"In case what? I don't follow."

"For example, Gretchen Ellis, who just blew through here in a whirlwind of beige is Byron Ellis's wife."

"The tech mogul who runs B. A. Ellis Industries?" Rue asked. "The one Spencer has been complaining about for the last year?"

"The same," he answered. "If anything comes to light that confirms they are, in fact, pilfering information from SpencerTech, and you share it over dinner, there's no guarantee that Spencer won't confront them, half-cocked, and blow our entire operation."

"You must think I'm really dumb," Rue folded her arms.

"I don't think that at all, Ms. Brennan." He offered her one of the unoccupied chairs. She sat. "I do, however, question your boyfriend's reasoning behind suggesting you come and work for me, considering the delicate nature of this work."

"And yet, you hired me," Rue shook her head slightly.

"I did," he confirmed. "Sometimes, I question my own reasoning as well. Should we move on to the work you'll actually being doing for me?"

"Please," Rue agreed. "But then can we get back to why Gretchen Ellis was here in the first place?"

"Certainly, but first..." Darwin outlined Rue's weekly salary. She held a poker face after the announcement, since it was a good bit more than what her current contract work was offering. There was the usual answering the phone and responding to emails and the occasional fax, sending and tracking invoices to clients, and so forth.

"I think I can handle all that," Rue answered, confidently.

"Well, good," Darwin replied. "But there is a bit more to it."

"Such as..."

"Such as, I need to train you on basic encryption and security operations here. Data is sensitive and we do our damnedest to protect it. This won't happen overnight, but over the next three months..."

"Three months?" Rue questioned.

"Well, yes? Did you not expect the training to be that involved, or not to be working for me for that long?"

Rue wrinkled her nose and shrugged her shoulders.

"It's both, isn't it?" Darwin let out a long sigh, clasping his hands to his hips.

"I'm sorry," Rue smiled, a bit apologetically, "but I'm still trying to wrap my head around this whole scenario."

"Understood," Darwin answered. "Er, there is one more thing..."

"And that would be?"

"Everyone I work with is vital to my team. And no one is on the sidelines. There are times where I may ask you to get in the trenches, so to speak."

"What does that mean?" Rue asked.

"It means that beyond being an assistant, I may ask you to be on the scene for some investigative work. Can you do that?"

Rue felt something in her heart do a flip-flop. The vibration traveled from her heart to her lungs and finally bubbled into her throat. She swallowed, hard. There was something exhilarating about the prospect of 'getting in the trenches.' After a moment, she answered, "Yes. I can do that." After a moment of silence, she added, "Is that all?"

"Just one more thing, Ms. Brennan," Darwin said. "A question, really."

Rue leaned in, curiously. "Yes?"

"Just how good are you at keeping secrets?"

CHAPTER 5

Training

Tuesday Morning in Battery Park

~

While the rest of Rue's first day on the job was very basic and somewhat bland, she was intrigued to learn that they would be investigating Astor Ellis while also gathering intelligence on B.A. Ellis Industries. Rue wasn't sure how to describe the new excitement she was feeling about the work. It was almost as if she could feel warm blood coursing through her veins for the first time in a very long time, and she liked it.

"So," Rue smiled coyly as she took her seat in front of Darwin's desk computer in preparation for her first lesson in logging sensitive data. "Are you looking forward to your date with Midge?" She hadn't forgotten that Midge and Darwin had plans Wednesday night.

"Midge?" Darwin remembered. "Oh, yes. Of course, I am. Your friend seems like..." he thought a moment, "a lot of fun."

Rue's expression darkened. "She's more than just 'a lot of fun', mister. She's probably my best friend, despite her unnatural clinginess," Rue considered. "But never mind that, just be respectful is all." If Rue were being honest with herself, she would have been more concerned with Midge's behavior around Darwin.

"I'm hurt that you think I would be anything but." Darwin's face dropped.

"Frankly, I am a little surprised."

"At?" Darwin leaned a hand on the desk. Rue could feel his energy as he stood behind her. She shuddered for a moment but then shrugged it off. She never felt odd like that when Spencer was near her. But then, she'd known him for a year, so maybe she just got used his proximity? She drew her mind back to the conversation.

"You just seem like an odd couple, is all," Rue confessed. "Forget I said anything. Let's focus." She looked at the dark screen that was Darwin's computer. "What are you going to teach me today?"

"Glad you asked." Darwin pulled up a chair and sat next to her. "See those filing cabinets over there?" He pointed to the two tan columns that sat in the corner of the room.

"Yeah?"

"They're pretty much just for show."

"What?"

"I mean," Darwin held his hands up, "not entirely. They contain take-out menus and a few office expenses. But let's just say there's nothing overly sensitive in there."

"Then, why do you keep it locked?" Rue asked. "You specifically gave me a key for it yesterday so I could grab a Rolodex with a phone number on it you were looking for."

"Well, part of that is out of an abundance of caution with regards to people's personal information. But the other part is to create a red herring."

"A red herring?" Rue was confused.

"Yes, a misdirection," Darwin explained. "For example, the other day, the lovely Gretchen Ellis, who you had the great fortune of meeting, had some of her thugs break into this place. They got nothing...except for what I wanted them to get."

"From the locked cabinet," Rue confirmed.

"Which they had broken into," Darwin finished.

"Did they not get anything off of your computer?" She motioned with her eyes back toward the screen at her desk.

"They couldn't," Darwin answered. "And sadly for them, not sure they would have been able to even if I hadn't password-protected and encrypting everything...not the brightest bulbs in the pack, I'd say."

"So, what did they get?"

"Well, if memory serves...there were about a hundred ski ball tickets left behind from when I took my friend's son to the arcade, the newest Dim Sum menu from Chang's restaurant..." He paused for a moment, as if pretending to think. "Oh, yes. And a few working animation grids and a blueprint of SpencerTech's animation software."

"What?" Rue sat up.

"From three years ago," Darwin finished. "B. A. Ellis Industries might very well assume that Spencer's designs are outdated given the old-style programming. And, if they didn't, they will have fun spending the time working through the bugs he took years to work out."

"Clever," Rue acknowledged. "So, where do you keep the actual info about your cases—clients, clues, evidence, etc. I assume they live...somewhere?"

"Yes, of course," Darwin answered, eagerly. "That's what I want to show you. May I?" He once again leaned over her shoulder to power up the computer. "You can go ahead and drive," he told her once the screen had awoken to reveal a blinking curser.

"Drive what?"

"Oh," Darwin hadn't realized quite how green Rue was about technology. "Take the mouse and keyboard and I'll walk you through everything. But you're in control."

"Ooh," Rue nodded, "I get it."

"Let's start with the login for information surrounding a bogus family I created for training purposes, okay?" Darwin suggested. He pointed on the screen to a little obscure icon in the lower-left-hand corner. "Click on that," he commanded. Rue clicked on it. "Now, the username is..."

Rue stopped to pull out a pen and paper from the desk in which she was sitting.

"What are you doing?" he asked, part annoyed and part surprised.

"I figure you're gonna give me a username and password for the account, right?"

"Wrong," Darwin corrected. "I'm going to give you a few back-end codes that you can use to access this information. But I don't want you writing any of it down."

"Why not?" Rue asked.

"Security. We were just talking about it, remember?"

"But then, how will I remember once I start working on several accounts?" Rue protested. "Surely you don't expect me to memorize them all. Or do you?"

"While that would be nice...no. But what I do want you to remember is *the pattern*."

"I'm afraid I don't follow."

"That's okay," Darwin answered, patiently. "I can give you an example using the mock-up file I created to train people. Go ahead and type in the letters, numbers, and symbols I give you." Darwin rambled off an odd sequence which Rue struggled to find on the keyboard and type in quickly. "That username is assigned to all the cases surrounding our fictional John Doe. Now, type this in." He went on to provide an entirely new set of codes.

Within moments, the file of a John Doe popped up, presumably with a fake photo and detailed information about the person including basics such as approximate height, weight, hair and eye color, all the way to details about where they had been and why, preferences on food and beverage choices and any interesting factoids that seemed irrelevant to the average person.

"What do you notice about this file?" Darwin asked.

"Well," Rue was hesitant. "Not entirely sure what you're after, but I notice his headshot and bio at the top, his physical features on the left, preferences on the right, and below that, you have photos, notes, and timestamps about where he's been."

"Excellent," Darwin praised. "Anything else?"

Rue looked closer. "I see that you have a hypothesis section with ideas as to what might be happening next to a confirmed list with these blue, underlined words."

"Click on one of those underlined words," he told her.

Rue was not particularly computer savvy, but she knew enough to click the mouse over the link. Nothing happened.

"Double click," he instructed patiently. Unsure, she clicked twice, and a new screen opened up connecting him to a Jane Doe. "See all those underlines?"

"What about them?" Rue asked.

"They either connect to other people or to relevant evidence."

"Oh," Rue was impressed. "That's amazing. On the few times I've been on the Internet, I seem to go in circles."

"This isn't the Internet," Darwin explained, "it's our private server." Rue's face was blank. He was using terms that she had heard Spencer use, but since Spencer got impatient when she asked questions, she simply stopped asking them. To Darwin, she merely nodded.

He motioned to the screen. "If you click on the Xs in the corners, you can close out these screens. Just one click."

She carefully clicked them and watched with amusement as they vanished.

"Now, go back to the home screen." Darwin folded his arms and waited, giving Rue a moment to figure it out. Finally, she did.

"Good. We're going to try a different client. Let's go to Jane Doe." He rambled off new codes which Rue typed in quickly. As with John, Jane popped up. "Now, let's pretend we've just learned that Jane had been in contact with John at 10:57 p.m., using the phone in her apartment. We want to note the time, phone number, and any other information that could be relevant. Click on that plus sign." He motioned to the corner of the screen, and what looked like a pad of paper popped up. "Click your cursor in the box."

Rue followed along.

"Type your note...just make something up." Rue typed in the time, a made-up phone number, and decided to add that Jane Doe sounded as if she were crunching on potato chips at the time and the sound of the rustle of the bag. "I applaud your imagination," Darwin laughed. "Now hit the save button," he pointed. "Always save after every bit of information."

Rue clicked the "save" button, turning to Darwin who was silent for a few moments as if letting the information sink in. "What now?" she asked.

"Now, I'd like you to spend the next couple of hours clicking on buttons and becoming familiar with the interface." Rue looked apprehensive. "Don't worry, it's just a sandbox," he explained.

"Sandbox?"

"Yes, a learning platform. Pretend you are adding and deleting info, looking up people, and connecting accounts. If you get stuck, write down your question and we'll go over it when I get back."

"Where are you going?" Rue wanted to know, slightly nervous.

"I need to do a little digging into the first case I am going to enlist your help on...finding out more about Astor Ellis's romantic liaisons." Darwin grabbed a jacket off the back of his chair and put it on. "I'll tell you more after you've gotten spun up on how the system works. For the time being, if anyone calls, you can jot down the message there," he pointed to the notepad and pen by the phone. "If someone comes in enquiring about anything, just get their information and tell them that I'll get back to them later today. Understood?"

Rue nodded, a lump forming in her throat. Part of the allure of being a journalist and a figure model is that in both cases, you worked alone and if you did have to interview someone for an assignment, it was on your terms because you had reached out to them. She was a little daunted by the simple task of having to answer the phone without knowing who was on the other end and what they wanted. She had the same apprehension about someone walking through the front door.

"You'll be fine," he smiled. "I won't be gone long." He started to leave but circled back. "By the way, notice anything about the username and password patterns?" he asked.

Rue thought a moment. A lightbulb went off in her head. "All the usernames had two letters, two numbers, two symbols and then one of each, in that order. All the passwords looked like phrases with numbers in place of vowels. Can't figure out the pattern for the symbols though."

"That's okay," he encouraged. "You're on the right track. Play with that pattern and see whom else might be on the server. Perhaps Jane and John Doe have little Does running around, or even a dog named Rover Doe."

With that, he closed the door and Rue went back to her studies. Truth be told, until last year, Rue didn't even have her own personal computer, relying on reserved time at the local library or in the offices of one of her freelance locations. When work finally became steady enough, it was Spencer, in an uncharacteristic show of support, who bought her an Intel computer and dial-up service that gave her access to the Internet. Frankly, she wasn't sure the whole Internet and email thing would ever take off, but the computer was a huge time saver compared to her old electric typewriter.

Spencer had made a show of it, bragging that he'd managed to get her a $1,400 computer for $750 at wholesale. Somehow, Spencer, showing how frugal he was did not impress her. Him actually showing an interest in her work, for once, however...did.

Rue returned her attention back to the task at hand. She tried a few random passwords, struggling to figure out Darwin's pattern for organizing them. She randomly glanced around the room—one small window, the front door, the small kitchen with three appliances placed neatly across the countertop. In her mind, she replaced objects with numbers and symbols, almost seeing them float up in front of her.

"Wait a minute," she smiled, excitedly. She typed in a username and password. Sure enough, the video of a wagging dog showed up with the words "congratulations" written at the top. "Now, go find the cat." Rue thought a moment, used the same username with a new password and an image of a purring cat named Rufus popped up. Rue was determined to find all the members of the Doe family before Darwin returned when she noticed something—they all had specific notes tying them together. Some were questions like, "Where is Rufus's collar?" and "Why was Jane Doe meeting a man named Jack at the bowling alley on Sundays?" And while it was all a game to get Rue actually interested in solving the puzzle, she dove into it with all the enthusiasm of someone who once had dreams of becoming an investigative reporter.

CHAPTER 6
The Theater

Wednesday Evening at the Theater

A frantic call came in from Midge at 5:30 p.m. just as Rue was returning from her third day of training at work. Today, Rue learned how to upload and move files around, send encrypted emails and the basics of preparing legal documents should a case have to go to court. Her brain was hurting, but oddly exhilarated at the same time.

"Hey," Midge responded as soon as Rue picked up the phone. "Glad you're home. I remembered to call first, instead of just stopping by... which, apparently, you hate...you're welcome."

It took a moment for Rue to respond as she'd barely gotten her jacket off and locked her front door. She stretched the phone's cord so she could deposit a small bag of groceries on the kitchen table as she talked.

"Uh, okay. What can I do for you, Midge?" Rue asked hesitantly. "Aren't you supposed to be getting ready for your date with Mr. Fennec?"

"Mr. Fennec," Midge laughed. "Listen to you, Miss Formal. Actually, my tall drink of water cancelled on me at the last minute. I don't wanna sit in a lonely private booth all by myself, so would you be a doll and be my plus one for the evening?"

"Sure," Rue answered, confused. She seemed to remember Darwin actually leaving early to beat rush hour traffic because of his plans that evening. "That's so odd. He was talking about meeting you tonight."

"Well, he called my cell phone—something I suggest you invest in, by the way. It would be way easier to get ahold of you. Anyways, he said he started feeling off when he returned home and bailed on me. But the tickets are at the box office in my name if you wanna meet me there."

"Hmm," Rue thought. "I hope he's okay."

"So, you'll come with me?"

"Uh, sure. Why don't you meet me downstairs at 6:30 and we can take a cab together?"

"No can do," Midge answered. "Still at the library researching somethin' for work. But I can meet you at the box office at 7ish. Just grab our tickets if you get there first."

"Okay, I can do that," Rue agreed.

Rue really didn't mind. She liked the theater, though she rarely had the funds to go unless Spencer took her, which wasn't very often as Broadway "wasn't his scene."

At that moment, a siren blared outside her apartment just as the phone went dead.

"Midge?" There was nothing but a dial tone. Rue hung up the phone and then went to drag a little, black cocktail dress from her closet, the one she wore when she wasn't sure what to wear, and then sifted through a pile of shoes on the floor, pushing aside sneakers, boots, and flats and settling on a pair of one-inch beige heels, the only pair of dress shoes she actually owned.

"Eat your heart out, Gretchen Ellis," she joked to herself.

Rue reached the theater at 7:15 p.m. thanks to traffic jams and a rough time hailing a cab. She assumed Midge would have already arrived, but she was nowhere to be found. Finally, she gave Midge's name at will-call.

"Oh, yes," the woman at the will-call booth answered, passing Rue a single ticket. "A woman left a message for you." She pulled it close to her nose to read it. "Hate to do this to you, but I've decided I'm not feeling theater-y after all. Not to worry, though. I sent someone else to accompany you so you wouldn't be alone. Have fun, M."

"What the heck is she talking about?"

"Hey, don't shoot the messenger." The lady at the window raised her hands up, defensively. "I got this call a half hour ago and am just passing it on."

"But she mentioned two tickets when I spoke with her earlier," Rue clarified. "Where's the other one?"

"Sorry, I only have one ticket on file under a Midge Pasternak." The woman's eyes peered over Rue's shoulder, leaving the not-so-subtle message that there was a large line forming at will-call. "Maybe the person she was sending has it already?" she suggested.

"Thanks," Rue answered, absentmindedly accepting the ticket.

Rue had just enough time to present her ticket to the usher at the entrance, find the nearest ladies' room, grab a whiskey sour and make her way to the balcony for the show.

By then, it was nearly time for curtain call. She showed the usher her ticket stub. "Oh, wonderful," the round woman smiled pleasantly, displaying a row of uneven teeth where one was distinctly missing. She was dressed in a crisp white shirt with black pants and a suit jacket with a colorful red cravat around her neck. It was one of the few distinguishing clothing choices that set her apart from the other ushers who stuck with the basic black and white ensemble. Her hair was a peppery gray and black, combed straight to her shoulders, the ends a little split and frizzy. "You've got my favorite box." She leaned in as if telling a secret. Her breath smelled of burnt cigarettes. "The famous Ellis family, you know—B. A. Ellis Industries—has Box 12 reserved exclusively for them all year long. It's just next door. But I think Box 11 is much nicer. The view is perfect. Right through here," she lifted the red curtain separating the private box from the hallway.

Seems the Ellis family is everywhere I turn lately, Rue thought to herself.

After adjusting to the light, Rue noticed there were four padded, upright chairs in the box, unlike general theater seats where they were locked together with fold-down bottoms. The box was rather spacious with a red carpet and the railed balcony overlooked a full view of the stage from a slightly off-center angle.

It was only then that she realized that there was another person in the box, and he was already standing when she'd arrived. His expression showed that he was just as surprised as she was, and yet in some ways—not at all. He politely pulled out a chair for her, not that it needed to be pulled anywhere, and motioned toward it.

Mr. Darwin Fennec.

Midge had set them up.

CHAPTER 7
Balcony

Wednesday Evening at the Theater

~

Despite the company she had inflicted on her that evening, Rue had to admit that the show was rather remarkable: the set design, costumes, musical numbers, the dancing, the singing. Honestly, she couldn't remember the last time she had enjoyed herself this much (and she thought about this really hard, but she was at a loss for coming up with a single date between her and Spencer that was this entertaining).

Her unintended escort actually surprised her as Darwin offered her his opera glasses to get a closer look at the stage, even though he only had a single pair. Instead, they took turns handing the glasses back and forth during varied performances. He also made sure that she had an unobstructed view of the stage since she was rather short, while the balcony rail was rather high. He even asked if she were comfortable. Not used to such questions, she merely nodded awkwardly, her shoulders shrugging in an "I guess so. What does that even mean?" sort of way. She was having a difficult time separating Darwin the boss vs. Darwin the cad and Darwin the...date?

At that moment, the lead singer for the evening launched into a modern performance of the 1930's classic, "If I Didn't Care." Rue leaned forward, resting her arms on the balcony rails of the lower wall and let out a blissful sigh (which was, fortunately, muted by the sounds coming from the stage). Dressed in a red, ruffled, evening dress with a long hem and a revealing open back, the singer swayed slightly in her scarlet, slip-on high-heeled shoes while delivering her final notes from the stage below. She even did a gratuitous spin for emphasis and to show off her well-toned back muscles and arms. Her hands and forearms were adorned with black, elbow-length silk gloves.

Darwin went to hand Rue the opera glasses for her turn when he noticed how transfixed she was. Rue was almost out of her seat, pitching as far as she could without actually leaping from the balcony toward the stage. He smiled to himself. *You know,* he thought, *if she weren't so determined to be disagreeable, she might actually be a pleasant person to be around.*

Darwin had seen this show before with a different lady friend just several nights prior. Therefore, he knew, even without surveying his program, that it was near the intermission. To avoid the crowds of people in the hallway vying for bathrooms, drinks, and bar snacks, he thought he'd dart out early. "Be right back," he whispered to her, who merely nodded as if he were a fly buzzing in her ear, somewhat annoyed that he'd interrupted the song she was trying to enjoy.

Darwin disappeared behind the curtain where the usher sat at the ready by the entryway between their box and the one just next door. She leapt to her feet, shining a flashlight at the floor so he could see his way to the exit. It was too dark to see her, save for a shadowed outline and a flash of white teeth as she smiled politely at him.

Fortune was with him (or so he thought) as he was quite alone in the hallway and opted to make a beeline for the men's room first. *Good thing the ladies' room is on the other side of the corridor,* he laughed to himself, *or this hallway would be considerably more crowded right now.*

Sadly, he didn't realize the gravity of this small fact.

APPLAUSE FOLLOWED the final act of part one and the lights dramatically went out for what seemed like an unusually long time. Murmurs could be heard from the crowd. But then, just as the house lights went up again, Rue heard a loud wail coming from behind the box's curtain. Jarred, she instinctively jumped from her seat as a woman, none other than the one who had just been on stage singing her most popular aria of the evening, burst forward, lunging straight at her.

Up close, it was clear that the dress didn't fit the woman as well as it appeared from the far-away stage. She was too tall and thin, and her costume was too wide around the middle and short, with the exception of the train that dragged on the floor. Her Spanish-heeled shoes brought her height well above Rue's petite 5'3" frame. Unfortunately, that wasn't what Rue was concerned about at that very moment. As the woman sailed into the balcony rail, her heel got caught on the hem of her dress. She spun around in an attempt to free her heel from her dress, revealing a large knife protruding from her belly and dark blood soaking the front of her stomach and beginning to drip slightly down one leg.

The woman looked down in horror as if she had only just now realized that she had been stabbed. Somehow, she seemed oblivious to the pain and distracted by some other thought. She backed up toward the balcony wall.

Fearing the tall woman was about to pitch herself over the edge, Rue reached to grab her arms.

"The baby," the woman gasped, reaching toward her belly.

"No, that's not a good idea," Rue tried to warn her about pulling the knife out with no way to stop the blood.

By this time, the woman's lower back hit the rail and she was now falling backward over the ledge. Rue tried to grab a leg, the hem of the dress, anything really. But all she managed to secure was the knife. It slid out of the woman as she tumbled from the balcony. Rue watched in horror as the woman landed across several orchestra seats on the ground floor, some of which were still occupied, injuring a few theater-goers unlucky enough to be there at that exact moment.

Several patrons rushed to the aid of the theatergoers, while security guards fought through the crowds and forced everyone to move away from the fallen woman. The dead woman lay draped across the chairs, blood spilling over them. There was no question about her state of "deadness" as the guards refrained from moving the body. What they had on their hands was either an accident, a suicide, or a crime scene.

It was only when they peered upward that Rue realized that she was still holding the knife, which was, fortunately, obscured by the balcony wall. She dropped it on the floor, nervously, just as Darwin emerged from behind the curtain.

"I didn't..." Rue tried to explain.

"I know," Darwin replied, shaken. "Clarissa stumbled into me, almost knocking me over as I reached our box. She was facing away from me, so I didn't even realize..." He held his hand to his mouth, queasily, as he noticed a few droplets of blood on the balcony rail and wall.

From outside the box, Darwin and Rue could hear a commotion as loud steps thundered in their direction. It was then that they looked at each other with a sudden realization.

Darwin had been alone in the hallway, coming back from the restroom. Meanwhile, Rue had been alone in their theater box when the woman burst in. The usher was suspiciously absent, meaning that neither person had an alibi at the time the singer burst into the private box and fell clumsily to her death.

Darwin bolted toward Rue, all but knocking her into one of the chairs. "Hey," she protested.

He pulled out a handkerchief, knelt to pick up the knife from the floor and wiped the handle haphazardly, placing it back on the floor and tucking his handkerchief back into his pocket. He then stood and quickly pulled Rue into his chest, hugging her tightly.

"What the..." Rue mumbled, instinctively trying to push him away with her hands.

"Rue, you're trembling," he said, wrapping his arms around her a little tighter. "It's okay, there's nothing you could have done."

Peering past Darwin's tall frame, two armed security guards fumbled through the curtain, opening it wide to reveal a host of onlookers behind them, watching the scene with wide-eyed fascination.

Rue took the cue and wrapped her arms around his waist and crinkled her face up. She buried her face into his chest and sniffed a little, as if sobbing.

"Were the two of you the only ones here when it happened?"

"I'm afraid so," Darwin lied.

The guard looked to Rue for confirmation, who merely sniffed and nodded.

"We're going to need you to remain here until the police arrive."

"We understand," Darwin answered, calmly.

Just then, the pepper-haired usher returned, the smell of burnt menthol cigarettes wafting after her. She sucked on a mint, nervously. "What happened?" she demanded of the guards.

"Clarissa is dead," the oversized, bulky one answered with some annoyance.

"Clarissa?" The woman was taken aback. "*Our* Clarissa? What the hell was she doing up here?"

"Dying," the smaller-framed guard answered simply. "Fell over the balcony. Where have *you* been, Loralei?"

"Went out for a smoke break. The other guy was supposed to cover for me," she defended. "Highly unprofessional of him to not wait for me to return, even if we are just volunteers."

The two merely shrugged their shoulders. They hadn't seen the other man who was supposedly on duty.

"Well, don't go nowhere," the large guard commanded. "The police detective will be here any moment for questioning."

The woman took a seat, crossing her ankles and shrinking like a small child in her chair, wringing her hands nervously. "I only left for a few minutes," she sulked. "Why does stuff like this always happen to me?"

Darwin's brow furrowed a moment in disbelief before he regained composure.

Rue finally broke the embrace, pulled her face from Darwin's chest and rubbed her eyes a little harder than necessary. She peered up, red-eyed, as the police detective, several officers and a few crime scene detectives arrived on the scene.

"Police Detective Ortega," he announced, flashing his badge so fast that he almost smacked Rue in the face as she leaned in to look at it. "You two witnessed what happened here?"

"Yes," Darwin answered quickly before Rue had a chance to react. "I was just about to get my lady friend and I some drinks at intermission when a woman pushed past me and stumbled over the balcony. Rue tried to catch her but..." He ran his hands through his hair.

"Right," the detective eyed him suspiciously. "Lady friend, you say?"

"Yes," Darwin confirmed quietly. "We're friends, and as you can see, she's a lady."

The detective eyed Rue up and down with disinterest. To the officer next to him he ordered, "Clear the scene and separate the witnesses."

Rue looked up at Darwin fearfully as she was escorted in one direction, he in the other. "I'll call you later, Rue," Darwin said over his shoulder. Rue nodded.

And just like that, Darwin and Rue's lives became intertwined, both suspects in a murder, and both one another's fictitious alibi.

CHAPTER 8
Questioning

Late Wednesday Evening at the Theater

"Please, have a seat, Ms. Brennan." Police Detective Ortega motioned toward a very ordinary and uncomfortable-looking folding chair.

Ortega had taken over a small upstairs office in the opera house accessible for theater personnel only and this one was sparse, containing a table and a few folding chairs, along with a poster of last year's fall lineup of shows that was half falling off the wall. There were a few random cables on the floor in the corner and an abandoned computer monitor that probably belonged to someone who worked there a very long time ago. Obviously, this room wasn't used very often.

Rue sat across from Ortega, clutching the underside of her chair, uncomfortably.

"Want to explain to me what happened tonight?"

"Er," Rue was confused, "starting from which part?" Really it felt like a loaded question, from the part where she was getting dressed for the show, where Midge stood her up or...

"How about the part where Clarissa Sauer took a tumble off the balcony from the private booth where you were standing?" Detective Ortega interrupted her thoughts.

"Oh," Rue thought a moment. *Why was that name familiar?* It was then that she remembered something curious. Darwin said the woman's name. She replayed it in her mind. *Clarissa stumbled into me.* And then she had another thought that made the hairs on the back of her neck stand up. It was when Darwin asked her, *how good are you at keeping secrets?*

"Something the matter, Ms. Brennan?" Detective Ortega rubbed his eyes uncomfortably. He hadn't expected on working late on a Wednesday evening.

"No," she answered cautiously. "I was just so shocked when it happened that I'm trying to remember it accurately."

The detective cocked his head to one side with curiosity and waited.

She had no opportunity to compare stories with Darwin to make sure they lined up. So, she decided, she would stick to the truth...mostly...and keep it as simple as possible. It had to be something she would remember, and that Darwin would most likely say as well. She replayed his earlier statement in her head. *I was just about to get my lady friend and I some drinks at intermission when a woman pushed past me and stumbled over the balcony. Rue tried to catch her but...*

"It was intermission," Rue began. The detective leaned in with interest. "Mr. Fennec ...the man I was with...went to get us drinks when the woman who had been singing on stage a short time earlier stumbled into our box."

"And what did you do when that happened?"

"Her behavior was erratic," Rue remembered. This part was very true, and the memory disturbed her. "Her eyes were wide, and she moved so clumsily, I'm not even sure if she realized at first that she had a knife in her stomach."

"Because she'd been stabbed," Ortega finished.

"Yes," Rue answered. "I assume so. Not like someone would do that to themselves, right?" She chuckled awkwardly. She hadn't meant to, but somehow, she couldn't help it. At that moment, her brain couldn't seem to come up with the appropriate response.

Ortega did not laugh.

Rue cleared her throat. "Anyway, she fell onto the balcony rail. She was so tall," Rue paused as her face crumpled at the memory. She didn't like the memory. She wanted it to go away. "I don't know whether it was the shoes..."

"What about the shoes?" Ortega asked.

"Well," Rue was careful. "When she was onstage, I noticed that her dress seemed long and her heels ridiculously high. Seriously, I couldn't even walk in heels that high," Rue offered.

"Focus, Ms. Brennan," Ortega cautioned.

"Right," she continued. "What I mean to say is, she was so tall that when her back hit the railing, she immediately started to topple. I tried to grab her arms, but it was too late." Rue teared up, for real.

Detective Ortega paused for a ridiculously long time.

"What's your relationship to the man you were with this evening, this Darwin?"

"Oh," Rue knew this wasn't going to land well. "He's my friend..."

"And..." Ortega sensed more.

Rue sighed. "He's also my boss."

"Oh, really?" Ortega's eyebrows went up. "Do you often accompany your boss to the theater after work, reserving a private box for the two of you?"

Rue's face became flushed. *Should she tell him about Midge? No,* she thought. *Why drag her friend into this?* Still, the question made her indignant.

"Is this relevant to your investigation?" she bristled.

"I don't know," he answered, "is it?"

Rue took a deep breath and waited a beat to calm down. "No," she finally answered. "I don't believe that it is."

"Then I just have one more question for you, Ms. Brennan...for now," he couched his comment. "The knife that stabbed Clarissa Sauer was lying on the floor of your booth and not in her belly. Wanna explain to me how that happened?"

Rue turned red. She remembered Darwin wiping the fingerprints clean from the knife before the detective arrived. It was to protect her...or was it? There was no way to realistically claim the knife had "accidentally" fallen out of a woman's stomach.

"An answer, Ms. Brennan," Detective Ortega was insistent.

"Well," she answered cautiously. "As I mentioned, it all happened so fast. I reached out to grab Clarissa...as you said her name was... but I was too late. I honestly don't know if in my attempt to grab her arms, I grabbed the knife or knocked it free...somehow."

Ortega looked down at Rue's arms. "And yet," he said, "from what we can tell so far, there were no fingerprints on the weapon. And you, Ms. Brennan, do not appear to be wearing gloves."

Rue thought a moment and suddenly it hit her. "No," she answered in a measured tone. "But now that I remember, Clarissa was wearing long black gloves." She sucked in a breath. "Is it possible that in the mayhem, she panicked and pulled the knife out herself?"

"Did you actually see that, Ms. Brennan?"

Rue thought of Darwin. She had no idea what he may or may not say. So, she didn't want to begin spinning any tales. Instead, she answered, "No, I didn't. As I mentioned before, it all happened so fast."

"Care to tell me how it is you know Clarissa Sauer...knew?" Detective Ortega corrected himself. It was Astor Ellis's turn to be interviewed by Ortega after Rue had been dismissed for the evening. After all, unbeknownst to Darwin, the entire Ellis family: Byron, Astor, Gretchen and the soon-to-be wife of Astor, Portia LaMonte, sat in a private box just next door.

Astor Ellis pulled a handkerchief from his suit jacket and coughed into it, fighting off a gag reflex. Unlike his imposing father, Byron Ellis, Astor was a thin man of average height with a soft-spoken, nasally voice and a far less commanding presence than his father. At 39-years-old, he was soon to be one of the youngest men to be placed at the helm of his father's multi-million-dollar company—something which his father, 40 years his senior, was fond of pointing out.

"Well," Astor answered, hesitantly. "I didn't really know her all that well."

"But you did know her?" Ortega persisted.

"Vaguely," he answered. "Portia, my fiancé, is a true patron of the arts and often visited the Artist Atelier school to support its fundraising efforts. Clarissa, being at art model at the school, met Portia at one such event." Astor paused for Ortega to ask a question that did not come. After a moment of awkward silence, Astor somehow felt the need to fill it. "In fact, that's why we're here tonight. Clarissa mentioned to Portia that she had a lead role in the show. And since Portia and I just announced our engagement to the world, we were simply enjoying a night out as a family to celebrate while also supporting Clarissa's debut."

"I see," Ortega tapped his fingers on the table as he thought. "So, Clarissa was a model *and* an actress?"

"Apparently," Astor answered. "As I said, I really didn't know her." Astor let out another cough into his handkerchief, sniffing uncomfortably as if he'd suddenly developed an acute case of sinusitis.

"Interesting," the detective answered.

"Why is that interesting, detective?" Astor used his handkerchief to wipe his sweaty brow.

Detective Ortega retrieved a notepad from his back pocket. "We are entering a handwritten note into evidence that was found on the body of the victim." Astor coughed, placing the handkerchief over his mouth with one hand, and placing the other on his stomach to calm the queasiness. "A note that appeared to be signed by you, Mr. Ellis."

"I don't know what you're talking about, detective. A note, you say?"

"Yes, from you." Ortega eyed him suspiciously.

"Perhaps, I should refrain from saying anything further until I talk to a lawyer."

"So," Ortega conveniently ignored him. "You didn't send Clarissa Sauer a note asking her to meet you at Box 11, the one your family has exclusively reserved for the season?"

Astor sat upright in his chair with a hopeful expression across his face. "No, I did not," he answered triumphantly. "And besides, if I had written such a note—which I didn't—I most certainly wouldn't have sent her to Box 11. The family box is Box 12."

"I see," Ortega acknowledged. "And who else was accompanying you in Box 12 this evening?"

"Portia LaMonte, my fiancé, as I mentioned, my father Byron Ellis, and my mother Gretchen."

"Any chance you know the people who were occupying Box 11 tonight, a Rue Brennan and Darwin Fennec?"

Astor thought a moment before shaking his head. "No, neither of those names mean anything to me."

"All right," Ortega answered. "You're free to go...for now. But you are a person of interest. To your earlier comment about talking with your lawyer? Well, I'd say that's a very good idea. Don't leave town until further notice, Mr. Ellis. Is that clear?"

"Crystal," he answered miserably.

PORTIA LAMONTE WAS UNFLAPPABLE. Called in directly after Astor, her energy floated through the room like a calm breeze—counter to Astor's sweaty nervousness.

"I'm told that you knew Clarissa Sauer quite well," Ortega sought the woman's face for recognition. Portia was a good five inches taller than Astor and much thinner, too. Her features were narrow and sharp as if she'd stepped out of a Charles Addams cartoon.

"I wouldn't say well," Portia corrected. "But I did know her, yes."

"Was she the reason you were at the theater this evening?"

"What an odd question," Portia observed, eyeing Ortega curiously. After a long pause, she answered, "Indirectly, yes. I'm sure my fiancé told you that we are celebrating our engagement."

"Congratulations," Detective Ortega muttered gruffly.

"Yes, well, this isn't exactly how I had expected the evening to go. Very inconvenient."

"I'm sorry a woman being stabbed to death has been so inconvenient for you, Ms. LaMonte." Ortega tapped his notepad with the small ballpoint pen that he kept fighting with.

"No need to be rude," Portia retorted, nonplussed. "I'm sorry the girl is dead, but I can't say that we were friends."

"What was your relationship to the deceased?"

"As you probably know, my family has always contributed a great deal to the arts. It just so happened that I was hosting a gala at the Artist

Ateliers several months ago when Clarissa Sauer approached me about a job."

"A job?" Ortega clarified.

"Yes," Portia confirmed. "She asked me to get her an audition for this very show even though she is not a member of any actor's union and has very little theater experience to speak of."

"And what did you say?"

"Well, naturally I was eager to help a rising star."

"Naturally," Ortega was unconvinced.

"Are you always this passive-aggressive, Detective Ortega?"

"No, usually I'm just aggressive, but I've been warned that I'm too mean to witnesses and suspects. I'm trying to be better." Ortega took out a handkerchief from his jacket pocket and wiped his moist brow. The theater felt warm to him, but maybe it was the fact that he was wearing a suit. Either that or his blood pressure was up again. "Please tell me why it is you were willing to help Clarissa Sauer even though she was unqualified?"

"Well, if you had ever heard her sing, you would understand. She was quite exquisite this evening. Once I heard her voice, I was sure to introduce her to all the right connections in the industry. She became a protégé, of sorts."

"I see." Ortega paused as if weighing the next question in his mind. "Any idea who might have been an enemy of this protégé of yours?" He eyed her suspiciously. After all, he may not have known Ms. LaMonte very well, but her fiancé's wandering eye was pretty common knowledge in the tabloids.

"No idea," she answered simply.

It didn't take long for Detective Ortega to understand how it was that Astor Ellis came to become engaged to Portia LaMonte. Money and connections aside, she was eerily like her future mother-in-law, Gretchen Ellis. The older woman may have been slightly heavier with cheeks that were unnaturally stretched through cosmetic surgery, but they each looked down their nose at the world in the exact same way.

"How long is this going to take, Detective Ortega?" Gretchen Ellis complained. "As you can see, I'm not a young woman and I am very tired this evening."

"Yes, I can see that," Ortega answered in a deadpan expression. Gretchen shot him a disapproving look. Usually, that was someone's cue to tell her how fabulous she looked, not a day over 40 (She was 67). Then she noticed Ortega biting back a smirk and realized he had set her up for a reaction. She crossed her arms over her already crossed legs and leaned forward, waiting for him to stop sniggering and ask her a question.

"Did you know the woman who fell over the balcony to her death this evening?"

"Vaguely," she pursed her lips.

"How so?" he pressed her for an answer.

"I met her briefly at my future daughter-in-law's charity event at the art school some months ago, a detail I forgot until Portia reminded me that she was performing this evening."

"So, you met her, but she wasn't very memorable," Ortega confirmed.

"I meet a lot of people, detective," Gretchen Ellis sighed. "And most are quite forgettable."

"You didn't share Ms. LaMonte's appreciation of her singing?"

"I wasn't aware of such an appreciation, nor had I ever heard the girl sing before this evening."

"And what did you think?"

"Of what?"

"Of her singing."

"Is this relevant to your investigation, detective?"

"I'll ask the questions, if you don't mind, Mrs. Ellis."

"Fine, if you must know, I didn't think all that much of her performance...not enough to kill her, if that's where you're going with this," she chuckled.

Ortega didn't laugh.

"Just one more question, Mrs. Ellis," Detective Ortega leaned in from his chair, placing his elbows on the table that sat between them. "I don't suppose you know the couple in the next box over? A Ms. Rue Brennan and a Mr. Darwin Fennec?" Gretchen Ellis sucked in her breath. "I can tell from your expression that you do."

Gretchen Ellis said nothing. Unlike Portia LaMonte, Gretchen Ellis was very flappable.

"I want my lawyer present before I answer any more of your questions, Detective Ortega," her face became flushed.

"I think that's a very good idea, Mrs. Ellis."

CHAPTER 9
Breaking the Silence

Late Wednesday Evening in a Taxi

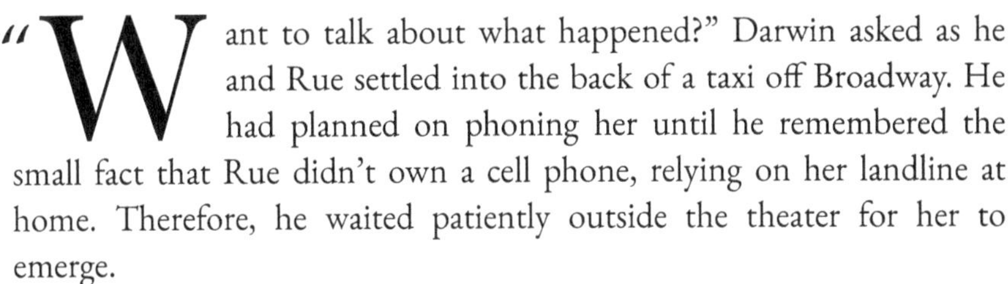

"Want to talk about what happened?" Darwin asked as he and Rue settled into the back of a taxi off Broadway. He had planned on phoning her until he remembered the small fact that Rue didn't own a cell phone, relying on her landline at home. Therefore, he waited patiently outside the theater for her to emerge.

"Not really," Rue confessed, "but I guess we should." Rue was exhausted and her head was pounding.

"Perhaps, I could tell you what I saw and what I shared with Detective Ortega?" Darwin glanced at the driver in the front seat. He was playing what sounded like Bollywood music and clearly not paying attention to their conversation, which was just as well.

"Please do," Rue wrapped her arms around herself in a comforting hug. "Because I had no idea what to say...or not say. I felt guilty even though I don't think I did anything wrong." She thought about this for a moment. "Except for pulling the knife out of her stomach, of course."

The taxi driver glanced up, momentarily.

"D&D role-playing game," Darwin explained to the driver. "We were at a throwback party."

The driver merely nodded and turned his music up a little louder. He had no idea what a 'throwback party' was, but he was fairly confident that he didn't care.

Darwin leaned a little closer to Rue, speaking in a hushed voice. She got a momentary chill. Something about his nearness made her edgy, though she couldn't figure out exactly why. "That was an accident," he reassured her. "Besides, by the way she went over that balcony, she would have broken her neck, regardless."

The driver furrowed his eyebrows but kept his eyes on the road.

"Perhaps we should talk at my place," Rue suggested, "since you insisted on dropping me off first, anyway?" Darwin was in midtown, Rue near the Bowery. It didn't make sense for Darwin to travel all that way only to have the taxi circle back to his home, but he insisted.

He nodded, eyeing the driver. "That's probably a good idea."

Rue wasn't sure if Midge would make one of her unwelcome appearances outside her window and she wasn't up for explaining what happened to her "not really feeling like the theater" friend that evening. Rue figured she'd fill her in the morning. Once Darwin was inside the tiny studio, she quickly drew the pillowcases functioning as curtains.

Darwin raised an eyebrow, curiously.

"Midge," she explained. "She has a bad habit of always showing up via the fire escape."

"Why does that not surprise me?" Darwin commented. He glanced around the tiny apartment. From his estimation, her entire apartment could fit in his living room. His condo was about three times the size which wasn't saying much in Manhattan as rent-controlled apartments, and more inhabitants to habitats, meant that everything was overpriced and underwhelmingly small.

"I know what you're thinking," Rue sighed. "I'm such a loser for living in such a tiny hovel...at my age. This is the apartment for a college student, right? Clearly, I'm not living up to my potential."

"I wasn't thinking that at all," Darwin eyed her, quizzically. "I know little about you, Ms. Brennan, but something about you tells me you're a go-getter. There's nothing wrong with where you live, though I do sense this is a stepping-stone to something more to your liking."

Rue wasn't sure what to make of this as Spencer always had less than kind things to say about her studio.

"Want something to drink?" she asked, opening her refrigerator. "I've got filtered water and..." She glanced at the leftover wine that Midge had bought her for her birthday, but since Spencer also had a thing or two to say about that, she didn't mention it. "So, I've got water," she finished, letting out a disappointed sigh. Had she not drunk all of the juice Midge brought, she could have at least offered that.

"I'm fine," Darwin answered. "Perhaps we could just sit and talk?" He motioned to the kitchen table. Rue set her purse down, wrapping her evening jacket around the back of her chair and sat. Darwin took the chair opposite her, closest to the door.

While Rue was convinced that Darwin was a womanizer, she had to admit that his presence was somehow comforting. She felt safe around him. That only served to annoy her. *After all*, she thought momentarily to herself, *what's wrong with me that I'm not worth hitting on?* She pushed that out of her mind, clearly, not a priority this evening.

"Someone bumped into me briefly before I returned to our box," Darwin finally shared. "A moment later, I saw Clarissa Sauer stumbling through the curtain heading toward you. By the time I got there, you were trying to stop her from going over the ledge."

"But you didn't tell the police that, did you?"

"Of course not," he admitted. "How could I? Then both of us would be suspects, or at least accomplices...one of us doing the stabbing, the other doing the pushing."

"How do I know *you* didn't stab her, Mr. Fennec?" Rue asked, candidly. She didn't really believe that, or else she wouldn't have invited him up to her apartment in the first place.

"If I did," he replied, "which I didn't, of course, why would I have gone through great pains to wipe the knife down so your fingerprints weren't on it?"

"Because if you stabbed her, your fingerprints would have been on it," she reasoned. "Maybe you were just covering up for yourself."

"Is that what you really think, Ms. Brennan?"

Rue thought a moment, "No, but if you had told the detective the truth, you would have sooner been a suspect than me."

"Would you like me to call him up and set the record straight?" Darwin offered.

After what seemed like an eternity, Rue answered, "No. At this point, it will just make matters worse. They'll still wonder how I came to pull the knife out of her and how she managed to take a topple over the ledge while I was standing right there."

"Agreed. And for the record, had I not wiped the knife clean, your prints would have been on them, possibly connecting you with the killing."

"And so would the killer's prints," Rue reasoned.

"Pardon me for saying so," Darwin offered, "but I suspect killers are better at this than we are. I'm pretty sure they would have been wearing gloves."

"Hmm," Rue thought.

"What is it?" Darwin asked.

"It just has me curious if the police stumbled upon anyone with blood-stained gloves this evening...or anywhere on their clothing, for that matter."

"If they did, I doubt they'd share it with us."

"Why not? You are an investigator, after all," Rue pointed out.

"Yes, but I'm also a person of interest. I don't think Detective Ortega has any intention of enlisting my services."

Rue nodded. For the next half hour, they clarified their stories. Fortunately, they were largely similar and equally cryptic.

"Just one more thing," Rue asked, "how did you know Clarissa Sauer?"

Darwin let out a sigh. "Well, I was planning on getting you a little further along in your training, but..." He paused for a moment. "Remember Gretchen Ellis's visit on your first day?"

"Yeah?" Rue nodded.

"She hired me...well, us...to look into her son's extracurricular activities."

"Clarissa Sauer being one of them?"

"Exactly. And a woman named Emma Post."

"Emma?" Rue was surprised.

"You know her?"

"Only in passing. She's another model at the Atelier. Don't think I've said more than three words to her over the past year."

"Well, according to Gretchen Ellis, both were pregnant with Astor's baby."

"Oh!" Rue sat upright.

"What is it?" Darwin was concerned.

"I forgot all about it under the stress of this evening. But the only thing Clarissa said to me when she came flying into the box was 'the baby.' I didn't realize it at the time, but she must have been worried about her unborn child—hence why she was trying to remove the knife right away instead of waiting for help.

"Did you happen to tell that to Ortega?" Darwin asked.

"No, it completely slipped my mind. Do you think I should have?" Rue was concerned.

"No, because I spent the better part of the evening trying to pretend I was with you at the time of the murder. Had you said that it would have made it quite evident that I wasn't in the box at the time."

Rue thought a moment. "So, Astor knocked up two women while being engaged to someone else...nice."

"Only his mother seems to think that's impossible. It seems that Astor cannot have children."

"Then who do you think the father, or fathers, are?"

"No idea," Darwin confessed. "Hmmm, Clarissa Sauer and Emma Post...one singer and one figure model. You've never crossed paths with Astor Ellis, have you?"

"Never met the man," Rue shook her head. "I've heard of his name, along with his fiancé, Portia, in art circles. And I know Spencer used to be friends with him before their falling out several years ago, but that's about all."

"Do you know what the falling out was about?" Darwin asked.

"Spencer hasn't told me much, honestly. Heck, you probably know more than I do," Rue paused to gauge Darwin's reaction...there wasn't one. "I only know it had something to do with intellectual property."

"Strange that the very people we're investigating happened to be in the next box over during a murder."

"Strange, indeed."

THE NEXT MORNING, the New York Times had a front-page story about the murder. It read, "Pregnant Diva Dies at Theater after Falling from Balcony." Unfortunately, not only was the Ellis family and Portia LaMonte named in the article, but so were she and Darwin. Fortunately, however, Spencer Hargrove's name wasn't linked to the event at all, which Rue thought would have been bad for SpencerTech. "Thank goodness for that," she said to herself, breathing a sigh of relief as she finished her morning tea before heading into the office.

CHAPTER 10
Searching for Clues

Thursday Morning at the Theater

~

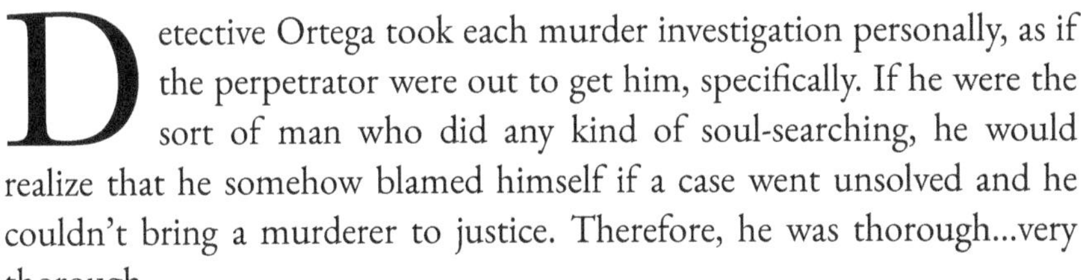

Detective Ortega took each murder investigation personally, as if the perpetrator were out to get him, specifically. If he were the sort of man who did any kind of soul-searching, he would realize that he somehow blamed himself if a case went unsolved and he couldn't bring a murderer to justice. Therefore, he was thorough...very thorough.

"Detective Ortega," the lead forensic scientist on the case called as soon as he'd reached the crime scene at the theater that morning.

"Good morning, Penelope," Ortega greeted, walking over to where another officer was taking photos of what appeared to be a large footprint on a chair.

No one questioned the impropriety of him referring to Dr. Penelope Washburn by her first name. If they had a shared history, no one else knew about it. And since Detective Ortega had been happily married for more than a decade now, no one asked.

"What have you found?" Ortega asked, peering at the chair. Penelope was considerably taller than the short and round detective. She reached over his shoulder and pointed.

"You see this very large dusty footprint on the chair?"

"Clearly," he replied, staring at the soot-covered plush chair, now adorned with a very obvious boot print.

"Well, first it seemed odd that someone would be standing on a chair in the theater at all."

"Perhaps they were short and needed to reach something overhead." Penelope waited for Ortega to look up toward the ceiling and realize that there was nothing to reach for. "Moved from another location?" he offered.

"Doubtful," she answered. "This chair hasn't been touched since last night. This was the same chair the usher sat in when working."

"You'd think she would have noticed the dirty chair and brushed it off," Ortega reasoned.

"Exactly," Penelope answered. "Which makes me think it was left after she went to take her little smoke break."

"So, you think this was left by Clarissa Sauer's killer?"

"It's a stretch, but a possibility."

"Why would her killer stand on a chair to deliver a knife wound to the woman's stomach? Seems impractical?"

A couple feet from where they stood a few officers listened in on the conversation. A rookie whispered to Officer Dennis, "How'd he get to be head detective? He's as dumb as a rock."

Officer Dennis was offended on his supervisor's behalf. "He most certainly is not," he defended. "It's part of their process."

"Process?"

"Yes," he explained. "One person shares the clues they found while the other asks the most basic questions that no expert would think to ask."

"Why?" the rookie wanted to know.

"Because according to Detective Ortega, sometimes the experts get so tangled in the overcomplicated clues, that they miss the obvious."

The rookie looked at Ortega with new appreciation. "Fascinating." The two watched the continued exchange between Penelope and Detective Ortega.

"Here's the thing," she offered. "Look at the mild indentation on the chair. The weight doesn't match the shoe size. It's as if—"

Detective Ortega's eyes lit up. "The person was wearing shoes far too large for them."

"Exactly," she nodded. "Maybe a men's size nine or nine-and-a-half. And according to the coroner, the knife wound in her belly matched someone tall."

"Tall," he answered, "or, standing on a chair."

"Why would the killer want to stand on a chair to stab our victim?" Now it was Penelope's turn to play the dolt.

"To frame someone else," Ortega concluded.

"If I had to guess based on the footprint alone, the person wearing this shoe was either a woman or possibly a man with very small feet."

"Realistically?" Ortega asked.

"I would have thought a woman, except—"

"Except that the usher, Loralei, mentioned a man who stood in for her while she went for a smoke," Ortega finished. Turning to Officer Dennis, he said, "Did she give a description of the man in her statement?"

Officer Dennis tapped the rookie's shoulder who handed over the appropriate folder from the heavy stack he'd been holding for a very long time. The rookie struggled not to drop the lot of them. Officer Dennis groaned as he prevented the stacks of folders from falling to the floor. "Careful, man!" Dennis complained. Officer Dennis was annoyed by the fact that he always seemed to get saddled with the newbies. To Detective Ortega, he said, "Nah, Loralei complained that she was having a nic fit and was getting the shakes. The only thing she clearly remembers was that he was wearing a red cravat, like her, which she thought was odd. She considered it her 'signature style'," Dennis added with air quotes. "And..."

"Yes?"

"He seemed to have a loud shuffle to his feet."

Detective Ortega and Penelope looked at one another. "From someone wearing shoes at least two sizes too big," Ortega's eyes lit up at the realization. "And clearly the person who stepped in knew about Loralei's style choice."

"Assuming Loralei is telling the truth," the rookie called over Officer Dennis's shoulder.

Detective Ortega eyed the young man who seemed to shrink behind officer Dennis from drawing attention to himself.

"What's your name, son?" Ortega asked.

"Ernest," he answered, shyly.

"Ernie," Ortega replied, automatically shortening the man's name, "what makes you think she was lying?"

"Just a thought," he answered sheepishly. "It was stupid."

Officer Dennis nodded in agreement.

"No," Detective Ortega answered. "It's not. Officer Dennis, do we have confirmation that anyone saw Loralei Stephens leave for her smoke break?"

"There were at least three other actors who confirmed they snuck out for a smoke and saw her outside." Officer Dennis glared at Ernest, annoyed.

"That's okay, son," Detective Ortega eyed Ernest. "It's good to question everything and explore all possible scenarios."

Ernest lifted his chest with pride and then immediately dropped it. He now regretted having called his boss *dumb as a rock. In fact*, he thought to himself, *perhaps that's why Officer Dennis was so impatient with him now.* It became clear that while Detective Ortega appeared a little rough around the edges, most everyone working with him held him in high regard. Ernest vowed to do better going forward.

"And what about the single witness to the crime...Ursula Gorky?" Ortega asked.

Officer Ernest shuffled through his notes. "When we interviewed her, she claimed to have only seen Rue Brennan on the balcony when Clarissa Sauer toppled over the ledge," he announced. "She was in the booth on the opposite end of the theater, waiting for her part in the show."

"She had a part from the balcony?" Ortega was confused.

"Yeah," Officer Ernest confirmed. "Kind of a kitschy thing theaters are doing these days. There was going to be a scene where she started singing from off stage. Only, Clarissa was murdered before Gorky's big number. She was so excited about her part that she always sat through the intermission just to make sure she didn't miss her grand entrance."

"So where does that leave Darwin Fennec?" Ortega wondered aloud. "Says he was in the booth the whole time, but Gorky says he wasn't."

"Could he be the killer?" Officer Dennis asked.

"Except that it seems the killer may have been short, trying to pretend they were tall," Penelope added. "Darwin Fennec has got to be almost six feet tall."

"Fennec also said he's never met the victim," Ortega offered. "But Astor Ellis, in the next booth over, had. In fact, he's the one named in the note Clarissa received."

"And," Ernest chimed in, now eager to be useful. He shifted the heavy stack he was holding to his other arm. "I read through all of these reports. There's a good chance the killer accidentally sent Clarissa to the wrong booth. Maybe Astor was the one being framed? Perhaps the note wasn't sent by him at all."

"Nah, that doesn't add up," Ortega shook his head. "Astor's too short compared to the height the imposter was obviously going for."

"But both Portia LaMonte and Gretchen Ellis, on the other hand..." Ernest offered.

"Both taller than Astor Ellis and his father, Byron," Officer Dennis confirmed, looking at the reports before giving a nod to Ernest. "Not bad, rookie," Officer Dennis admitted.

"Hypothetical wrench in the works," Penelope chimed in. "At this point, we're assuming Astor Ellis did not write the note and we're assuming that someone was trying to frame one of these two women, or at least someone tall. And we're also assuming that Clarissa ended up in the wrong booth."

"Lot of assumptions," Ortega admitted.

"Any chance it could simply be that one of the Ellis men did it and stood on a chair to throw suspicion off of them."

"No," Officer Dennis shook his head. "I don't think so. Of the fourteen ushers on duty that night, one is unaccounted for."

"Oh?" Ortega raised an eyebrow.

"Fourteen ushers reported for duty that night. But a fifteenth stood in for Loralei. No one saw that usher during the show, except for Loralei. But they all confirmed seeing Loralei out having a smoke during the break."

Detective Ortega rubbed his forehead. "This is a needle in a haystack search. There had to be more than 1800 people in the theater that night."

"Yes," Ernest confirmed, "1500 theater goers, 14 ushers, 45 staff members and 37 members of the cast and crew."

Detective Ortega noticed that Ernest was not referring to a single document that he was holding. "How is it that you remember all that, Ernie?" he wanted to know.

"Well," Ernest answered. "I did say that I read all the reports...three times, if I'm being honest. And, I guess I just have a head for numbers."

"Any chance someone on staff or the theater troupe had a chance to change out of costume and then return without being noticed?" Officer Dennis stepped in front of Ernie, upstaging him so that he was now blocked from making eye contact with Detective Ortega. *After all*, he reasoned to himself, *he's making me look bad.*

"Doubtful," Ernest answered, peering around Officer Dennis. "The lights went up at precisely 9:13 p.m. Clarissa fell over the balcony just after the lights were turned on, and by 9:17 p.m., the security guards were alerted, and the theater was on lockdown.

Penelope held her camera at her hip as she gazed out one of the long windows outside of the private theater box. She had a clear view of the street below. It was bustling with lots of small alleyways and clusters of people vying for space on the sidewalk. Several pedestrians darted between cars on the main stretch as they honked, annoyed at pedestrians not using the crosswalks. She then lifted her chin to look to her right, spotting a clearly marked "exit" door.

"What is it, Penelope?" Detective Ortega asked.

"Do we know what time the main doors would have opened to the outside for intermission?" she asked. "You'd think they would open them just beforehand in anticipation of some theater goers wanting to step outside during the break."

"Don't know," Ernest offered, "but I'll bet we could find out."

"What are you thinking?" Ortega pressed her.

"Well, there wasn't really time for someone to change out of their costume or suit, commit a crime and then change back in time, no matter how fast the transition. But..."

"Yes?" Ortega's eyes grew wider.

"During an intermission, who really cares who comes and goes? I mean, really, who's going to try and sneak into a theater halfway through a performance? What if the killer snuck in during intermission, already dressed as an usher? No one would think anything of it."

"And," Officer Dennis caught on, "they could have slipped out the exit just after the crime, before the theater was locked down."

"Exactly," Penelope nodded.

"All right," Detective Ortega announced. "Officer Dennis, see if you can find out when the doors were opened for intermission and if anyone spotted an usher coming in just before the break. In the meantime, let's pause for lunch."

"C'mon, rookie," Officer Dennis poked Ernest in the arm. "Wanna hit the deli on the corner with me? They make a mean Reuben sandwich." Officer Dennis wasn't often gracious, but he realized that Ernest might actually turn out to be useful for the team. And, if he was staying, it's best if they got along.

"Sure," Ernest agreed. "But can we lock these in the squad car first? My arms are killing me."

"Here," Officer Dennis finally intervened. "Give me those. We can drop them off for sure."

"Not that way!" Ortega stopped them at the exit. "We still need to sweep that for clues. Penelope and I will block it off before we break, but I don't need either of you accidentally mucking up the crime scene."

Dennis and Ernest rolled their eyes at one another and grinned, but they were smart enough not to say anything. They retreated toward the carpeted theater steps leading to the main entrance.

"What'll you say, Penelope? Join an old friend for lunch?"

"I suppose," she answered, packing up her camera and boxes marked for evidence. "Let's drop these off at the precinct first."

"Here, let me." Ortega picked up one box while she slung her camera bag over her shoulder and grabbed the other. Detective Ortega let out a sigh. "I'm getting too old for this shit," he muttered.

"Who are you kidding?" Dr. Penelope Washburn teased. "You *live* for this shit."

CHAPTER 11
Artful Dodging

Thursday Morning in Battery Park

The reporters were already surrounding the office of Darwin Fennec, cyber forensic consultant and private investigator, when Rue arrived Thursday morning for work.

"Rue Brennan?" A woman from the local news shoved a microphone in her face while several other competing stations surrounded her and did the same. It was only then that Rue discovered that she was highly claustrophobic and struggled to catch her breath. She could feel her heart racing.

Rue regretted wearing a very bold patchwork, multi-patterned jacket as she realized she stood out like a sore thumb.

"Yes," she answered instinctively. "I mean, no," she countered. "Please, let me through. I'll be late for work." She pushed her way past them while photographers flashed cameras in her face.

"Did you know the woman who fell to her death at the theater last night?" one reporter asked.

"If you didn't kill her, who do you think did it?" asked another.

And then the most dreaded question of all, "We heard a rumor that you're dating your boss, Darwin Fennec. Can you confirm that for us?"

"No," Rue answered, annoyed.

"No, you're not. Or, no you can't confirm it?" the reporter persisted.

"No, I'm not dating Mr. Fennec."

"Then why were you at the theater with him last night?"

"What, I—?" How was Rue to explain that she ended up on a date with Darwin by accident. She suspected the story would have gotten twisted somehow, anyway. Once again, she thought of Midge. *No sense bringing her into this,* she reasoned.

Just then, the door to Darwin's office swung open, briefly. An arm grabbed her, pulling her inside. Darwin slammed the door shut and drew the blinds on a photographer who was snapping photos of them from the outside window.

"Good morning, Mr. Fennec," Rue caught her breath. Somehow, that was the only thing she could think of to say.

Darwin smirked and furrowed his brows at her, quizzically. "Good morning, Ms. Brennan. How are you this fine morning?"

Outside, the reporters pounded on the door and screamed as if they could be understood from the other side of the wall. The desk phone began ringing incessantly. Somehow, it sounded even louder than usual, each ring followed by an odd buzzing.

Darwin just realized something and motioned for Rue to keep talking.

"Oh, fine, thank you, Mr. Fennec. And you?"

"Just lovely. I decided to take in a show."

"Really?" Rue played along. "And how was it?" He unscrewed the receiver and transmitter on the phone and frowned...nothing.

"Absolutely delightful, until about halfway through, when the lead performer fell from the balcony."

Darwin flipped the phone over. *Sloppy work, if you ask me,* he thought, as he pulled back a small piece of black electrical tape holding a tiny microphone. He pinched the microphone between his thumb and forefinger. *Police issue,* he realized.

"Why, that sounds dreadful, Mr. Fennec."

"Believe me, it was."

Darwin removed his shoe, placed the bug on the table and smashed his heel over it so hard the table shook, and Rue jumped at the sound.

"Sorry," Darwin apologized, placing a finger over his lips.

Rue fell silent.

Darwin did a cursory search of the rest of the desk, but knew a thorough check would take more time than they had.

Outside, reporters grew restless, and the sound of voices grew louder. More people were arriving. One turned on a boom box and faced the speaker at the window. It was a heavy metal song Rue didn't recognize. They turned the volume up.

Are they trying to force us out, with...noise? Rue wondered.

Darwin reached in his pocket and pulled out what Rue could only assume was a portable phone as he punched the keypad on it and held it to his right ear. He pushed his forefinger in his left ear to muffle the sounds from outside.

"Yes, I'd like to order two pizzas to be delivered to the fox hole...the under fifteen minutes or it's free deal. Yes, swiftly." He held a button down on the keypad and slipped it back into his pocket.

Rue shrugged her shoulders, questioningly. Darwin didn't even try to explain. Instead, he reached into a desk drawer and pulled out two sets of ear plugs, handing Rue a pair.

Exactly how often does this happen? Rue wondered, accepting the foam plugs and pushing one in each of her ears. Unfortunately, they didn't help much.

Moments later, a car horn could be heard from outside, honking in a very distinct pattern...long, long, short...pause...short, short. Long, long, short...pause...short, short.

"Time to go," Darwin yelled. "Keep your head down."

As soon as he opened the door, they were flanked by two very tall, very large and intimidating men. One took Rue's arm, the other Darwin's, as they were escorted to a black stretch limousine with its emergency lights on, blocking a one-lane road in the alley between Darwin's office and an accounting firm. The guard gently, but with considerable pressure, pushed Rue's head down as she climbed into the passenger seat. Darwin jumped in the opposite side. Then, the men merely turned their backs on them, standing at the trunk-end of the limo with arms crossed as a barrier to the vehicle.

A single photographer had figured out the arrangement and stood defiantly in front of the limo, snapping photos at the driver.

The driver seemed nonplussed. Instead, he darted out of the driver's seat with the swiftness of a fox, grabbed the man's camera, holding it over his head with one long arm. With the other, he pushed into the man's chest, holding him at arm's length. "What's more important to ya," the driver asked the photographer, "the camera, or your life?"

The photographer grew wide-eyed. "You wouldn't," he dared.

The driver grinned. "Nah, I know how crappy a photo-journalist's salary is," he laughed. "But I'm gonna need the film." With that, he tugged the back of the camera open and pulled out the reel.

The photographer let out a few expletives.

The driver handed him back the camera. "You have 15 seconds to clear out so I can leave."

"I'm not going anywhere," the reporter grabbed his camera, standing disobediently a few paces in front of the limo.

"Suit yourself," the driver crinkled his lips and hopped back into the vehicle, slamming the door behind him. He revved the engine and put one foot on the break and one on the gas. The limo squealed mournfully as the now terrified photojournalist jumped to one side. The driver wasted no more time as he removed his foot from the brake and the limousine lurched forward and then sped through the alley to the street on the opposite side.

It wasn't until they were halfway through the Lincoln Tunnel that anyone spoke. "You guys okay back there?" the driver asked.

It was only then that Rue caught a glimpse of their rescuer. He had round cheeks in an otherwise long face, an olive complexion, and a five o'clock shadow around his chin and lips. He wore a plaid cabby cap with bits of a dark brown hair creeping out from underneath it.

"We're fine, Bristol, thank you." The driver nodded. "May I introduce you to my new assistant, Ms. Rue Brennan?"

"Nice to meetcha," Bristol nodded, eyeing Rue curiously through the rearview mirror. Before Rue could answer, he added, "What happened to Ashley?"

The pit of Rue's stomach gave a small, bitter lurch.

"Leave of absence," Darwin answered, simply.

Bristol merely nodded and kept driving. It wasn't until about thirty minutes later that he announced, "We'll switch cars once we reach Hoboken and circle back to the fox den."

"Excellent," Darwin answered. "Thank you, Bristol. It's nice to know that even when we lose touch for a few months, I can always count on you."

"Sure thing, Finn," Bristol answered. "You know I've always got your back."

Rue looked at Darwin, questioningly. "We need to relocate," Darwin read her expression. "I'll explain later. But don't worry, Ms. Brennan. You're in safe hands."

THE "FOX DEN," Rue would come to learn was Darwin's one-bedroom condo in midtown, while the "fox hole" was the office. By Manhattan standards, the condo was spacious with a large, three-paned window overlooking the city with a faux brick wall on one side and a pale gray wall on the other. If Rue had to guess, the entire space was likely around 900 square feet or so. There was a clearly defined office area with one desk flush against the window, providing the best view overlooking the city, and a second desk against the brick wall. When facing away from the office, Rue observed what she assumed was the living room. It had a plush, black, wrap-around couch and small glass coffee table facing the back wall where a large TV screen was mounted to the wall. It was the largest and flattest TV Rue had ever seen outside of a movie theater and Rue thought it remarkable that anyone could have a mini-movie theater in their own home.

Next to the office area was an efficiency kitchen with a small table and two chairs beside a tiny window. Adjacent to that, was the entryway to what Rue assumed was Darwin's bedroom.

"Sorry about today," Darwin apologized, "but given our perceived involvement in Clarissa Sauer's death and the uncomfortable reality that everyone is going to make lots of assumptions about a detective dating his assistant—"

"We're not dating," Rue jumped in.

"Clearly not," Darwin cleared his throat, "but that's what everyone will infer given our appearance at the theater."

Rue let out a sigh. *Damn it, Midge! Why couldn't you have just met Darwin at the show like you were supposed to?"* She brushed the thought aside. After all, that would have meant that Midge might have been in her place when all this happened instead of Rue. She felt guilty for even having had the thought as she sensed the next few weeks of investigations and interrogations were not going to be pleasant.

"So, what do we do now?" Rue asked.

"Well," Darwin sighed. "If you are amenable to it, I suggest we work from here for the time being, just until the case is solved, and the reporter intrigue dies down a bit."

"You want me to work in your apartment?"

"Condo, actually," Darwin corrected her. "But, why not? It's a little further for you to get to work, but the view is nice, and I can convince the building manager to let us use the service entrance, so it'll be easier for us to come and go undetected."

"But," Rue paused, "you *live* here."

"I am aware of that, yes."

"Won't that just feed into people's perception that a boss is dating his assistant if and when they find out?"

"We can't go back to the office, at least not right now. Between the cops bugging the place and reporters surrounding it, we have no hope of solving Spencer's security leak or the status of Astor Ellis's romantic liaisons for Gretchen. Furthermore, we won't get a moment of peace until Detective Ortega discovers who really murdered Clarissa Sauer."

Rue wasn't sure what to make of this suggestion. After all, she had her own thoughts about Darwin and none of them were particularly flattering.

"I suppose it's fine, but what do we do after hours? I mean, do you think the press will be hanging outside my apartment?"

"Probably," Darwin admitted, pointing to the ground level of the building, seven floors below. There was a small gathering of reporters, photographers, and a camera crew (not much more than action-figure sized at this distance) at the front entrance with the doorman, who was holding them at bay.

"Shit," Rue cursed under her breath. "Can I borrow your phone for a minute to call Spencer? I haven't even filled him in on what's happening yet."

"Sure," Darwin reached into his desk drawer and pulled out one of several burner phones.

"Why do you have so many cellular phones?" Rue asked.

"Security," he answered simply. "I'll explain later." Spencer handed one to her. "Just keep it short. Minutes are expensive and the longer the call, the easier it is to trace."

Rue accepted the phone, staring at it for a moment.

"Is there a problem?" Darwin asked.

"Just never used one before, is all." Rue, quite logically, found the "on" button. And, after a moment, figured out how to make a call. Meanwhile, Darwin disappeared into the bedroom and closed the door, taking another phone with him, presumably to make a call of his own.

Spencer picked up on the third ring, as usual.

"It's me, Spencer," Rue announced.

"Rue? Where have you been? I've been trying to phone you all morning. I even stopped by your place and witnessed a few reporters mulling about. Are you okay?"

"Hmmm," she answered. "Don't remember seeing anyone when I left. They probably only just now figured out where I live."

"What's going on?" Spencer demanded.

"I was at the theater last night and witnessed a murder. And," she paused a moment, "there's a good chance that I'm a suspect."

"What?"

"Listen, I can't talk for long. I just need to stay at your place for a couple days until reporters lose interest."

"Oh," Spencer answered quietly. Rue heard a shuffling sound as if he were shifting papers around.

"Don't sound so thrilled, Spencer," Rue answered flatly. "The truth is, very few people seem to be aware that I'm your girlfriend. It's the best option until this blows over."

"Well, okay," Spencer relented. "I suppose a couple of days will be okay."

"Thanks for making me feel so...welcome." And there it was, that gnawing in Rue's belly. It was the one that told her something was not quite right.

"It's not that, darling," Spencer answered quickly. "It's just that I'm so focused on work right now, that I don't want you to feel...lonely, is all."

"Don't worry, Spencer," Rue read between the lines. "I promise not to distract you from your precious work. I can feel equally lonely in your place as in mine."

"Well, now you're just being snarky."

"Whatever," Rue answered curtly. "Listen, I've got to go. See you tonight."

"Uh, okay. Just phone me when you're heading over. So, I can be prepared."

Prepared for what? Rue wondered. "Sure," she answered finally. "Phone you when I'm off work."

Rue hung up the phone just as Darwin re-emerged from the bedroom. He eyed Rue's expression, curiously. "Everything okay?" he asked.

"Just peachy," she forced a smile. "I'll just be staying with Spencer for a couple of days until all this blows over. I already have a few changes of clothes over there, so it shouldn't be a problem."

Darwin cleared his throat uncomfortably and nodded. Despite his keen awareness that Rue was Spencer's girlfriend, somehow hearing about the fact that she had clothes over at his place bothered him. He pushed those feelings aside.

He smiled at Rue. "Let's get back to your training, shall we?"

CHAPTER 12
The View

Saturday Evening at a Restaurant in Manhattan

"A little late, but hopefully worth the wait," Spencer held up a glass of champagne. "Here's to you, darling."

Tonight was her last evening at Spencer's place, since it seemed the press had stopped dropping by her downtown apartment. A fact that she confirmed with her at-home watch dog, Midge. Darwin's office, on the other hand, was still abuzz.

Rue blushed a little and raised her glass in return and clinked the edge of it to his before taking a sip.

"Veuve de Clicquot," he explained. "I hope you like it."

Just then, the waiter stopped by their table. "Nice to see you again, sir," he greeted Spencer.

Spencer shook his head. "You must be mistaking me for someone else," he replied carefully. "This is the first time my girlfriend and I have been here."

The waiter coughed awkwardly, embarrassed by his error. "My mistake," he smiled at Rue in a very practiced way. "Well then, welcome to

The View. The rooftop revolves every hour giving you the most spectacular view of Times Square. I'm your host, Andre." Andre was very polished, wearing a crisp, white dress shirt and black pants with matching vest and a starched service towel hanging over his arm. "I see that our sommelier has already brought you champagne. For the lady," he offered Rue a menu. "And for the gentleman," he handed Spencer the other.

"Uh, thank you," Rue answered glancing at the menu that was handed to her.

"I'll give you a few moments to look it over and will be back to answer any questions you may have and take your order." With that, Andre tiptoed away with the stealth of a silent ninja.

"Spencer," Rue leaned in and whispered after glancing at the menu. "There are no prices listed. Are you sure you can afford this?"

Spencer leaned in and touched her hand. "Relax, Rue. And don't worry. I'm not exactly poor, you know. And once SpencerTech rolls out its latest digital animation software in a few months, we'll be eating caviar for breakfast, lobster for lunch, and bluefin tuna for dinner."

"That's a lot of seafood Spencer."

"The point is, we'll be in a much better place. And who knows? Maybe you won't even have to stay an administrative assistant for long. You could do something else like..." He paused to think of something.

"Write?"

"Write? Write what?"

"A novel, Spencer. Or, I don't know, maybe become an investigative journalist." Come to think of it, Rue realized she sort of *fell into* writing, somewhat by accident. But somehow, it suited her. She felt privileged to share people's stories, and loved the back and forth between conducting interviews and then holing up for the weekend, crafting her words in solitude. *I wonder what else I could write?* she thought to herself.

"Hmmm," Spencer answered, pulling her back into the moment. Somehow, he hadn't thought of that. "Well, whatever. You'll figure it out." He paused to look at the menu. "Grilled steak in a miso-truffle butter," he said out loud before peering over his menu at her. "What are you having?"

"It looks like I'm supposed to pick three courses so..." Rue scrunched her nose and was still deciding when the waiter showed up.

"Do you have any questions about the menu?" he asked politely.

"Nope," Rue smiled, her eyes suddenly growing bigger than her stomach. "I've got it." She shifted in her seat, excitedly. *Spencer did say not to worry about it.* "I'd like the scallops to start, then the sea bass and the sorbet for dessert."

"Excellent."

"Nope," Rue grabbed the waiter's arm as he went to take her menu. Spencer glanced around the room, slightly embarrassed by her enthusiasm. "Scratch the sorbet. Make that the cheese plate."

"Excellent selection, miss," Andre finished. She suspected he'd have said the same thing no matter what she'd picked. It's probably good for business to compliment the diners on their choices as it reassured them that they made the right food decision.

Spencer placed his order so quietly that Rue could barely hear anything other than "medium rare." She took another sip of her champagne. *Maybe I could get used to not being poor,* she decided, sliding back in her chair and peering out the window at Times Square.

"Speaking of work," Spencer returned to their previous conversation and waited for a moment while Rue caught up with the shift. "How is it going working with Darwin Fennec, particularly after the..." he lowered his head and coughed a little, nervously, "incident."

"Well," she answered hesitantly. For some reason, Spencer was reluctant to talk about Clarissa Sauer's death, even though he wasn't at the theater and as far as Rue could tell, would have no reason to know her. The best he could muster was the occasional check-in to see how Rue was handling the trauma of witnessing the event and her guilty feelings about not being able to save the woman. Aside from that, he was largely absent, coming home late for the past two nights, usually just when Rue was already curled up underneath his 1000 thread-count Egyptian cotton sheets.

"After the...incident...we were questioned by the police; that much you know."

"Yes," Spencer shook his head. "I'm still annoyed with Midge for getting you into this mess in the first place. If she liked the man, why did she back out?"

"I dunno," Rue answered, biting her lip. In her mind, she *did* know.

Midge had been playing matchmaker, despite Rue reminding her that she already had a boyfriend. She did her best to dissuade Midge, but once her friend got an idea in her mind, it stuck there like Gorilla Glue. "But the next morning, the office was swarming with reporters, so we had to relocate to Darwin's home office in midtown."

"Home office?" Spencer was curious.

"Yeah," Rue answered. "I told you all this Thursday night."

"I'm sorry, my darling...just focused on work is all."

"Well," Rue was annoyed, "far be it from me to let a murder investigation get in the way of your work," she whispered angrily.

"There's no need for attitude," Spencer leaned in, giving her a warning look as he peered around the restaurant. Above all, Spencer was all about keeping up appearances. "Let's just try to enjoy the evening, shall we?"

Rue relented. After all, he was trying to make up for the fact that he had forgotten her birthday. "Anyway," she continued, "Mr. Fennec had to send in some of his buddies to relocate the computers to his condo after we clawed our way past the media. Fortunately, he has a friend in the limo business...Bristol, I think he said his name was."

"Bristol?" Spencer clarified.

"Yes," Rue confirmed, "Bristol."

"What kind of a name is that?"

"I dunno," Rue was flustered. "Maybe he's from Bristol, Pennsylvania, or New Jersey, or New York. Whatever...the point is, he's the guy who picked us up and drove us there."

"To Darwin's condo?"

"Yes, exactly." Rue thought about this. "You know, for a cad, he sure does seem to have a lot of friends."

"Bristol?"

"No, Darwin!" Rue let out a huff. Spencer just wasn't listening.

"So, you'll be working from his living quarters from now on?" Spencer clarified.

"Bristol?" Rue asked.

"No, Darwin." Spencer let out a huff.

Communication is hard.

"It looks like it, unless that bothers you and you want me to quit?"

"No, not at all. I trust him," Spencer decided, sipping his champagne.

"Really!" Rue thought about this. "Why? I got the impression he was a bit of a womanizer."

"Nah," Spencer laughed. "Frankly, I suspect he's a little light in the loafers."

"Light in the—" Rue shook her head, confused.

"Gay," Spencer whispered. "I suspect he's gay. He's a little too sensitive and charming. And, as you said, he seems to date a number of lady friends...probably a cover."

"Oh," Rue answered quietly. Somehow, the thought of him not being attracted to women bothered her. *I mean,* she considered this to herself. *I certainly don't like him and it's best if we're working together that I don't have to worry about him putting the moves on me.* But still... She brushed the thought away as their appetizers arrived.

THE EVENING ENDED with Spencer presenting Rue with her belated birthday gift just as the cheese plate and a glass of a Willamette Valley pinot noir arrived.

Spencer was disappointed that she chose an Oregon wine over a more popular French Bordeaux or California cabernet. But Spencer seemed to be concerned about lots of things that didn't really matter, Rue decided.

"Here," he handed her a shoebox-sized gift.

She looked lovingly at the camembert, Roquefort and gruyere plate that was perfectly accompanied by melba toast and both red and green seedless grapes before catching a glimpse of Spencer's excited eyes as he handed her his present. She pulled her attention back toward his gift, accepting it graciously. Rue unwrapped it carefully to reveal a rectangular phone with buttons and no chord.

"Nokia cell phone," Spencer explained. "That way, I won't have to phone Midge to get ahold of you anymore. And check this out." He pulled a similar device from his jacket pocket and used his thumbs to awkwardly type at the keypad. A moment later, Rue's new phone buzzed. She looked down to read the first text message she'd ever seen in her life. "Happy birthday, darling," it read. "You are my favorite star stuff."

CHAPTER 13
Love Notes

Sunday at the Police Station

~

"It seems sad, really," Penelope commented to Detective Ortega as they were writing possible clues they had gathered so far on the large whiteboard they had bolted to the wall in Ortega's office.

"What does?" Detective Ortega asked, re-reading the message from the note they found tucked underneath the bra strap of Clarissa Sauer's dress after they found her dead, sprawled across several theater seats in the orchestra section following her fall.

"Well, if she and Astor Ellis *did* have a relationship, that she wouldn't recognize his handwriting," she explained.

"I'm afraid I don't follow," Ortega confessed.

"I mean, that evidence would suggest—at least so far—that the letter did not come from Astor Ellis himself, but someone just pretending to be him. Which means that in all the time that Astor and Clarissa knew each other, she most likely had never received a love note from him...not even a card. Otherwise, I would think she'd know if it was his handwriting or not."

Detective Ortega thought about this for a moment. "Did I never write you a love note?"

Penelope was so surprised by the personal question that she gasped a little.

"Not unless you count pathology reports," she finally grinned, wryly.

"Well," Detective Ortega replied after a long and uncomfortable silence, "that was wrong of me."

"No use getting sentimental now," Penelope answered, adding a few more notes to the board with a green dry erase pen.

"What happened to us?" Ortega asked, seriously.

Penelope let out a sigh. She knew this question would come someday. Yet somehow, she thought 'someday' would have been more than a decade ago. Not now that Ortega had married and they'd both moved on. "Your work happened to us," she finally answered. "It's still happening to us," she confessed. "Only, it really doesn't matter anymore, does it?"

Detective Ortega thought of his wife. Nancy was a wonderful woman. Was he slowly pushing her away, too, in his quest for social justice? Maybe he was as bad a husband as he'd been a boyfriend when he and Penelope were together. Things at home had been strained lately.

He assumed they were normal stressors: finances, demanding relatives, Nancy's unruly teenage son who was not too keen about his mother being married to a police detective, and of course, work. Work was always stressful. There was no getting around that.

"It's so strange," Penelope drew Ortega out of his mind wandering.

"What is?" he asked.

"It's strange how there is nothing on the body or the scene—no stray hairs, no dandruff flakes, fingerprints, nothing to help connect us to the killer."

"They left the knife and the note," Ortega reasoned.

"Yes," Penelope acknowledged. "If I didn't know any better..."

"What is it?" Ortega persisted.

"It's almost as if the killer only left clues they wanted us to find." Penelope cycled through questions in her mind. *Had the killer accidentally sent Clarissa to the wrong box? Or were they trying to frame Darwin Fennec and Rue Brennan? But Darwin and Rue didn't know her. At least, that's what they said in their statements. What if they were lying?*

"Clever," Ortega acknowledged. "But if that's true, they'll make at least one critical mistake."

"What makes you say that?" Penelope wondered.

"Clever murderers are often narcissistic, at least the ones I've seen," Ortega answered. "They'll have to brag about their brilliance to someone."

Penelope paused for a moment "I know it's a long shot, but is there any chance that Clarissa was sent to that booth to discover Rue and Darwin together? Perhaps they were being outed and Clarissa Sauer and Darwin Fennec actually did know one another and quite well?"

"I suppose anything's possible. But then how does that explain how Clarissa ended up with a knife in her belly?"

Penelope pointed to the "weapons" section of the dry-erase board. "The knife was a prop from backstage. Though, I can't understand why a sharp kitchen knife was being used as a prop. Maybe Clarissa brought it with her?"

"What? To murder Astor Ellis? The note supposedly came from him and it sounded reconciliatory: 'I miss you. Can I see you? Meet me at Box 11 during the intermission. I made a mistake. Love, Astor.'" Ortega re-read the note, peering off into space. "Did I *really* never send you a love note, not a single one in three years?"

"Focus, Jose," Penelope called Detective Ortega by his first name. "Detective Ortega," she corrected as several officers passed the office door.

"Sorry," Ortega apologized. "It's just that...I'm trying to be better." He paused for a moment. "Nancy complains I don't listen to her. Did you feel that way, too?"

"Sometimes," Penelope admitted. "And only when you had your head buried in a case...which, now that I think about it, was most times."

"I'll bet your boyfriend, Garth, is a better listener."

"Gareth," she corrected.

"His name isn't Garth?"

No," she grinned. "It's always been Gareth."

"Hmmm," Ortega acknowledged, "maybe Nancy is right." Ortega scanned the dry-erase board trying to connect the dots.

How were Clarissa Sauer, Darwin Fennec, Rue Brennan, Astor Ellis, Byron Ellis, Gretchen Ellis and Portia LaMonte connected, other than being in neighboring booths during the show? An idea suddenly struck him.

Penelope recognized that look. "What is it?" She stood upright in anticipation.

"Rue Brennan is Spencer Hargrove's girlfriend," Ortega stared off into space. "I remember reading it recently in the tabloids, but she was at the theater with her boss, Darwin Fennec. Spencer Hargrove runs Spencer-Tech, while the Ellis family runs B. A. Ellis Industries. They hate one another."

"Do you think the murder is related?" Penelope asked. "Of course, you do, or you wouldn't have mentioned it," she shook her head at her own silliness.

"Let's just say my spidey sense is tingling," he joked, referencing the famous words of Spider Man. "Somehow, I feel this has less to do with Clarissa Sauer and more to do with Rue Brennan."

CHAPTER 14
SpencerTech

Monday at SpencerTech

"Thanks for meeting me here, Darwin." Spencer met Darwin at the back of a co-workspace ThinkLab building. "Let's take the stairs," he suggested, unlocking a door marked "members only."

It wasn't enough for Darwin to move his business to his home office, he still had to skirt the media. Fortunately, it seemed they had quickly lost interest in Rue and given up stalking her at home. She was still relatively unknown, whereas Darwin had been involved in several high-profile cases over the years.

"Did you know Clarissa Sauer?" they asked. *"Who was the woman you were with that evening on the balcony?" "An anonymous tip said the woman of interest is named Rue Brennan. Can you confirm that?"* It was relentless. Darwin and Rue began taking the service elevator and leaving his condo through the employee entrance and exits. The building's superintendent wasn't too thrilled about it, but he agreed with the investigator's reasoning that the attention was causing concern from the other residents of the

building. Their poor doorman faced the brunt of the onslaught and ceased to answer or acknowledge a single reporter's presence. On three occasions, security had to ask them to stop loitering or they would call the police.

SpencerTech was comprised of a large suite on the fourth floor, complete with three private offices, a common area, a room dedicated toward housing servers and equipment, a shared bathroom and a small utility closet, expensive by New York standards, but modest for a tech company trying to make itself appear bigger than it actually was.

"Hey dudes," a small, thin-framed man in his early twenties greeted the men as they passed his office. He was wearing a gray earflap beanie and a checkered flannel shirt over a plain black t-shirt and jeans.

Darwin gave a two-fingered salute, touching his forehead as if he were tipping an imaginary hat. "Hey Max," he acknowledged.

A taller, bulkier, and older man almost bumped into Darwin before catching himself. He had his nose in a pile of papers he'd just printed out. "Whoops, sorry D," the man touched Darwin's shoulder.

"No worries, Zain," Darwin responded. Zain was in his late thirties and still wore a dress shirt and tie to the office, regardless of whether they were seeing investors that day. He had dark skin and a thick accent and chronically had his head either in his books, paperwork, or behind a computer. Zain nodded and kept going. He was a busy man and the new lines of script he was formulating weren't going to code themselves.

Darwin and Spencer continued down the long hallway to Spencer's office—the largest and with a window view of the city. The room was sparse with one long chrome-colored desk and white leather chair lit by several overhead fluorescent lights.

The desktop was filled by two side-by-side full-sized computers with external speakers and a computer tower that stood between the two displays. On one corner of the desk sat a telephone with a small notepad, pen, and Rolodex. On the other was a stack of printed papers waited to be filed in one of the three file cabinets on the opposite wall.

There wasn't much in the room by way of personal memorabilia, though Darwin did note that Spencer had taken the time to put up exactly three framed pictures—one featuring a "Best in Innovation" award from B. A. Ellis industries, one with his Computer Science degree from NYU and an old photo of himself as a young boy with his arms around a long-haired Australian Shepherd. He was smiling as the dog's tongue hung out to one side, staring straight ahead with excited eyes.

A picture of his old dog, Darwin noted. *But not a single photo of Rue, not even a small one on his desk...interesting.*

"Well..." Spencer began.

Darwin held up a finger to his lips and Spencer fell quiet, nodding.

Darwin nimbly moved around the room, feeling under the desk and around the photo frames, taking parts of the phone receiver off and peering inside, looking for any signs of a bug.

Finally, he gave an all-clear sign and Spencer let out a sigh.

"Any new incidents?" Darwin asked.

"No," Spencer answered. "We've been shutting everything down each night after encrypting our data and backing it up to the server. The new security software, firewalls, and blockers your guy put in place seems to have our computers on lockdown."

Darwin wanted to tell him that the "guy" was actually a "gal," but kept his mouth shut.

"What about your home computer?"

"I've been really careful," Spencer explained. "I'm the only one able to remote in given your new protocol, not that I worry about Zain and Max. Zain I've known since we were kids and Max is my nephew who I practically helped raise. I trust them both completely. But..."

"But what?" Darwin pressed him.

Spencer crossed his arms. "When I was meeting with a potential investor the other evening, he very candidly told me that it was between supporting my new project, or a similar one being developed by my old employers at B. A. Ellis Industries."

"What's odd about that?"

"It's something he said." Spencer thought a moment. "While he had signed a non-disclosure agreement, he let something slip about the design software project they are ready to launch just two weeks after mine, unless I can get mine to market sooner."

"What was it?" Darwin stood upright.

"He said something about it having a stardust feature."

"Well, it is graphic design and computer animation software.

Wouldn't it be likely that there would be a few built-in applications for the sun, moon and stars?"

"But he said stardust," he confirmed. "Stardust has been the name we thought about giving our product. Except, no one outside of the team knows that, and at this point, it's just an internal nickname."

Darwin let out a sigh. "Well then, I'd better get a couple of my team members to scour this place and your condo to make sure they're clean."

"Er, not the condo," Spencer hemmed and hawed.

"We have to secure your computer and make sure there's nothing compromising your outgoing or incoming messages."

"Look, I'm happy if you want to have your guy hack into my home computer, ethically of course, to see if they need to shore up any security issues, but I can assure you I don't talk business with anyone on my land-line or cellular phone and the only one in my condo at present is me. And," he let out an awkward laugh, "I'm certainly not talking to myself!"

"Obviously, you're my client and I'll honor your wishes," Darwin conceded. "Though, I definitely think we should ensure that we investigate all sources that in any way send and receive info—either through your internal system or via external wires."

"Yeah, about that 'we'."

"Yes?"

"How is it going with Rue?"

"Oh, Rue...well, fine," Darwin stammered. "I'm beginning to teach her the basics of encryption and making sure confidential content is protected beyond simply usernames and passwords. She really is a quick study."

"Well," Spencer answered, "don't feel obligated to teach her too much."

"Eh, why's that?"

"I don't anticipate you needing to have her in your employ for long," he answered.

"Oh?"

"No, I just need you to...distract her, for a few more weeks, just until I secure the investments I need and beat B. A. Ellis Industries to market."

"Distract her? You mean...keep her out of your way?"

"Exactly," Spencer's smiled dropped when he saw Darwin's questioning expression. "Oh, don't get me wrong, she's a great girl. But she's not exactly the sort to make a good impression among investors, the media and future buyers...particularly not now with the recent spotlight on her."

Darwin ground his teeth but said nothing until he'd carefully framed his words. "I don't understand how she threatens to make a bad impression."

"Oh, come on. You've seen her!" he chortled. "She dresses like a bohemian, says whatever comes to her mind. Hell, she even eats green beans with her fingers...not even using a fork. Who does that?"

I do, Darwin had to admit to himself. *What's wrong with eating food with your fingers? Lots of countries around the world do that.*

Spencer interrupted Darwin's thoughts. "Just give her something to do to make her feel useful, as if she's helping me in some way by working for you. Understood?"

"Perfectly," Darwin answered, between clenched teeth.

THAT DAY, Darwin called Bristol from a spare Tracfone after walking down several flights of stairs, two at a time. He held his foot between the door and the frame to keep it from locking behind him.

"Hey, Finn, what's the word?" Bristol answered the phone in a huff. "Finn" was Bristol's nickname for Darwin, but it only made sense to the two men, as it came from a story from their somewhat murky past. Behind him, the sound of loud banging and a bandsaw could be heard.

"Need you to get our two trusted buddies to meet me at the dorm rooms to inspect the place for mice."

"You got it, Finn. You there now?"

"Just outside," Darwin answered.

"Great, I'm sure I can get them there in a jiffy."

"Oh, and Bristol?"

"Yeah, Finn?"

"Tell 'em to ignore the termites."

A snort could be heard on the other end of the line.

"Whatever you say, boss," he laughed.

"One more thing, just do me a favor and do your shimmy in about ten minutes? I need a distraction for Frat Boy."

"You got it, boss."

With that, Darwin hung up the phone.

He made his way back up the steps, winded this time. Darwin reminded himself that he should get more exercise. He did a fair bit of walking during the day, but he'd gotten lazy about taking the stairs instead of the elevator, a situation that had only gotten worse with the recent publicity and wanting to stay out of sight.

"Two of my team members should be here to secure the place in a few minutes. In the meantime, mind if I do a cursory search?" Darwin asked Spencer.

"Suit yourself," Spencer agreed. "Hey guys?" Spencer stood between the two rooms where Zain and Max were glued to their respective computers. "Mind if Darwin here scans your offices for bugs? He's also got a couple of his men stopping by, too."

"Nah," Max knew the drill and went to follow Zain to the common area for coffee, leaving behind their personal satchels and backpacks for inspection. Just for fun, Max turned suddenly to Darwin, contorted his face, and proceeded to pull up his black t-shirt, flashing his bare chest. "See? No wires!"

Zain flicked him on the arm. "Dweeb," he laughed.

Max dropped his shirt and beat his chest like Tarzan.

Darwin shook his head and smiled. *Inside every male web developer, programmer and cybersecurity nerd lives a 12-year-old boy just dying to get out.*

Just then, Spencer's phone rang.

"Hmm," Spencer furrowed his brow. "Excuse me," he told Darwin. On the other end, Bristol's boisterous voice could be heard. Except, it was distinctly more Jersey sounding than his usual voice. "Hey man, when you gonna come pickup your caw (car). I ain't got all day, ya know?"

"Who is this? I think you have the wrong numb—"

"Is this..." Bristol repeated the number.

"It is, but..." Spencer was flustered.

Darwin quickly made the rounds, planting a few cutting edge "termites" not available to the general public, in each of the "dorm" rooms, to include one in the bag Spencer left in his office. *For people so concerned about security, that was far too easy,* Darwin grinned as he once again, took the steps to ground level two at a time. He met his backup—the two young women Rue mistook for Darwin's paramours that day at the pier.

"Darwin, honey," the dark-haired woman cooed in her sultry voice, "we gotta stop meeting like this."

"Just lock the door behind you when you leave," he smirked, waving a finger at them. "And no funny business."

"Sure thing, Finn," the blonde answered, winking at him.

"Define 'funny business,'" the brunette demanded.

"The boys are off limits as are wallets and all things bright and shiny."

The blonde pouted. "When did you stop being fun, Finn?"

"I was never fun," Darwin countered. "Which reminds me. May I please have my wallet back, Candice?"

"What? I didn't..." the blonde appeared offended.

"C'mon, Candy," the brunette slapped her friend's arm. "Hand it over."

"You too, Monica." She was going to protest, but knew it was useless. Monica handed over Darwin's Breitling Chronograph watch.

"It's Monique now," the dark-haired woman protested. "And your watch is a knock-off, about as fake as my name...and yours."

"I am aware of that, thank you...Monique."

"You shouldn't carry this much cash on you, Finn," Candice handed him his wallet. "That's what banks are for."

"Thank you for the tip," he paused a moment, his wallet extended. "Ahem," he coughed.

Candice rolled her eyes and forked over the wad she'd already procured from his wallet.

"It was for expenses," she wrinkled her nose at him. "You think I wake up this beautiful?"

"I am very certain that you do," Darwin shot her a practiced smile.

"Glad not everyone is as much of a gentleman as you, Darwin," Monica who goes by Monique now explained, opening the employee door wide just as an older, balding man walked past, eyeing the women with interest. She purposefully shifted her hip to one side so the gawker could get a better look. "It'd be bad for business."

"As I mentioned," Darwin reiterated.

"We get it," she interrupted. "No touching the boys. C'mon Candy. We got work to do."

With that, Darwin put on a ball cap, lifted his shirt collar and did his best to slink his way through midtown unseen.

CHAPTER 15
Merriam Hall

Friday Evening at a Dance Hall

~

"I can't believe I let you talk me into this ridiculous dress, Midge." After a long work week, Midge insisted that she and Rue needed to 'let their hair down' and go clubbing.

"And the boots," Midge pointed a red lacquered nail toward Rue's faux leather, lace-up ankle boots with high heels. "If you're going to credit me, you gotta include the shoes."

"I wasn't crediting you, Midge," Rue replied, lining up behind a dozen other people at ten o'clock at night, waiting to get into Merriam Hall, Manhattan's premier dance club...for those just barely of legal drinking age through those who hadn't realized that they weren't in college anymore.

Midge fell into the latter of those categories but refused to be pigeonholed by age. It seemed to work for her as her red hair, white powdered face with black lipstick, and her lime-green cocktail dress caught the admiration of a number of men a good decade her junior as they eyed the other women in the queue. "I was blaming you," Rue finished, tugging at the form-fitting leather mini-dress with a silver zipper that ran the length of it.

"Oh," Midge waved a hand at her. "Trust me. You'll thank me later. You look sexy as hell. If I went that way, I'd be all over you by now." Midge licked her forefinger and held it in the air like a barometer. "Gonna get chilly tonight on account of the winds."

"You are the weirdest person I have ever met."

"Why, thank you, Rue," Midge beamed proudly.

"That wasn't a compliment."

At that moment, a burly security guard mumbled a few words into a walkie-talkie as he surveyed the line. He eyed Rue from head-to-toe curiously. Midge smiled seductively, putting a hand on her thigh and thrusting her hip to one side. He was taken aback, but merely wrinkled his nose and moved on.

The security guard motioned to two women further down the line from where Midge and Rue waited for the doors to open. The two young ladies, falling into the "just barely legal" category, walked by proudly in their spiked heels and thigh-length dresses toward a roped-off door. The guard un-roped it as another attendant opened the door to the club and ushered them inside. The door was closed and the rope replaced.

"What the hell was that about?" Rue complained. "We've been standing here a half hour, and they got to waltz right past us!"

"Eh, don't worry about it," Midge replied. "They let the trampiest girls in first because it draws the men to the club. The more men there are, the more they spend on drinks for themselves and the ladies."

The guard walked down the line again, past a few college boys ogling the women around them, a few of these men cat-calling to several young ladies who were passing by. One of whom flicked them a finger. One particularly distasteful young man, standing just in front of them, followed the long line of Rue's zipper from top to bottom as if unzipping it with his mind. The guard took the cue.

"You can go on inside," he told Rue in a deep voice.

"Me, too!" Midge grabbed Rue's arm. "It's a package deal."

The corner of the guard's mouth started to twitch until he beat the smile down and returned to a frown. "You girls enjoy your evening."

Apparently, the two were fairly high on the trampiest looking list.

"Catch you inside," Midge told the young man who had been eyeing Rue, fingered the collar of his dress shirt and winked, never losing his gaze. He grinned back as one his friends jabbed him in the ribs as if egging him on.

"What was that about?" Rue whispered when they'd reached the door.

"Two things, really," Midge explained. "Once he realizes that one, your legs are closed and are not open for business, and two, that acne-prone face isn't gonna get him too far, he'll fall right into my web."

"That's disgusting, Midge," Rue chastised. "And I thought you had a new boyfriend." Rue vaguely remembered Midge recounting her latest trip to Atlantic City, but she tuned out the details of the man she supposedly met at the roulette table. Midge did a lot of dating...a lot of gambling...a lot of drinking...well, a lot of everything, really.

Once Rue reached the door, she pulled out cash and the attendant inside stamped her hand with a green, glow-in-the-dark logo.

Midge fished around in her purse for money and a few coins spilled out over the floor. "Sorry," she apologized to the impatient attendant, kneeling down to pick up the change she had strewn. Rue couldn't even lean over to help her because the dress was too tight and so short, she really didn't feel like revealing her underwear to the world.

Midge finally resurfaced, handing the attendant the change and ever-so-slowing dipping into her purse and digging for a few more dollar bills.

"You know what?" the attendant forced a smile, peering at the fresh crop of women trying to get in followed by the few men that they were finally admitting. "Don't worry about it. You just go on inside and enjoy yourself." The attendant stamped her hand.

"Thank you," Midge tipped an invisible hat, grabbing Rue's arm and leading her toward the first bar they could find. "Works every time," she yelled above the pounding mix of rock and metal music.

"What does?" Rue wanted to know.

"I only paid $5.75 for admission instead of $15. That's a bargain if you ask me."

"That was a scam?"

"More like a grift," Midge explained. "C'mon, if they're gonna rob us by charging $6 for a bottle of Corona, then I think I should at least get my first beverage on the house."

"Alabama Slammer," Midge called to the bartender who nodded before turning his eyes to Rue.

"Uh," Rue fumbled.

"She'll have the same," Midge finished. The man nodded, wiping out a few glasses and then pulling a bottle of Southern Comfort off the shelf.

"What happened to the Corona?" Rue was confused.

"What?" Midge was distracted. In fact, she looked as if she were twitching and ready to jump out of her very skin. "By the way," she continued. "I think your white lace panties would have gone better with this dress, just sayin'," Midge offered helpfully.

Rue was dumbfounded until she realized that with her friend crawling on the floor gathering her change, she had gotten an intimate look at Rue's...well, intimates. "Do I even want to know how you know what's in my underwear drawer?"

"Probably not," Midge confessed. "Let's just say it was laundry day and I would have been going freestyle if I didn't."

"Midge!" Rue held up a hand. "Boundaries! No rifling through my drawers anymore, got it?"

Just then, the bartender set the drinks down with a smirk. He winked at Rue. Rue grabbed the drink and took a large gulp. "You're getting this round," she commanded of Midge. "It's the least you can do for violating my underwear drawer."

"Deal," Midge plopped a twenty-dollar bill on the counter. "Keep the change," she said to the bartender.

"There isn't any," he grumbled, swiping the bill and delivering it to the cash register.

Midge didn't seem to notice, nor was she inclined to leave a tip. "Let's dance," she finally suggested, grabbing Rue's arm and dragging her to the main dance floor. There were three others, one on the lower level, one on the second floor, and another down the hall. This room was the largest and featured a series of long stone steps leading all the way up to what one would assume was an altar if it were Aztec times. Instead, the DJ sat on his thrown on high, strobe lights flooded all around him with a movie screen behind him flashing odd abstract images.

Rue was a lightweight and within minutes on the dance floor was already beginning to feel the effects of her beverage. However, she noticed, the alcohol dulled the obnoxiously loud music and sounds from the crowd, so she kept drinking.

Two men slinked up to the ladies and Rue suddenly had a dance partner who reached out and gently touched her hips with his hands and began swaying. Instinctively, Rue, in turn, put her hands on his shoulders as the two continued to move in an awkward side-to-side motion. Occasionally, her new dance partner would take a step forward or back and Rue would follow.

At some point, he took her hand and led her through a twirl, but halfway through it, another woman grabbed the forearm of Rue's dance partner and he willingly dropped Rue's hand to go off with the new woman. Rue turned, surprised, standing alone on the dance floor, surrounded by a crowd, some couples and some dancing in a group.

She drained her drink and deposited her plastic glass in a bin near the bar. As Rue spun around, it seemed she already found herself with a new dance partner. This man was much shorter than the first and a bit grabbier. He wrapped an arm around her waist and pulled her to his chest, lifting her right hand with his and hugging it to his shoulder. This man smelled like whiskey and Marlboros and made her nose itch. He was also a little too sweaty.

Rue tried to politely back away, no easy feat with the dance floor so packed that many were shoulder-to-shoulder. She gazed around the room trying to find Midge, but despite her obvious bright red hair, Midge somehow blended in with the strobe lights and smoke machines obscuring everyone's features.

"Where ya goin', darlin'?" The man pulled her aggressively toward him.

Rue shook her head, pulling away. "I can't hear you!" she explained in vain. "But I don't want to dance anymore!"

He couldn't hear her either as he merely smiled and tugged her in a hug, planting a kiss on her cheek—a sweaty, whiskey and Marlboro one. "Where ya goin' darlin?" he said again, blinking as if in slow motion.

This time, Rue pushed her hands against his chest. "Sorry!" she yelled, pointing toward the DJ, "but I can't hear you above 'Smells Like Teen Spirit!'"

The man obviously misinterpreted her gestures, smiling and turning toward the DJ, holding up a clear plastic cup with a lingering piece of ice melting at the bottom. "I feel stupid and contagious," he started yelling the song lyrics and smiling. He thought she just really liked the song.

Rue took it as her cue. As he gazed up the steps at the DJ stand, singing at the top of his lungs, she pushed her way through the crowd until she came to a dark hallway leading to another room. Grateful to get away from her dance partner and the noise, she followed the hallway which opened up to a smaller room that was slightly less crowded. In it, a live band played a combination of reggae and funk.

"You look like you need a drink," a well-muscled man with long dreadlocks handed her a glass filled with ice and clear liquid. He smiled. "Go ahead, I didn't take a sip yet, and can get me another."

"What is it?" she asked curiously. To be clear, Rue most certainly did *not* need another drink, and had she been right of mind, she wouldn't have accepted this one.

"Oh, just a gin and tonic," he smiled, signaling to the bartender standing behind a nearby counter for another. This dance hall seemed to have a three-to-one ratio of bars to dance floors.

"Thanks," Rue smiled, taking a sip. This man already seemed more polite than the last.

"What's your name?" he asked, flashing his pearly whites.

"Rue Brennan," another woman answered, agitated, slinking up next to the man and taking his arm, possessively—Ursula Gorky.

Ursula was a fellow figure model at the Artist Atelier. She had a slightly larger frame than Rue and her long brown hair cascaded over her shoulders. She flashed her blue eyes at Rue. "I saw you at the theater the other night," she stated coldly. "I saw what you did."

"I don't know what you're talking about," Rue answered, taking another sip of her drink. Her head was starting to feel a little fuzzy which she attributed to having two drinks, dancing, and possibly being a little dehydrated.

"You pushed my best friend over the balcony," Ursula clarified.

"Whoa, ladies," the man put one arm around each of them, detaching from Ursula's grasp. "Let's not argue. You're much prettier when you smile. Let's have a smile." Ursula was unresponsive. He tried again, "Let me get you a drink," he offered.

"No thanks," she spat, but he'd already retreated to the bar to pick up his replacement beverage.

"I didn't push her," Rue explained, "I tried to catch her."

"Then why did you lie to the police?" she challenged.

"What are you talking about?"

"You told them your date was there with you when it happened, but I saw you from the opposite balcony. You were alone with Clarissa." Her eyes grew red with anger.

"Listen, I can't say anything about the case while it's being investigated..."

"You mean while *you're* being investigated."

"And," Rue realized, "how could you possibly know what I did or did not tell the police?"

Someone bumped into Ursula from behind. "Excuse me." It was Midge. Attached to her like lichen on a tree branch, the acne-ridden boy from the line clung to her, his arms wrapped around her waist as he sniffed her hair and smiled. To Ursula, she commanded, "Just shut your pie hole. You don't know what you're talking about."

"Freaky," the muscular man returned, offering a beverage to Ursula who turned it down a second time. He was staring at Midge's hair and lime green dress with admiration.

"I'll take that," she grabbed it from him and gulped it down in under ten seconds. "Thanks, I was parched."

"No problem," he smiled at her.

Just then, an athletic-looking woman with short brown hair and blonde streaks in it bounced in.

"Ursula," she called loudly.

For a moment, Ursula put her aggression on hold. "Emma!" she squealed, giving her friend a huge hug that involved rocking from side to side for an uncomfortably long time. "You made it!"

"Let me introduce you to Jordie, my...new friend."

Jordie, the smooth-talking man who liked delivering drinks like Santa during Christmas, flashed a toothy grin at Emma.

"Nice to meet you," he almost growled, surveying the woman from top to bottom.

Emma noticed and didn't appreciate it.

"Get you a drink?" he asked, winking.

"Long Island iced tea?" she asked. He may have been lechy, but drinks at the club weren't cheap, so...

"My kind of girl," he grinned, while Ursula shot him her best, 'you're supposed to be with me look.'

The fogginess in Rue's head worsened. She grabbed Emma's arm and asked, "Sure you should be drinking...in your condition?"

Emma pulled her arm back. "What the hell are you talking about, freak? Condition? I'm not pregnant!"

"Sorry, I just..."

"Hey, listen, Rue," Midge interrupted, "can you find your own way home? Tommy here invited me back to his place."

Rue's brain fumbled to make sense of what Midge was asking as the strobe lights and loud music further confused her.

"I can see to it that your friend gets home safely," Jordie offered.

"No, you can't," Ursula jumped in. "She can find her own damn way home." She dragged the man reluctantly to the dance floor in time for a slow song. Over her shoulder, she called, "I told the cops I saw you with that man. Even if you didn't do it, you're hiding something."

Midge flicked her middle finger at Ursula.

Rue put her hand on Midge's arm to steady herself.

"Hey, you okay?" Midge asked, concerned.

"Yeah," Rue answered. "Think I need some fresh air. I'm gonna head out. I'll catch a cab or something."

Tommy nibbled on Midge's ear. Unlike the whiskey and Marlboro man, Tommy smelled like Nag Champa and possibly weed.

"Okay, catch you later," Midge turned and planted her lips onto Tommy's and the two remained lip-locked as they headed to the dance floor.

Emma, it would seem, was left abandoned by everyone, so she approached the bar to order her own Long Island Iced Tea. She let out a sigh as she took a sip. *Sometimes, I wonder about my life choices,* she thought to herself.

Meanwhile, Rue stumbled to the nearest exit sign. The cold wind hit her in the face and she accidentally dropped her empty cup on the ground. It tumbled quickly away, but she was too dizzy to go after it. Instead, she hung onto the outside wall of the club as the door behind her slammed shut. She gazed groggily around at the back alley where she landed. It smelled of sewage and urine. Large trash bags were piled up in varied spots on either side of the narrow walkway. She jumped as a large rat darted past her in search of its next dinner. She heard a noise behind her and turned to see two men making their way toward her. It was dark and she couldn't see their faces in the shadow.

"Hey, lady," one of them called to her.

The hairs on her neck stood up. *This can't be good,* she thought to herself.

She went to tug at the club's door, but there was no handle. She was locked out.

She moved as quickly as she could toward the other end of the alley where she had a partial view of the streetlights and road.

"Don't be afraid of us, bitch," the second man yelled, picking up speed. They could have caught her easily in her state, but they seemed to enjoy watching her terrified reaction as she fled and were careful to keep just enough space so she had the lead. Like two cats cornering a mouse, they were playing with her.

It wasn't until she'd reached the street that one of them grabbed her arm. "What's your hurry?" he asked, pulling her toward him and pushing her against the wall of the club.

"Get away from me," she called, raising a knee to his groin. He doubled over in pain and let out a few expletives as she shoved him into his friend. The friend pushed him aside and lunged for Rue.

She began running, as fast as she could in clunky, high-heeled shoes and a form-fitting leather dress. She regained some of her balance, probably due to sheer adrenaline.

Despite the millions of people living in New York City, they appeared to be the only ones around on this desolate stretch of road at this time of night. There were several lanes going in each direction, divided by a small concrete island. The wind howled as the temperature dropped. Rue shivered.

The men were gaining on her, this time not intent on letting her get away.

Just then she heard a car horn blaring as a yellow cab darted across multiple lanes of traffic, navigating expertly around the island, and stopping at the curb in front of her. The passenger door clicked open.

"Get in," the driver commanded through the open window.

She obeyed, slamming the door behind her just as one man reached through the window and tugged at her hair.

He yelled a few more derogatory words at her as his friend slammed the trunk of the cab with his fist as it sped off, leaving the two of them alone in the middle of the street, one holding a tiny clump of Rue's hair.

It was only then that Rue realized who the driver was.

"Bristol?" she asked.

"Guilty as charged," he grinned. He was wearing a cabby cap and chewing on a toothpick. He eyed her dress curiously. "Eh, nice dress." He left it at that.

"How did you know I was here?"

"Well," he stammered. "Let's just say it was my turn to look after ya."

"Look after me?" She heard and felt her stomach growl. Rue was feeling a little queasy.

"GPS tracker in your phone," he explained. "Say, are you all right?" The sound of her stomach did not escape his attention.

"I feel a little funny," she cringed as her stomach cramped.

"We're only a few blocks from your place, hang tight." He hit the gas and picked up speed, strategically taking a few little-known side roads to get there faster. Fortunately, traffic was not as heavy as it usually was in the Greenwich Village area.

Rue's head was pounding. "How do you know where I live?" she wondered aloud. She'd always taken the subway to Darwin's place, walking the final few blocks in an attempt to avoid reporters who appeared to have gotten bored with *her* story after only a few days, but seemed overly curious about her interactions with Darwin Fennec. "The tracker thingy?"

"Exactly."

"I didn't know phones had them."

"Most don't," he explained. "But give it a few years and every phone will have one."

"Why would people want the ability to be tracked through their phone?" Rue doubted the logic of this invention.

"Well, tonight's a good example."

Rue moaned. "I don't feel so hot."

Bristol parked on the corner of Rue's apartment complex in a handicapped zone. He quickly hung a paper tag on the mirror.

Rue was feeling too sick to argue, but Bristol could read the judgment in her eyes.

"What?" he defended. "It's for emergencies."

He helped her out of the car, but she pushed her way passed him. She managed to climb the steps at lightning speed as Bristol was still grabbing the door at the base of her complex so he didn't get locked out. He followed her, taking the steps two at a time.

She burst into her studio apartment and ran to the bathroom, just in time to vomit into the toilet. In her kitchen, she heard Bristol opening cabinets and the refrigerator.

Embarrassed, she flushed the toilet. Fortunately, she was otherwise unsoiled as she brushed her hair back and rinsed her mouth out. She then took the time to brush her teeth and rinse with mouthwash.

"Better?" Bristol asked when she returned.

On the table, he laid out a glass of ginger ale and a few salted crackers he found in the cabinet.

"Yeah, just embarrassed." She took a cracker and nibbled on it. "I didn't think I drank that much."

"What'd you have?" Bristol asked, curiously.

"An Alabama Slammer," she thought a moment. "And then someone gave me a gin and tonic."

"Someone?" Bristol raised an eyebrow.

"Yeah, just some guy who was trying to get a few of us drunk, I guess."

"I'd say he was doing more than that," Bristol shook his head. "Listen, sweetheart, and I say this with respect. Never, *and I mean never,* accept a drink from a stranger, unless it goes directly from the bartender into your pretty little hands."

Rue nodded.

"And furthermore," he continued. Apparently, the lesson wasn't over yet. "Never leave your drink unattended, capisce?"

"Understood. Thanks for rescuing me, Bristol. Though I'm really uncomfortable with the fact that you were tracking me. Was that Darwin's doing?"

Bristol held his hands up. "Look, you didn't hear it from me, but I happen to know he's very concerned about you being in the center of a murder and all. Plus, with your boyfriend's new product launch..."

"Do you think they're connected?" This was the first Rue was hearing of this. Up until this moment, she assumed they were two separate events.

"Look, I've already said too much." Bristol put his forefinger and thumb to his lips as if turning a key to lock his lips.

"Tell you what..." Rue took a sip of the ginger ale. After all, she reasoned, Bristol wasn't a stranger, and he proved to be trustworthy so far.

"What's that?" Bristol folded his arms.

"You don't tell Darwin about my awful state tonight and I won't mention that you spilled the beans about SpencerTech's connection."

"Alleged connection," he corrected.

"Alleged connection," she confirmed, "between Clarissa's death and SpencerTech's launch. My lips are sealed unless Darwin brings it up himself. Deal?"

"Deal," he smiled.

"And thanks again," Rue whispered, quietly.

"Aw, tonight was nothing," Bristol laughed, walking toward the door. "If you saw how many times I had to all but carry Darwin home after he got shit-faced when we used to live..." He caught himself again. "Eh, never mind."

"Thanks again, Bristol," she acknowledged.

"No problem. You just get some rest." Bristol quietly closed the door behind him and made his way back to his cab. A few bystanders eyed him, annoyed. Realizing why, he adopted a limp. "Had to get my mother up three flights of stairs and neither one of us walk none too good," he explained.

They nodded, sympathetically, and kept walking.

Once inside the cab, Bristol made a phone call. "Yeah, not sure if they're still there, but you may want to check out two mugs in the back alley of the Merriam. They seem to be preying on those without their wits about 'em. Not too sure what's going on inside, neither. I suspect there's some funny business with the drinks." He paused to listen to the person on the other end. "Yeah, no problem, Dennis. Happy ta help."

With that, Bristol removed the handicapped sign and made his way toward his garage.

CHAPTER 16
Hangover

Saturday Morning at Rue's Apartment

A tiny beam of sunlight sliced its way through the curtained window, hitting Rue in the eye. She rolled over and shielded her eyes. She had a splitting headache, and she had a taste in her mouth that made her sure something crawled in and died there while she was sleeping.

Rue pulled back the sheets of her bed and dragged herself to her feet, shuffling her way to the bathroom to rinse her mouth out for what became the fourth time since she was sick last night. She still felt queasy, so Rue went back to the kitchen for more of the ginger ale and a few crackers. There were a few gaps in last night's events, but she seemed very clear on Midge ditching her for a boy named Tommy, men chasing her down the alley and Bristol bringing her home where she was finally sick. Rue also remembered what he'd said about Clarissa's possible connection to SpencerTech, but she couldn't let Darwin know. But why wouldn't he have told her? Was he worried she'd talk too much to Spencer? Or that whatever it was would put her in danger? Was Spencer in danger?

She rubbed her head and stopped thinking. Every time she did, the throbbing became worse. How much did she have to drink last night?

Rue left the ale and crackers on the kitchen table and went to cover the window in her bedroom completely and climb back into bed.

Before she did, however, she saw the sliver of a flash of red through the edge of the cloth cover. This was followed by a tap on the window...Midge.

"Good, you're up," she leaned over, peering in the window. "C'mon out on the ledge, I've got Bloody Marys to help recover from last night. Or, I can come in...either way."

It was then that the rest of the evening came flooding back...the grabby dance partner who smelled of cigarettes and whiskey, a well-spoken muscular man who handed her a drink that she now knew had likely been laced with something, and Bristol telling her that she was on "his watch," that night—presumably another thing that she wasn't supposed to know.

Midge finally paused to take stock of her friend. "Wow, you look like crap. What happened?"

"Someone drugged me at the club, two men almost raped me and were it not for one of Darwin's friends intervening, I'd probably be lying dead in a gutter by now."

"Huh," was all Midge could say before finally adding, "Sounds about right for one of my Saturday nights. Glad you're okay, though."

Rue eyed her friend with a mix of bewilderment and anger. This was the same woman who insisted on accompanying her to meet Darwin about a job in broad daylight. Yet somehow Midge was apathetic about today's news. Why? She was beginning to question Midge's mental health.

"So, can I come in?" Midge was wearing jeans and a sweater and already had one leg over the ledge, her clunky leather shoe dangling in mid-air.

"No, Midge, you can't," Rue stopped her.

"Well, why the hell not?" Midge protested, eyeing her curiously after realizing that Rue hadn't called her by her affectionate friend term "Mensa." She pulled her leg back and then squatted down on both feet, waiting for an explanation.

"Why?" Rue rubbed her bloodshot eyes, the pounding in her head matching the pounding of her heart. "Because every time I'm near you, bad things have a way of happening. You try and set me up with Darwin and now I'm a suspect in a murder trial. You drag me to a club and abandon me for a fling with that pimply-faced kid."

"Tommy Marcuzzo," Midge finished. "And he was sweet," she reminisced.

"Men groped me, and I was attacked."

"How was that my fault?" Midge was offended.

Rue let out a long sigh. "It's not your fault, Midge. It's just that these are just two of a long history of catastrophes that all seem to have one common denominator—you."

"Well, gee, if you feel that way about it," Midge pouted.

"I just think I need a little space from you. No knocking on my window any time you feel like it. No messing with my love life, and certainly no rifling through my lingerie drawer."

"Fine," Midge's eyes grew dark. "Go back to your boring life with your boring Spencer. I won't interfere." Midge began her ascent back to her apartment, somehow expecting that Rue would feel bad and stop her. When she didn't, she doubled back. "Oh, and by the way, Tommy used to be an intern at B. A. Ellis Industries a while back. That lady who took a tumble off the balcony? Clarissa Sauer?"

Rue's ears perked up. "What about her?"

"Astor Ellis was having a not-so-secret affair with her while dating his now fiancé, Portia LaMonte. Tommy constantly had to cover for Astor. Turns out, he dumped her once the papers got wind of it. Didn't you say his family was in the next booth over at the theater? Sounds pretty fishy to me. But, whatever."

Rue felt like a heel, even more so given that she was already well aware of Clarissa's involvement with Astor, but that was information garnered at work and she couldn't share it with Midge.

"Look, Midge, I'm..."

"No, no," Midge waved her hand. "I get it, no more interfering from me. Except you should also know that he somehow convinced his former lover to hooch up to someone at SpencerTech and do a little snooping."

Rue thought about this. As far as she knew, Zain was still married to his high school sweetheart, so that left young Max. He might just be gullible enough to be swayed by a pretty, older woman with a lilting voice.

"Why would she help him after he broke her heart?"

"Apparently, he was having second thoughts about Portia who didn't understand him as well as Clarissa. The usual bullshit when a man wants to make sure he's got a plan B lined up in case things don't work out with the current one."

"Or he was just using her."

"Either way, I'm encroaching on your personal space, so I'll just be going." She turned to go. "Oh," Midge circled back, "and just one more thing."

"Yes?"

"Your boyfriend Spencer supposedly signed an intellectual property agreement with B. A. Ellis Industries when he worked for them ten years ago. Astor and Byron Ellis pitched a fit when Spencer launched his company. From their perspective, all of his current ideas came while he worked for them. So..."

"They think he stole from them on a technicality."

"Don't know. Sorry, I'm still invading your personal space." Midge sniffed the air indignantly. "You're just like my *former* friend Louisa. Fixed her up with a perfectly good man. But did she appreciate it, no...insisted on staying with her deadbeat husband. Neither you, nor she, have any appreciation for the lengths I go to help my friends."

"C'mon, Midge. Try to understand."

"Oh, I understand all right. You're forgetting...146 IQ and all. But you know where I am when you realize that life is way more exciting with me in it, than without." With that, Midge climbed the emergency fire escape, stomping as hard as possible along the way, making the metal rails vibrate. Upstairs, she could be heard closing her window—loudly.

CHAPTER 17

Not a Girl

Monday Morning at Darwin's Condo

~

"How was your weekend, Ms. Brennan?" Darwin asked when Rue arrived for work on Monday morning. Three days later and her head still hurt.

"Fine," she answered. "Pretty quiet," she lied. "And you?"

"About the same," he answered. There was a thickness in the air, the kind you feel where you suspect that neither person is telling the truth, but you don't want to call them out on it.

It had been nearly two weeks since Clarissa's death and reporters had since gotten bored with them. Unfortunately, their stalking had not been without incident, as vandals not only made a mess of Darwin's downtown agency, but they managed to bust a plumbing pipe on the premises, causing considerable water damage. He was still sorting out the mess with his landlord. So, they continued to meet at Darwin's condo, for now.

Rue walked into the kitchen to store a tuna sandwich in the refrigerator for lunch, setting it on the shelf below one of Darwin's dark-green beverage containers and store-bought Mediterranean salad.

"Do you eat anything for lunch that isn't green?" Rue asked.

"Do you eat anything that isn't sandwiched between processed white bread?" He motioned toward the tuna sandwich she just put in the frig and then turned to point at the bagel she had sitting on her desk along with a cup of tea. "I picked up breakfast for you, as promised."

"Fair point," she acknowledged. "And...thanks."

"Spirulina is good for the little gray cells," Darwin explained, even though Rue hadn't asked. He pointed to his temple.

"You've lost me," Rue admitted.

"My green drink," he explained. "Made up of blended kale, apple, celery, cucumber and a bit of Spirulina...good for the body and brain."

If she hadn't been hung over just two days prior, she might not have looked as queasy as she did at that moment.

"Mind shutting the refrigerator door?" Darwin pointed to where Rue stood with the door to the frig hanging wide open. "Energy is expensive... and, are you okay?" he asked. "You look a little green around the gills."

Rue nodded and closed it haphazardly. "I'm fine. I must have stood too close to your drink," she joked, returning to her desk. *Probably should get a little food in me, though,* Rue thought. She sat and nibbled a few bites of her breakfast bagel and took a tentative sip of her tea, still too hot. Meanwhile, Darwin took her place in the kitchen to pour himself a cup of coffee. He had his own routine, coffee for breakfast and a green smoothie and salad for lunch.

Moments later, Darwin's front door burst open. "I knew you'd come calling when that plain little assistant of yours didn't work out. Second time in less than a week." Monica (who goes by Monique now) sashayed her way across the threshold of Darwin's home office wearing a tight black dress that only reached mid-thigh with 4" red-spiked heels and a matching scarf wrapped around her neck. The scarf was longer than her dress and nearly reached her knees.

It was then that Monique saw Rue and wrinkled her nose a little.

"Oh," she offered flatly. "You're still here. Hadn't seen you since that day at the Seaport and assumed..." Monique didn't feel the need to finish the sentence. It was only then that Rue recognized her. She was one of the two women cooing over Darwin at her interview.

Darwin ignored the exchange, returning from the kitchen with two cups of coffee. "Good, you're here," he said to Monique as he handed her one of the cups. "Tall, no cream or sugar, right?"

"That's right, baby," Monique accepted the cup. "Just the same as I like my men—tall, dark, and bitter."

"Monique, may I introduce you to Rue. You met Rue at the pier two weeks ago, remember?"

"Oh, I remember," Monique shot Rue a fake smile before taking a sip of her coffee, leaving a bright red lipstick stain on the rim.

"I have an assignment for you both. Monique, I'm afraid you're going to need a different outfit for today, of the jeans and t-shirt variety."

"Boring," Monique set her coffee cup on the table next to Rue and began unwrapping the scarf that was around her neck.

"Candy secured press passes for you both." Darwin walked over to his desk, procuring two clip-on passes. He handed one to each of the women.

"Passes for what?" Rue was curious.

"B. A. Ellis Industries is having a small press event with a behind-the-scenes tour of the company. It's part of their 'transparency' initiative to embrace the media. This works out perfectly for us." Darwin leaned against the back of the couch. "Rue, I need you to play journalist for..." he motioned for her to hand the pass back so he could look at it, "*The Tech Boom Times*?" He shook his head. Candice was having a little too much fun being creative. "Monique, they are expecting a male photographer so..."

"Why can't she be the man?" Monique whined. "It's much easier for a woman to play a man versus the other way around. I can fix her up in no time."

"I like her better as a woman, thank you."

"Oh, I'll bet you do," Monique winked.

Rue was perplexed. Monique smiled and finished unwrapping her scarf, revealing a very large Adam's apple. She proceeded to tug at her hair and a well-fitted wig came off in her hands. Monique then dug into her purse for a cloth makeup wipe, expertly removing her eye, cheek and lip makeup in one swift motion. Rue watched, mesmerized.

"Darwin, honey, help me with the back." Darwin obliged, unzipping the back of Monique's dress part-way, just enough so that she could reach behind her back to unzip it the rest of the way.

"You can change in there," Darwin pointed to the spare bathroom on the other side of the room, next to a closet.

But Monique couldn't resist pulling the top of her dress down and tugging at the heavily padded bra. She turned her back toward both of them, dropping the bra on the floor as she made her way to the bathroom, pausing at the closet with her dress hanging around her waist, to fish out a pair of jeans and a t-shirt that Darwin had left for her.

Once she'd closed the door, Rue asked, "So, I guess Monique stays here a lot, seeing as you have a spare wardrobe for her....er, or him?"

Darwin cleared his throat and walked over to the now-open closet. He pulled out several hangers to show them to her—a dress, a pair of pants, a long-sleeved men's shirt. "Much like an array of costumes you might find at the theater, I have several on hand for a few contractors who do work for me."

Rue paused, taking the information in.

"So, no," Darwin clarified, "I can assure you that Monique does *not* stay here a lot or at all, for that matter."

"Your loss," Monique answered as she re-emerged from the bathroom wearing a black t-shirt and blue jeans, barefoot. Only this time, she was a *he* and the timbre and pitch of his voice were noticeably deeper.

"By the way, it's Monte," he offered Rue his hand as if meeting for the first time. "My given name is Montgomery, but no one but my mother ever called me that. Call me Montgomery, and I'll have to scratch your eyes out."

"Nice to meet you." Rue shook his hand, cautiously, watching as the Adam's apple bobbed up and down.

"What, haven't you ever seen a man this stunning before?" He winked. Frankly, Rue thought Monte looked better as a man with wavy, black hair that reached about an inch below his earlobes. Without the fake eyelashes and presumably, green contact lenses, she could see that his eyes were a deep brown. Honestly, she didn't know why he would want to cover them up. He had a square jaw that seemed more pronounced without the scarf.

"Just surprised is all," Rue choked out. To Darwin, she asked, "So, what's my disguise? Anything in that wardrobe for me?"

"Why would you need a wardrobe?" Darwin asked. "What you're

wearing is fine. And you have experience as a journalist. You'll blend right in."

"But I'm Spencer Hargrove's girlfriend," she explained. "Won't someone at B. A. Ellis Industries recognize me and find it odd that the competitor's girlfriend would be taking a behind-the-scenes tour?"

"Funny," Darwin explained. "I guess I hadn't thought of that given that I've never actually seen you and Spencer out in public together."

Come to think of it, neither had Rue. At least not at public events, usually just dark movie theaters and restaurants.

"We could give her a goth-look black wig, white makeup and lipstick. I can fix her up in a jiffy," Monte offered.

"No, then she'll stand out *too* much."

"Then leave her as she is. I promise you; no one will notice that little scrap of a thing in whatever this is," he made a sweeping motion over Rue's plain black knee-length flair skirt and tan sweater. Spencer always criticized her colorful wardrobe, and she was doing her best to dress more demurely for work.

"You realize I'm standing right in front of you, *Montgomery*," Rue hissed.

"Trollop." Monte stuck his tongue out.

"Ladies, please," Darwin chastised. He paused to look at Rue's face, making a little too much eye contact. She felt her cheeks getting warm. "Hmmm," he said.

"What, hmmm?"

Monte stood beside Darwin and began eyeing Rue in the same way.

"Maybe we make a few subtle adjustments, so she looks different enough not to raise any eyebrows."

"Like actually filling out her eyebrows a bit more," Monte suggested.

"Exactly. We can line her lips a little more, so they don't look so thin." Darwin pointed.

"It's rude to point," Rue complained. *And what was so bad about having thin lips? No one had ever complained about them before.*

"A few hair extensions," Monte added.

"Do we have time for that?" Darwin asked.

"Probably not. Perhaps just a beret or hat to tuck her hair in?"

"Excellent idea."

Over the next fifteen minutes, Rue sat miserably as the two men fixed her hair and makeup and added a few pieces of silver and beaded jewelry that a journalist on a budget would wear. Then, she caught a glimpse of herself in the mirror, and realized that maybe she should let other people dress her up from now on. She looked pretty darn cute if she said so herself.

"Now for the important part," Darwin told them. "The assignment is two-fold. One, we need to keep an eye out for Astor Ellis. As head of Research & Development and next in line for the Ellis Industries throne, he will certainly make an appearance. His office is on the third floor overlooking the research lab below. You're going to need to see if you can access his office, either during the tour or when he steps out to lunch, which is almost always at noon sharp."

"What are we looking for?" Rue asked.

"On behalf of our contract with Spencer, we need to survey what his computer setup is, and any clues as to who might be sending him intel and how. And at Gretchen Ellis's request, see if there's a little black book or some evidence as to who else he might be seeing. Personally, I think he's going to behave himself for a while, at least until he takes over the company and he and Portia LaMonte marry."

"But that's still three months away," Monte pointed out. "Men like that can't keep it in their pants for that long, even with a hottie like Portia LaMonte on their arm."

"Perhaps," Darwin acknowledged. "Just be careful. Keep an eye out for surveillance cameras and if it seems too risky, bow out and we'll find another way."

CHAPTER 18
B. A. Ellis Industries

Monday Afternoon at a Press Gathering

Monte and Rue blended with relative ease on the tour. To their surprise, no one actually asked for any form of ID. They merely flashed their press badges and that was enough for the guard at the front desk to motion them to join the rest of the group which consisted of about a dozen other reporters and photographers from local newspapers and TV groups.

A tour guide wearing a sharp blue and white suit jacket and skirt greeted them. She had a small red cravat around her neck and looked more like a stewardess then a host at a tech company.

"We're so excited you've decided to join us today," she beamed a row of perfectly straight and obviously whitened teeth at them. "A few housekeeping rules before we begin our tour," she began. "Photography is permitted everywhere except within the lab itself," she cautioned. "Due to proprietary concerns, the lab is off limits. But our publicist will happily provide you with pre-approved photos should you wish to write an article about your experience today, and," she winked, "we hope you do."

Rue reached into the small hip purse Darwin's wardrobe provided her and pulled out a wintergreen Lifesaver, popping it into her mouth. She offered Monte one just as the tour guide looked at her.

"No food or beverages are permitted in the lab," she smiled sweetly.

Rue tucked the offending mint between her cheek and teeth instead of sucking on it. The woman continued to tick off a list of other rules that Rue was only half paying attention to as she put her mints away, something about touching things in the lab that were hands off, smoking, and well, that's about all Rue heard.

Rue, however, perked up once they'd gotten past the blah, blah, blah history of the company and entered the lab. To Rue, it seemed endless, beginning with the area dedicated toward the future of cell phone technology, then moving on to the next wave of high-speed Internet and something called a "blue tooth" which made no sense to her. There was one section she paid extra attention to, and that was the computer graphics development area where the guide bragged about how they were revolutionizing the way movie animation was created, leading to better graphics and special effects. She remembered hearing Spencer say something like, "One day, entire movies will be played out using the computer animation technology that SpencerTech built." Funny, as this woman was saying about the same thing—almost word for word, except she was crediting Ellis Industries for such inventions.

Just then, they passed Astor Ellis's office, the Astor Ellis who is the current head of Research & Development and next in line as CEO of B. A. Ellis Industries once his father retired and he had secured the hand of the pet supply heiress and influencer Portia LaMonte.

"Will Mr. Ellis be making an appearance today?" Rue asked, casually pointing toward Astor's door so there was no confusion as to which Ellis she was referring.

The guide smiled at her. "Unfortunately, the Ellis family it out of town on business today and won't be joining us. But with any luck, one of our developers will pop by to greet us before our tour has concluded."

That didn't interest Rue, but she tried not to appear visibly disappointed.

It was then that the group was directed to the most awe-inspiring area of all. It was the future of something they called "virtual reality." Rue, feeling as if she had enough trouble with "real reality" followed Monte's lead when he tugged at her arm so they could quietly peel away from the group.

Once the tour had moved on, Monte wasted no time in breaking into Astor Ellis's office. She expected him to use a nail file and a credit card like what she'd seen so often on TV. Instead, he pulled out some small, square device that seemed to magnetically connect to the front of the door, just next to the door's handle. He leaned in and listened, for what, Rue couldn't be certain. Then, at just the right moment, Monte smiled and turned the knob. And just like that, the door to Astor's office was unlocked. They quickly crept inside, closing and re-locking the door behind them.

Monte surveyed the room, murmuring senseless words like, "Intel processing unit, HP tower, DSL line and multiline connectors," as if committing all of it to memory.

"I'll handle the tech if you dig through the desk and see if you can find anything interesting."

Rue merely nodded. After all, she was an events writer. Investigative journalism was new to her, and therefore, she wasn't entirely sure what she was looking for. But somehow, she wanted to prove herself a worthy assistant to a boss who she really didn't want to work for anyways...did she?

Just then, they heard someone breathing heavily, followed by the jiggling of a door handle.

"Who's in here?" a security guard demanded, fumbling with the lock before bursting into Astor Ellis's office. Monte was sitting at the desk, taking inventory of the computer monitor, computer tower, printer, and related equipment including floppy disks, CDs and external hard drives. His prop camera sat precariously on the edge of the desk. Just as the man entered, Monte spotted a sticky note with a few numbers and letter on it.

Rue looked up. She had been about to rifle through one of the desk drawers when the guard almost caught her red-handed. Monte looked at her, eyes widening as if to ask, *what do we do?* After all, when it came to quick thinking, he typically relied on Candice. Too bad she wasn't there.

In a moment of desperation, Rue did the only thing she could think of. She plopped herself into Monte's lap, wrapped her hand around the back of his head and pulled him in for a kiss. She expected to meet resistance. Instead, he kissed her back, a little more forcefully than was necessary, wrapping an arm around her waist and hugging her to him. She could feel his chest and abs. *Strong*, she thought briefly, allowing her other arm to wrap around his shoulder as she melted into the kiss.

With his free hand, Monte reached forward and palmed the sticky note, slipping it into in his shirt pocket, never losing his lip-lock with Rue.

"Knock it off, lovebirds," the security guard demanded. His eyes started to fall toward the drawer that Rue had opened. Desperate times called for desperate measures. With her toe, she nudged Monte's camera to the ground and heard it shatter. As the guard's gaze fell toward the floor, she shut the drawer.

Monte stifled back a few expletives as they broke from their embrace. As a final act, Rue unclipped her press pass, jamming it into her small purse. Monte followed suit, stuffing his into his back pocket.

"I'm so sorry," Rue sniffed. "We're in the middle of a messy divorce." She crumpled her face. "And working with my husband again," she eyed Monte, lovingly, "was the first real connection we've had in a long time."

"And what does that have to do with your being in Mr. Ellis's office?"

Monte eyed Rue for a moment before answering in the manliest way possible. "We haven't had sex in a year and the broom closet was locked."

"And this room wasn't?" The guard peered at the door handle.

"No," Monte answered.

"No matter. Take your business elsewhere. I'm not going to report seeing you as I don't want to come between a couple trying to work on their relationship, but you most certainly can't stay here, and you're no longer welcome at B. A. Ellis Industries. That clear?"

"Crystal," Monte squatted down to pick up the camera. The front lens had shattered.

"Leave it," the guard motioned to the pieces on the floor. "I'll have maintenance clean this up. Just take what's left of your camera and get out of here."

Just as Monte began standing from his kneeling position on the floor, he spotted something on the underside of the desk—the same police-issue bug taped to it, just like the one Darwin had found recently in his office.

"C'mon honey," he wrapped his arm around Rue's waist and pulled her toward him, once again, a bit closer than necessary. "Let's go home."

"Sorry, again," Rue murmured as she passed the guard. "I promise to write something nice about today's tech tour at B.A. Ellis industries."

"Never mind," the guard gruffly answered, pointing toward the elevator. Once they'd disappeared behind the doors, he placed a call to the front desk. "There's a female writer wearing a beret and a photographer with a broken camera on their way out. Make sure they actually leave the premises. Nah, not necessary. Thanks."

With that, the guard let out a sigh and called maintenance.

"BROKEN CAMERA ASIDE," Monte acknowledged, "I have to give credit where it is due. That was some fast thinking back there."

"Thanks," Rue beamed proudly. "You know," she laughed, "you sure are a good kisser for someone who isn't attracted to women."

Monte was offended. "Who says I don't like women?"

"Well, I mean…the wardrobe, the 'I like my coffee like I like my men' comment."

"So, because I like to dress as a woman, it automatically means I'm not attracted to them?"

"I guess not?" Rue fumbled. "Forget I said anything. You're a cross-dresser who likes women, not men, got it."

"And who says I don't like men?"

"You're very confusing," Rue admitted.

"Actually, honey," Monte shifted his shoulders. "I'm not confused in the slightest." They took a few back roads toward Darwin's condo, just in case they were being followed. "Exactly how long have you lived in Manhattan?"

"Just over a year," she answered, "why?"

"That explains it."

"What does it explain?" Rue demanded.

"I'm guessing Spencer Hargrove has been your only boyfriend upon arrival?"

"So, what of it?"

Monte stifled back a laugh. “That explains the kiss.” He smiled, proud of himself.

“What’s that supposed to mean?” The pitch in Rue’s voice was creeping up.

“It means you have a lot to learn about living in Manhattan. Honey, you need to get out more.”

“I think you’re out enough for the both of us,” Rue teased.

“Trollop,” Monte wrinkled a nose at her. “But I tell you what? If things don’t work out with you and Spencer, give me a call. I'll show you what it’s like to date a real man.”

“No thanks, Montgomery. My ego can’t take the idea of dating anyone prettier than me.”

“I am pretty gorgeous, aren’t I?” Monte acknowledged.

“Exquisite.”

Darwin had not yet returned from…well, wherever he was, when Monte and Rue got back from their adventure. Rue felt terrified, and yet exhilarated, at the same time. Her first assignment undercover and it went far better than expected, even when getting caught.

Rue and Monte were laughing about today’s turn of events when Darwin finally arrived, carrying a leather satchel and an underarm full of mail, most of it junk.

“You two seem awfully happy,” Darwin observed. “Did you kiss and make up?”

Rue’s face turned red as she fought back an awkward laugh. Monte merely looked at his bare, buffed fingernails as if he found his cuticles spectacularly interesting. Given that it was Monte, that may have been the case.

Finally, Monte chimed in. “We got interrupted mid-search,” he explained.

“Oh?” Darwin was concerned.

“Don’t worry, we talked our way around it okay. However…” Monte reached into his pocket and pulled out a small yellow post-it note. “The dumb-ass boss's son at a high-security tech company actually had his username and password stuck to the side of his computer monitor."

Monte then went on to explain, in detail, the computer setup in Astor's office, information which was still largely over Rue's head. She nodded with pretend interest.

"Great work," Darwin snagged the note.

"Oh," Monte continued, "and the place is bugged a la Detective Ortega style. Guess he's still a person of interest in the Clarissa Sauer case."

"Indeed," Darwin answered before turning to Rue and asking, hopefully, "and what was your experience like, today? Discover anything interesting?"

Rue suddenly felt deflated. After all, Monte now knew the soup-to-nuts of Astor Ellis's computer network, his login info, and that he was being hounded by the police. Rue had a whole lot of nothing to contribute.

"Sadly, no," she dropped her gaze. "I'm afraid I wasn't much use at all."

Monte chimed in, "Are you kidding?" He looked first at Rue and then Darwin. "She was...magnifique...truly," he praised. "I couldn't have gotten the intel I did if she hadn't provided a good cover and been quick on her feet."

Rue smiled to herself. She couldn't recall ever being called *magnifique* before. It was kind of nice.

Darwin glanced oddly between Monte and Rue. After all, aside from Candice, Monte was never particularly keen on praising anyone but himself which told Darwin that in one short afternoon, Rue had managed to earn something that Monte didn't give away freely...his respect.

Moments later, Candice arrived, looking as if she'd had a rough night.

"Look at what the cat dragged in," Monte commented.

"Screw you, Montgomery," Candice chastised, eyed Rue for support and winked. "Just a tough time getting to sleep last night, is all," she explained.

"Oh, I'll bet," Monte spoke in his Monique voice.

Candice was dressed in a pink tank top that was so tight, Rue was certain her breasts were going to pop out at any moment. She also had on a very short, very tight, red leather miniskirt that made it impossible for her to bend over without revealing her thong. And given that Rue knew the woman had a thong on, meant that Candice wasn't even trying to be delicate. Her eye makeup was smeared, giving her a raccoon look, and her concealer appeared to have been applied with a trowel. In short, she was a train wreck that Rue couldn't help but be fascinated and horrified with at the same time.

"What are you lookin' at?" Candice demanded.

"I think she's trying to tell if your boobs are real or not, or if you're even a girl."

"Why would she—" Candice glanced at Monte, still buffing his nails. "Oh," she smiled. "I get it." She walked over to Rue, pulling her shoulders back and thrusting her chest out. "You can feel 'em if you want. I can assure you; I am all woman."

"I'm good, thanks." Rue backed away.

"Ahem," Darwin interrupted. "Candy, would you mind changing out of your...uh...work clothes into...well, your *other* work clothes?" He motioned toward the bathroom.

"Sure thing, boss," she answered, winking at Rue before leaving the room. She turned the bathroom light and fan on and closed the door behind her.

"Hey, Candy!" Monte called in after her, moments later.

"What? I'm on the toilet! Can't it wait?"

"Uh, yeah. It can wait."

After what seemed like an eternity later, Candice emerged from the bathroom, wearing a pair of blue jeans and a casual blouse. The makeup had been removed and her hair had been combed.

"Much better," Monte commented.

By this point, Rue was already updating notes from today's events into the computer while Monte filled Darwin in on their adventures. He was gentleman enough to soften the part about the kiss, reducing it to a mere peck on the lips. And yet, Darwin still raised an eyebrow and glanced at Rue.

"I can feel your eyes burning into the side of my head, Mr. Fennec," Rue typed. "It was necessary to maintain our cover...no big deal."

"So, what was so urgent that you had to yell at me while I was on the toilet?" Candice asked Monte.

"I was reminding you that Bristol has a gig at the coffeehouse tonight. Are you gonna be up for it?"

"Sure," she answered. "I doubt my assignment will take more than a few hours and I'll have a chance to get a nap in before tonight."

"Well, you missed me telling Darwin how brilliant Rue was today on the investigation."

"Really?" Candice pinched her lips together.

"I think we should bring her along to celebrate her first undercover work."

"You always remember your first," Candice winked.

"A small reminder that you're technically in the office," Darwin cautioned.

"Sorry, boss," Candice answered. To Rue, she said, "Monte is not easily impressed. So, if you got by his overly critical judgment, then you're okay in my book. You should definitely hang with us tonight."

"Okay," Rue agreed. The queasiness from the morning was now replaced with a bundle of nerves and energy. "Are you going, too?" she asked Darwin.

"No," Monte answered for him. "He doesn't fraternize with the help," he laughed. "To be honest, I wouldn't want to be seen with us, either. Our collective hotness is a little too much for most people to handle."

"About today's assignment," Darwin turned back to Candice, ignoring Monte's comments. "I need you to do a little digging into Astor Ellis's personal life. His mother is concerned that his dalliances might interfere with his upcoming nuptials."

"Nuptials," Candice snorted. "You and your big words."

Darwin eyed her, curiously.

"Okay, you got it boss. I'm on it."

CHAPTER 19
Kaffeehaus

Monday Evening at a Coffee House

~

Rue had been in the city for over a year now and still hadn't scratched the surface of all that was Manhattan. Of course, part of that was because Midge and Spencer were the few people she socialized with on a regular basis. And while Midge was the adventurous one, always taking Rue to questionable places just for the fun of it, Spencer was pretty...*status quo.*

Were it not for a journalism gig that required she interview entertainers and review special events, there was a good chance that Rue wouldn't have made it much past her block, save for Midge's odd outings. Still, Monte had a point. She was pretty green when it came to understanding the Big Apple. And, if she were being honest with herself, she was flattered that he and Candice invited her to the coffee house to hear Bristol's set. She suspected they didn't typically invite people into their little circle, a fact that she didn't take lightly.

She arrived at 8 p.m. wearing a long-sleeved, brown knit dress, faux-leather ankle boots, along with ridiculously large gold-plated hoop earrings that Midge had given her. Somehow, she was distinctly aware of them, making her feel as if her ears were twice as large as her head.

Rue felt a moment of anxiety walking into the crowded coffee house alone, seeing groups and couples all swarming together while the house music played over the loudspeakers. The smell of freshly ground coffee and sweet caramel filled the air. She felt oddly conspicuous despite the fact that no one seemed to actually be looking at her.

In fact, she was about to turn around and walk out when... "Hey, Rue, honey!" Candice waved her arm frantically. "Over here!"

Rue inched her way over to them, turning sideways and slipping between people until she'd made it to the deep-seated, espresso-colored leatherette couch where Candice and Monte sat. Monte's long arms were spread across the back of the couch, legs sprawled out in front of him, ensuring that he and Candice had claimed the entire space including the small coffee table in front of them.

"Cute earrings!" Candice gushed when Rue sat down. "Take a load off. Bristol should be on any minute."

Moments later, a server stopped by the lounge area, placing a small Turkish coffee pot and cup in front of Monte and a raspberry danish and cappuccino before Candice.

"Get you something, hun?" the server asked Rue.

"Uh, yeah. How about a double espresso macchiato...if you have that," Rue ordered, hesitantly.

"And a raspberry danish," Candice called. "Get her a danish, on me!" The server nodded as other patrons quickly began vying for her attention, no one wanting to abandon their comfy couches or pub tables lest someone take it while they were at the coffee counter.

"You sure know your coffee," Candice complimented. "Hope you like raspberry, but if not, I'll eat it. Their pastries here are to die for."

Monte laughed. "She says the same thing about the red bean sticky buns from Chinatown. The girl likes her pastries."

"And it's startin' ta show," she pinched a roll of flab across her midsection. "I can already pinch more than an inch," she complained before settling back into the couch.

Moments later, Bristol took to the stage, pulling up a chair and setting a music stand low in front of him while a man dressed all in black brought him a microphone with a stand. He relieved Bristol of his guitar case after Bristol pulled a Martin acoustic from it. Two other band mates took to the stage, one bearing a fiddle, the other a hand drum. After a few minutes, they each had microphones in front of them. Bristol didn't wait for anyone to introduce them. Instead, he started playing quietly. A wave came over the coffeehouse as the noise flowed into hushed voices and then applause, coupled with a few cheers, as they recognized him. Then, for the first time since Rue arrived, the place grew quiet.

The server placed her hyper-caffeinated beverage in front of Rue along with a sugar bowl, cream, and one raspberry pastry. She didn't talk, merely nodded and darted away.

Bristol began singing a slow and hauntingly sad ballad about lost love. Rue had never heard it before, but like everyone else, sat mesmerized. His voice was melodic and sounded much softer than his day-to-day speech. Just as everyone had settled into that warm glow, there was a long pause and suddenly the fiddler and drummer jumped in as the music transitioned into a Celtic jig. "We're the Clifdens. Thanks for being here," Bristol called. "Be sure to tip your servers. They're workin' hard for you tonight. And be sure to tip your musicians...we can really use the cash." The crowd laughed as several people dropped bills into the tip jar at the edge of the stage.

It was only then that Rue noticed something...his voice sounded Irish. But she didn't remember him sounding that way before. Maybe it was part of his stage persona?

"Seems to be a man with many talents," Rue commented to her new friends. "Great with the get-away cars and—" she paused to avoid mentioning her rescue from Merriam Hall. "And a talented singer, too."

"Not to mention a great songwriter, musician, and—" Candice motioned toward a little girl standing at the corner of the stage clapping her hands together gleefully, wearing a pink dress with bright aqua stockings, her blonde hair in curls, "a great dad," she finished.

The song ended and during the applause, the little girl who couldn't have been more than about five-years-old, bounded up the stage steps, her curls bouncing along with her. Without asking permission, she climbed into Bristol's lap. He set his guitar on the stand that had been set beside him. She settled in, facing the audience, her hands on each of her dad's knees, smiling as if the applause had been for her.

Bristol tousled his daughter's hair before leaning forward, placing his hand on the mic and saying, "No boundaries. Does whatever she likes... just like her mother." The crowd laughed.

The little girl turned her torso, holding her hand up to cup it around her dad's ear as if whispering him a secret.

"That one?" he clarified, still talking into the mic. The little girl nodded.

"And then you'll go sit quietly with your Aunt Candice until your mum arrives to pick you up?"

She nodded, enthusiastically.

"Well," Bristol addressed the crowd. "Seems Evie refuses to go to bed unless we sing her a lullaby. Do you mind?"

The crowd's applause indicated that Evie had them all wrapped around her adorable little finger.

With that, Bristol scooted his daughter off his lap. She stood, wrapping her arms around his neck and leaning into his side as he fetched his guitar. He launched into Edelweiss, his bandmates offering backup vocals. He rocked back and forth as little Evie, who couldn't possibly have understood the meaning behind the song's lyrics at such a young age, sang with him.

"Blossom of snow may you bloom and grow," they sang.

Pretty soon, the entire coffeehouse was singing. For all the people who claimed to have never seen the Sound of Music, Rue thought it an amazing coincidence that so many people seemed to know the words.

Toward the end of the song, one of the Clifden members unhooked his microphone and brought it over to Evie who released the grip on her dad's neck long enough to pull her hair out of the way and lean into the mic to finish the song. "Bless my homeland forever."

The crowd erupted. Evie waited for the noise to die down before she very purposefully grabbed the mic and said in a very rehearsed manner, "And don't forget to tip the band. It keeps me in curls and my dad really needs the cash."

The crowd laughed emphatically as more people dropped money into the tip jar.

"Little hoodlum," Monte shook his head. "Can't believe he's exploiting his daughter like that."

"Oh, c'mon," Candice waved her hand. "It's all in good fun."

"Says you. Just you wait until she grows up swindling men out of their money at the pool hall conning 'em with false tales of suffering so they pay her way to meet her family in Europe."

"I had no idea you were so cynical, Montgomery," Rue teased.

Monte leaned in and whispered, "Yeah, you just keep calling me Montgomery, would you? See how fast I let Darwin in on our little tête-à-tête at Ellis Industries the other day."

"I think you mean Spencer," she clarified, "my boyfriend."

"Do I?" He tilted his head toward her, a churlish grin on his face.

"Why would I care what Mr. Fennec thinks?"

"Why, indeed?" Monte crossed one arm across his chest, resting his other elbow on it and framing his face with his hand.

Rue felt her face grow hot. "Jerk," she scolded.

"Trollop," he countered.

"Hey, I resent that!" Candice chimed in, even though no one was talking to her.

The argument was interrupted when Bristol told Evie, "Why don't you go sit with Aunt Candice."

Candice's eyes lit up as Evie climbed down from the stage and ran over to her.

"Are you really her aunt?" Rue asked, finally remembering to take a bite of her gifted raspberry pastry.

"Honorary title," Candice answered as Evie climbed onto the sofa, planting herself beside Candice and leaning into her chest. Candice wrapped her arm around Evie and gave Bristol a thumbs up. He nodded as his band continued their set.

Just then, Rue caught sight of someone peering in her direction, but when she turned to look, he cast his eyes downward and turned his back on her. The man who sat next to him tucked his head as the two exchanged a few words.

Rue set her danish down, wiping her hands on her dress before standing up. Monte gave her a questioning look.

"Be right back," she said.

The two men remained huddled until she addressed them.

"Max, how nice to see you," she smiled widely as the SpencerTech employee feigned surprise. She turned to the other pimply-faced man. "Tommy? Is that right? I believe my friend Midge and I met you the other night."

Tommy's eyes brightened for just a moment. "How is Midge? She hasn't been returning my calls."

"Couldn't say," Rue answered, feeling somewhat sorry for the man. "Haven't spoken to her much since then."

Tommy looked crestfallen.

"So interesting," Rue commented. "Tommy, didn't you use to work at B. A. Ellis Industries?" Tommy tried to sink into his bar stool. She turned to Max. "And I'm assuming you are still working with my Spencer, else I'm sure I would have heard differently. Is this like a meeting between the Montagues and Capulets?"

"Listen, Rue," Max explained. "Tommy and I have been friends since Kindergarten, long before Spencer ever worked with the Ellis family. His feud with them has nothing to do with me."

"Understood," Rue answered bluntly, the double shot of espresso coursing through her veins. "Just wanted to come over and say hi, so hi!" Her voice pitched upward as a nervous energy overtook her. Her hands began to tremble a little.

Max put his arm out and stopped her as she turned to leave. "Hey, Rue," he spoke softly. "Would you mind not telling Spencer you saw us here? He'd pitch a fit given the current legal battles."

"What legal battles?" Rue asked.

Max's expression revealed that he thought she already knew.

"Perhaps I've said too much."

Rue thought about this a moment. She could walk away and pretend she didn't see Max and Tommy here and mind her own business. But would that make her deceitful to Spencer? She could betray Max, but how would that affect SpencerTech's production so close to product launch (not to mention making her feel like a heel)? On top of that, what good would it do? If Max was, in fact, leaking info to Tommy, he'd certainly be shoring up his accounts and deleting any paper trail following this encounter. Or she could tell Darwin, so they could collect as much info as possible before presenting evidence to Spencer."

Suddenly, Midge's hot-headed voice echoed through Rue's mind, *"Somehow convinced his former lover to hooch up to someone at SpencerTech and do a little snooping."*

Rue made a bold move as both Max and Tommy waited for her response.

"Tell you what, Max," she smiled. "Tell me more about these lawsuits and maybe I won't let Spencer know about your liaisons with Clarissa Sauer, where there's a good chance you spilled the beans about some of SpencerTech's upcoming technology."

Max exchanged confused looks with Tommy. Rue could see the wheels in Tommy's head turning as he calculated a response and figured out *she didn't know.*

"I think you should just tell her," Tommy finally said.

"About?" Max shot Tommy a curious look, eyes growing wide.

"About the lawsuits, of course," Tommy replied, cryptically. "She's working with a well-known investigator, after all. They'd figure it out eventually."

"Right," Max answered. "I guess I'm just surprised Spencer didn't tell you all this himself."

Rue had been wondering that very thing.

"It seems that Astor and Byron Ellis have been challenging a series of copyrights and patents that SpencerTech has on about a dozen different inventions. They claim that he drew up those blueprints while still working for B. A. Ellis Industries, even using their manpower and equipment to develop his ideas on company time."

That can't be, Rue thought. *Spencer was too noble to do something like that.*

Tommy chimed in. "I get where he was coming from," he defended Spencer. "If I were an intern working for minimum wage while helping make the company millions, I'd at least want to profit in some small way. After all, B. A. Ellis Industries showed an increased profit of 15% just six months after Spencer Hargrove began interning for them. Did they offer him a bonus for his efforts?" he asked. "No," he answered his own question. "Instead, they gave him a $100 restaurant gift card."

Rue thought about their recent dinner at The View. *Was Spencer living beyond his means, and not as well-off as he let on. If so, by how much?* she wondered.

"It was a bad rap," Max agreed. "But that's all gonna change in a few months. With SpencerTech becoming such a huge success, maybe the two companies will let bygones be bygones."

"I wish I could be as optimistic as you," Tommy shook his head, taking a sip of the coffee he'd let get cold before biting into a chocolate brownie.

"Which products are they suing him over?" Rue asked.

"A bunch," Max answered. "You might want to grab a notebook to write them down."

"Perhaps you could just tell me," Rue answered. "Slowly. Just one at a time."

Max was surprised by this but began rambling off the nature of each lawsuit. In Rue's mind, she started composing patterns not unlike the ones Darwin had taught her for unlocking accounts. She visualized each event as if it were a cartoon in front of her, giving each piece of data colors, shapes, numbers and images in her personal mind map. When he was finished, she answered. "Thank you, Max, you've been most helpful."

He grabbed her arm. "You're not going to tell Spencer, are you?"

I'm not, she thought. *But once this case is solved, Darwin might.*

"No," she answered as honestly as possible. "My lips are sealed."

Max smiled nervously, relieved. As she turned to leave, Tommy called over her shoulder. "Tell Midge I said hi?"

"Will do, when I see her," Rue answered, not that she had any intention of talking to Midge again anytime soon. Still, she felt a little sorry that Tommy ended up being another of Midge's casualties.

Once back at the couch, Candice announced. "There she is!" To Rue, she said, "We were wondering what happened to you."

"Candice, thanks for the danish and the invite, but I gotta go," Rue proclaimed.

Monte sat up, bending his knees and pulling his long legs in. "Where are you going?"

"To the office," she explained. "I've got to input some information on a case."

"To the office," Candice was surprised. "You mean Darwin's condo?"

"Exactly," she answered. "I can't access our files from my home computer."

"But it's after 9 p.m.," Monte protested. "Don't you think you should wait until normal business hours?"

"No, Mr. Fennec will understand."

Monte exchanged glances with Candice.

"Just get home safe, honey," Candice called after her.

"Guess I better phone Darwin and let him know that a whirling dervish is heading his way," Monte reasoned.

"Wonder what all that was about?" Candice asked, curiously.

"Aunt Candice?" Evie looked up, sleepily. "When's my mom going to get here? I'm really tired."

Candice kissed the top of the girl's head. "Any moment now, sweetie. You just rest your head in my lap until then."

Evie nodded, laying her head on Candice's lap. Candice rubbed the girl's back for a moment. Evie smiled and drifted off to sleep, despite the music, loud voices, and the whir of milk being frothed for lattes with the aroma of fresh roasted coffee filling her nostrils.

Since it was outside of business hours, Rue didn't use the key code to get in. In fact, she couldn't even get past the night security guard.

"Can I help you?" She stopped Rue at the elevator.

"Yes, I'm just popping up to see my boss, Mr. Darwin Fennec, on the seventh floor."

"You often visit your boss at this hour?"

"Well," Rue put a hand on her hip, "you know how it is." The rather plump security guard did not, in fact, seem to know. "He's actually my boyfriend," she lied.

"I thought you just said he was your boss."

"Just my nickname for him," Rue tried again. "Like Elvis is the King and Springsteen is the Boss?"

"Are you saying that Springsteen is your boyfriend?"

"Well, gee. Wouldn't that be nice?" Rue joked.

The guard was not amused. She picked up the phone and dialed. "Yeah, Mr. Fennec. I've got a lady here who claims to be your girlfriend."

She heard a muffled voice on the other end of the line, but Rue couldn't make out what he was saying.

The guard looked Rue over and pursed her lips. "Looks like the girl you described, but wouldn't it be easier if you tell me her name?" She listened for a minute. "Uh huh." She turned to Rue, "Your name Hildy? Hildy Johnson?"

Rue paused for a moment before it sank in. She bit her lip. "Yup, that's me."

"Go on," she motioned toward the elevator. "Crazy people and their weird role-playing. It's just sick," the guard mumbled to herself before returning to the romance novel she was reading.

Darwin met Rue at the door wearing white pajamas with blue pinstripes and fuzzy tan slippers.

"Hi, Walter," Rue answered, putting a hand on her hip in her best Rosalind Russell impersonation. "Didn't picture you as a fan of old movies." She brushed past him. "I can't talk now. I've got to record the notes in my head before they leak out!" Rue headed straight for her computer and powered it to life.

Darwin closed the door, standing there in his pin-striped pajamas, eyeing her curiously. He could see that she was pulling up Spencer's files and info on SpencerTech. What he couldn't understand was why she was creating a new file on someone named Tommy.

He wandered into the kitchen and retrieved a bottle of scotch from under the counter, added one ice cube to a small glass and poured. "You want..." he started to ask. He realized that she was too absorbed in her project, so he simply sipped and waited for her to finish her furious typing. He came back into the living room and leaned against the back end of the sofa.

"There!" she finally said, looking up. It was only then that she noticed the night clothes, slippers, and scotch. "Oh," she looked at him. "I'm sorry. Guess I should have called first, but you've got me so trained not to write anything down on paper that I had to get my thoughts archived and protected before I forgot anything!"

"That's okay," he grinned. "I think Monte tried to call and warn me you were coming but the cell reception was terrible, and the call was dropped."

Rue looked at him blankly. While Spencer had gotten her a cell phone, she still wasn't entirely comfortable using it and she had no idea what it meant to drop a call. "I discovered something," she proclaimed, eyeing the scotch.

"Would you like some?" he offered.

"Ew, no," she wrinkled her nose. "Besides, I'm still coming down after a caffeine high."

"I can see that," he answered.

"I'll let you read my notes in the morning," Rue explained. "But here's the Reader's Digest version. B. A. Ellis Industries has at least five lawsuits out against SpencerTech for 'stealing' proprietary information and selling it. Meanwhile, someone sent Clarissa Sauer to hooch up to Spencer's business partner, Max. Seems she was still loyal to Astor Ellis, even though he dumped her. Looks as if she and Max were having a fling."

"Really?" There was something gnawing in Darwin's chest about that one, but he wasn't sure yet what it was—a premonition of sorts.

"He as good as admitted it."

"What? When did you see him?" Darwin asked.

"Tonight, at the coffee shop with Monte and Candice. I saw Max hanging out with Tommy Marcuzzo."

"The Tommy who used to intern at Ellis Industries?"

"The same. And he even dated Midge for a short time. Small world, isn't it?"

"It would seem so," Darwin appeared unconvinced.

"Anyways, Max begged me not to tell Spencer, saying he and Tommy had been friends long before Spencer had a falling out with Astor Ellis over tech rights."

"So, Spencer doesn't know any of this?" Darwin asked.

"Of course not!" Rue was getting frustrated. "We can't let Spencer in on this until we have all the facts, otherwise, he can blow our investigation wide open if he lands into Max without...you know...having all the facts."

Darwin bit back a laugh. "If I understand you correctly," he clarified. "I'm the first person you're sharing this information with."

"Yes," Rue answered. "Why is that funny?"

"It's not," he smiled, shaking his head. "I must say, you're on fire tonight. We must remember to keep you overly caffeinated. Seems to help your sleuthing skills."

Rue let out a sigh. "I should probably leave," she said finally.

"Let me call you a cab, Ms. Brennan."

CHAPTER 20
Elektra

Tuesday Afternoon at the Artist Atelier

~

Rue found the whole idea morbid, but when the model coordinator called her out of the blue to take part in a draped modeling series being called "The Art of Death," Darwin encouraged Rue to participate.

"Why?" Rue demanded of Darwin at his home office that morning. "Is this revenge for my stopping by so late last night? That now you're visualizing me dead?"

"Now who's being morbid?" Darwin protested. "I just thought that it might get you in closer contact with Ursula Gorky, perhaps turn her into a character witness instead of just, well, just a witness."

"Given her friendship with Clarissa and how much she seemed to dislike me when we met up at the club last week, I doubt I'm likely to become her friend anytime soon."

"Club?"

Rue realized her mistake. She had neglected to tell him about Merriam Hall and Bristol, true to his word, kept his mouth shut.

"Let's just say, Midge dragged me to a dance hall and it didn't go so well. Ursula Gorky, and Emma Post were there. That was where Midge met Tommy Marcuzzo."

"Why are you just telling me this now?" Darwin asked, raising his voice in annoyance.

"Don't get your panties in a bunch," Rue defended. "It was a night I was hoping to forget, and Midge and I had a falling out, of sorts. Didn't think I had to share my whereabouts on my off hours," Rue pouted.

"But, just like last night, when you came barreling into my home with news, this is pertinent stuff surrounding our cases. What was different about that night?" Darwin eyed her suspiciously.

Rue cast her eyes to the floor, and Darwin realized...it might be something she didn't want to talk about lest he judge her. Darwin was very skilled at reading people. He softened his voice a little. "Why don't you get me up to speed about Ursula, Emma and this Tommy fellow? Leave out any personal details."

Rue relented, giving the bare-bones facts about Ursula telling the police she saw Rue push Clarissa over the balcony, Emma Post not really being pregnant, and that Midge and Tommy were over, but he still might be connected to the security leak SpencerTech was experiencing.

"So, Ursula and Emma are friends?" Darwin confirmed.

"Yes, and both figure models at the Artist Atelier like I am from time to time."

"That makes me even more convinced that you should take the modeling gig. Think of it as undercover work," Darwin reasoned.

"The Art of Death" series was the brainchild of Jaks Liebling, a dilettante who fashioned himself a great artist and instructor despite having no formal training. True, he had a natural talent, but it was his very large contributions to the Artist Atelier in the Lower East Side that garnered him admiration.

He was a legend in his own mind and the worst sort of narcissist. Jaks was the kind that did a fair job of feigning humility. He once held a wildly popular art exhibit featuring a series of "masterpieces" he supposedly painted during his time living in the Caribbean and invited freshman students to submit their tropical-themed works as part of a scholarship program. The student that won would have their tuition paid for one full year. But many claimed it was all for show and he did it to demonstrate how much better of an artist he was than they were and how his fame as a painter had garnered him the funds to support the less fortunate.

His most recent series involved models posing in the tragic death scenes from the world's most popular operas, including Tosca, Carmen, La Bohème, Elektra, and the Flying Dutchman. The opera has never been kind to women.

"Which scene did the model coordinator ask you to be a part of?"

"If I agree to do it, I get to be Elektra."

Darwin suddenly felt a lump in his throat as he unconsciously surveyed Rue from head to toe and then averted his gaze. "So, as a figure model, you have to dance around...naked?" Darwin banished the thought from his mind...eventually.

"No," Rue barked at him. "It's draped."

"What does that mean?"

"It means I get to keep my clothes on. I'll be in costume."

"Oh," was all Darwin said, trying not to sound disappointed.

"And I won't be dancing. I'll probably just be asked to hold a dance-like pose for an unbearably long time. Or worse, Jaks Liebling will have me lying in a dead heap on the floor for six hours a day for three days."

"Six hours? That sounds like a lot."

"It is a lot, Darwin. Being an art model is a lot harder than it looks."

"I'll bet. Well, then, never mind. It was just a thought." Darwin paused for a moment. "If you don't like modeling, then why do you do it?"

"That's just it," Rue explained. "I love it. I may not be an artist myself, but I love being around all that creativity and knowing that I get to be a part of it in some small way."

"But you seem averse to this project. Why?"

"I can't explain it," Rue answered. "There's just something creepy about posing for a death scene for an equally creepy Jaks Liebling."

"I see," Darwin acknowledged. "Well, don't do anything that makes you uncomfortable. We'll figure something else out."

Rue felt her stomach drop. There was nothing in Darwin's voice that sounded disapproving, and yet, just like with Spencer, she felt the need to not disappoint. It was bad enough that she was often disappointed with herself.

And, on the other hand, Rue thought to herself, *18 extra hours of contract work modeling, coupled with what Darwin would be paying me as his assistant on top of that and*...all that added up to the realization that Rue was going to be playing a dead Elektra.

CHAPTER 21
Box 11

Late Tuesday Evening at Darwin's Condo

Darwin was having a fitful night's sleep. His head hurt like it always did when he was missing something and an idea was trying pop out of it. He tossed and turned, rolling on his back, then his side, then his other side like a rotisserie chicken. Finally, he drifted back to sleep at 2 a.m.

It was one of those dreams where he was somehow inhabiting a foreign body without knowing who he was or why he was there.

He pulled back a black curtain and there she was...Clarissa Sauer, standing at the balcony in the same flowing red dress she wore the night she died, her fingers lightly stroking the top of the railing as she looked wistfully out toward the stage and the theater seats below her.

"You forgot your gloves," Darwin said to her, handing her the long black gloves she had been wearing the night she died.

She turned to him and smiled softly, her eyes falling toward the floor, tears streaming down her face. She sniffed them back. "He was using me, you know."

Darwin said nothing in return as she accepted the gloves.

She continued, "He thought dating me would make you jealous, and then..."

"He sent you in to spy on me," Darwin finished. Somewhere in the back of Darwin's dream state, he was asking himself, *who am I? Where did that come from?*

"Yes," Clarissa answered. "For a short while, I thought maybe he actually cared about me and that maybe I could come to care for him."

"And how did that work out?" Darwin asked, only this time, it wasn't his voice. It was that of someone else. *Who?*

She rubbed her belly, "You know how that worked out, Astor."

"You know I wish things could be different," he moved toward her.

Clarissa turned her back to him once again. "You don't know how many nights before the show, I'd come up here to your family's box and stand right here, wondering what life would be like if you'd chosen me over Portia."

"I didn't have a choice," Astor defended.

"Of course, you had a choice," she growled. "You're just using Portia for her money and influence, just as Spencer used me. Everyone is busy using everyone else." She paused. "I can't believe I actually started trying to feed you information, as if that would magically bring you back to me."

"You know I didn't ask you to do that," Astor told her, gently.

"Don't you realize," Clarissa sniffed, "that I would have done anything for you?"

"And you come up here, every night to Box 12, imagining a life that can never be?"

Clarissa's eyes furrowed, confused. "Box 12? No." She reached toward her chest to retrieve the note she'd had secured beneath a bra strap. "You mean box 11, don't you?"

With that, Darwin felt himself being pulled backward and out of Astor's body. As he was floating away, Clarissa turned to him, her voice muffled. It was then that he saw it, a bloodstain on the right side of her body—off center. "Did you ever think that maybe you're missing the obvious, Darwin Fennec? Just like me, you're letting your emotions cloud your judgment."

THE NEXT MORNING, while Rue was on her way to the Artist Atelier for several days of modeling that Darwin managed to convince her was part of her "undercover work" (not to mention the promise of extra cash), he put a call in to Detective Ortega. Surprisingly, Ortega was on the phone almost immediately.

"I know this is going to sound strange," Darwin told the detective, not bothering to exchange pleasantries, "but I need to ask you a question." Darwin didn't wait for permission. "Was Clarissa Sauer's stab wound fatal?"

Darwin could hear Ortega sucking in his breath on the other end of the line. Finally, he cleared his throat and asked, "Please tell me, Mr. Fennec, that you are not trying to investigate the very crime in which you are actually a suspect?"

"I'm not," Darwin defended. "It just so happens that your case seems to have some overlaps with one I'm working on for a client."

"Is that so," Ortega was interested. "And who might that client be?"

"I can't say," Darwin answered. "But—"

"Listen very carefully, Mr. Fennec," Detective Ortega interrupted him. "If you're withholding evidence..."

"I'm not," Darwin repeated. "But what I can tell you is that I think Spencer Hargrove was the father of Clarissa's unborn baby."

There was a pause at the other end of the line. "And how is it that, number one, you knew she was pregnant, and number two, that she was dating...Spencer Hargrove, is it?"

"Come now, detective," Darwin answered. "I'm sure you've already uncovered that Spencer Hargrove used to work for the Ellises and that Rue Brennan is his girlfriend."

"And the pregnancy?"

"Part of my investigation."

"And," Ortega lowered his voice in a whisper as if keeping information to himself. Darwin could hear him shut the door to what he assumed was Detective Ortega's office. "Was your being with Rue Brennan at the theater, the night of the murder, also a part of your investigation?"

"In a way," Darwin confessed. "Yes, except it didn't exactly go according to plan."

"Clearly," Ortega answered flatly.

"Listen, Detective Ortega," Darwin tried again, "what I propose is this —while I can't share specific information about my clients, I am happy to let you in on anything that might assist with your case."

"Well, gee, Mr. Fennec," Ortega mocked, adopting the voice of a young child. "That would be swell!" He coughed before growling into the phone, "You'll let me in on any information you have because you and your 'lady friend' are suspects in a murder investigation. And, for the record, it is highly uncustomary for a police detective to be working with an outsider...what did you say you were again, a cyber-something-or-other?"

"A cyber forensic consultant and private investigator."

"Right," Ortega answered, in a way that suggested he wasn't overly impressed with Darwin's credentials.

"The point is," Darwin sighed. "Should you wish to work together and exchange information, you know where to find me."

"I'll keep that in mind, Mr. Fennec. Is that all?"

"It is, except you haven't confirmed whether the non-fatal wound found on Clarissa's body was on the right or left side."

"Doesn't matter which side, does it?" Ortega raised his voice. "Since you're not on the case!"

"Thank you, Detective Ortega, for confirming my suspicions."

Ortega realized his mistake. "Crafty, Mr. Fennec. Very crafty. Well played." He paused a moment longer. "Okay, since you were good enough to put me on to Spencer and Clarissa's relationship, I can confirm that it wasn't Clarissa's wound that killed her. It was the tumble over the balcony. She broke her neck in the fall."

"And the baby?" Darwin pressed his luck.

"Too young and not far enough along...couldn't be saved, I'm afraid." Ortega could be heard breathing heavily into the phone. "Really strange when you think about it," Ortega finally said. "Penelope...er, Dr. Washburn, thought so, too."

"What was?" Darwin asked quietly.

"Everything about the murder was so well-planned, so calculated. And yet, it was as if they were purposefully trying *not* to harm Clarissa Sauer, nor her baby. Why would a murderer go out of their way *not* to kill their victim?"

CHAPTER 22
The Gala

Four Months Ago, Before Clarissa Was Murdered - At the Artist Atelier

For artists, entrepreneurs, and philanthropists who needed to donate a percentage of their wealth quickly into charitable causes just before tax season, The Gala fundraiser at the Artist Atelier was the event of the season.

The grand entrance and the three surrounding galleries on the main floor were decorated with thousands of white, glittering string lights artfully placed across the ceiling and down the walls. One wall displayed an indoor cascading fountain with a basin covered in ivy vines and a white cherub statue sitting at the edge. The lights were strung in a way that framed the resin, wall-mounted fountain. On the opposite end of the room, a living wall covered in greenery flowed from ceiling to floor, accented with twinkling, handcrafted porcelain fairy figurines and pixies appearing to be tending to a few strategically placed ornamental flowers. At the center of the room was a tall, metal sculpture made of hundreds of silver balls all melded together to look like a woman who was dancing. The artist standing in front of the sculpture posing for pictures and answering questions was presumably the creator of said work who was touting something about it "being on loan from the Guggenheim."

People dressed in evening gowns and tuxes meandered in and out of the galleries, often holding a program in one hand and a beverage in the other. Servers dressed in either all black or all white pants with matching jackets floated around the room, edging their way between patrons, offering up platters filled with hors d'oeuvres such as bacon-wrapped scallops, filet mignon bites, and shrimp on crackers.

The most popular area, of course, were the open bars situated by the living wall and fountain, respectively. The poor cherub sculpture had been accidentally stepped on or leaned upon so many times, it was unlikely to make it through the evening without a few scratches.

Spencer and his date arrived in a taxi. He asked the driver to drop them off a block away from the Artist Atelier, "to avoid getting stuck behind the loading and unloading of limos," he informed his date for the evening.

It's important to note here that Rue was *not* the woman who he helped out of the taxi that evening. Instead of making an appearance with his girlfriend of over a year, he had invited...Clarissa Sauer, who was at this time still very much alive.

Clarissa was wearing a floor-length, black evening gown with a low v-cut front delivering just enough cleavage for anyone who cared to look. Her spiked heels were a shimmering red. She would have been taller than Spencer who dressed in a rental tux and bow tie were it not for the fact that he thought ahead and wore platform shoes.

He opened the car door for her, and she took the hand he offered in a practiced way. After paying the driver, Spencer stood upright, adjusted his jacket and offered his arm to the long-haired beauty.

Clarissa's feet were killing her in those shoes, and she certainly didn't relish the thought of walking another minute in them, let alone a block, but she smiled back at Spencer and didn't complain. Unlike Rue, she never complained about anything and was always agreeable, two traits that Spencer liked best.

"Remember, darling," he reminded her, "only one glass of champagne unless you see me take a second or if we're separated and all of the ladies in the group are drinking. Drink slowly, and if your glass is empty, ask the bartender to refill it with ginger ale."

"Don't worry," she smiled, "I remember. And waive off the hors d'oeuvres unless you accept one first or if I'm in a group where I'm encouraged to eat."

"Exactly, and..."

"Stick with simple foods like watermelon bites and coconut shrimp and avoid potentially messy ones like short ribs or a braised...anything."

"That's right," he kissed her hand. "I promise to make it up to you later with a pepperoni pizza and as much beer to wash it down as you like."

Clarissa Sauer was college-educated. In fact, she was at the top of her class in the dramatic arts program and was on the music world's short list of up-and-coming opera singers of 1997. She preferred the finer things in life like good champagne and messy hors d'oeuvres topped with fancy truffle oils and garlic aioli. And unlike most people, she actually had a palate for it. But she let Spencer "educate" her because she learned early on, you got further in life if you smiled and didn't make a fuss.

What she wasn't counting on was Astor Ellis.

When they arrived, the very first thing Spencer did was survey the room and garner each of them a glass of champagne, presumably so their hands had something to hold while looking sophisticated instead of standing there awkwardly with their arms dangling in the air.

"This way," he guided his date.

For the first time, she balked.

"What is it?" he asked, uncomfortably.

Clarissa spotted Astor Ellis standing next to his reportedly, soon-to-be fiancé, Portia LaMonte. Portia LaMonte's family was the main sponsor for the gala, held to raise money for the elite art school—providing scholarships, renovations, and above all, a "knowledge and appreciation of the fine arts."

Clarissa sucked in a breath. "Nothing," she whispered. "I thought I caught my heel on my dress, but it's fine now." She smiled cautiously.

Spencer nodded as he continued his journey toward his nemesis. At one time, he and Astor had been friends, both working for Astor Ellis's tech mogul father, Byron Ellis. But after three occasions where his ideas were taken without giving him credit and a contract stating that anything he created at any time during his tenure at B. A. Ellis Industries was the intellectual property of the company, Spencer grew bitter. When he quit last year, Astor felt betrayed and so did Spencer. After all, it was Astor who leaked info to his father about some of Spencer's current creations which had been imagined off hours and while still under B. A. Ellis Industries' employ.

They threatened lawsuits, but in the end, the only thing that appeared at this time was cyber warfare. Spencer was certain Astor and his family were hacking into his system and stealing his tech as they had a bad habit of announcing new inventions always just ahead of his own launch. And then there were those inconvenient times when blueprints seemed to go missing as if someone were purposefully corrupting his data.

Initially, he wanted to hire Darwin Fennec and his team to hack into the Ellis family fortress and tech empire and garner a little intel of their own, but Darwin was adamant about ethics. The best he could offer was locking down Spencer Hargrove's computer network and servers, looking for vulnerabilities and sniffing out who might be pilfering information and why.

"Spencer Hargrove, how delightfully surprising it is to see you here this evening," Astor Ellis lied in his annoyingly nasal voice before laying eyes on Clarissa. "And who is your charming date for this evening?"

Astor knew who Clarissa Sauer was. After all, he had been sleeping with her for several months before finally ending it as the time of his stepping into his father's shoes as CEO of B. A. Ellis Industries grew closer, along with his engagement to his girlfriend of two years, heiress Portia LaMonte.

Spencer knew this, too, and so did Clarissa, obviously. The only one who presumably didn't, was Astor's bride-to-be, Portia.

"Ah," Spencer answered eagerly. "May I present, Miss Clarissa Sauer."

"How lovely," Astor acknowledged, taking her hand and holding it for about three-seconds too long. Portia didn't seem to notice. Clarissa, on the other hand, *did* notice. It was sweaty, like it always was when he felt guilty about something.

"Er," Astor fumbled a little, dropping Clarissa's hand. "This is my lovely date for the evening and reason we're all here tonight, Ms. Portia LaMonte."

"How nice to meet you," she greeted Spencer and then set her gaze on Clarissa.

Clarissa's face felt hot. *She couldn't know, could she?* And even more to the point, *did Astor regret his decision?* After all, what they had was special, wasn't it?

Spencer could barely contain his glee nor his contempt for his former friend. Arriving at tonight's most memorable event with the woman he knew for damn sure Astor preferred? Priceless.

Astor boasted, "Thanks to Ms. LaMonte's unwavering dedication, tonight's fundraiser is expected to bring in close to a half a million dollars to support the school."

Clarissa's face dropped slightly. But then, she thought a moment.

"Ms. LaMonte," Clarissa finally smiled, making eye contact with a nemesis of her own. "It's wonderful that you are such a patron of the arts and understand its value in our culture and society."

"Indeed, I do," Portia answered, warmly. "While not an artist myself, I appreciate the talent I see from the young men and women who graduate from this school."

"With that in mind...if I may be so bold?" Clarissa continued.

Spencer's face dropped and his skin went clammy. *What was she doing? This wasn't at all scripted.*

"Yes?" Portia asked. "What is it?"

"I would very much like to audition for the lead role in the off-Broadway production of *If I didn't Care*. Its scheduled opening night is in four months, but it seems I don't have the necessary memberships to allow me to audition."

"And," Portia asked graciously, smiling, "what does this have to do with me?"

"Well," Clarissa, a good 15-years-or-more-younger than Portia answered. "Given your dedication to the arts, young artists, and actresses and your influence, I thought you might...put in a good word for me with the director?"

Portia paused for a moment as Astor and Spencer both sucked in their breaths.

"What makes you think I have any influence over this particular production?" Portia asked.

"Well, it's at the Plymouth," Clarissa tread carefully. "I happen to know that's one of the theaters your family supports. I read that it's one of your favorites." Clarissa fell silent, awaiting Portia's answer.

Finally, Ms. LaMonte smiled. "Well, obviously, I have to hear you sing first," Portia answered. "Astor, my bag," she motioned to Astor Ellis who had been holding her pearl-beaded clutch purse on her behalf. He dutifully handed it to her. "Here," she dug out a business card and handed it to Clarissa. "Call my office in the morning and my assistant will schedule a time for you to sing for me. It's the most I can promise, but..." she paused, looking Clarissa over, judgmentally. "If you're as good as you seem to think you are, then you will have my full support."

"Thank you, Ms. LaMonte," Clarissa spilled, graciously. "I happened to have read in the papers...forgive me for mentioning the tabloids...but..."

Portia nodded in understanding.

"But I heard that you and Mr. Ellis are to be engaged very soon. I would be honored if you might attend the show one evening as a way of celebrating? Assuming it all works out and I'm cast, of course."

Astor's face turned a beet red. *What is she doing?* he wondered. *Is this a sick form of revenge?*

Spencer was confused as well and appalled at her arrogance. *Did she really think that she was as good as all that—she'd naturally be chosen if she got the audition?*

Portia, standing there in a creme-colored dress with black sequins that shouldn't have worked together, but did, along with gold-colored shoes complete with chunky heels, didn't miss a beat. She flashed her fake eyelashes and answered in a sultry tone of voice, "We would be delighted." She paused for a moment. "It's at the Plymouth theater, you say?"

"Yes, that's right," Clarissa acknowledged, nodding.

"Well, my family has box seats at many of the theaters in town. Rest assured, if you can impress me enough to get you an audition and top billing in *If I Didn't Care*, we will be there."

It didn't matter that Portia LaMonte was not an actress, singer, dancer, artist, or musician herself, nor that she possessed any skill as an art critic other than knowing simply what she liked and what she didn't. All that mattered is that she had a lot of money...and that meant that her opinion *did* matter...to everyone...and for more than it should.

Clarissa felt something settling at the center of her chest. *What was it? Grief? Jealousy? Sadness?* No, it was something much worse...*worthlessness.* No matter her education, her skills, or who she was as a person, the one she wanted was soon to be engaged to a woman she could never be. She wasn't a well-put-together blonde-haired debutante with razor-thin features and a bank account worthy of kings. She didn't have the confidence, either, at least not in anything other than one thing, her voice.

She clutched Spencer's arm a little tighter. Spencer merely looked over and smiled back. He observed Astor's expression as he clenched his jaw. By Spencer's estimation, despite this odd detour, things were going...perfectly.

It was unclear what Spencer hoped to gain by showing up with Astor's recent ex-lover that evening, not even to Spencer. Somewhere in the back of his mind, he thought perhaps it could serve as blackmail should Astor reveal another one of SpencerTech's creations as his own. But even more so, it was leverage if B. A. Ellis Industries followed through on their threats to sue him. He could take the story to the papers and they loved a good scandal, particularly when it involved prominent socialites in the business world.

"That would be wonderful," Clarissa bit her lip. "I'm honored."

"What have I missed?" Gretchen Ellis blew in like a breeze, touching Astor's elbow. "Sorry I'm late, but I had a dreadful time in traffic this evening."

"Mother," Astor greeted, "you remember Spencer Hargrove, don't you? He worked with Dad and I at the office?"

Gretchen gave Spencer a long once over...and again, smiled. "I'm sure if we'd met, I'd have remembered," she presented a hand to Spencer. "Nice to meet you, Mr. Hargrove."

Astor shuddered slightly. "Anyway, he's here with his lady friend, Clarise, is it?"

"Clarissa." Clarissa stewed under her breath.

"My apologies," Astor corrected himself. "Clarissa. Anyway, they have been discussing an upcoming show that she might be auditioning for, thanks to Portia's generous support. Eh, what was it called?"

"*If I Didn't Care*," Clarissa answered, loudly, accentuating each word. Ironic, as at that moment, she was confident that Astor Ellis didn't care about anything but himself.

"That's right," he smiled slightly. "Anyway, Portia has box seats at that theater, so perhaps the family could make a night of it when the show runs? Might be a nice way to celebrate a certain engagement?" He nodded his head toward Portia as if his mother were daft and unaware of the arrangement.

The only woman in the room more practiced in her demeanor was Gretchen Ellis who immediately responded with, "I'm familiar with your reputation, Ms. Sauer..." She paused while Clarissa sucked in her breath. "As an opera singer," she finished...eventually.

"Oh," Clarissa let out a sigh. "Yes, of course."

"It will be our great fortune to get to hear you sing."

"Assuming she gets the part," Spencer added, helpfully.

Clarissa nodded slightly and forced the tiniest of smiles on her face. But it was all too much. She took a sip of her champagne, handed the rest to Spencer and said, "I need to powder my nose for a moment. Will you excuse me?"

"Of course, my darling," Spencer gallantly offered. "Hurry back, though, won't you? The world is much emptier without you."

Clarissa shot back a practiced smile with loving eyes, willing herself not to look at Astor to catch his expression. She darted into the nearest ladies' room where she cried her eyes out in one of the stalls for the next ten minutes.

Astor and Portia were called away to prep for a presentation that including announcing raffle contests and the sponsors of the evening.

Meanwhile, Gretchen Ellis sidled next to Spencer. "She is lovely," Gretchen commented.

"Nice to see you again, Mrs. Ellis."

"Come now, Spencer. We're alone, no need to be so formal."

"Why did you pretend not to remember me? Or did you forget?"

Gretchen made certain no one was near them when she reached around and pinched Spencer on the bottom. "Of course, I didn't forget," she grinned, her eyes circulating the room and not meeting his gaze.

"What is it that you want, Gretchen?" Spencer eyed the ladies' room door across the floor, wondering when Clarissa was going to return.

"I'm curious," Gretchen ignored the question. "Since your girlfriend —Rue Brennan—your real girlfriend, not this imposter designed to make my son jealous, is actually one of the models of the Atelier, tell me," she leaned in and whispered in his ear, "why is she not here with you? All of the models were invited, free of charge."

"Well," Spencer backed away, sticking a finger in his ear to scratch the itch caused by Gretchen's breath. "She doesn't exactly present well, now, does she?"

"Really?" Gretchen was surprised. "Certainly better than a gold-digger like Clarissa Sauer, don't you think?"

Spencer grew defensive. "Clarissa's not a—" He caught a glimpse of Gretchen's snicker and realized he fallen right into her trap.

"Don't get testy, my dear." Gretchen touched his arm. "But when you've decided you've had enough of this running around with pretty little things that can't possibly help advance your career, look me up. We had a good thing together...once." She winked at him and waltzed away, quickly swarmed by a host of admirers and at least one photographer.

Gretchen was more than 25 years his senior—forceful, confident...and rich.

"Sorry about that," Clarissa apologized when she'd returned, taking Spencer's arm.

"That's okay, my darling," he patted her hand. "What say we get out of this place?"

"Without seeing any of the exhibits?" Clarissa questioned, trying in vain to stretch her toes in her uncomfortable pointed shoes.

"Are you in any of them?" he smirked.

"Of course not," she answered, "I'm a singer, not an art model." Clarissa seemed almost offended at the accusation. She momentarily thought of her friend, Ursula, who *was* in fact, a figure model. But there was a part of her that didn't want Spencer to know that, given his admissions about his own girlfriend's choice in occupation.

"Well then," he replied. "There is nothing here worthy of my attention." He leaned in, pressing his forehead to hers and smiling, as if sharing a secret. "Let's get out of here."

Suddenly, Clarissa felt something in her heart flutter, just a little. *Maybe...*she thought.

CHAPTER 23
The Art of Death

Wednesday Morning at the Artist Atelier

Rue arrived early for the second shift and decided to sit in on the early-morning set. It was the final day of Ursula Gorky posing as Tosca. The model was wearing a bright orange and white gown that trailed behind her on the floor. She was draped across a series of stools covered in gray drop cloths arranged to give the illusion of a castle's parapet. Rue's best guess was that this was the actual act of dying versus the death, with Tosca attempting to throw herself from the parapet. Ursula's arm was wrapped around her face with her opposite arm and leg dangling from the ledge. She was surrounded by a blue hue of dim lighting designed to imitate a moonlit night. On each side of the stage, space heaters whirred loudly, blowing toward the stand to keep the model warm given her limited attire.

Rue found an unoccupied folding chair at the back of the studio and quietly melted into it, trying not to disturb the students who were surrounding the model stand, diligently adding and blending paints to canvas on their individual easels.

At the center of the group stood Jaks Liebling. He was a small and thin man with shoulder-length brown hair that he kept pulled back in a mullet, a pale complexion, and a pointed chin. He wore a murky, chocolate-colored turtleneck and corduroy jeans that went out of style years ago.

While he was commissioning the project, he invited students to participate as well, with the idea that the final exhibit would showcase his work alongside students—which of course, was really to demonstrate how his painting far outstretched everyone else's. And yet, a very appreciative, hand-picked group of the Atelier's best art students were chosen to showcase their final projects.

Jaks glanced over at Rue momentarily and grinned from ear to ear, as if he knew a secret that he wasn't sharing, before returning to his canvas. Rue attempted to crane her neck to see his work and what she saw was somewhat disturbing. He didn't paint the scene with the gray, white, orange, and pale blue colors on the model stand. All of his colors were an ugly mix of black and red that swirled together, making Tosca appear more like a demon in the abstract than an unfortunate heroine who lost the love of her life.

Conversely, several of the students surrounding him had work that was promising, some focusing on the light that was hitting Ursula's back and shoulder, others capturing the fine details of her gown and the way her hair hung haphazardly forward with several unruly strands refusing to lay comfortably. Instead, they sprang upright in frazzled rebellion.

"She sure fidgets less than the last one," a female student commented on Ursula's rigid pose. From her experience, most models were 'squirmy,' making them hard to paint accurately.

The room was quiet, except for the occasional cough or the sound of someone cleaning off their brush by swirling it in a plastic cup of paint thinner. The room smelled of fresh paint and a combination of linseed oil and Liquin.

Finally, the great Jaks Liebling called the time and ordered a few students to help strike the set. The room came alive with bustling as students began to clear their spaces of canvas, brushes, pencils, and oil paints.

Rue stood, heading over to the unoccupied model changing area to see what costume Jaks had left for her. She passed the first station where

Ursula had draped her day clothes over the top of it and headed to the second station where the door was wide open. There was nothing in the small enclosed, open-air room except for a mirror, a chair, and a long gown on a hanger, hooked to the side wall of the station. Rue touched the fabric. It was coarse with noticeably less material than Ursula's costume.

Rue changed quickly as she waited for a fresh crop of students to arrive and for Jaks to decide how to stage the next set. When finished, she plopped her jeans and t-shirt on the chair, along with her phone and coin purse where she kept her apartment key tucked away. As she left the room, she paused by the model stand, waiting patiently alongside other students attempting to strike the set, for Ursula to break from her pose.

There was just one problem.

Ursula Gorky wasn't moving.

Someone thought to turn on the overhead lights above the model stand, while another student touched Ursula's arm and then quickly recoiled. "She's cold," the woman announced, horrified. The young man standing next to the woman moved toward Ursula, carefully rolling the model over and letting out a gasp.

Ursula's lips were blue and her body was stiff. Her throat appeared swollen with a frothy saliva forming around her mouth. Her fingertips were also cold and blue—something that escaped the artists given that there was a blue filtered light above the model stand. The long and short of it? Ursula Gorky was dead.

Detective Ortega rubbed his tired eyes from beneath his glasses. "You mean to tell me that the entire class, including the instructor, spent the last hour painting a dead girl and didn't know it?"

Penelope cleared her throat. "It would seem so," she answered calmly, the forensic scientist taking a few more close-up photos of the body.

"Normally, the models break after 20 or 30 minutes," Officer Dennis offered, "but we were told that Ursula always insisted on one-hour stretches of time so as not to break the 'mood' of the piece. Her last break was at noon."

"So, she died thanks to her work ethic?" Ortega scratched his head.

"Not necessarily," Penelope explained. "We found an open bottle of red wine in the model changing area. I won't know until further examination, but if my suspicions are correct, she died from manchineel poisoning."

"Manchineel?" Ortega was surprised. "You mean the deadly tree?"

"Exactly," she explained. "The sores around her mouth indicate she may have ingested the berry. You're the detective of course, but I'd bet any amount of money we're going to find that this wine is manchineel-berry infused."

"So," Ortega concluded. "We're looking at murder."

"It would seem so at this point," the forensics expert agreed.

"Anything else of interest?"

"Yes, we found scuff marks in the changing area, which could be Ursula's, but given the tread patterns, I'd be willing to bet they came from the same shoe we found on the seat cushion of the theater two weeks ago."

"The one at the crime scene?" Ortega asked for confirmation.

"The same, only this one has traces of cigarette ash on the bottom, as if they'd stamped a bud out before coming inside."

"But no sign of cigarettes or smoke actually in the room?"

"None," Penelope confirmed.

"Officer Dennis?"

"Yes, Detective?"

"Send in Ms. Brennan for questioning. And have Officer Ernie scout the grounds for nearby smoking lounges, both indoors and out. See if he finds anything of interest."

Students had already been separated in the hallway or placed into smaller classrooms, the remaining classes in the school being cancelled for the rest of the day.

"Certainly, Detective." Officer Dennis left to first fetch Rue who was, unfortunately, still wearing the gaudy Elektra costume she had just changed into. He didn't need to ask which one was Rue Brennan as this was his second encounter with the woman.

Also unfortunate, was that Jaks Liebling had reimagined what his exhibit's Elektra would wear, placing Rue in a dress that looked like shimmering lilac flower petals with long bits of fabric cut in strange places to reveal a little too much leg, torso, and cleavage. The shoes were pale-peach ballet flats that were two sizes too big.

Rue crossed her arms in front of her, uncomfortably.

"Ms. Brennan," Detective Ortega stated calmly, "it seems that you find yourself, once again, at the center of a murder investigation. Am I to assume that this is going to be a regular occurrence?"

"Of course not, Detective," Rue tapped her foot nervously. "I was merely early for my modeling shift." She hugged her arms tightly around her. Despite the heat in the building and the space heaters, she was freezing.

Ortega glanced at her costume with disinterest. He seemed unaware that she was shivering.

"Just seems awfully coincidental that the one woman who spotted you on the balcony the day Clarissa Sauer died is the same one who appeared to have been poisoned not two weeks later. Doesn't that strike you as odd?" He looked her over once more.

"Of course, it does," Rue agreed. "But I had nothing to with it and," she noticed that his eyes fell on her chest, "Detective, do you mind if I change out of this ridiculous costume before we continue this inquiry? It's a little...revealing, don't you think?"

"Aren't you a figure model?" he asked.

"Yes, what does that matter?"

"So, you pose naked?"

Rue felt her face turn red. Penelope looked up from her camera where she was taking shots of the crime scene from all angles, concerned.

"Yes, but I don't see how that's relevant."

"So, why would wearing a revealing outfit bother you?"

"Inspector Ortega..."

"Detective," he corrected.

"Detective," Rue raised her voice. "When, where, and under what circumstances I choose to pose nude is my prerogative. It doesn't get decided for me."

"I'm all done photographing the changing area," Penelope offered, sympathetically. "If we need to enter her clothes into evidence, then perhaps we can send Officer Dennis to fetch her a suitable change of wardrobe." She shot Ortega a warning look. "She looks cold."

Ortega beamed a practiced smile. "All right, Dr. Washburn," he nodded before turning back to Rue. "It seems our forensics expert sees your point. Officer Dennis, can you bring Ms. Brennan her clothes?"

"Er," the detective stammered, peering around the corner from the changing area. "I'm afraid they have already been entered into evidence," he explained, "along with all the other costumes and clothing in storage here."

"Great," Rue mumbled.

"Got your phone and coin purse though," he offered, handing them to Rue who accepted them awkwardly. "We went through your list of contacts and text messages, but there's hardly anything on your phone. Do you even use it?" Officer Dennis asked.

"Are you allowed to invade my privacy like that?" Rue wanted to know.

"Tell you what, Ms. Brennan," Ortega offered, ignoring her question. "You go home and put on suitable clothing. We'll call you to resume this discussion in the morning, if need be. But," he added, wagging a finger at her, "don't plan on leaving town until we do, or I'll have no choice but to drag your ass back here and throw you in jail."

Penelope shot him the second *what the hell* look in a manner of minutes.

Rue swallowed a response. "Thank you, Detective," she acquiesced. He turned his attention back to his notes which Rue presumed meant that she had been dismissed.

Just was she was leaving the Artist Atelier, her cell phone rang...Darwin.

"I was just down the block when I heard the sirens. Seems they were heading your way. Everything okay?"

"No, Darwin, everything is not okay," she darted into the nearest ladies' room on the ground floor of the school. "Could you please bring me a long coat or blanket or...something."

"Sure," he answered, confused. "Will my jacket do?"

"It'll have to," she sighed. "Meet you out front."

Darwin did a double-take when Rue made her way through the revolving door of the school's entrance to the street. He bit back a grin as he removed his jacket and handed it to her.

"Something amusing?" she asked as she accepted it, wrapping it around her. Fortunately, Darwin was tall, so it was rather long on her. Rue pushed the sleeves up to reveal her hands. She began flopping ahead in her oversized ballet flats.

"Nope, not a damn thing," he caught up with her, averting his eyes. "Let's catch the F train...unless you'd rather walk?"

"No, Darwin, I most certainly do not want to walk," she grumbled.

At that moment, the sky darkened as clouds quickly rolled in. There wasn't even time to say, "Looks like rain," before the floodgates opened, drenching them both in drops so cold they felt like ice pellets. Rue shivered, hugging her arms tightly around herself.

A few men whistled as she shuffled past, eyeing her legs. Darwin shot them his best aggressive look, which did very little as there was nothing about Darwin that screamed anger and aggression. Therefore, he wrapped an arm around her, shielding her from onlookers, the cold, and the rain as they hurried toward the train.

CHAPTER 24
Emma Post

Wednesday Afternoon in Detective Ortega's Office

~

The hardest thing about working with your ex, Detective Ortega decided, was less about the residual chemistry, or about the intimate knowledge you knew about one-another (that everyone else seemed well aware of, too), but was more about the awkwardness of being involved with the very thing that split you up in the first place. In this case, it wasn't infidelity, not another woman. Ortega was obsessed with his work. And every time he and Penelope worked on a case such as this one, he was cruelly reminded of the fact that the one thing that once drew them together (the thrill of solving crimes) was also the very thing that drove them apart.

Even worse was the sad realization that it was happening all over again in his marriage. He knew it and he was pretty sure Penelope's keen observations had witnessed it too. She was just too classy a lady to point it out to him or lord it over him. *What if?* Ortega allowed his mind to momentarily wonder, *what would have happened if I hadn't screwed it up with*

Penny? No, he pushed the thought away. He was happily married to Nancy now. No reason to ruminate on the past.

Except he did ruminate. He also wondered why, every time he thought of his current marriage, he felt this bitter twisting in the pit of his stomach. Ortega couldn't be certain if it was over the guilt of feeling as if he were a terrible husband, if there were unresolved feelings for Penelope, or if it were simply the unfortunate truth that he and Nancy were incompatible. The sad reality was, no matter what the cause, it only added to Ortega's self-loathing.

"You're doing it again," Penelope interrupted Ortega's thoughts.

"Was I?" he answered. He didn't need to ask. He knew that his mind had wandered again, and he also knew that it was obvious.

"It's okay, but you should know that this is really weird," Penelope continued.

"What is?"

"The fact that this is the same scenario as the theater. Instead of 1500 theater goers, we have that many students with little or no way to monitor their comings and goings."

"Any accounts of new people being here who shouldn't?"

"Nope," Penelope answered. "We interviewed the model coordinator and all the men and women modeling have been with the school for at least a year and the students all check out, too."

"So, in the case of the theater, there was an unexpected extra usher who is unaccounted for. But here, there's no odd man out."

"Not that we can see," Penelope acknowledged.

"And the manchineel juice found in the wine? Anyone in the group recently traveled to the Caribbean or the Gulf of Mexico?"

"Literally, all of them," Penelope sighed. Ortega raised an eyebrow. "Okay, slight exaggeration, but who doesn't go to Florida in the winter or just to visit Disney World? And the school prides itself on inclusion and diversity, and has an entire exchange program dedicating to ensuring that students from other countries have the opportunity to attend."

"So, another needle in a haystack?"

"Another needle in a haystack," Penelope confirmed.

"There is one odd thing," Officer Ernest interrupted them, standing just outside of Ortega's office.

"And what's that, Ernie?"

"Well, I reviewed the statements from the students several times and three students had the same observation."

"Yes?" Ortega motioned for him to continue.

"They thought the lighting was off on the model stand. Jaks Liebling was particular about stuff like that, so they were surprised he didn't adjust it. They all chalked it up to his unique artistic vision."

"What was so odd about it?" Ortega asked.

"It's beyond me," Ernie admitted. "But supposedly it left a shadow across her face and arm and cast more light on her torso which seemed an odd focal point."

"That isn't the only oddity," Officer Dennis stood beside Ernie. "I just got back from meeting with the model coordinator. It seems Ursula Gorky wasn't the model scheduled to play Tosca. It was Emma Post. The coordinator asked Ursula why she was signing in for Emma's session and she said that Emma called her and asked her to sub for her last minute because she wasn't feeling well."

"Without running it by the model coordinator first?" Ortega asked. "Is that usually how it's done?"

Officer Dennis's head dropped. "Honestly, I hadn't thought to ask that."

"No matter. I think we should pay a visit to Ms. Post."

"Even though she's sick?"

"She could have been a hell of a lot sicker had she showed up for this gig," Detective Ortega reasoned. Penelope shot him one of those *you're being insensitive* looks again. "Er," he re-thought his next statement. "We won't keep her long. What's her address?"

~

Visiting Emma Post

Police Detective Ortega and Officer Dennis stopped by Emma Post's tiny apartment in Greenwich Village, passing through Washington Square Park along the way. A few pedestrians stopped to eye them curiously, trying carefully not to make eye contact. An odd man bundled in a tattered jacket, scarf, and knit hat stood on one of the benches. Upon closer inspection, it was evident that he was wearing an elephant nose. Just after the two men walked by him, he lifted his nose in the air and let out his best impression of an elephant roar.

Officer Dennis stopped. "Should we do something about that?"

Ortega eyed the people around him. No one seemed to notice the man, nor care. "Nah, doesn't seem to be disturbing the peace."

Officer Dennis shrugged his shoulders and the two kept walking. Once they'd reached the street where Emma Post lived, there was a distinct aroma of cheap marijuana and incense, presumably to cover up the weed's pungent aroma.

Officer Dennis looked around but there was no obvious source of the smell.

"Stay focused," Ortega cautioned him. "I'm much more concerned about catching a killer than I am about arresting someone for their recreational habits."

They'd reached Emma's complex and rang the bell for her apartment on the second floor.

"Yeah," a woman's voice called through the intercom.

"Emma Post?" Ortega asked.

"Depends on who's asking," she retorted.

"Police Inspector Ortega," he replied. "I'd like to ask you some questions about Ursula Gorky."

After a long pause, he heard the intercom click again. "You wanna come up or should I come down?" she offered.

"With your permission, myself and my assistant, Officer Dennis, would like to come up if you're feeling up to it."

"Why wouldn't I be?" she seemed flustered. "Never mind, c'mon up."

The officers took the stairs, finding the petite woman waiting on the landing wearing a gray jogging suit and seeming slightly out of breath and pink in the face.

"So, guess you're feeling better?" Ortega asked, flashing his badge. She ignored the question as she touched the edge of the badge with her fingers. "Yours too," she motioned to Officer Dennis. "I didn't stay alive in this neighborhood for 36 years by being stupid."

"Interesting choice of words," Ortega commented. Emma's flushed faced seemed to turn redder.

After peering closely at Officer Dennis's badge, she was satisfied. "C'mon in," she stepped back into her studio apartment, revealing an old white tile floor about three shades grayer than it stood be with several noticeable cracks in it, along with missing grout. Two fold-out chairs sat on each side of a small round table. To the left was an efficiency kitchen. To the right was the bathroom and an accordion-shaped screen that seemed to section off the sleeping quarters. What was most noticeable, however, was how low the ceiling was. The very tall Officer Dennis felt like Alice in Wonderland after eating the cake that turned her into a giant.

"Well, what did you expect for $750 a month in a rent-controlled apartment building?"

"Ms. Post, we're not here to discuss your living arrangement. We were curious about why you called in sick for your modeling gig, sending Ursula Gorky in your place."

Ortega paused to gauge her reaction before adding, "When it appears that you are not sick and that you may have actually been out jogging?"

She looked back and forth between the two men.

"What are you talking about?" she demanded. "I never called in sick." Emma was visibly annoyed. After a long pause while the two men waited for her to continue, she added, "Bernice, the model coordinator called *me*. She said Ursula had a last-minute opportunity to be the understudy for the show our friend Clarissa had been in and needed to swap days to fit her rehearsal schedule. I was happy to help, so Ursula was supposed to take my shift while I covered over the weekend."

"So, the model coordinator...Bernice...called you. Not the other way around?"

"No," Emma shook her head. "Though, I thought it was odd that Ursula hadn't asked me to cover for her herself, but she was pretty shaken up over Clarissa's death, so I didn't think much of it. I was happy for her, though sad as to why the opportunity was suddenly available." Emma's eyes started tearing up and she fought back a few sniffles. "Seems like they were finally resuming production after her death."

Officer Dennis looked helplessly around the meager apartment, noticed a roll of paper towels by the kitchen sink and grabbed a sheet.

Handing it to Emma, he said, "I'm sorry for your loss…well, losses. Seems you were friends with both Clarissa and Ursula."

Officer Dennis, while not known for being the brightest bulb in the pack, was not without feeling. And from what he could tell, Emma was sincerely grieving.

"Thanks," she sniffed, accepting the paper towel. "I heard on the news that someone died at the school, but it wasn't until another model I know phoned that I knew it was Ursula."

"I know it's a difficult time for you," Ortega said in a practiced manner. He really wasn't good at situations where feelings were concerned. "But we were told that when Ursula showed up in place of you, it was because you phoned her telling her that you were sick."

"Did Bernice say that?" Emma was surprised.

"She did," Ortega confirmed.

"But that doesn't make sense," Emma answered. "I don't think she's lying, mind you. It's just that when we need to miss a shift, we call Bernice to arrange it. Even if I had phoned Ursula to replace me…which I didn't, I would have followed up with a phone call to Bernice to let her know that I had to miss the sitting, but had a replacement if she needed it. The whole thing sounds a little fishy to me."

"So, you never called Ursula claiming to be sick?"

"Absolutely not."

"And Bernice called you asking you switch days with Ursula."

"Yes, well, I think it was Bernice."

"What do you mean, 'think?'" Ortega pressed her.

"Her throat sounded all froggy on the call, like she had a sore throat or something. Wouldn't have known it was Bernice if she hadn't told me."

"I see," Ortega answered. "Anything else unusual about that call?"

"Not at all," Emma answered. "She just confirmed the day and time of my next session and offered me time and a half for changing the day on such short notice."

"Is that typical?"

"Yeah," Emma nodded. "They always do that if they have to make changes to the schedule in under 48 hours."

"And was there any communication with Ursula from the time

Bernice called you until the time—" Ortega caught himself before adding, "of her death?"

"No," Emma shook her head. "In fact, the last time I saw her was at Merriam Hall."

"Merriam Hall?" Ortega was curious.

"It's a nightclub," Officer Dennis and Emma said in unison.

"Yeah," she answered, eyeing Officer Dennis, curiously. He seemed a little too stiff and proper to hang out at Merriam Hall, she decided. And she would have noticed. He wasn't good looking in the Brad Pitt sort of way. In fact, Officer Dennis was a little pudgy around the middle for someone so young, and had a round, boyish face and sandy brown hair parted in the middle in such a way that she could clearly see exactly how his head would develop a bald patch in about fifteen to twenty years. She smiled to herself, but then pushed that thought aside. *After all,* she decided, *can't really trust cops, can you?* She brought herself back into the moment. "I met up with Ursula and some guy she hooked up with."

"Hooked up with?" Ortega asked.

Officer Dennis and Emma Post let out a sigh. Ortega clearly wasn't from their world.

"She was out with some guy she met on some new dating site."

"Dating site? I'm afraid I don't follow. Is this another place in Manhattan?"

"Well," Emma thought how best to explain it. "You know how people meet one another through newspaper ads...posting a bit about themselves and hoping someone will call or write back?"

"Yes?" Ortega was intrigued.

"Well, Ursula discovered this new way of dating, except instead of the paper, people find one another on the Internet."

"That seems strange," Ortega answered.

"How is that any stranger than meeting someone you don't know via a newspaper ad?" She put her hands on her hips.

"I see your point," he admitted.

"Anyway, she called me to meet her there, just in case he turned out to be a creep."

"Was he?" Ortega asked.

"I dunno," she confessed. "Seemed a little too slithery to me and quick to pass around drinks. But," she laughed, "don't go by me. I have the worst taste in men." She eyed Officer Dennis for a moment, before blushing and dropping her gaze toward the floor, immediately regretting her comment. He lowered his gaze and tapped the tip of his shoe on the tile. All of this escaped Ortega.

Emma thought a moment, interjecting a comment before Ortega could say anything, "There was one odd thing, though." She looked into the distance as if recalling the image to mind.

"What is it?" Officer Dennis encouraged.

"Well, we ran into Rue Brennan," she answered. "You know, the girl that was thought to have pushed Clarissa off the ledge at the theater?"

"We are aware of her, yes." Ortega sucked in his breath, impatiently.

"Well, Ursula was all upset. She was convinced that Rue had something to do with Clarissa's death."

"Did you think that as well?" Ortega asked.

After a moment, Emma answered, "Nah." She shook her head. "Ursula was one of my best friends, don't get me wrong, but she was also a hot head. Always seeking justice for any cause that happened to get her attention that week. Nah, I think if Clarissa got stabbed, Rue was legit trying to help."

"I see," Ortega answered. "Any idea who might want to kill Clarissa Sauer?"

Emma bit her lip.

"Emma?" Officer Dennis coaxed her, as if he knew her better than he actually did. Yet somehow, it worked.

"If Ursula was the social activist, Clarissa was the instigator," she admitted. "Don't get me wrong, Clarissa was smart, classy and had a heart of gold, but she sure knew how to manipulate men to get them to do what she wanted."

"So, you think a man killed her?" Ortega asked.

"I dunno," Emma shook her head. "I just know that girl had a million schemes. She used to say, 'I may have been born a pauper, but by God, I'll die a princess.'"

"What an odd thing to say," Ortega mused.

"With all due respect," Emma eyed Ortega from head-to-toe. From the looks of it, he was well-dressed, well-manicured and well-fed for man of his position. So, either he came from money, or he married well. "But women have gone from being told to marry someone financially stable and be good wives and mothers, to get a job and not be such gold diggers. Except, jobs are a bit harder to come by for poor women and we're paid significantly less than men."

"That's a shame," Officer Dennis wrinkled his brow in sympathy. Ortega shot him an irritated glance. Officer Dennis snapped back to attention.

"Anyway," Emma continued. "Clarissa was a sweet person, but I can't say for certain that she didn't make any enemies along the way."

"And what was so odd about the evening?" Ortega reminded her.

"Well," Emma bit her lip, "Rue showed up which was surprising enough because she seemed a little too square for the likes of Merriam Hall.

Ortega started to mouth the word "square," when Officer Dennis shook his head. Ortega shut his mouth.

"And what happened after she showed up?" Ortega asked, instead.

"Well, I ordered a Long Island Iced Tea and Rue asked me if I should be drinking in my condition?"

Officer Dennis was crestfallen.

"Nah," she chastised him. "Don't look at me that way. I'm not knocked up or anything. I just don't know where she would have gotten an idea like that. I mean, sure, I gained a couple of pounds over the past year...thank you aging!" She looked to the sky. "But that don't mean I'm pregnant. Hell, at my age, I'm not even sure that's possible."

"That is curious," Ortega admitted, clearing his throat. "So, I have one last question."

"What is it?" Emma wanted to know.

"Any reason someone would want you dead?"

"Well, gee. That was morbid."

"You *were* on the schedule to model at the Atelier," Ortega reasoned.

"Nah," she shook her head. "I recognize that I'm not all that and a bag of chips," she pointed to herself, "but, I try to live on the straight and narrow and don't cause problems for nobody. I'd never once consider that the target was me, never."

CHAPTER 25
Rootkit

Wednesday Afternoon at Darwin's Condo

~

"The shower's just through there," Darwin motioned. "You'll have to go through my bedroom, I'm afraid."

Rue stood in the doorway of Darwin's condo awkwardly. At this point she was used to working there, but most times she was far less...soggy. Rue looked absolutely miserable, wet, cold, and...scared. He hadn't even gotten an update as to why she left the school so abruptly.

"Uh," he eyed her sympathetically. "Give me a second and I'll see if I have something you can change into." Darwin disappeared into his bedroom while Rue remained stock-still on the doormat, not wanting to drip on the floor.

In the distance, she could hear him opening and closing drawers, the shuffle of papers, a loud thunk followed by some expletives. It was almost as if Darwin were less looking for a dry change of clothes and more trying to cover up the mess that was his bedroom before Rue had to pass through it to the shower.

"Okay," he finally emerged, pulling a dry t-shirt over his chest and tugging it in place. "I left a fresh towel in the bathroom along with a warm bathrobe. It's mine. I hope you don't mind." He paused by the hall closet and pulled out an oversized sweatshirt and a pair of small gym shorts out of the wardrobe, handing them to Rue. "Have no idea if any of it will fit you, but it's temporary and," he added, trying not to grin, "still more comfortable than what you're currently wearing. You can rifle through here later to see if something fits you better."

Rue stuck her nose in the air, accepting the clothing as she darted past him. "Thank you, Mr. Fennec." The truth was, she was freezing, so she scurried through his bedroom, merely glancing with a passing interest at a king-sized bed with books stacked on the nightstands that flanked it.

Given the built-in lights above the headboard on each side, it was evident that Darwin was an avid reader. Across the room was a club chair and footstool which sat beside a small dresser. Above it was a large window, black curtains drawn, surrounded by shelving units with more books, an odd collection of model cars, motorcycles, collectable beer steins, and a smattering of action figures, some still in their original casing.

Rue found this amusing as she shut the bathroom door behind her and turned the shower on. Unlike her apartment, Darwin's condo had water that actually ran hot on demand. She let the water run over her and let out a brief sigh of relief. It was momentary, as her mind quickly shot back to the eyes of Ursula Gorky as she lay dead on the model stand.

Back in the main living room, Darwin's phone rang, but it wasn't his cell phone. It was a burner phone, one of several lying in his desk drawer. He retrieved it from his desk.

"Hi, sunshine," he smiled. "Anything new to report on the baby front?"

"No," Ashley sighed. "I swear, if these two don't pop out soon, I'm going to ask the doc to evict them!"

Darwin laughed. "Then why the call...on this phone?" Somehow, this small detail had only now occurred to him.

"Listen, I'll send an encrypted text with more details. But I discovered something interesting on Frat Boy." Frat Boy was Ashley's code name for Spencer Hargrove. She gave all of his clients and even some of his colleagues secret nicknames, often unflattering, unless she particularly liked them.

"We'll get back to why you're working on maternity leave in just a moment," Darwin chastised. "What can you tell me?"

"There was an odd VPN login to his account not ten minutes ago, not at his office, mind you. This one appeared to be someone trying to connect from an address in Ukraine, but after a bit of threat-hunting, it turned out they only wanted it to *look* that way. It was...get this...someone logging in directly from Frat Boy's home computer. And they installed a Rootkit that attacked data on his company network."

"So, either someone broke into his home, he's self-sabotaging his own work for some reason, or..."

"There's someone else staying in the frat house," Ashley confirmed. "Any chance it's your Gal Friday?"

"No," Darwin glanced toward his bedroom. The sound of water from the shower could be heard. "Not a chance. She's in my shower."

"Oh, really," Ashley's ears perked up. "What aren't you telling me, Darwin?"

"It's all completely innocent, I promise," Darwin answered.

"Disappointing," Ashley let out a sigh.

"Is that my brother?" A male voice from behind Ashley called.

"Yeah," Ashley answered. "He's got a woman in his shower, but it's all completely platonic." To Darwin, she said, "Ryland's off to a baseball game, again. If he misses the birth of our sons, I tell you what I'm gonna do with his autographed Yogi Berra Louisville Slugger. I'm gonna stick it where the sun don't shine."

"One, I didn't need that visual, and two, you married the wrong brother. You should have picked me when you had the chance," he joked.

In truth, Ryland and Darwin met Ashley on the playground in grade school. Ryland and Ashley were eight, Darwin was ten. Ryland pulled Ashley's pigtails. All Darwin ever did was plant a kiss on her cheek and stuff a Valentine's Day card in her Wonder Woman lunch box. Still, Ryland won out as he and Ashley ended up marrying fourteen years later. The ten-year-old Darwin had long-since recovered, but he couldn't pass up a chance to remind her about it every so often. "And why are you working? Aren't you on strict bedrest?"

"Yeah, and I'm going nut-balls here. These kids must be doing gymnastics in there. Had to do something to distract me. Hey, listen, hate to cut this short, but lemme send you what I've got before we run out of time."

"Thanks, Ashley. Have Ryland call me if anything changes on the baby front."

"Oh yeah," she remembered. "Just one more thing... that girl Emma? The one who supposedly emailed Beige?" 'Beige' was Ashley's nickname for Gretchen Ellis.

"What about her?"

"The email was sent from the public library. Seems legit, so it really could have been sent from anyone, unless we could somehow track what computer it came from at the exact day and time the message was sent."

"And find out who might have checked into the library and reserved a computer at that time."

"Exactly," Ashley confirmed.

"Thanks, Ashley. Now go get some rest."

Moments after they ended the call, Ashley sent the encrypted messages. Darwin made a few mental notes before dropping the phone on the floor and smashing it, unceremoniously, beneath his heel.

"What did that phone ever do to you?" Rue joked, emerging from the bedroom in Darwin's burgundy terrycloth robe, towel-drying her hair. It may have been calf-length on Darwin, but on Rue, it skimmed the floor.

Darwin grabbed a dust bin from the hall closet and scooped up the mess. "Sorry, you're not the only one having a rough day," he confessed, tossing the remnants of the phone into a small blue bin next to the trash can, for proper disposal later.

"At least you weren't on the scene for a second murder," Rue finally blurted out.

Darwin's face dropped as if she'd socked him in the jaw. "What are you talking about?"

Without thinking about it, Rue took a seat on the couch and folded one leg under her, sinking into it. *Comfy,* she thought. To Darwin, she answered, "Ursula Gorky, the one who saw us from across the balcony at the theater?" She waited for Darwin to nod in acknowledgment. "Dead," she finished.

Darwin's complexion grew sallow.

"Are you okay? I didn't realize she meant anything to you." Rue leaned forward, concerned.

"*She* doesn't," Darwin rubbed his forehead. "But *you* do." Rue searched his face, surprised, but said nothing. After all, she'd made up her mind about Darwin Fennec straight away, and then double-downed on that opinion, no matter what evidence suggested the contrary. To her, he was a womanizer...a cad. Not faithful like her very predictable Spencer.

Darwin took a seat on the club chair adjacent to where Rue sat. "Tell me everything that happened today in as much detail as you can remember."

CHAPTER 26
Everything That Happened

Wednesday Evening at Darwin's Condo

~

Rue did a fair job of recapping the day's events, though there were so many pieces she didn't know. She began by describing the room, and then the people, and then the unfolding of events from start to finish. Rue also attempted to interject a bit of what she and Darwin had already discovered in case it was useful.

For example, they suspected from their investigations that Clarissa was blackmailing Gretchen Ellis, and they presumed Ursula Gorky was the one person to come forward as a witness that Rue was, in fact, alone in Box 11 with Clarissa before she tumbled from the balcony. The irony that Ursula, too, died from a staged balcony did not escape Rue nor Darwin.

Darwin was able to fill in about Emma Post's email being sent from the library after having spoken with Ashley but left out the small detail of someone else being in Spencer's condo pilfering information. This weighed heavily on his mind. On the one hand, Rue was his assistant, and should be informed. On the other, since Spencer was a paying client, he assumed Spencer would want him to keep this knowledge to himself.

Until Rue was out of earshot, this was a conversation he was unable to have with the man, short of sending an encrypted message. This seemed to be a man-to-man conversation though, not something to be sent through email.

And on that same hand was the fact that getting into their personal life was really none of his business. And back on the other hand was the fact that he was really starting to like Rue. He didn't want to see her get hurt, didn't want to be the one to reveal Spencer's affair, and most importantly, didn't want to let his feelings cause him to make any rash decisions. So, he remained quiet.

"What I don't understand," Rue dragged Darwin back from his thoughts, "is how I got mixed up in both murders. Seems awfully coincidental." Darwin tended to agree. "I mean," Rue joked, "it's not as if someone were jealous of me being seen with you so that they tried to take me out at the theater and then at the college, right?"

Darwin's face grew even more serious, if that were possible. "Actually, that thought has not escaped my attention."

"Huh? Why?" Rue whined, slapping the couch with her hands. "I said that as a joke."

"I know you did," Darwin paused to think. "But the fact that you were so close to both murders leads me to think that you are either guilty, which I know you're not..."

"Tell that to Detective Ortega," Rue snorted.

Darwin continued, "Or, you are the scapegoat and someone is trying to frame you, or..."

"Someone is trying to kill me?" Rue finished, solemnly.

"I'm afraid of that possibility, yes."

"For knowing you? Do you have a jilted lover or something who'd have it out for me?" Rue wanted to know.

"Doubtful," he admitted. "But we can't rule out that it's not tied in some way to Spencer's rivalry with B. A. Ellis Industries."

Rue thought a moment. "Can we convince Ortega to put me under some kind of police protection?" Rue asked.

"While he's convinced you're involved in the murders?" Darwin answered. "We can try, but I'm not sure how that'll fly."

"Then, what should I do?" Rue's unfortunate name was living up its reputation and she was falling victim to its built-in paranoia.

"Well, you can't go back to your apartment, that's for sure," Darwin reasoned. "Besides, the reporters are certain to, once again, be all over this."

"Maybe I can stay with Spencer again for a bit. His condo is like a fortress with an armed security guard at the door and everything."

Darwin tried not to shudder at Spencer's name, but he couldn't help it, given what he knew. But he couldn't tell Rue. No, that was Spencer's responsibility.

"That might be the best idea," he relented. "I'd rather us be overly cautious and have it be nothing. Why don't you give him a call?" Darwin motioned toward a spare burner phone sitting on his desk.

Rue nodded, an odd sense of dread coming over her. *What was that about?* She slowly picked up the phone and glanced in Darwin's direction. He took the hint.

"Oh, right," he pointed absentmindedly toward his bedroom. "It's about time I had a hot shower after being out in the rain, too. I'll just be..." he pointed again, "in my room for a few minutes."

Rue nodded and dialed Spencer's number.

As expected, he picked it up on the third ring...always the third ring, never the first, second or fourth.

"Spencer Hargrove," he answered, not recognizing the number.

"It's me," Rue answered.

Spencer paused for a moment. "Oh, hello, darling," he finally answered in what Rue always called his Cary Grant voice, even though the accent wasn't his. Come to think of it, she wasn't sure if it was Cary Grant's either. There was something insincere about his voice, Rue noted. Why had she not noticed that before? It was as if there was a filter over her mind that was slowly lifting, and she was beginning to see things with more clarity. *Well, that's silly,* she chastised herself. And the filter was firmly back in place.

"Spencer," Rue began. "I have some bad news, I'm afraid."

"What is it?" Spencer sounded concerned. "Are you okay?"

"Yes," she assured him. "I'm fine, but...there's been another murder."

"What? Where?"

"At the Artist Atelier, where I was modeling. One of the models I know was murdered."

"Which model?" Spencer asked quickly.

"Ursu—" Rue caught herself. "Wait a minute, why does it matter which one? Do you know them?"

Spencer coughed, awkwardly. "No, of course not. That was a stupid of me," he countered. "Don't even know why I asked it."

"The point is, Spencer, I have now been on the scene of not one, but two, murders."

"Oh, darling. How terribly frightening for you. Are you home? Perhaps you should draw yourself a nice hot bath with those fancy salts you like, and I'll stop by later to hold you and remind you that everything is going to be okay."

Rue could sense a disconnect but reconnecting was a challenge. In the past, she would have blamed herself for this lack of communication. Now, she wasn't sure. She just knew that she was...tired...tired of trying.

"Well, Mr. Fennec is concerned that perhaps I was the target of those murder attempts."

"What? No, that can't be," Spencer reasoned. "Who would want to hurt you? You're too sweet a gal."

"I dunno, Spencer, but Mr. Fennec is concerned about me staying in my apartment. Could I stay with you for a bit? Sorry to do that to you twice in one month, but...it's just not safe."

There was a long pause on the phone line. "Now that I'm thinking this through, I don't think that would be for the best."

"Why not, Spencer, do you not want me there? Or are you worried that I might put you in danger?"

"Not at all," he proclaimed with bravado. "But given that I hired Darwin Fennec to investigate those trying to steal my multi-million-dollar plans, I can't help but wonder if they are trying to get to me—through you."

"Really? I'm not sure..."

"No," he answered quickly. "I'm quite certain that the safest thing you can do is stay far away from me for a while."

"What?" Rue's voice trembled a little. "But I don't want to stay away from you."

"No," he answered quietly. "I can barely stand the thought of not holding you in my arms tonight and reassuring you that everything is going to be okay. But I'm only thinking of your safety."

"What about *your* safety?"

"Nobody will harm me," he was convinced. "They need my brains to keep stealing ideas from me."

Rue ignored the implication that her brains weren't worth anything. Instead, she answered, "But, where will I go?"

"Hmmm," Spencer thought a moment. "Maybe stay with Midge for a while?"

"No," Rue sighed. "That won't work. For one thing, I'm not talking to Midge right now. For the other, she's only two floors up from me. How will that protect me?"

"I could hire a bodyguard for you?" Spencer's voice stretched in the way it does when he was uttering something that made him uncomfortable. And as a man who's invested everything he owned into his business, he likely didn't have wiggle room to procure a full-time security guard for his girlfriend, no matter how affluent he seemed to like to pretend to be.

"No, I'm not sure that's necessary. Honestly, I have no idea what I need right now," Rue's lips quivered a little.

"Tell you what," Spencer caught the waiver in her voice and had to think quickly. "Put Darwin on."

"Er, Mr. Fennec is..." She stopped herself before saying that he was likely in the shower. That wouldn't sound right. At that moment, he emerged from the bedroom wearing a fresh pair of dry jeans and a thin cardigan over the t-shirt he had been wearing. He was busy drying his wet hair with a towel. "Just a moment," she told Spencer. "Mr. Fennec," she whispered, "can you talk to Spencer for a moment?"

He eyed the phone quizzically before accepting it. "Hello, Mr. Hargrove," he greeted. "Yes, yes. She's doing okay. Understandably, just a little shaken up." He listened for a minute. Rue could hear Spencer's muffled voice on the other end, but not what he was saying. "So, no family close by," Darwin acknowledged looking momentarily at Rue.

Rue was beginning to feel as if she were a lost puppy that people were trying to figure out what to do with.

"No," Darwin agreed. "We can't put anyone else in potential danger, either." He paused to listen. "Well, invariably, it's up to her. Though, I'm not sure this is wise or appropriate." He looked at Rue again as Spencer spoke. "Yes, I understand. I'm concerned about her, too. Why don't the two of you discuss it. If she agrees, then I suppose a few days would be all right." Darwin handed the phone back to Rue. "Perhaps the two of you should chat about this. I'll just be in the kitchen." He didn't really have anything to do in the kitchen, but it was the farthest space away in the condo without going back into his bedroom. *Hmmm, maybe dinner,* he thought to himself.

Rue took the phone. "What's going on?" she asked Spencer.

"I just had a nice talk with Mr. Fennec and he and I agreed that it would be best if you stayed there for a couple of days. After all, there's full-time security and cameras in that complex and he has enough associates already working with him that can help look after you. I really think that is the smartest solution."

"Stay with Mr. Fennec? But there's only one bedroom...and he's my boss...and, Spencer, I really don't think this is a good idea at all."

"Are you worried he might put the moves on you? Because I'm pretty sure..."

"No! That's not it. It's just," Rue tried to find the right words, "for someone who is so big on keeping up appearances, it seems odd that you're okay with your girlfriend working and living with her boss. Kinda strange, don't you think?"

"I'd rather that then have anything happen to you," he reasoned.

Rue relented. "I suppose if he's okay with it," she glanced toward the kitchen, where Darwin was pretending to wipe down the counters and not eavesdrop.

"There's a good girl. Just lay low for a couple of days and I'll check on you in the morning."

Rue thought she heard a strange shuffling in the background. "What's that noise, Spencer?" she asked.

"Oh, nothing," he answered, "just...taking off my shoes and trying to balance the phone at the same time. Talk to you tomorrow, my darling." He rapidly hung up the phone before Rue could say goodnight.

"Everything okay?" Darwin called from the kitchen. By this point, he was pulling a box of pasta from the cupboard.

"I'm not sure," Rue answered. "I think so."

"Any dietary restrictions?" Darwin let out an awkward cough.

"Uh, no," Rue answered.

"You okay with pasta and a salad then? It's a compromise between your love of enriched white flour and mine for things that are green," he tried joking.

"Sure," Rue replied. "Though, I'm not really hungry."

"Well, maybe by the time it's ready. You should try and eat a little something." He put a pot of salted water on the stove and turned the burner on to bring it to a boil.

"Need any help?" Rue offered.

"No, thanks. But uh," he pulled a large jar of crushed tomatoes from the pantry. "Perhaps you'd like to pour yourself a glass of wine and fill me in again on everything that happened at the school today, maybe see if there are details you haven't told me yet? If you need something stronger to settle your nerves, I've got a decent Scotch in the cupboard." He pointed. "Oh," he remembered how Rue wrinkled her nose at the suggestion once before, "never mind."

"Wine is plenty strong enough," she answered. The wine rack was sitting in plain view. "Which one should I open?" She touched a hand to one of the bottles.

"Well, what do you like? There's red, white, sweet, dry."

"What's good with pasta?" Spencer usually made these types of decisions for her since she didn't consider herself particularly well versed in wines. The corkscrew opener was hanging on a hook beside the wine rack.

"Well, if you're not opposed to something dryer, go with a chianti or pinot noir. If you want something a little heavier and bolder, try the cabernet sauvignon."

Rue settled on the chianti. She wasn't feeling particularly bold. She fumbled with the corkscrew for a moment but managed to remove the wine bottle's foil and lever the cork. She reached for two stemmed glasses hanging upside-down above the wine.

"Oh, none for me," Darwin shook his head as he poured dry rotini pasta into the now-boiling water. "Probably best if one of us is clear-headed on the off chance something happens."

"What do you think will happen?" Rue asked.

"Hopefully nothing. But just acting out of an abundance of caution." He reached under the counter to retrieve a small food processor. "The larger glass might be better," he indicated. "Brings out the aroma of the wine better."

Rue hadn't realized there was a distinction between the small and large wine glasses other than one probably held more wine than the other, but she swapped the glass and poured herself a modest serving.

Within a short while, Darwin had a simple salad and pasta on the table, along with two forks and two plates. He'd even taken the time to provide a small dish of freshly grated parmesan cheese.

While Rue sipped her wine, Darwin settled on water, pouring a second glass of water for her, just in case she wanted it.

"This is really good," Rue commented after taking a bite of the rotini.

"Thanks," he smiled. "Nothing fancy, but I figure pasta is easy enough to have on hand for a quick meal during emergencies. I mean, one never knows when one's assistant is going to need a safe house." Rue took a larger sip of wine. "Sorry," he apologized. After a long pause, he added, "I think I should send Candy to your apartment tomorrow morning to retrieve some of your clothes...at least enough for a couple of days."

Rue nodded. "Not sure how she'll get past Midge though. I told her to back off, but she's as nosey and clingy as...well, her name!"

"Don't worry about Candy," Darwin was confident. "She's pretty good at getting in and out of places undetected. And, if Midge does spot her, we'll have a story ready."

"Well, if you think it's safe."

"It'll be daylight," Darwin reassured her. "And I can get Bristol or Monte to go with her as backup."

"So, uh," Rue looked around the room. "I'm guessing that couch is a fold-out bed?" She motioned to the living room.

"Uh, yeah but," he took a sip of water, "I figured you could take my room, to give you some privacy. I'll take the couch."

"No, I couldn't impose like that," Rue objected.

"Nonsense," Darwin disputed. "Besides, if anyone's gonna get in here, it's likely to be through the front door instead of the windows at this level. Best if I'm in the living room."

"What would you do if someone did break in?" Rue wanted to know. "Do you have a gun or know karate or something?"

"No, but I can booby trap the front door and scream like a toddler that's dropped their ice cream if someone trips it. Don't you worry about me," he sat back in the kitchen chair and smiled.

Rue fumbled with the salad tongs, nervously dropping a few bits of lettuce, coupled with diced cucumber and tomato onto her plate. She turned out to be hungrier than she realized.

"Perhaps if we talked about something other than murder or the cases we're working on, this...situation might be a little more comfortable for us?"

"Okay," Rue agreed hesitantly. "What did you want to talk about?"

"I dunno. Something about you, personally," he offered. "Might help me to get to know you better. And I'm happy to do the same."

Rue bit her lip. She almost preferred to talk about murder again instead of her past. "Well, okay. But here's the thing, Mr. Fennec..."

"I wish you would call me Darwin outside of work. No need to be so formal."

"Well, okay." Rue paused, refraining from saying his name altogether. "I'm not super fabulous at talking about myself or overly private stuff from my past."

"Fair enough," Darwin agreed. "How about if I ask you a question and if it makes you uncomfortable, you just say, 'pass.' Would that work?"

"Sure," Rue agreed.

"Do you have any brothers or sisters?" Darwin asked to get the conversation started.

"Pass," Rue answered, forcefully.

"Oh, okay. I thought that was a soft-ball question but..." He thought a moment. "Are your parents still alive?"

"Pass."

Darwin was visibly confused.

"Okay, clearly we're not talking about your family. How about something simple. Where were you born?"

"Pennsylvania," Rue folded her arms, defensively.

"Oh, okay, great. We're getting somewhere. Where in Pennsylvania?"

"Pass."

"Oh, come on, Rue. How the hell am I supposed to learn anything about you if you keep every detail about your life locked up?"

Rue tucked her chin to her chest like a chastised child who was sulking. She sank into the kitchen chair.

"Fine," she thought a moment. "Yellow is my favorite color."

"Is it? Well, that's something..."

"No!" Rue covered her face with her palms. "That's a lie. It's really aqua, like the ocean."

"Then, why did you say yellow?" Darwin was confused.

"I don't know!" Rue wailed. Her eyes were red as if she were ready to start crying. Instead, she bit her lip and sucked in her breath. No tears emerged. "I guess no one's ever taken enough of an interest in me to ask what my favorite color was."

"I had no idea color was so important to you."

"It's not, it's...never mind."

"No, not never mind," Darwin answered calmly. "Surely Spencer takes an interest in you?"

Rue leaned forward and looked him squarely in the eyes. "If he did, then why am I sitting here with you?"

After what felt like an eternity. "Understood," he nodded. "I have another idea."

"Yeah, what's that?" Rue asked.

"Perhaps tomorrow, we can sneak out of here for a bit and take a day out. I can get Bristol to drop us somewhere and I am pretty good at disguises, if I say so myself."

"Wouldn't it be safer to stay put if there's a murderer on the loose?" Rue reasoned.

Darwin tilted his head slightly. "While I cherish the idea of hibernating in my home with you, particularly with the weather being as cold as it has been, I'm fairly certain that one or both of us might go stir crazy for too lengthy a time. Maybe just a short outing?"

"Where would we go?" Rue wanted to know.

"I dunno. Anything you have an interest in seeing in Manhattan that you haven't seen yet?"

"Well," Rue thought a moment. "Monte and Candy were talking

about some bakery in Chinatown that had the best sticky buns on the planet." She used air quotes for emphasis. "Maybe there?"

"Ah, I think I know the place," Darwin nodded, wiping his mouth with a napkin and taking another sip of water. "Chinatown is a good place to visit that won't likely be on anyone's radar. Let's plan on that in the morning. In fact, since your apartment is on the way, maybe we can have Candy meet us en route to drop off some of your clothes."

"And for the rest of the evening?" Rue looked around nervously.

"Settle in with a good book and more wine?"

"That sounds like the best plan of all," Rue smiled. "Hey," Rue realized, "when do I get to ask you personal questions?"

"What did you want to know?" Darwin asked.

"Did you ever date Monte?"

"Of course not. What made you think that?" Darwin was surprised.

"No reason." She paused a moment. "So...you like...girls?"

Darwin choked back a laugh. "If you're trying to ask if I'm gay or not. The answer is no." He took a sip of water. "And for the record. Yes...I prefer women."

"Hmm. Well, what about Candice? Did you ever date her?" Rue fired away.

"No, are you crazy? She's young enough to be my daughter!" Darwin cringed. "You know, for someone who doesn't like me, you seem awfully interested in my personal life."

"You're right, I don't like you," Rue said in a lighthearted way as she chomped down the last of her salad and went back for more pasta. "But do you like me?"

Darwin eyed her for a moment. "Pass."

CHAPTER 27
Chinatown

Thursday Morning in Chinatown

Candice came through, meeting Darwin and Rue just a few blocks from her apartment with assorted clothing and toiletries.

Frankly, Rue was a little embarrassed at having someone else see her modest living quarters, sparse clothing selection, and even sparser collection of makeup, hair products and other accessories. Unlike Midge, Candice was discreet enough to not mention the need to retrieve bras and panties from Rue's underwear drawer. In fact, of all the people that could have been sent, Candice seemed to have a knack for what's needed in a pinch, having picked out just the right assortment of mix and match clothes, jackets, shoes and the like.

She also managed to fit it all into a tiny bag that would be small enough to store in the overhead of a plane. All this led Rue to the conclusion that Candice was used to having to pack and leave town in a hurry.

"Thank you," Rue whispered as Candice threw the bag in the trunk and hastily made her exit. She wasn't sure about how well she could, as Darwin called it, "get in and out of places undetected" while wearing the oversized, pink feathery jacket and the long dangling earrings she currently had on, but she was grateful, nonetheless. This only reaffirmed her belief that bold was the new beige in Manhattan, and the weirder you seemed, the less you stood out.

"No problem, sweetie. Just stay safe," Candice answered, interrupting her thoughts, before disappearing down the steps of the nearest subway line.

Bristol had arrived in the most boring looking blue sedan she had ever seen, but it worked. They blended in with traffic, and before long, Darwin and Rue emerged in Chinatown, Bristol dropping them off on Mott Street.

Rue, for the first time ever, had her hair tied back and tucked under a wig and hat. Her face was powder white with pink cheeks and bright red lips. She overemphasized her eyebrows with a little brush and makeup kit that was stashed in Darwin's hallway closet. He was wearing padding under his sweater and a deerstalker hat pulled over his ears.

Darwin led the way to a small corner bakery with nothing inside but a modest counter and a handful of baked goods. The place could hold no more than around five people at a time before it seemed too crowded. He motioned toward the sweet buns.

"Can I help you?" the young woman behind the counter asked as if on autopilot, eyeing over Rue's shoulder as several more people lined up behind them, the door now held open to accommodate the foot traffic. "Please close the door," she said loudly. "Heat is expensive." With that, the last unfortunate person in line was forced to wait outside in the cold, standing impatiently as those inside made their selections.

"I'll have two of the red bean buns, please," Rue asked. The woman grabbed two from the shelf.

"Heated?" she asked.

"Yes, please," Rue smiled in anticipation.

The woman was annoyed. Heating required an extra minute in the oven. Meanwhile, a few more people gathered outside. While the sticky pastries were heating, she rang them up.

Darwin went to pull out his wallet.

"No, let me," Rue offered, digging through the small backpack she was carrying. "How much?" she asked the woman.

"$1.75 for two," she answered.

Rue's jaw dropped. "That's it?" Had she known, she might have ordered a few more, but the woman's icy stare warned her against making any additional changes to her order. Rue handed her exact change and a minute later, the woman handed over the goods.

Outside, Rue pulled one of the pastries from a small wax bag, and handed the bag holding the other bun out to Darwin. She broke the small, warm sticky bun in half and took a bite.

"Oh, my God," her eyes grew wide as she spoke between chewing. "This is like the most awesome thing ever!"

"I know, right?" Darwin devoured his food. "You got the water, I think?"

"Yeah, reach in my bag," she turned her back. "There are two small bottles in there." Darwin unzipped the backpack, pulled out two tiny plastic bottles, and zipped it back up.

The two made a small toast with the bottles of water, pretending to clink them together.

"How have I lived this long and not tried Asian pastries like this?" she wanted to know. "What am I saying?" she kept talking before Darwin could speak. "Spencer would thumb his nose at anything this cheap."

"Good food is good food," Darwin reasoned. "Doesn't all have to be expensive. Wanna wander?"

"Sure." Rue finished her pastry and licked her fingers, wiping them on her jacket. (Spencer would have hated that, too.)

Unfortunately, Rue discovered that the divine smell of pastries wafting from the bakery did not last once they made their way down the street, where the smell of the fish market smacked them in the face. Rue wrinkled her nose. On display with ice and hanging in windows were every variety of sea life: snapper, bass, raw prawns, crabs, dried silver fish and more. As an omnivore, she'd eaten fish plenty of times, but somehow, seeing so many dead ones in one place made her a little sick to her stomach.

"What kind of fish is that?" Rue pointed to a large hanging gourd with spikes all over it. "A pufferfish?"

Darwin looked up. "No, that's durian. It's a type of fruit. I'd recommend staying away from pufferfish if it's ever served you. Done wrong and it'll kill you." As they walked by the row of fruit hanging in the booth. "Though, in my opinion, durian fruit is not much better," he frowned.

"Not a fan?" she asked.

He shook his head. "Not a fan." Darwin observed Rue's face looking a little sallow.

"Maybe a different part of Chinatown?" he suggested.

"Yes, please," she confirmed, averting her eyes from a worker chopping the head off a large fish.

They darted down the next block and walked until the smell of sea life subsided.

Outside a Chinese grocery sat rows and rows of flowers: delphinium, lilies, roses, carnations, snapdragons, peonies, crocuses and more. Rue leaned in to smell them...definitely better than fish, she decided.

"After the color incident, I hesitate to ask which one is your favorite," Darwin joked...very, very carefully.

Rue laughed, "What, no bird of paradise?"

The woman behind the flower cart merely smiled at them but said nothing.

"Ooh," something in the next shop window caught her attention.

It was a gift shop and in the window sat rows of bonsai trees, a few ceramic cats, multi-colored plastic bowls, tea sets, and a few hanging red ornaments of which Rue was unfamiliar and deeply curious about.

The bell clanged loudly as they entered, but no one bothered to look up. The place was bustling for a weekday.

Rue touched her finger to the top of the tiniest tree she'd ever seen and smiled.

"Serissa Bonsai," Darwin explained. "It gets pretty white blooms."

Rue leaned in for a closer look. "How do you take care of it?"

"Well, instead of traditional watering, you soak the base once a week, add a few drops of nutrient, and trim it when it needs it. They can be a bit temperamental though," he cautioned.

"Hmmm," was all Rue said.

"You like?" A small, older Chinese man asked, pointing to the Bonsai.

"Very much," Rue answered.

"You see," he pointed to the layers on the leaves. "There are three lines —this branch Earth, this one Man and this one Heaven."

Rue nodded. "And how much is this Bonsai tree?"

"This one very special...$35. Plus, you need small shears to trim it and food, yes?"

Got it. Rue thought to herself. *I can afford red bean sticky buns, but definitely not Bonsai trees.*

"We'll take it," Darwin answered. "And the food and clippers, too."

"No," Rue protested. "That's too expensive."

"In all the time I've known you," Darwin answered, "which admittedly isn't very long, there are only two things that I've seen make you light up like a kid at Christmas, red bean buns and this Bonsai tree. It's worth the investment."

"Very good," the man smiled, carefully taking the little tree. "Follow me."

At the counter, he cautiously set the Serissa Bonsai in a padded cardboard box along with a small green tube of liquid and tiny metal shears rolled in bubble wrap for safety.

A glimmer of light caught Rue's eyes, just above the shop's doors. She looked up to see an odd-shaped wooden octagon with lines all around it. At its center was a small round mirror. "What kind of mirror is that?" Rue pointed toward the strange, hexagon-shaped mirror.

"A Bagua," he answered. "Very good luck above your door. But must keep heaven on top."

"Heaven?" Rue was curious.

"Yes," he shuffled over to a shelf beside the cash register and pulled out a large box. Inside, he retrieved a small, eight-sided yellow, black, and red mirror with long and broken lines imprinted all around it. He pointed to the three solid lines at the top. "This heaven. It faces up. Hang in your home for protection."

"I'm afraid to ask," Rue pursed her lips, thinking of the Bonsai.

The man read her thoughts. "$2.99."

"We'll take that, too," Darwin chimed in. "$2.99 is a small price to pay for protection."

"Yes," the man smiled, adding it to their spoils.

Rue grabbed the door on their way out. "Well, thank you for that, Mr. Fennec. I didn't expect you to buy me anything today."

"Who says it's for you?" Darwin smirked. "It's for the office. We'll both enjoy it."

"Guess we should head back soon and not press our luck," Rue reasoned. "Plus, you shouldn't have to lug that around the rest of the day."

One thing that Rue discovered about Chinatown were the many scents. They reached the corner where the street smelled of sweet incense. Midway down the block, sandwiched in the middle of other buildings was a Buddhist temple.

"Maybe one more stop?" Rue followed the scent, curiously. She paused in front of the temple where she eyed a large statue through the glass window—a shrine. In front of the Buddha were rows of sand, tea-light candles, and sticks of incense. She noticed someone take one of the sticks, light it, and kneel on a red pad on the floor. After a moment of prayer, they stuck the bottom of the incense into the sand, leaving the top to continue smoking. They pressed their hands together and shook them lightly. Bowing slightly at the Buddha, they then took a seat along one of the rows of chairs running on each side of the statue. Several other people sat there in silence as well as if soaking in the scent during a silent, shared meditation.

The door was propped open so Rue peeked her head inside as if testing the waters. One of the monks, wrapped in an orange and burnt red robe smiled and extended an open palm, welcoming her inside. "Can I?" She pointed to the incense.

"Please," he smiled.

Darwin raised an eyebrow, curiously, but took a seat on one of the chairs, propping the Bonsai tree and other purchases on his lap.

Rue slowly approached the Buddha. She noticed that next to the altar was a bowl full of tiny scrolls marked, "Fortunes, Take one." Behind it was a box with a slit for bills or coins marked, "Donations."

Rue dug through her backpack and pulled out a meager dollar, rolled it up and put it in the donation box. She knelt in front of the altar, took a stick of incense and lit it as she'd seen the previous person do. She held the stick between her palms and looked up at Buddha. His palms were in his lap, a serene look on his face. Rue felt this overwhelming sense of calm, the likes of which she hadn't remembered feeling in a very long time.

Okay, Buddha, she thought to herself. *I'm not Buddhist. I'm not even particularly spiritual. But you seem like the understanding sort. I seem to have bad luck follow me wherever I go on account of my name. Maybe you can help? If you or some other helpful spirit is listening, maybe send a little good fortune my way? I guess what I can really use is...clarity."*

With that, Rue placed the incense in the sand, stood and took one of the scrolls from the "Fortunes" bowl. She turned to leave and then remembered. Spinning around, she placed her palms together, sandwiching the tiny scroll in her hands. She shook her hands slightly and tipped her head toward the Buddha. "Thank you," she whispered.

The monk merely smiled at her as she also waved her hands in his direction. He pressed his palms together and bowed in return.

"Well, Ms. Brennan," Darwin commented after they had left the temple. "You are full of surprises. Never pictured you as a Buddhist."

"I'm not," Rue confessed. "Not sure what drew me in there." She unwrapped the scroll.

"What does it say?" Darwin asked.

"It says," Rue read, "'only when the veil has been lifted will you see things clearly.'"

"Odd," Darwin commented.

"No," Rue disagreed, remembering her prayer. "Makes perfect sense."

Just then, Darwin's cell phone rang. He shifted the box to his left arm.

"Here, let me." Rue relieved him of the box. He pulled his phone from his jacket pocket and hit a button.

"Yes?" he answered.

"I have good news and bad news. Which do you want first?" It was Monte.

"How about the good news?"

"They caught the murderer. Some guy named Tommy Marcuzzo confessed to everything. You guys don't need to go around in disguise anymore."

Really? As in the Tommy who had dated Midge and was friends with Max? "Wonderful," he finally answered. "And the bad news?"

"Just hacked into junior's computer remotely." *Junior* was their new nickname for Astor, Byron Ellis's son.

"And?" He eyed Rue, pointing a finger that he'd be just a minute more.

"Someone sent him an email with a bit of proprietary information that was suspiciously similar to the tech Frat Boy was going to unveil from his company next month."

"Do you know who sent the email?"

"No, but there's more."

"What is it?"

"Bristol just spotted Frat Boy entering Il Cortile in Little Italy with some woman."

"Who?"

"Dunno, but I don't want to be the one to break it to Gal Friday...er, Rue," Monte corrected himself. "Just letting you know since you're in that neck of the woods."

"Thanks, we'll check it out. Catch you later."

Darwin hit a button and ended the call.

"Everything okay?"

Darwin weighed his decision very carefully. On the one hand, they had just had what could be argued was the perfect day. Why spoil it? On the other, if she discovered Spencer on her own, then he couldn't be accused of revealing it, now could he?

"Actually, yes." Darwin flashed a practice smile, taking the heavy box back from her. "Good news. They caught the killer."

"What? Who?"

"Tommy Marcuzzo, of all people."

"Tommy? Really? Somehow, that young pimple-faced boy didn't seem smart enough to tie his shoelaces let alone execute a murderous plan."

"He confessed," Darwin shrugged his shoulders. "Why would he confess to something he didn't do?"

"Exactly," Rue put her hands on her hips. Something didn't add up, but she couldn't quite figure out what it was.

"Hey, let's discuss it over a meal. It'll be the perfect end to our outing. And—" he nodded toward his belly, "I can lose this ridiculous stomach pillow." He paused at a bench to set the Bonsai tree down. Once he was certain no one was looking, he tugged the pillow from under his sweater, tucking it next to the Bonsai food. He picked the box back up.

"Yeah," Rue smiled back. "What did you have in mind?"

"There's a bistro I heard about in Little Italy. How about a meal that's better than the boxed pasta and canned tomato sauce I subjected you to last night."

"Well, Mr. Fennec, that sounds awesome." Without thinking, she took his arm in her hands. Then, she remembered herself and pulled her hands back, tucking them awkwardly in her jacket pockets. She was hoping he hadn't noticed, but he had. Darwin was just smart enough to pretend he hadn't. "But I would argue that last night's dinner was plenty good."

"But not as good as red bean buns?" he joked.

"Let's not get crazy," she smiled up at him. "Lemmee just check on Midge real quick? She did actually go on a date with this joker. I need to make sure she's okay." She hit the contact list on the cell phone Spencer had gotten her, clicking on Midge's number.

After a moment, Midge answered, pretending to be an answering machine. "I'm not in for traitors posing as friends," she droned. "Please leave your message after the tone. Beep!"

Rue smiled in spite of the fact that Midge was an utter pain in the ass at times. She played along. "Sorry to have missed you, Mensa. But I heard the news about Tommy Marcuzzo. Just checking to make sure you're okay. I guess I'll try back at another time." After a pause with no response, she ended the call. "Okay," she said to Darwin, "I'm ready!"

"It's just this way," he motioned an elbow since his arms were now re-occupied with a small Bonsai tree that seemed to get remarkably heavier the longer you held it.

After a short walk, they reached the restaurant. If Spencer were still there, he was at least discreet enough not to sit by the window. They ventured inside and requested a table.

"Certainly," the host answered. "Right this way."

He was leading them toward a table at the far end of the room when suddenly, Rue heard a chuckle. It was one Spencer used when he was trying to sound interested in something you'd said but really wasn't.

"Hang on," she instructed Darwin. "Be right back."

Rue meandered around tables, finding one in the opposite corner of the restaurant.

There, with his back toward her was Spencer. She could recognize that preppy haircut and neckline anywhere. And he was, quite obviously, holding someone's hand. The woman's head was leaning in as if sharing a secret, so all Rue could see was a suit jacket of beige and a swarm of gold necklaces hanging around her in varied lengths.

The woman, becoming aware of Rue, merely leaned back and smiled, gently releasing Spencer's hand.

"Miss Brennan," she said. "How unexpected to see you...looking like that," she motioned to Rue's wig.

"What?" Spencer pulled his hand back and leapt to his feet. "Rue, I—"

Just across from Spencer was none other than Gretchen Ellis.

Rue's face grew hot. All this talk about being so busy and being so concerned about her safety that she should stay far away from him. Pawning her off as Darwin's responsibility.

"Rue, should you be out in public?" Was all that he could think to say.

She opened her mouth to speak, but no words came out. For the slightest of moments, she thought to yell, but there was a small part of her that didn't want to make a scene, not to preserve Spencer, mind you, but technically, both Spencer and Gretchen were their clients. More importantly, Darwin was waiting anxiously at their table, eyeing the scene but trying not to interfere. She couldn't hurt his business or embarrass him after the nice day they'd just had. She gazed momentarily at a few of the tables surrounding her, mostly couples waiting with baited-breath at what they anticipated happening.

"No," she finally smiled sweetly. "Probably not." Rue left out the part about Tommy's confession. She turned to leave.

Spencer caught her wrist. "Please, let me explain," he whispered.

"Be back at your condo in an hour," she muttered between gritted teeth. "You can explain then." With that, she flicked her wrist to release it from his grasp. She didn't wait for his reply.

At this point, Darwin was already by the front door.

"Let's go," she said curtly.

Darwin merely nodded and followed. Outside, she said, "Sorry to do this to you, Mr. Fennec, but it seems I have some business to attend to. Namely, I have a boyfriend to break up with. Any chance we can have Bristol pick us up and drop me by Spencer's condo?"

"Yes, but are you sure that's wise?" Darwin had a flood of emotions coursing through him at that moment. Joy at Rue's mention of Spencer being an 'ex,' guilt over having her discover Spencer's infidelity in this way, concern over her feelings, and something else which he'd yet to define.

"Yeah," she answered. "I need to have a word with Spencer and then I'll be back at your place, if you don't mind. I know it was supposed to be an off day, but there's more to this than just my relationship at stake. This has to do with our cases. Just not exactly sure how, yet."

Darwin was surprised. He had expected her to be so overcome with emotion that work wouldn't have been a concern. Her focus on their cases was both admirable...and confusing.

As requested, Bristol was there to pick them up and deliver Rue to Spencer's condo in advance of Spencer's arrival. She hadn't a key, mind you. So, she waited on a couch in the lobby. "You gonna be okay?" Bristol asked, sympathetically.

"Yeah." She fought back a tear. "It helps that I'm more angry then heartbroken at the moment."

"Okay, I'm gonna drop Darwin off and be back waiting for you outside in a jiffy."

"Thanks, Bristol," she sniffed. "You're the greatest."

"Aw, we both know that's not true, but you're welcome." He tipped his cabby hat at her and backed into the revolving door, almost falling over in the process. "I'm okay!" he called back, laughing.

Moments later, a very flushed Spencer shot through the same door. The door couldn't move fast enough, despite his speed.

"Rue," he whispered, eyeing the guard who merely shot him a glance and nodded in recognition of Spencer being a tenant. "Could we go upstairs and talk about this?"

"Of course," she smiled sweetly. "Let's do that."

Spencer was surprised at Rue's calmness, something which both disturbed him and impressed him, all at the same time. What was she up to?

CHAPTER 28

The Slut, the Mother, and the Professional

Thursday Evening at Spencer's Condo

Rue's calm demeanor cracked as soon as they reached Spencer's condo. It didn't help that there was an obvious scent of Gretchen's perfume wafting in the air, along with a beige scarf she'd left hanging on the edge of his couch.

"Does she have her own drawer too?" Rue growled, pacing back and forth, eyeing the room for more evidence. "Do you divvy up the space between lovers?"

"Darling, would you please calm down and let me explain?" Spencer attempted to take Rue by the shoulders, but she shrugged him away.

"Don't you 'darling' me you Cary Grant wannabe!" Rue spat.

"So, now we're resorting to childish name-calling?" Spenser chastised.

"Oh, no, you don't," Rue pointed a finger at him. "Don't you *dare* turn this back around on me, you man-whore."

"Again with the name-calling." Spencer's face turned red. "Are you at least going to let me explain my side of things?"

"Oh, forgive me, my sweet," Rue mocked. "By all means, please explain your side of the story, so I can understand how your sleeping with Gretchen Ellis is in any way not cheating on your current girlfriend," Rue pointed to herself, in case Spencer needed reminding.

"What makes you think I'm having an affair with Gretchen Ellis? Did it ever occur to you that it may have been a business meeting?"

"A business meeting in a dark little corner of an Italian bistro where you were holding hands?"

"That wasn't what was happening at all. She was upset. Byron is having another one of his affairs again and I was just comforting her, as a friend."

"Comforting her?" Rue clarified.

"Exactly. So, you see—"

"Then explain this," Rue interrupted, reaching over and lifting a lace bra from the couch and holding it up. "This is at least two sizes too big for me and costs more than half of my entire wardrobe. Is this how you comfort all your friends?"

"Okay," he held up his hands in defeat. "But for your information, Gretchen and I had a minor relationship before you and I ever met."

"So, this was a little stroll down memory lane despite the fact that you're supposedly my boyfriend. Oh, and by the way, she's already married...to your former *boss*! Or did you forget that?"

"Please try to understand. She's just a means to an end. Gretchen has been helping me figure out who at B. A. Ellis Industries has been stealing scripts for the intricate programming that took us years to write and rework and then has been repeatedly trying to infect my system with malware. I suspect his entire business is corrupt."

"Helping...you?" Rue bit her lip. "Let's put infidelity aside for a moment, shall we? Why on Earth would Gretchen Ellis help you damage her husband's business by siding with SpencerTech?"

"Because she believes in me," Spencer whined, just a little. "She knows her husband is a self-absorbed, overweight, misogynist bastard who, I might add, is a chronic philanderer."

"So, that makes whatever the hell this is, okay?" Rue challenged.

"We were going to take down B. A. Ellis Industries together."

"You and I?"

"No, silly. Me and Gretchen."

"She was working with you to sabotage her own husband?" Rue was shocked.

"It was revenge, of sorts."

"For what?"

"For his infidelity, of course."

"And what about your infidelity, Spencer?"

"C'mon Rue," Spencer reasoned. "It's not as if we're married, now, is it?"

Rue's eyes widened. "Forgive me, Spencer," her voice squeaked in a high-pitched tone. "It was silly of me to assume that if you and I were sleeping together, then it meant we weren't sleeping with other people! After a year of being together, I clearly expected too much from you."

"Well, what about you and Darwin?"

"What about me and Mr. Fennec?"

"Mr. Fennec, please," Spencer scoffed. "Don't give me that formal 'Mr. Fennec' shit."

"I assure you, Spencer, my boss has been nothing but professional. And you were the one, after all, who called him 'light in the loafers.' Did you expect there to be some innocent flirtation on the off chance he wasn't enough to pique my interest and distract me from your affair? Is that why you wanted me to work with him? To keep me waiting in the wings for when you were ready for me again?"

Spencer held his hands together in a prayer position and waved his hands in front of his chest as if trying to explain. "You don't understand," he reasoned. "The world doesn't fit into this neat little package that you've created for it. *Relationships* don't follow the Rue Brennan system of how the world is supposed to work."

"Are you trying to suggest that I'm the problem here? That I'm supposed to be okay with all of this?"

"Just think about it for a moment. Look at it from my perspective. I'm trying to create a better life for us."

"You and Gretchen?"

"No, silly. You and I!" he chastised. "But a person in my position needs to keep up certain appearances and have the right connections."

"What is that supposed to mean?"

"Gretchen's influence opened a lot of doors for me. I got to meet with potential investors who otherwise wouldn't have given me the time of day."

"And appearances? It's not as if you could be seen in public with Gretchen, not with her husband's fame and influence."

Spencer coughed and tugged at his tie.

"Oh," Rue answered softly. "But you couldn't be seen with me either, could you?"

Spencer's face dropped. "Listen, darling, I love your free-spirited Bohemian style and that you laugh in the face of societal expectations placed upon us, but when it comes to getting one's foot in the door, it's much easier if I...fit in."

"I see," Rue felt that gnawing in the pit of her stomach. Suddenly, a lightbulb went off in her brain...clarity! "The day you went to the Gala for the Artist Atelier—the one that I, as a figure model, was invited to by the model coordinator and then unceremoniously uninvited by you..."

"I told you I was sick that day."

"But you didn't want me to go alone." Rue thought on this some more.

"I was worried about your safety without an escort."

"You've never been overly concerned about my safety before, not even now, when I was on the scene of two murders and might have easily been the intended target."

"You're being unfair."

"And you're lying again, aren't you, Spencer?" Rue searched Spencer's eyes. He put up a momentary front, but then slumped his shoulders and dropped his gaze. "You took someone else to the Gala that night, didn't you? Someone more...professional...polished...less *Bohemian*?"

"Yes," he finally answered.

"Who?"

"Does it matter?"

Rue thought on this a moment. "If I'm so embarrassing to you, Spencer, why are you still with me? Excuse me, why *were* you with me?"

"Perhaps our timing was just off," Spencer explained.

"And what does that mean, exactly?"

"Let's be honest, Rue. I'm a hot-blooded male. We're hardwired that way."

"So, society would have you believe."

"Don't go all Gloria Steinem on me now."

"Screw you, Spencer."

"Classy. Very classy, Rue." Spencer held up a hand. "Would you let me finish?" He waited a moment while Rue crossed her arms and bit her lip. She leaned up against the side of Spencer's living room table for what she knew would be the last time. "There are three types of women in my world, Rue—there's the kind you marry and have children with, the kind you bring to professional events—the colleague who doubles as your pretend wife—and—"

"The slut you sleep with while you're sowing your wild oats."

"Your words, not mine. But in a manner of speaking, yes."

"Which one is Gretchen Ellis...the professional or the slut?"

"I wish you wouldn't talk about her that way."

"Fuck you, Spencer. I don't give a shit about Gretchen and how my words might offend you."

"Again, classy."

"And which one was I, Spencer? The one you take home and introduce to mother? Did I just arrive at the scene a little too soon?"

"Kind of," Spencer admitted. "Though with the mouth on you, I'm starting to wonder."

"Well forgive me, your horniness, for not fitting into the appropriate girl-box you've put me in. I guess I was just supposed to be quiet and sweet, keeping my legs together for everyone but you, while you whored your way through Manhattan. Then, when you were finally ready to settle down, good 'ol Rue will be there, ready and waiting to make a good home for you and pop out a few babies when the time was right."

"I think you're being a little dramatic."

"I think you and I are finished."

"You don't mean that."

"Oh," Rue protested, "but I do. Goodbye, Spencer."

Spencer cleared his throat after Rue had made her powerful march across the floor to the front door. "And your belongings?"

"The one pair of pajamas in the drawer you cleared out for me and my toothbrush? I think I can live without those. You can donate my extra space to Gretchen." Rue opened the door. "Oh, and by the way. Your next quarterly payment is due to retain Mr. Fennec's services. I'll see to it that you have the invoice in the morning."

Spencer stood upright, surprised. "You're not telling me that you plan to stay on as Darwin's assistant after all this, are you?"

"Of course, I am. Unlike you, I'm very adept at keeping my personal life and my private life separate. I'm helping Mr. Fennec with your case and plan to continue doing so until it's resolved."

"What if I were to tell Darwin that I don't want you on the case anymore," Spencer threatened.

"It's not up to you."

"If I'm paying his company, it is."

"That's fine, Spencer. Though, you may want to look at the fine print on your contract with us."

"Us? You and me?"

"No, you idiot. Mr. Fennec and me."

"What fine print?"

"Given our investment in time, materials and resources, and the fact that we're past the halfway mark on our proposal, you're too far into the contract. So, by all means, cancel. But you'll still be required to pay our fee in full."

"That's highway robbery!" Spencer complained.

"No, Spencer," Rue corrected. "That's business. Try reading your contracts before signing once in a while."

With that, Rue slammed the door to Spencer's apartment for the last time, rushing to the elevator before the tears started flowing like a river.

Darwin wasn't there when Rue arrived back at the condo. But Monique and Candice were. Candice had been half-sitting on the edge of one of the desks, flipping through one of Darwin's books on code-breaking when Rue burst through the door. Monique was at Darwin's computer, typing rapidly on the keypad. Bristol, while sympathetic to her situation, had Evie and her younger sister at home fighting off a stomach bug and had to relieve his wife of parent-duty so she could get some rest. Consequently, he dutifully dropped her off at Darwin's place and left in a hurry. His heart sank a little. He knew she was hurting, and was hoping the rest of the team could be there, even if he couldn't.

Rue had done her best to wipe away the tears with the back of her hand and smooth her hair back before returning to what had become both her workspace and her temporary home. Unfortunately, as soon as she saw them both, the tears began flowing.

"Uh oh," Candice stood. "Here come the waterworks." Candice walked over and wrapped her arms around Rue. Rue sniffed back a sneeze. Candice's perfume was a little intense. But at least it overpowered Eau du Gretchen. "Lemme guess, you had it out with that asshole boyfriend of yours. Darwin told us about the incident at the restaurant. Sweetie, I'm so sorry."

Rue nodded, wrapping her arms around Candice and hugging her back, sobbing.

"Men are such a disappointment," Candice offered.

"Hey," Monique protested.

"Present company excluded, of course. Darwin, too."

"That's a little better," Monique hit enter on the keypad and looked up from the screen. "What about Bristol?" he wanted to know.

Candice thought a moment. "Yeah, I'll give him a pass, too, but only cuz that wife of his sorted him out. I also think having two daughters was karma's best revenge."

Rue thought about this a moment. "Do you have a family?" She chastised herself for not having thought to ask sooner.

After a short silence, Candice answered, "These chumps are the only family I got."

Monique nodded. "I was disowned the day my uber-religious father caught me trying on my mom's Sunday dresses. Candy is the closest thing I've got to family. She's like a sister to me."

"The point is," Candice hugged Rue a little tighter. "You didn't deserve what he did to you. But we gotchu. You're part of the Fennec family now," she smiled, leaning back to look at Rue's tear-stained face.

"Fennec family?"

"Yeah, Darwin and Ashley."

"I'm afraid I don't follow."

"Ashley? The gal you probably assumed was Darwin's one-time girlfriend?"

"What about her?"

"Well, that part was true," Monique corrected, laughing. "When he was *five*!" After a few more chuckles, Monique continued. "Ashley's married to Darwin's brother, Ryland. In other words..."

"Sister-in-law?" Rue finished.

"The girl is a quick study," Candice joked. "Well, let's just say, Darwin and Ashley have a knack for picking up orphans and adopting them, in a manner of speaking. And no matter how much time has passed...three months...six...a year, even if we go our separate ways for a while, we always come back to the tribe. And it's like no time has passed at all."

"How did you come to meet him?" Rue asked, immediately regretting it.

"Okay, but don't get all judge-y." Candy pointed a lacquered finger at Rue, closing her book and setting it down on an end table. "Nothing like what you're thinking."

"I thought you were a call girl and Darwin gave you a respectable job."

"Hmm," Candice wrinkled her lips. "Okay, so it is what you're thinking," she confessed. "But not to the *level* that you're thinking."

"Huh?" Rue was confused.

"I was—" she stopped herself. "I *am*...an escort. But I draw the line at funny business."

"Funny business?"

"Use your noggin', Rue," Candice explained. "I still am a part-time escort...a companion, of sorts, to men...er, and some women, if I'm being honest."

"Oh," Rue answered.

"Again, stop with the judge-y!" She wiggled a finger at Rue. "Well, let's just say, one day, things were starting to get desperate in the finance department. So, I thought I'd kick it up a notch. And the first guy I try to hooch up to on the street was—"

"Mr. Darwin Fennec," Monique answered.

"So, he was your first..."

"No!" Candice answered. "I offered him my body. Instead, he offered me a job."

"What would inspire him to do that?" Rue wanted to know.

"I was also really good at picking pockets. Except he caught me trying to steal his wallet. Asked if I wanted to put my skills to better use. He was on a case at the time, and I happened to be in the right place at the right time."

"So, you and Mr. Fennec..."

"Nothin' has ever happened," Candice confirmed as she and Monique exchanged glances. Candice leaned in as if sharing a secret with Rue. "Ya know," she confessed, "you could do worse than Darwin Fennec...as tonight has clearly illustrated."

Rue let out a sigh.

Just then, they heard someone fumble with a keypad and Darwin emerged from the outer hallway carrying what looked like an envelope.

"How are you doing?" he asked Rue. It was only then that she noticed he'd already placed the Serissa Bonsai in the window between their two desks.

"Okay," Rue answered. After a pause, she added, "I told Spencer—" She stopped herself. "I told Mr. Hargrove that we'd have his quarterly invoice to him in the morning." She sniffed a little and then started laughing so hard the tears began rolling down her face.

After a moment's pause, Monique, Candice and Darwin began laughing with her, Monique wrapping his arms around both Candice and Rue in solidarity.

Darwin waited for the trio to break their group hug before he asked, "Er, Candice?" Darwin held up the envelope. "Can I speak with you privately for a moment, in the kitchen?"

Once again, the sad thing about condos in Manhattan, even luxury ones, is that the living room, kitchen, and dining area are often one large, inescapable place. Short of asking her to meet him in the bedroom or bathroom, there weren't many options.

Monique and Rue attempted to occupy themselves at the computer before realizing it was fruitless.

"You didn't actually get to eat a decent meal today, did you?" Monique finally asked.

"No," Rue confessed, her stomach grumbled in confirmation.

"Well, since it's safe for you to go out again, seeing as they caught the killer, why don't you and I pop around the corner for something to eat? I know of a really good Thai place."

"Perfect," Rue answered, gratefully. "I'll grab my coat."

"Heading out for Thai food!" Monique called. "Buzz me if you want us to bring you back something."

Darwin waved an acknowledgment but refocused his attention on the letter he was holding for Candice.

Outside, Rue asked, "What was that about?"

"Darwin trying to reconnect Candy with her family."

"So, she does have a family...outside of the Fennec family, of course."

"Yeah," Monique answered, patting back her windblown hair. "Not my place to say more than that, though. Candy can fill you in when she's ready. Let's eat!" She changed the subject, grabbing Rue's hand and half-dragging her along. Monique was a master at walking in heals, but even the flat-footed Rue had trouble keeping up with her friend's long strides. Fortunately, the restaurant was only two blocks away.

INSIDE DARWIN'S KITCHEN, he and Candice stood, her eyes glued to the floor as she tapped her toe against the tile. Sometimes, everyone forgot that Candice was only in her early twenties. With her makeup, dress and demeanor, people often assumed she was a decade or more older.

"You contacted my parents," she whined. "Without telling me?"

"It wasn't like that, Candice," he answered. "Your dad hired a private investigator who I happened to know. He reached out to me before reporting anything back to your parents."

"Do they know I'm in New York?"

"They know you're safe," Darwin answered. "But they don't know where you are. Here." He handed her the envelope.

"What's this?" Candice sniffed.

"It's a letter from your mom. She sent it to my colleague's post office box, requesting he get it to you."

"Did you read it?" she asked, accepting the letter.

Darwin let out a sigh. "I'm not gonna lie...yeah, I read it."

"But it's a personal letter," she protested.

"And I didn't want to deliver anything potentially harmful to you without at least being prepared…or preparing you."

"What does it say?" she asked, crossing her arms.

"It says they love you and want you to come home."

"And school?"

"They're open to discussing a trade school instead of a business degree if that's what you want."

"Why did it take running away for them to listen?" Candice furrowed her eyebrows.

"Not having kids," Darwin admitted, "I have no idea. Point is, there's a ticket back home with your name on if you decide to use it."

"What if I get back there and it turns out to be a mistake?" Candice sobbed.

"Well, then, you know you've always got a second home in Manhattan. Pretty sure Monte isn't planning on replacing you with a new roommate anytime soon."

"Heh," Candice laughed. "There's no one else but me who'd put up with him leaving his makeup, cologne, and undershorts all over the place. No boundaries, that guy."

Candice took the letter and opened it. After a few minutes, she set it down on the counter.

"Well?" Darwin asked.

Candice didn't say another word. Instead, she ran toward Darwin and wrapped her arms around him in a bear hug. He awkwardly hugged her back. Having little experience in the mentoring department, he didn't really feel equipped for this sort of thing.

"I love you, Darwin," she sniffed. "In a strictly familial and not hitting on you sort of way," she clarified.

Darwin chuckled. "Likewise."

CHAPTER 29
The Truth

Monday Morning at Darwin's Condo

~

"Good morning, Mr. Fennec," Rue called out cheerfully after tapping the entry code to Darwin's condo and barreling inside. With the murderer caught, Rue felt safe returning to her apartment after she and Monique returned from their Thai food adventure. She tried knocking on Midge's door, but her friend was obviously still avoiding her. But, having heard her voice on the phone being as sarcastic as usual, she felt good knowing that at least Midge hadn't been one of Tommy's victims.

Rue had taken Friday off and had the long weekend to recover and take some time to process her emotions. Since she was not far from Chinatown, she even made a special visit back to the Buddhist temple just to sit for a few minutes, taking in the warm aroma of incense and clearing her head. The following day, she walked along the pier at the Seaport, smiling to herself as she passed the park bench where she had originally met Darwin...which somehow seemed like a lifetime ago.

She pulled herself out of her thoughts and back to the present.

Darwin wasn't home when she arrived. Rue looked around the room, curiously. But given the open container of trail mix and a half-filled glass of one of his green smoothies at his workstation, she figured he'd be back soon. It also appeared that he left his personal cell phone behind, too.

She slung her backpack on the seat of her chair. The chair creaked a little as she settled into it. Rue glanced out the window. The city looked pretty from this height, she decided, particularly since today was the first day they had a light snowfall.

It was only then that she noticed something. Darwin's desk and computer was on the opposite side, facing the faux brick wall. He had given her the view. *Curious*, she thought. *Why would he have done that?*

She paused for a moment to admire the Bonsai tree on the windowsill and the Bagua mirror that Darwin dutifully hung above his door, heaven-side up.

Just then, something beeped on Darwin's computer. Rue was all prepared to ignore it, but it began beeping again, rather persistently. She walked over to his desk. There, on the screen, was an email alert, blinking rapidly. Something was wrong with the server he was using to back up their data. "That can't be good," she said to herself. Her first instinct was to phone Darwin, until she once again noticed his phone staring back at her.

Well, she reasoned, *isn't this what she was being trained for? What's the worst that can happen?* If she did nothing, there was a good chance the data would be lost either way.

Rue typed in a few bits of command lines that Darwin had taught her and waited.

Something was wrong.

"Wait a minute," she realized. Someone was trying to hack into their system. Hence the rapid alert. First, she took steps to secure their computers and remote server. Then, she set up a ghost account from what appeared to be Guam (it was the first place she'd thought off, for whatever reason) to pursue whoever was poking around their accounts. *Wait a second,* she recognized that IP address—Spencer!

"Oh no, you don't, you cheating bastard!" Rue did the virtual equivalent of a drop and kick, tossing him offline. She then blocked him. Rue had momentary thoughts of sending some malware to his address but stopped herself. Unlike Midge, Rue stopped at having the devilish thought before ever acting on it. And, of course, Midge was sometimes bat-shit crazy. Rue wasn't.

"What the heck are you looking for, Spencer?" she asked aloud. She systematically began plugging in the code combinations, following Darwin's instructions to memorize the patterns of the codes versus the actual passwords. She logged into the profiles they had set up for Byron, Astor, Gretchen and Portia, but all the notes were current. She moved on to Ursula, Emma and Clarissa, still nothing new and interesting. She went through every profile she had access to, beginning to actually enjoy herself. What used to be a source of frustration had now become easy for her, logging in and out and putting the cryptic codes together so quickly.

"Wonder what my code would look like?" she laughed to herself. Rue typed in the sequence that, to the best or her understanding of Darwin's made-up algorithm, would match a profile for one Rue Brennan. She hit "enter" and that's when she saw it. Her face dropped.

There, in front of her, were detailed logs about her life, including photos of Rue and Midge standing outside of Merriam Hall, Rue and Monte heading to B. A. Ellis Industries, and one image of her stopping for tea at a cart outside of Spencer's condo. On this one, the caption read, "prefers Earl Grey with light sugar."

There were lists of where she went after she left work, including stops at the bodega around the corner from her apartment and visits to the laundromat across the street. It even noted that she most frequently did her laundry on Sunday mornings at around 8 a.m.

In a separate document was a list of "likes:" theater, art museums, being on the water, writing," and more recently, "Chianti, bird of paradise flowers, Bonsai trees, Buddhist temples, and red bean buns." There was even an extra note that read, "seems to be highly sensitive to caffeine."

The hairs on the back of her neck stood up as she quickly scrolled through pages and pages of her life over the past month, horrified. Somehow, it was fine to keep tabs on who she deemed were the "bad people." They were the greedy, disreputable Ellises and LaMontes of the world. But why had Darwin been keeping such tabs on her?

Then, she saw it, a zoomed in photo of Spencer through the window of an obscure little Japanese steakhouse on the opposite side of town where he lived. Even at a distance, she could make out Gretchen Ellis's pointed nose and smile, as if the photographer had caught her mid-laugh. The timestamp read 6:24 p.m., two weeks prior to her discovery of them.

And then there were two other folders, one marked "Invoices," the other "Receipts." She clicked on "Invoices," and discovered that Darwin had been charging Spencer weekly for services marked as "Monitoring support." It identified the hours when Rue was at work, and the couple of times, off hours, such as their excursion to the theater and Chinatown. Her stomach sank deeper.

She clicked on "Receipts." There, she saw an ongoing log that included a number that distinctly matched her weekly paycheck.

"You're early," Darwin's voice startled Rue. She jumped from her chair. He walked all the way to the kitchen countertop without her even noticing. He dropped a pile of office supplies he'd just procured from a local shop. "I didn't expect you for another hour."

"What is this?" Rue choked.

Darwin gazed at the computer, opened his mouth and then closed it again. "I could ask what you're doing at my computer," he challenged.

"Security breach, and don't change the subject!"

Darwin's eyebrows shot up, curiously as he attempted to peer over her shoulder at the screen.

"Don't bother," she spat. "I fixed it. The larger question is, why do you have a file on me, Mr. Fennec?"

"Oh, crap," he answered, running a hand through his hair. Rue rotated in the chair, wrapping her arms behind her as if hugging the back of it, waiting for an answer. "Look," he put his hands out to his sides as his head swayed back and forth as he formed his words. "I wanted to tell you. In fact, I had every intention of telling you."

"When?"

Darwin sighed. He sat on the arm of the living room couch, crossing his long legs in front of him. He crossed and uncrossed his arms, as if not sure what to do with them but not wanting to come across as defensive. Finally, he jabbed his fingers uncomfortably into his front jean pockets.

"First of all, I had to make sure you weren't involved in either of the two murders," he explained.

"Bullshit, Darwin," Rue answered, angrily. "These records began before you and I officially met. Why were you keeping tabs on me?"

"I can't—"

"Why can't you?" Rue stood, her eyes beginning to well up.

"Client privilege. It would be unethical," he all but whispered, his voice cracking a little at the end. His eyes dropped to the floor.

"Who was the client? Spencer? What does helping him uncover who's stealing tech secrets from his company have to do with spying on me?" She whirled around on the chair and punched in a few codes. Darwin resisted the urge to stop her, secretly worried she was going to delete the files out of spite or discover something new she had missed.

Instead, she began typing. "It was Gretchen, this whole time, wasn't it?" she asked. "She pretended to be on his side, but she's been feeding their inventions to her son and husband, hasn't she?"

"I suspect so, yes," Darwin confirmed.

"And Spencer's affair with Clarissa?"

There was a long silence.

"How did you—" Darwin began.

"I'm an investigator's assistant," Rue retorted. "It's my job to know." She looked down at the computer and began sobbing. "He tried sending her in to seduce Astor, didn't he? To make Astor jealous that Clarissa was with him after Astor left her for Portia LaMonte? She was supposed to steal intel, wasn't she? But instead, she was trying to get back together with Astor."

"I suspect that you're right about that, too." Darwin walked over and rested his arms on her shoulders. She shrugged them off. "Don't try to comfort me, Mr. Fennec. You knew he was cheating on me. Why didn't you tell me? And furthermore, I still don't understand why you were watching me."

Darwin let out a sigh and remained silent during another one of his ruminations. "He paid me to watch you."

"What?" Rue tilted her head back to stare up at Darwin. "So, those receipts for my paycheck? Spencer actually paid you to hire me?"

"Please," Darwin stepped aside and motioned toward the couch. "Perhaps we can sit and talk for a moment."

Rue relented and relocated to the couch, never taking her eyes from

Darwin, as if trying to read his thoughts. She wanted to make him say something that would magically make it all right, but she couldn't think of any scenario where that would be possible.

He sat next to her, leaving a good four feet between them, lest she start replaying false scenarios of him being a playboy again, despite all evidence to the contrary. "Spencer did hire me to find out who was stealing information and releasing similar product lines just ahead of SpencerTech. That part was true. What you didn't know was—"

"Yes."

"He wanted me to keep you out of the way until he did."

"Why?"

"I assume it was so he could pursue Gretchen Ellis without fear of your discovering it."

Rue stood. "You helped him cover up his infidelity!"

"I didn't know that at the time, I swear." This time, both hands went to pull back his hair—a sign that he really was stressed. "He told me he was concerned for your safety, a ruse that was conveniently reinforced when Clarissa Sauer and Ursula Gorky died in your presence."

"So, he paid you to babysit me?!"

"Well, it sounds awful when you put it like that."

"Because it is awful, Darwin! And if he truly was concerned, did it not occur to you that he could have told me and hired a bodyguard for me? Why would he send me to work for someone poking their nose into the world of people he deemed dangerous?"

"Well, when you put it like that—"

"Some investigator you are!" She eyed him over, distastefully.

"Hey," he whined. "That was unnecessary."

"And yet completely justified," Rue stood and went to grab her backpack.

Her back was toward Darwin when he said quietly, "It's because I liked you."

"What?" She turned her chin in his direction.

"I thought it was odd too, but the truth is, I liked you...right away, even before I'd met you at the pier that day."

She turned to look at him. "How is that possible?"

"The way Spencer described you. All the things he thought were annoying about you, the way you dress, how you say whatever is on your mind, when you eat with your fingers instead of using a fork—"

"I use a fork, when necessary," Rue retorted. Somehow, that seemed the least relevant thing to say in this moment and she immediately regretted it.

"The point is, all those little things that bothered him, I thought were completely endearing. And when I saw you and Midge out on the balcony during on your birthday—"

"You were spying then, too!"

"For the record, I didn't know it was your birthday or I would have reminded Spencer. The point is, I liked you, and I kinda wanted an excuse to have you around." After an unnervingly long pause, he added, dropping his gaze to the floor once again. "I still like you," he whispered.

Rue was boiling over on the inside, and the words formed before she could stop them. "Well," she answered quietly, "I don't like you."

He threw a hand in the air. "So you keep reminding me."

Rue headed for the door, pausing before unlocking it. "Just tell me one thing,"

"Anything."

"Did you purposefully take me to that Italian restaurant to discover the two of them?"

"I had to do something," he explained. "Ethically, I had to keep my client's information confidential. But personally..."

Rue let out a sigh.

"Where are you going, anyway?" Darwin was concerned. "I know they arrested Clarissa and Ursula's killer, but that doesn't mean I don't worry about you. Besides, you yourself said that something didn't seem right about it. Perhaps going out alone, for the time being, is a bad idea?"

The realization that he was probably right sank in.

"I'm going for a walk. Probably Central Park. They'll be lots of other people out at this time of day. Maybe I'll ask Midge to go with me, even though I vowed never to speak to her again and she has yet to answer my phone calls when I *did* try and speak with her again."

"Just be careful," he cautioned. "I'll keep my cell phone on me should you need me. And, when you come back perhaps you can tell me about the security breach you encountered? Kinda important for me to know, don't you think?"

Rue nodded. "It was Spencer. I backed up the logs. You can access them on the shared drive." She paused for a moment before leaving, looking over her shoulder. "Tell me something, Mr. Fennec. Did you think I would dump him and come running into your arms after I found out?"

"Only in my fantasies," he confessed. "In reality, I just wanted more than anything for you to know the truth."

"Well, thank you for that, at least. It seems I can't trust anyone anymore, not Spencer, not Midge...and not you."

CHAPTER 30
Central Park

Monday Morning in Central Park

Rue walked at a brisk pace, and it had nothing to do with the cold and everything to do with the hopes that she could somehow out walk her anxiety. It wasn't working.

She walked around the turtle pond, eyeing a few small, remote-controlled model sailboats on the water. It was cool enough for her to see her breath as she exhaled and somehow the cold air was a pleasant shock to her face. After all, she needed to cool down.

Rue didn't know what to think. If she were being honest with herself, she and Spencer had been drifting apart for some time, but every time she'd brought it up in the past, he dismissed it, citing work and reassuring her that "everything would be different once his new computer animation software hit the market." They would have more time together, instead of the long nights he'd spent working. It was only now that she understood how he was really spending those long nights.

And what about him pawning her off on Darwin Fennec, as if she were a small child needing a babysitter, filling her with all this crap about finding a suitable career "at her age?" What about any of this seemed like a good idea to Darwin? While it may have been flattering that he paid more attention to her than Spencer ever had, and that she was actually enjoying what she was learning on the job, how dysfunctional would it have been if she'd entertained the idea of dating him? He was only a few years older than her, but he was still her boss and furthermore...he had lengthy records about her, her likes and dislikes, her routine.

Sure, she thought to herself, she could make the argument that it was part of what Spencer asked him to do. She could further deduce that he had at least some reason to think she might be a murder. *But no.* She shook her head. Rue couldn't get past the fact that Spencer was actually paying her salary. That hurt, considering that she thought she was being useful on the job. *Wonder if he expensed the Bonsai tree,* she thought, miserably.

No, she decided. Everything that Darwin did was stalker-ish and unacceptable. He had clearly crossed a line.

She approached the large Alice in Wonderland statue, still deep in thought. *And speaking of boundaries, there was Midge...*who she only just now realized was leaning against a magic mushroom kissing a man not much taller than she was...*Jaks Liebling? The art teacher?*

"Oh, Rue," Midge broke away, wiping her mouth. "Fancy meeting you here," she said, nonchalantly.

"I left you a message and *told* you I would be here. I just didn't say *exactly* where in Central Park I'd be."

"Well, still a coinkydink if you ask me," she smiled. "I think you know Jaks from the Atelier, don't you?"

Jaks grinned at Rue in a way that gave her the chills—and not in a good way. "Ah, yes. Almost didn't recognize you without your dancing Elektra dress on."

It seemed odd that he'd choose that reference, considering that the last time she saw him was the day Ursula Gorky died via what they now publicized as an allergic reaction due to drinking manchineel juice-spiked wine that caused her throat to swell up so badly that she suffocated to death. Rue pushed the horrible thought away.

"You two are...dating?" Rue was surprised.

"You caught me," Midge laughed, and twirled a lock of her red hair.

"Let's walk. I'm chilly," she commented. Rue fell in step beside Midge with Jaks keeping pace on Midge's opposite side. "Got your message," Midge confessed. "Don't worry, I accept your apology."

Rue hadn't apologized for anything. She just called to check on her friend. She decided to just nod and say nothing.

"Thanks for worrying about me," Midge continued, "but Tommy and I were done a long time ago."

It was only two weeks ago, Rue thought to herself. Again, she remained silent.

"And, as you can see, I'm with someone way better."

"And, uh," Rue stammered. "How did you two meet, exactly?"

"Well, after you so rudely left me, I took my sorrows to Atlantic City, where I met Jaks on a beach walk outside the casinos."

"Interesting," Rue answered, "that you both live in Manhattan and yet happened to meet on a beach in Atlantic City...New Jersey."

"I thought so, too," Jaks grinned, kissing the side of Midge's neck. Rue made a sour face, but quickly recovered before he'd noticed. "Kismet, I guess."

"I just wish you'd told me about this guy sooner," Midge grabbed Jaks' face, giving it a playful squeeze. "How long have you worked with Jaks at the school?"

"Actually, I believe I've only modeled for you," she referenced Jaks, "on a handful of occasions. Honestly," she paused, "it hadn't crossed my mind."

"Just look at that face," Midge smiled at Jaks who grinned back at her, eyeing her like a hawk who just spotted a rabbit.

Rue *was* looking...and she didn't get it.

"So, what did you want to talk to me about?" Midge asked. She paused to rifle through the small-beaded purse that was strapped across her chest and hanging at her side. She pulled out a packet of menthol cigarettes and a lighter. "Come to think of it, you seem a little off today. You okay?" She lit it and took a deep inhale.

"I'm fine," she answered. "And when did you take up smoking?"

"What? I've always been a social smoker."

"I've never seen you smoke and we're social."

"Well," Midge explained. "I've cut back a lot. But Jaks reminded me that there are no guarantees in life, so we should just enjoy ourselves as much as possible.

"By giving yourself cancer and polluting the environment?"

"Ladies, please," Jaks interjected. "Don't let me be the cause of your fuss. Call me a hedonist, but I would rather live for today, rather than get old and be full of regrets."

Rue didn't quite get the logic as you have less of a chance of growing old if you're unhealthy. And, if you do manage to live that long, but feel like shit all the time, then you likely would be full of many regrets.

"Hey, Earth to Rue," Midge waved a hand in front of her face. Rue's nose tickled from the smell of smoke and she let out a sneeze. "Bless you. You were about to tell us why you're acting so weird today?"

There was no way she was going to share any personal information with Midge, not with her creepy new boyfriend around. "Just recovering from a stressful couple of weeks...being on the scene of two murders and all. It was a little...jarring."

"Oh, I'll bet," Midge paused a moment, furrowing her lips. "But, at least, they caught the guy who did it. Our guy Tommy. Who knew? Maybe now the police will stop bugging you."

Rue stopped in her tracks. "Who said the police were bugging me?" She eyed Midge, suspiciously.

"Nobody needed to tell me nothin'," she answered. "Reporters and cops were swarming our apartment complex last week asking all kinds of questions about you before the news report about Tommy's confession. Where were you, anyway?" She eyed Rue, curiously. "Staying with Spencer?"

"Exactly," Rue lied.

"Well, probably for the best. Anyhoo, you'll get a kick outta this, Jaks and I pelted them with cherry tomatoes from the fire escape. Freaked one cameraman out who didn't know what was happening. I think he thought he had blood on him from an attack."

While she sympathized with the cameraman, Rue had to admit, that was a little funny. "Well," she laughed, "few people expect assault by cherry tomato."

Jaks let out a hearty laugh, too. Apparently, he approved of this sentiment as it backed up his hedonist logic.

"Wanna join us?" Midge offered. "We're gonna hit a new martini bar for lunch."

Rue eyed her watch. It was only 11 a.m.

"No thanks," she answered. "I gotta get back to work. Told Mr. Fennec I'd be a little late this morning—taking personal time, but that I'd be in before noon."

"Listen to you," Midge laughed. "And how are things going with you and Mr. Fennec?" Midge wiggled her eyebrows.

"We have a great working relationship," Rue lied for the second time. "Jaks, nice to see you again." That was her third lie. "You two enjoy yourselves."

"Oh, we will," Jaks said, placing his hands on Midge's thighs and pulling her in for a kiss.

"Down boy!" Midge joked, flicking the cigarette ash in the snow behind her. She kissed him in a way that suggested he was not at all adverse to a tongue that tasted like tobacco. She then held up the lipstick-stained cigarette for him to take a drag.

Rue wrinkled her nose again. "Okay, well, bye!" She waved a hand, moving away from the couple as quickly as possible.

At least most of Midge's relationships were short term. She was relieved by the fact that this one would likely fizzle in two weeks. She could wait it out.

~

15 Minutes Prior at Darwin's Condo

One of Darwin's spare track phones rang from his desk—Ashley.

"Tell me you're calling with good news and you just forgot my cell number."

"Just shut up and listen, Darwin," Ashley yelled into the phone, taking several labored breaths in and out.

"What's going on?" Darwin answered. "Are you okay?"

"What's going on is that I'm in labor, but I've got info you need to know before we reach the hospital!"

The sound of ambulance sirens could be heard.

"Are you in an ambulance?"

"Shut it, Darwin, or so help me I'll punch Ryland right in the gut. That's about how I'm feeling right now!"

"I'm pretty sure she means it," Ryland called over her shoulder, laughing. Somehow, Ryland was so overjoyed about becoming a father, that he was willing to overlook his wife's verbal assault.

"Talk," Darwin finally answered, simply.

"Tommy Marcuzzo is innocent. I know he confessed, but something wasn't sitting right with me about it. I did some digging." She paused to suck in a deep breath. "The guy was in debt up to his eyeballs and made a lot of enemies delivering intel on B. A. Ellis Industries to people he shouldn't have." Ashley paused again to rapidly blow in and out a few times before continuing. "Right after he turns himself in and confesses to two murders, $500,000 mysteriously shows up in his bank account and all his credit cards are paid off. Best I can tell is that the money was wired from an offshore account in the Cayman Islands. The point is, a killer is still on the loose, and I got a bad kick-in-the-gut feeling that has nothing to do with babies. You need to look out for Gal Friday."

With that, Ashley hung up the phone. Darwin immediately phoned Rue. Not having used it much, it took her a moment to remember how to answer her cell phone. "What do you want, Mr. Fennec?" she asked, annoyed. She was standing at the front of a food truck and had just retrieved a hot chocolate after waiting endlessly for the man in front of her to make up his mind when there were only four beverage choices on the menu. She nodded to the attendant, plunked her change on the counter and walked away.

"Rue," Darwin sounded anxious. "Are you still in Central Park? Where are you?"

"Just leaving, why?" Rue asked suspiciously, holding the beverage to her lips.

"I need you back here as quickly as you can. Or I can come and get you."

"I don't know..."

"You're not safe," Darwin all but yelled into the phone.

"What are you talking about?" Rue looked around, nervously, lowering the drink before having taken a sip.

"Tommy Marcuzzo's confession was bogus. There's still a killer on the loose."

The hairs on the back of Rue's neck stood up as she remembered Ursula Gorky's blue face and swollen lips.

"I'll be there shortly. No need to come get me," she answered. After she hung up the phone, she glanced back at the food truck, where a loud commotion could be heard. There, on the snow-covered ground, lay the older man, the one who had just been standing in front of her. Two people began CPR as a police officer and medic arrived. On the ground next to him, was a spilled cup of a hot liquid. She didn't know what kind as she hadn't bothered to pay attention to that detail.

Her heart began racing. She dropped her untouched cup into a trash can and all but ran back to the main street, where she made it back to Darwin's condo in record time. This time, however, she opted to go back to their old protocol and retreated to the employee entrance in the back, taking the service elevator up to the seventh floor.

Darwin saw Rue's frazzled expression as she arrived. "Did something else happen?"

Rue huffed and puffed for a minute, struggling to catch her breath after her rapid sprint to the office. Meanwhile, Darwin popped his head out the door, instinctively, looking down the hall on each side before bolting it. Unlike Rue's pillowcase curtains, Darwin's setup was more sophisticated. He flipped a lever and a tan shade dropped from the ceiling, stopping at the bottom of the windowsill, effectively shielding them from view, while still allowing light into the room.

Despite her nerves, seeing something so simple and yet so sophisticated versus what she had in her little studio apartment, made her feel distinctly less than...adequate.

"I'm not sure if it's related or not," she glanced at the window shades, swaying side-to-side nervously, "but after I got my hot chocolate at a food truck, you called. Just then, I saw a man on the ground with people around him. Looked as if he had a heart attack. He had been in line in front of me. Could have been a coincidence, but it spooked me enough to run home...er, I mean, here." Rue caught herself. After all, this was Mr. Fennec's home, not hers.

"Where's the hot chocolate?" Darwin asked.

"What? I threw it away. Why does that matter?"

"Because we could have analyzed it for traces of poison. You didn't drink any of it, did you?"

"Not after what I saw."

"Where was the truck? I'll see if Monte has time to go down there undercover and find out what happened."

He picked up his phone to make the call while Rue removed her gloves, stuffing them into the pockets of her coat before hanging the coat on a clothing hook by the door. She wrapped her scarf around it and sat her knit hat on top. Rue rubbed her hands together, still feeling the chill from being outside, and eventually sat down at her desk and powered up her computer.

"What are you doing?" Darwin asked after hanging up the phone with Monte.

"Did you ever think," Rue created a new account in her logs, "that instead of following Spencer's idiotic attempts at finding the person or people responsible for stealing his intellectual property..." She turned to Darwin. "Kinda funny, when you think about it."

"What is?" Darwin was confused at her pleasantry, particularly given how angry she had been at him not three hours earlier.

"The irony of it all. He's worried about intellectual property when it's become largely apparent that the doofus gave it away himself when he hooked up with Gretchen Ellis and Clarissa Sauer." She turned and continued typing. Darwin waited for her to continue. "Well, instead of researching him, or finding out the chain of women Astor Ellis has bedded recently, which," she glanced up at Darwin's perplexed face before turning back to the keyboard, "from the looks of Portia LaMonte's tight leash and prenup agreement, hasn't been anyone since Clarissa."

"Prenup?" Darwin was suspicious.

"Yeah, that day Monte snagged Astor's login credentials, we logged in remotely and found an electronic version of a rock-solid prenuptial agreement. They get divorced and she's taking him to the cleaners."

"And where are you going with all of this, exactly?" Darwin crossed his arms, scowling like a disapproving parent.

"That we should be trying to figure out who actually murdered Clarissa and Ursula ourselves, since I seem to be oddly mixed up in it without knowing why. Therefore, Mr. Fennec, I'd like to retain your services."

"I'm sorry, what?" Darwin folded his arms. He was sure he misheard her.

"You pay me well enough, or should I say, Spencer pays me well enough that I've got money in reserve to cover my rent for a couple of months. I'd like to return a portion of that back to you in exchange for your help investigating murder suspects, provided you keep paying me, of course. I think it's only fair Spencer foots the bill since there's probably a connection between B. A. Ellis Industries and SpencerTech behind all this. We just can't see it yet."

"I'm not sure I follow your logic," Darwin admitted. "And I doubt that Detective Ortega would appreciate us meddling in his case." Darwin peered over her shoulder. "Jaks Liebling," he read the bio. A photo of a younger Jaks with a full beard and mustache flashed on the screen. "The instructor who was there the day Ursula was murdered?" He put his hand on the back of her chair. Rue could feel the warmth of his stomach near her back, even though he kept a proper distance from her. She was unsettled by the fact that his presence was both comforting and distracting, at the same time. She tried to focus.

"Yeah," she finally answered. "He was at the park today with Midge."

"What was Midge doing there? Did you call her?"

"I did. But I didn't expect her to show up with *him*," she shuddered at the thought. "Apparently, they met on her last casino run. But something about it is fishy."

The wheels in Darwin's head were turning, but he was having trouble getting all the gears in sync. "Tell you what," Darwin offered, "you start pulling together final reports that we can present to Gretchen Ellis and your boy—," Darwin stopped himself, "and Spencer Hargrove, and I'll see what I can dig up on this Jaks Liebling. It might also be worth my trying to reach out to Ortega one more time. I still think we can help one another out."

"Okay," Rue agreed. She stretched her fingers over the keyboard. They were finally starting to warm up after having been outside in the cold.

Darwin retreated to his own desk computer and started pulling the public records for Jaks Liebling. With Ashley on maternity leave, he would have to rely on his limited hacking skills and Monte's. Monte was decidedly better at ethical info-gathering than he was.

As if on cue, one of Darwin's burner phones rang. It was Monte.

"Whatcha got?" Darwin asked.

"False alarm," Monte answered. "Seems the guy legit had a heart attack. No foul play suspected, but..." he continued.

"But what?"

"But I gathered up a bit of the snow where he spilled his beverage in a container so we can have it analyzed, just to be sure."

"Good thinking," Darwin praised. "I've got another assignment for you if you're up for it."

"You know I am. Lingerie isn't cheap and you're helping keep this gal living in the style to which she would like to become accustomed." It sounded strange when Monte wasn't exactly Monte nor Monique, like now, when he was speaking as Monte with words that Monique would use. Darwin wasn't sure whether he just forgot to add the inflection, or it was his way of messing with people.

"Excellent." Darwin decided to ignore it. "I'll send you an encrypted email with more details." He hung up the phone. "Good news," Darwin told Rue who was now pulling together their reports to begin compiling final evidence packets for their clients. It was a tedious process, but she found it helped turn the focus away from herself, her anger, and her fear.

"Looks like the man at the food truck was most likely unrelated, but we should have confirmation soon."

Rue nodded while she kept typing feverishly on the computer. Darwin noticed that, unlike when she first started, she had already doubled her typing speed. He'd also noticed how quickly she became skilled at navigating the client portals, catching and correcting security breaches, and doing boots-on-the-ground detective work. In fact, she was turning into quite the generalist. He'd have to figure out a way to keep her on after Spencer was no longer a client. Darwin turned back to his computer.

"Hey, Darwin?" Rue finally spoke.

"Yes?"

"I'm still mad as hell at you. But if it's all the same to you, I'll stay here tonight for safety reasons. But to be clear, I think it might be best if you didn't speak to me for a while, unless it's about a case. Understood?"

Darwin would take what he could get as long as Rue remained safe. "Understood," he answered quietly.

After Rue left the room, he picked up the phone. He got Detective Ortega's answering machine where he began to leave a detailed message. Halfway through explaining how Tommy Marcuzzo was a scapegoat, someone abruptly lifted the receiver.

"Just what kind of game are you playing, Darwin Fennec?" a very tired Detective Ortega spit into the phone.

"Just thought you should know, Marcuzzo wasn't the murderer. And given that you're in the office late makes me suspect that you know it, too."

"Offshore accounts," Ortega said simply.

"Exactly," Darwin answered.

"Don't suppose you happen to know who the real killer is, do you, Mr. Fennec?"

"No," Darwin admitted. "But despite your protests, I think it's high time that you and I had a talk."

CHAPTER 31
Darwin and Ortega

Tuesday Morning at Darwin's Condo

~

"I must confess..." Darwin told Ortega. Ortega's eyebrows shot up, curiously. "Not *that* kind of confession," Darwin clarified. Detective Ortega's shoulders slumped, just slightly, disappointed but not surprised. "I didn't expect you to agree to meet with me regarding Clarissa Sauer's and Ursula Gorky's deaths."

Detective Ortega eyed Darwin's condo with interest. He had intended on meeting Darwin in his office in Battery Park until he'd learned about the unanticipated publicity surrounding the case, not to mention the vandalism. The fall-out had died down for a short time, only to be reignited by Ursula's murder.

The police precinct, Ortega decided, would be too intimidating and might put Darwin ill at ease, as if he were being accused of the crimes. Not to mention the conflict of interest their meeting might cause. And finally, Ortega no longer trusted their ability to meet at a local coffee house or some public outdoor location without security concerns. Since cybersecurity was Darwin's forte, he assumed that meeting at his home would be the safest bet.

"Coffee?" Darwin offered. Ortega shook his head, unwrapping the long scarf he'd had around his neck. The weather that day was bone-chilling with wind tunnels between the buildings making it feel a good ten degrees colder than it would normally.

"Nah, I'm good," Ortega answered, hanging his scarf on the back of a chair. He turned toward Darwin, rubbing his hands together, trying to warm them.

Darwin poured himself a cup of coffee and joined Ortega in the living room. "Please, have a seat," he motioned toward his office chair. Somehow the living room couch seemed a little too informal, though he didn't think much of it every time Rue decided to sit there when she was reviewing paper files.

"Nah, I'll stand if you don't mind," Ortega stood akimbo, looking around the place. "Nice setup," he complimented.

"Thanks," Darwin answered, opting to lean on the back edge of the couch as if half standing and half sitting. "But I'm pretty sure you didn't come here to compliment my taste in furniture or my office design."

"You are correct, Mr. Fennec." Ortega paused to brush at his itchy chin. For the third day in a row, he'd forgotten to shave, and the stubble was starting to irritate him. "It's highly uncustomary for a police detective to meet with a person of interest. Truth be told," Ortega continued, "it can be the end of my career if anyone finds out, so if you're recording this, I will politely ask now that you stop."

"I will if you will," Darwin smiled, pausing first to remove the small wire he had attached to his arm before walking over to the footrest set in front of the couch and lifting the top open to reveal the recorder. He switched it off. "Oh, and—" he made his way over to his desk, where Ortega was now standing, "let's not forget this one, too." He pulled the small 'termite' Ortega had just planted there.

"Busted," Ortega laughed. "Anything else I should be worried about?"

"That's it," Darwin answered. "I may be many things, but a liar isn't one of them. Gentleman's agreement that whatever we discuss today stays between us?"

"Agreed," Ortega answered roughly. "It just so happens that I was about to phone you and take you up on your offer to exchange information when your call fortuitously came in. Would you like to start, or shall I?"

"You go ahead, Detective," Darwin encouraged. "Since these are your cases."

Ortega let out a long sigh before continuing. "There are just too many gaps between them, and I hate to admit it, but I'm stumped. When Clarissa was murdered, my first thought was that either you or Ms. Brennan was the killer, and you were covering up for one-another. You were one another's alibi, of sorts." He paused to gauge Darwin's reaction, but his face was neutral. "Then I thought Ms. Brennan might actually be setting you up," Ortega paused again as Darwin's left brow lifted in surprise, just a little. "Given the shoes and the knife angle."

"What shoes? And, what about the knife angle?" This was news to Darwin.

"I'll get to that in a minute, Mr. Fennec. What I'm trying to determine is what Ms. Brennan would have had to gain from killing Clarissa Sauer. And then when Ursula Gorky was murdered, the only person in that entire theater to claim to have seen Ms. Brennan push Clarissa Sauer over the ledge—"

"Allegedly," Darwin corrected.

"Allegedly," Ortega agreed. "Well, since the one person to witness the event, Ursula Gorky, ended up dead, too, and Ms. Brennan was among the last person to see both women alive, stands to reason—"

"What does?" Darwin played ignorant.

"That Rue Brennan might be a murderer and you're covering up for her."

"I thought this was an exchange of information, Detective Ortega," Darwin challenged, turning a little red in the face. "This feels a little more like an inquiry."

Ortega paused to choose his next words very carefully. "I'm sorry, Mr. Fennec. But please listen to what I'm about to say, very carefully." He leaned in as if there were other people in on the conversation. "Based on the evidence at the scene, the shoes the murderer wore were at least two sizes too big for them and they likely stood on a chair to commit the crime. It's looking more and more that your lady friend Ms. Brennan might have murdered Clarissa Sauer and was trying to set you up. You could be protecting someone who has it in for you."

"Well, that's just not possible, Detective Ortega," Darwin answered simply.

"Why's that?"

"Well, for one thing, when I returned from the men's room, Rue...er, Ms. Brennan, was trying to prevent Clarissa Sauer from falling off the balcony. How the hell would she have had time to stab Ms. Sauer, and then get changed back into an evening dress in time to 'push' her over the ledge?"

"I'm aware of the logistics," Ortega agreed, then crinkled his forehead. "Though you neglected to mention that you were returning from the bathroom in your original statement." He waited for Darwin to explain, but he remained silent.

"Never mind," Ortega continued. "Originally, I thought you did the stabbing, but I'm still convinced someone was trying to make it look as if it were you. Maybe Ms. Brennan didn't know the perpetrator and was just trying to make the most of a situation that presented itself. Or maybe they were in it together. I don't know." Darwin's expression appeared to Ortega as a tortured man caught up in his own thoughts. He eyed Darwin from head to toe as if sizing him up. "What else aren't you telling me?"

Darwin thought long and hard before answering, a lump gathering in his throat. "From what I could see, it appeared as if when Ms. Brennan tried to assist Ms. Sauer, she reached out to grab the woman, but only succeeded in grabbing the knife."

"Did you witness Clarissa Sauer getting stabbed?" Ortega asked candidly.

"No," Darwin answered, "I did not."

"See anyone leaving Box 11?"

"No."

"And how is it that the knife was free of fingerprints, Mr. Fennec?"

"Gentleman's agreement?" Darwin reminded him.

"Gentleman's agreement."

"I wiped them off to protect Ms. Brennan because I knew how it would look."

"And Ursula Gorky's statement?" Ortega seemed unaffected by the confession.

"She was correct that Rue Brennan was, technically, the only one in the booth when Clarissa Sauer fell over the balcony, except that I arrived just at that moment. It makes sense that I wouldn't have been visible to her in Ms. Sauer's last moments. She would have been distracted by her friend's death and wouldn't have seen me."

"Let's overlook the fact that you tampered with evidence for the moment, Mr. Fennec. What makes you so certain that Rue Brennan is not a murderer?"

"What could she possibly have to gain from killing two women who she didn't know personally?"

"As you said, because her boyfriend got Clarissa pregnant. Thanks for the tip, by the way. We confronted him and he confessed that he was the father. Surprised he didn't mention it to either of you."

"Must have slipped his mind," Darwin answered, considerably irritated. "But Rue wasn't aware of this. I'm certain of it. And Ursula?"

"Well," Ortega scratched his head. "Other than being a friend of Clarissa's, the only motive that makes sense is that your lady friend didn't like having her as an eyewitness to the crime."

"Or," Darwin couched his words carefully, after all, Gretchen Ellis was a client, "perhaps someone in the Ellis family wanted Clarissa and Ursula out of the way since we know Astor had a wandering eye. Ursula was Clarissa's best friend and knew too much."

"As did Spencer—the wandering eye bit," Ortega added. "Two peas in a pod. No wonder they used to be best friends before the tech feud. And which family member might this be?"

Darwin was silent. "I really shouldn't—"

"Gretchen Ellis?" Ortega guessed.

"But I suppose if you figured it out on your own. Well, that would be all right then." Darwin confessed, rolling his eyes.

"Paying for the women's silence would make more sense than murder, don't you think? Affairs in that family aren't exactly uncommon," Ortega reasoned.

"Unless there was more that we've yet to discover," Darwin added.

"Well, there's more to the crime scene, that's for sure," Ortega added.

"More?"

"Yeah. It seems Penelope, er, Dr. Washburn, my forensic scientist, confirmed that the same shoe prints were found at the scene of the second murder at the art school, along with dirt and ash presumably tracked in from outside. And I'm sure you already know about the manchineel poisoning?"

"From leaks to the papers, yes," Darwin confirmed.

"So, there were the same footprints at each location, but in the first murder, it was as if the killer were trying not to cause fatal harm Clarissa or her baby; but in the second location, they were dead set on offing Ursula."

"Interesting choice of words," Darwin commented. "But first things first. You would think that if jealousy were a motive, it would also be less pre-meditated and more spur-of-the-moment. And, as you said, it was as if the killer really wasn't trying to kill Clarissa...perhaps just threaten her? But I agree that Rue seems to be the lynch pin here. How do we know she wasn't the target all along, and maybe the killer messed up...twice?"

"Why? Because I happen to know that Ursula Gorky wasn't supposed to be modeling that day. A lady named Emma Post was. Pretty sure Ursula was the target though, and not Emma."

"Emma Post?" Darwin was surprised.

"You know the name?" Ortega questioned.

"Yes, supposedly she sent a letter to Gretchen Ellis claiming to be pregnant with Astor's baby."

"Another one?" Ortega scratched his head.

"But one of my colleagues traced the email as having come from the local library. But Gretchen also had a blackmail letter that was handwritten, allegedly from Clarissa."

"Think Emma was trying to piggy-back off of Clarissa's blackmail attempt?" Ortega asked.

"No, because she told Rue point blank that she wasn't pregnant."

"She said as much when we interviewed her," Ortega confirmed. "So, who sent the email? And furthermore, who sent the other handwritten note to Clarissa and the letter to Gretchen and why? Because I'll be willing to bet, they weren't the names signed on those letters. In fact, I suspect they were written by the same person. But who?"

"No idea."

"Can I get a copy of that email, along with a copy of the hand-written letter?"

"Certainly." Darwin set his coffee cup on his desk.

"Speaking of which," Ortega continued, "I was hoping you had a sample of Rue's writing, perhaps? Since you work together. Just to rule her out if she is, as you believe, innocent."

Darwin thought a moment. He reached into Rue's desk, pulling out one of her notepads. He settled on a page that had nothing more than her grocery list on it. He then retrieved a flip phone from his desk, snapped what appeared to be a photo of it, and emailed it to himself.

"What did you just do there?" Detective Ortega was surprised. "Is that a camera or a phone? Did you just take a photo on that little thing?"

"It's a prototype of both," Darwin explained. "Not on the market yet, but it's a flip phone that takes photos that people can text to one another."

"Text?" Ortega may have been upper in years, but he liked to pride himself on remaining current on technology trends.

"Uh, yeah," Darwin explained. "A message that you type, or take a photo of, and send without needing to hand-write a physical note or take a picture of it with a professional camera and have it printed at a studio. It's all digital."

"Fascinating," Ortega admitted. "How can I get one? It would help a lot with my investigations."

"As I said, it's not on the market yet." Darwin saw Ortega's face looking somewhat crestfallen. "But perhaps I can see about getting you one in advance of public release after this case is over."

"I'd appreciate that, Mr. Fennec."

Darwin already had copies of Emma's email and Clarissa's note photographed and uploaded to his server. Now, it was just a matter of printing the samples up.

He walked over to his computer and waited as the energy-savor mode switched off and the computer whirred back to life. He dialed into his email account and the two listened to the annoying whir of the server connecting. Moments later, he retrieved the email with the photo of Rue's writing and clicked for it to send the image to a printer located on

Darwin's desk. He then clicked to print the other samples he had already uploaded.

Ortega was impressed. "My computer at the precinct takes three times as long to log in."

"DSL line," Darwin explained. This meant nothing to Ortega.

Instead, Ortega smiled. "If it turned out that Ms. Brennan is innocent...well, that would make you very happy, wouldn't it Mr. Fennec?"

"Well, of course, it would, Detective Ortega. She's my assistant and—"

"Nah, that ain't it," Ortega's grin grew wider. "I'm not the most observant of fellows where emotions are concerned. And yet, I can see that your face lights up every time I mention her name. Just how is it that she came to work for you, Mr. Fennec?"

"Her former boyfriend, Spencer Hargrove, recommended her to me."

"Really? Does she have cybersecurity and investigative skills?" Ortega was interested.

"She's learning," Darwin answered.

Ortega paused, staring out the window at the city below. Darwin recognized that deep state of inner brainstorming as one tried to connect the dots and politely remained silent for an unbearably long time. Eventually, Detective Ortega spoke, "I never did find out how you came to be at the theater with Ms. Brennan that night. Frankly, you seem to be too upstanding a guy to take another man's woman out, particularly one who works for you."

Darwin cleared his throat. "Actually, I was asked on a date by one of Ms. Brennan's friends."

"Really?" Ortega's eyes shot up. "And why is this the first time I'm hearing of this?"

"Because I didn't think it was relevant."

Ortega's face turned beet red. "Not really your place to decide what is or is not relevant to my investigation now, is it?"

"Please, Detective. This was before I had gotten to know you. But now that you bring it up, there is something odd about the whole thing."

"Tell me," Ortega ordered.

"Midge Pasternak, Ms. Brennan's friend, cancelled on me at the last minute and sent Ms. Brennan in her place. I think it was an innocent game of matchmaker."

"But Rue Brennan already had a...match."

"Maybe Ms. Pasternak didn't know that. Or maybe she didn't care," Darwin reasoned. "The odd thing is, Ms. Pasternak appears to now be dating Jaks Liebling."

"The instructor at the Artist Atelier who was there when Ursula was murdered," Detective Ortega confirmed.

"The same. I don't know that it's a coincidence. Perhaps it's worth questioning Mr. Liebling again and doing a bit more digging?"

"Indeed," Ortega nodded his head in agreement before looking down at his watch. "I'll tell you what, Mr. Fennec. I need to get back to the precinct before it seems odd that I'm not there. I'm going to overlook the fact that you lied to me and tampered with evidence. I'm further going to overlook the fact that you had within your possession potential evidence that you kept from the police. Only because I need your help and I believe you and Ms. Brennan may be innocent after all. But you need to be straight with me from now on, or I can't help you. Understand?"

"Perfectly," Darwin acknowledged.

"I know you sent Ms. Brennan and another guy to sneak into Astor Ellis's office. I'm going to pretend I don't know that, provided you keep me posted about what you find."

Darwin began to protest.

"I know, I know!" Ortega answered. "Client confidentiality and all, but we're talking about the murder of two women. I will do my best not to soil your precious reputation. But in the future, you should choose your clients more carefully, Mr. Fennec."

"What do you mean, Detective Ortega?"

"Since you've been so helpful today, I'm going to offer you a little tip."

"Yes?" Darwin leaned in, eagerly.

"I advise you to spend some time looking up the names listed on SpencerTech's patents and copyrights. Or should I say, one name in particular?"

"What name?"

Ortega lifted his scarf from the back of the office chair before leaving. "You just do your homework, is all I'm saying." Ortega touched his two fingers to his forehead as if to tip an invisible hat. With that, he made his way down the hall. He opted for the staircase instead of the elevator, since

Nancy had been complaining that he'd put on a couple of pounds and needed to exercise more. He reasoned that going down seven flights would at least be easier than walking up them.

Once out in the street, Ortega pulled out a tiny tape recorder, no larger than a slim TV remote and clicked play. The micro cassette inside whirred and the conversation with he and Darwin could be heard. He smiled to himself. He may not have Darwin Fennec's fancy phone-camera combo or a DSL line (whatever the hell that was), but he made do with what he had available to him. He tucked the recorder back in his pocket and headed back toward the precinct.

"I THINK it's safe to come out now," Darwin called into the bedroom where Rue had been holed up during Ortega's visit.

She opened the door. Behind her, he could spot the recorder and headphones Rue had set up on the end table next to his bed. She stared at him, momentarily.

"What?" he asked.

"Rue Brennan," she repeated her own name.

"What are you doing?"

"Just trying to see if your eyes really light up every time you hear my name," she teased.

"Well, now you're just being mean," Darwin complained, turning his back on her. "Did you get all that?"

"I did," she answered. "Are you sure it was wise to confess to wiping off the knife though?"

"I had to confess something big or else he wouldn't have trusted me," Darwin reasoned.

"Well, let's just hope all of this doesn't come back to bite us in the ass." Rue sat at her computer. "Alright, I need some help getting the audio from your meeting uploaded to Ortega's file. Give me a hand?"

"Sure," Darwin answered. "You drive." He went into the bedroom to grab the recorder, before pulling up a chair next to her and placing the recorder on the table. Rue logged into the new file they created for Detective Ortega, linking relevant information to the Ellis and Hargrove files. "And for the record," Darwin paused, "they do."

"Do what?" Rue was busy typing. "What are you talking about?"

"My eyes light up every time you enter a room and every time someone mentions your name. You just never notice."

Rue felt her face get flushed, her fingers held over the keyboard, trembling slightly. "Well, Mr. Fennec." She hit the wrong keys, cursed under her breath, hit delete, and tried again. "It's a shame because I don't like stalkers and hate men who lie to me."

"Hate?" Darwin was surprised. Rue's eyes remained glued to the computer screen. He smiled and put one hand on his hips. "Dislike, to intense dislike, to hate? Frankly, when you say you hate me, I can't help but think that maybe you really like me an awful lot."

"That's cuz you're delusional." Rue finished typing. "There, it's set up. How do I get the audio from this," she pointed to the cassette tape, "to here?" She pointed to the online file.

"Might be easier if I demonstrate." He took a moment to hook up a cable to the side of the recorder and then to the back of the computer tower. "This is not publicly used technology yet...eat your heart out, Spencer Hargrove."

Rue found this interesting. In all the time that Spencer bragged about his tech savvy, he never actually expounded on any of it—never bothered to teach her anything.

"May I drive?" Darwin asked.

Rue backed up while he took the mouse and dragged and dropped a file that had miraculously shown up on the desktop like a ghost. She saw a twirly image, as if the computer was thinking about it. "Wanna try for yourself? We can delete the duplicate later."

"Sure," she answered.

Darwin unplugged the cable from the computer and recorder and closed out all files. "Okay, from start to finish. You try."

Rue admitted that she had to fiddle a bit to find the right input on the side of the computer, along with the one to the recorder. "What happens if I accidentally choose the wrong port?"

"You'll blow up the entire computer?"

"Really?" Rue was horrified.

"No," he laughed. "But you might bust the cable connector or damage the port. So, let's try not to do that."

Rue went through the motions and within minutes, she had successfully transferred the audio files and managed to encrypt them to prevent a security breach.

"Thank you, Mr. Fennec." She smiled proudly. "I still hate you, but I'm grateful for the training.

"Hmmm," Darwin stood, making his way to the kitchen to grab a salad for lunch. He rifled through the refrigerator, calling into the living room. "Frankly, if you ever claim to detest me, then I'll start to suspect that you're actually falling in love with me."

"Not gonna happen, Mr. Fennec," Rue protested, putting her computer in sleep mode. "I stand by my sentiment."

CHAPTER 32
Jaks Liebling

Thursday Morning at Jaks Liebling's House

~

When Jaks Liebling failed to show up at the precinct after Detective Ortega's polite request for a follow-up interview, he and Officer Ernest decided to make a special trip to Liebling's house in Newark to pay him a visit.

They sat in the cul-de-sac of his New Jersey neighborhood for a good fifteen minutes before a black-striped, red Dodge Viper drove slowly down the street, pulling into Jaks' place of residence. They watched as his garage door opened and he parked his car inside. It was only when they had confirmed he was there, that they drove their police vehicle into the drive, blocking the garage.

They made their way up a paved path to the front door and rang the bell.

Moments later, Jaks threw the door open vigorously and gushed, "Did you miss me already?" His smile quickly dropped, however, when he saw Ortega and Officer Ernest standing there.

"Golly, we sure did, Mr. Liebling," Detective Ortega mocked in a childlike voice. "Especially since you neglected to show up for questioning yesterday, despite our request."

"Did I?" Jaks feigned ignorance. "I'm sorry, I didn't receive any such message. Please, come in," he stepped aside, allowing them to enter.

Once inside, he shut the door and escorted them to his living room. It was clear from his decor that Jaks Liebling thought very highly of his own work. The sofa, chairs, console table with built-in wine rack, and even the carpet were a stark white. By contrast, every painting on the wall was black and red, or bright orange. The one exception was a rather large self-portrait which seemed to capture his macabre smile. In short, all of the paintings were ones of his creation.

"Please, have a seat," he offered. Officer Ernest removed his hat and sat on the plush couch.

"I prefer to stand," Ortega answered, eyeing Ernest, who immediately popped back up.

Jaks positioned himself in front of a long white window seat, shielding his face from the sun as he peered outside.

"You were hoping for someone else?" Ortega asked.

"Well," he turned and smiled. "If you must know, I just dropped my girlfriend off at the train station. Hence, why I must have missed your call."

"Midge Pasternak?" Ortega confirmed.

"How did you—" Jaks began, while frowning, before catching himself. "Yes, that's right."

"I see," Officer Ernest chimed in. "You were entertaining."

"Yes," Jaks' eyes widened mischievously. "You could say that."

"If you dropped her off, then who are you expecting to show up here?"

Jaks let out a sigh. "She's a feisty one, that girl," he confessed, "I half-expected Midge to catch a cab near the station and turn right back around and come back to me."

"Why not just call you and ask you to pick her up?" Officer Ernest was confused.

Jaks let out a sigh. "Not well-versed in the art of romantic gestures, are you, son?"

Ortega cleared his throat. "We have a few questions for you, if you don't mind, about Ursula Gorky's murder."

"Certainly, detective," Jaks answered. "Whatever you need."

"Did you know Ursula Gorky or Emma Post?"

"I know they were models at the school. I've worked with them both on many occasions, if that's what you mean."

"And yet you seem oddly unaffected by Ursula's death."

"That doesn't make me a murderer, detective, if that's what you're implying." Jaks sat in a lounge chair by the window, trying not to make it obvious that he was still keeping watch, obsessively sneaking a glance out the window every few moments. "Besides, I read in the papers that they caught the killer. So, why are you here?"

"Not implying anything, Mr. Liebling," Ortega answered. "Just trying to tie up loose ends. Can't just assume the guy we've got in jail was working alone. Not even sure how he slipped onto campus unnoticed. Officer Ernie, if you would be so kind—"

"Of course," Ernest stood, pulling out his notepad and pen. "According to statements, at least three students noted that the lighting on the model stand was off, and they were surprised you didn't adjust it. We're curious as to what they might be talking about?"

Jaks burst out laughing. "Seriously? That's your evidence? The lighting? Was anyone ever killed by *bad* lighting?"

"Someone would have been more likely to notice a poisoned woman on the stand a bit sooner had the light been on her face, don't you think?" Ernest was somber.

Jaks stopped laughing. "I see. Forgive my impertinence, officer. The truth is, I was hoping one of the students would point that out before we began the session."

"So, it was a test, of sorts?" Ortega confirmed.

"Exactly," Jaks nodded. "A test. But since no one did, I thought it might be a fun experiment to see what the students would do with the existing setup." After a long pause, Jaks asked, "Is there anything else?"

"Actually, yes, just a couple more questions." Ernest referred to his notes. "Were you aware of the victim having any particular habits?"

"Habits, officer? You mean like, addictions?"

"Exactly," Officer Ernest nodded. "Like drinking or smoking."

"Can't say that I was. I didn't know any of those girls outside of class. To me, they were just subjects."

"So, you don't know why there would have been a half-empty bottle of wine or cigarette ash in her dressing area?" Ortega asked.

"I'm sorry, I do not. A model's changing station is private. No idea what might have been in there."

"It's so interesting to me," Ortega motioned for Officer Ernest to follow him to the front door.

"What is?" Jaks asked as he followed them.

"Well, I'm not known for being particularly..." Ortega struggled to find the right words, shifting his shoulders from side-to-side.

"Compassionate? Empathetic? Emotionally available?" Officer Ernest offered, helpfully.

Ortega pointed toward Ernie. "Exactly, Ernie," he answered. "Emotionally available. But I can't help but notice that you seem awfully hung up on your lady friend returning, but not the slightest concerned over... what did you call them...your subjects?"

"Once again," Jaks ticked his head slightly as if a bug had landed on his nose. "That doesn't make me a killer."

"True," Ernest answered. "But it does kinda make you sound like a jerk."

Ortega fought back a laugh but quickly recovered. "Officer Ernie, your manners."

"Sorry, Detective Ortega," Ernest lowered his eyes.

"Thank you for your time, Mr. Liebling," Ortega said.

Officer Ernest and Detective Ortega were outside when Jaks went to shut the door behind them. Ortega caught the door mid-swing. Jaks looked up, surprised. "Just one more thing, Mr. Liebling."

"What is it?" Jaks tried in vain to cover up his annoyance, his calm exterior now being replaced with some other emotion bubbling under the surface.

"What size shoes do you wear?"

CHAPTER 33
Golf Game

Friday Afternoon in Florida

"What's the temperature in New York?" Byron asked as he set up his golf ball on the tee and took a few practice swings.

"Last I checked, it was 38 degrees and cloudy," Gretchen answered, climbing out of the golf cart. This time, she actually wore something other than beige. Today, she was sporting a pleated white golf skirt and matching polo top. On her head was a bleached white visor to protect her face from the sun.

"Maybe we should consider staying in Florida for a few more days?" Astor suggested, taking a swig of water from a bottle he pulled from a cooler attached to the back of the cart. He pinched his thumb and forefinger to his chest, tugging his golf shirt back and forth as if trying to air it out. He was sweating more than the Florida heat warranted that day.

"Not possible, I'm afraid," Portia chimed in as she selected her club for the next shot.

Everyone fell silent as Byron swung. After the ball went sailing, they continued the conversation.

"You were saying, my darling?" Astor's syrupy voice dripped.

Portia hid her distaste. He was a fine enough catch to marry, but his romantic overtures, she thought, were irritating. Perhaps, over time, she could teach him how to sound more genuine, at least when dealing with the public.

"Apparently," Portia continued. "We have a meeting with Darwin Fennec on Sunday."

"You mean that flat foot that has been poking his nose around B. A. Ellis industries?" Byron asked.

"The same," Gretchen finished, stepping in front of Portia in a way that suggested that she'd just been upstaged. Portia retreated, opting instead to reach into the cooler and pull out a single-serve chardonnay bottle and a plastic stemmed wine glass. She poured herself a drink while Gretchen explained.

"And he's not a flat foot. He's a cyber something-or-other investigator. Seems he's asked us if we'd be willing to meet along with Spencer Hargrove for a discussion."

"Discussion?" Astor was aghast. "Why would we want to meet with that traitor?"

Gretchen held up her hands. "Don't ask me, but I think we should take the meeting." She winked at her husband Byron, who winked back before giving room for Portia to take her turn.

They waited as she placed her wine glass on the roof of the golf cart and then moved to set up her shot, club in hand. Portia drew her arms back and rotated her torso as she took her swing.

"Maybe he wants to negotiate a settlement," Astor blurted out as Portia dug her iron into the grass, pulling up bits of soil with it.

"Mulligan!" she yelled, glaring at Astor. He looked back at her, baffled by her reaction. She quickly softened her face and added sweetly, "Astor, honey, you know I love you. But please shut up while I retake my shot."

Astor played along, putting his thumb and finger to the side of his lips and sliding to the right as if to zip them up.

Everyone was silent as she took her do-over shot. They proceeded to the next hole.

"Did they ever find out what happened to that theater gal and the model they questioned us about?" Byron asked.

"Did you not hear?" Astor was surprised. "Tommy Marcuzzo confessed to both."

"Little Tommy," Byron furrowed his brow. "Well, that can't be. He was always such a nice kid." This seemed to bother Byron so much so, that his reaction annoyed his son.

"Either way, it gets the detective and those reporters out of our hair," Astor said.

"Agreed," Byron nodded. "Still seems out of character for Tommy." He shook his head, muttering for the second time, "Such a nice boy..."

CHAPTER 34
Infidelity

Sunday Morning at the Ellis Estate

~

"Sure you're ready for this?" Darwin asked as he escorted Rue to the front door of a rather large mansion.

"Yes," Rue smiled, appreciatively. "Thank you for this," she whispered, leaning in, "but I still hate you."

"Noted," Darwin answered, ringing the bell.

Everyone arrived at the Ellis estate almost on schedule, like something from a Whodunit Thin Man or Hercule Poirot Mystery. Rue always thought of those movies as silly and unrealistic. *I mean, really,* she thought. *In what world would a bunch of suspects actually sit around a table just waiting to be accused?*

And yet, here they were.

When Rue and Darwin were ushered into the main library, Gretchen, Byron and Astor Ellis were already seated on a large red, wrap-around couch surrounding a low-lying table with nothing on it, but an oversized vase filled with fake gardenias. Portia LaMonte was also present, sitting at the edge of a large, dijon-colored high-backed chair next to the couch. Her legs were crossed at the ankles and while Astor leaned his body towards her from his end of the couch, she was purposefully positioned so that she threw a cold shoulder in his direction. It was obvious that she had no intention of giving him the attention he wanted.

Darwin and Rue were offered chairs across from the table, two leather-backed ones that were surprisingly stiff and uncomfortable. Perhaps Gretchen had planned it that way.

The one person still missing? Spencer Hargrove.

When he finally arrived, he looked both perplexed and nervous as his eyes darted around the room between Gretchen, Rue, and then everyone else. "May I ask what this is about?" Spencer furrowed his brow, instinctively leaning over to give Rue a kiss on the cheek before she recoiled, instead directing him to the couch, where Astor reluctantly moved away from his position closest to his fiancé in order for Spencer to have a seat. It was that or have Spencer sit next to his father, Byron Ellis, and he feared that might lead to fisticuffs. Spencer sat on the edge of the couch, resting his hands on his knees, leaning forward awkwardly, making the couch appear about two sizes too small for his tall frame.

Finally, Gretchen nodded to Darwin who stood uncomfortably and cleared his throat. Despite everything, Rue felt sorry for Darwin. He may have been dishonest with her, she reasoned, but as far as deceitfulness went, he was the least deceptive of the bunch. It's sad that in her mind, this was a high compliment.

"I suppose you're all wondering why I've asked you here today," Darwin began (straight out of a whodunit).

"You think?" Spencer held his body tight as if trying not to make any physical contact with the Ellises to the right and left of him as if whatever they had was contagious. Spencer eyed Rue, questioningly. She offered him the briefest of smirks that let him know, in no uncertain terms that one, they were over, and two, this was payback...sort of.

"Spencer," Darwin addressed Rue's now ex-boyfriend. "You hired me because you believed the Ellis family was stealing secrets from you and planning to pass off SpencerTech inventions as their own before yours had a chance to make it to market."

"What's this about?" Spencer stood, angrily. "That was confidential. What kind of an investigator are you, anyway?"

"A tired one," Darwin replied calmly.

"Sit down, Mr. Hargrove," Gretchen ordered.

Spencer sat.

"But you were wrong," Darwin acknowledged. "They weren't stealing anything." He eyed Portia LaMonte, who merely shrugged her shoulders. "There was no way that an heiress was going to marry into this family without some guarantees of continued success and influence, so it was she —a devoted patron of the arts—who thought to send Clarissa Sauer to strategically intercept you, Spencer, on one of your nightly coffee trips to the cafe just across the street from your office."

Spencer's eyes lit up in surprise. He turned his gaze to Portia, who merely averted her gaze.

"You see, Spencer," Darwin explained. "They didn't need to steal secrets to take a product to market before you did. You gave it to them."

"See here!" Spencer protested.

"Shut up, Spencer," Gretchen ordered. Spencer fell silent. To Portia, she said, "I underestimated you, Ms. LaMonte." Gretchen eyed her future daughter-in-law approvingly. "It seems you're going to fit in with this family after all."

Portia turned the corner of her mouth up in a slight smile and the two women shared the oddest familial moment that Rue had ever witnessed.

"Ahem," Darwin cleared his throat in order to regain their attention. "It wasn't Astor Ellis who got Clarissa Sauer pregnant," Darwin paused for emphasis, "it was you, Spencer."

Rue bit her lip and fought the quivering feeling in her stomach. Darwin had prepped her for this. She knew what was coming, but it still hurt.

Spencer looked first at Rue, shaking his head, then systematically at everyone around the room. There was no denying it. It was true and with today's modern science, very easy to prove. An autopsy could still match the DNA from Clarissa's unborn baby to him. Refusing a paternity test would only further reinforce his guilt.

"But—" was all he could think to say.

"Save it, Spencer," Rue chastised. "You already confessed as much to the police."

"The police? But how..." he continued, helplessly.

Darwin cleared his throat. "May I continue?" The group gave a mournful nod, wishing the family had stayed in Florida after all. "Clarissa fed all of your ideas, the ones you bragged about all those late nights while Rue was waiting for you, to Astor—who, in turn, shared it with his father."

"I could sue you," was all Spencer had to say. "What happened to client confidentiality?"

"I'll get to that," Darwin brushed him aside. "Let's move on, shall we? But Clarissa was a smart woman. You, a young man with a start-up, didn't have nearly as much money and influence as you pretended to have, so she did what she thought she had to...she went to Gretchen Ellis, demanding money to keep the pregnancy—which she claimed was Astor's fault—a secret. But Gretchen knew that this was impossible, given that Astor is sterile."

"Hey, now!" Astor chimed in, standing. For the briefest of moments, his pants stuck to the couch, and then peeled away as he rose. Sweat began to pour off his brow. Portia looked up, surprised. This was news to her. "It's not true," he protested.

"Yes, it is, and sit down," Gretchen ordered.

"Mr. Fennec," Portia finally interjected. "Is there a reason why you feel the need to drag the Ellis family name through the mud and my name in the process?"

"I'm getting to that, Ms. LaMonte," Darwin answered. He paused to take a deep breath, resting a hand on the back of Rue's chair. Without thinking, she touched it, looking up at him supportively—a look that did not go unnoticed by Spencer.

"Clarissa Sauer was murdered before she could collect on her bet, but not before she told her plan to her best friend, Ursula Gorky, who in turn mentioned it to another art model, Emma Post. Several weeks ago, I would have hypothesized that Emma worked independently, trying to ride Clarissa's coattails to success by sending an extortion letter to Mrs. Ellis."

"Vermin," was all Gretchen had to say.

"Financial desperation does funny things to a person," Darwin offered.

Gretchen was offended. "What? Am I supposed to feel sorry for someone because they had the misfortune of being born poor? Or that they didn't have the where-with-all to drag themselves out of squalor as some of us have?" Everyone turned to look at Gretchen, who suddenly felt very conspicuous. She pulled the edges of her cardigan sweater together as if trying to hide behind it.

"The point is," Darwin continued, "Emma Post was not pregnant and most likely did not send the email."

"Then who did?" Gretchen asked.

"We still don't know," Darwin answered.

It was only then that they noticed that Spencer had turned an odd shade of pale. His face giving off a sallow, sickly hue. He seemed, for once, almost remorseful. "I heard on the news that Tommy Marcuzzo confessed to Clarissa and Ursula's murders. Is that true?"

"I don't think it is," Darwin answered honestly. "I think Tommy was just a scapegoat for someone else." He glanced around the room.

"Are you implying that it was one of us who killed her?" Byron Ellis asked, taking a sip of Scotch that had just been delivered to him by the housekeeper. Everyone started for a moment, having forgotten that he was actually there.

"I am not," Darwin answered simply. "I'm just filling everyone in on the pieces of the puzzle that I know about."

"Why the sudden unveiling, Mr. Fennec?" Gretchen Ellis asked, amused. "What happened to your code of ethics?"

"More of a 'who'," Darwin glanced at Rue whose cheeks turned a little pink. Spencer eyed Rue and Darwin. It was then that he realized that when he hired Darwin to also keep tabs on his girlfriend, that he might be handing over the heart of the one woman who he could have actually counted on to support him. His heart sank a little at the realization. "And sadly," he continued, "I ceased to be ethical the moment I took on Mr. Hargrove as a client...and you, Mrs. Ellis."

Spencer was surprised. This seemed to be happening a lot lately. "What is he talking about, Gretchen?"

Gretchen? Both Astor and Portia were visibly surprised. *Since when did Spencer Hargrove address their mother and future mother-in-law as... Gretchen?* Somehow, it seemed perfectly acceptable for her, a considerably older women, to refer to Spencer by his first name, but not the other way around.

Suddenly, Byron Ellis began laughing uncontrollably, so much so that a deep, phlegmy cough erupted from his lungs.

"May I ask what you find so amusing?" Spencer demanded.

Gretchen began laughing as well, standing and walking over to her husband, ruffling what was left of his thinning hair and giving him a peck on the side of his temple. She shook her head as she and Byron exchanged knowing glances.

"Spencer, my boy," Byron Ellis choked, "you made stealing your ideas so much easier when you began sleeping with my wife!"

"What?" Astor and Portia sat up. Spencer eyed Gretchen questioningly before remembering Rue and shooting her an apologetic look. She met his gaze with eyes like daggers.

"Oh, don't look so surprised, Spencer," Gretchen chuckled. "You didn't honestly think I was going to leave my husband for you, did you? You certainly are a young and supple thing, but I can assure you that young and hungry men with big dreams are a dime a dozen in this town." Spencer looked hurt. He opened his mouth to speak, but then closed it again.

"Come now, Spencer," Byron Ellis tried to soften the blow. "I know you had no intention of running off with my wife. You were just using her to get intel on me. It was just business. I get that."

"But, I..." Spencer protested, "liked you," he said to Gretchen, a look of betrayal on his face.

"Oh," Gretchen pouted her lips and leaned over to grab Spencer's face in her hands. "I know you did, you sweet boy." She planted a faint kiss on his lips. "I could just eat you up."

Spencer pulled away, looking to Rue as if for support. Rue, who he had cheated on with not one, but two women...that she knew about. He tried to explain. "I never meant to hurt you. In fact, I hired Darwin to protect you from all this."

"Protect me?" Rue was incredulous. "Did you think we'd end up a happy little couple after you'd introduced SpencerTech's new software to the world? We'd ride off into the sunset as the tech world's newest power couple?"

"Well, kinda," he admitted. "After you'd given up modeling and taken on a respectable job—which I lined up for you, thank you very much."

"So Darwin could babysit me!" Rue yelled. Spencer looked at Darwin, betrayed. Rue caught his gaze. "I figured it out for myself," she explained. "When it comes to investigative work and cyber forensics, Mr. Fennec is a very good teacher."

Darwin smiled in spite of the circumstance. From his best recollection, that was the only time Rue had actually something nice to say about him.

"That doesn't change the fact that you failed to keep my business a secret, client privileges and all," Spencer, of all people, spat angrily at Darwin at the betrayal. "I will sue you for damages and make sure you never work in the investigative industry again."

"I'm still working out the bit about you sleeping with my mother!" Astor's face crumpled as if he ate something sour. He sniffed a few times, as if he'd suddenly come down with postnasal drip.

"Not to mention the fact that you and Spencer were both sleeping with Clarissa Sauer," Portia added, helpfully.

"That's not the point," Spencer sulked. "I trusted him!"

Rue sucked in her breath. She knew what was coming.

"That's all right," Darwin answered. "I'll see to it that you and Ms. Ellis are refunded for everything I charged you...to include the money you gave me to keep Rue in my employ." Spencer's mouth dropped. Every time he thought everything he'd done had been exposed, there was one more nail in the proverbial coffin. Darwin put a hand on Rue's shoulder. She merely smiled. Spencer looked back and forth between the two of them.

"Wait a minute," he darted a finger back and forth. "You two aren't..."

"No, Spencer," Rue finished. "We are not sleeping together, nor are we a couple. Believe it or not, some men and women can work together without sex becoming an issue."

Darwin coughed a little and removed his hand from her shoulder. Instead, he began pacing. "As I was saying," he continued, "I'm refunding all of your money. No use making a good income if you can't go to sleep at night with a clear conscience."

"Oh, don't play all victim with me," Spencer's voice dripped venom. He had a lot of indignation for being a chronic philanderer.

"Shut up, Spencer," Gretchen interjected. She said it so often that Rue thought to have it made into a t-shirt. To Darwin, she answered, "You'll do nothing of the kind. Byron and I will pay your fee in full, so will Spencer."

"What fee?" Astor sat up, rubbing his head. He was very confused.

Gretchen and Byron shared a smile. "My crafty wife," Byron beamed, giving a playful pinch on the bottom, "knew you couldn't keep it in your pants, son," he offered, indelicately. Astor shrank into the couch. "She wanted to make sure there were no other lingering skeletons before you and Portia tied the knot. Had to make sure you were B. A. Ellis Industries material."

Astor eyed Portia, pleadingly.

She took his hand, affectionately. "Don't worry, Astor," she reassured. "I don't give a shit what you do on your free time as long as the press doesn't find out about it. Your mother and I had a long talk about it yesterday and worked everything out." She kissed his hand briefly and forced a smile, as if kissing him were the very last thing she wanted to do at that moment.

He smiled back, weakly. "But what does my mother—"

"You did us a huge service, Mr. Fennec," Gretchen praised, interrupting her son.

This time, Darwin was caught off guard. After all, he was ready to return all the money and expenses he incurred over the past few months for their cases, just to walk away with peace of mind. He fully expected to leave the meeting far poorer than going into it.

"How so?" Darwin asked.

"You've made it easier for Spencer and me to talk, businessman to businessman!" Byron stood, answering for his wife. He walked over to Spencer who shrank a little as if expecting an attack. Instead, Byron grabbed him by the back of the shoulders and shook him with pride. "Spencer, quit fighting the inevitable. You've got a great invention there... several, really. Why make me take it back from you when we can work together? Particularly, since I owned it from its inception? On your own, you'll only garner a small percentage of what we can accomplish with my backing. Together," he made a fist, "we can move mountains!"

"Just a moment...how did you own it first, exactly?" Spencer asked, indignantly.

"Spencer, my boy," Byron asked. "Don't be coy. Where did you do your college internship all those years ago?"

Spencer's face turned gray. "Ellis Media Group," he finally answered.

"And what technology clause did you sign in your work agreement?" Spencer shrank into the couch. "I can tell from the look on your face that you remember. Anything you created while working for any of my companies is the intellectual property of B. A. Ellis Industries."

"But these are my ideas," Spencer whined. "I spent endless nights working for minimum wage, developing plans, only for you to sue me for them later. When all you needed to do was offer me proper compensation and credit!"

Byron's face grew sour. Spencer was not nearly as appreciative as he thought he should be, particularly given that he had been sleeping with his wife and all. And he, from his perspective, tried to run off with his intellectual property, too. "I don't think you realize the length of the olive branch I'm offering you, my boy." He gripped Spencer's shoulder tightly in one hand, pinching it like a vice.

Spencer winced. "So, am I to understand that you're offering to back my inventions and share in the profits?"

"Exactly! It'll be under B.A. Ellis Industries, of course, but what does that matter if it makes you one of the wealthiest men in the country?"

"Perhaps Father would consider starting an offshoot 'doing business as' company?" Astor offered. "The headline would read, 'B. A. Ellis Industries Merges with Up-and-Coming SpencerTech for a Revolutionary New Invention.'"

"Ooh," Portia praised, flirtatiously. "I like it, honey."

"Thank you, darling," Astor leaned in and kissed her cheek. Portia didn't praise him often, and so he relished these moments. She didn't even seem to bristle at his lips, or that his breath was hot on the side of her face.

"Take the offer, Spencer," Gretchen advised. "I promise you, it's the best you're going to do in our world."

Spencer mulled on this for a moment. The thought did have merit.

Byron hemmed and hawed for a moment. "You know, perhaps I'd been selfish. Should have acknowledged you more. But let's resolve this silly dispute and find a way to work together!" He held his arm up like Rosie the Riveter in an overly dramatic display.

"Excuse me," Rue interjected. Everyone looked up, surprised. Aside from Spencer and Darwin, everyone else seemed to have forgotten that she was there. "There's just one small matter we still need to resolve."

"And what's that, my dear?" Gretchen pursed her lips, eyeing Rue distastefully.

"The software that you all are talking about is copyrighted under my name." She paused as everyone let that sink in. "And so are all the patented inventions."

Spencer sucked in his breath and rubbed his forehead. Beads of sweat began to form, almost immediately. Without thinking about it, Darwin rested a supportive hand on Rue's shoulder once again as he stood behind her as if he was her personal security guard. To Spencer, she added, "C'mon Spencer. Did you really expect me to believe that you were having Darwin look after me so that we could actually be together when all this was said and done? Don't—" she cautioned as he opened his mouth to protest, "lie to me."

He closed his mouth.

"You wanted to keep an eye on me because I was your workaround," Rue continued. "You knew that Byron would lay claims to your inventions because you thought of everything while still working for Ellis Media Group. Rather than avoid a legal tangle, it was easier to put the copyright and related patents, under my name."

"How did you...but I changed them!" Spencer suddenly protested.

"And how did you do that?" Rue asked quietly.

"Not another word, Spencer!" Gretchen warned. "Not until we speak with our lawyers."

But Spencer was fit to be tied. He stood, pointing an angry finger at Darwin. "You did this!"

Darwin held his hands in the air. "I did nothing of the sort. I didn't even know about any of this. It was Ms. Brennan who figured it out."

Spencer's eyes fell to Rue. "You?" He was visibly shocked.

"Turns out you were right, Spencer," Rue smiled. "Administrative assistant to a cyber forensics expert really was the career boost I needed." She leaned in and motioned for him to come closer. He bent over so she could whisper a secret in his ear.

"I changed them back..." she offered softly, adding before standing back up, "star stuff."

It was clear who was now running the show. Rue stood. "Mr. Fennec," she addressed Darwin.

"Yes, Ms. Brennan?"

"I think we should go now."

"I think you're right."

They stood to leave.

"You'll hear from our lawyers," Byron reiterated his wife's earlier sentiment. "You won't get away with any of this!" To Spencer, he spat out, "Stupid boy."

"Don't worry, Mr. Ellis," Rue answered. "I can assure you that I have no interest in being entangled in this mess any longer than necessary and I have no intention of raking you all through the coals, although you probably deserve it. Just see that Mr. Fennec and my fees and expenses are paid, along with a small inconvenience fee for putting me and my name in potential legal jeopardy, and we can make this all go away."

"Are you blackmailing us?" Gretchen asked, horrified. "What about your code of ethics?"

By then, they had reached the front door, which a servant opened for them.

"His code," Rue motioned to Darwin. "Not mine. And besides, this isn't blackmail. Legally, my name was added to everything. I own it...all of it."

"But you know it's not yours," Spencer protested.

"Do I?" Rue asked. To Gretchen, she countered, "This legal battle would present quite a black eye on your family name. All I'm asking for is a small fee in damages. Then, I'll see to it that everything goes back in Spencer's name and you all can duke it out from there."

"I suppose something can be arranged," Byron growled.

"Of course, this still doesn't solve the very obvious problem still looming over this family's head," Portia LaMonte piped up. Astor looked at his fiancé, bewildered. "We still don't know who murdered Clarissa Sauer and Ursula Gorky, or why."

Both Astor and Spencer shared one last moment of sorrow...the small, human parts of them that actually felt bad that the two women were dead.

And then, the group merely looked at one another and shrugged before returning to business as usual and how Spencer's company would be absorbed into B. A. Ellis Industries.

Darwin and Rue exchanged glances and took their leave. Aside from the two of them, no one else really seemed to care.

~

"DETECTIVE ORTEGA, you need to see this," Officer Dennis descended on Ortega's office with a level of ambition the likes of which the detective had never seen.

"What is it, Officer Dennis?"

"I had a hunch about that email and the notes you asked me to trace." Officer Dennis was bobbing up and down as if he'd downed thirty cups of coffee. "Turns out, we were able to confirm the person who reserved the computer at the library to send that fake email to Gretchen Ellis, the one that supposedly came from Emma Post?"

"Really?" Ortega was impressed.

"Yes," Officer Dennis nodded, seemingly about out of breath. "But there's more. The handwriting on the note that was found on Clarissa Sauer, supposedly from Astor Ellis, was suspiciously similar to the handwritten name of the very same person...it was the signature on the library card that gave it away."

"Who's signature was it?" Ortega enquired.

"Detective," Penelope Washburn burst into the room. Ortega and Officer Dennis looked up, surprised.

"We think we got a lead on who left the bottle of wine in Ursula's changing room," she nodded to Officer Dennis.

"Same person?" Office Dennis asked.

"Same person," Penelope confirmed. "And as you would say, Detective. My spidey sense is telling me we've gotta get to their apartment complex now before they strike again."

CHAPTER 35
Wine

Sunday Afternoon at Rue's Apartment

Darwin dropped Rue off at her apartment complex after their meeting with the Ellis family.

"Sure you don't want me to come up?" he asked.

"I'm sure," Rue smiled, oddly touched that he was still so concerned about her safety. "Besides, there's no place to park around here. You'll be driving in circles for hours. Thanks, though. Just circle back in ten minutes. I should be ready by then."

Rue was still staying at Darwin's home but needed to stop back to check her mail and gather a few necessities. Honestly, while she felt bad about Darwin taking the fold-out couch, his place was far more comfortable then her own. She denied admitting that it had to do with the fact that he was there and not here.

"Just be careful," he cautioned. "We solved one mystery today, but there's still a murderer on the loose."

"I will. Besides, we just left the Ellis house. If it was one of them, they couldn't get here in time." Rue slammed the car door shut a little harder than was necessary. She just wasn't used to riding in cars that often. Subways, after all, didn't have doors that you could slam.

Darwin watched until she reached the front entrance of her building. A series of angry car horns blew behind him, indicating that he was holding up traffic. Reluctantly, he began driving.

Rue stopped at the post office boxes on the ground floor to retrieve her mail. Aside from a few random grocery store flyers and clothing catalogs, there wasn't much else. She tucked her mail under her arm, pausing to throw her backpack over her shoulder and trudge up the three flights of steps that led to her apartment. Once there, she fumbled in her bag for the key, finally retrieving it from the farthest corner at the bottom.

Inside, she absentmindedly dropped the mail and her backpack on the kitchen table. That was when she saw it...a bottle of wine, the same twist-top one Midge brought her for her birthday. Next to it, sat three long-stemmed wine glasses. They weren't there when she last left her apartment a week ago for the safety of Darwin's condo.

"Surprise!" Midge called, as Rue jumped and then spun around, all but walking into her friend who was now only a few inches from her face.

"Midge," Rue grabbed her heart. "You scared the shit out of me! How did you..." Then she glanced at the open window by the fire escape. "I keep that locked. Did you break into my apartment?"

"I had to! How else was I going to surprise you with exciting news!"

"What news?"

With that, Midge revealed the newspaper she'd been holding behind her back.

"SpencerTech was listed as the top up-and-coming startup, voted most likely to unseat the current high-tech mogul, Byron Ellis of B. A. Ellis Industries."

"Why would you be happy for Spencer. I thought you hated him." Rue was suspicious.

"Kinda do," Midge admitted. "But if he's your boyfriend and stands to make a shit ton of money, then I'm for it, just so he takes good care of my bestie." She slapped Rue on the arm. "In another coinkydink, the tabloids are all the buzz after someone leaked that Astor Ellis fathered two kids while engaged to Ms. LaMonte."

"But that can't be," Rue took the paper, perplexed.

Midge opened the bottle and poured two glasses of wine, leaving the third. She walked back over to Rue and handed her a glass which Rue accepted, absentmindedly.

"Why can't that be?" Midge eyed her curiously.

Midge didn't know about Astor's inability to have children, nor that she'd just had a conversation with the Ellis family, and that Portia LaMonte didn't seem to give a rat's ass about Astor's infidelity so long as it didn't affect the family business and he did a better job keeping it out of the press.

Like watching a video on fast-forward, scenes from the past month started flashing through Rue's mind, starting with the wine glass she was holding. She glanced at it, as the connections started forming. The wine bottle found in the changing area was from the same vineyard as the one now sitting on her kitchen table, a common brand that no one could track to one particular buyer. The scuff-marked chair at the theater from shoes that were obviously too big for the wearer. The strategic setup for Darwin to be there at the theater that night instead of Midge. The falsified letter from Emma Post, the ease at which the killer managed to get onto the Artist Atelier campus. The cigarette ashes...

Midge's eyes lit up, waiting patiently for her less-smart friend to make the connections.

"Have a sip of wine, Rue," Midge encouraged, smiling.

"I don't think I will, Midge," Rue set the glass down, calmly, the hairs on the back of her neck bristled.

"I'll drink mine first, if you like." Midge put her glass to her lips and took a sip. "See, no poison."

"Why, Midge?"

Midge let out a laugh. "Isn't it obvious?" She waited for Rue to figure it out, but she didn't. Finally, she continued, "I saw how disappointed you were when Spencer forgot your birthday and I had my suspicions that he wasn't entirely on the up and up—call it intuition. So, when I saw the chemistry between you and Mr. Darwin Fennec, I devised a plan to get the two of you together."

"Your plan was to murder two women?!"

"Of course not," Midge defended. "My plan was to create a traumatic scene that was emotionally charged enough to throw you two together.

Given his detective work, I thought I was being poetic. It was a non-lethal stab wound."

"So, the note that told Clarissa Sauer to meet Astor Ellis was from you—only you directed her to our private booth instead of the Ellis's booth next door."

"Now you're catching on," Midge smiled, gulping down the rest of her glass.

"The usher who went on a smoke break? That was your doing, too?"

"Precisely. I had just enough time to take her place. I stood on the chair to make it look like a taller person had stabbed her. I just didn't have time to wipe off the chair, really didn't see Detective Ortega figuring that one out."

"And you pushed her through the curtain at me."

"Yeah, except Darwin shoulda been there, too. I didn't account for him having a weak bladder. But once she fell over the balcony, he did the debonair thing of trying to cover for you."

"And Ursula Gorky? She was the one eyewitness that recognized both Darwin and I, and she was set to testify that we were not together when Clarissa fell to her death."

"Another unanticipated glitch," Midge went to pour herself another glass of wine. "Would you feel better if I drank from your glass next? I assure you, nothing here is poisoned."

"No, thank you, Midge." Rue knew she had to call the police and Darwin, but she had no idea how to do that with a murderer in her apartment. She eyed the door.

"Going somewhere?" Midge asked.

Rue tried diverting Midge's attention back to the conversation. "How did you get into the school? Did you apply as a model, or..." Rue's eyes fell to the third wine glass on the table, "did you have help?"

Suddenly, she felt the heat of someone standing directly behind her. She turned to face Jaks Liebling. He was leering at her. "You're right, Midge," he smiled, never taking his eyes off of Rue. "She's not very bright, but she eventually catches on."

"What purpose could the famous Jaks Liebling have for wanting Ursula Gorky dead?"

Jaks smiled. "For the art, of course."

"A little different for me," Midge explained. "I didn't like hearing how she publicly accused you of killing Clarissa Sauer. And given that she was the only eyewitness to the event, she had to go."

"You killed her…because of me?" Rue was horrified. Yet, Midge somehow took this as appreciation.

"It was easy since Ursula was an alcoholic," Midge explained, ironically sucking down a second glass of wine before pouring a glass for Jaks. "I left a half-opened bottle in the dressing room with a love note directed at Emma Post from her 'boyfriend.' Really, I just made up a name as Emma's legs are closed tighter than Fort Knox, at least according to what I've heard. Anyways, Ursula assumed Emma left it behind and thought nothing of drinking her friend's gift before her set. Honestly, I thought she'd be a goner long before you arrived, but she must have held off until the final sitting…no pun intended." She and Jaks smiled at the joke. Jaks leaning in to plant a kiss on Midge's lips.

"All in the name of romance," Midge sighed. "You and Darwin were meant to be together."

"To romance," Jaks held his glass and clinked it with Midge's now-empty one. She went back for a final refill, but then decided against it.

"Look," Midge pointed to her feet. "I'm even wearing the shoes I did on both nights, a size nine when I'm only a six-and-a-half. Even had them on the morning after Merriam Hall, but you were too hung over to even notice," she laughed. "I'll leave the last glass for you, Rue." They paused for an eternity. Finally, Midge asked, eyeing Rue's horrified expression. "What's wrong?"

Jaks' eyes grew dark. "I told you she wouldn't understand."

"What?" Midge defended. "Of course, she understands. I did it for her." She searched Rue's face for confirmation.

"I don't think she does," Jaks moved closer to Midge. "I told you we should have cut our losses in Central Park and taken her out then."

"I'm not comfortable killing my best friend, Jaks," Midge held her hand up in protest. "Not after I went through such lengths to get her and Darwin together."

Suddenly, the cell phone from Rue's purse began ringing.

"Speak of the devil," Rue joked. "He's supposed to be picking me up in a few minutes for a…work event." Her breathing was labored. She had to remind herself to take long, steady breaths, but they were still coming out choppy.

"Then, by all means, take it," Midge motioned. "But don't," Midge held up a small .22 Beretta Tomcat and positioned it at Rue's forehead, "make me have to kill you," she finished. Jaks' face lit up in a creepy way as if watching his favorite porn video.

Rue fumbled through her purse, almost dropping the phone. She caught it on the last ring.

"Hello, Darwin," she forced a smile.

"I've circled the block a few times. Everything okay?" he asked.

"Yes, Darwin, I am almost ready. Just have to grab my business suit and I'll meet you out front," Rue continued, "Midge is here." Midge shuffled from side-to-side, pushing the gun against Rue's forehead as a warning. "She brought me wine to celebrate."

"Celebrate?" Darwin asked, carefully.

"Yes, it seems SpencerTech is getting rave reviews in the tech world." Rue forced as much enthusiasm as she could muster. "I can fill you in on it in a moment."

"That is wonderful," Darwin answered cautiously, speaking a little louder than necessary. "Good for him. Perhaps I can take the two of you out to dinner to celebrate."

"That sounds lovely, Darwin." The mark from the barrel of the gun was beginning to leave an imprint on her forehead. "Just finishing a celebratory glass of wine with Midge. Can you wait for me out front? I won't be but a moment more." She hung up the phone before he could answer.

"Well done," Midge lowered the gun. "Though, I was really hoping you were going to tell me you ditched that lowlife for Darwin Fennec. He's a much better catch if you ask me. Still, that's what best friends do, don't they?" She shook her head before peering closely into Rue's eyes. "Look out for each other?"

"My darling," Jaks chimed in. "How can we let her live now that she knows everything?"

"Relax, Jaks," Midge smiled. "I have a plan." To Rue she announced, "Give Jaks and me a 48-hour lead time to get out of town before you contact the cops. It's the least you can do as a show of gratitude for your closest friend. Deal? After all, I was doing all of this for you."

Rue knew she had to sell it. She also knew that Midge could smell bullshit a mile away. "Okay, Midge," she answered finally, cautiously moving toward the wine bottle and pouring a few ounces into the one untouched glass. "While I disapprove of what you've done, in a show of trust and friendship, I promise not to contact the police...not now, not ever." Rue took a sip of wine and waited expectantly...nothing.

Midge smiled. "I told you it was just wine!" But that settled it. If Rue was willing to trust the wine, then she was willing to trust that Rue would keep her word.

"Let's go, Jaks," Midge motioned toward the window.

"Wouldn't the hallway stairs be easier?"

Midge let out a sigh. "Call me sentimental, but since this is my last time climbing out of Rue's window, let's go this way. It's sort of...ceremonial."

Jaks wasn't happy with this solution, but Midge seemed to be his weakness. He wrapped an arm around her and kissed her neck hungrily. They climbed through the window and began their descent. It was only when they'd reached the second floor that Midge realized her mistake.

She looked up to see a team of police officers swarming Rue's fire escape above them. On the ground level, several sirens rang out as the police also covered the street.

Officer Dennis and Detective Ortega had burst into Rue's apartment moments earlier, just as Darwin arrived. Darwin ran over and wrapped his arms around her. "Are you okay? Are you hurt?"

Rue eyed the wine. "Out of an abundance of caution, I believe we should call an ambulance and take that bottle of wine on the off chance I've just been poisoned."

Hours later, Rue learned that while Midge had been taken into custody, Jaks Liebling got away.

"How is that possible?" she wanted to know, as the nurse wheeled her to the entrance of the hospital, "you had them surrounded."

Darwin put his hand out to help Rue to her feet.

"Apparently, Midge pulled her gun and started firing. She's lucky they didn't open fire on her. It just so happened that she tripped on the last rung of the fire escape ladder and landed face-first on the gravel which was enough to save her. They tackled her and took her in. Guess those shoes ended up being her undoing."

"And Jaks?"

Darwin shook his head. "Somehow, in the commotion, that weaselly little man managed to escape."

Rue signed the papers releasing her from the hospital. As it turned out, the wine was just wine and she hadn't, in fact, been poisoned. Guess Midge really did value their friendship, in her own twisted way. Fortunately, her lack of symptoms meant that she also avoided having her stomach pumped.

"Just one more question, Mr. Fennec," Rue asked as they made their way on foot toward his condo. "How did you know I was in trouble?"

"That was easy, Ms. Brennan," Darwin replied as the doorman opened the door for them at the entrance. "Despite multiple requests, I've never been able to get you go call me by my first name. When you called me 'Darwin' three times in a single phone call, I figured you must have been in trouble."

"Good catch, Mr. Fennec," she punched number seven on the elevator. Moments later, they were standing outside of Darwin's condo. Darwin typed in the key code to his home.

"But just so we're clear," she smiled. "I still hate you."

"Duly noted, Ms. Brennan." He followed after her as she made her way inside. "I'm perfectly comfortable on the fold-out couch and you're welcome to stay as long as you need to until Detective Ortega clears you to return to your apartment."

"That's very thoughtful of you, Mr. Fennec," Rue acknowledged. She set her purse on her workstation, instinctively. *Funny,* she thought. *Under normal circumstances, Midge and Spencer would have been the first people she would have turned to for a place to stay and for support when she needed it. Darwin Fennec would have been the absolute last.* Funny how life turns out.

CHAPTER 36
Incarceration

Wednesday Afternoon in a NYC Correctional Facility

~

Midge arrived wearing a hunter-green uniform, something that only she could pull off with her bright red hair and freckles. She was actually attractive in the most unattractive suit possible. In fact, had she instead been out on the streets of New York, onlookers might have described her as...adorable. An adorable murderer.

Her eyes lit up when she saw Rue.

"I knew my bestie wouldn't let me down," she beamed after picking up the phone and peering through the bullet-resistant glass that separated inmates from visitors.

Rue was less than enthusiastic as she held the phone to her ear, wondering if she should have used a disinfecting wipe on it first and if psychopathic behaviors were in any way contagious.

"How are you doing, Midge?" was about all that Rue could bring herself to say.

Midge's face dropped. "It's Mensa," she reminded her, "and, hey, I'm the one stuck in here. Why are you so glum?"

"It's because of *why*, Midge. You murdered two women."

"Allegedly," Midge corrected. Rue shot her a look. "Okay, fine. But you would have done the same thing for me."

"No, Midge!" Rue corrected. "No, I would *not* have."

"Really?" Midge tilted her head sideways. "But I was just trying to bring you and Darwin together."

"Well, we're not together," Rue answered. Though, something about this statement felt wrong to her, but she couldn't quite figure out why.

"After everything you've been through?" Midge was incredulous. "How the hell not?! I went through a lot of trouble causing that accounting glitch at Garnet Media so you'd lose your job and have to go work for Darwin."

"That was you?!" Rue stood, eyed the guard on high alert, and sat back down.

"Of course. Darwin's not the only security expert, remember? Why are you so hung up on that man-whore, Spencer, anyway?"

"Spencer and I broke up," Rue confessed, clenching her teeth. She didn't have the energy to ask how Midge knew about the infidelity. "You're missing the point, Midge," Rue explained. "While I appreciate that you were trying, in your weird sort of way, to help me out, murder is not an acceptable way to meet that goal. Do you not understand that?" Rue was on the verge of tears. Midge had been her best friend for over a year now. How did she not know about her homicidal tendencies? What did that say about her assessment of people? Hell, what did that say about *her*?

"Not really," Midge confessed. "Maybe if they were good people to begin with—" she reasoned.

"Who gets to be the judge of that?" Rue wanted to know.

"Obviously, me," Midge smirked. "Though, to be fair, I hadn't intended on Clarissa dying. I was so careful about leaving her a non-lethal wound that wouldn't significantly harm her or the baby. But she freaked out and then you pulled out the knife when she went over the ledge. Mighta worked out differently if everyone had remained calm."

"Calm? Would you be calm if you were pregnant and someone stabbed you in the stomach?"

"Yes, I believe I would be," Midge was confident.

"And Ursula? You're going to tell me that she was an accident, too?"

"No," Midge smiled to herself. "When Jaks dreamed up 'The Art of Death,' I thought it was absolutely brilliant. He has a 152 IQ, you know, and is smarter than me."

Rue noticed the guard looking at her watch. They didn't have a whole lot of time to left to chat.

"But you killed her, in as horrific a way as possible."

"Oh, don't be so melodramatic," Midge waved her hands. "There are lots worse ways to die."

"Her mouth, esophagus and stomach burned as her throat swelled up and suffocated her to death," Rue reminded her former friend.

"I didn't say it was pleasant," Midge defended. "Just that I can think of worse ways."

"I'll bet you can," Rue sighed, standing up.

"Wait," Midge looked around frantically, as if buying time. "She was ruining everything," Midge explained. "She recognized you and Darwin, and her testimony could have blown the whole plan up. She had to go."

"You didn't need to murder her. I was innocent."

"Look, no one was supposed to die, but then Jaks convinced me that it's way more interesting when someone actually *does* die. We even planned it so that she was on a balcony, too. So poetic!" She smiled as if this explained everything. "It certainly spiced up our romantic life, if you know what I mean." Midge wriggled her eyes, suggestively.

Bile began to rise in Rue's throat. She didn't want to imagine how murdering someone could be construed as an aphrodisiac. She tried a different tack. "And you're not the least bit angry that Jaks Liebling betrayed you? You're taking the heat while he's run off to who knows where?"

Midge smiled to herself and let out a contented sigh. "You can't understand genius." She sat back in her chair, wrapped her arms around herself. "I'm sure he'll come back for me when he's ready."

"Just a couple other questions, Midge," Rue was curious.

"For you, I am an open book," she spread her hands wide to illustrate.

"Am I right in assuming that you sent all the letters? The one to Clarissa Sauer for her to meet Astor Ellis in Box 11, the one to Gretchen

Ellis announcing the baby, and the follow-up email to Gretchen supposedly from Emma Post."

"Guilty, on *two* counts," Midge beamed with pride. "Pretty sure Clarissa sent that handwritten note herself. She was a bit of a schemer." She paused a moment. "I know Darwin did a fair bit to train you...not that I was spying or nothin'." Rue was unconvinced. "But I like to think I helped a little. Nice investigative work, overall. For your first attempt, I'll give you a B+." Midge sat backed and hugged herself, beaming about a job well done.

"Managed to even make it look like that email actually came from the library. Great misdirection on my part, if I say so myself...except for the part where they tracked it to my library card. That was unfortunate," Midge mused.

"Take care of yourself, Midge." Rue started to hang up the phone.

"Wait," Midge stood, all but yelling into the phone. The guard looked up, concerned. "You will come back and visit me again, won't you, Rue?"

"I'm not sure, Midge," Rue confessed.

"It's Mensa!" Midge stamped her foot. "You have to come back." Midge thought a moment. "Did you have the wine I brought you tested?"

"Of course, I did."

"And what did you discover?"

"That it was just wine."

"Exactly," Midge was proud of herself. "I'd never harm my best friend. Friends look out for each other, don't they Rue?" Midge searched Rue's face for some spark of connection but found none.

Rue sucked in her breath. "Goodbye, Midge." She hung up the phone, turning her back on her former best friend, her heart sinking.

"You have to come back!" Midge screamed angrily into the phone and pounded the window before the guard stopped her. "You're my best friend!"

But Rue couldn't hear her. She exited the jail for the first, and hopefully, last time.

CHAPTER 37
"I Know What You're Thinking"

Sunday Morning at Rue's Apartment - One Week After Everything

A knock at the window drew Rue away from the last chapter of *The Alchemist*. She was at the part where the boy realized that the treasure he was looking for was right where he started and in front of him the entire time. "Well, he was pretty short-sighted," Rue had murmured to herself before looking up to see Darwin crouched outside her window. She was startled for a moment, as in a moment of déjà vu, she had expected Midge.

Rue went over to the window, struggling to lift the heavy glass up just high enough where her voice could clearly be heard, leaving about a three-inch gap between the windowsill and the glass. "What are you doing here, Mr. Fennec?" she demanded. "More specifically, what are you doing crouched outside my bedroom window? It's creepy."

Darwin folded himself up as much as possible in order to get his face low enough to talk through the open air so that she could hear him above the traffic outside. "I know," he acknowledged. "Sorry about that, but I had to tie up loose ends with the remaining evidence in Midge's apartment. It was easier to climb down the escape than knock on your door, given that she had pretty much taken over the fourth floor with multiple computers, servers, filing cabinets and all manner of electronic equipment. No disrespect, but maybe I hired the wrong Gal Friday."

"I knew she did something with IT, but really, the entire fourth floor?"

"It would seem so. By the way, we found records upstairs of Jaks Liebling wiring money to Tommy Marcuzzo's bank account. Another piece of the puzzle solved...Er, so, can I come in?"

"Huh," Rue pondered the news. "Uh, yeah...Not sure a peeping Tom outside my bedroom window is any better than Midge's intrusions, though."

"Perhaps not. But have you ever thought of blinds?"

"These are perfectly good window covers. Know what? Never mind." Rue lifted the window the remainder of the way. Even still, Darwin had to crumple his tall frame like a contortionist to fit through it. Graciously, Rue put out her hands as Darwin gripped her forearms to climb the rest of the way inside, his pure white polo shirt getting tinged with dust as it brushed the window frame. Once inside, Rue directed him. "C'mon into the kitchen. I don't need Darwin Fennec, world's greatest cyber-investigator, snooping through my underwear drawer."

He dusted off his shirt and jeans as much as possible, closed the window and followed her. About four steps later and they were in the kitchen. Darwin peered around the room with interest. It was only the second time that he'd been here.

"Yeah, I know what you're thinking," Rue commented. "It's not at all like your digs, but it's all I can afford at the moment. And yes, I realize that at my age, I should have accomplished more with my life. You don't need to tell me."

Darwin leaned against the wall separating the bedroom from the kitchen, crossing arms and legs as he looked at Rue with interest.

"What is it?" Rue tugged at her crocheted cardigan, wrapping one side over the other, and hugging herself, nervously.

Darwin tilted his head, giving her one of those devilish smiles that Rue was, obviously, immune to. "It has come to my attention," he answered quietly, "that you rarely, if ever, know what I'm thinking, even when I think I've been pretty forthright about it."

"Really? Because right now, I suspect you must be thinking I'm pretty stupid, letting Spencer use me like that." Rue wrinkled her brow, leaning back against the adjacent wall, just to the left of the refrigerator. Rue fought the urge to actually put her forehead against the side of it to cool her face, which was feeling warmer by the minute.

Darwin took a step toward her, sidestepping the kitchen table. "Quite the contrary," he offered quietly. "You're one of the smartest people I know, even more so than your psychopathic friend Midge who thinks she's wiser than the rest of the world."

"Why are you here, Mr. Fennec?" Rue sucked in her breath, nervously. Everything about him suddenly made her nervous and she didn't know why. It had only been a week since they last saw each other. It was when Midge was arrested. And yet, it seemed like an eternity. Her heart did this little buzzing thing. She took a deep breath.

"I wanted to apologize."

"For what?" Rue barely choked out the question. She felt her face getting flushed and her eyes beginning to water, ever so slightly. "The fact that you spied on me as if I were a common criminal, keeping detailed notes about my daily habits, my likes and dislikes. I didn't bother to read everything, I couldn't. I was too angry." Rue thought she had forgiven him for all that, but clearly it was still bothering her. And now, it just came pouring out, despite the fact that her heart was in her throat just at his being in the same room with her. "For all I know," she continued, "you followed every bit of my life like a stalker, down to what salad dressing I like, to my time of the month."

"I have no idea what type of dressing you like," Darwin recounted quickly. "And, if I'm being honest, you're cranky a lot of times, so it's really hard to tell when you're being hormonal."

"Screw you," Rue grumbled.

"See what I mean?" He grinned. Rue let out a snort, smiling in spite of the fact that she was still angry.

Darwin reached into the pocket of his jeans and pulled out a flash drive. "I should have just shown it to you from the get-go," he admitted, holding it up. "Here's everything I have on you."

"What the hell is that?"

"A flash drive," Darwin explained.

"My question remains." Rue wrinkled her nose.

"Okay," Darwin tried again. "It contains all the data I've collected on you. You can review it whenever. In the meantime, I've deleted and purged any records I have on you."

"Purged? That sounds..." Rue gagged a little at the thought of the incident after Merriam Hall, "permanent."

"It is," Darwin admitted. "So, if you decide to destroy this, then I no longer have any records about you."

Rue thought about this a moment, "So, you won't remember what kind of tea I like?"

"Earl Grey," Darwin answered, without hesitation.

"Or what flowers I prefer?"

"Bird of paradise, for starters. But you also seem to be drawn to blue delphiniums."

"Or my favorite color?" she challenged.

"When under stress, it's yellow, probably because it's such an optimistic color. But other times, it's more like a sea green."

"So, you pretty much remember everything," Rue noticed, quietly. There was that buzzing again. It seemed to start around her heart and then vibrate up around her neck and ears.

"Yes," Darwin admitted, whispering back. His eyes drifted closed for a moment. "Everything."

He let out a sigh as he walked over to the pub table in the corner and set the flash drive down. "Perhaps I should just leave this with you," he offered.

"Any questionable photos of me in my underwear or in the bathroom?"

"Please," Darwin held his hands up. "Nothing remotely like that. You already saw most of it."

"Okay, well, thank you for this, Mr. Fennec."

Darwin paused before asking, "Do you really dislike me as much as you pretend to?" He took a step toward her.

"You're changing the subject again, Mr. Fennec. Of course, I do." Rue scanned the room uncomfortably, as if looking for an escape. "Pretending?

Really? Why would you think otherwise?" She touched the fingers of her left hand on the cool refrigerator while her right hand rested gently on the kitchen table as if she wasn't quite sure what to do with these extra limbs. Somehow, the coolness on her fingertips was relaxing, or at least enough of a distraction as to not leave her completely unnerved.

Darwin took another step closer, now just two feet away from Rue who appeared to have noticed this simple fact but said nothing.

"It's the little things, really," he spoke quietly, forcing her to almost lean in to hear him. "For example, you had no trouble confronting Spencer the other day at the Ellis estate and I'm pretty sure you're not terribly fond of him, and yet..."

"And yet, what?" Rue whispered, sucking in her breath.

"And yet, here I am, a man you intensely dislike, hate even, standing in your kitchen. You haven't told me to get lost, and..." he tilted his head in an attempt to lock in on her averted eyes, "you can't even seem to look me straight in the eyes, why is that?"

"Clearly, it's because I am offended by your very presence," Rue blurted out. She didn't mean it. She didn't even know why she'd said it. And yet, she couldn't stop it. Something in her heart did something weird again. She'd have to remember to talk to a cardiologist about that.

"I see," Darwin took another step. "You sure have a funny way of showing it. The truth is, I can't help but think that maybe you really like me an awful lot." He paused, directly in front of Rue, resting his fist and forearm against the wall above her, leaning in for support.

"And what evidence do you have to support such claims, Mr. Fennec?" He was now close enough where she could feel a slight warmth kicking off of his body and an annoyingly pleasant smell of a lavender aftershave.

"In addition to the aforementioned lack of eye contact and a command to leave, I've noticed that you catch your breath every time I take a step closer to you, and..."

"And what?" Rue whispered.

"You don't have your arms crossed in a defensive position. One hand is on the refrigerator and the other on the table, with your torso exposed. And," he added, "the closer I get, the more you seem to lean ever so slightly toward me."

Slowly, Rue lifted her eyes to meet Darwin's. "I'll ask you one more time. Why are you here, Darwin?"

"I told you. To apologize and leave your file with you." It had not escaped him that she, once again, addressed him by his first name, usually that only happened in the midst of what she perceived as danger.

"Is that all?" she challenged.

"No," he finally answered, wrapping one hand around her waist and the other cupping the side of her face. "I wanted to see if there was the slightest chance that..." With that, Darwin leaned in to kiss her, except Rue seemed a bit preemptive, capturing his advance mid-kiss with one of her own. He opened his eyes with surprise as she finally rested her mouth on his. He kissed her back, fervently, following up with a light kiss on the side of her neck. She rolled her head back and looked at the ceiling.

"Darwin?"

"Yes, Rue."

"We should probably just flush that flash drive down the toilet. I don't need to see it."

"It's probably for the best."

"And Darwin?" Rue whined at the sudden realization. By then, Darwin was giving equal time to the other side of Rue's neck, as she leaned in, instinctively.

"Yes, Rue?"

"There's a good chance that I might detest you."

"Well, that's just fine," Darwin smiled, kissing Rue again.

Epilogue

One Friday Morning in Prison

It was the most unlikely of escapes. It happened at precisely 5:33 a.m. on a Friday in Brooklyn. The women at a nearby correctional facility were supposed to be heading to a worksite for an assignment, but only one of them would actually make it.

Instead of a random prison break, which would normally send dozens of inmates scrambling to see how far they could get, this one was strategically planned to include built-in safeguards to ensure that no one returned.

One team of female escapees found themselves on an old Volkswagen bus headed toward the Jersey Shore. It caught fire while passing through a toll lane, only to explode moments later, sending shards of debris and female remains everywhere.

Another group sailed past the turnstiles of the R subway line toward Penn Station, only to have several members of the group suddenly drop to the ground with inexplicable food poisoning. None of them recovered.

And then there was Midge.

"Hey, baby!" She smiled, climbing into the front of an oversized cement truck just off of Bedford Avenue.

Jaks Liebling, appearing ridiculously small considering the gigantic vehicle that seemed to envelop him, leaned over for a kiss. "Hey, baby," he said in return, planting a hard kiss on Midge's lips. He looked her over. "Oh, what I would do to you if we had the time."

"Eyes on the road, pal," she laughed. "There's time for that later."

Jaks grinned.

Several police cars rushed past them, sirens and lights blaring.

"Do you suppose they're looking for me?" Midge asked, innocently.

The police expected the usual escapes via car, on foot, even by public transportation. But no one expected soon-to-be-convicted murderer, Midge Pasternak, to be escaping from a maximum-security women's prison in, of all things, a slow-moving cement truck.

Jaks pulled into a construction site. One of the workers, presumably the project manager, motioned for him to stop. He rolled down the window.

"What are you doing here today?" the man demanded. "We're not ready for you until Monday."

Jaks was ready, adapting his generally neutral accent into a Bronx tongue. "Hey, don't shoot the messenger, pal. I was told to be here by 6 a.m. sharp, no excuses." He thrust a work order through the open window into the man's face. The man didn't touch it.

"Well," the man sniffed, removing his hard-hat and scratching his head. "I don't know what to tell you, *pal.* But you're going to be sitting here for three days. We don't need you until Monday."

Surprisingly, Jaks merely smiled and rolled up the window and waved his fingers at the project manager as if to say, "bye, now."

He and Midge could think of plenty of ways to pass the time on a construction site until they needed to move out before the actual cement truck driver commissioned for the job arrived. By then, no one would expect that an escaped inmate was so close to the prison site, and they could slowly amble their truck down the road, catch a train and be on their way.

The project manager was about to bang on the window when a loud hammering on the other end of the worksite got his attention.

"What the..." the worker yelled. "You guys are killing me!" he called above the noise as he made his way over to yell at his crew for whatever it is they were doing that they should not have been.

"You are so brilliant," Midge cooed, leaning over to kiss the side of Jaks' neck. Jaks returned his attention to Midge. "How did I get so lucky?"

Jaks pulled her in close, running his hands roughly across her chest and down her thigh. "Musta done something really awful," he smirked, catching her mouth and forcing his tongue inside.

"Where to, now?" Midge asked when they'd finally come up for air.

"I dunno," Jaks thought a moment. "How do you feel about...Florida? Need to stock back up on manchineel berries."

Pennies from Heaven

With each book I write, I am reminded of how lucky I am to have the support and friendship of so many wonderful people in my life. These are the people who helped bring Pennies From Heaven to life...

Thank you, Lisa Ramirez, for painstakingly editing for me and loving my characters as much as I do! To Cindy Readnower, for her ongoing advice, beta reading and publishing support. Thank you, Graham Mack, for co-narrating all of my books with me and giving each character a unique voice. And thank you to my partner in love and life, John Palli, supporting this book through beta reading, lending technical and historical knowledge, and always encouraging me to pursue what I love.

I also need to send a special thanks to Mike Costello, tour guide extraordinaire, on my recent trip to Ireland. Mike shared much about the rich history of Ireland, and these wise words, "Never let the truth get in the way of a good story." Thank you, Mike.

Prologue

The year is 1998 and still at the height of the tech boom. Startups are all the rage, and a select few have access to inventions that won't be readily available to the public for several more years. The Internet is considered a passing fad, and only a small percentage of people carry cell phones.

Emma Post is a force to be reckoned with. Living in a run-down studio apartment in the Lower West Side of Manhattan, and earning a modest living as a figure model, she has a general "punch first and ask questions later" approach to life. She distrusts technology and people, particularly cops. The recent death of her two friends only reinforces her inherent belief that the world is a dangerous place.

She might be right...

CHAPTER 1
"Because You Just Can't Trust Cops"

Nine Months Ago in Manhattan; 1998

"Why are you here, Officer—" Emma Post struggled to remember his name.

"Dennis," he answered awkwardly, police hat in hand as he shuffled nervously from one foot to the other. "But you can just call me Dennis."

"That's right," Emma remembered. "You were one of the cops who interviewed me a few months ago, after my two best friends were murdered."

The last time Officer Dennis had paid a visit to Emma's apartment complex, it was to help investigate the murder of a singer named Clarissa Sauer, and her art model friend and actress, Ursula Gorky.

Not much had changed since he'd last visited... she still occupied the same bland-white studio apartment with noticeably low ceilings, cracked tile, and an efficiency kitchen that melded into the bedroom. Frankly, while Officer Dennis' digs were not that much bigger, he had to admit to himself that his living arrangement was far better.

What had changed, however, was Emma Post's hair. He remembered. The last time, it had been a short brown-haired cut that curled under once it reached her shoulders, coupled with a few blonde streaks through it. He smiled to himself. While she still retained the same athletic look today, she had obviously bleached her hair blonde and had it permed. Officer Dennis decided she looked just as pretty both ways. He even thought that her plain gray hooded sweatshirt and jeans, with no makeup on, suited her.

"Yes." Officer Dennis glanced sheepishly at the floor. "I guess I just wanted to see how you were getting on... er... seeing how you lost two people who were close to you."

"That seems highly uncustomary for a police officer, doesn't it?" Emma answered. She had let him in her apartment, nonetheless, and Officer Dennis' husky frame took up an enormously large amount of space, made evident when he sat on a small metal chair with a tiny plastic seat that was one of Emma's two kitchen seats. They looked as if they once were used in an elementary school classroom... they probably had been.

Officer Dennis thought a moment, as he shifted his weight uncomfortably in the chair. "How would you know that?" he asked curiously. "I mean, what makes you think it's uncustomary?"

"It just seems like a nice thing to do and —"

"Cops aren't nice?" Officer Dennis finished.

"Your words, not mine," Emma answered flatly. While Officer Dennis sat, she began unpacking the groceries she had procured just prior to his arrival. She paused for a moment as she put a carton of milk, eggs, and fresh vegetables into her refrigerator. Emma let out a sigh. "The truth is, I've been better. It's like there's this giant hole in my heart. And sometimes—" she paused at the door and looked over at Officer Dennis. "I forget they're gone, like when I get good news I want to share or feel like catching a movie. I pick up the phone like old times and then it hits me. I've no one to call." She closed the door of the refrigerator. Then, as if remembering, "You want some coffee or juice or anything?"

"Nah, I'm good," Officer Dennis answered. "Thanks, though."

Emma returned to the kitchen counter and reached into a second paper bag, pulling out two pink candles, a round rose quartz stone, and what looked like a small bag of dried rose petals. The name on the bag read, 'Elementals Magickal Gift Shop.'

"You know," Officer Dennis suggested, "I wouldn't be opposed to catching a movie with you sometime." He coughed slightly. "Just so you wouldn't have to go alone and all." He eyed the objects Emma was holding curiously.

Emma blushed. "They're for a money spell," she lied, disappearing behind the large accordion screen that separated the kitchen from the bedroom. Officer Dennis couldn't see much into the room, but it appeared as if she placed them on a little table that sat low to the floor. On it, was what looked like an incense burner, several gemstones and a small gold ring. He couldn't see what else was there.

"Officer Dennis—" Emma called from behind the screen. "Er... Dennis." She peered around it like a curious cat. "Were you just asking me out?"

"Well, that depends" He grinned cautiously. "If you were accepting, then definitely yes. If you weren't, then definitely not."

"Hmm." Emma returned to the kitchen and hoisted herself up onto the counter, sitting with her legs dangling below her as she rested her hands on each side of her hips. "What did you have in mind?" She eyed him suspiciously.

"Well, there's a really great steakhouse near the movie theater on—"

"I'm a vegetarian," she interrupted, pursing her lips distastefully.

"Oh." Dennis recoiled slightly. He wasn't entirely sure what vegetarians actually ate, mind you. He assumed a lot of lettuce. But he was quick on his feet. "Well, there's a nice vegetarian Japanese restaurant in Midtown that we could try... at least, I think it's good. I've never been there."

"And the movie?" Emma asked. "What would we see?"

"Anything you like, really." Dennis sat up optimistically. "A romantic comedy, a foreign flick—"

"What makes you think I want to see either of those?" she challenged. "Because I'm a woman?"

"Fine, an action movie?"

"Too violent."

"A drama?" Dennis tried again.

"Too depressing." Emma bit back a laugh. It was then that Dennis realized that Emma Post was having a little too much fun messing with him.

"You know, Emma," he said, leaning forward, resting his elbows on the table. "Your love spell might work better if you don't shoot down every guy you meet."

Emma's face dropped. "What? How did you?" She glanced toward the altar in the bedroom and back at Dennis.

"My little sister, Rose, got herself kicked out of Catholic school on account of practicing witchcraft." Dennis laughed at the memory. "My folks were fit to be tied, the only one out of the six of us to have to go to public school." For some reason, Dennis thought this was hilarious.

The color drained from Emma's face. "So you're—"

"Roman Catholic, yes," he confirmed.

"And you're one of six—"

"Kids," he nodded, finishing for her.

"Officer Dennis," Emma began, suddenly appearing woozy. Dennis sat upright. Her reverting to addressing him by title set off alarm bells in his head. He had pushed too hard and said too much. "I really don't think you and I would make a good match at all."

"Well, I wasn't asking for your hand in marriage or anything. Just a dinner between friends."

"We're not friends," Emma scowled, sliding off the counter and standing. "It was really nice of you to check in on me, but—" She moved toward the front door and held her hand on the doorknob leading out of her apartment.

Dennis stood. "So, you're going to shoot me down because my family is Roman Catholic?"

"Do you have any idea what the Catholic Church did to Wiccans throughout history?"

"Not really," Dennis confessed. "But I can tell by your expression that it wasn't good."

"No, Dennis," she answered anxiously. "It wasn't good. They were tortured and brutally murdered—"

"But I wasn't there *then*," Dennis pleaded. "And I hardly ever set foot in a church... except for Christmas and Easter."

Emma sighed again, this time more loudly. Dennis was quite a bit taller than she was and a little chunkier around the middle. He obviously didn't exercise regularly and probably visited that steakhouse he mentioned a bit too much. From what she could tell, he was also several years younger than her. Honestly, Emma wouldn't have given him a second glance if she passed him on the street. And yet, after two brief encounters, she sensed there was something really… sweet… about him.

"How old are you, Dennis?" She eyed him curiously.

He knew where this was going. "What does that matter?" he answered defensively. "How old are you?"

"None of your business," she retorted. Then she remembered, she told him her age the last time she met, when he and Detective Ortega, his boss, were investigating the murder of her two friends. "Thirty-six," she finally answered.

"Well, I'm thirty-one. Now that we've gotten that out of the way—"

"Officer Dennis, I have been nothing but difficult since the time you arrived. Why on Earth are you so set on taking me out on a date?"

"Well," he thought about this. "You just seem really put together is all."

Emma's face became flushed. "What do you mean 'put together'? You mean my body?!"

"No, no," he tried again, holding his police hat in his hands and rotating it awkwardly in a circle. "I mean, as an overall person. You seem to know what you're about. You're obviously smart and independent and… will I get tossed out on my ear if I tell you I think you're kinda cute?" Dennis turned his head away, glancing sideways sheepishly.

Emma smiled despite her attempts to be as disagreeable as possible.

"If I'm remembering correctly," Dennis cleared his throat, "the last time I was here, you told Detective Ortega that you, and I quote, 'have terrible taste in men.'"

"Yes," Emma nodded. "That is true."

"Well, have you ever thought of going against the grain — trying someone different?"

"Like you, you mean?"

Dennis nodded. "Yes, I'm an omnivore who comes from a long line of Catholics. I'm a little younger than you and am obviously not as athletic as you are. And… drum roll please… I also happen to be a cop, which you hate. In fact, I'm probably the last person on Earth who would be considered your 'type'." Dennis put the word 'type' in air quotes. "And yet I'm asking you, Emma Post, will you go on a date with me?"

Emma couldn't recall the last time anyone made that much of a fuss over her and couldn't believe he hadn't given up at the start. He was definitely a determined young fella, that was for sure. Finally, she smiled. "Okay, Officer Dennis. I will go out with you. Vegetarian Japanese food, then? With a movie to be determined?"

"Perfect," Dennis smiled back, placing his police cap on his head. Emma cringed a little out of habit, but quickly recovered. He reached into his shirt pocket and procured a small pen and notepad. He scribbled a note, peeled off the slip of paper, and handed it to her. "Here's my number. How does Saturday at 6:30-ish sound? I can meet you here and we can catch a cab together?"

Emma opened the door for him, reaching out to take the paper. She smiled with the tiniest glimmer of hope. "Saturday at 6:30-ish," she agreed. "See you then."

She closed the door behind him and leaned against the door, glancing at the note, wondering if this was a good thing or the biggest mistake of her life.

CHAPTER 2
The Call

Two Weeks Ago; 1998

"Detective Or—" Detective José Ortega caught himself. "This is José," he said as he answered his cell phone. It was given to him by Cyber Forensic Consultant and Private Investigator Darwin Fennec after the two men became unlikely allies in solving a multiple-homicide case in Manhattan nearly a year ago.

"Detective Ortega," Dennis could be heard on the other line. "It's me, Officer Dennis. It's good to hear your voice, Sir."

Ortega smiled despite his typically sour mood. "It's good to hear from you too, Officer Dennis. But you can call me José now. As you know, I am retired."

"I know," Dennis clucked into the phone. "I know all too well. The detective they assigned to us after you left is a real pain in my ass, if I'm being honest."

"I have it on good authority that you said the same thing about me when you and I first began working together years ago," Ortega laughed. Dennis' awkward silence on the phone let Ortega know his suspicions had been correct, and that Dennis was embarrassed about it now. "Just give the new detective a little more time. I'm sure it will work out."

"Er, maybe... But, Sir?"

"Yes, Dennis?"

"I'm not staying in New York. I'm in Florida."

"Really?" Ortega was surprised. When his wife Nancy insisted he retire early in an effort to 'save their marriage,' she also got it in their head that they should move to a warmer climate and get away from the crime-ridden city. Ortega agreed, and had since spent the last nine months bored out of his skull.

No longer conducting murder investigations, he became one of their HOA's worst nightmares, always reporting to the Home Owner's Association in their sub-division if someone parked on the street during a weekday, watered their lawns on non-approved days, or failed to pick up after their dogs at the poop station at their community dog park. He'd even once wrongly accused his 83-year-old neighbor, Bob, of stealing his *Tampa Bay Times* from his front porch, only to find that Nancy had already retrieved it — leading to a very uncomfortable apology to Bob.

"What business do you have in Florida?" Ortega asked. "Are you on vacation?"

"No, actually, I requested a temporary exchange with another officer to see what it's like down here for a bit. I think I'm near you. We've moved into a small house in St. Pete."

"We?" Ortega was curious.

Dennis paused. Ortega could actually feel him blushing on the other end of the phone. "So, you remember the woman we interviewed during the murder of the singer Clarissa Sauer and the figure model Ursula Gorky?"

"Of course, I remember. It was my last case before retiring. Emma... Emma Post, I believe, was her name."

"That's her."

"What about her?" Ortega was suspicious.

"Well, we've been sort of... seeing each other."

"I'd say it's a bit more than that if you're living together, wouldn't you?"

"It's not like that," Dennis explained. "We're living in the same house but have separate bedrooms. It's temporary... unfortunately."

"Things not working out?" Ortega was sympathetic. There was a lot of that going around lately.

"It's working out just fine... though, a little slower than I'd like, if I'm being honest. I'm never 100% sure how Emma really feels about me. But that's not why I'm calling."

"You want to plan a double date with Nancy and me? We're close. Parrish is only about an hour from you."

"Well, no," Dennis admitted. "I mean, yes. But that's also not why I'm calling."

Ortega gave Nancy a quick peck on the lips as she headed out for her weekly tennis lesson. Nancy gave a playful twirl to show off her new pleated white skirt as she headed out the door, blowing him another kiss. Ortega smiled. *Gotta take in the good moments when you got 'em*, he thought to himself.

He drew himself back into the conversation. "So, why *are* you calling Officer Dennis?"

"Emma has suddenly come into some money... a *lot* of money."

"Oh?" From what Ortega could remember, she was a woman of very little means, living in a tiny hovel on the Lower West Side of Manhattan. He shuddered to even think of it.

"Yeah," Dennis explained. "She had been modeling for this artist and philanthropist Erasmus Vandenberg."

"The tycoon whose family fortune came out of selling vitamins?"

"The same, though I'm told they prefer to refer to them as nutritional supplements or nutraceuticals. Probably some hoity-toity rich thing," Dennis reasoned. "Must have worked for him, though. Seems to have died in his sleep just shy of his 89th birthday... heart failure."

"That's a pretty good run," Ortega admitted. Ortega wasn't sure he wanted to live that long. His joints were already a little achy, and he couldn't imagine thirty or more years with bad knees. "So, am I to assume that he left Emma something in his will?"

"Nearly everything," Dennis answered.

"Everything? As in... his entire fortune? Were they having an affair?" Ortega blurted out before he could stop himself.

"They most certainly were not!" Dennis all but yelled into the phone. "He was like a grandfather to her!"

"But his *entire* fortune?" Ortega was incredulous.

"*Nearly*," Dennis clarified. "He donated much of his wealth to some charity that supports women in crisis, another for at-risk youth, and a third to provide mental health services to men and women who can't afford them."

"Sounds like a pretty upstanding guy," Ortega had to admit. He rarely thought fondly of those with money, Nancy's family being the exception. He had spent too much of his career uncovering the shady dealings of wealthy men doing their best to cover things up.

"That amounted to only 30% of his fortune. The rest... his estate on Treasure Island, his high-rise in Manhattan, and his manor in Leitrim... he divvied up between Emma, his nephew, and one granddaughter. Emma got the house in Florida and the remaining 70% of his financial assets."

"That doesn't make sense," Ortega insisted.

"I agree. So does Em. I think she's a bit overwhelmed by it all."

"I'll bet." Ortega cleared his throat. "Might wanna talk to a good accountant and hire a lawyer."

"She's done that... only, they were Erasmus Vandenberg's accountant and his team of lawyers. I recommended she talk with someone without close ties to the family."

"Smart thinking, Officer Dennis. But what does any of this have to do with me?"

"The thing is," Dennis lowered his voice, "I don't think Erasmus Vandenberg died in his sleep at all. I think it was murder."

"Who would murder a nearly 90-year-old man who probably didn't have that many years left, anyway?"

"I don't know, but the family is acting all fishy if you ask me."

"Wouldn't you act fishy if your family fortune was handed off to an art model that their dearly departed Erasmus couldn't have known very well?"

"That's just it," Dennis answered. "You would think they would contest the will, call her a gold digger and tie the estates up in court."

"Exactly."

"But that's not what they're doing," Dennis explained.

"It isn't?"

"No, they've already been all over the news celebrating her new fortune. They say that dear old Erasmus had a heart of gold, through and through, and who more deserving of his fortune than the one woman who gave his life purpose and was a friend to him in his older years?"

"That's surprisingly... generous of them," Ortega eventually found the words.

"It's bullshit, if you ask me... er, sorry Sir," Dennis apologized.

"Dennis, I'm no longer your boss. You can curse any damn time you want to. I don't care. And please, call me José. Call me Ortega. Call me whatever you want, but don't refer to me as 'sir' or 'detective' anymore. Okay?"

"Okay... Jo." Dennis thought carefully and decided he liked that nick-name (even though it likely only made sense to him). Ortega didn't, but since he gave him free range to call him 'whatever,' he'd have to learn to accept it. "As I was saying, it's bullshit if you ask me. I believe Erasmus Vandenberg was murdered, and the family is being agreeable because they're all hiding something."

"Did you report your suspicions to the proper authorities in each district?"

"I did," Dennis sighed. "But no one believes me. And, if they do, they're not willing to disturb the potential hornet's nest that is the Vandenberg family."

"So, I'll ask you again. What does any of this have to do with me?"

"I wanna hire you, Jo," Dennis answered simply. "You can't be happy being retired. Help us figure out what's going on here, else Em won't be able to accept the fortune with a good conscience."

"Did she know you had plans to contact me?" Ortega asked.

"Of course," Dennis answered. "It was Emma's idea."

CHAPTER 3
Erasmus Vandenberg

Two Months Ago in Manhattan; 1998

"Beautiful, my Dear," Erasmus complimented. "But could you lift your chin just a smidge upward... yes, perfect," he praised. "Now the light catches the side of your face, just so.

Emma Post had been the private model of wealthy philanthropist Erasmus Vandenberg for the past six months. While she was hesitant about accepting the position at first, the model coordinator at the Artist Atelier, an art school where Emma had been a figure model for years, vouched for his character. Several models, both male and female, had sat for him over the years in his home studio on the Upper East Side of Manhattan — always draped, never nude.

In fact, Erasmus was typically fond of Rococo-era art, often renting ball dress replicas for Emma to wear during her sessions. While it was a far cry from her everyday jeans and sweatshirt, she found that she rather liked it.

More than the dress, she appreciated that Erasmus treated her like a lady and never felt the need to call attention to the fact that he was wealthy and had plenty of money, whereas she had almost none. He was respectful and kind and, in Emma's world, that combination was rare.

On this day, Erasmus had his back to the window, where the sun beamed brightly over his shoulder. The light landed directly on the model stand where Emma lounged across a gold-trimmed, light blue sofa with stiff padding and ornate patterns across it. She was wearing a contrasting indigo ball gown with a base so wide that it was literally impossible for Emma's slight frame to fall over, even if she tried. Frankly, she had no idea what she'd do when it was time to take a bathroom break.

Erasmus hunched over his easel, as he had done for over six decades. It was a little harder for him to hold the paintbrush now, the knobs on his arthritic hands becoming more prominent with each passing year, but he learned to be patient, waiting for his hands to stop trembling before he applied the next stroke. His vision was challenged too, and while his earlier work was a precise mix of complex lines, colors and subtle light shifts, he'd learned to adapt his later work to meet the needs of his aging body. For example, there were fewer lines on the canvas, but they were purposeful. Any intricate shading he would work on after the model had gone home, where he could take as much time as he needed waiting for the natural light in the room to shift just so. His brush strokes were larger and his colors bolder.

"Do you have time for a late lunch today?" Erasmus asked, absent-mindedly humming for a moment before catching himself.

Emma waited for him to finish his tune before answering. "Sorry, Raz. I promised Dennis I'd meet him for an early dinner since he's working late tonight." *Raz* was Emma's pet name for Erasmus, since it was the only logical one she could come up with for someone with a name like Erasmus. It should be noted that Emma was the only person permitted to give him a nickname. He hadn't even let his late wife do that.

"Ah." Erasmus nodded, glancing up for a moment, holding his paintbrush at arm's length to measure. "The police officer. How is it going with Officer Dennis?" He fought back a knowing grin.

"Good, so far." Emma resisted the urge to scratch the unfortunate itch under the folds of her gown. She didn't know how she'd reach it, anyway.

The muscle behind her left shoulder ached, but she dared not move. Instead, she took a deep breath, as if willing it to soften. It did, slightly.

"Well, that's encouraging," Erasmus smiled. "Though I am a little cross at the young man for interfering with our late lunches."

"Next time," she smiled. "I promise."

"Yes," he nodded. "And one of these days, I'll have you and your par amour to dinner so I can size him up properly. Make sure he's good enough for you."

Emma thought this was sweet. Her own father had skipped out on her mother at a young age, and unfortunately, her mother's love life comprised a revolving door of men, each one worse than the last. That's why Emma was so particular now. In all matters of the heart, she kept her wits about her. Though, if she were being completely honest with herself, Officer Dennis was carving out a neat little spot in the center of her chest that seemed to flutter slightly when he was around. But she'd never tell her boyfriend that, lest he get the wrong idea.

Erasmus began humming again. Emma immediately recognized the tune and began singing along softly. It was 'Pennies from Heaven.'

Erasmus stopped humming, surprised. "You know the tune?"

"Yes," Emma chuckled. "You sing or hum it almost every time I sit for you."

"Do I?" Erasmus mused, taking out a white cloth and wiping a small spot on the corner of the canvas. "I had no idea. Sorry, my dear."

"Don't be," Emma smiled. "I like it."

After a moment's pause, Erasmus hummed and sang quietly under his breath, *"Hmmm... hmmm... each cloud contains..."*

Emma joined in, *"Pennies from Heaven."*

There was a knock at the door. They both stopped singing, their smiles dropping simultaneously at the interruption.

"Ex... ex... excuse m... m... me... gra... grandfather." A mousy young woman peeked a nervous head around the large mahogany door. Her hair was raven black, cropped short and framing her round face, her dark bangs a stark contrast to her pasty complexion.

"Elsbeth." Erasmus was delighted. "How nice to see you. Please come in." The young woman cautiously entered the room and shuffled her feet toward her grandfather. "Shut the door behind you, please. It's drafty."

She turned to obey.

"Emma, have you met my granddaughter Elsbeth before?" Elsbeth looked as if she'd rather fade into the deep blue painted walls, a little challenging as she had on a plain toffee-colored dress. Elsbeth eyed Emma's gown and then glanced at her own, blushing a little.

"I have not," Emma smiled pleasantly. From her estimation, Elsbeth had to have been in her early twenties, probably not much more than a decade younger than Emma. And yet, she carried herself like a small child. "It's nice to meet you, Elsbeth," Emma offered softly.

"Hi." Elsbeth curtsied, tucking her head as she absentmindedly clung to her dress with both hands, rocking nervously from side-to-side.

"Elsbeth is visiting with her mother, my daughter, Edwina, from the Hamptons."

Apparently, the family liked names that began with the letter "E."

"What is it, Elsbeth?" Erasmus persuaded.

After a pause, she said, "M... M.... Mother... w... wants to know if y... y... you'll be taking us to a B... Broadway... sh... show this w... w... weekend." She kicked the side of the very expensive couch where Emma was posing.

"Emma." Erasmus turned to his model. "Why don't we break for today? We can continue on Thursday." Emma nodded, standing up with some difficulty. Her joints were stiff, and she attempted to stretch her arms overhead. Unfortunately, the dress was as stiff as her joints, and wouldn't allow her to raise her arms more than about shoulder high. Instead, she twisted her neck from side-to-side and then lowered her arms.

"You're b... b... beautiful," Elsbeth blurted out and then shrank back, clasping her hands over her mouth.

Emma smiled at the young woman's abruptness but was careful with her reply. She realized Elsbeth was a bit... different.

"Well, thank you, Elsbeth," she offered. "But I'm certain it's the dress."

Elsbeth furrowed her brow, confused.

"Elsbeth," Erasmus addressed his granddaughter gently, while putting his paints away. "Are you quite certain it's not you who really wants to go to the theater and not your mother?" Elsbeth turned a beet-red and fought back an embarrassed giggle. She wrapped an arm around her face as if to hide herself. "It's okay, my dear. Tell your grandpa what it was you were hoping to see."

Elsbeth looked at Emma for a moment, her mouth dropping in a frown. She dared not say it aloud. Instead, she ran over to her grandfather and motioned for him to bend over. She cupped her hands around his ear and whispered.

"Really?" Erasmus confessed. "I'm afraid I don't know that one." He shook his head. "But maybe Emma does. Why don't you ask?"

Elsbeth was unsure, looking down at her Mary Jane shoes and simple, ankle-length dress and then over at Emma, whose hair had been pinned up to reveal long, toned shoulders and a gown fit for royalty. Elsbeth seemed to have difficulty understanding fantasy from reality. She lost the concept that Emma was only pretending to be from the Rococo time period and hadn't actually magically appeared from the past so that her grandfather could paint her.

Still, she let Emma in on her secret. But instead of answering aloud, even though there were only the three of them in the room, Elsbeth suddenly darted over to Emma, having taken her into her confidence. She tugged at her arm until the slightly older woman leaned over to listen, the folds of the gown making a crinkling sound as she bent. Elsbeth cupped her hands over Emma's ears, as she had done her grandfather's, and whispered.

"Beauty and the Beast?" Emma clarified. At first, Elsbeth was embarrassed that Emma had said it out loud. She backed away, slowly, catching the heel of her shoe on the carpet. She toppled backward until Emma caught her arms and righted the girl. "Well," Emma smiled encouragingly, "that's a very good musical. I had a friend who was an understudy for it—"

Emma caught herself, her face dropping. It was her now-deceased friend, Clarissa Sauer, who had been in that show. Clarissa had been murdered last year and, for a short while, Emma was a potential suspect in the investigation. It was how she met Officer Dennis. And while she would have given anything to have her friend back, the one bright spot was that the tragedy brought her and Dennis together, something for which Emma would always be grateful. *Well*, she thought, *at least so far.*

Emma found her eyes beginning to well up at the memory. "I should change," she announced to Erasmus, who had finished packing up his tools and was now manually turning the lever of a knob on one of the tall windows behind him to let a little of the crisp New York air in to help rid the room of the smell of harsh oil paints.

She darted past Erasmus before he could see her expression, one that had fortunately been lost on Elsbeth. At the far corner of the room was a doorway that led to a very large private bathroom, which served as her changing area. She closed the door, almost catching the hem of the dress behind her.

"Elsbeth!" A woman's voice yelled from the foyer before bursting into the room like a gale force wind. "Where are you, simple girl?"

Elsbeth ran to hide behind her grandfather. She clung to the back of his shirt with her hands as if to shield herself.

"She's with me, Edwina," Erasmus addressed Elsbeth's mother, his daughter.

Edwina had a short, cropped haircut that almost matched Elsbeth's, except that hers had been dyed brown with streaks of blonde added in strategic places. She wore a white, pin-striped pant suit with a large gold chain that had been double-looped around her neck. At the end of it was a very noticeable, diamond-encrusted, golden cross. Her heavy French perfume was a scent that did not mix well with the smell of paint and solvent.

"I'm sorry, Father," she apologized on her daughter's behalf. "Elsbeth, come out from there and leave your grandfather alone. He's very busy!"

Erasmus' gray brows knit together in a solid line. "I'm never too busy for Elsbeth," he answered simply as he gently nudged Elsbeth toward her mother. "Nice to see you again, Edwina," he answered, formally.

"You too, Father." She took Elsbeth by the hand, just as Emma emerged from the bathroom wearing jeans and an oversized light pink sweatshirt, a fanny pack wrapped around her waist. Edwina eyed Emma distastefully before turning her attention to Erasmus. "I've instructed Cook to plan for dinner at 6 p.m.," she announced. "I hope that's alright. I know it's late for you, but I need to stay on a strict dietary schedule."

Edwina was a tall, thin woman who didn't really need to stay on any sort of schedule at all. She liked everything just so and felt anxious when life's events were out of her control. Therefore, she attempted to control… everything.

"I'll adjust," Erasmus sighed. Unlike Edwina, who was about thirty-five years younger than he, old Erasmus wasn't put off by little things such as when dinner was served, or if someone interrupted his work. He didn't even bat an eye that his daughter had only just arrived that morning, and she had already taken hold of the house schedule and re-arranged it, even though the house was solely… *his.*

Edwina grasped Elsbeth's hand so hard the young girl winced a little, as she dragged her daughter out of the room, accidentally slamming the door behind her as a gust of wind blew in from the window.

A darkness fell over the room as a few storm clouds blew through Manhattan, casting a shadow over the city.

"She seems nice," Emma bit her lip, sarcastically, and suddenly a laugh erupted from the depths of Erasmus' belly. She had heard plenty of stories about Edwina. Though, surprisingly, few about Elsbeth other than a passing reference.

"She certainly is… something," Erasmus concurred. "Give me a moment, and I'll have Ferdinand meet you out front to take you home." He glanced at the window.

"Thank you, Raz," she agreed. For the first month working for Erasmus, Emma insisted on taking two subway stops from his three-story luxury condo and walking the rest of the way before she finally relented and agreed to be chauffeured to and from her apartment. It was more at the behest of her new boyfriend Dennis. As a cop who'd seen a thing or two in the city, he wasn't comfortable with her having to take any unnecessary risks when Erasmus was perfectly willing to provide a safe escort for her.

At first, she felt funny at the looks she received from her neighbors when she arrived home in a stretch limo, but she didn't even try to explain. She let them think whatever they wanted.

"Same time Thursday?" Emma confirmed.

"Same time Thursday," Erasmus smiled.

Just then, they heard the briefest sound of thunder, followed by a light rain on the roof. Before Emma could close the door behind her, Erasmus hummed pleasantly. Only, the tune had changed to something more sinister, "*No one here can love and understand me... Oh what hard luck stories they all hand me...*"

After years of hob-knobbing with friends in the arts, Emma recognized this song too. Just before the closing line, she jumped in to finish the tune, "*Blackbird Bye-Bye.*"

CHAPTER 4
Baxter Baker

Two Months Ago in Manhattan; 1998

Emma waited in the front lobby of their building for Erasmus' private driver, Ferdinand, to retrieve her, sitting on a stiff white couch that seemed a poor choice of both color and material considering the foot traffic that must have gone through there regularly. The floor was adorned with gold-trimmed white carpet runners. Overhead hung an oversized and overpriced crystal chandelier. To amuse herself, she tried to imagine what a carpet and chandelier like that would look like in the entrance of her apartment complex, but decided it was so large that it wouldn't even make it through the front door.

The traffic was heavy on the avenue outside, which meant that it might take Ferdinand a few extra minutes to drive the short distance from the private garage to the front door of their building; but Erasmus wouldn't hear of her actually walking down to the garage to meet him. "That's no place for a lady," he reasoned. He was particular like that.

So, she sat.

"Sit down, you simple girl," a voice barked. Edwina had emerged from the elevator and was now yelling at Elsbeth. They stopped several feet away from Emma. Edwina was now wearing a cream-colored wool walking cape and thin, black-leather gloves. Elsbeth obediently took a seat, not on the next couch over, but rather the opposite end of where Emma sat. Edwina caught Emma's expression and softened her voice. "There's a good girl," she praised her daughter. "Don't move, and I'll be back in a jiffy." She shot Emma a furtive glance before walking back to have a talk with the security guard standing just inside the lobby's entrance. There was another positioned outside too, just under the awning by the front door. It was a well-protected building.

Emma caught the glance but had no idea why Edwina would even care about the opinion of a low-income, working-class girl from the Lower West Side, but guessed that appearances were important to Edwina.

Elsbeth was busy fidgeting with the long coat she had strewn across her lap as she sat, waiting for her mother. Emma caught her glance and smiled. Leaning over, she whispered. "I hope you *do* get to go to the theater this weekend."

Elsbeth returned the smile with a small, close-lipped smirk, appreciatively.

"Is that my favorite cousin?" A voice boomed, startling the women.

Emma looked up to see a tall man with bleach blonde hair parted on the side, hanging in ear-length locks, coupled with a tan complexion too perfect to be real. He wore a striped, long-sleeve polo shirt, black jeans and the swagger of someone with all the confidence in the world.

"H... hi... B... B... Baxter," she stammered, staring at the floor.

He took her by the shoulders and pulled her enthusiastically to her feet. "Here. Give your cousin a kiss." Before she could respond, the man leaned over and planted a kiss on Elsbeth's cheek. She returned with a light peck on his opposite cheek. "Kissing cousins," he joked before noticing Emma sitting on the couch. "It's alright," he reassured Emma. "We're thrice removed." He winked.

Emma didn't find him amusing.

"And who is this charming lady you're sitting with, Elsbeth?" He nodded toward Emma, releasing his cousin's shoulders.

"This is... E... E... Emma... gra... grandfather's... m... model."

Emma was surprised Elsbeth remembered her name. She wasn't sure the young woman had been paying that much attention.

"Oh, really?" His eyebrows shot up.

"She means portrait model," Emma quickly explained. "Her grandfather Erasmus hired me to sit for one of his paintings. I'm Emma." She extended her hand to shake his.

He took her small hand in both of his and just... held it, looking into her eyes. "Well, my grandfather has excellent taste." He looked her over briefly, from head to toe. "Perhaps you'll sit for me one day?"

"Are you a painter?"

"For you, I would become one," he countered, smiling devilishly.

"May I have my hand back, please?" Emma retorted sourly.

"Certainly." He released her palm.

A man in a black suit and driver's hat cleared his throat behind them.

"Ah, Ferdinand." Emma smiled gratefully. "Thank you for giving me a lift." To Elsbeth and Baxter, she said, "Nice to have met you both."

"Just a moment, Emma." Baxter touched the inside of her forearm, careful not to appear too grabby. "Let me take you to dinner tonight."

"Oh." Emma pulled her arm back. Behind her, Ferdinand stood, rocking back and forth on his heels impatiently. "Thank you, but I have a boyfriend."

Emma felt something in her stomach lurch. Did she, in fact, have a boyfriend? She knew she wasn't dating anyone else, and she didn't think that Dennis was either. He always seemed so eager to see her. But then, she really didn't know for certain. And, since their dating was *mostly* innocent — a few heated kisses at the end of the evening — there was no real reason to push the issue... except in situations like this one. But Emma had dated her share of "Baxters," and they were all the same... self-absorbed, dishonest, charming when they needed to be, and, unfortunately, sexy as hell.

"Should I take your silence to mean you are considering it?" Baxter was hopeful.

"No!" Elsbeth stood and stamped her foot. She was loud enough for a few onlookers to pause. She quickly turned red and retreated inward, casting her eyes to the floor. "Sh... she already t... told y... you. She has a boyfriend. Dennis." Elsbeth crossed her arms defiantly.

It seemed that Elsbeth had been eavesdropping.

"I see… Dennis," Baxter repeated. "And what does your boyfriend do for a living, this… Dennis?"

"What does that matter to you?" Emma demanded.

"He's… a c… cop," Elsbeth answered, lifting her chin. For reasons which Emma could not understand, Elsbeth already seemed to be 'team Emma and Dennis' and definitely not 'team Baxter.'

"Oh, a cop," Baxter smiled. "Must take you on some lovely dates… on a cop's salary. Dinner on the Riviera? Spontaneous trips to the Maldives?"

"There's nothing spontaneous about an 18-hour flight to the Maldives," Emma snapped back. "And what is it that you do, Baxter… exactly?" Emma wasn't sure why she asked, as she really didn't care.

"I'm the Vice-President of Operations for the Vandenberg nutraceutical company. Nutraceuticals are—"

"I know what nutraceuticals are, Baxter. Thank you."

"We have one manufacturing plant in the U.S. and one in Ireland, as well as relationships with over 100 private organizations. I oversee all of it."

"So, you watch *other* people work all day?"

"There's a bit more to it than that," Baxter smirked.

Ferdinand cleared his throat again.

"I'm thrilled for you."

"No need to be snarky, Emma." He shook his head, grinning. "You asked."

"Right." She nodded. "I did."

"I can do better than the Dallas BBQ for dinner," he whispered, leaning toward her.

"I'll keep that in mind." She turned to leave.

"At least…" He stopped her one more time. "Take my card?" He held a business card in front of her face.

Emma didn't move. She just stared at him, her nostrils flaring.

Suddenly, quick as lightning, Elsbeth snatched the card and tucked it into her coat.

"I'll keep it s… safe f… for Emma." Elsbeth dutifully nodded.

"Thank you, Elsbeth." Emma smiled at her new friend before turning to Baxter. "But I won't be calling."

Before Baxter could try again, she darted around him to Ferdinand, who produced an umbrella, seemingly out of nowhere. The sound of thunder erupted outside as the rain came down in buckets. "I parked as close to the building as I could," he explained.

"Don't worry," she told Ferdinand. "I won't melt." Ferdinand let out a laugh. "And, sorry to keep you waiting."

"Not at all, Miss Post." He shrugged as they made their way awkwardly through a revolving door that forced everyone to stand a little too close for comfort. "It was worth it to see Baxter's face when you turned him down. That doesn't happen often."

Once in the limo that Ferdinand was driving, Emma asked, "Who *is* Baxter, anyway?"

"He's the great nephew of the late Esmee Vandenberg, Erasmus' late wife and great-grandson of her older sister, Katherine."

"Oh," was all that Emma could think to say.

"Oh, indeed." Ferdinand shook his head. "Not my place to say, of course. But Baxter is used to getting his own way. If he bothers you again, be sure to tell Erasmus. He'll put it right."

"Thank you, Ferdinand." Emma sank back in her seat. "But I've dealt with far worse than the likes of Baxter... What's his last name?"

"Baker," Ferdinand answered.

"Well, as I was saying," Emma finished, "I've dealt with far worse than the likes of Baxter Baker."

CHAPTER 5
Thursday

Two Months Ago in Manhattan; 1998

As promised, Emma returned to the Vandenberg household for her next modeling session. Only this time, Elsbeth was there, too.

"I'm afraid I'll have to miss the theater this weekend, dear Elsbeth," Erasmus broke the news to his granddaughter, who, after having met Emma, decided she quite enjoyed being there during her modeling sessions with Erasmus. Other than Erasmus' random humming, or the rare day when he had classical music playing softly in the background, most times, it was quiet in the room. This delighted Elsbeth because, then, she could hear with crystal clarity the other sounds that normally got overshadowed, such as the gentle movements when Erasmus was mixing oil paints on a palette, or the creak of the couch as Emma made a slight adjustment, and even the crisp rustle of Emma's oversized ball gown when she stood to stretch on her breaks. And the best part of all was sitting behind her grandfather and watching as a blank canvas morphed into art.

"Oh." Elsbeth was pulled from her trance. Her lip quivered a little.

She was very much looking forward to seeing a musical with her grandfather. Unlike her mother, who typically hovered over her like a helicopter, criticizing her every move, Erasmus was the typical doting grandfather. To him, Elsbeth was perfect in every way. Elsbeth wasn't sure how her mother, Edwina, had gotten to be so ill-tempered and cross. Her grandfather wasn't like that at all. She assumed that she must have taken after her grandmother, who died long before Elsbeth was born.

"Don't fret, my Dear. I promise we'll go next weekend." Erasmus tried to reassure the young woman.

Elsbeth's face crumpled like a piece of paper about to be thrown in the trash. "W... why... n... not... th.. this w... w... weekend?"

Erasmus stopped and set his paintbrush on the easel momentarily, surveying his granddaughter. "Emergency trip to my production plant in Florida, I'm afraid. It's an urgent matter that can't be handled by telephone. I have to be there in person."

Emma took advantage of the momentary distraction and reached over her shoulder to scratch an itch, pushing on her elbow with her opposite hand so she could reach it more easily. *Finally, relief!* She thought. That had been bugging the hell out of her for the better part of fifteen minutes. Of all the costumes she had to wear, this one was by far the itchiest. *Funny, all the little things we take for granted until they become a challenge to do,* Emma's mind-wandering continued. *Something as simple as scratching an itch, when you have to hold still on the model stand, suddenly becomes the most important thing in the world when you can't do it.* She drew her attention back to the room. Noticing that Erasmus had picked up his brush again, she all but snapped to attention.

"M... m... maybe... I... c... could... g... g o... w... with you?" Elsbeth suggested. Suddenly, her face brightened. "M... maybe w... we c... could g... go to D... Disney... W... World instead?"

Erasmus thought on this a moment. He was getting up in years; he reasoned. Who knows how many more excursions he and his granddaughter would get to enjoy together?

"M... Mother... w... won't... c... care," Elsbeth continued. "S... since I w... was... g... going to be spending the w... w... weekend w... with y... y... you, anyway."

From what little Emma saw of Edwina, Elsbeth's mother, she imagined she'd be delighted to have Elsbeth be someone else's problem for the weekend. It was almost as if Edwina saw her daughter as a burden. And it was obvious that Erasmus did not.

Just then, there was a loud jingle of the tall French door leading into the room, followed by the obvious vibration of someone tugging and pushing the door back and forth, willing it to open. This was followed by a loud knock. "Father, are you in there?"

It was Edwina.

"Yes, just a moment," Erasmus called. To Elsbeth, he said, "Go let your mother in, won't you?" Elsbeth reluctantly nodded and went to unlock the door.

Edwina burst in, all but knocking her daughter over. "Why was the door locked?" She demanded, eyeing Emma on the model stand, as if she had something to do with it.

"I locked it because some people don't know how to knock before entering a room," Erasmus chided, never lifting his eyes from the canvas.

"What?" Edwina grew annoyed. "Hmm... never mind." She thought for a moment. "Now I forgot why I came in here... oh, right," she remembered. "Butler let me know that you and some of the staff are taking the private plane to Florida tomorrow."

"Yes, that's correct," Erasmus confirmed. 'Butler' was his personal companion, Ferdinand. Edwina had trouble remembering their names, so instead she referred to them by their job titles.

"May I ask why?" Edwina crossed her long arms, her deep red lips dropping in a grimace.

"Yes," Erasmus answered simply.

"Yes, what?" Edwina replied.

"Yes, you may ask why," he chuckled.

"You are an impossible man!" Edwina complained. "Fine. Why are you suddenly taking a trip to Florida?"

"It's a business—" Elsbeth started to answer before her grandfather interrupted.

"I'm taking Elsbeth to Disney World. Kind of a spur-of-the-moment thing."

"But I thought you were going to the theater this weekend? I had it on my calendar."

"We were, but then we agreed it would be more fun to visit Belle and the Beast in Disney World instead of seeing them on Broadway."

"Why wasn't I informed of this?" she demanded. "I'm only the girl's mother, after all."

"It w-was m-my f-fault M-Mother," Elsbeth choked. "I asked g-grandfather to take me."

Before Edwina could protest, Erasmus continued. "Grant an old man a trip with his only granddaughter while he's still healthy enough to do it?"

Edwina thought on this a moment, tucking her chin, her sharp nose pointed toward the floor. If Emma wasn't mistaken, she could have sworn the tiniest of smirks crossed the woman's lips and her eyes flashed as if she'd suddenly had an idea.

"Please, M-Mother—" Elsbeth began.

Edwina held up her hand and Elsbeth fell silent. "I agree. In fact, Father, you must let me help you pack. I'll arrange for Chef to go with you too and call in a security guard to accompany you."

"Please, Edwina," Erasmus protested. "Why would I need a personal guard for a simple weekend trip?"

"Because you're one of the richest and most important men in this town, even bigger than that blowhard, Astor Ellis. And," she added with as much feeling as she could muster, "I worry about you."

Emma cringed at the mention of Astor Ellis. At one time, the young business executive had been secretly seeing one of her friends, before her friend met with an untimely death. It was right before Astor married his socialite fiancé, Portia LaMonte, and stepped into his father Byron's role at B. A. Ellis Industries. *Erasmus was nothing like that family,* Emma decided. She didn't like him even being compared to them.

"Fine," Erasmus agreed. "I'll let you arrange everything, my dear. Just make sure Ruth doesn't forget my health bars and tea. She'll know which ones I like."

"Ruth?" Edwina thought a moment. "Oh, right... Chef." Edwina made a mental note of her name, though she was likely to forget again. Much like Astor Ellis' mother, Gretchen Ellis, Edwina found most people unimportant and quite forgettable. *Must be a strange dementia among the wealthy,* Emma thought, absentmindedly letting out a snort. Suddenly, everyone in the room was focused on her.

"Ahem," Emma coughed slightly, averting her eyes.

Edwina opened the door and yelled, "Chef!" loudly, before adding, "Ruth! Could you come in here please?"

"Yes, ma'am." A small, rotund woman with gray hair and a large mole on her cheek bounced in the room. Her hair was tucked in a hairnet. She held a wooden spatula in her hand.

"There's been a change of plans," Edwina barked.

"Oh?" Ruth questioned. Emma couldn't help but hone in on the mole as Ruth spoke. It bobbed up and down as Ruth moved, as if it had a life of its own.

"Yes, Father is going on an unexpected business trip. He says you are aware of his preferred health snacks?"

"Oh, yes, ma'am," Ruth answered, shooting Erasmus a pleasant smile. "The purple berry ones at midday, and the green almond cherry bars at bedtime." She tapped a finger on the side of her temple. "I remember everything."

"Thank you, Ruth," Erasmus praised. "Knew I could count on you... Oh," he remembered, "And could you make sure Ferdinand picks up a valerian root tincture for me before I leave? I always have trouble sleeping the first couple of nights after traveling."

"Certainly, Sir." Ruth smiled, awaiting further instruction.

"Eh, Ruth," Edwina paused as if the name were somehow inconvenient. "That will be all."

"Yes, ma'am." Ruth nodded and quietly left the room.

"Elsbeth," Edwina commanded. "Come along so Maid can help you pack your bags." The maid's name was Ivy, but Edwina hadn't bothered to learn her name, either.

Elsbeth nodded, reluctantly following her mother out of the room like a shadow.

"Oh, one more thing, Edwina," Erasmus remembered.

Edwina stopped suddenly, and Elsbeth almost walked right into her mother. Annoyed, Edwina stepped around her.

"Yes, what is it?" she growled impatiently.

"Since you're going through the trouble of packing for me, can you please ensure that Ferdinand compiles my favorite records to bring along?"

"Records?" Edwina was confused, as her mind went toward documents and bank statements.

"Yes," Erasmus confirmed. "Records... Harry James Band, Bing Crosby, and Georgie Stoll... Just ask Ferdinand. He's got them all organized."

"Why on Earth would you need your record collection for such a quick trip?"

"Because I find them relaxing," his voice cracked. "What does it matter to you?" The raised pitch of his voice let Edwina know she had gone too far.

"Very well," she agreed. "But you *will* be back in time for your birthday dinner Monday night, won't you? Chef and I are planning a very special menu."

"Yes, we'll be back in time." Erasmus paused to admire his work. *One of my better pieces,* he mused. Edwina eyed her father, impatiently ringing her hands.

"Can I at least see what you're working on that seems to consume all of your attention these days?" Edwina asked as she shot Emma a look. Something was bothering her. Emma wasn't sure what the woman thought of her, but she suspected it wasn't good.

"Of course," Erasmus answered, surprised. "I didn't think you had an interest. Here it is, then." He backed away so that Edwina could lean over his shoulder for a closer look. "In fact, we should be finished after today's sitting. Probably just need to put the finishing touches on it this evening," he mused.

Emma was crestfallen. It was less about the impact of what not working for a wealthy man would have on her dwindling bank account. She was more disappointed about not getting to spend time with Erasmus, of whom she'd grown very fond.

Edwina eyed the painting critically, peering back and forth between Emma and her portrait. "Lovely," she began optimistically before adding, "You flatter her."

Emma bit back a response.

"No," Erasmus answered. "I don't think I did her beauty justice at all."

That only served to annoy Edwina more. She quickly grabbed Elsbeth's hand.

"Ow!" Elsbeth complained. Her mother ignored her, dragging her out of the room and all but slamming the door behind her.

Erasmus smiled at Emma. "I think we're good for today. But I'm afraid I will need to take a raincheck on lunch."

"That's okay; I understand," Emma answered, standing and stretching her arms over head before twisting from side to side to get the kinks out from hours of sitting in one position. "Maybe we can plan to meet up when you get back in town next week."

"I would like that very much," Erasmus answered. "And perhaps your gentleman friend will join us, too." Emma nodded as she headed toward the adjacent room to change back into her street clothes. "Oh, and Emma?"

"Yes?" She doubled-back.

"Perhaps we can discuss my retaining your services for a new project... if you have the time?" A sigh of relief rushed over Emma.

"Of course," she beamed gratefully. "I would like that very much."

As she left the room, there went Erasmus, humming again, occasionally breathing out a few of the lyrics, starting with 'Pennies from Heaven' before morphing into 'Bye, Bye, Blackbird'. *"Pack up all my cares and woe, here I go, winging low..."*

"Bye, bye, Blackbird." Emma sang out from the other room.

Erasmus turned back to Emma's portrait and smiled.

CHAPTER 6

Friday Flight

Two Months Ago on a Flight to Florida; 1998

Erasmus Vandenberg; his personal servant and butler Ferdinand; Elsbeth's private cook and personal companion Ruth; Elsbeth Ions; a contract pilot named Bernie; a flight attendant and licensed co-pilot Vivian; and a security guard named Hugo all boarded Erasmus' private jet at around 4 p.m. on Friday.

Bernie was a pleasant enough, tall fellow who insisted on wearing an official pilot's uniform from his commercial airline days, even though no one asked him to. A man of few words, he settled into the cockpit, and no one heard from him for the remainder of the journey.

Vivian, a medium-sized, Barbie doll-shaped woman with hair tied back into an uncomfortable-looking bun, offered Erasmus an arm to guide him to his oversized seat. Not needing assistance, he grasped her arm because it wasn't often that a woman sixty years his junior took an interest in him. "I'm turning 89 in a few days," he smiled at her.

"Well, happy birthday, Mr. Vandenberg," she smiled sweetly at him, flashing a row of perfectly whitened teeth as she ushered him to his seat.

Elsbeth clunked her carry-on bag, hitting each of the seats on each side of the aisle despite the wide space between them. This included her grandfather's aisle seat, and her own. She finally settled into her spot across the aisle, next to Erasmus. Ferdinand followed behind her with Elsbeth's oversized travel bag and Erasmus' customized rolling record case, followed by Ruth, who actually pushed a serving cart up the ramp and onto the plane so that Erasmus could have a home-cooked meal, even though the flights to and from Florida and New York were only a few hours each way. Ruth liked to be prepared and even had an extra supply of groceries so that Erasmus could stick to his strict diet while staying in his Florida home. The plane's kitchen was tiny for the rather round woman, but she pre-prepped the proteins, grains and vegetables and could make it work. She quickly put all her food items away, with the help of Ferdinand, before the two took their places in seats behind Erasmus and Elsbeth. Ferdinand kept Erasmus' precious record collection, which held a dozen of his favorites securely at his feet.

Then there was Hugo. No one knew anything about Hugo except that he came highly recommended at the Steele Security Service company, and he seemed particularly large and formidable for someone with a small and humble-sounding name. He wore sunglasses on the plane, though it wasn't sunny, and insisted on a place behind all the travelers where he had a clear eye on them, as well as all the plane exits.

Elsbeth took one look at Hugo and furrowed her brows. Everyone else on the plane was very pleasant, but Hugo wore a chronic and intimidating grimace.

Erasmus let out a yawn as he settled into his seat. He smiled pleasantly at Elsbeth, who smiled warmly in return.

Not long afterward, they received an all-clear and departed. Once in the air, Ruth set to work in the kitchen, making a hearty fish stew with Vivian serving the passengers. Ferdinand, while skilled in many areas, was useless when it came to food prep, and got to sit back and catch up on the latest issue of the *New York Times*. Elsbeth clenched her seat nervously. Despite her apprehensiveness on planes, she couldn't look away and found herself watching the city below, through her window with an odd fascination, as the tall buildings became smaller and smaller.

Not more than an hour and a half later, Elsbeth remembered something and quickly removed her seatbelt. She spun around, kneeling into her seat to address Ruth, who was sitting directly behind her. "You forgot grandfather's snacks," she whispered. Oddly enough, the further away she got from her mother Edwina, the better her speech became.

"Ah," Ruth smiled, remembering. "Got them in the back, along with his nightly tea. Why don't you help me fetch them for him?"

Ruth took no time in preparing his evening tea, held in a small, Japanese-style ceramic cup. She added a few drops of valerian root, just as Erasmus preferred. She unwrapped his nutrient-rich, company branded green snack bar, placing it on a matching plate. Vivian joined them, but Elsbeth insisted, "No, let me." Without the assistance of a serving tray, Elsbeth carefully carried Erasmus' tea and evening snack from the back of the plane to his seat in the front. She paused while Vivian, close at her heals, opened a small, fold-out table for the older man. Elsbeth put the items down carefully before returning to her seat.

"Thank you," he smiled, tugging at a small cotton blanket he had settled around his lap. *Why are planes always so cold?* He wondered.

Within about fifteen minutes of his evening snack, he yawned a second time. Vivian quickly removed the food items, closed the serving table, and helped recline his seat. As if on cue, Ferdinand produced a small pillow from his seat behind Erasmus.

"Excuse me, Sir," Ferdinand whispered as Erasmus looked over his shoulder.

"Oh, thank you, Ferdinand." Erasmus lifted his head gently while Ferdinand tucked the pillow under his master's head.

"Can I offer you a nightcap, Sir?" Vivian asked. "A martini, perhaps?"

"Oh no," Erasmus shook his head. "Never touch the stuff."

"I'll take one," Elsbeth chimed in. Vivian was surprised, looking to Ruth for confirmation that it was okay to serve Elsbeth a cocktail. People seemed to forget, given her childlike nature, that Elsbeth was in her early twenties.

Ruth nodded. "She'll be less fidgety that way."

"Vodka martini?" Vivian asked.

Elsbeth nodded. "With an olive," she added.

"Certainly," Vivian agreed, disappearing into a small bar area in the back of the plane. She returned minutes later with Elsbeth's cocktail.

Elsbeth took a sip and wrinkled her nose. She wasn't entirely certain she even liked alcohol, but it seemed to calm her nerves, so she endured the unpleasantness of it.

"Elsbeth," Erasmus addressed his granddaughter, tiredly, as she lifted the toothpick housing a large olive and sucked on it. "You won't mind if I close my eyes for a short nap, will you?"

Elsbeth shook her head as she gnawed at the olive. In fact, a nap sounded like a very good idea to her, too. She handed Vivian her now-empty glass and reclined her own seat, settling beneath a cotton blanket similar to her grandfather's.

Bernie's voice suddenly chimed in from the speakers overhead as the plane shook gently. "We're experiencing a few unexpected weather conditions," he explained calmly. "Nothing to worry about, but it may take us a bit longer to land. Might want to strap in with your seatbelts fastened for the next fifteen minutes or so, just to be on the safe side."

Ferdinand and Ruth obliged. Elsbeth, who would have normally been alarmed, nodded off groggily. Erasmus appeared sound asleep across the aisle. Vivian took a free seat behind Ruth. On a commercial flight, she might have asked Elsbeth and Erasmus to return their seats to an upright position during these weather conditions, but she knew how fussy private plane owners could be and silently strapped herself in. Hugo, who everyone almost forgot about, hadn't moved the entire flight, silently keeping watch over the passengers.

In a three-hour flight that took almost four-and-a-half due to bad weather and vying with other small crafts for a runway in which to land, they finally touched down in Florida.

The humidity hit them full force as Vivian opened the cabin's main door.

Elsbeth untangled herself from her blanket, and upon noticing that her grandfather was still asleep, slipped her seatbelt off and bounded to her feet.

"Grandfather," she whispered, touching his arm. "We're here." She recoiled at its stiffness. She shook it again gently. His arm was ice cold. It was only then that she noticed his lips were an odd blue. "Grandfather!" she yelled louder, alarmed.

Hugo pushed his way past the other passengers and shook the older man gently before checking his pulse, just to be sure. "He's dead," Hugo proclaimed in surprise.

The last sound everyone remembered before a swarm of medics and the police arrived was Elsbeth's blood-curdling scream.

CHAPTER 7

Edgar

Two Months Ago in Ireland; 1998

Edgar Vandenberg had an unusual love of reptiles, amphibians, and arachnids, but not just any kind. He preferred the dangerous ones, such as the Western Taipan snake, the golden poison dart frog, and the Brazilian wandering spider. Sadly, none of them existed in Leitrim. You might stumble upon a false widow, but Edgar didn't find those particularly interesting.

And so, when he was tending to his uncle Erasmus' Ireland estate, he had his collections especially flown in. Most were now well-preserved under glass, having met with untimely deaths years prior, and were of no danger to others. But Edgar enjoyed having his collection with him — some under glass countertop cases and some in shadow box displays he had installed in the wall of the main study. He found them sort of... comforting.

Edgar was only in his early sixties but, between his hunched shoulders and the way he shuffled his feet when he walked, most people assumed he was Erasmus' brother, not his much younger nephew. Edgar didn't care.

Appearances meant nothing to him, and he was content to wear the same outdated tweed jacket that he'd had for the better part of four decades. He had a long white beard that he remembered to groom once a month, usually about the time the footman, Isaac, offered to draw him a bath to "relax his weary shoulders from all those long hours in the study." It was Isaac's polite way of telling him that his hygiene habits — or lack thereof — were beginning to offend the other servants in the house.

"Well, Myrna." Edgar went over to a long cage, where the one other living thing in the room resided. "Guess it's feeding time... again," Edgar laughed as he poured a bag filled with assorted dried spiders, crickets and beetles (that he also had especially flown in) into the cage. From its burrow under a pile of dirt, twigs and dried out leaves, a little pygmy shrew emerged, eagerly attacking the delicacies.

Edgar had rescued Myrna after a peregrine falcon accidentally dropped her from a great height on the lawn. Since shrews rarely live more than a year anyway, Edgar saw no need to return her to the wild in her injured state, instead choosing to care for her for the remainder of her days... an oddly compassionate thing to do for someone obsessed with toxic predators.

There was a knock at the door.

"Come in," Edgar called, smiling one more time at Myrna before replacing the lid to the cage.

"Sorry ta interrupt yer work," Isaac said in his thick Northern Irish accent upon entering the room. He was wearing a wool jacket and cap, both soggy from the rain. His coat dripped a little onto the floor, but neither of the men seemed to notice it. Isaac removed his cap and began twirling it uncomfortably.

"That's alright," Edgar replied. "I was just about to break for lunch, anyway." Edgar grew up in New York but spent most of his adult life dividing his time between Leitrim and County Kerry. His accent was a little more subtle than Isaac's. Edgar closed a few dusty books he had open to chapters about the mating rituals of the funnel-web spider. "Care to join me?"

Isaac eyed Edgar curiously. He'd worked for five households in his long lifetime, and this was the only one where the master deigned to dine with the help. Isaac found Edgar's informality both refreshing and slightly uncomfortable. Still, the two men had developed a kind of working-friendship over the years.

"Eh, no, t-ank yew," Isaac replied. "Em... I'm afraid I have some rather bahd news for ya. It's about yer uncle, Erasmus."

Edgar nodded. "He's dead, isn't he?"

His matter-of-factness took Isaac aback.

"Yeah," he answered sadly. "But, how'd yew know?"

Edgar thought a moment. "He's up in years. I suppose by the way you came in here twirling your cap and looking forlorn. I surmised that the news wasn't good when you mentioned Uncle Erasmus by name."

"Are yew, okay, Sir?" Isaac asked, concerned.

Edgar sighed, surveying his collection of reptiles, amphibians, and arachnids. "Yes," he finally nodded. "Uncle wasn't a young man, and—" he tapped the glass overtop the displayed taipan snake, "everything dies eventually."

A small tear formed in the corner of Edgar's eye. He tipped his head and brushed it away, lest Isaac witness his display of emotion.

"Still sahd though, yeah?" Isaac persisted. "He was a gewd man."

Edgar tapped the glass once again and nodded, his back toward Isaac. "That, he was," he agreed. Edgar seemed lost in thought for a few moments.

Isaac cleared his throat uncomfortably. "T-ere's a bit more, I'm afraid," he continued.

Edgar rubbed his forehead. It was much easier dealing with dead insects, reptiles, amphibians, and the like. Feelings attached to people were far more complicated. "What is it?" He turned to face Isaac.

"Yer presence is requested at the reading of ta will," Isaac explained. "It's being held at the end of next month at the Manhattan residence.

"Oh, that will never do," Edgar protested, closing his books. "I have far too much to do here with my research. Erasmus would have understood."

"Erasmus no doubt would," Isaac agreed, scratching the underside of his chin. "But what about yer family, yeah? Your cousin Edwina will be there. So will your cousin Baxter—"

"That boy," Edgar objected, "is *not* part of the Vandenberg line. As for my cousin Edwina... horrid woman. Why can't she just mail out copies of the will instead of being so melodramatic by hosting an official reading?" he scoffed.

"Cousin Elsbeth will be t-ere," Isaac tried again.

Edgar's face dropped. "Oh," he answered quietly. He had a soft spot for Elsbeth. She was a lot like him... introverted, stuck in their own little fantasy world most of the time. He always imagined that if he had had a daughter, she would be quite a bit like Elsbeth. "Poor girl," he mused. "Erasmus was more than her grandfather. In many ways, he raised her when Edwina's deadbeat husband ran off with that hoochie coochie dancer from Vegas."

"Aye." Isaac held back a grin. "But knowing Edwina, could yew exactly blame 'em?"

Edgar snorted. "Do I feel sorry for that Bible-toting, holier-than-thou, control freak cousin of mine? Absolutely not. But he didn't need to abandon Elsbeth. She was innocent in all of it."

"I agree wit yew, Sir," Isaac answered. "But surely you'll go... far her sake?"

"Isaac," Edgar chastised. "When did you become such a softie?" He made his way to the door.

Isaac patted him on the back. "I've always been a softie, Edgar. T-at's why I've put up wit yew for so long."

Edgar laughed. "Well then, I insist that you join me for lunch. Formalities be damned!" He paused, eyeing Isaac for emphasis. "You'll hurt my feelings if you don't."

"Well, we can't have t-at, Sir," Isaac finally agreed. "Ya know some-tin', Edgar."

"What is it, Isaac?"

"Yer just like yer dad, God rest his soul. And even more like Erasmus."

"Well," Edgar thought it over, closing the door. "That's a fine compliment, indeed."

CHAPTER 8
Protection Spell

Two Months Ago in Manhattan;1998

"Emma." Dennis fumbled with the key to her apartment.

Emma looked up from her place on the kitchen floor as Dennis fought with the copy of the key she had given him 'for emergencies only.' She had forgotten about it. Instead of standing, she crossed her legs under her and buried her head in her hands, sobbing. Around her was a circle of stones that took up nearly her entire kitchen floor: black tourmaline, clear quartz and obsidian. In front of her was a bowl of burning white sage.

"Everything okay?" Dennis continued, finally getting the lock to budge. He swung the door open wide, concerned. "Why did you cancel our date? Why didn't you answer the door? And why—" He stopped when he saw her crying from the center of the room, "are you surrounding yourself with lots of gemstones?" He bounded toward her.

"No!" She stopped him. "Not over the circle," she warned. "Use the entryway."

Off to the side of the circle, nearest the stove, was a small gap in the stones. That was apparently the way in. He crossed the gap, pausing to grab a paper towel from the roll sitting on the kitchen counter. He knelt down next to her, putting a hand on her back. "Em?" he asked quietly. "What's going on?"

Emma sniffled. "What's going on is that I'm a jinx!"

"What are you talking about? Does this have something to do with Erasmus?"

"Yes," she blurted out. "You should stay as far away from me as possible, Dennis... Dennis—" She peered up at him. He handed her the paper towel. Accepting it, she said, "I just realized that in the two months we've been dating..."

"Seven," Dennis corrected.

"Seven?" Emma sniffled. "Has it really been that long?"

"It has definitely been that long," Dennis sighed. He refrained from pointing out that in that time they hadn't gotten much past kissing and some over-the-clothes fondling, but things were going so well otherwise that he didn't want to press the issue. Although, the lack of sex was sometimes agonizing.

Emma seemed unaware of this. "Well," she continued. "In the seven months we've been dating, I realize that I have no idea what your last name is." She wiped her eyes and then nose with the paper towel.

"McCleary," he answered hesitantly.

"Irish?" Emma asked.

"Yes? Are you going to hold that against me, too?" He joked, lightly, considering how much she disapproved of lots of things about him.

"No," she sniffed. "That's fine."

He sat down next to her, folding his legs under him, and hugging his knees to his chest so as not to disrupt the circle of stones, nor accidentally burn himself on the incense burner. "So, what's all this about you being a jinx?"

"Well, Ursula's dead. Clarissa is dead. And now Erasmus! Everyone I get close to ends up dead!"

Unfortunately, they had gotten wind of Erasmus' death nearly two months ago from the tabloids. No one from the family thought to phone Emma and let her know, but maybe that was too much to expect. After all, she was only a contracted art model. Still, she thought it might have been nice of someone to reach out, particularly since she had previously been coming to the house weekly.

The story disappeared as quickly as it came to light. All six people on the flight the night Erasmus died, somewhere between New York and Florida, were interviewed, and his death was quickly ruled as age-related heart failure. He was cremated a month later, and that was that.

Just yesterday, a Mr. Lundy, one of Erasmus' lawyers, reached out to Emma and asked if she would be present for the reading of the dead man's will. No one in the family was privy to its contents and had received no copies prior. It seemed to be something Erasmus had been adamant about when he drafted it. Emma couldn't understand why she would have been included and thought maybe Erasmus left her one of the portraits he'd painted of her over the past six months.

Which would have meant that Erasmus musta amended his will quite recently, Emma thought to herself. *Why would he do that?*

"Em," Dennis reasoned, drawing her out of her thoughts. "Erasmus was nearly 90 years old. Maybe it was just his time."

"Just seems strange that it was not long after he hired me to model for him, is all," Emma reasoned.

"I'm sure that was just a coincidence." Dennis paused as he surveyed the stones. "So, what's all this about?"

"Protection spell," she explained.

"Ah," he nodded. "Well, you see? I'm in the circle with you. We're safe."

"We'll see," Emma answered miserably. Somehow, this new communication from Mr. Lundy sent Emma back into a tizzy.

Dennis put his arm around Emma's shoulders and pulled her toward him, resting the side of his cheek on the top of her head. "I promise you, Emma, everything is going to be okay."

CHAPTER 9
The Will

Three Weeks Ago in Manhattan; 1998

Finally, the day arrived when family and friends gathered at the late Erasmus Vandenberg's luxury condo in the city for the reading of his will. Emma wore an uncomfortable black business suit over a cream-white polyester shirt, along with a distinctly out-of-place pair of yellow, all-weather boots. Perhaps the woman at the Macy's counter misunderstood that she was looking for something people wear to the reading of a will or maybe a funeral. Instead, the woman set her up with something called a 'power suit.' Emma did not feel powerful. In fact, she felt very awkward. The boots didn't help.

The weather was terrible and unusually muggy for a summer day, even by New York standards. Her face dropped when she saw that everyone else in the room had dress shoes on. There was a neat line of boots in the doorway, along with an umbrella rack filled with soggy umbrellas. She hadn't thought to bring a change of shoes because she didn't really have anything else, other than sandals and sneakers — neither of which would have been appropriate for this setting. She didn't think to ask the lady at Macy's about footwear.

Even Dennis, who had taken the day off from work to support her, had on a pair of faux-leather shoes. He had the good sense to roll up his trousers before they arrived and unroll them before she rang the bell to Erasmus' suite. Save for a few wrinkles around his ankles, it didn't look *too* bad.

Ferdinand eyed her curiously as she wiped her feet on the doormat before entering, and then quickly snapped to attention. "Good to see you, Emma," he greeted her. "You must be Dennis," Ferdinand smiled. "Nice to meet you... though, I wish it were under better circumstances."

Dennis' eyes brightened as he glanced at Emma. It was nice to know that she had been talking about him. She shot him an annoyed, *Don't let it go to your head or nothin'* look.

"Nice to meet you." Dennis put out his hand.

Ferdinand eyed it, bowed slightly, and said, "Right this way."

Dennis dropped his hand. Coming from a blue-collar family, he had no idea what to expect from the upper crust of society, particularly people who had their own year-round servants.

Emma and Dennis followed Ferdinand quietly into the room. It was the library, just at the other end of the hall of the spacious room where Emma used to model for Erasmus. The library was set up with several long couches, armchairs, and a few upright dinner chairs that had been relocated from the kitchen and dining area to accommodate the more than a dozen family members in the room. The walls were lined from side-to-side and top-to-bottom with books, along with a sliding ladder on each wall, making the books on the highest shelves accessible.

Emma and Dennis took a seat next to the least intimidating person in the room... Elsbeth. She furrowed her eyes slightly before moving over to give them space on the couch beside her. Elsbeth rocked nervously back and forth. She didn't like this many people in one place and kept staring at the clock above the mantle on the opposite wall, as if counting the minutes until it would all be over.

Her eyes brightened when her second cousin, Edgar, arrived. She was about to rise to greet him when her mother clamped a hand on her arm.

"Stay where you are," Edwina hissed from her high-backed armchair situated right next to the young woman. "Don't make a scene."

Elsbeth nodded and dropped her eyes. She had no idea how getting up to give her cousin a hug was a 'scene,' but, as usual, she found it best not to argue.

Edgar, accompanied by Isaac, shuffled into the room and spotted Elsbeth sitting there with down-turned eyes, flanked by her mother and two people he didn't know. Isaac motioned toward a seat on the couch adjacent to them, and the two men sat. Edwina eyed Isaac as if to protest. After all, there was a clear order of things — at least in her mind. The primary family came first and branched outward based on blood relatives versus relations by marriage only, and how far removed people were from her father, Erasmus Vandenberg. Friends sat behind the relatives. The 'help,' however, stood behind those who were seated. Or, if they were getting up in years, they took a seat far behind the family circle. By Edwina's estimation, Emma and Dennis should have been at least two rows back, but she was trying not to make an already uncomfortable situation worse. That was exactly how she described the death of her father in her mind, too... uncomfortable. She fidgeted with the gold cross around her neck.

Ferdinand took his place next to Ruth, the chef, and Ivy, the housekeeper. There were other servants standing behind various relatives, but Emma didn't know who they were nor what function they served.

Several whispers ensued as family members eyed Emma curiously. Finally, one rotund woman leaned forward and asked, "Forgive me, my dear. But who are you?"

"Emma Post," a boisterous voice called from the entryway. Everyone's eyes shot up, startled. There stood Baxter Baker, next to a tiny twig of a woman wearing a low-cut, skin-tight, wrap black dress that hung about mid-thigh, with three-inch heeled shoes and a ridiculous fascinator hat that should only surface during the Kentucky Derby, at Royal weddings or on Halloween. The woman eyed Emma suspiciously and wrapped a tiny hand around Baxter's arm, gripping it possessively.

"Who's she?" The woman asked, flicking a strand of her long brown hair over her shoulder with her 'non-possessive' hand.

"That's what we were wondering," another older man in the room answered before squinting his eyes at her. "Lisa?" he asked.

Baxter cleared his throat. "No, Uncle Morris," Baxter explained. "This is Rachel. Surely, you've heard me talk about her… many times."

Morris cleared his throat. "Oh yes," he played along. "Now I remember. Nice to see you."

Baxter and Rachel took a seat in chairs across from Elsbeth, Emma and Dennis and behind Morris and the woman who was presumably his wife.

"We still don't know who this woman is," another young woman sitting behind Edgar said, "nor the man sitting next to her. Were you a friend of our dear Erasmus?"

"Yes—" Emma began.

"This is Emma," Edwina interrupted. "She was Erasmus' art model… a protégé of sorts."

"Protégé?" Morris's wife eyed Emma suspiciously. "Are you an aspiring artist?"

Emma's face grew warm as everyone in the room turned their gaze in her direction. Dennis took her hand and squeezed it supportively.

"No," she admitted. "At least I have no plans to become an artist at this moment."

"Then… why are you here?" The woman asked.

"Stella, please," Morris whispered. "Leave it alone."

"Why should I leave it alone?" his wife answered. "I'm a member of this family, aren't I? Certainly more than this protégé of Erasmus'! Why shouldn't I be able to ask questions?"

Dennis clenched his jaw angrily, fighting back a response. In relationships past, he would have attempted to defend his partner's honor. But Emma was different. She preferred to fight her own battles, and he knew it.

"She's here because I asked her to be here." A very large and formidable looking man, wearing a three-piece suit and carrying a briefcase, entered the room. A younger man, also in a suit, stood at his heels.

"Mr. Lundy," Edwina acknowledged. "Thank you for coming."

"Of course." He tipped his head slightly to one side. "And may I present Mr. Adani? He is assisting me today with the reading of the will."

"Oh!" Stella's eyes widened. "Your Erasmus' lawyer. Is that it?"

"One of them, yes," Mr. Lundy answered simply.

Ferdinand sat Mr. Lundy and Mr. Adani on two upright dining chairs sandwiched between the couches where Emma and Edgar sat. Mr. Lundy set his briefcase on the glass coffee table and clicked to open it.

"As I was saying." He motioned his head toward Emma. He seemed to make a lot of gestures using just the nod of his head. "I asked Miss Post to be here as today's reading of the will pertains to her, too."

Once again, the attention fell on Emma. Elsbeth eyed Dennis holding onto to Emma's left hand for support and watched as Emma clenched it in return, sucking in her breath. It was then that Elsbeth did a curious thing. She took Emma's right hand in hers and squeezed it. Emma looked at the young woman, surprised. But Elsbeth merely pursed her lips and nodded at her, as if she understood exactly how Emma was feeling. Emma's heart lifted slightly as she gripped Elsbeth's hand lightly and smiled.

Edwina slapped Elsbeth's arm, motioned toward her hand, and Elsbeth quickly retrieved it, setting both her hands in her lap. She looked apologetically at Emma, who merely smiled warmly back and furrowed her brow as if to say, *It's okay. I get it.*

"If everyone is ready?" Mr. Lundy asked, retrieving the will from his briefcase.

"Not just yet, Mr. Lundy." Edwina stood. "We are a God-fearing family," she began.

Edgar rolled his eyes. Baxter stifled a grin, covering his mouth so no one could see. He then turned his gaze toward Emma with eyes that suggested he was thinking less than godly thoughts about her. Rachel pinched her fingers into his arm until he winced, returning his gaze to the small woman at his side. To Edwina, Rachel nodded, removing one hand from Baxter's arm long enough to make the sign of the cross.

Edwina smiled approvingly. She wasn't Catholic, mind you. But the girl was behaving acceptably. *She can be molded,* Edwina thought.

"Everyone, join hands." Edwina insisted, and like it or not, those in the room attempted to join hands, as well as they could sitting in varied circles. Edwina took Elsbeth's hand, and Elsbeth, once again, took

Emma's. This time, her mother did not protest. Her mother had a strange order of things, Elsbeth decided.

"Dear Lord, we come to you as humble servants, here to carry out your will—" Edwina began. Most in the room bowed their heads. Edgar's knee bobbed up and down uncomfortably. Elsbeth resisted rocking back and forth lest she hear about it from her mother later. Dennis bowed his head and closed one eye, using the other to glance at Emma, gauging her reaction. Emma stared straight ahead, expressionless. "We know we are sinners who do not deserve your mercy—" Emma shifted in her seat but remained silent. "But through your grace, we will move through this darkness and into the light."

After what seemed like an eternity, Edwina ended the prayer with an "Amen."

Everyone in the room said, "Amen," except for two people: Edgar, who sort of grunted, and Emma, who didn't even attempt to mouth the words. Everyone dropped their hands.

"I didn't hear you say Amen, Emma," Stella pointed out. "Are you an atheist?" she asked.

"No," Emma answered. "I have my beliefs."

"And what does that mean?" Stella challenged.

"It means just that," Emma answered simply.

"But are you a friend of Jesus?" Ruth leaned over Emma's shoulder, whispering helpfully into her ear as if encouraging the woman.

Emma glanced back toward Ruth. "Can't say that he and I are acquainted, no," she answered flatly.

There was a collective gasp from the room.

"Then, what are you?" Stella persisted.

Baxter fought back a laugh. Unlike Dennis, he *did* feel the need to intervene. "Oh, come on, people! Are we really here to interrogate this poor woman and find out her religious perspective, or are we here to find out what's in Uncle Erasmus' will?"

Emma looked at Baxter gratefully before casting her eyes toward the floor. Inside, Dennis' heart boiled. *Should he have said something?* It now bothered him that Baxter had come to her rescue when he had not. Emma was unaware of Dennis' internal struggle.

"Now, may I begin?" Mr. Lundy asked tiredly.

"Of course." Edwina motioned to him. "Please go on."

"I, Erasmus Vandenberg, being of sound body and mind—" Mr. Lundy began.

For the next several minutes, the family sat, mesmerized. Mr. Lundy began with the charities to which Erasmus was leaving some of his fortune, and how much.

"Such a generous man." Stella nodded at Morris, approvingly. Several nodded in agreement.

Then, they reached the critical part...

"Now, I'll read the rest of the will, leaving out sensitive information, such as personal social security numbers, and such—"

Edwina nodded in understanding.

"I leave my New York estate to my granddaughter, Elsbeth Ions, along with a trust fund in an amount to be disclosed on her twenty-fifth birthday. I name Edwina Vandenberg the executor over my New York estate until the time she decides to turn over such executorship to Elsbeth Ions, or when Ms. Ions reaches her twenty-fifth birthday — whichever comes first."

Edwina clenched her jaw but said nothing.

"To my nephew, Edgar Vandenberg, I leave my Leitrim estate in Ireland, along with $500,000 dollars to renovate the property in any way he deems necessary." The lines around Edgar's eyes softened, his face dropping in a way that suggested he was both surprised and touched. Isaac touched his arm supportively. Then, upon seeing several people eye the gesture quizzically, he pulled his hand back.

Edwina put her arms on each side of the armrests on her chair and dug her fingers into them like talons.

"And finally, to my cherished friend, Emma Post, I leave my St. Petersburg, Florida estate and all of my remaining wealth, including all property, vehicles, money, and assets in my name."

"What the hell?" Morris, Stella, and several family members stood angrily. Rachel, who was not even a family member, looked at Baxter, infuriated. Baxter merely shrugged his shoulders.

"What did you do?" Stella pointed an accusatory finger at Emma. "Were you sleeping with him?"

Emma's face grew red and contorted. "No! I most certainly was not!"

"Then why else would Erasmus leave the bulk of his estate to you?" Morris challenged. "Why not Edwina?"

Edwina wondered the same thing, though, she had her suspicions. Elsbeth and Edgar looked up at each other briefly. Elsbeth was terrified, but Edgar merely gave her a gentle smile. She took in a deep breath and sat back in her chair.

"There's a bit more," Mr. Lundy explained as his assistant, Mr. Adani, handed him another paper.

"More?" Edwina asked. "I assume this has something to do with Vandenberg Nutraceuticals?"

"It does," Mr. Lundy agreed. "Ms. Post is now the primary shareholder of the company and technically in charge of both manufacturing plants and their operations."

Baxter sat up, a look of surprise and amusement across his face. He and Emma locked eyes for a long moment, something that escaped neither Dennis nor Rachel.

"I can speak with you privately about the best way to proceed," Mr. Lundy assured Emma, who now had a lump in her throat that felt so large she assumed it was visible on the outside of her neck. "But my law firm and all of Erasmus' personal accountants and advisors are at your disposal. You might also want to speak with Mr. Baxter Baker over there about company operations." Baxter, upon hearing his name mentioned, smiled in Emma's direction. It was as if he were thinking, *Looks like I'm getting that dinner date with you, after all, Ms. Post.*

Emma's eyes widened in fear. Mr. Lundy leaned in and whispered, "Don't worry, Ms. Post. It'll be all right."

At that moment, an unusual hush fell over the room. It was as if they all realized something at the same moment. They could contest the will if they wanted to, but for the time being, this stranger, Emma Post, had access to nearly all of Erasmus' fortune and, consequently, their future.

"Well," Edwina finally stood and addressed the room. "We did open in prayer and put our faith in the Lord," she smiled. "And we know he works in mysterious ways."

~

Outside of what was now Elsbeth's condo, several reporters hovered, snapping photos of the black limousines that lined up out front. They swarmed Erasmus' family and friends as they emerged from the lobby of the high-rise.

"What happened?" One reporter shoved a microphone into Mr. Lundy's face, who merely answered, "Client-lawyer privileges, I'm afraid." Mr. Adani swatted at the reporters like flies, trying to get them to back away. He clearly wasn't as polished at dealing with the press as Mr. Lundy was. Mr. Lundy glanced over his shoulder, watching as Emma and Dennis slunk away to the parking garage around the corner. He smiled to himself, satisfied, before getting into one of the limos. No one recognized the two, and so blending in with pedestrians on the busy sidewalk at midday was easy.

One reporter spotted Edwina as she purposefully strolled toward Ferdinand, who opened the door for her. "Edwina Ions!" He shoved past the others and blocked the entrance to the passenger seat.

Her eyes narrowed. "It's Vandenberg," she hissed. "Ions is my ex-husband's name, and he's dead to me."

"Sorry, Ms. Vandenberg," he corrected before pressing on. "Can you tell us what happened today at the reading of your father's will?"

A short distance away, Morris' indignant wife whispered, "How did they know what was happening today?"

"I dunno. Maybe the limos out front gave it away?" Morris shrugged.

Baxter walked slowly behind them, giving Rachel ample time to tiptoe along with her tight dress and impossible-to-walk-in heels. She eyed her companion curiously. Sure, he was handsome, but somehow not as handsome now that he seemed far less affluent at this moment than he was before the reading. Baxter glanced at her and grinned, as if reading her thoughts. Her face grew pale. Baxter turned his attention momentarily toward Edwina. Baxter Baker was more than a pretty face. He was far shrewder than anyone gave him credit for, assuming he got by in life on his looks and his family's money... or his late aunt's money, as relatives were so fond of pointing out.

He knew exactly who alerted the press. He turned his back on Edwina as soon as she began her obviously practiced reply to the media, "Obviously, some members of our family were surprised. However, given Erasmus' generous spirit, and how much he cared for the less fortunate, we couldn't be happier for Ms. Post..." Baxter helped Rachel into one of the limousines, shutting the door after she'd finally settled inside. "Yes, that's right." He could hear Edwina clarifying. "Emma Post... spelled just as you'd expect... P... O... S... T."

CHAPTER 10
Murder?

One Week Ago in Florida; 1998

~

Ortega wasted no time reviewing the case that Emma and Dennis had now dropped into his lap, all of which began after that unexpected phone call from Dennis just a week prior. But he had to tread carefully. After all, he'd promised Nancy that once he'd retired, there'd be no more late nights, no more abandoning her on holidays and special occasions, and particularly no more pacing the house drinking and smoking a cigar while he berated himself over what clues he may or may not have missed. Most importantly, he promised to be there for her.

On the other hand, he reasoned to himself, it hadn't escaped his attention that Nancy had managed to fill up her social calendar quickly once they'd moved here. At first, she tried to include him, but he wasn't particularly interested in bridge games, golf, cocktail parties... or people, in general. He liked his solo lifestyle with one or two people he could reach out to if he ever felt lonely... which was almost never. After a while, Nancy just stopped inviting him. He would have been fine with that, except there was something distant about her lately. He couldn't put his finger on it.

Well, he decided. *I think a special moonlit dinner on Anna Maria Island might be just the ticket.* He made a mental note to phone a bistro he knew and make reservations.

But for now, he justified his agreeing to help Emma and Dennis. After all, he wasn't supposed to officially retire for at least another six years. So, there should be some easing into retirement, he felt. Plus, he wasn't technically a detective anymore, either. This was just a one-off instance where he was helping a young couple out.

He just had to make sure Nancy didn't find out about it.

Ortega poured himself several ounces of bourbon on the rocks, while he reviewed the notes he'd fervently taken following the newest and rather arduous phone call, this time between both Emma and Dennis. He laughed as he recalled bits of the conversation just one hour earlier...

"WOULD YOU GIVE ME THE PHONE?" Emma had protested. "That's not what I said at all!"

Dennis reluctantly handed her the phone, only to interrupt a second later. "I don't want you anywhere near Baxter Baker!" Dennis grumbled at her suggestion, grabbing the phone and stretching it over his head so Emma couldn't reach.

"Oof!" Ortega heard Dennis proclaim as something clattered to the floor. There was a shuffle before Emma returned to the call after she had presumably punched him in the gut in order to retrieve the phone.

"Detective Ortega," Emma huffed into the phone. "Wouldn't you agree Baxter is the best person to shed light on this situation?"

From Ortega's perspective, the couple was approaching this case like amateurs. He would have expected this from Emma but not from Officer Dennis. *The boy is letting his Johnson get in the way of solid police work,* he thought to himself.

"Listen," Ortega interrupted them. "Put me on speaker phone," he ordered.

"Uh," Emma replied. "This is a landline, and I have no idea if it can even do that. I'll have to call you back on the cell phone thingy."

"You do that," Ortega suggested. "Then, call me back." He didn't wait for a reply before hanging up. Moments later, his cell phone rang.

The first thing he heard was Dennis' impatient voice saying, "Not that one, this one." Eventually, both Emma and Dennis had figured out how to use the speakerphone feature on Dennis' still relatively new cell phone.

"Can you both hear me?" Ortega confirmed.

"Yes, we can hear you," the two answered.

"Good, because I'm only going to say this once. If I'm going to help you, I need to glean as much information as I can from the both of you. Therefore, we're treating this like a formal investigation."

"Well, that's good—" Dennis began.

"Let me finish, Officer Dennis." Ortega reverted to the old days. It worked. Dennis fell silent. Ortega continued. "I want to interview one of you—and I mean only one of you — at a time. While I do that, I want the other of you to go somewhere else, someplace out of earshot."

"My apartment is a studio," Dennis complained. "And it's raining outside!"

"I don't care where you go... hide in the bathroom with the fan on for all I care," Ortega raised his voice in annoyance. "All I care about is taking a statement from each of you without the other interrupting."

Dennis sighed. "I'll go first," he relented. He shut the speaker phone feature off and handed his phone to Emma. "Call me when it's my turn." Dennis retreated into their bathroom, turning on both the fan and the shower radio. Once Emma was certain he was out of earshot, she told Ortega everything she knew.

THE CALL TOOK MORE than an hour, but Ortega refused to hang up until he was certain he'd gleaned every possible bit of information about Erasmus and everything surrounding his death.

Erasmus Vandenberg was as healthy as a horse and scheduled to turn eighty-nine just three days after he died. He had no known cardiovascular issues, no diabetes, nothing.

The coroner ruled the cause of death congestive heart failure given his age, and since he had fallen asleep at such a high altitude, no one would have noticed if he had any breathing issues. Therefore, the informal ruling was that he, quite simply, died of old age.

There had been no formal investigation and no autopsy.

"So, who would have cause to off old Erasmus?" Ortega said to himself. "And why?"

On his short list of possible suspects was someone from the Vandenberg family. Edgar and Elsbeth were named in the will. *What if they knew they stood to collect a lot of money once he was gone? But why chance it at Erasmus' age? And what about Edwina Vandenberg? How was she to know she had been left out of the will? Or did she? Even worse, what if she had an inkling it was going to be amended, but she got to him too late?*

"I'm missing something obvious," he chastised himself aloud, taking another sip of bourbon. "Why on a plane?"

He heard Nancy's car pull up the drive. He quickly hid his notes in his desk drawer and left his office to head out to the kitchen to greet her.

"And what have you been up to, my dear?" Ortega smiled at the assortment of shopping bags Nancy carried in, all from the nearby Ellenton Outlet stores. He gave her a peck on the lips.

"I needed a new tennis outfit and bathing suit," she answered. "And I know what you've been up to," she laughed. "Already hitting the booze?" She set the bags down. "You're not working on a case, are you?" She teased.

He let out a cough. "No, just pacing the floor until my lovely wife returned home... Didn't you just buy a new tennis outfit last week?" He eyed the purchases curiously.

"Yes, Mr. Nosey Pants." She touched his nose playfully. "But Dominic says I have real potential if I practice, so I've added in a few more lessons. You don't mind, do you?"

"Potential for what?" Ortega wanted to know. "Are you trying for Wimbledon?"

Nancy rolled her eyes. "I know it may not mean much to you," she answered. "But I wouldn't mind competing in some local tennis matches, just for fun. Gives me a sense of purpose."

"The whole raising a child and having a husband doesn't give you purpose?" He stopped himself before pointing out that she had made him give up his purpose when he was forced into retirement. Ortega saw the look on her face and instantly regretted it. "I'm joking, my Dear." He wrapped his arms around her and gave her a kiss on the cheek. "Of course, I support anything that makes you happy."

"Did you remember to pick up some lettuce and chicken breast at the store today?" She broke from his grip and walked over to the refrigerator.

"Uh," he tried to cover. "I'm sorry, I forgot."

"Well, what have you been doing all day?" She eyed him suspiciously, opening the refrigerator and finding it in the same condition, with the same contents, as when she left.

Ortega thought quickly. "Actually, I didn't forget. I was going to surprise you later, but the truth is... I was hoping to take you to that French bistro on the island tonight."

"Well, that will never work," she answered. "You have to book well in advance for that place." Ortega knew that too, but it was that or admit he was working on a case. "Besides, what's the occasion?"

"Can't my loving you be occasion enough?"

"You're hiding something." Nancy squinted at him.

"Nancy, I'm wounded." He gripped his heart melodramatically.

"Never mind." She waved a hand at him, chuckling. "Let's just order a pizza and watch a little TV tonight. There's a new *Sex & the City* on."

"Gre-e-at," he answered unenthusiastically. He couldn't understand why Nancy, who was so adamant about getting out of New York, was enthralled with a very unrealistic show about single women living in Manhattan, who could afford very large living accommodations and an ostentatious lifestyle on what — a writer's salary? At least, he seemed to remember one of them was a writer. But then, Nancy was born into money, so it's likely she never did have a clear sense of what 'normal' people could or could not afford.

Ortega picked up the phone to dial for a pizza. He eyed one of Nancy's many bags, one of which had 'factory outlet' written on it.

"That's it," he accidentally said out loud. "It had something to do with his visit to the factory."

"What was that, Honey?" Nancy asked.

"Er, nothing," he lied. "Just thinking about a story I read in the newspaper."

Someone didn't want Erasmus visiting his Florida factory, but why?

CHAPTER 11

The Disagreement

Present day in Manhattan; 1998

~

"If there's nothing going on, then why am I not invited?" Dennis grumbled loudly so she could hear him on the other side of the apartment.

"Because," Emma explained, inserting small pearl earrings into each of her pierced ears. "You're a cop. He's not going to speak freely if you're there."

"Right, that's why Baxter Baker specifically asked you to come alone." Dennis crossed his arms, leaning into the counter in Emma's kitchen while she finished getting dressed on the other side of the divider that led to her bedroom. "What makes him think you wouldn't just come home and fill me in on everything that happened?" Emma emerged from behind the screen. Dennis' eyes widened when he saw her. "And *that's* what you're wearing?"

She looked down at her jeans questioningly. "What the hell is wrong with what I'm wearing?"

"You don't need to dress so... provocatively," he accused.

"Dennis," she chastised, "I'm wearing stonewashed jeans and a black t-shirt. And look," she pointed to her feet. "Flats… I don't even own heels… which you probably already have noticed. How is this provocative?"

"It's just in those jeans, you look a little…" Dennis struggled to find the right words. "Curvy."

Emma snickered, swaying her hips seductively as she sauntered over to him and gave him a playful kiss on the lips. "You are cute," she said.

"And you're trying to distract me." He touched her nose with his forefinger. Although, if he were to admit it to himself, he was suddenly having trouble catching his breath.

"Did it work?" she asked.

"No." He was adamant. "Okay." He blushed. "Maybe a little… But that's not the point. I don't trust him."

"Then we agree on something," Emma pointed out. "I don't trust Baxter Baker either, but he's the best person to shed some light on the Vandenberg family business and why the hell Erasmus left me most of his fortune."

"What makes him the best person?" Dennis challenged.

Emma pursed her lips. "Because he's the only one who will talk to me, except for Elsbeth, but I'm not sure she'll be much help. And he said there's stuff I should know about the family."

"Fine," Dennis relented. "But at least take this." He handed her a large, handheld cassette recorder. "What the hell am I supposed to do with that?" She looked at her outfit.

"Well, don't you have a purse you can hide it in?"

"And what, leave it sitting in my bag, recording the entire time? Not sure how that'll work getting a good audio recording, and besides…" She hit the record button and waited while it beeped loudly. The gentle whir of the cassette wheels turning could be heard. "Kind of obvious. Anyway, even if you follow us, you still won't be able to hear what's going on inside."

"Fine, then we go back to my original plan. I like that one better, anyway."

"Sitting in a van outside and listening in?" Emma's voice went up in pitch. "What's with the cloak and dagger bullshit? And don't you think a wire is a little extreme?"

“You said yourself, you think Erasmus was murdered. I would much prefer to be close by in case anything happens. And the wire was Detective Ortega’s idea. You *were* the one who asked me to reach out to him.

After multiple telephone calls over the course of the week, it came to light that while the Vandenberg family may have publicly praised Erasmus’ decision to leave most of his fortune to her, they completely shut her out of their life. The closest she got to them was the lobby of the suite, now owned by Elsbeth Ions.

“W... what does she w... want?” Elsbeth’s voice could be heard over the intercom.

“Elsbeth,” Emma had leaned over the counter, while the concierge eyed her with a mixture of surprise and annoyance. “I need Baxter’s number.”

“Why?” Elsbeth demanded.

“If you let me come up and see you, I can explain.”

Suddenly, Edwina’s voice boomed through the intercom. “That won’t be possible, Ms. Post,” she answered curtly. “We don’t even have Baxter’s number and couldn’t give it to you if we wanted to.”

That wasn’t entirely true, and later that evening, Emma received an anonymous message on her landline. The voice was disguised. It told her to stop by the lobby in the morning and that Baxter Baker’s business card would be left with the concierge, along with instructions to give it to her. Sure enough, his business card, the one he had tried to give to Emma, but that Elsbeth had intercepted, was waiting for her at the counter.

Well, at least one member of that family likes me, she thought. Though she couldn’t understand why Elsbeth felt the need to disguise her voice. But who else might have phoned her? Emma chalked it up to the young woman’s fear of her mother finding out.

Meanwhile, Dennis tried to voice his concerns to the police detective that replaced Ortega, but the response was that there was simply not enough evidence to support opening an investigation. Dennis made the mistake of suggesting that this is exactly the reason for investigations... to find the evidence, and nearly got himself suspended.

Instead, he asked for a temporary transfer and made plans to move with Emma to her new estate in St. Petersburg, Florida.

Baxter Baker appeared to be the only family member willing to talk to her and only if she agreed to a date. Ortega suggested the wire and that Dennis be close at hand. Ortega wasn't fond of potentially putting Emma in harm's way, but she was adamant. He had to admire her for this. After all, why not just take the money and keep your mouth shut? She had a level of integrity that few possessed.

DENNIS WAITED for an eternity for Emma to respond to his question.

Emma sighed, "Okay. Okay. I'll wear the damn wire. We'll at least be able to play the audio for him afterward... assuming I get anything useful. So how do we do this? Better get moving, so I'm not late for my 'date with destiny.'"

"That's not funny, Emma," Dennis sulked. "And, as far as the process..." He blushed again. "Er..."

"What?"

"I'm gonna kind of need you to take your shirt off?"

"And you think Baxter Baker is a player? This is the best line I've ever heard." Before Dennis could protest, she stripped her black t-shirt off to reveal a lacy matching bra.

Dennis paused for a moment, staring at her. His chin nearly dropped before he caught himself.

"Hey, Dennis McCleary." Emma snapped her fingers at him. "My eyes are up here!" She bit back a grin as Dennis, very *uncomfortably*, taped a wire to her. She giggled. "That tickles," she complained, squirming a little.

"Sorry," Dennis answered, trying to focus. "Kind of hoped my first time seeing you in lacy underwear would be under different circumstances."

"Don't worry, Dennis," she smirked. "There will be plenty of time for that soon enough."

CHAPTER 12
Date With Destiny

Present Day in Manhattan

Frankly, Emma was expecting something a little more upscale for her 'date with destiny' with Baxter Baker, particularly after he made such a point of bragging about his money and influence when she'd first met him. Instead, they sank into the booth in the corner of a very ordinary Irish pub in lower Manhattan.

He'd told her to dress casually, but somehow she expected to be whisked away on a private boat or something. She was mildly disappointed. Somehow, that made her feel guilty, as if Dennis could hear her thoughts from the police car he had parked outside. He would have rather used an unmarked van, but the car was the only way to ensure he could stay in one place for any length of time on the busy New York strip without causing suspicion.

Meanwhile, inside, Baxter asked her to meet him early and, as such, the pub wasn't crowded, save for a few early drinkers at the bar and several men playing cricket, occasionally arguing as they scratched out numbers on the chalkboard. There were hundreds of holes in the wall around the dart board from players who thought they played better drunk instead of sober — they were wrong. A small, skinny man with an oversized guitar case strapped across his back paused at the bar to grab a few unshelled peanuts. He glanced in their direction momentarily before turning his attention back toward the small stage in the corner. It was only a foot high and barely large enough to fit more than about five musicians on it at a time. He cracked open the peanuts and popped them in his mouth and then dropped the shells directly on the floor before stepping on stage.

Emma looked at the shell-covered, dusty floor distastefully. No one but her seemed to notice or care, except for Baxter, who merely slunk back into the corner of the booth, covering his mouth so she couldn't see him grinning at her.

A server came by with menus and to take a drink order. Baxter settled on a Guinness on tap.

"Iced tea," Emma ordered, just as the guitarist launched into an acoustic version of Eric Clapton's *Change the World*.

"Long Island Iced Tea?" the server confirmed, talking above the music.

"Wow," Baxter nodded approvingly as the server dropped the menus on the table. "I like your style, Emma Post."

"No," Emma corrected, "regular unsweetened iced tea." The server looked visibly disappointed. Non-alcoholic drinks and non-drunk patrons rarely led to overwhelmingly high tips.

Baxter waited patiently as Emma eyed the menu. Between the burgers, Shepherd's pie, bangers and mash, there was nothing on the menu that she could actually eat. Even the salads were smothered in turkey and bacon.

"Excuse me a moment," Baxter said. "You look at the menu. I'll be right back." Emma nodded as he slid out of the seat and approached the bar. He whispered to the bartender as he slipped something across the counter. The bartender nodded, turned quickly and retreated to the kitchen behind him.

"What was that about?" Emma asked accusingly.

"Oh, nothing," Baxter replied innocently.

"You should know that I have a lead stomach and strong constitution," she answered fervently. "So, if you're trying to sneak liquor, or worse, into my drink—"

"I'm not." Baxter held up his hands. "I promise."

Moments later, the server arrived with Baxter's Guinness and Emma's iced tea. She silently grabbed the menus and left.

"Why did she do that?" Emma asked. "We didn't even order."

"And what off that menu would you have ordered?" Baxter asked.

"Iceberg lettuce, hold the... everything," Emma admitted.

"Give me a little credit, Ms. Post. I chose this location for anonymity, not for the cuisine. And I promise you, if given the chance," he leaned in and whispered, "I can do better."

At that moment, the server returned, setting down two plates. "Cauliflower and potato soup," the server announced, "soda bread and a side of hummus. Anything else?" she asked.

Baxter shook his head. "I think that will be all, thanks." She turned on her heels and walked away.

Emma looked up, surprised. "This wasn't on the menu."

"I know," Baxter smiled, adding a pinch of salt to his soup without even tasting it first. If it had been Dennis, she would have chastised him for his salt consumption, and for adding it without checking first to see if the dish even needed more salt. But Baxter wasn't Dennis, so she bit her tongue. "Again, give me a little credit, Ms. Post. I specially requested it based on what I assumed they'd have in the kitchen. You're vegetarian, correct?"

"Yes," Emma's eyes narrowed. "But how did *you* know that?"

"Unfortunately," Baxter confessed. "I probably know a lot more about people than is good for me, yourself included."

"What is that supposed to mean?" Emma asked, finally taking a sip of her soup. She hated to admit it, even to herself, but it needed more salt.

Baxter leaned in for his quiet confession. "It means that I'm taking a big risk in being here with you, Emma Post."

Emma eyed him suspiciously. "Is that a line?" she finally asked.

"No." He leaned back, once again pressing his forefinger against his mouth to hide his amusement. "But I wish it were."

"And what is *that* supposed to mean?" She tried again, agitated.

Baxter took a moment to slide his hands underneath their table, as if searching for something. He even bent his head awkwardly to survey the underside.

"Did you misplace your chewing gum?" Emma asked sarcastically.

"Saving it for later?" But she knew why he was looking. He was searching for a bug or some other listening device. She fidgeted slightly, absentmindedly touching the left side of her shoulder, where the wire was taped to her, recording everything for Dennis, and eventually Ortega, to hear. Baxter eyed her curiously, his gaze falling on her shoulder. Emma sucked in her breath, worried that she'd given herself away.

"Erasmus went to Florida to shut down the production plant for Vandenberg Nutraceuticals," he finally confessed, averting his gaze.

"Why on Earth would he do that?" Emma was curious.

Baxter leaned back in the booth, taking a long breath in and out before continuing. "Because he suspected that our biggest client, the Church of Infinite Love, was taking Vandenberg health bars, beverages, and other snacks and infusing them with their own..." he cleared his throat, "special sauce."

"Special sauce?" Emma asked.

Baxter sighed. "Think, Emma," he chastised. "What do you *think* I mean?"

"The Church of Infinite Love," Emma thought a moment. "Didn't they have a show that aired on Sundays? Seemed to have a stadium-sized audience."

"Yeah, and that was filmed during one of their 'Holy Days' where members from nearly a hundred locations across the United States and Europe met at a rented-out arena in Texas."

Suddenly, images of the church's early-morning TV broadcasts, which often featured people magically being healed of pain from old war injuries, flashed before her eyes.

"You mean, like... drugs and potentially mind-altering substances?"

"Now the witch is catching on," he smiled. "Thought that, given your bent for magic, you would have figured that out sooner."

Emma huffed as she used a spoon to scoop some of the hummus onto a piece of bread. "Why the heck does everyone assume I would — obviously — know about such things?"

"Well, being a pagan and all—"

"Kind of a broad category," she explained. "Just cuz I don't fit into the Judeo-Christian belief systems, doesn't mean that I necessarily smoke peyote, drink ayahuasca or take hallucinogens. And it certainly doesn't mean I'm a witch."

"Well, are you?" Baxter asked curiously, taking a sip of his beer.

"I prefer the term animist."

"And what does it mean to be an animist, exactly?"

Emma took a bite of her food, careful not to chew too loudly, given that the microphone was so close to her mouth.

"It means I have respect for the natural world and see all energy as sentient."

Baxter knocked on the table. "Even this table?"

"In a way... look, Mr. Baker, while I'd love to talk at length about my fundamental beliefs, don't you think it's best if we focus?"

"My apologies," he offered, taking a sip of his soup. "I can't help it if you're fascinating."

"Why shut down the plant?" Emma ignored him, instead, changing the subject back to the reason they were both there. She ignored the flushed feeling in her face, hyper-aware that Dennis was on the other end of the microphone, probably turning red with anger and fit to be tied. "Why not just cut them off as clients, if his morality was getting the better of him?"

"I'm not sure," Baxter confessed, rubbing his forehead tiredly, before taking a sip of his soup. "Most of the churches were clean... I mean, as clean as a money-hungry cult *can* be. Erasmus himself used to make large donations at the end of the year... I assumed for tax purposes," he smirked. "To my knowledge, there were only a few locations with questionable practices. Maybe it was penance, or maybe he wanted to ensure that his legacy wasn't marred. Whatever the case, Erasmus was taking no chances that we would continue to turn a blind eye to the church's practices. He even went as far as to publicly denounce the church."

"Continue?" Emma asked, biting into her soda bread.

"You are very curious, Emma" He shook his head. "I'd be lying if I said I didn't have the tiniest inkling of poor practices... easily justified as we, technically, had nothing to do with what happened to our product *after* it sold."

"And that didn't bother you?" Emma questioned.

Baxter paused for a long time, as if sizing Emma up as a person.

Finally, he answered, "I am exactly what you think I am, Miss Post. Did it bother me? Yes. Was it enough to turn down a fortune? No. Turning a blind eye is easy when it doesn't affect you personally."

"So, what changed?" Emma asked. "Why are you telling me this now?"

He leaned toward her, taking one of her hands for emphasis. "Because now? Now it affects me personally."

Emma slipped her hand out of his. "I believe I told you, Mr. Baker, that I have a boyfriend." The heat in her cheeks rose enough to where she was sure it was visible.

"I meant, Elsbeth," he grinned, leaning in toward her shoulder. "And I'm aware of your relationship with the flatfoot." His eyes lifted to meet hers… he knew.

"What about Elsbeth?" Emma asked, blushing.

"Surely you've noticed that she's… different?"

"Yes, I assumed she had some sort of developmental or neurological disorder?"

"She might," he admitted. "But no one knows for sure because Cousin Edwina refuses to have her tested."

"Really? Why?" Emma was surprised.

"Because the Church of Infinite Love frowns on pesky little things like doctors and scientists." Baxter suddenly pulled a cell phone from his back pocket, glanced at it momentarily, and cringed before putting it away again. Emma recognized it because Dennis had acquired the same Nokia variety at the behest of Ortega. She really didn't understand the need to have a phone attached to one's hip at all times.

"You mean Edwina is—" She drew his attention back to the conversation.

"A very high-ranking leader within the church," he finished. "No doubt she feels she is being judged for having a daughter with mental challenges. She either failed as a mother, failed as a Christian, Elsbeth is possessed by a demon, or a combination of all three."

"Are you being serious right now?" Emma asked. "Demon possession?"

"I'm afraid I am," Baxter sighed. "Listen, as it turns out, I can't stay long. So, here's what you need to know. And if you speak to the authorities, remember that none of this... I repeat... *none of this*... came from me."

Emma leaned in. Baxter did the same. She could smell his aftershave... *Damn it!* She thought to herself, annoyed. *He smells... really good.* She pushed the thought away.

"Erasmus denounced the church about a month ago and, no doubt, stopped making 'charitable donations' to them. There's a good chance Erasmus was also planning to shut down *both* factories, the one in Florida and the one in Dublin. But it's the factory in St. Pete that you want to look into. That's the one selling to select congregations of the church... all of which happened to be under Edwina's district."

"Quite a coincidence." Emma shook her head.

"Indeed," he agreed. His eyes fell to her lips for a moment before he lifted them to meet her gaze, holding it there for a little too long.

"Well, should be easy enough." Emma tapped her fingers on the table. "Since I'm the main shareholder now."

Baxter shook his head, "Oh, Emma... Adorable, Emma. It's not going to be that easy. You're not going to be able to waltz right in and ask to see the books nor the facilities. You'll need to be a bit more discreet than that."

"Well, aren't you the Vice-President of Operations? Surely, you can help me."

He leaned in even closer, his face only inches from hers. "I'm afraid I can't."

"How are we doing over here?" The waitress returned with a paper bag filled with, presumably, take out.

"Ah, thank you. We're just fine — a check when you have a moment." He eyed Emma's half-eaten plate. "Did you want to take the rest of that with you?"

Baxter appeared to be in a hurry, suddenly, because he checked his watch... twice, only seconds apart, just to confirm he'd gotten the time right.

"You don't worry about me," Emma answered. "If you have somewhere to be."

To the server, Baxter confirmed, "Shepherd's Pie and a side of sausages to go?"

"Yes, that's right," the waitress nodded, handing him the bill. Without looking at it, he pulled a large wad of cash from his pocket and sandwiched it between the billfold. "I believe that should cover it."

The server's eyes grew wide and then immediately narrowed. Without leaving the table, she pulled out a marking pen and began checking off each bill now in her possession, as if looking for a fake. When she was satisfied, she smiled enthusiastically, flashing a large mouth with seemingly very thick teeth. "Well, thank you very much!" After a dramatic pause, she finally added, "Have a good night!" And all but ran away before he could change his mind.

"Shepherd's pie and sausage." Emma eyed him coldly.

"As I've already told you," Baxter explained. "I am exactly what you think I am. I've never tried to hide that from you."

Emma had no idea what to make of Baxter. He was a conundrum. He flaunted his money and then took her to the most mediocre pub in the city — a place that had not a single vegetarian dish, so he could gallantly order up something special for her — only to leave with a meat on a meat takeout platter. If he was trying to woo her, his courting methods were the oddest she'd ever seen.

Baxter leaned in. "Oh, don't take it personally, sweet Emma." He caught her gaze again, as if reading her thoughts. "I just need to make a hasty exit for a while." He paused a moment before adding, "I don't think you realize the risk I've taken talking with you this evening."

He slid out of the booth, brown paper dinner bag in hand. Before Emma could say anything, he leaned over and pressed a soft kiss on her lips, lingering for a moment. Emma was so surprised she didn't react. At least, that's what she told herself. If she were being honest, she would have admitted that, while he caught her by surprise, she leaned into it and kissed him back... and liked it. It was a momentary lapse of judgment that someone like Emma rarely made.

"Please be careful, Emma," he whispered earnestly, pulling away. "I don't think Erasmus' death was due to natural causes any more than you do, and I wouldn't want anything to happen to you."

She nodded dumbly. *Exactly how much of that had Dennis picked up on?*

"If things don't work out with your cop friend..." Baxter put his mouth near her shoulder, where he knew the wire to be. She shuttered a little as the warmth of his breath sent a few chills down her spine. "You give me a call."

For once in her life, Emma was speechless.

Before leaving, Baxter whispered, "You'll be the death of me, Emma Post."

CHAPTER 13
The Second Disagreement

Present Day in Manhattan

"What the hell was that about?" Dennis angrily removed his gun and holster, all but tossing them on the kitchen table of Emma's apartment.

"Hey!" she complained. "Be careful with that. I'm not exactly keen on having guns in this place to start with."

"Oh, I'm sorry." Dennis' face turned red. "Was I insensitive? Like you, when you were sucking face with some rich guy born with one silver spoon in his mouth and another up his ass."

"That's not at all what happened!" Emma protested.

"Then what did happen?" Dennis challenged.

"He leaned in to kiss me, and—" Emma paused.

"And what?" Dennis spat, sweat beginning to form around his brow. "Please don't give me the 'I was just playing along' crap!"

Emma had to think quickly. She wasn't keen on lying, but she was worried about what would happen if she told the *exact* truth. The *exact* truth was that Baxter Baker had kissed her, and — despite her better judgment — she liked it... a *lot*. But when she kissed him back, she remembered that she wasn't chronically single anymore. In fact, she most definitely... probably... had a boyfriend. This was a relatively new phenomenon for the fiercely independent Emma, so that exhilarating moment was coupled with... guilt.

"No," she answered carefully. "He kissed me... on my cheek," she lied. "I didn't push him away, which I probably should have. But, I was trying to get information from him so—"

"So... what?"

"So, I let him kiss me on the cheek and did my best not to flinch." She paused to gauge Dennis' reaction. "That's what you must have heard over the wire... his ridiculous breathing in my ear." She smiled, as if she and Dennis shared an inside joke.

He took the bait, which only made Emma feel worse.

"Okay." He put his hands in the air. "I'm sorry. I'm not the jealous type, it's just—"

"Just what?" Emma asked.

Dennis rapped his knuckles lightly on the table before looking up at Emma seriously.

"What are we Em?" he asked, sincerely.

"What do you mean?" Emma knew. A lump formed in the back of her throat. She wasn't ready for this conversation, and it had nothing to do with Dennis. She was gripped by a sudden fear that made her worry that she might never be ready.

"I mean..." Dennis hesitated. "Are we boyfriend and girlfriend? Are we exclusive? What are we? I heard you tell him you had a boyfriend, but you've never actually let *me* in on this small detail."

Emma thought fast, pulling from her mental directory of all the excuses men had given her over the years until a few helpful nuggets surfaced.

"Do we have to give it a label?" she finally asked.

"I'm sorry... what?" Dennis was confused.

"Why do we have to be confined to everyone's definitions of what relationships are? Can't we just enjoy each other's company?" The words flowed easily, but they didn't come from her. She couldn't remember which past love interest they came from, but they were definitely not *her* words.

It took Dennis a moment to gather his thoughts and harness his emotions. Finally, he answered, "Listen, Em. I don't want to rush you into anything you're not ready for. But the truth is, I *like* those labels." He moved toward her and pushed a strand of her hair away from her face and traced the line of her cheek with his finger. "I want nothing more than to be your boyfriend, exclusively." He paused to gauge her reaction. Dennis sensed fear. "But if you're not ready, I understand. I just hope that someday you will be."

Emma opened her mouth, but no words came out. She was having a difficult time understanding the heart-pounding rush of emotions she felt when Baxter kissed her, unexpectedly, to the warm, safe glow she felt every time Dennis was near her. The energy was different. That much she knew. But she didn't understand *how* or *why*.

"I should go," Dennis finally said, picking up his gun and holster. "I'll go through the recordings tonight and forward them to Detective Ortega... Er... Jo." Emma nodded as Dennis opened the door to her studio apartment. She opened her mouth to say something, but finding herself at a loss for words, she shut it again.

"Goodnight, Em," Dennis whispered. He leaned in to kiss her. Emma kissed him back. She wasn't trying to compare his kiss to Baxter's... she really wasn't. But she couldn't help it. Baxter's had this electric, lusty... let's-do-this-now vibe. But Dennis' kiss was different. His lips were warm, fleshy, and lingered in a comforting and warm way that said, "I'm in this for the long haul. And I'm here for you, no matter what."

Emma had never experienced this kind of kiss before.

CHAPTER 14
Rue and Emma

Present Day in Manhattan

Emma wasn't happy about meeting up with Rue Brennan and Darwin Fennec at their condo in Midtown Manhattan, any more than Rue was interested in having Emma Post in both her home and workspace. Rue Brennan and her former boss-turned-partner, Darwin Fennec (an unlikely love interest, cyber forensic consultant, and private investigator) were once again having issues with their official place of business in Battery Park. This time, there had been an electrical fire. Darwin was beginning to suspect that the landlord was planning these little emergencies for insurance purposes, but he couldn't be sure.

Rue met Darwin back when her then-boyfriend, Spencer Hargrove, hired Darwin Fennec to investigate a tech company that was competing with his own, unexpectedly dragging an unsuspecting Rue into the middle of a murder case in which she had been the primary suspect.

Under normal circumstances, Darwin might have requested that Emma and Dennis meet him at a new, up-and-coming co-workspace on the Lower East Side. It was one of the first of its kind and promised to be a great solution for small start-up companies and those displaced because of workplace disruptions, such as the one he and Rue were currently experiencing.

However, he'd developed an unlikely friendship with the newly retired Detective Ortega over the last year. While older and decidedly more jaded about life, Ortega had grass roots skills and powerful deductive reasoning that few could match. Meanwhile, Darwin understood the value of new technology to compensate for human error and had this chameleon-like ability to adapt to people and environments. Darwin had connections to, let's just say, the seedier side of town with people who would talk to him but never let a former cop in their confidence.

Had Nancy not convinced her husband to move to Florida, Darwin and Ortega would have been an unbeatable team. Therefore, when Ortega made a special request for Darwin and Rue to help Emma Post in her time of need, Darwin found it impossible to say, 'no.'

Rue was hoping for a redemption of sorts, as she was reminded that Emma still blamed her, in some way, for the death of two of Emma's closest friends. Even though Rue was an innocent in the events, she still felt the need to prove herself.

"Please, come in." Darwin welcomed Dennis and Emma into their home and make-shift office.

"Thank you, Mr. Fennec," Dennis acknowledged, pausing for Emma to enter the room first.

Emma bristled when she saw Rue.

"Please, make yourself comfortable." Rue motioned toward the couch, clenching her jaw ever-so-slightly.

Emma eyed the room hesitantly, wondering exactly how much one would have to earn to get to live in a place like this. She settled on *a lot.* Finally, she sank into the dark plushy couch. It was comfortable... much more so than the small, hard minimalist chairs in her kitchen and the bean bag sack in her bedroom. *Heck*, she thought. *It was even more comfortable than her twin bed.*

Most times, Emma didn't feel insignificant, not even when modeling for multi-millionaire Erasmus Vandenberg. But today was one of those days. If she'd only realized that less than a year ago, Rue had lived in a place that was only moderately nicer than Emma's current digs, she might have felt less insecure. Emma was also aware that money would be forthcoming, but she didn't entirely trust the news — at least not until some of it actually hit her bank account. Dennis took a seat beside Emma and placed one hand over hers. She usually disliked public displays of affection, but given her emotional state lately, first at the reading of the will, and now, she allowed it.

"Can I get you some coffee?" Rue asked with forced politeness.

"I dunno. Is it poisoned?" Emma retorted.

"Not usually, but I can add some if you like," Rue smiled sweetly.

"That's enough, kids," Dennis chastised in a joke that didn't land quite as well as he'd hoped. The two women glared at him. He coughed a little. "Uh, no coffee for me, thanks. I'm good."

Rue wasn't particularly fond of Dennis either, after his one investigation where he confiscated her clothes, sending her home scantily clad in a costume and oversized shoes from a modeling gig that got interrupted. *Boy,* she thought. *Emma can sure pick the winners.*

Darwin was too busy retrieving the audio recording from Emma's date with Baxter, while also setting up the Tandberg camera and video conference with Ortega, that he'd missed the exchange.

"I think we're about ready," Darwin announced.

Suddenly, the former Detective Ortega appeared on Darwin and Rue's oversized plasma TV like the magical Wizard of Oz.

He was in his living room, sipping what appeared to be a tumbler of bourbon. He was also smoking a Cuban cigar. Dennis found this amusing.

"Can you see and hear us okay, Ortega?" Darwin asked, lining up his webcam to capture the sitting area in the condo.

Rue took her seat in an easy chair beside the couch, crossing her legs and leaning forward, curiously. She still couldn't quite fathom how you could have a video conversation with someone hundreds of miles away. To her, it was as if she were having a conversation with one of the actors from a movie. This was only the second time she'd experienced this phenomenon, as Darwin was still working out the bugs in the system.

"I can see and hear you just fine." Ortega took a puff of his cigar. "Especially you, Officer Dennis." He pointed a meaty finger toward the camera. "I can see the judgment in your eyes to see me drinking on the job. But may I remind you, I don't technically *have* a job anymore. Mr. Fennec is taking the lead on this case. I'm just here to support when possible."

"I wasn't judging, Jo," Dennis protested. "It's nice to see you relaxing a little, for once."

"Well, I dunno about relaxing." Ortega fidgeted in his chair. He was going stir crazy with all this retirement crap. "But let's just say, I'm trying not get as wound up about things as I used to."

"Well, that's just fine, Sir." Dennis smiled pleasantly. Somehow, a face-to-face video call, while not in person, had a deeper connection for Dennis than a disembodied voice on the phone line. Despite having multiple conversations recently, this was the first time that he felt truly connected to his ex-boss.

"What say we begin with a replay of Emma's conversation with Baxter Baker, a nephew by marriage and the VP of Operations for Vandenberg Nutraceuticals?"

Emma and Dennis exchanged glances. At Emma's behest, Dennis edited out the last part, where there was a kiss that was less innocent than what Emma let on.

Just then, the buzzer rang. Darwin, the only one in the room still standing, went to open the door. "Ah, Monique," he greeted one of his assistants. "You're just in time. We're about to review the audio from Emma's meeting with Baxter Baker last night. Please, come in and have a seat."

Monique was dressed demurely by 'Monique standards' wearing black slacks and a white blouse with a bright red scarf wrapped around her neck that matched her high-heel shoes. Before taking a seat beside Rue on the couch, she peered at the plasma screen and blew Ortega a kiss.

"Is that really necessary?" Ortega replied gruffly. Monique merely winked.

This was the first time Emma and Dennis had ever met Monique, so they didn't realize that on alternate days, he went by 'Monte.' He dressed according to his gender preference for the day, switching it up only when necessary for undercover work. All Emma knew was that something was different about Monique, but she couldn't quite figure out what. Monique sensed her confusion and found it highly amusing.

"Bi-gender," Rue leaned in and whispered, saving what she thought might be a considerable waste of time.

"You take the fun out of everything," Monique pouted.

"Don't start, Montgomery," Rue chastised, using his given name — which he hated.

"Trollop," Monique retorted.

Emma mocked, "Well, Rue Brennan, you appear to make friends everywhere you go, don't you?"

"Oooh." Monique flicked a wrist at Emma, showing off a perfectly manicured set of candy apple red nails and enough sparkly bracelets to light up Central Park at night. "Feisty! I love it!"

"Ahem," Darwin cleared his throat. "Shall we?"

Darwin replayed the audio from Emma's meeting with Baxter. Ortega pulled out a notepad and pen and began feverishly jotting down details of the call. Rue and Darwin had already logged their observations on their private server, and so they waited patiently for Ortega to finish.

"Thoughts?" Darwin finally asked. If he didn't know any better, he could have sworn that Ortega's eyes lit up at the prospect of a new case.

"Lots," Ortega answered, taking a sip of his drink before continuing. "Obviously, Junior here is afraid of what might happen to him for talking with Emma... Do we have any idea why he was suddenly in such a hurry to leave, though? Seemed rather abrupt."

"No," Emma answered. "He pulled a cellular phone out of his pocket... like the one Dennis carries. I'm guessing he saw the number of someone calling or received a text message? Anyway, he looked at his watch seconds later and then rushed us through dinner."

"Hmm," Ortega thought.

"Maybe whomever was on the call was letting him know they were on to him?" Darwin suggested. "After all, he was pretty convinced Erasmus Vandenberg was murdered, and was essentially outing the company for unethical practices."

"Or maybe he had a getaway plan in place, and once he was told it was time to go... he went?" Rue added.

"Maybe," Ortega nodded. "Or maybe someone was looking out for him and trying to warn him."

"Well, he knew I was wearing a wire," Emma offered. "But that didn't seem to bother him."

"What?" Dennis sat up abruptly. "Why didn't you tell me that?"

"Because," Emma lowered her voice. "You were already mad. Besides, what does it matter?" Dennis' face turned a little pink. He sucked in a deep breath and sank back into the couch, hands balled into fists and resting on his knees.

"Strange," Ortega furrowed his brows, "that he'd be fine with being recorded, but suggested that he was putting himself at risk being there."

"Not if he planned on vanishing," Darwin reasoned. "If this ever turns into an official case and it goes to trial, and we can't find Baxter to testify, then this is all we've got."

"Same is true if someone offs him," Monique suggested, sucking on a nail.

Something in Emma's stomach dropped. She didn't like Baxter Baker, but she somehow didn't like the idea of something happening to him even more.

"So, where do we go from here?" Dennis asked. He was all about the practical next steps.

"May I?" Darwin asked Ortega.

"Please," Ortega handed the proverbial floor to Darwin.

"I think we start off visiting one of the main Northeastern branches of the Church of Infinite Love. It's located in a small town in rural Pennsylvania. Rue and I can manage that. Then, perhaps when Emma and Dennis make it to Florida, your team can investigate the main nutraceutical factory that Baxter suggested... undercover, of course."

"Wait," Monique protested. "Then what am I supposed to do?" She pouted a little. "I could go undercover at one of the church's special healing ceremonies they are so fond of sharing on Sunday morning television. They would love me," Monique smiled seductively. "I can ask them to pray the gay away and then transform into Monte, right before their eyes!"

"While we all appreciate your flare for the dramatic," Darwin answered. "I've got research I need you to do."

"Boring," Monique sighed. "But fine. I'm the best researcher you've got at the moment, since your sister-in-law, Ashley, got herself preggers again."

Rue bit her tongue. She was mighty fine at investigative research herself... though no one had Ashley's mad ethical hacking skills. But after giving birth to twins, she ended up pregnant again soon afterward, leaving her little time to support the team at the moment.

Darwin ignored the 'preggers' remark and continued. "I need you to see what you can dig up on the church. Specifically, if they were adding a 'special sauce' to their supplements, drinks, and energy bars. We need to find out who was affected by it, any legal troubles, illnesses, lawsuits, that sort of thing."

"I'm on it, boss," Monique agreed.

"What am I missing?" Darwin asked Ortega.

"Not much, from what I can tell so far," Ortega answered. "Except one vital question."

"What's that?" Darwin asked, surprised. He thought he'd been thorough.

"Why take him out on an airplane to the factory?" Ortega asked. "Why not at home or in Florida?"

"To cast suspicion on the passengers on the flight?" Rue suggested.

"But no one suspected foul play," Darwin replied.

"To make it harder to investigate? You'd be looking at a federal investigation versus a state one." Ortega offered an answer to his own question.

"But wouldn't that draw more attention?" Darwin suggested.

"Ahem," Monique coughed politely. "May a gal offer an opinion?" Both Rue and Emma found this mildly annoying. None of the other gals in this room felt they needed to ask for permission to speak.

"Spit it out," Ortega answered brusquely.

"Only sometimes," Monique winked. Ortega's expression let Monique know he was not amused. "Well," she continued. "Maybe that was the only time the murderer would have had access to Erasmus."

"Actually, that's good thinking," Ortega had to admit.

Suddenly, keys could be heard jingling in a lock from a door behind where Ortega sat. "Shit!" he exclaimed, snubbing his cigar out in an ashtray sitting on the table in front of him.

"Are you smoking again?" A woman's voice asked as Nancy could be seen entering the main doorway and now stood behind Ortega in their kitchen.

"Yes, but it was a special occasion," Ortega lied. "Darwin and Rue are expecting. We were just having a celebratory smoke. You remember I told you about Darwin Fennec and Rue Brennan — the last case I was on before our move?"

Nancy peered over Ortega's shoulder and smiled into the camera. "I remember," she answered. To the camera she bellowed, "Congratulations guys!" But then the corners of her mouth dropped. "Why are you the only one smoking, dear?" She shot a suspicious glance in her husband's direction.

"Uh, Rue has terrible allergies, and we thought the second-hand smoke might be bad for the baby," Darwin lied in an attempt to cover for Ortega.

"Hmm, interesting," Nancy answered. "And here I thought that was a ritual saved for men pacing outside of a hospital nursery."

"Well, times are changing?" Darwin tried again, the pitch in his voice shifting slightly.

"Oh, Darwin. Stop covering for my husband. I know when he's full of shit." She paused. "So why are you really on this call... It's not a case is it, because you promised—" her voice raised as she squeaked out the last bit.

"No, Honey," Ortega tried to calm his wife. "It's not like that. Officer Dennis just asked me to share a bit of knowledge with him based on my experience. It's for a case *they're* working on... has nothing to do with *me*, I promise. Come here." He pulled Nancy into his lap. Sitting on one of Ortega's thighs, she peered into the camera and asked, "Is this true, Dennis?" She leaned so far forward that her face took up the entire screen. "I know you wouldn't lie to me."

Dennis cleared the lump that was forming in his throat. This time, Emma took his hand for support. Technically, it was *mostly* true. He had been hoping Ortega would take the lead on the investigation, at least on the Florida side. But since nothing much had happened yet, he wasn't *exactly* lying. "That is true, Mrs. Ortega," Dennis nodded emphatically. "This is my fault. I asked for Detective Ortega's advice."

Nancy squinted at Ortega and wrinkled her nose at him. "That better be all you're doing," she warned, before playfully giving him a kiss on the bridge of his nose. "I'll leave you to it, then." To Ortega, she added, "I'll be upstairs if you need me."

Once Nancy was safely out of earshot, Ortega continued. Beads of sweat now formed on his brow. Instead of wiping them away, he took another sip of his quickly dwindling bourbon. Little of the ice remained frozen.

"As I was saying," Ortega whispered loudly. "There's not much missing except... you might wanna find out more about Baxter's relationship with Elsbeth. Seems to have a soft spot for her. Curious if his sudden change of heart is truly related to her, or someone or something else."

"Good thinking," Darwin answered.

"And I'd like to find out why no one I contacted from the precinct in Manhattan agreed to investigate his death. They were convinced it was simply 'his time' and not the least bit open to the fact that it might not have been. I'm also befuddled as to why no one in the family is contesting the will."

"Let's gather what we can first," Ortega suggested. "Give them a reason to pay attention."

Dennis nodded.

"I'd like to propose one more question," Emma piped up. "Seeing as I'm the reason we're all here?"

Always about her, Rue thought. Though that wasn't entirely true, and she knew it. Rue was just feeling disagreeable.

"Of course," Darwin answered.

"Why is it you two," she pointed toward Darwin and then Rue, "are the ones visiting the Church of Infinite Love instead of sending Dennis in undercover before we head to Florida? Are you worried someone will connect him to me?"

"That's part of it." Darwin shot Rue a glance. "But, there's something else."

Rue sighed. She knew this was coming. She just wished she could have stalled a bit longer. Finally, she explained: "I happened to have spent nearly the first three decades of my life living at the Church of Infinite Love campus in Pennsylvania as a member before finally escaping to New York. And that was only because the police stormed our campus one night back in '96 after two young women went missing. I know exactly what to do, when we get to the church, and how to do it." After a long pause, she added, "I'm counting on Darwin here to make sure I don't get stuck there again." Even as she said it, chills ran up her spine. The thought of returning made her nauseated, but she had to go. In her mind, she had a strange sense of duty. She felt a duty to help Emma out of guilt over what happened to the woman's friends and a larger mission. She hoped her actions might help other women break free from the church, too. Rue's nausea was coupled with dizziness, so she let go of her thoughts for a moment and forced her attention back into the room.

For once, Emma was dumbfounded. Somehow, she had this story in her head about Rue that included having life handed to her on a silver platter. It certainly didn't include growing up in a cult known for its less-than-stellar treatment of women.

"I'm sorry," Emma finally answered. "I didn't know that."

And for the first time, Rue and Emma shared a look. It was one of mutual respect.

CHAPTER 15
Nyla Sprightly

Present Day in St. Petersburg, Florida

~

Emma and Dennis arrived at Erasmus' mansion on Treasure Island in St. Petersburg after a ridiculously long flight because of unforeseen weather and mechanical issues. *Correction: It was now Emma's mansion. Something she needed to remind herself of regularly.*

Not two days after their visit to Darwin and Rue's 'fox den' to discuss a game plan for investigating Erasmus Vandenberg's likely murder, they were addressing part two of that plan... getting Emma set up in her new home and working out the details of her inheritance. Frankly, she was surprised that no one asked what she thought would have been a logical question. "How do we know you didn't murder Erasmus yourself, Emma, after learning of his will?" But she wasn't aware of the will. Nor did she have the means to kill him. And, even if she had both, why risk it when there was a good chance that he was going to die of old age soon enough, anyway? But somehow, it never occurred to them she could have been responsible. This unearned trust only made her that much more motivated to figure out who killed her friend, Erasmus. In her heart, she knew it wasn't old age or 'just one of those things.'

Emma paused in front of the two-story waterfront property, surrounded by royal palms and an entranceway paved with polished stones leading up to a set of blue and white-painted, double-wood doors. For the first time since learning of her inheritance, she felt woozy, and stopped to take in a deep breath. Dennis caught her as she swayed from side to side, wrapping one long arm around her shoulders.

"You okay?" he asked.

Emma nodded. "Quite a bit different from my old digs, huh?" She eyed the two suitcases and carry-on that the taxi driver dropped next to her before making a hasty exit. Storm clouds were rolling in, for what promised to be a miserable, rainy night. "Half my life so far can fit into one of those cases. How sad is that?"

He hugged her tightly. "Not sad, at all." He motioned across the expansive property. "Look at this as the beginning of a new life for us... er, you." He corrected himself, not wanting to be presumptuous. He was just thrilled that she was letting him accompany her and that his request for a temporary transfer at the precinct had been approved.

"I've never had a lawn before," was all that Emma could think to say, daunted as she eyed the property. "I don't even know how to take care of it. Have you ever mowed a lawn before?"

Dennis laughed a little. "Pretty sure I can manage. Hey," he motioned to the sky. "Let's get inside before the floodgates open, huh?"

Emma nodded.

After fighting with the two keys for the upper and lower locks of the front door, Emma eventually pried it open. She barely had time to breathe a sigh of relief when a shrieking alarm began to sound, reverberating through the house, piercing through the air like an ice pick.

"What the hell?" Emma covered her ears.

Dennis cringed, squinting as if walking through a blizzard. "I don't suppose the property manager said anything about an alarm code, did they?

"No!" Emma yelled. "I'm sure I would have remembered."

The shrill was so loud, it began feeling as if the very pulse of it replaced their heartbeats, and the high-pitched tones pierced their brains. Emma felt a dull pain forming behind her eyes.

At that moment, Emma witnessed a slim, ebony arm reach past her and punch a few numbers on the keypad next to the front door. Moments later… silence.

With the noise, neither Emma nor Dennis heard a slim, dark-skinned young woman wearing a patchwork sundress and brown, spaghetti-strap sandals slip past them and disable the alarm.

"Uh, thanks—" Emma turned to the woman, startled, as she spun around to find the woman's face not three inches from her own. She tried to back up, almost tripping over the threshold of the now open doorway. The woman flashed a large toothy grin, so wide it caused her eyes to crinkle around the edges. She looked at Emma as if expecting something. What, Emma had no idea.

From Emma's best guess, the young woman couldn't have been more than in her early twenties, tops… probably Elsbeth's age.

"Hi! I'm Nyla," the woman declared enthusiastically. "But my friends call me 'Sprightly.' Nyla-Sprightly seemed to carry with her a lot of pent-up energy. She looked as if you took her by the shoulders and gave her a good shake, she would take to flight like a rocket.

"Why do they call you—" Emma paused, watching as the girl restlessly swayed from side to side, swinging her arms. One of them almost slapped Dennis in the abdomen, but he sidestepped just in time. The wide-eyed grin remained plastered on her face as if frozen that way. "Never mind. Nice to meet you, uh…" Emma's head was still throbbing from the alarm and the effects of a long travel day. "Nyla Sprightly."

"Oh," Nyla corrected. "Sprightly isn't my last name, it's—" Suddenly, the gears in Nyla's brain clicked into place. She decided she rather liked her new name. In fact, the more she thought about it, it was much nicer than her actual last name, and it wouldn't require her to give up the pet name people seemed to use around her. "That's right," she finally answered. "Nyla Sprightly, at your service!" She saluted.

"I'm sorry, I don't follow," Emma confessed.

"Oh, didn't Erasmus tell you?" She seemed surprised. "I'm the house manager slash house sitter." She made a cutting motion in the air to represent the slash between her two job titles.

"And what exactly does a house manager slash house sitter do?" Emma asked, repeating the slashing motion in the air, for emphasis.

"Well," Nyla Sprightly thought a moment. "I do a few overnights here, every once in a while, to make sure there's no funny business with burglars… to give the place a presence, you see."

"I see," Emma answered. But she really didn't. She'd heard of pet sitters and babysitters, but never house sitters. But then, Emma never really owned a house… or much of anything, for that matter.

"And I make sure the lawn service comes weekly to mow and trim the trees and bushes, and that the bug people spray regularly."

"Bug people?" Emma asked.

"Yeah, you know, so you don't get overrun with roaches, ants, and spiders… this is Florida, after all. Plus, you're near the water, so if you see any snakes, don't engage. Just call me, and I'll take care of them for you."

"I promise you," Emma smirked. "I won't be engaging with any snakes, that's for sure."

"Well, good." Sprightly swung her arms from side to side again as she shifted from one foot to the other. "Sorry about the alarm, by the way. Erasmus only recently had it installed. Guess not everyone knows about it, yet."

"Don't worry about it," Emma answered, jiggling her pinky finger in her ear as if washing water out of it. It still rang, slightly, from the piercing noise just moments ago.

Dennis began lifting one of the suitcases. Sprightly rushed to his side. "Oh," she smiled. "I can help you with that."

"No," Dennis protested. "That's a man's job, I can—"

He stopped when Emma shot him an, *Oh no, you just didn't* look.

"Fine," he corrected. "But it should be the job of the strongest and most capable."

Before he had a chance to lift a single suitcase, Sprightly already had them stacked inside the front door.

"I agree," Emma chuckled. "It should go to the strongest and most capable." She turned to follow Sprightly inside the house.

"Now that was just mean," Dennis complained.

"So, how long will you be staying Miss—" Sprightly's eyes grew wide. "Oh! I just realized that I don't even know your name!"

"I'm Emma, and this is my—" She paused, trying to find the right words. "Dennis."

Sprightly curtsied. Emma raised a curious eyebrow.

"Well, it's nice to meet you, Miss Emma and Mr. Dennis." She nodded approvingly. "I'm also available to run errands, schedule appointments, and do light housekeeping, though when Erasmus is here, he usually brings people with him." Sprightly paused again, the wheels in her head ticking. "Come to think of it, no one told me you were coming. Usually, Mrs. Edwina has her secretary phone me to let me know who in the family is on their way. So... who are you?"

Emma tried to ignore her pounding head. All she wanted was a long hot bath and to maybe to have a veggie pizza delivered. "I'm the new caretaker of this home," Emma finally said.

Sprightly was crestfallen. "Oh." She rolled her eyes away, embarrassed. "I see. Were my services unacceptable?"

Dennis realized the confusion and stepped in, putting out a hand as if to calm her. "No, you misunderstand," he explained. "Emma is not replacing you. She's the new owner of this house."

Sprightly brightened for a moment. "Oh! Er... but what happened to Erasmus?"

"He's dead, I'm afraid," Emma blurted out.

Dennis shot her a *What is wrong with you?* look.

It was too late. Sprightly's face crumbled like a discarded piece of paper. Her lips began quivering, and soon she began sobbing uncontrollably. "Dead?!"

Dennis put a supportive hand on her shoulder. "I'm sorry," he explained. "If we had been told you'd be here, we would have made sure you were informed."

Sprightly's shoulders shuddered as she continued sobbing. "Such a nice man!"

Dennis patted her shoulder. Emma, feeling like a jerk, rubbed the girl's back in as comforting a way as Emma knew how. Her bedside manner needed work. Empathy was Dennis' area of expertise, she decided.

"There, there," Dennis continued. "He had a long and good life."

Sprightly nodded. "He was rather old. Did he die in his sleep... natural causes?" She looked up, hopefully.

"Exactly," Dennis confirmed. He had his doubts about the '*natural causes*,' but he figured this shock was about as much as Sprightly could handle in one day. "Didn't suffer a bit."

Sprightly sniffed back a few more tears, absentmindedly grabbing the hem of her dress to wipe her eyes. Dennis dutifully looked away so as not to accidentally see the woman's unmentionables as she hoisted the fabric up to her face.

"I can't believe Ms. Edwina's secretary didn't call to tell me," she sobbed.

"I'm sure she meant to," Dennis offered. Sprightly nodded.

"Sprightly." Emma dropped her hand. "I hate to be rude, but we are exhausted. Could we pick this conversation up another day?"

"Oh." Sprightly's eyes grew wide. "Of course, Miss Emma. I can be here bright and early tomorrow at—"

"How about Monday?" Emma suggested. "It will give me a chance to settle in and figure out exactly what I need here."

Sprightly nodded. "Of course. Whatever you need." She thrust a hand into her dress pocket and pulled out a plastic card-holder with a mini pen attached to the side. The woman yanked a card from the case and scribbled something on it with the pen. "Here." She handed it to Emma. "Good thing I always keep these handy. I've added your alarm code on the back for next time. Also, I run a small concierge business and manage a few houses in the area. It has my direct phone number on it." She pointed to the number on the card. "If I don't pick up, it means I'm working, but just leave me a message and I'll call you right back as soon as I can. I've got one of those fancy new answering machines built right into the phone... so I can check my messages from almost anywhere." She beamed proudly.

Emma had no idea what the young woman was talking about. She had a landline that she hardly ever used and couldn't be bothered with answering machines. If it was important, she reasoned, people would call back. Dennis had tried to persuade her to use a cellular phone, but at the moment, it was still in its original casing, nestled in one of her suitcases.

"Thanks." Emma accepted the card and waited for Sprightly to make her exit.

Instead, Sprightly stood there, kicking the edge of the door frame.

"Is there something else?" Emma asked.

"Ohhh, no... it's just—"

"What is it?" Dennis encouraged.

Sprightly wrinkled her nose uncomfortably. "It's just that it's payday."

Emma sighed. She knew money was coming soon, but she didn't have her inheritance yet — aside from the house. She had no idea how to pay the woman.

Dennis chimed in. "And how much are you usually paid?" he asked.

"Well," Sprightly answered. "My going rate is $11 an hour, but Erasmus always insisted on paying me $18 dollars an hour. I put in about 20 hours over the past two weeks, so... $360?" She cringed. "If that's too much—"

"No," Dennis answered. "It's not that. We've just arrived and don't have any money on us at the moment."

Sprightly's eyes shifted back and forth from the house, back to Emma and Dennis as if mentally trying to get them to notice something, but it was apparent to no one except for the young woman.

Emma crossed and uncrossed her arms. "What? What are you motioning toward?"

"Erasmus keeps cash in the cookie jar in the kitchen. He usually just tells me to pay myself and then, when Miss Edwina or another family member arrives, they refill it and make sure I didn't pinch more than I should... which I'd never do," she reassured them.

"Then why don't we see about paying you?" Dennis led the way inside. To Emma, he whispered, "I can take it from here if you want to have a look around."

Emma sighed gratefully. She wasn't used to having support in domestic matters, and she kind of liked it.

Dennis marched through the main entryway, past the living room and down the hall into the kitchen, as if he'd lived there all his life. In truth, he was pretty much just guessing. He eyed the layout of the kitchen with interest. It was the first he'd ever seen with an island in the middle for prepping food, not to mention stainless steel appliances.

Sprightly reached for a colorful tin on the counter. Apparently, Edwina had refilled it recently, because it was full to the brim with cash in a variety of bills.

"I can just take $220 and give you my normal rate, if you prefer," Sprightly offered. "Seeing as this is an unexpected change of events and all."

"No," Dennis insisted. "Take what you're usually paid."

"You can check with Mrs. Edwina," Sprightly offered. "She can confirm I'm telling you the truth."

"I don't have to check with anyone." Dennis crossed his arms. "I have a pretty good sense about people."

"Really?" Sprightly asked, counting the bills and tucking them into her dress pocket. "How's that?" She wanted to know.

"I'm a cop," he confessed. "It's my job to have a good sense about people."

Sprightly's eyes grew wide. "Do you carry a gun and all?"

"Sometimes," he confessed.

"Ever shoot someone?" Sprightly was fascinated.

"No." He shook his head. "See you in a few days, Nyla Sprightly," he smiled. Dennis knew that Sprightly wasn't her last name but saw how Nyla's eyes lit up when Emma referred to her as such.

Sprightly's wide, toothy grin returned.

"Sure thing, Mr. Dennis."

"Just Dennis," he answered, showing her to the door. "'Mister' is my dad's name," he laughed.

Sprightly laughed as he escorted her out. He watched her all but skip down the driveway and climb on a little green bicycle that was sitting by the curb. Nyla Sprightly waved and hit the bell on it as she pedaled away.

LATER THAT EVENING, Edwina Vandenberg was plagued by two annoying phone calls. While Dennis claimed to have a 'good sense about people,' Emma was not as trusting. She phoned Edwina to confirm that Sprightly was who she said she was, and that she could be trusted. Edwina, who couldn't be bothered with the woman who, in her mind, stole the family fortune, barked messages to Ferdinand, who calmly delivered them as if echoing Edwina.

"Tell her that—that girl has been with us for several years now, and her mother took care of the Florida home for two decades before that," Edwina called over Ferdinand's shoulder, forgetting Nyla's name as quickly as Emma read it from the business card.

"Miss Nyla has been with us for several years now—" Ferdinand began.

"Thank you, Ferdinand," Emma interrupted. "I got that." She bit her lip.

"Tell her that I trust that girl more than I trust a woman who ran off with the Vandenberg fortune!" Edwina added, bitterly.

"Madame Edwina says—" Ferdinand tried, again, reluctantly.

"I heard her, Ferdinand," Emma answered, a hint of sarcasm creeping into her voice. "I just wanted to make sure Nyla was truly the property manager. Thank you for confirming."

Not ten seconds after Ferdinand hung up the phone, it rang again.

"What does everyone want from me?" Edwina complained loudly from the couch as Ivy brought the woman her nightly cream sherry and the latest copy of *Vogue*.

This time, it was Sprightly on the other end.

Ferdinand listened with a mix of confusion and patience while the hyperactive woman explained. "I didn't even think about it until after I'd let them in that maybe I shoulda made sure they were who they said they were—" Nyla began.

"Miss Nyla—" Ferdinand tried in vain to gently interrupt.

"I would just feel awful if I let strangers into the house and, come to think of it, maybe I should go back there now and check on the place—"

"Miss Nyla—" Ferdinand tried again.

"I mean, they seemed trustworthy, with Mr. Dennis being a cop and all… assuming that was even true! What if it wasn't—"

"Miss Nyla!" Ferdinand all but yelled into the phone.

"Yes?" Sprightly answered softly.

"Miss Emma was telling you the truth. She is the new owner of the Florida estate. Perhaps you should consider contacting her for all future concerns related to the property."

"Oh, I see. Okay," Sprightly acknowledged. "Could you at least tell Miss Edwina that it was lovely working with her and—"

"I will do that, Miss Nyla," Ferdinand cut the girl off once again. He knew if he didn't, she would keep talking non-stop for another twenty minutes. "Good night."

CHAPTER 16
The Church of Infinite Love

Back in Pennsylvania

~

Rue and Darwin swerved through the twists and turns of the mountainous road in upstate Pennsylvania. Darwin was at the wheel of the rental car. Meanwhile, Rue was clenching both the hand-rest and her teeth, trying not to be ill. Her face was visibly sallow.

It had nothing to do with motion sickness.

Rue was afraid.

"Talk to me, Rue." Darwin glanced at her and then back at the road as he expertly maneuvered their rental car along the long and winding road. "Are you okay?"

He knew she was nervous about returning to a church that took her so long to flee from. But there was more to it than that. He was certain of it. Darwin suspected it had to do with her family... a topic that, even after being together for nearly a year now... was a touchy one, and largely off limits.

"It's just that—" she began.

"Yes?" Darwin encouraged.

"I know it's silly, but — whenever I'm back in this neck of the woods, I get all panicky."

There was a long pause while Darwin waited for an explanation that didn't come. "Why?" he finally asked. He suspected he knew.

Rue let out a labored sigh. He was going to figure it out sooner rather than later, anyway. "Because it took me so long to escape from this town, that being back here sets off an irrational fear that somehow I'll get sucked back in and won't be able to leave."

"Do you mean that they'll imprison you? Not let us leave?" Darwin asked, alarmed.

"I don't think they'll physically detain us, no," Rue answered. Though she wasn't a hundred percent sure this was correct. "But it doesn't stop the fear."

The two pulled into the parking lot of the Church of Infinite Love.

There was nothing spectacular about the church itself. In fact, the building looked like a large, gray wooden barn about to collapse in on itself. The most remarkable features were the new white sign that had been recently placed by the roadside with an arrow to the church, and a large, red glass heart that someone hung on the front door of the entryway. It looked like one of those old sun catchers that people painted for fun… it probably was.

"I would never let that happen," Darwin reassured her. "Besides, Monique outdid herself with your makeover. Any members there who knew you back then aren't likely to recognize you."

It was true. Monique helped her sift through their hall closet, where Darwin kept an assortment of costumes and disguises at the ready for cases requiring they go undercover. Monique fitted her with a passable auburn wig that was long and curly. "Don't mess it up," she cautioned. "It's my favorite." Rue knew that. She wore it all the time. Since she remembered that the church didn't permit women to wear makeup (it was deemed a sign of vanity), but she needed some to adequately change her appearance, they settled on a self-tanning cream, green contacts and oversized, prescriptionless glasses. For the pièce de résistance, Darwin suggested a brown corduroy skirt that reached her ankles and an ugly white polyester blouse with ruffles around the neckline that furrowed down the front where the buttons were.

"Perfect," Monique praised. "You look hideous."

Now at the church, Rue unlocked the passenger side of the car and pushed the door open, sticking a leg out and stepping to the ground. "We'll see," Rue shrugged. "Let's go."

As they approached the doorway, it swung open, as if they were expected. Rue couldn't help but think this was the setup to a bad horror movie. Her stomach lurched a little.

A pear-shaped, middle-aged woman with hair that ran the length of her back (about a foot of it, a tangled mess of split ends) greeted them. "Welcome," she smiled, reaching into a shallow straw basket that she was holding and producing a brochure. "Are you here for today's service?"

"We are," Darwin answered simply, accepting the brochure. "Thank you."

The woman cautiously looked them over. "I don't believe I've seen either of you before," she confessed. "Is this your first time at the Church of Infinite Love?"

Darwin opened his mouth to answer again, more out of habit than anything else. Rue put her hand out and touched his chest to silence him, as if to say, "*I've got this.*"

"Haven't been here since I was a kid," Rue explained. "But we regularly attend the sister church in Hoboken."

"Oh," the woman nodded. "The one in New Jersey?"

Rue nodded. *Was there any other Hoboken in the world*? Rue wondered.

Just then, a family made their way to the door, waiting for their turn to enter. The woman wore an all-white cotton dress, while the man wore a light tan suit with a fat, burnt orange tie. The two kids, one boy and one girl, were dressed in similar colors, with a matching yellow dress and ruffles for the girl and a white suit with a wide yellow tie for the boy.

"Right this way." The woman motioned toward the rows of chairs. "Take a seat anywhere."

"You let Monique know our exact location, right?" Rue whispered.

"Yes," Darwin tapped his cell phone. "Tracker," he answered simply. Rue wasn't certain she completely trusted the tracking feature on Darwin's cell phone out in the middle of nowhere. She hadn't used one long enough, and thus, she doubted their effectiveness, despite the fact that his friend Bristol had used it to rescue her one fateful night outside a nightclub in Manhattan some months prior.

Inside the church, Darwin expected to see a series of church pews lined up in front of a podium. Instead, there were rows and rows of ordinary folding chairs. The floor appeared to have old basketball patterns on them, now worn away and scratched. The most interesting aspects of the room were the high, V-shaped ceiling with interlocking wooden beams, and the tall stage in the front of the room where the podium stood. In front of the podium was a large gold medallion featuring a lion, a leopard, a young lamb, a wolf, and a small child. It was probably the most ornate object in the room.

Rue planted herself in the back row, in the farthest corner where she could survey the entire room. Darwin took her cue and sat next to her, eyeing the room curiously. "Have you never been to a church before?" Rue whispered.

"Oh, I have," Darwin answered. "It was a cathedral, actually. And I was only there once... on my wedding day."

Rue's chest dropped. "Wedding day?!" she whispered back, visibly shaken. After all, they had been living together now for the past four months. She even gave up the lease on her apartment. Why had she not heard of this sooner?

Several people a few rows up turned to look at them, puzzled by the noise. But instead of saying anything, they merely smiled politely, in a way that suggested, *"You know you're in a church, right?"*

Rue sat back and crossed her arms while Darwin finished surveying the room. It was only when he glanced at her to say something that he saw her expression. "Oh," he realized his mistake. "That was over a long time ago, decades really."

"You didn't think it pertinent to mention that you were married before?" Rue leaned toward him. A few more people looked in their direction. Rue smiled back sweetly.

By now, dozens more people had arrived, and the seats in front of them began to fill up quickly. A few sounds of babies crying and children being fussy echoed against the high ceilings as their parents tried to hush them.

"Not really," Darwin admitted. "I don't pry into your past because I know you don't like it. Didn't seem to make sense bringing up mine." Rue let out a huff. "But if you want to discuss it later, we can. It was a mistake that only lasted a few years."

"So, you're divorced?" Rue confirmed.

"Yes," Darwin answered. "Have been for quite some time. Wasn't in a hurry to do *that* again," he joked, saw her expression, and promptly fell silent.

Rue wasn't sure how to take this news. On the one hand, it further disrupted her previous beliefs that Darwin was a playboy afraid of commitment, as he was committed enough to marry someone, and then went on to invite Rue to move in with him. So, that's something. Still, there was a childlike part of her that didn't like to think that there had ever been a 'someone else' even though he was in his early forties, and it stood to reason that there had been many 'someone elses' along the way. *Come to think of it*, she thought. *I don't even know exactly how old Darwin is or even when his birthday is. We've known each other nearly a year now, and the topic has never come up? Did it pass without him mentioning it? It must have!* It was becoming increasingly clear to Rue that the two might consider spending less time working on cases and more time actually getting to know one another.

Just then, a woman stepped from behind a black curtain that hung on each side of the stage and stepped slowly, rhythmically even, toward the podium. "Welcome friends," she smiled sweetly. "Please rise." The congregation stood. "I invite you to turn to page 137 in your hymnals. A second woman stepped from behind the curtain and made her way to the far corner of the stage, where an old upright piano stood. Once seated, she opened her hymnal and placed it in front her, set her right foot on the sustain pedal and began plunking the ivory keys.

The church sang, "*A mighty fortress is our God...*"

The pianist hit the piano chords angrily, as if trying to adjust to the fact that the congregation didn't get the timing right on their words, so she kept modifying her rhythm.

Rue felt flushed and her hands began trembling. She handed the hymnal to Darwin, who quickly grabbed it out of her unsteady hands. Holding it open with one hand, he circled his free arm around her waist for support. "You okay?" he mouthed. Rue nodded.

Darwin didn't know the song, of course, so he just mouthed the words and occasionally emphasized an end note as attendees around him smiled and nodded.

"Please be seated," the woman at the podium said, after the song had finished.

The congregation sat. The woman was shorter than Darwin had first realized, concealed by the fact that she was on stage and wearing very high, chunky-heeled shoes. Her peach dress flowed down around her ankles, and the collar was cut high around the neck. The gossamer sleeves reached all the way to her wrists and were tightly buttoned on each arm. It was clear that the dress was going nowhere and was revealing nothing.

"For those who don't me, I am Deaconess Frances. Before Reverend Simon gives his sermon for today, I'd like to welcome out-of-town guests and first-time visitors. I'll begin with first-time visitors." Her gaze honed in on Darwin. "If you are a first-time visitor, would you stand, please?"

Darwin was about to stand, but Rue grabbed his arm and shook her head. He stayed firmly seated.

Frances seemed a little unnerved. "In that case, any out-of-town visitors?" This time, she stared directly at Rue. That was their cue. Rue motioned for Darwin to stand first, and she followed. Rue dutifully tucked her head shyly and allowed her gaze to fall to the floor. "Ah, welcome," Frances called. "Which church are you visiting from?"

Darwin waited for Rue to answer. Instead, she elbowed him in the ribs. "Hoboken," he coughed out.

"Hoboken." Frances' smile remained plastered to her face. "One of our... newer churches, no doubt. Please, share your names with us so we may greet you properly."

Darwin thought a moment. "Mr. and Mrs. Swift," he answered simply.

To the congregation, she said, "Let's give Mr. and Mrs. Swift," as she eyed Rue again, "a warm welcome."

"Welcome Mr. and Mrs. Swift," the church droned.

After what seemed like an eternity, Reverend Simon took to the stage. He was a tall and bulky man with a broad chest and belly. He wore a black suit and tie, and had his hair slicked back with what looked like men's hair cream that went out of style in the '50s.

"Where will you be on that fateful day?!" Reverend Simon boomed. Rue slouched in her chair and did her best to tune it out. Darwin, on the other hand, found the entire experience completely fascinating. He choked back a laugh somewhere in the middle where Simon reminded the wives to obey their husbands, and husbands to cherish their wives as the 'weaker vessel.' Darwin glanced at Rue, who uncrossed her arms as soon as she saw him, and instead rested her hands lightly in her lap. She smiled lovingly back at him, holding his gaze just long enough for her to witness a few church goers smiling approvingly in her periphery.

Weaker vessel? Darwin laughed to himself. *And good luck getting Rue to do any obeying. That woman has a mind of her own, and I prefer it that way.*

"Now it's time for the healing ceremony," Reverend Simon announced. "If there is any among you feeling physical or emotional pain, please come forward so that we may pray over you."

Finally, Rue thought. This is why they were here. The healing ceremony was a double-edged sword. On the one hand, there were a small group of people who actually believed in faith-healing. For some newcomers, it was their last option when they had exhausted all others. Mixed in were those with a victim mentality, who showed up for every service with a recurring injury or a new ailment-of-the week. They claimed to feel immediately better after each prayer circle, but the effects didn't always last as long as they'd hoped. And then there was the *other hand*. If you admitted you had any physical or emotional pain (and really, who doesn't?), then you were clearly doing something wrong spiritually. So, many would clam up and feign perfect health. Meanwhile, the martyrs had no trouble admitting their 'weakness,' and paying a weekly financial offering to the church in the hopes that *this* time would be the time they were cured of all ills.

Rue turned to Darwin, rolling her eyes at the number of people lining up in the long row down the center of the church. It was only then that she realized he was no longer sitting next to her. *Where did he go?* She peered around frantically for a moment before she saw him in line, limping slightly as the line progressed. *What was he up to?*

The young woman in front of Darwin approached the front of the stage. Deaconess Frances motioned for her to walk the steps that led to the podium where Reverend Simon stood. "What ails you, my daughter?" Reverend Simon asked, having retrieved the microphone from its stand on the podium and holding it in front of her. The young woman rung her hands, embarrassed. "It's okay, you're among friends."

"I've been feeling... sad," she answered simply.

"Really?" Reverend Simon peered at her sympathetically. "And why are you sad?"

"I just—"

"It's okay." He touched her shoulder. "We're all here for you."

"I just feel like my life is pointless," she finally admitted. "And then I feel guilty for even thinking that because, after all, I am one of God's children." She began to tear up.

"Indeed, you are, my daughter." He motioned for Deaconess Frances to bring over a cup and plate. She placed them on the podium. "And you are among the chosen," he continued. "God has a special plan for you, and today we shall pray that he reveals it to you." He handed the deaconess his microphone. She, in turn, offered him a tiny vial, opening it and placing a few drops of oil into his palms. He rubbed his hands together before placing them on the young woman's bowed head. Without the microphone, the congregation could only hear mumbling. And it was quite possible that it was gibberish. Although onlookers would have asserted that he was speaking in tongues.

After a moment of prayer, Frances handed him a small yellow plate with what looked like a cookie. He held it up, and the young woman opened her mouth as he placed it on her tongue. "Let this morsel represent manna from heaven, blessed by God." She chewed whatever it was and swallowed before he followed up with a small yellow cup. "Let this holy water complete your healing." She drank the water and smiled.

"Better?" Reverend Simon asked gently.

She nodded gratefully as the church said in unison, "Amen." The woman was quickly escorted offstage by another church attendant.

Frances returned the microphone to Reverend Simon.

Darwin was next. When he reached the front of the stage, he, too, was invited up the steps to the podium. The minister asked, "What is troubling you, my son?" Reverend Simon thrust a hand-held microphone in front of Darwin's face.

It should be noted that Reverend Simon was at least a decade younger than Darwin. Darwin bit the inside of his cheek lightly to avoid laughing. He let out an awkward cough. "It's my knee, you see." Darwin pointed. "Old sports injury. Doctor says I need surgery."

There was a gasp from the audience. Rue crossed her arms and pursed her lips, shrinking into her chair. Surgery and doctors were generally frowned upon, and the church had to make special allowances for those with cancer who needed chemotherapy or radiation. But it was always mixed with a bit of judgment. After all, it was easier to blame the cancer patient for not being right with God. Otherwise, you might have to admit that God wasn't listening or, even worse, that he didn't care.

"I can assure you, my son," Reverend Simon furrowed his bushy brows. "That won't be necessary. Deaconess—" he addressed Deaconess Frances.

Once again, she returned with the small bottle of anointing oil. Given his height, Reverend Simon had to all but stand on his toes to reach the top of Darwin's head. The minister went as far as to push Darwin's head forward roughly, encouraging him to bow his head a little further.

After the prayer, Frances handed Darwin a small, macaroon-shaped morsel that sat on a green plate. It was larger than the one offered to the young woman, so Reverend Simon suggested, "Perhaps you could put your palms out, my son."

"Certainly," Darwin obliged, placing his cupped palms out in front of him. Once handed the macaroon, he took a bite before coughing awkwardly. He pulled a handkerchief from his pocket and spit the morsel into it.

"Is something the matter, my son?" Reverend Simon touched Darwin's arm, concerned, and possibly a little annoyed.

"Forgot to mention a peanut allergy. There aren't any peanuts in this, are there? Should have thought to mention that first. Sorry." He slipped the handkerchief back into his suit jacket.

"No peanuts," Reverend Simon confirmed. He waited while Darwin ate the remainder of the macaroon.

Next came the beverage in a matching green cup, except when Reverend Simon went to offer it to Darwin, he sipped it so fast that he spilled half of it on his shirt.

"Geez, I'm sorry. I'm such a klutz." He looked down at his stained shirt, laughing awkwardly. "Oh, and sorry for swearing."

"That's quite all right," Reverend Simon reassured him, motioning for Frances to bring over another cup... another green one. "You seem to be having a rough day, aren't you?" He joked.

"I'll say," Darwin laughed, again, jovially. This time, he downed the beverage without incident. It tasted like the sugar water they give small children when they have the hiccups.

Reverend Simon repeated the ritualistic words he had used for the woman who stood for healing before Darwin.

"And how is your knee?" Reverend Simon finally asked.

Darwin played along, shaking out his leg, surprised. "Better!" he proclaimed.

"Amen!" the congregation called enthusiastically.

Darwin was escorted off the stage and made sure to limp, just slightly, on the way back. After all, he didn't want to oversell it.

The healing ceremony continued for a good thirty minutes before they were called to pray once more and close with another hymn.

After the service, a few members of the church politely stopped to greet Rue and Darwin.

"Hello, dear," an older woman wearing an enormous hat said. "So lovely to meet you." She put out a hand. Rue tried to shake it, but it went limp in hers. Instead, they held hands for an awkward moment while Rue answered, "Nice to meet you as well, Mrs.—"

"Grail," she finished. "Mr. and Mrs. Harold Grail." Apparently, the women didn't get a name of their own. Rue felt a chill up her spine and neck. It took her a moment, but then she recognized the longtime member, Mrs. Grail. *Let's hope she doesn't remember me,* Rue thought.

Harold was a boatload of enthusiasm. "Hope you'll both join us in the reception room for fellowship," he stated. It seemed more a command and less a request. He eyed Darwin's soiled shirt and let out a chuckle.

"Yes," Rue quickly answered, before glancing downward, embarrassed. "After I visit the ladies' room, of course."

"Oh, it's just through there." Mrs. Grail pointed toward an archway on the side of the stage. "We'll catch you both in a few minutes, then?"

"Of course," Rue lied. She had no intention of fellowship. In fact, after they had gotten the information they came for, Rue planned to be back on the road and heading straight to New York.

"You know," Mrs. Grail paused. "There's something about you that is familiar to me. You've never been to our church before, you say?"

"No," Rue interrupted. "Never been to the Pennsylvania campus before today."

"Oh," Mrs. Grail nodded. "Well, then you have a twin somewhere. Your voice is just so familiar." The woman mulled on this for a moment. Finally, at Mr. Grail's hurried request, they made their departure. He seemed to be in quite a hurry for refreshments.

Damn it! Rue thought to herself. Somehow, she'd never thought to adopt an accent or in some way disguise her voice.

Just then, the rumble of thunder could be heard outside.

The congregation quickly dispersed to the reception room, where coffee cakes and fresh brew awaited. Lightning flashed through one of the small, square windows at the top of the church. It was as if the Red Sea were parting as people moved aside. And that's when Rue saw her. Deaconess Frances now standing directly in front of them, as if appearing out of thin air. She smiled sweetly and waited until the room was empty, and she, Darwin and Rue, were the only remaining people.

"Hello, Rue." The woman eyed Rue up and down, almost amused. She wasn't fooled by the disguise. "It's nice of you to visit."

Rue swallowed hard before answering, "Hello, Mother."

CHAPTER 17

Private Quarters #5

Present Day in Pennsylvania

"You might have told me she was your mother," Darwin whispered as he and Rue were led down a long hallway toward Frances' private quarters.

After Rue and Darwin's unexpected encounter with Rue's mother, the deaconess excused herself, but not before requesting the two meet with her in private after she'd been given 'a few minutes to collect herself,' following the shock of her daughter's unexpected visit.

"I wasn't sure she'd be here, and by the time I saw her, it was too late," Rue whispered back.

"Still, a little heads up in the car would have helped."

The usher, who escorted them, politely walked in front of them, pretending not to eavesdrop.

"Could we talk about this later?" She nodded toward the woman leading them.

Darwin nodded. Between her mother and his undisclosed divorce, the list of things they needed to discuss was adding up.

The attendant rapped on the door at the end of the hall in a very distinctive pattern… three rapid hard knocks, followed by a pause and then two very light taps. It was one of many doors they passed, but this one was labeled, 'Private Quarters #5.' Across the hall was a door labeled, 'Private Quarters #6.' From the looks of it, this particular wing appeared to have about a dozen or so such rooms.

"You may enter," Frances' voice called from inside the room, recognizing the knock.

The attendant quickly opened the door and motioned for Darwin and Rue to follow. Like the deaconess, this woman was also covered from neck to ankle, with little skin showing, but was wearing a stiff black blouse and a long black dress. She had gray-brown hair, no makeup, and a mole that was almost as dark as the dress. Had they not been opposed to doctors, Rue might have suggested that the woman have that looked at by a dermatologist.

"You may go," Frances addressed the attendant, and waved at her as if to shoo her away. The woman merely nodded and, despite Rue's hope that the door would remain open, she shut it quickly, and from the sound of it, locked it behind her.

Darwin heard it, too, and found that quite curious. He let out a yawn, oddly tired after the service, coupled with a strange sense of calm. *Maybe I should give this faith healing thing more of a chance?* He thought to himself.

Frances was still in her church dress, sitting at a small round table off to the side of the door, and motioned for them to sit in the two upright, uncomfortable-looking chairs across from her. Glancing behind the woman, Rue could see a small single bed and pillow, with a nightstand and lamp next to it. There was a thin clothing rack on the far wall.

"Can I offer you some tea?" she asked. "Or perhaps a snack? We have our own signature nutrient-rich fruit and nut bars that I'm sure you'll like. Rue, you remember?"

It was then that Rue noticed that her mother had what looked to be a small efficiency kitchen behind her, with a utility sink, mini refrigerator, and even a tiny stove and oven. *I guess the deaconess role comes with privileges,* Rue thought.

She remembered her parents having to share a room smaller than this one at their old campus, but there was no private kitchen. Everyone ate together in a common area, and no food was permitted in the private quarters. She learned that the hard way when she and her three roommates, sharing a room about this size, but with matching bunk beds, tried to sneak extra fruit snacks back from dinner. As punishment, they were all sent to the infirmary and forced to drink something that made them vomit. They were then given lots of water to re-hydrate but denied a regular breakfast the next morning... only a slice of whole wheat bread and a glass of water for each of them. And none of the other children were permitted to speak with them for 72 hours.

"Something the matter, Dear?" A rumbling could be heard outside, the signal of a storm brewing.

"No, Mother," Rue answered, "just taking a private stroll down memory lane."

Darwin stood next to her awkwardly. His head felt a little muddled, as if he were standing in the middle of a dream.

After an inordinately long pause, she asked, "Aren't either of you going to sit down?"

"I think I'll stand, if you don't mind, Mother. We won't be long."

"Oh." Frances seemed surprised. "So, this isn't a social visit? How disappointing. I was going to have rooms prepared so that you could both stay the night."

"We definitely won't be staying the night," Rue announced, not realizing that she was now shouting above the rain and thunder that began violently pounding the roof.

"Unfortunately, you may not have a choice," Frances answered.

"You can't keep me here, Mother." Rue growled.

"*I* have no intention of keeping you here." She pointed to the ceiling. "But given the weather, perhaps *He* does." She was, of course, referring to God. "Listen to that storm. The roads here are prone to flooding, and do you really want to be driving on a winding mountain road in this weather? I wouldn't advise it."

She looked at Darwin. "Please have a seat, Mr. Swift. You look very uncomfortable."

Darwin eyed Rue apologetically, really not wanting to be caught between whatever it was that was happening between Rue and her mother. All he knew was that it was big enough where neither woman felt the need to even hug one another nor share more than the most basic of pleasantries upon their reunion.

He finally concluded that he could win more bees with honey, and if they were going to get any information out of Frances, he should attempt to be amenable, particularly if Rue was not. Plus, he was feeling a little groggy and sitting seemed the best option.

As he sat, Frances added, "Or should I call you Darwin Fennec? That is the name you are going by these days, isn't it?" She flashed a devilish smile at him.

"How did you—" Rue began.

"Oh, hush my dear. I'm a mother; I worry. When you left the sanctuary again, in the middle of the night, without telling anyone where you were going, I had to send some of our protectors to find you."

"Protectors?" Rue asked. "Is that what you're calling your prison guards these days?"

"You're being overly dramatic. Are you sure you won't have some tea? It always relaxed you when you were anxious, which—" she laughed as she looked up at Darwin, as if sharing a quaint childhood story, "... was all the time, it seemed."

Darwin didn't laugh. Nor did it escape him that Frances referred to her leaving 'again.' *Exactly how many times had she tried to leave and failed before?* He rubbed his forehead, forcing himself to focus.

"No thank you, Mother. And that was two years ago. Once you'd discovered where I was, which it seems that you clearly did, why did you keep tracking me? You could see that I was alright."

Frances cleared her throat. "If by alright, you mean living in that little hovel of yours and posing nude, then I suppose you were alright—"

"Now she sounds like Spencer," Rue joked to Darwin.

"Well now, that man had potential—"

"What do you know of it?" Rue retorted angrily. "And my hovel was a lot better than the cramped dorm rooms the church had me in."

"Well," Frances explained. "If you had worked your way through the ranks as I did, or not run away when you did, that would have changed." Rue opened her mouth to speak, but after seeing her mother's eyes narrowing as if to challenge her, she closed it again. "After all," her mother continued, turning to Darwin. "Off she went into the night, and on the eve of her wedding—" Frances paused to witness Darwin's surprised expression. She was enjoying this.

"That's enough, Mother," Rue interjected, shooting Darwin a look, as if to say, *"Add this to the things we need to discuss later."* Thunder boomed again as the lights in the room flickered, as if threatening to go out at any moment. "We're here because we need to ask you some questions. But perhaps you already know that, too."

"Questions?" Frances appeared surprised, but it was nearly impossible to tell whether or not she was acting. "Whatever do you mean?"

"Darwin and I are investigating a murder."

"Murder?" Frances' eyebrows lifted in disbelief. "Who was murdered?"

"Erasmus Vandenberg," Rue said loudly, waiting expectantly for a horrified reaction that didn't come. A slight shuffling could be heard on the other side of the door as someone passed by.

"Is that name supposed to mean something to me?" Frances blinked innocently.

Rue repeated his name. "You know... Erasmus Vandenberg... wealthy nutraceutical and vitamin tycoon who made his fortune by largely selling custom-branded products to churches such as yours."

Frances thought a moment. "Oh," she finally answered with a start. "You mean the teas and snacks and such?"

"Yes, Mother," Rue answered blandly. "That's exactly what I mean."

"It's *his* company manufacturing our healthy foods? I had no idea. I always assumed the church made them in house."

"Really?" Rue was suspicious. "You, who know where I live, who I date, and what kind of work I do, and yet you were unaware of who made the 'miracle' foods that you pimp out to the congregation at a pretty penny for cures for everything from arthritis to depression?"

"First of all," Frances corrected, "I resent your suggesting that I'm pimping anything, particularly coming from you. And second, I trust the church and have no reason to look into their business dealings. That's none of my concern."

Rue crossed her arms and all but stamped her foot. "In other words, you don't trust me and... what the hell do you mean by that 'pimping' remark, anyway?"

"Well, you were never known for your sound decisions... except maybe for Spencer, but you screwed that one up, didn't you?"

"He was a liar and a cheat!"

"Judge not, lest thou be judged," Frances retorted.

"That's rich coming from you, one of the most judgmental people I have ever met!"

Darwin sat up, alarmed.

"Keep your voice down, Dear," Frances hushed her daughter. "Noise travels here."

"About the pimping?" Rue couldn't let that one go.

"Just seems odd to me that your boss suddenly became your lover, is all. Is that part of your work arrangement?"

Rue was about to respond, telling her mother exactly what she thought of her when Darwin held out his arm, as if to say, *"Just wait a moment."*

"Frances—" he began.

"I'd prefer it if you addressed me as Deaconess," she replied. Darwin bit back a response. He was beginning to share Rue's sentiment about her mother.

"Deaconess," he tried again. "I am not your daughter's boss. It may have seemed that way at first—" Darwin tried to frame his words carefully. After all, it was Spencer that commissioned him to hire Rue on the pretense of a job to keep her out of the way while he pursued other work and personal interests — a fact that Darwin discovered too late. "But we are currently business partners who run our investigative agency together."

"Oh, is that so?" Frances nodded.

"Yes," Darwin confirmed. "That is so."

"But you are lovers?" Frances asked.

"Darwin and I are dating, Mother," Rue explained. "So, yes. I wouldn't have put it as crudely as you just did. But we are, in fact, intimate."

"Who live together and work together?" she confirmed.

"What does that matter?" Rue demanded.

"It matters not at all... if you don't mind living in sin and potentially being cast out into the Lake of Fire and damned for all eternity."

"With all the murderers, pedophiles, and abusive people in the world, I hardly think any God will give a rat's ass if I, a grown woman, am having sex with my boyfriend out of wedlock."

Darwin cringed. He really didn't enjoy being in the middle of this. Frances turned to him. "Do you have any intention of marrying my daughter?"

"You don't have to answer that, Darwin," Rue told him.

"But I want to," Darwin replied calmly. "Yes, Deaconess. While it's still early in our relationship, that thought has crossed my mind."

Rue's expression froze, as if someone had just slapped her in the face. She had no idea he was that serious about her, and the thought was both electrifying and terrifying, all at once...the idea of being a Mrs. Fennec. But then her face dropped when she thought about it. *That would make me Rue Fennec or Rue Brennan Fennec. Both of those sound like terrible names!*

"My husband and I married two months after we met," Frances explained to Darwin. "There's nothing wrong with early." After pausing for a moment, she eyed Rue up and down. "Of course, why buy the cow when you can have the milk for free?"

"Am I supposed to be the cow in the scenario?" Rue all but yelled.

"Once again." Frances motioned with her hand to indicate Rue should lower her voice. "Please keep your voice down."

"And may I remind you, Mother," Rue whispered vehemently. "That Father *did* buy the cow *and* still got his milk for free?"

"And you saw where that got him." Frances waved her hand, as if this were old news. "Excommunicated and paying child support for some poor bastard." Frances' eyes drifted away for a moment as she curled her nose distastefully. "Ah well," she returned with a small grin. "He'll get what's coming to him, and at least he brought me two things." She touched Rue's hair in what felt very fake and very forced. "You and the church."

"Mother," Rue said, as she tried returning to the subject at hand. "That's all very sweet, but we still have a crime to solve. Can you help us?"

"I don't see how I can possibly be of any help to you." She eyed the two of them quizzically.

"We have reason to believe that Erasmus Vandenberg's death has something to do with the Church of Infinite Love," Rue stated emphatically.

"Why on Earth would you think that?" Frances asked, surprised.

"Because Erasmus Vandenberg was not only selling large quantities of his nutraceuticals, and protein bars, and vitamins, etc., but he was also a large donor to the church."

"Oh, I hadn't realized he was a member." She thought a moment. "Funny, I've never heard his name mentioned before now."

"Well, he was," Darwin chimed in. "But just a month before he died, he denounced the church and cut off funding. And, we have reason to believe he was trying to cut off all ties with the church, even though it meant giving up Vandenberg Nutraceuticals' most prestigious client."

"The Church of Infinite Love," Frances finished quietly. Rue could see her mother putting connections together in her mind, and it appeared that she was not happy with the results. "That couldn't be—"

Thunder and lightning struck again, and the room went dark. Rue sucked in her breath, realizing that she was having trouble inhaling. She started panting in and out like a small dog overheating in the sun.

"Rue, are you alright?" Darwin stood, knocking his knee against the small table. "Dammit!" He rubbed his knee, which ironically, hadn't been sore before today's service, but now it was. He felt his way through the dark until he reached her, wrapping an arm around her.

"She's fine," Frances answered flatly. "She just gets like that sometimes."

Rue continued to pant rapidly.

"I've never seen her get like this!" Darwin hissed. To Rue, he said calmly, "Slow breaths... calm down. The power went out; that's all."

"We're not... staying... here... tonight," Rue forced out.

"No," Darwin promised. "Definitely not."

"Well, where are you planning on going with weather like this?" Francis was incredulous.

"We'll sleep in the car if we have to," Darwin reasoned. The lights flickered back on. Rue's knees started to buckle under her. Darwin wrapped his other arm around her waist, pulled her up, and drew her tightly into his chest, adrenalin now coursing through his veins, replacing the earlier grogginess. She sank into him, her hands and the side of her cheek pinned against his chest. “Don’t worry,” he whispered. “I’ve got you.” Rue’s breath slowly returned to normal. To Francis, Darwin said, “It’s been lovely meeting you, Deaconess. We’ll just be going now.”

“Rue,” she interjected. Rue raised her eyes slowly to meet her mother’s gaze. “Do you mean to tell me that you’d feel safer sleeping in a car in a flooded parking lot, during a major storm with dangerous thunder and lightning, instead of a comfortable room, not unlike the home you spent nearly your entire childhood in?”

“Yes, Mother,” Rue answered quietly. “That’s exactly what I’m suggesting.” Their eyes locked for an additional moment. Rue saw a flicker in her mother’s eyes. It was the tinge of an emotion she couldn’t quite place — at least, not coming from her mother. It almost felt like... regret.

Darwin began guiding Rue carefully to the door. He grasped the knob, only to remember that the door was still locked — from the outside.

“Oh, just a moment, Mr. Fennec.” She stood. Frances darted over to the efficiency kitchen and rifled through her cabinets. She plucked two different snack bars from the shelf and walked over to Darwin, quickly stuffing them into his pocket. “In case the two of you get hungry later,” she whispered. “The red one is good for energy in the morning. The purple one is best before bed. It has valerian root, used for calming purposes.” She held his gaze several seconds longer than necessary. “Both contain very powerful nutrients, so space them out by at least six hours...” Frances deliberated on something before adding, “They’re different from the macaroon you ingested earlier. We’re not typically supposed to have snacks outside of the common area, but it will be our little secret.” Darwin wasn’t sure how that explained the miniature kitchen behind her, but nodded, nonetheless. To Darwin she added in a whisper, “The walls have ears.”

She then turned to Rue, and said, “You’ll come back and visit me again, won’t you Rue? After all, you are my only child.”

Rue felt a sudden flash of heat, and her heart sped up again, just for a moment. It triggered a memory, the one where she was talking with her friend Midge under the most unpleasant of circumstances. She pushed the thought aside.

Francis pulled on a chord hanging next to the door, summoning the same attendant who, once again, purposefully rapped on the door in her signature pattern.

Frances unlocked it. "Please escort our friends to the front door," she instructed.

"But it's raining cats and dogs out there!" the attendant protested. Maybe the deaconess didn't realize that.

"Then give them an umbrella," Frances responded curtly.

"Yes, Deaconess," the woman replied meekly, biting her lip as if fighting back a response. To Rue and Darwin, she said, "Right this way."

After Darwin made certain that Rue was settled as comfortably as possible in the back seat of their rental car, he climbed into the front, stripping off his suit jacket and shirt.

"Aren't you going to be cold in just an undershirt?" she protested.

"I'll survive," Darwin answered, rolling up the pieces of clothing and tucking them under the front passenger seat side. "Besides," he grinned into the rearview mirror, "I can always climb back there with you if I need to warm up."

Rue forced a groggy smile. The evening was turning out to be cold, damp, and anxiety-producing. She tugged off the itchy wig that was now beginning to lose shape and stick to her cheeks in a damp mess. Rue fluffed her hair underneath and combed it with her fingers.

"Probably best to remove the contacts, too," Darwin reminded, reaching into the center console and retrieving a small contact case. "They're not really meant for long-term use."

A clap of thunder and the boom of a tree getting struck by lightning sent them both jumping toward the ceiling of the car. Darwin nearly dropped the case before Rue snatched it with both palms as he leaned over the backseat.

Rue caught her breath before settling in again, curling up on the seat and wrapping her arms around her for warmth. "Can you put the heat on?" she suggested. "Just for a few minutes?"

"Yeah, I can do that," he agreed. "But we can't leave it running too long or we won't have enough fuel to get back into town in the morning."

"Darwin?" Rue yawned.

"Yes, Rue," Darwin answered.

"Why didn't you tell me you were married?"

"Probably the same reason you didn't tell me you ran away on the eve of your wedding."

After a long pause, Rue asked, "Do you think I'm crazy?"

"No, of course not." Darwin was surprised. "Why would you think that?"

"Well, because of my panic attack, running out on my fiancé, and then disappearing to New York."

"No," Darwin reassured her. "I don't think you're crazy." After a pause, he added, "Why don't you try to get some rest, and we can talk about it during our long ride back to New York in the morning?"

Rue let out a groan as the rain pelted the roof of the car and fogged up the windows. "Darwin?"

"What is it, Rue?"

"Now I really *do* have to go to the bathroom," she whined.

CHAPTER 18

Long and Winding Road

Present Day in Pennsylvania

Rue was so hungry by morning that she was tempted to eat one of the snack bars her mother had given them. But she couldn't. She knew they were evidence. What she didn't realize was that Darwin had a little evidence of his own tucked under the passenger seat that she now occupied.

"We can stop for a quick bite to eat," Darwin reasoned. "But we have to get these samples to the forensic scientist Ortega recommended. I forget her name—"

"Penelope," Rue offered. "She was on the scene when one of the art models died before my session at the Atelier school." Rue remembered that while Ortega and Dennis were being... well, very stereotypically male and seemingly unfeeling... Penelope had been kind, advocating for Rue. That type of kindness somehow didn't match with her work investigating potential homicides.

"That's right," Darwin nodded. "Penelope."

"But what's the hurry? There are just two snack bars for her to send to the lab to analyze."

"That's not all," he smiled, glancing at her. "Under your seat are the remains of that spilled sugar water on my shirt and a half-eaten macaroon in my suit jacket."

"You devil," Rue laughed, sitting back and shaking her head.

"Oh, you don't know the half of it." He wriggled his eyes suggestively.

"I have some idea," Rue smirked.

After a long silence, with nothing but the sound of the windshield wipers going back and forth, cutting through a light drizzle, Rue finally asked, "So about that marriage?"

"Yours or mine?" Darwin's eyes remained on the road.

"Yours, obviously," Rue answered. "I've never been married."

"Right." Darwin tapped the steering wheel. "So, what would you like to know?"

"Uh, the usual... Who was she? How did you meet? Why didn't you stay married?"

"You're missing one vital question in that," Darwin replied.

"And, what's that?"

"Why we got married in the first place?"

"Well?" Rue motioned for him to continue.

Darwin thought a moment. "I was around twenty-three at the time. She was a bit younger."

"How much younger? What was her name?" Rue interrupted.

"Twenty-one, and why does it matter?"

"Just curious."

"I was in Ireland at the time—"

"Really? Why?" Rue sat up.

"If you'd stop interrupting me, I'll tell you," Darwin chastised.

"Well, excuse me for living," Rue pouted. "Go on."

"Let's just say I had fallen in with some bad people — story for another time. But the point is, I was about to get my proverbial goose cooked were it not for a young lass that took pity on me."

"What did she do?"

"She prevented her very influential father from feeding me to the fishes on a grift gone bad."

"You? And here I thought you were a pillar of society," Rue mocked. "But, that sort of explains Bristol."

Bristol was a contractor Darwin hired periodically for his special skills as a bodyguard, 'project manager,' and getaway car driver. He owned a chop shop in Jersey that posed as a car repair and detail service center. Now married with kids, he appeared to be making a slow transition into respectable living. She was still waiting on the 'origin story' of how he and Darwin met. But, one reveal at a time.

"Well, funny you should mention Bristol," Darwin laughed.

"Why is that?" Rue wanted to know.

"Cuz I married his sister."

"What? How did I not hear about this sooner?" Rue leaned so far forward, she all but hit her head on the windshield.

"Careful," Darwin warned. Rue sat back, folding her arms. After a moment, Darwin relented. "I was orphaned at a young age but discovered I had the gift of gab... managed to support myself by small grifts here and there. By the time I was seventeen, I had several mates working for me."

"Bristol being one of them?" Rue asked.

"Ours was more of a collaboration. Only, we chose the wrong mark."

Rue put the connection together. "The 'mark' being Bristol's dad?"

"Exactly," Darwin confirmed. "The man had more money than God, and we thought if we could nick a bit of it, we'd have enough to flee to America and start a real enterprise."

"Only you got caught."

Darwin nodded. "Only, we got caught. His dad let him off with a warning, but I wasn't about to be so lucky."

"Until Bristol's sister took a shine to you?"

"Er, something like that."

"What does that mean?!"

"It means we sort of had a... thing... before that."

"What kind of 'thing'?" Rue wanted to know.

"C'mon Rue. I was a young lad with nothing in this world who suddenly had this pretty red-head making googly eyes at me. What do you think?"

"Oh." Rue was somewhat disappointed. "I see."

"Don't look so disappointed. That was over two decades ago!"

Darwin could sense her doing the math. "I'm forty-four," he finally answered.

Rue shook her head. "How is it that we're living together and still know so little about one another?"

"Maybe neither one of us is particularly proud of our pasts?" Darwin offered.

"Hmmm, maybe," Rue agreed. "But so far, your past sounds far more exciting than mine. So, let's skip ahead to the marriage part."

"Not much to say after that." Darwin confessed. "I was adopted into Bristol's family and became part of a larger grift. Molly got pregnant."

"Her name was... is... Molly?"

"You were right the first time," Darwin sighed, pushing back emotion.

"She's dead?" Rue confirmed.

"Yes. I'll get to that," Darwin paused for several minutes as he swerved carefully down the mountain road toward the Pennsylvania Turnpike. "She got pregnant. We were convinced that getting married was the 'right thing to do,' even though we soon learned that we had almost nothing in common. She had a miscarriage, but we decided to try to give it a go for a few years."

"And then got divorced," Rue confirmed.

"Yes... stayed friends though. It was just one of those things."

"How did she die?"

"Like me, she decided to go it on her own. Only, I wasn't there to save her like she did me. Got in with the wrong crowd... ended up dying of an overdose at age thirty-three."

"Shit, Darwin." Rue folded her arms. "And here I am feeling sorry for my life."

"Yeah, but it didn't need to be that way," Darwin answered. "I mean for Molly, not you. Like you, she was born into the family's... way of thinking. But Bristol and I did our best to protect her. But we were too late."

"I'm sorry," Rue answered quietly.

"Well, the silver lining, if there is one, is that it convinced Bristol that he and I should try using our talents for good. I arrived in the States first, changed my name and set up my business as a private investigator. Been on the straight and narrow ever since... mostly."

"That explains my mother's comment about the 'name you're going by these days.'"

"You caught that, huh?"

"Yup. So, what *is* your name?"

"Could we just leave it as 'Darwin Fennec' for now?"

"Sure," Rue answered.

After another long pause, they approached a roadside diner.

"Wanna grab some breakfast here?" Darwin asked.

"Works for me. I'm so hungry, I could eat a horse."

"I've never heard that expression said where somehow it didn't disgust me," Darwin confessed.

"But eating chicken-fried steak with a side of ham is okay?" Rue challenged.

"I didn't say it was logical," Darwin confessed.

"Besides, you know as well as I do, you're going to settle on granola and yogurt.

"You are probably right, Ms. Brennan," he joked, reverting to a time when they used to refer to one another by their surnames. After parking the car, Darwin and Rue made their way to the entrance of the Red Eagle Diner. He opened the door for her to pass first. "Why, thank you, Mr. Fennec."

"So," Darwin asked when they'd finally slid into a cracked red vinyl booth, "When do I get to hear about the time you skipped out on your fiancé and escaped to New York?"

A waitress wearing a pale blue dress and white apron and bonnet handed them menus. "Howdy folks," she boomed pleasantly. "Start you off with some coffee?"

"Sounds great," Rue answered. After the server had nodded and disappeared, Rue leaned over to Darwin. "Soon. Story for another time?"

Darwin nodded. He felt a little exposed, though he hated to admit it. But then, Rue had just faced her mother, and a cult she tried for years to get away from, and a panic attack that she was embarrassed about and would rather forget.

"Story for another time," Darwin agreed.

~

The ride back to the city was an uneventful one... until the last leg when they were about three miles shy of the Lincoln Tunnel.

Darwin had been sulking, just a little, about the realization that he knew so little of his now live-in girlfriend. More unsettling was the fact that he had been so forthright about his past, always answered her questions honestly, and yet, when it was Rue's turn, she'd always clam up. Having met her mother and visited the church, he was beginning to understand why, but what would he have to do to earn her trust? *Time,* he thought to himself. *Maybe she just needs a little more time.*

Suddenly, a deer leapt into the road. Surprising for this time of day. Darwin hit the brakes, except the peddle felt mushy, as if he were stepping into mud or melting snow. He swerved, just missing the beast, who — after stopping in terror — seemed to regain its wits and scamper away. Car horns blared as he pulled off the road to avoid getting hit from behind. The car behind him jammed on the brakes while the car in front was smart enough to speed up, avoiding a near collision. Meanwhile, Darwin's rental spun around 180 degrees and stopped roadside, facing the wrong direction. Thanks to last night's storm, the car got stuck in a thick pool of mud. He quickly pulled the key from the ignition and sucked in a breath.

He looked over at Rue, who stared straight ahead of her as if in a trance.

"Rue?" he asked, touching her shoulder. "Are you okay?"

Rue blinked several times before turning her head toward Darwin and muttering, "I hate Pennsylvania."

CHAPTER 19
Penelope

Somewhere in Brooklyn

It was half-past one when Darwin and Rue finally arrived at forensic scientist Penelope Washburn's Brooklyn apartment complex.

"Sorry," Penelope sniffed as she let the two into her home. "Seems the elevators are chronically out of order in this place."

Rue was used to it from her former life living in a Lower East Side walkup. Darwin, on the other hand, was a little out of breath. "That's okay," he huffed. "Just a reminder that my green smoothies are not going to do my cardio for me."

Penelope didn't understand the comment and decided to nod politely but otherwise ignore it. She shut the door behind them.

It was only from the glow of the hallway light that they could see that her eyes were puffy. She had been crying.

"Are you alright?" Rue asked sympathetically. She, herself, was exhausted from the encounter with her mother and the church, spending all night sleeping in a car, and almost dying in car accident near the Lincoln Tunnel. Frankly, she felt she could really use a shower. But Penelope's worn-out expression pulled Rue out of her own feelings of self-pity.

"Mmm, hmm," she lied. Penelope used the back of her hand to wipe away a few tears. That seemed to bother her, so she darted behind her kitchen counter to grab a paper towel from the roll. She blew her nose, threw the paper towel in a foot-operated trash can, and then quickly washed her hands. Years of collecting data from a crime scene made her highly aware of fingerprints, germs, and why one should not stick one's fingers near their eyes. Just then, the phone above the counter rang. "Excuse me a moment." Penelope grabbed the phone while Rue and Darwin stood awkwardly in the entranceway. Darwin was still holding his balled-up shirt and suit jacket from the church service just the day before.

"I can't talk now, Gareth," Penelope whispered. "I have company." She paused while they could hear the muffled sounds of a male voice on the other end. "None of your darn business. Don't call me again tonight. Goodbye." She hung up the phone, abruptly, despite protests on the other side. Moments later, the phone rang again. Penelope lifted the receiver and quickly hung it up again. Then, she unplugged the phone from the wall.

"Sorry about that, too," Penelope said, eyeing the clothes in Darwin's hands. "Whatcha got for me?"

"A shirt stain from some kind of sugar water, a half-eaten macaroon in the right jacket pocket, and two snack bars from the Vandenberg Nutraceuticals company... any or all of it may be laced with something. What? I don't know."

"Fascinating." Penelope's eyes lit up slightly. Ortega had notified Penelope that Darwin might need to stop by, but she didn't know the details. It was better that way in case she got caught using the crime lab for outside private cases.

Penelope reached under the counter and pulled out what looked like an oversized plastic freezer bag and a pair of blue latex gloves. After putting the gloves on, she pulled open the bag and stood in front of Darwin. "Here, drop them in the bag for me."

He obliged, and she quickly sealed the bag, removed the gloves, and grabbed a permanent marker that was attached by a magnet to the side of her refrigerator. She quickly scribbled a few letters on the bag before setting it on the counter with lightning speed.

"Wow," Rue commented. "Efficient."

"I try to be," Penelope answered modestly. "I'll phone Detective Ortega with the results, if it's all the same to you?"

"That's just fine," Rue answered. "We can check in with him about next steps. In the meantime, thank you for letting us barge into your personal home on your day off. We appreciate the help."

Penelope wasn't risking her neck and her job for them, and they knew it. But, she was ever-polite, nonetheless.

Rue opened the door. "We'll just see ourselves out. Thank you." She motioned for Darwin to go first. Before closing the door, she turned and whispered to Penelope, "Whomever they are, they are an idiot for making you cry and don't deserve you."

It was only then that Penelope recognized Rue. "Wait a moment." She waved a finger into the air. "You were the gal at the Artist Atelier school during our investigation months ago. The one wearing that weird costume... Oh!" The lightbulb went off in her head.

"Yes, few recognize me when I'm not dressed as a scantily clad Electra," Rue joked.

"I knew the name Darwin was familiar when José mentioned it, but I didn't piece it together until just now. Funny—"

"What is?" Rue was curious.

"That you both went from being suspects in a murder investigation to investigating murder." Penelope thought a moment about the irony. "Oh," she finished. "And you're right, Gareth is an idiot who doesn't deserve me." Penelope held her chin up proudly.

Rue didn't know who Gareth was, but she nodded supportively. After all, Penelope seemed the kind sort. And in this world, that breed of human is sometimes hard to find.

~

A BURNER PHONE rang just as Darwin and Rue entered their condo after a harrowing couple of days.

"That was quick," Darwin greeted Bristol pleasantly, as he answered. It was someone from his team who towed Darwin's car after the near-accident in Pennsylvania.

"Who'd you tick off?" was all that Bristol could say in a down-played Irish-turned-New York City accent. "I've seen a lot of funny 'mess with the breaks' situations, but this here was a little too clever for me."

"What do mean by clever?" Darwin wanted to know.

"They didn't slash the brakes. That would be too obvious," Bristol answered. "They drained the brake fluid just enough to where you'd have troubles an hour or so down the line but not immediately, and—"

"And?"

"You did say this was a rental car, right?"

"Right," Darwin confirmed.

"The brake pads are so worn thin they might as well be rice paper. What rental company would send a car out in that condition?" Darwin could feel Bristol shaking his head from the other end of the phone line. Meanwhile, the sound of welding and a chainsaw could be heard in the background. Darwin decided not to ask why.

"So, we're presuming someone messed with the brake fluid and pads while we were attending Rue's old stomping grounds?"

Bristol let out a huff loudly into the receiver. "It's an easy enough job - they probably only needed an hour or so, tops. Whoever did this, well, if they didn't wanna kill ya, they certainly wanted you messed up a bit."

"Well, thank you, Bristol. Do I need to come and get the car to take it back to the rental agency?"

"Nah!" Bristol answered, as the sound of grinding in the background continued. "I'll take care of it for ya."

"I don't know what that means, Bristol," Darwin answered.

"Probably best that way," Bristol answered, hanging up the phone before Darwin could ask any more questions.

Moments later, the phone rang a second time... It was Ortega.

"Please tell me your day is going better than mine," Darwin greeted.

"Why? What happened?" Ortega demanded.

Now out of harm's way and safely back at their condo, Darwin filled Ortega in on the day, ending with their near-accident.

"Shit!" Ortega answered. "I don't like this. I don't like this at all."

"I wasn't too fond of the idea of dying either," Darwin joked.

"Want me to make some calls at the precinct?" Ortega offered.

"Absolutely not," Darwin answered. "Ever since you and Officer

Dennis left, we've been hitting nothing but brick walls. Between the Church of Infinite Love and the Vandenberg Family, the two seem to have their fingers in many pies. Seems hard to find support from law enforcement in Pennsylvania and New York."

Ortega sighed. "Running into the same deal in Florida," Ortega confessed. "But I've got a few tricks up my sleeve. You and Rue need to lie low for a couple of days. I'll follow up as soon as I a can."

"What are you going to do?" Darwin asked, before catching himself. "Never mind, don't tell me. Probably shouldn't have had told you as much as I did over the phone." Time for Darwin to bust another burner phone and set up a replacement. While security on cell phone calls had gotten better over the past year, he still wasn't taking too many chances.

There was a long pause on the line. Darwin could hear Ortega breathing unsteadily.

"You okay?" Darwin asked.

"Uh, yeah," Ortega answered. "Listen, I have a favor to ask outside of the case. Do you mind?"

Darwin was intrigued. Ortega wasn't one to ask for help and was somewhat flattered that he trusted him for it. Finally, he answered, "What do you need?"

CHAPTER 20

Ortega and Nancy

Back in Florida

Nancy arrived home to witness her husband slamming the house phone down, only to pick it up and slam it down a second time.

"Rough day?" Nancy asked, swinging her tennis racket slightly from side to side.

Ortega began to pace angrily. "I used to be able to snap my fingers and get what I needed to do my job. Now that I'm retired, it's like I'm invisible and powerless. I have to ask 'Mother, May I?' for every blessed thing!"

She glanced at the cell phone on the counter quizzically. "So, you're resorting to violently attacking our landline?"

"Somehow, pushing the little button on the cell phone is not as satisfying when you're trying to hang up on someone," Ortega huffed. "Call it... catharsis."

"Oh, I'd call it something all right," Nancy chuckled. "But that wouldn't be the 'c' word I'd have chosen."

"I'm sorry, Honey." Ortega gave Nancy a peck on the lips. "How was your day?"

"Obviously, better than yours," Nancy retorted. "This is why I didn't want you wrapped up in detective work anymore. Look at what it does to you."

"I couldn't tell Officer Dennis 'no,' not after all our work together."

"Bullshit," Nancy answered. "I could see the gleam in your eye the other day on that video call. You were champing at the bit to get back into solving crimes."

"Is that so terrible?" Ortega challenged. "I was actually a useful, productive member of society before moving to Florida. Now I'm just—"

"My husband?" Nancy offered. "Maybe if you were a little more social... volunteered somewhere—"

"But this is what I love," Ortega protested.

"Can't you try loving something else, for once?" Nancy all but yelled, before catching herself. She set down the racket, defeated. "Fine."

"What do you mean, 'fine'?" Ortega asked angrily.

"Tell me about your case." Nancy waved her hand at him.

"I told you. It's not my case. I'm just helping Officer—"

"Tell me about your case," Nancy tried again. "You're up to your eyeballs in it. So, what's the problem?"

Ortega paused for several moments, assessing whether she was serious. Finally, he answered, "Might want to have a seat." Ortega guided his wife over to the couch, where files were strewn everywhere on the coffee table in front of him.

Ortega took the next half hour getting Nancy up to speed on everything he knew so far. When he was finished, he waited, expecting Nancy's eyes to be glazed over with boredom. But it was just the opposite. She had a fire in them the likes of which he'd never seen before.

"I can help you," Nancy proclaimed suddenly.

"Come again?" Ortega was certain he'd misheard her.

"I can help you," she grinned from ear to ear. "Our next step is to snoop around Vandenberg Nutraceuticals, right? We can ask my father. I'm sure he's got connections with someone there—"

"No," Ortega shook his head fervently. "We're not dragging your father into this. Besides, it's got to be undercover, otherwise, they'll just hide the evidence before we get there." Suddenly, Ortega realized something. "And what's this 'we' all of a sudden."

"If you're not going to take an interest in my life, then, let me take an interest in yours." Ortega was about to protest both her involvement in the case and the fact that she'd assumed he had no interest in her day-to-day goings on. She held up a hand, "I'm not taking 'no' for an answer, José." After a dramatic pause, she added, "I can go undercover."

"What?! No you can't!" Ortega barked.

"Why not? I did a little theater in college."

"Did a little theater in college? Nancy, would you listen to yourself?" Ortega stood, and went back to pacing across the living room floor. "There's been a murder—"

"*Alleged* murder," she corrected him.

"Pretty sure it was murder." He tilted his head, sideways. *Alleged my ass,* he thought. "And you're not a trained agent!"

"But it seems that since Officer Dennis can't get the New York or Florida police departments to look in on the case, trained agents are in short supply, wouldn't you say?" Nancy raised an eyebrow, the one she always raised when she knew she had won.

"And if I did enlist your services, how exactly do you plan on getting in?"

"Well, you said yourself," Nancy rummaged through his files, pulling up one that outlined a map of the Vandenberg factory and security procedures for getting in and out of the place, "someone has to go in undercover. Perhaps a new employee? I can do that."

"When have you ever work—" Ortega caught himself under Nancy's fiery gaze. She hadn't ever had a traditional job, from what he could tell. Ortega was her third husband. Nancy had gone right from graduate school to marriage and motherhood, volunteered here and there, but she always had her father's money and two exes who made significantly more than Ortega ever did. Both paid her a decent settlement to end their marriages quietly and without media attention. Frankly, Ortega wasn't sure why Nancy had even picked someone like him in the first place. He certainly didn't fit into any of her social circles, something that had become increasingly evident with their move to Florida.

Ortega tried a different tactic. "You'd be willing to perform tedious factory work for eight hours a day, for an indeterminate amount of time, just to potentially dig up clues?"

"I know what's going on in that brain of yours, Honey. And yes, I am fully capable of handling a job. Plus, it sounds exciting! I've never worked on a case with you before!"

"Yeah, well it's not nearly as romantic as you think it is," Ortega reasoned.

"Well, you seem to love it," Nancy retorted.

"And, how do you suggest we get you past security with any recording devices or tracking equipment?" Ortega asked. "Even if we manage to get you on the payroll, you'd have to go in clean." *Once Nancy makes up her mind about something*, he thought to himself, *there's no changing it.* One of the things he loved the most about her was her fierce determination and strength. Unfortunately, also, on occasion, these were traits that he liked the least.

"Don't you worry about that." Nancy winked, standing and tossing his thinning hair as he paced by her. "I've got a plan. Theater, remember?"

~

"YEAH, NO PROBLEM, JO," Dennis told Ortega, who phoned the officer not long after his conversation with Nancy. "Let's plan on meeting here tomorrow, if that works for the two of you. Say, 8:00?"

Dennis heard a quiet shuffle behind him as he assumed that Emma had returned from a grocery store run. The two were pleasantly surprised to find that waiting in the garage at their new residence was one of Erasmus' 'old' cars, a sleek, shiny black Porsche 959. But this one had a customized upgrade... an automatic transmission. He was surprised he hadn't heard the garage door open or the rev of the car's engine, but he had been a little distracted today.

Dennis listened to Ortega's remarks on the other end of the phone line, nodding to no one but himself as he moved around the house, visiting each indoor plant with a watering can. "I agree. We need to send someone in undercover, but I'm hesitant to use civilians. Let's talk about it tomorrow. Maybe, then, we'll get closer to understanding what really happened to Erasmus."

Dennis ended the call, tucking the cell phone in his pocket and setting the can above the kitchen sink. He swung around and all but body slammed Sprightly, who stood right behind him with a fabricated grin plastered on her face that didn't match the concern in her eyes.

"What really happened to Erasmus?" Sprightly asked.

"Sprightly, how long have you been here?" Dennis enquired.

"For about three minutes," Sprightly answered honestly. "Right about the part where you said you needed to investigate Vandenberg Nutraceuticals to get to the bottom of Erasmus' death."

"Well, I'm sorry you heard that, but you shouldn't go sneaking up on people. What are you doing here, anyway?" Dennis demanded.

Then he saw her, a small woman standing silently in the open doorway… Elsbeth.

"Have you guys met?" Sprightly motioned toward the girl in the doorway and then to Dennis.

"Yes," Dennis answered. "Elsbeth, nice to see you again." He began grinding his teeth nervously. To Sprightly, he said between grit teeth, "Sprightly, remind me that you and I need to discuss your letting yourself in and out of the house unannounced. That may have been okay before, but it's not okay now."

"Roger that," Sprightly saluted unapologetically. "But it seems Elsbeth is here for the same reason you're having a meeting tomorrow."

"Is that so?" Dennis asked cautiously.

"Yes," Elsbeth answered simply. "S… s… someone m… murdered Grandfather Erasmus. And, I'm here t—t-to help find out who."

Dennis was taken aback by her response. Far from the timid young woman he met at the reading of Erasmus's will, this one appeared like a solid block of granite at his doorstep. She had clearly set her intentions and would not be moved.

A car could be heard coming up the drive, followed by the electric whirring of a garage door opening. Moments later, Emma appeared carrying two large brown paper bags.

Sprightly immediately went to retrieve them from her. "I coulda gone shopping for your, Emma. But I was picking up—"

"Elsbeth?" Emma was surprised. "What are you doing here?"

"Nice to s… see you, too," she mumbled. At that moment, the facade broke, and the girl began sniffing back tears.

"Oh, Elsbeth," Emma's voice softened. While not as good at the whole touchy-feely thing as Dennis, she rushed to the girl's side, wrapping her in an awkward hug that was not returned by Elsbeth, who valued her personal space. This hug was not on her terms. Elsbeth stood there coldly, save for a single tear that trickled down her cheek. Eventually, Emma caught on, smiled awkwardly, and released the girl.

"As I was saying," Sprightly set the bag on the kitchen counter, "I would have gone shopping for you, but I got a call from Ferdinand about picking up Elsbeth from the airport."

Emma looked around the young woman. "Elsbeth?" she asked. "If you just flew in, where is your luggage?"

"On it!" Sprightly circled a finger in the air as if whipping up some magic. "Got it in my car."

Emma had wondered who was driving the unsightly beater car sitting to one side at the end of the driveway. She'd almost hit it accidentally when turning, with great speed, heading toward their garage. Emma was having a little too much fun with her newly acquired vehicle.

"Elsbeth, why don't you sit down in the living room and I'll get you something to drink. An iced tea, perhaps?"

"Got any vodka?" she asked abruptly, gently wiping her eyes with her fingertips.

"Well, no," Emma answered.

"Too bad," Elsbeth replied, marching into the living room and sitting on the edge of one of the couches.

Moments later, Sprightly returned with her single bag. "Shall I put this in one of the spare bedrooms?" she asked.

"Uh, yes," Dennis chimed in quickly. "The first one on the left, just next to the main bedroom." He didn't want her wandering into his room at the far end of the hall, lest she, for one thing, see how messy he was, and secondly, notice that he and Emma were sleeping in separate bedrooms. He had a reputation to uphold... for some reason.

"Sure thing," Sprightly called, as she made her way down the hall. "By the way, I'm in!"

"In?!" Dennis called back. "In for what, exactly?"

Sprightly bounced back in the room. "The coup you're planning at the factory. I'll go undercover for you. No problem."

Emma and Dennis glanced first at Sprightly, then at each other, and then at Elsbeth, who was now eyeing them all with odd fascination. She saw Dennis and Emma exchange glances once more.

"I know w-w-hat you're thinking," Elsbeth answered. "I m-might be a s... suspect. But if you w-w-ant to get into that f... factory, you are going t... to have t... to t... trust m... me."

CHAPTER 21
The Plan

Florida

It was almost as if the word "ragtag" was invented after seeing Ortega's team gathered at Emma and Dennis's residence the morning before their 'factory coup.' Sprightly was the first to arrive, wearing a paisley-patterned, spaghetti-strap dress and flip-flops. She also donned a hat and sunglasses, furtively looking around, as if to make sure no one in the neighborhood noticed her arrival, even though her telltale blue bicycle was sitting out front.

"Coffee?" Dennis offered, once Sprightly had made her way to the living room inside their home.

"No thanks." Sprightly rocked back and forth on her heels, excitedly. "Makes me too jittery."

Ortega arrived with Nancy next. Dennis had only met Nancy in person, briefly, on two occasions, one was at a station Christmas party thrown when Ortega was still a detective with the precinct. The other was the time she stopped by their station to drop off Ortega's lunch one day. (Though many suspected it was really so she could see what Penelope,

Ortega's old flame, looked like.) She has gained a bit of weight since he first met her several years ago. Her hair was also now dyed a dark red and cut short.

"Nice to see you again, Mrs. Ortega," Dennis greeted. "Coffee?"

"No thanks," Nancy answered. "We brought our own." She held up a thermos that was hiding behind her back. "And you can call me Nancy."

"Decaf," Ortega whispered to Dennis, shaking his head sourly.

"I heard that!" Nancy answered. "Caffeine isn't good for your nerves. You're lucky I don't make you drink herbal tea."

At that moment, Emma made her way down the hallway carrying a small plate of cookies.

Ortega almost didn't recognize her. Her usual sweatshirt and jogging pants had been replaced with a short-sleeved red blouse and flair skirt that covered her knees. Her hair was now a curly bleach blonde that she somehow pulled off despite her olive complexion. Emma still wore red running sneakers though, he noticed.

"Nice house," he said absentmindedly.

Nancy hit him in the arm. "Where are your manners?" To Emma, she said, "I'm Nancy Ortega. It's nice to meet you."

"Likewise," Emma greeted. "Won't you sit down?" The words felt funny coming from her mouth. She'd never had enough furniture to invite guests to sit down... or to even entertain.

"Are we waiting on anyone else?" Nancy asked.

As if on cue, Elsbeth arrived in the room, appearing almost out of thin air. Nancy was taken aback. Despite her small frame, it was almost as if Elsbeth was a vacuum and could suck the energy out of the room just by her presence. Today, she wore an all-black blouse and slacks, a stark contrast to her excessively pale complexion.

"Everyone, this is Elsbeth Ions, granddaughter of Erasmus Vandenberg," Emma quickly introduced her.

"Elsbeth, why don't you have a seat next to Nancy?" Emma suggested. With the stealth of a ghost or quiet ninja, she floated across the room and sat down. Nancy was confused by Elsbeth, looking to her husband for clarity. Ortega seemed unaffected by the woman's odd behavior. Nancy sighed. Ortega seemed emotionally unaffected by lots of things. So, there she sat, with Elsbeth to her left and Ortega to her right.

I'm surrounded by emotionally unavailable people, Nancy thought. *Story of my life.*

"Shall we begin?" Dennis offered pleasantly, standing at the front of the room. "Jo, do you want to lead this or should we?" He motioned to Emma, who had been leaning up against the wall, arms folded. She stood upright, taken aback. She wasn't used to being a 'we' and wasn't entirely certain how she felt about it. Meanwhile, Ortega cringed at his new nickname. *Surely Officer Dennis could come up with something better?* He thought.

Ortega was used to leading, barking orders for everyone else to follow. Frankly, he was surprised Dennis had even questioned who was in charge. But then, he was retired now, and one side-long glance at Nancy reminded him that she was only there trying to be supportive but wasn't really keen on him taking a case. This was a departure from her excitement just yesterday. Ortega was beginning to recognize that, after more than a decade of marriage, he didn't seem to know Nancy very well at all.

"Why don't you kick it off, Dennis," Ortega finally answered. "And, I can just fill in where necessary."

"Uh, okay," Dennis was surprised. "So, Elsbeth arrived yesterday insistent on..." Dennis reconsidered his words, "... convinced that her grandfather's death was suspicious, and she wants to help use her influence as a member of the Vandenberg family to get her and Emma inside."

"They're... h... h... hiding... s... s... something," she stammered. Elsbeth shook her head and pounded a fist into her thigh. Nancy raised an eyebrow but said nothing.

"It's okay, Elsbeth," Emma jumped in, sensing the girl's frustration that her stutter had returned. "You're just upset. We all are."

Dennis continued, "With Emma being a key shareholder, it makes sense that she'd want a tour of the facility. But it's going to be hard to convince them of that without a team of lawyers present."

"Which would make it nearly impossible for us to carry out a normal investigation," Ortega added.

"Exactly," Dennis agreed. "But, as Elsbeth pointed out to us upon her arrival, they know her. If she asks for a tour, they may be more inclined to accommodate the request and let their guard down."

"So, what's your plan?" Ortega asked.

"Well," he looked at Emma. "Why don't you tell him?"

"I found out from Mr. Lundy, Erasmus' lawyer — now *my* lawyer, as it turns out — that the three key players at the factory are Baxter Baker, the general manager who is now absent until further notice—"

"What happened to him?" Nancy asked, sitting up as if alarmed.

"He said he had to disappear for a little while. I suspect it had to do with the fact that he was trying to warn us about Erasmus' death not being an accident," Emma answered.

"Oh." Nancy leaned back into the couch. "Right," she chastised herself. That was in yesterday's brief. *Remembering all these details is harder than I thought,* Nancy mused.

"The next two are Victor Newberry, vice-president of operations, and Mordecai Sanzani, chief operating officer. Mordecai is reportedly out of town on business this week; but we'll still have to skirt around Victor Newberry."

"How do you plan to do that?" Ortega asked.

Elsbeth smirked devilishly, "I can handle Uncle Victor. Don't worry." Oddly enough, the stutter was momentarily gone.

"Where do we come in?" Sprightly was dying to know.

"First," Emma replied, "Elsbeth and I visit the factory tomorrow. We're fairly confident we can get Victor's okay between Elsbeth's family connection and the threat of me bringing lawyers, if he doesn't play nice. We don't entirely know what we're looking for yet..."

"Anything linking Vandenberg Nutraceuticals with questionable products being shipped to the Church of Infinite Love," Dennis chimed in. "Not entirely sure I'm buyin' it that everything that left that factory was on the up and up and ingredients were added later. Else, why would Erasmus be so upset?"

"Plus, Darwin Fennec phoned to give us an update on what his friend Monique found," Emma chimed in.

"What?" Ortega was almost offended. "Darwin called... you?" He'd never been sidelined before. And while he'd protested up and down to Nancy that it was Dennis' case, he really didn't expect Darwin to share with Dennis first. *But then,* he reasoned to himself, *it was pretty obvious from that call that Nancy had been purposefully kept in the dark about the details. Maybe in his strange way, he was trying to protect our marriage?*

Nancy, Sprightly, and Elsbeth all tilted their heads at once, like curious puppies, waiting for the update.

"That's right," Dennis answered uncomfortably. "It seems there were three deaths linked to the church within the past decade — all young women whose stories vanished as soon as they hit the news. It was amazing Monique found what she did."

Emma, suddenly remembering, darted from the room, returning later with manila envelopes, handing one to Nancy, one to Sprightly, and one to Elsbeth. "Inside are newspaper copies of the news stories. You can read up on the women before you visit the factory."

"So, we *are* going to get to do some sleuthing." Sprightly rubbed her hands together, excitedly.

"Don't get so excited," Dennis answered. "I'm still not keen on sending civilians in to do an officer's job. It just so happens that I can't get anyone at the precinct to believe me—"

"I think they believe you, Dennis," Ortega answered. "They just don't care."

"Money talks in this town," Dennis nodded. Then, noticing the known-to-be well off Nancy, he cleared his throat awkwardly before continuing. "We're hoping Elsbeth and Emma can do a cursory search. And, if makes sense, we'd like to send you, Nancy, and you, Sprightly, in for a few days as factory workers. We'd set you up as new hires and give you back stories."

"How exciting!" Sprightly bounced up and down in her chair.

"Unless you give yourself away," Elsbeth answered flatly. "Then, you're dead."

Sprightly stopped bouncing.

"All we're asking you to do," Emma explained, "is go through a typical day. You're not asking questions, not rifling through anything. You'll just share what you observe, if anything."

"So, how are you going to get us in?" Nancy asked logically. "Do you have access to company IDs?"

"That's what we still have to find out," Emma answered. "Let's regroup after Elsbeth and I do the rounds tomorrow."

"What do you think, Jo?" Dennis asked.

"Frankly," Ortega answered, "I think it's a terrible plan. I don't like the idea of sending this girl," Ortega motioned toward Sprightly, "and my wife into that factory. I'd much rather you send me in to go undercover first."

"No can do, Jo," Dennis answered. "One, you've been on too many high-profile cases that have gotten international attention, and two... all of their factory workers are either boys, between the ages of fourteen and seventeen, or women."

"You mean there's not a single adult male in that factory? What about Victor and Mordecai?"

"They don't count. They are executives in the company."

"I see; so why is it that there are no men actually working on the production line?"

"Good question," Dennis answered. "But look at the photos in the news stories we provided." He pulled one out and pointed. "Get a magnifying glass for a closer look... see any men there?"

"Well, I'll be—" Ortega scratched his head. "This whole case is getting weirder by the minute."

"Good thing you have us." Nancy put a hand on her husband's knee and shot an excited glance toward Sprightly. To Ortega, she added, "Don't worry, Honey. I was best in my class at improv."

"I still think this is a terrible idea," Ortega complained.

CHAPTER 22
Factory

Florida

Victor Newberry seemed visibly surprised when a female attendant escorted Emma and Elsbeth into his office first thing on a Monday morning.

"They're here about the tour sir," she explained sheepishly. Her gaze fell toward the floor.

"Elsbeth, how nice to see you" He plastered on a fake smile as he quickly closed the ledger he had open on his desk.

"H... h... hello, Uncle Victor," Elsbeth answered softly, shrinking behind Emma. Her behavior was so strange... confident around some people and a shrinking violet among others.

Victor eyed Emma up and down before holding her gaze intently. Whereas Baxter had a modicum of charm about him, something about Victor's gaze was somehow... letch-y. Victor was a rotund man with a double chin. He stood to greet them, his tall form towering over the women.

Elsbeth shrank a little further.

"And who is this charming young lady you have with you, Elsbeth?" He took one of Emma's hands and cupped it between his two sweaty palms. It took everything in her power not to pull away. Instead, she smiled sweetly. "I'm Emma Post. Nice to meet you."

He dropped her hand. Victor's eyes darkened for a moment before he recovered his plastered-on smile. "Not the Emma Post who was left the entire Vandenberg fortune?"

"Not the entire fortune," Emma corrected.

"But enough," he grumbled.

"Uncle Victor," Elsbeth spoke softly. "I w... w... wanted to sh... show E... m.. ma the f... factory where Uncle Erasmus worked."

Victor paused for an unbearably long time, as if deciding to be in a sour mood or a sweet one. He tried settling on sweet. "You know that I'm not really Elsbeth's uncle," he explained, smiling coyly, as if Elsbeth weren't standing right in front of him. "But Erasmus began bringing her here on business trips. I have fond memories of little El running around with her pigtails and t-shirts with horses on them."

"Unicorns," Elsbeth corrected flatly.

"Yes, that's right," he smiled. "Unicorns. While not a Vandenberg myself, I like to think I'm an honorary member of the family." Emma smiled politely but said nothing. To Elsbeth, Victor said, "My dear girl. Don't you remember? We give tours on Tuesdays, not Mondays."

Elsbeth scratched her head absentmindedly. "Oh, that's right. Well, could you m... make an exception for Em... mm.. a s... since she's c... come all this way?"

There was something inconsistent about Elsbeth's speech patterns, but Emma couldn't quite figure out what it was. Instead, she turned her attention to Victor.

"Or," Emma suggested, "we could look around ourselves. We promise not to be in the way."

"No, that won't be necessary," Victor answered quickly. "Given that you're a shareholder and have traveled all this way to be here, let me see what I can do." He picked up the phone on his desk and hit the intercom button.

"Celia? Could you come in here, please?" The same attendant who escorted them into Victor's office returned.

"Yes, Mr. Newberry?"

"I'd like you to give my adopted niece, Elsbeth, and her friend Emma a private tour. Could you do that, please?"

It did not escape Emma's attention that he was both distancing himself *from*, and ingratiating himself *with*, the Vandenberg family, at the same time, while also diminishing Emma's position within the company, by referring to her as simply 'Elsbeth's friend.'

He's a special kind of chauvinist. Emma thought to herself but said nothing.

"Of course, Mr. Newberry," Celia answered, bowing her head slightly. After a long pause, she asked, "Now?"

"Yes, now would be perfect," he smiled, lips pursed like a cat that just ate the canary. "Now, if you don't mind, I'm very busy. But Celia will take care of you. You girls have fun." He used his fingertips to physically push Emma and Elsbeth on their backs, just between their shoulder blades, as if guiding them to evacuate his office as quickly as possible.

Once the three women were on the other side of the door, he closed it. Emma heard a loud 'click' as Victor locked them out. Next to the door was a thin glass window. Before he could turn his back on them, Elsbeth waved cautiously at him. He bent over, waving his fingers back at her. "Bye!" he could be heard saying, as he backed away.

Celia cleared her throat. She stood there, knees and ankles pressed together tightly. She was wearing a gray polyester skirt and a cream-colored blouse. Pantyhose covered her legs. Her shoes were a simple black with uncomfortable looking points on them. It was only then that Emma realized something. Celia, while polished in every other way, wasn't wearing any makeup.

That's odd, Emma thought. *I know I'm not terribly keen on the stuff, but most professional women seem pretty hung up on having their appearance 'just so.'*

"Right this way," Celia invited pleasantly. "Let me give you a brief history of the Vandenberg legacy," she began. Celia launched into Erasmus Vandenberg's early days of being a self-made man who 'pulled himself up by his bootstraps' to make a name for himself, even though he came from a family of potato farmers. At varying points during Celia's tour, Elsbeth could be seen mouthing Celia's words, metered almost exactly to Celia's speech patterns. It was uncanny… and made it clear that Elsbeth had heard this tour… a lot.

They took the stairs, not the elevator, to the lower factory floor. Celia said it was because they valued physical activity for better health. Emma wondered why, if they were so concerned about physical health, Celia was forced to go up and down the steps wearing close-toed, heeled shoes certain to cause lower back pain and hip and knee issues. But, Emma decided, maybe that was a choice, given that all the factory workers seemed to be wearing the same ugly gray pant and v-neck shirt combination. On their feet were thick black orthopedic sneakers.

Unlike the upstairs carpeted area, the floor here felt springier, like something someone would find on a running track. Emma bounced lightly.

"Synthetic rubber," Celia offered. "That's the spring you're feeling. Better than concrete when having to be on one's feet or walking back and forth for long periods of time."

The room appeared to be a giant warehouse, with assembly lines carved out, some for using machinery to assemble the packaging for products, others to systematically churn the ingredients for snack bars before sending them on the conveyor belt to the baking area. While parts of the work were manual, a large percentage of the factory consisted of specialized areas where a worker would repeat the same task, over and over.

It was as if Celia could read Emma's mind. "The difference between the use of specialized machinery and manual labor is that the product efficiency and output is one hundred times faster than if someone were to do everything by hand."

They paused by a woman who was busy loading macaroon wracks into a heating unit.

"Sounds… mind-numbing," Emma admitted.

"It's honest work," Celia smiled sweetly. "And purposeful work."

"How do you figure?" Emma asked blandly.

"We make the world a healthier place by feeding its people nutrient-rich foods they might not otherwise, normally, get in their diet. Our factory workers understand that, while their job might not *feel* glamorous, their work is very meaningful and important."

Emma searched Celia's face for sincerity. Somehow, Celia appeared to believe her own hype.

"Don't touch that!" Celia suddenly called out, just as Elsbeth was fingering the lever on one of the conveyors. Elsbeth quickly drew her hand back as several factory workers looked up from their tasks. "I'm sorry for yelling," Celia apologized. "But we have a well-oiled system in place. Any disruptions could put production back for weeks."

"Sorry," Elsbeth said absently. Emma was fairly certain that she didn't mean it.

They passed a sign that read 'Research and Development.'

"What's that about?" Emma asked.

"Oh," Celia answered, brushing past the sign and the hallway leading toward a different wing within the factory. "That's our R&D department, where they test out new recipes, do market research, and bring new product to market."

"Fascinating," Emma lied. "Can we see it?"

"Oh, I'm afraid that's not part of the tour." Celia shook her head.

"Even for a primary shareholder in the company?" Elsbeth suddenly chimed in. Celia was taken aback.

Finally, she answered, pursing her lips, "I'd have to run this by Mr. Sanzani. But, unfortunately, he's not here today."

"Then, he'll never know," Elsbeth tried again.

"Sorry, no," Celia was adamant.

At the end of the hall was a supply closet. The door was open, revealing stacks of folded uniforms and what appeared to be name tag holders on lanyards.

"Can I t-t-take t-t-two uniforms for Halloween?" Elsbeth asked suddenly.

"Hallow—" Celia was confused. "Sorry, no. And Halloween is a long way off."

Elsbeth pouted, shrinking behind Emma for the second time today. Emma took the cue.

"Celia," she leaned in, as if sharing a secret, "Elsbeth has been having a rough time adjusting to her grandfather's death. Any chance you can check with Victor and see if he might allow her a uniform... as a way of remembering Erasmus?"

"Two uniforms," Elsbeth corrected. "We need a s... slightly bigger one, too, s... so Ruth can take me trick-or-treating."

"You seem a little... old... to be trick-or-treating." Celia eyed her curiously. "And, Halloween is the Devil's work, if you ask me." She held her chin up, haughtily.

"We didn't a... ask you," Elsbeth pouted. "I'll a-a-ask Uncle Victor m-m-myself."

Suddenly, Celia's face dropped. She couldn't very well have Mr. Newberry's adopted niece upset, now, could she? "Wait here a moment. I'll just check."

As Celia made her way to a nearby intercom, Elsbeth snagged two lanyards from the closet with red stripes across the place where name badges are slipped inside. She hid one in each of the pockets of her dress and returned to the hallway. She held up a finger to her lips as a caution to Emma as Celia returned.

"It seems that Victor has approved you to take two uniforms in whatever size you like, as long as you don't bother him again while he's trying to work."

Elsbeth grinned proudly, rushing into the closet to retrieve one small and one medium-sized women's uniform. "Which ones are w-w-women's sizes versus m—m-men's," she called loudly.

"Oh, they're all women's sizing," Celia confirmed.

"That's odd," Emma observed. "Don't men work in the factory?"

Apparently, Celia had an answer for this, too. She motioned for them to keep walking... conveniently toward one of the doors marked, 'exit.'

"Oh, they do, but they typically hold higher positions."

"Why is that?" Emma asked innocently.

Celia let out a knowing sigh. "I know, you're probably one of those feminists who feel like men and women are equal in every way."

Emma bit back her initial response. "And you don't feel that way?"

Elsbeth had a look of death across her face and hovered behind Emma like a vulture. She even slunk her shoulders forward and tilted her head downward like the carnivorous bird.

"Of *course* men and women... are equally important in the eyes of God." *Oh shit,* Emma thought. She hadn't realized she'd stepped into Jesus land. Emma bit her lip. "But most of the women here are either single gals just working until they find a good husband to care for them, single mothers whose husbands have died or abandoned them, or empty-nesters looking for purpose in their lives now that their children are grown."

"And which one are you?" Emma asked.

Celia was obviously *not* prepared for this question. She lowered her head, unnerved. "If you must know, it just so happens that I had a child out of wedlock. But Mr. Newberry saw something special in me, took me under his wing. Through hard work, I rose to the ranks of executive assistant."

"That's... wonderful," Emma smiled politely. She tried, but Emma lacked the acting chops to pull it off. Celia became distracted a moment by something along the assembly line. Behind her back, Elsbeth pretended to stick her finger in her mouth as if about ready to vomit. Emma reached around her back and attempted to slap Elsbeth's hand from her mouth. The young woman glared at her but stopped gesturing. Celia's attention returned to them with the slightest hint of impatience crossing her face.

"Where will you go from here?" Emma mused. "From executive assistant to—"

"Wife, if I'm luck," Celia smiled dreamily.

"I was going to say, chief executive officer," Emma finished.

"Oh, no." Celia shook her head as if Emma were daft as a dodo bird. "Women are the nurturers and mothers. We don't have the same minds as men to handle the stress of all that—" she fought for the right words.

"Information? Power? Responsibility?" Emma threw out a few guesses.

"Information," Celia finished, nodding. "Our wisdom is different from a man's." She waited for Emma and Elsbeth to agree with her. Both women began eyeing the exit door with extreme interest.

"Celia," Emma finally said. "You've been so kind. We couldn't possibly take any more of your time. Perhaps Elsbeth and I can show ourselves out?"

"Thank you for your understanding." Celia nodded. "I *am* quite busy." She walked to the door and pressed hard on the bar lever that opened up to the parking lot.

Suddenly, Elsbeth turned to Celia. "Thank you... C... Cousin... C...

Celia," Elsbeth stammered, wrapping her arms around the woman in an uncharacteristic show of affection. Celia was taken aback, patting the young woman cautiously on the back. "You must be a wonderful mother," she sniffed.

Elsbeth could feel Celia's body soften as the woman embraced the girl.

"Bless you, Child," Celia whispered.

Elsbeth wiped her downwardly cast eyes as they made their way to their car. Both Elsbeth and Emma felt the heat of the Florida humidity as it smacked them in the face. Emma was growing accustomed to the temperature, but Elsbeth swatted at the air as if she felt her muggy surroundings were trying to attack her.

Celia let the one-way door slam, effectively locking the women out of the factory.

Elsbeth smiled. There it was again, that Cheshire cat-like grin.

"What is it?" Emma asked.

It was only when they'd reached their car, where Sprightly was waiting behind the wheel, with feet up on the dashboard and eyes closed as she leaned into the seat, that Elsbeth flashed it... Celia's badge. "Might help us recreate what we need to get Sprightly and Nancy in this week."

At the sound of her name, Sprightly sat upright, lowering her legs. "Musta dozed off, but I'm ready!" she assured them, as Emma and Elsbeth clamored into the sports car. Elsbeth and Emma had many skills, but having lived in Manhattan for so long, driving wasn't one of them. Emma realized that the moment she almost took out Sprightly's car in the drive just two days prior. For this longer journey, she enlisted the help of Sprightly, who was only too happy to chauffeur them in Emma's Porsche.

"You little devil." Emma shook her head at Elsbeth, grabbing the badge and eyeing it.

Elsbeth put her hands behind her head and leaned back in the passenger seat, still grinning.

And suddenly, it all made sense: Elsbeth's stutter, her appearing as if autistic or in some way challenged, the way she went from meek to fierce depending on the circumstances. It was all an act... and she had the entire Vandenberg family eating out of her pretty little hands.

CHAPTER 23
Elsbeth

Florida

~

"Why the lie, Elsbeth?" Emma asked the young woman when they were safely back at Emma's residence on Treasure Island. "Your entire family thinks there is something wrong with you."

"There was," Elsbeth answered simply, taking an apple from Emma's refrigerator and biting into it without asking if she minded. Emma waited while the girl munched a large piece of it and swallowed. "By the time I was seven, it was assumed I had a neurological disorder and debilitating speech and memory issues."

"But you don't now?" Emma questioned.

Elsbeth took another bite of her apple. "Nope," she answered simply.

"Why do you let everyone believe that you do?"

Elsbeth sighed, tossing the apple core in a trash can. "Unless you compost?" Elsbeth offered, after-the-fact.

"I've been here less than a week. What do you think?" Emma asked. "And quit changing the subject."

"Well, for the longest time, I really did think something was wrong with me. But one week in private school, I traded those stupid nutritional bars. Mother always made me eat for Airheads and M&M's. For some reason, Sally, one of my classmates, was mad for them. I thought they tasted like tree bark."

"And what happened?" Emma was beginning to put two and two together.

"Sally had an inexplicable seizure — only one time; no one knew why."

"But... you did?" Emma asked cautiously.

"I was only eight at the time, and not a hundred percent sure, but I suspected."

"And what did you do, Elsbeth?"

"I started ditching the bars any chance I could, just to see what happened. And within a month, my mind sort of... cleared up."

"Why didn't you tell anyone, Elsbeth?" Elsbeth was silent. Emma tried again. "Why didn't you tell anyone?"

"At first, it was for selfish reasons," she admitted. "I was worried I'd get in trouble if I told. And... because I talked funny, Mother stopped making me go to church ceremonies with her. She thought I was an embarrassment. Then, she pulled me out of school and began homeschooling me, which I preferred. Don't know if you've noticed, but I'm not the most social of creatures."

"Oh, I noticed," Emma nodded.

"And then—"

"And then, what?" Emma coaxed.

"I heard a buzzing around the house that a woman from the Church of Infinite Love died of an overdose, and they thought it was linked to grandfather's nutrition bars. I wanted to tell grandfather but—"

"But—"

"I heard him fighting with Edwina one day about it. I wasn't a hundred percent sure he wasn't in on it."

"Did you go to the police?"

"No, I didn't go to the police!" Elsbeth yelled. "I was only eight, for Christ's sake, and just got my wits about me! I didn't even leave the house again until I was eleven, and that's only because I had an appendicitis.

Mother actually asked her superiors' permission for them to operate to save my life."

"Geez, Elsbeth," Emma rubbed her forehead. "Alright, so, we need to tell Officer Dennis and —"

"No!" Elsbeth was adamant.

"Well, we have to share this information. Maybe then he can get the authorities to—"

"No!" she reiterated. "Not unless you're trying to get me killed, too." Elsbeth eyed her with a seriousness she'd never before seen in the young woman.

"So, your plan is just to pretend to have a learning disability for the rest of your life?"

"No," she corrected. "My plan was to wait until my 18th birthday and legally leave home. Only when I was out of that place could I think about reporting what I suspected. But then, a story surfaced about two more girls dying under suspicious circumstances, and I... chickened out."

"There was no one you could talk to about this... not Ferdinand, Ivy, or Ruth? Or maybe make your grandfather realize the side effects of his creation?"

"You really don't get it, do you?" Elsbeth was incredulous. "They are all members of the Church of Infinite Love. More than members... the Evangelicals." Her eyes grew wide.

"What do you mean the Evangelicals?" Emma had never heard the Vandenberg family referred to in this manner before.

Elsbeth thought a moment. "Oh," she said quietly. "I forget that outsiders wouldn't know that. The Evangelicals are the church founders. They meet in secret, and most members don't even know who they are. If they showed up at a random campus, it's unlikely anyone but the elders and deacons would know who they were."

"But Ferdinand, Ivy and Ruth... they are not family members. Are they Evangelicals, too?"

"Not exactly," she answered. "They're considered private ambassadors for the Evangelicals. It's a glorified way to refer to the servants of our house."

"So, being a member is a prerequisite for working at any of the Vandenberg residences? What about the factory?"

"Yes, to the first question. And, I'm gonna guess the factory is more of a recruitment center," Elsbeth cringed.

"So strange, though," Emma mused. "How is it that your mother is an Evangelical? I thought only men rose in rank."

"I guess the rules don't apply to those in the bloodline," Elsbeth suggested. "And even she answers to people I don't know about." She paused for an unbearably long time.

"What is it?" Emma coaxed. "You suspected Erasmus of being her superior... despite the illusion she seemed to give that she was head of the household."

Elsbeth nodded. "When I got wind that grandfather was going to close the factories and come clean, I thought maybe I could finally talk to him, but then—" Elsbeth broke down, sobbing.

"You really did love him, didn't you?" Emma put an arm around the girl. *I wish Dennis were here,* she thought. *He's so much better at this than I am.*

Elsbeth nodded. "I tried making excuses for him, but deep down I didn't trust him."

"Elsbeth," Emma considered her next question. "Was that the real reason you wanted to go with Erasmus to Florida... to come clean, yourself?"

Elsbeth nodded.

"And the others on the plane... the pilot, the flight attendant, the security guard?"

"I can't say for certain, but it stands to reason they were somehow linked to the church. They liked to surround themselves with their own, you know?" she sniffled, smiling to herself. "I think the only innocent in all this is Uncle Edgar. But he's locked away in his castle in Ireland. What could he do, even if I had a chance to tell him? Besides, we get it drilled into our heads early on not to trust outsiders."

"So, who can you trust?" Emma asked absentmindedly.

"You," Elsbeth suddenly answered. "I'm trusting *you*."

~

Elsbeth was on the next available flight out of Tampa heading home before her mother returned from her latest church-related business trip. Edwina had taken Ruth with her, leaving only Ivy and Ferdinand behind. Fortunately, Ivy was preoccupied with her kids visiting from out of town and had taken a few days off to give them a tour of the Big Apple. As a single mother with grown children, it was rare for Ivy to get a chance to escape the confines of the Vandenberg high-rise for something other than grocery shopping and visits to the dry cleaners. Meanwhile, while Ferdinand insisted on driving Elsbeth to and from JFK Airport, he promised not to inform Edwina of her daughter's departure unless she expressly asked where Elsbeth was. And since Edwina forgot that Ivy was away, she assumed Elsbeth had two remaining chaperones.

"Did you have a fruitful trip, Elsbeth?" Ferdinand asked, while dragging the young woman's suitcase from the baggage claim area.

"Y... y... yes... F... Ferdinand," Elsbeth stuttered. "E... m... ma was v... very k... k... kind to m... me."

"Well, I'm glad. And you'll be happy to know that your mother hasn't phoned yet, so your secret appears to be safe with me." Ferdinand opened the door of his black sedan and Elsbeth climbed in. "Seatbelt on," he commanded. Elsbeth obeyed. It was only after he'd settled into the driver's seat that he dared to ask. "I know it's not my place, Elsbeth. But may I ask why you needed to go to Florida in such a hurry?"

"I w... wanted to m... make sure E... m... ma was okay in her new home," she answered simply.

"Well, that was very thoughtful of you," he mused. "But wouldn't a telephone call have been easier?"

Elsbeth hugged herself and shook her head adamantly. "Y... you know I h... hate phones."

Ferdinand nodded. "Ah, the whole idea of a disembodied voice on the other end."

"It's creepy," Elsbeth added. She fought back a smile as she sank into the passenger seat. Her goal was to make sure Emma got into the factory, and she knew if she were there, Victor wouldn't put up a fuss. Everything was going according to plan.

CHAPTER 24
Four Women, All Dead

Manhattan

"I'm telling you, Honey Bear," Monte winked into the web cam set up in Darwin and Rue's condo, where a visibly uncomfortable Ortega and his wife, sitting beside him resting one hand on his knee, were once again displayed on a large television screen. "You should let me come down there and visit the factory as Monique. I've been undercover before, and—"

"No," Ortega interrupted him. Monte placed one hand on his hips in protest, shaking his head and neck from side to side as if to say, *"Oh no, you just didn't."*

"What do you mean, 'no'?" Monte challenged.

"These people are church-loving devotees wearing no makeup and nothing that would be perceived as vain."

"So?" Monte crossed his arms indignantly. Today, he was back to his typical "Monte" wear — black jeans and a matching t-shirt. While Monique had a flair for the dramatic, Monte kept it simple.

Ortega tried again. "While I'm certain you could pass for a sufficient woman in New York—"

"Sufficient?!" Monte looked to Darwin and Rue for support. Rue stifled back a laugh. It was nice to be on the sidelines for once, where Monte was giving attitude to someone else for a change. "Let me tell you something, Honey Bear—"

"My name is former Detective José Ortega!" Ortega snapped. "Not Honey Bear, not Sweetheart, or any other term of affection!"

Nancy rubbed her husband's knee supportively. She didn't like to see him so upset, concerned that his anger would cause a spike in his blood pressure... or worse.

Monte was smart enough to know when he'd pushed too far. "Never mind." He waved a hand. "I'm not interested in flying into Tampa, anyway. Florida is absolutely grizzly this time of year."

No one was quite sure why Monte seemed to be suddenly fond of bear references, but they decided to let it go.

"Listen," Ortega tried again, eyeing Darwin and Rue for support. "I mean it as a compliment. The women in that factory aren't... shall we say... as glam as you. No makeup, no frills, and frumpy uniforms. Could you pull it off without all the... accoutrements?"

Monte surveyed his cuticles, his go-to reaction when he wasn't sure how to respond.

"Not sure, to be honest," he finally admitted.

"Then, I think it's best we send Nancy, my wife—" he motioned toward Nancy. "And Emma's helper-gal, Sprightly. No one will even notice them."

"Well, gee Honey Bear," Nancy chided, annoyed. "Glad to be so plain that I can just blend right in."

Monte stifled back a laugh.

"You know that's not what I meant," Ortega fumbled.

"Isn't it, though?" Nancy crossed her arms defiantly.

"Look." Monte held up his arms. "I get it. But let me at least share more on the case files I dug up on the three women who mysteriously died while being devoted members of the Church of Infinite Love. The church must have some pretty kick ass lawyers and publicists because it was a bitch uncovering this."

"What did you find out?" Nancy leaned in, intrigued, before Ortega had even gotten the words out. He looked at his wife, surprised at her continued interest. He'd never seen her this interested in anything... other than maybe tennis. "I mean," she continued, "beyond what you've already sent us. I read your case files several times."

Ortega, Monte, and Darwin looked over at the unassuming Nancy quizzically.

Dennis got pulled into a separate case and was stuck working late, while Emma had not yet returned from the airport with Sprightly after Elsbeth's departure. That left Ortega to collect details to share with the Florida team later.

"Help me out here?" Monte looked to Darwin who nodded. Darwin had a separate small screen set up to share images of the photos and documents Monte had secured copies of after spending hours sifting through outdated microfiche and taking rudimentary shots from the cell phone Darwin provided him.

Within minutes, Darwin had the images on display. They were grainy, having been blown up ten times their size, but good enough for their needs.

"The first is Marnie Watson," Monte began.

"The woman in her early twenties who tried to run away just days after being married off to a church deacon nearly two decades her senior." Nancy filled in.

"Very good." Monte put his hand on his hip and nodded, impressed. "She was the first reported death, of course... back in 1988. But on my first pass, it seemed the reported cause of death was 'inconclusive'." Monte put the word 'inconclusive' in air quotes. "But with the help of your friend Penelope—"

Ortega became flushed at the reference, glancing nervously at his wife. She bristled slightly but said nothing. After all, they had been married for more than a decade. That was water under the bridge, and... she trusted her husband... for the most part.

"We're hoping that she'll be able to confirm what conspiracy newspapers have been alluding to—"

"And what might that be?" Ortega asked.

"That there were antidepressants and stimulants in her system at the time of her death," Monte continued.

"Self-medicating or—" Ortega asked.

"From what we're told, she was secretly seeing a psychotherapist who was prescribing her meds for depression."

"Secretly?" Nancy asked. "Why would a 23-year-old see a shrink in secret?"

Monte cleared his throat. "Because the church frowned on outside medical interventions — physical or mental."

"I see." Nancy shook her head, disturbed. Ortega eyed his wife admirably. He'd never seen her display this kind of empathy before (not that he was an expert on the subject). To him, it was... refreshing.

"Well, there's more than reasonable evidence to suggest that the church was supplying their devotees with Vandenberg Nutraceutical bars with similar ingredients as her prescription."

"So, she accidentally overdosed?" Ortega offered.

"That's what we're trying to confirm," Monte nodded. "Unfortunately, it's been a challenge trying to recover records from a decade ago. Penelope has been trying to tap into her connections in the Pennsylvania area, as well as internal records. But so far, she's coming up empty."

"Yes, and we can't have her digging too much," Ortega squirmed in his seat. "I don't want her losing her job, or worse, getting in harm's way." He eyed Nancy, who had her eyes cast toward the floor, as if she were lost in her own thoughts.

As they continued to talk, Rue slunk away into the condo's kitchen. While out of sight from the video camera, and Ortega, Nancy and Monte's view, Darwin had a clear line of Rue hovering by the stove, hugging herself uncomfortably.

"You okay?" he whispered.

"Yeah, just bringing back a flood of memories I worked very hard to forget."

"Why don't you wait in the bedroom while we finish up here?" Darwin suggested.

"No," Rue rubbed a tired eye. "I'm okay. I just need a moment."

"Right." Darwin rubbed her shoulders, supportively, before returning to the living room.

Monte had since moved on to the next two victims, Jessica Jones, age 17 and Linda Parker age 16. "Both of these women drowned in a lake near the church grounds in Pennsylvania... about two hours north of the church you and Rue recently visited."

"I remember those girls... vaguely," Rue piped up from the other room. "They had just transferred into our church campus and dorms right before I bolted. I know the area you're talking about. How on Earth could they have drowned in a shallow lake that couldn't have been more than four feet deep at its very center?"

Monte thought a moment, eyeing Rue quizzically with a modicum of sympathy. "So many questions."

"Story for another time," Darwin interjected, stepping in front of Rue as if to shield her from everyone's gaze.

Monte nodded before continuing. "But to at least answer your question... they were inebriated."

"What? They were drunk?" Rue asked. She had read the same file they did, but it merely listed the cause of death 'accidental drowning.'

"Another case where we only have a few conspiracy channels to go by. The toxicology reports are sealed tight at their parents' requests and because they were underage."

"How drunk do you have to be to drown in a shallow, calm lake?" Rue pondered out loud. "And given the fact that there were cameras and security all around the compound, how the heck did no one see them out there?"

"Good question," Dennis said. "And unless we can get those cases reopened, I'm pretty sure the church isn't going to hand over camera footage from that evening. They probably destroyed it a long time ago, anyway."

"But most of this information was in the files you sent us several days ago," Ortega reminded him. "So, other than a few new conspiracy theories about the real cause of their death, we have nothing new to go on? Is that it?"

"My, we are negative, Honey Bear," Monte teased. Before Ortega could respond, Monte waved his fingertips at the camera. "Hang on, I have one more photo to show you."

With that, he clicked over to an outdated portrait of a woman who'd obviously had her photo taken at one of those cheap mall studios.

Rue gasped. Darwin's face lit up in alarm.

"What about this woman?" Rue choked out.

"So, you know her?" Monte confirmed.

There was an old photo of Deaconess Frances... Rue's mother.

"She's my mother," Rue finally answered. "Darwin and I just spoke with her several days ago. What happened?!"

"Oh, shit, Rue." Monte looked from side to side as if seeking a place to hide. Monte rarely lost composure, but this was one of those times. "I'm... I'm sorry. I didn't know." His eyes grew red. He covered his mouth, as if shocked beyond words.

"What happened?!" she demanded. Darwin tried to put his arm around her, but she shrugged it off.

"She was found dead last night in the church's library," he answered softly.

Rue gasped. An emotional numbness overtook her, and her voice continued talking as if on autopilot. "How — how," was all that came out of her mouth.

"They found an overturned ladder with her at the bottom. The news report was vague, but forensics believe she somehow fell from the ladder while reaching for a book, hit her head, and broke her neck in the fall."

"But the ladder was overturned," was all Rue could say, as if her voice were disconnected from the rest of her body. She struggled to put a logical thought together.

"Yes," Monte confirmed. "Rue, I'm so sorry—"

"It's okay," Rue answered, her voice emotionless and seemingly very far away.

From the other end of the call, Ortega chimed in. "I'll call Penelope right away and see if she knows anyone on the forensics team out that way. I'll see what I can find out."

It was almost as if they forgot he and Nancy were still there remotely. Nancy looked at Ortega incredulously. She knew he was trying to help, but one look at Rue's face told her that this seemed as if it should be a secondary reaction, not a first.

"Rue," Nancy offered gently. "You're in shock. And you may not know what you need right now, but we are here for you."

"Thank you," Rue nodded, staring at her mother's image on the small screen, as if mesmerized by it.

"Oh, for God's sake, man," Darwin grumbled to Monte. "Shut that off, would you?" Except he didn't wait for Monte to respond. He walked over to the camera and quickly disabled it.

"Until we know what happened for sure," Darwin looked up at Ortega and Nancy grimly, "I would be very careful about your factory investigation in the morning. It seems awfully coincidental that this comes after our recent visit to the Church of Infinite Love."

~

OFFLINE, Ortega turned to Nancy. "I feel like we're missing an opportunity here."

"What do you mean?" Nancy answered.

"Well," Ortega thought a moment. "If Emma's new friend, Elsbeth, is related to the Vandenberg family, and her mother has strong ties to the church, is it possible she knows more than she's letting on?"

"I doubt it," Nancy answered. "You saw how flaky she was."

"But if they have a history of drugging their members..." Ortega thought on this. "What do you think?"

"Are you actually asking my opinion about your case?" Nancy was touched.

"Yes," he answered. "I'd really like to know what you think."

"Do I think it's possible that the girl is being fed a diet of drugs to keep her in that state? I suppose it's possible, but unrealistic. Why would they want to?"

"Control?" Ortega offered.

"No." Nancy was adamant. "I can see them accidentally damaging her — and an adverse reaction and such. But no, I can't see them purposefully keeping her drugged. Who would do that to their child?" Even the thought of it made Nancy cringe.

"And Rue Brennan," Ortega continued.

"What about her?" Nancy answered.

"She and Elsbeth both grew up in the same cult. Both have high-ranking mothers. It would be interesting to get them talking—maybe interview them to see what they both know?"

"Not a bad idea, Honey Bear—" Nancy teased.

"Don't start," Ortega wagged a finger at her.

"But, given Rue's state tonight, I'd say we need to give her a few days. Not to mention the fact that Elsbeth just lost her grandfather."

"Perhaps you're right," Ortega sighed. "But I'm afraid we may not have that kind of time."

"We should get to bed," Nancy suggested, slipping into a nightgown and draping her clothes over a chair in their bedroom. "I've got a big day sleuthing tomorrow."

Ortega nodded, pulling down the covers from the bed. After stripping down to his boxer shorts and undershirt, he climbed under the covers and pulled them up over his head. He was trying hard not to compare the two. He really was. But all he could think of was how these brainstorming sessions were far more productive with Penelope as a thought partner. Ortega knew he wasn't being fair. After all, his wife was not trained for police work, and was doing a pretty bang-up job despite her lack of experience. Still, he secretly wished he could have this conversation with Penelope instead.

CHAPTER 25
Blindfolds

Florida

With Elsbeth now back in New York, Emma expected to enjoy a little alone time with Dennis. Unfortunately, she quickly learned that she'd be settling in for round three of her ongoing spats with him instead.

"Damn it, Emma!" Dennis bolted into the kitchen. He had just returned from work and made the mistake of rifling through the mail before walking through the door. "What the hell's it gonna take for you to finally trust me?"

Emma looked up from the blackened tilapia she was about to throw on a small electric grill.

"What brought this on?" she asked, surprised. "Elsbeth is on a plane heading back to New York, by the way, for anyone who cares."

"This!" Dennis answered, all but shoving the document into her face, ignoring her comment. Emma peered down at it. Her cheeks became warm as her heart flooded with a mix of anger and guilt. "... Is what brought this on!" he finished angrily.

"Where did you get that?" she demanded.

"Does it matter?" Dennis' face turned pink around his cheeks and nose.

"It does when you're asking me why I don't trust you?" she defended.

"So, I'm right?" Dennis answered triumphantly.

"About what?" Emma was confused.

"That you don't trust me," Dennis continued.

Emma turned off the grill and tossed the tilapia on a plate to avoid burning the filets.

"I'm afraid I'm going to need you to be more specific." Emma's clipped tone let Dennis know that she was about to become annoyed... very annoyed, unless he did some explaining.

Dennis rubbed his forehead, searching for the right words. "It was an accident," he began, phrasing his words carefully.

"What was?" Emma was suspicious.

"If you give me a minute, I'll explain!" Dennis was frustrated.

"Stop yelling at me!" Emma whined.

"I'm not..." Dennis paused before letting out a long sigh. "Just, please give me a minute to explain."

Emma, for once, said nothing. Instead, she covered the tilapia with the lid from the frying pan and tossed it into the refrigerator for safe keeping. It seemed they weren't likely to be having dinner anytime soon, and she hated to waste food, particularly if it was fish that sacrificed their lives for their evening meal... Emma always thought about stuff like that.

After a long pause, Emma's eyes grew wide, and she motioned her hand into the air as if to say, *"Well, get on with it, then."*

"I stopped to pick up the mail just now," Dennis began.

"Oh, thanks. I forgot—"

"Found this blank envelope mixed in and opened it without thinking. Wanna explain what this is?" His cheeks and nose grew redder. She glanced at it, a sinking feeling in her chest.

"It's a prenuptial agreement," Emma answered softly.

"Emma, why?" Dennis demanded. "We're not even sleeping in the same bedroom yet because I assumed you wanted to take things slow... which is—" he ran his hand through his hair, "frustrating, but I was okay with it because I wanted to see where this was going. And, I figured you were worth... waiting for," he answered sheepishly.

"Well, obviously I'm planning for the long-term, else I wouldn't have contacted Mr. Lundy to draft that up."

"But we've never talked about marriage. Hell, there are some days when I can't even tell if you even like me all that much!"

"I like you," Emma protested. "What makes you think I don't like you?"

"Maybe because I followed your heels from New York to Florida like a lost puppy and am still sleeping in the guest bedroom, as if I were your roommate."

"Well," Emma defended. "Maybe I just wanted to be sure that this—" she motioned a finger between the two of them, "was going somewhere, and that you weren't the love 'em and leave 'em sort."

Dennis let out a sigh. He took her by the soldiers. "Emma, you've got me eating tofu and jogging... me, jogging! I had to eat meat in the garage twice already, so I didn't have to bear your look of disdain—"

"You eat meat in the garage?" Emma was surprised.

"That's not the point." Dennis changed the subject. "I think that I've more than proven myself over the past nine months. I'm not going anywhere."

"Then why are you so upset about a prenuptial agreement... assuming you're in this for the long haul?"

He dropped her shoulders and began pacing the tiny kitchen. "For one thing, we've never talked about marriage or even... well, us. 'Why do we need to put labels on it?'" he reminded her, putting his words in air quotes. "Sound familiar?"

"Well, that was before..." Emma reasoned.

"Before what?"

"Before you actually got on the plane and came down here with me."

"You thought I'd bail? I got a temporary transfer and everything."

"Yeah," she reminded him. "Temporary!"

"But, I've been helping you with the case. Obviously, I'm putting a lot on the line for our relationship."

"Well," Emma back pedaled. "I appreciate that."

But Dennis hadn't gotten everything off his chest yet.

"Up until now, I had no idea if you were interested in a long-term commitment or not, and I certainly don't love the idea that you trust me so little as to think we need to guard our money, particularly since you bring in far less than I do."

"You're forgetting about the inheritance," Emma pointed out. "If Erasmus' will holds up, I stand to be a good deal better off than I have been in the past."

"And you really think that that's what I'm about?" Dennis was hurt.

"No," Emma admitted. "But then, I've made really bad decisions about men before. What if I'm wrong about you and in two years you run off with some young redhead at work named Amber who teaches yoga on the weekends?"

"That was... oddly specific," Dennis pointed out.

Emma shook her head. "Look, I'm sorry. It was a stupid idea."

"No," Dennis' voice softened. "What was stupid was you not talking to me... about any of this? That's kinda what couples do, right? Talk about hopes, fears, and that sort of thing?"

"So, we're definitely a couple then?" Emma asked.

"I don't know," Dennis admitted. "You tell me."

"Well," Emma answered after what seemed like an eternity. "I'd like to be."

"Well then," Dennis replied. "So would I."

"Kinda convenient since we're already technically living together," Emma reasoned, her gaze falling to the floor, a little embarrassed.

"And I'm nothing if not practical," Dennis laughed, circling his arm around her waist and pulling her in for a kiss. Emma lifted her eyes to meet his. She took his face in her hands and kissed him back fervently. With the case looming over them, it was their first moment of real connection since they had arrived in Florida.

"Come with me," she smiled seductively, taking him by the hand and leading him toward her bedroom.

"Where are we going?" Dennis was afraid to get his hopes up.

"Thought maybe you might wanna finally see the inside of my bedroom... Unless you want me to go back to making dinner?"

"No!" Dennis answered and then let out a cough. He hadn't meant to yell.

Emma pushed the door to her room open. From the hallway, Dennis could see a plush brown carpet with a queen-sized bed covered in a pink blanket and pillows. Frankly, Dennis didn't see Emma as the sort of woman to like pink anything. She seemed more like a gray sweatshirt and baggy pants kinda gal, with linens to match.

"Just one more question, Dennis," Emma looked up at him innocently.

"Yes, what is it?"

"What are your thoughts on... blindfolds?" She winked at him.

Dennis' face felt flushed again, but this time, for a completely different reason. "Should I be worried?" he asked, his voice cracking.

"Probably," she grinned, closing the bedroom door behind them.

CHAPTER 26
New Recruits

Florida

Nancy and Sprightly were filled with nervous excitement as Dennis and Ortega dropped them three blocks from the factory on a Friday morning in two separate vehicles where they were instructed to enter the Vandenberg factory at least five minutes apart. Friday was "new hire" day, as it turned out. They were wearing the uniforms Elsbeth had procured for them and name badges recreated by some guy named 'Moolah' that Darwin had recommended to Ortega. The badges matched Executive Assistant Celia's... without her title, of course. Moolah dropped them at Ortega's door at the ungodly hour of 5 a.m., along with a white delivery van with a large photo of baked bread on the side of it. Moolah made sure Ortega knew it was 'only a loan.' Ortega had no idea why the man thought he'd want to keep a battered old bakery van that had seen better days. He arrived with Nancy while Dennis dropped off Sprightly in her old Chevy Citation, which, not unlike the bakery van, had also seen better days.

"Remember," Dennis reminded them. "They'll make you pass through a metal detector and won't allow you in with any cell phones or recording devices. Nancy, you remember the plan?"

"Of course, I remember," she answered haughtily. "It was my idea!"

"Right," Dennis nodded. "But Sprightly, we're not going to have any way of tracking you. So, try to stay close to Nancy, if possible; but don't make it obvious."

Ortega sat in the borrowed van that, to him, actually felt sad from neglect. He feared the couch on wheels that Nancy bought him might be too obvious. Now, he wasn't so sure. He stationed himself in an open parking area of a neighboring print shop factory, just north of the Vandenberg factory at its back entrance. He had a recording device set up so he could listen in on what Nancy's microphone picked up.

Emma was nowhere near the factory, not with the surveillance cameras they appeared to have surrounding the place. Instead, she waited impatiently at an outdoor coffee shop a good half-mile away, sipping a latte as slowly as possible, while pretending to read a book. She had finally unwrapped the cell phone Dennis had bought her and had practiced using it last night. While it was fairly straight forward, she preferred landlines where you could very clearly tell when you'd picked up and hung up the phone. This little contraption, she didn't entirely trust.

But Emma was there merely if she needed to suddenly show up at the factory and cause a distraction. She had no idea what that might be and silently rehearsed possible scenarios.

She recalled her earlier phone call to the security desk at Vandenberg Nutraceuticals. "Hi," she said in what she thought was a Florida accent. (Really, she had no idea.) "This is Marla from HR. I've got two new employees heading your way for the R&D department—"

Emma paused while the woman on the other end expressed annoyance that HR never seemed to comply with Vandenberg procedures.

"Cut me some slack," Emma added in a bit of her own attitude. "I'm only two days on the job on account of some deadbeat getting arrested on a DUI. I'm the replacement. At least I showed up sober!" She waited while the woman on the phone expressed her apologies. "No matter," she continued. "You've got a Nessa O'Conner due in at 9 a.m. today... a fresh transfer from our Emerald Isle office... never worked in the Florida office before. And, there's also a Susan Brown. She's a Florida resident who's a new hire—" Emma listened at the employee's concern. "Yeah, I get that new hires don't usually get placed in Research & Development!" she all but yelled into the phone. "Maybe she's sleeping with your boss Mordecai. What do I know?!" A long silence made Emma realize she'd gone a bit too far with her act, particularly when dealing with, what appeared to be, a 'faith-based' company. Emma dialed it back with, "I apologize for my bad attitude. The truth is, I don't know why she was assigned to R&D out of the gate. Not my place to decide, is it? I mean, if that's what Mr. Newberry requested?"

And now the Research and Development department of Vandenberg Nutraceuticals, the area where Emma, the major shareholder, and Elsbeth, the granddaughter of the founder, Erasmus Vandenberg, couldn't seem to get access to, was open to their two moles... Nancy and Sprightly. Emma continued sipping her latte and waited...

Meanwhile, Nancy arrived at the front desk first. Dressed in an ungainly gray uniform with a lanyard hanging around her neck, she stepped through the security station.

"Beep! Beep! Beep!" The metal detector chimed.

"Just one moment," an overgrown male security guard motioned toward Nancy.

"Probably my pacemaker, Hugo," Nancy explained, reading the guard's name tag. "Heart attack last year."

The guard read her name badge, "Nessa O'Conner. Just let me check." The guard typed her last name into the small computer at his desk. "That checks out... funny, you don't sound Irish. Where are you from originally?" he asked, curiously.

Nancy remembered the pacemaker part, but forgot she was supposed to be a new transfer from Ireland. She did her best to add in what she thought might be a passable accent, "Originally from New York," she explained in a poorly blended accent. "But me dad got a job in Dublin when I was a wee thing, and I guess it's been back and forth for me between the States and Ireland ever since." She shrugged her shoulders and smiled innocently.

"Down the hall and to the left," he directed. "They should be able to get you situated from there," he finished gruffly.

"Thank you." Nancy curtsied awkwardly before heading down the very long hall that Emma and Elsbeth traveled not days earlier. Only, unlike those two, she would actually get to see what happens in the R&D department. Additionally, her 'pacemaker' was, in reality, a very tiny bug that enabled her husband and Officer Dennis to hear what was happening behind-the-scenes. This was the most fun Nancy could remember having —ever. Now, she sort of understood why Ortega loved it so much.

Moments later the guard called after her absentmindedly. "Oh... Sorry 'bout your heart attack!"

Nancy turned and nodded but kept moving.

About five minutes later, Sprightly arrived on the scene. "Susan Brown reporting for duty!" she proclaimed enthusiastically.

"Well, we'll just see about that," the guard answered. He lifted her badge from her chest and eyed it, and her, suspiciously. Sprightly shifted from side-to-side uncomfortably. He motioned her to proceed through the metal detector. Unlike Nancy, Sprightly didn't set off any alarms, and yet he still felt the need to phone the R&D department. "Yeah," he said to the person on the other end of the phone. "I've got a Susan Brown here, brand new and yet assigned to your department. I dunno—" He paused and held his hand over the phone's receiver. "They wanna know why you were recommended for a department meant for employees with tenure?"

"Don't know," Sprightly answered innocently before adding on a whim, "someone I met at church recommended I apply, and so... here I am?!"

"The Church of Infinite Love, you mean?" the guard asked. "The one in Tampa?"

"That's the one." Sprightly's eyes grew wide. "Don't tell me you're a member, too?" She feigned surprise. "I only just started going. So, I don't know too many people yet."

"Just one moment." The guard held a hand up to silence Sprightly. "I think she's okay. Got a referral from the church. Right." He hung up the phone. "Down the hall and to the right," he instructed.

Sprightly sprinted away before he could change his mind or ask her anymore questions about who referred her.

As soon as she'd arrived at the glass door leading to the Research & Development lab, she found it locked. Confused, Sprightly eyed Nancy through the glass, who was already in a factory line up, adjusting some type of syringe that appeared to be automatically infusing products in the chain as they went by. Sprightly waved emphatically. Nancy's eyes widened to suggest, *"Cut that out! You're being too obvious."* Sprightly dropped her hand. After a cursory glance to make sure no one saw her, she tipped her badge and glanced toward it. A lightbulb went off in Sprightly's head, and she held up her badge to unlock the door.

Once inside, another woman, dressed in the same drab gray onesie uniform, approached her. The only difference was that this woman's badge had some sort of star on it... possibly to indicate rank. "You must be Susan," she asked politely. "I'm Rita."

"Pleasure to make your acquaintance!" Sprightly held out a hand. The woman looked at it but made no move to return the gesture. Sprightly lowered her hand.

"This way please," she told the young woman. "We just had someone phone in sick, so your arrival today happens to be a good one."

Sprightly passed Nancy's station with disappointment. *So much for she and Nancy getting to stick together.* Instead, she passed through another set of doors with a sign marked, 'Private Shipping and Receiving.'

"Your job is pretty simple," Rita explained. "Shipments come in through there." She pointed to the receiving area where two young boys were loading boxes onto a conveyor, while two others pulled them and lined them up on a long aluminum table. She pulled an oversized brown log book and opened it to today's date. "You read each box and note what's in the box and where it's from. You've got plenty of pens in the tin." Rita motioned to a tin box filled with pens at the workstation. "Open each box to confirm you received the right product and quantity, then put the open box on this conveyer." She gestured. "So they can be added to our stock. Box cutters are next to the tins. Be careful not to cut yourself." She eyed the thin Sprightly and asked, "Some of these boxes are heavy. Think you can handle it?"

"No problem, Rita," Sprightly answered excitedly. "I'm strong as an ox. I won't let you down!"

Rita wasn't used to this much enthusiasm. She answered flatly, "The bathroom is just through that door." She motioned to a corner of the room. "Make sure you notify the manager before you leave the shipping floor. Is that clear?"

Sprightly was about to ask exactly who the manager was before her attention was drawn to a man sitting on a high-backed chair on what looked like a stage above the workers. At the word "manager" he lowered the newspaper he was reading and nodded in their direction before returning to his paper.

"Lunch is at noon. You have 45 minutes. Any questions?"

"Just one," Sprightly confessed. "Everything gets logged into that big book over there. I get that. But it seems strange that I wouldn't be logging inventory directly into a computer. Wouldn't that be more efficient?"

Rita sighed. She hated when newbies questioned the system. "Your job is not as an efficiency expert, Ms. Brown. Just fill out the logs as I've instructed. Follow the sample at the top of the page, and you should be fine."

Sprightly nodded. But the question remained bouncing around in her brain. Just beneath the counter where she stood lived stacks of old log books that must have gone back at least two decades. Another worker eyed her curiously, so Sprightly set to work at her designated station and began the mind-numbing task of opening boxes, counting bottles, and notating where they were from. Most were from medical facilities she'd never heard of in South America. They all had long names that seemed as if they were variations of popular Western medications. Sprightly's best guess was that they seemed to be a combination of sedatives, anxiety meds, and caffeine-infused energy tinctures. She carefully eyed the manager on high. He seemed to know instantly when someone's eyes were on him, as he looked up from his paper and stared back at her. Sprightly merely smiled and drew her attention back to her work.

After what seemed like an eternity, Nancy made a surprise visit to Sprightly's station, which meant that the woman had to pass from her production line, through the double doors to the Private Shipping & Receiving area that was an extension of the Research & Development area.

"Are you Susan?" Nancy asked innocently. Sprightly paused for a moment before remembering her undercover name.

"That's me!" she answered. "What can I do you for?"

Nancy showed her an invoice from a factory in Guatemala. "I was asked to see if you could check your logs for when this might have arrived. It was supposed to have come in two months ago, but we can't find it in storage. They were holding it for some new tea they're introducing."

"I'll look," Sprightly lowered her voice. "Any idea what it is?" she asked under her breath.

Nancy kept her voice at a normal level. Unlike Sprightly, she was doing a far better job at keeping a low profile. "Just check the invoice number and location." She pointed to the paper. Sprightly eyed it. Unlike the ingredients she had been checking in, this one seemed to be a cocktail of just about everything. Sprightly dug into her record book from two months back, and that's when she noticed it... a random page was missing. There were the tiniest of remnants of where someone had taken a blade and sliced it from the book. Whomever it was used enough pressure that the page beneath it was also slightly cut. It was the page between September 16 and 18.

"Sorry," Sprightly answered apologetically. "I don't see a record of it."

"Nessa!" Rita popped her head through the door, just as the lunch bell was signaled, and everything and everyone came to a grinding halt. "Never mind; we found it. Someone accidentally put them in storage cubby five instead of four. Would have been quite a mess if it got added where it shouldn't," she grimaced. "We can pick up again after lunch." Rita let the door slam behind her.

The manager promptly folded his paper and climbed down a set of wooden steps, making his way outside, presumably for lunch. He didn't wait until the floor was clear, because it seemed that no one there wanted to stay in the building a moment longer than was strictly necessary.

"Heading out for lunch, Susan?" Nancy asked. "I'll walk out with you." Sprightly caught on.

"Sure thing, let me just close out this last log." Sprightly eyed the room. When she was convinced no one was looking, she scanned the stack of log books shelved under the counter where she had been working. On the spine was the year. Sprightly sifted through her mind like a Rolodex.

Finally, she grabbed two of them, 1988 and 1996, and began quickly flipping through them.

"What are you doing?" Nancy eyed over her shoulder.

"First day on the job," Sprightly answered calmly, shaking her head from side to side in case there were unseen onlookers. "I just wanna make sure my entries are consistent with the way they do things around here."

She grabbed a pen and flipped through the first book. Sure enough, there was a missing page between March 13 and 15. She took a pen and marked M14 on her hand. Then, she turned to the second book, flipping until she found another inconsistency. There was a page missing between April 8 and 10. So, she marked A9 on her hand.

"Someone's coming." Nancy heard the shuffling of feet. She helped Sprightly stash the books as Sprightly added one final mark on her hand, S17.

The two exited through the Research & Development lab as the manager returned early to his station on high, surveying the floor below as he was certain he heard voices.

Back on the R&D's main factory floor, Nancy slowed to a crawl at one of the cubbies near her workstation. There were dozens of them from floor to ceiling. The one she was looking for was labeled with a simple #5 above it, and it was at her feet on the lowest shelf. She bent to snag one of the tiny vials while Sprightly stood behind her.

"Finished tying your shoe yet?" Sprightly asked as Nancy bent over.

It was then that Nancy was hit with a sad truth... their uniforms had no pockets. *How was she supposed to get past security on their way out? They check your purses and everything?* It was the first time since grade school that she regretted having small breasts. Larger ones would have come in handy. Therefore, in a moment of desperation, she dropped the vial down her shirt, wiggling a little and catching the lump as it made its way down her leg. Then, with some difficulty, she tucked it between her legs and squeezed as if doing a Kegel exercise... and held it.

"Let's go," Nancy said, straining. Sprightly followed at her heels. "Walk with me out front?"

Ortega heard the signal and messaged Dennis with one simple word, 'Now.' From the car he'd borrowed from Sprightly, Dennis sat three blocks away. He started up the engine once he received the text. Ortega did the same in his vehicle, waiting anxiously for his wife to return safely.

Nancy was the first through security. Once again, she beeped. "Pacemaker," she responded hurriedly. She was worried she might drop the vial and have it slide down her leg and shatter on the floor... blowing her entire cover.

"You seem to be in a hurry," the guard commented.

"Just have to use the bathroom *really* bad," she lied. "Thought I could hold out until lunch, but—"

"Go on, then." The guard motioned.

Once outside, she waved frantically for Ortega to pull in closer. Surprised, he drove right in front of the building as Nancy awkwardly climbed into the passenger seat, her upper thighs locked together. "Drive," she ordered. He didn't question her. He just drove.

Next, Sprightly went through security, politely opened her purse, and waited while they searched it.

"What's on your hand?" the guard asked, pointing to the notes she made for herself marked M14, A9, and S17. "Don't remember seeing that this morning."

"Ah," Sprightly thought quickly. "Bible verses," she answered.

"Which ones?" He wanted to know.

"You know, the popular ones from... Malachi, Acts and... Solomon," she quickly answered, trying to recall verses she had been forced to learn as a child that she had long since forgotten. Moreover, she doubted they would line up exactly with the numbers on her palm. She hoped the guard wasn't in the habit of memorizing scripture.

"Song of Solomon?" The guard raised an eyebrow. "Interesting."

"Uh, yup. That one." She squirmed nervously.

The guard bit back a laugh. "Go ahead." He motioned, noticing the growing line of antsy workers still eager to get out of the building in the hopes of having at least 30 minutes left to eat their lunches.

Sprightly darted through the door and made her way toward the main road, where Dennis pulled up alongside her. She hopped in quickly.

"Crap," Dennis said. "I think we've been spotted." He eyed a black van pulling out of the Vandenberg lot and following slowly behind them.

Its windshield was splattered in one corner with bird droppings. Otherwise, it was immaculate.

"Does it matter?" Sprightly asked, eyeing the rearview mirror. "Not like I'm going back after lunch."

"Yes, it matters," Dennis growled, angry at his carelessness. "It not only puts us all in danger but could mess up any chances of getting the police to conduct a proper investigation."

"Will this help?" Sprightly reached around the back seat of her car and pulled out a magnetic police light.

"Where the heck did you get that?" Dennis asked.

"There's a reason I've never gotten a speeding ticket," she answered proudly.

"That's illegal!" he chastised. The car was getting closer.

"Wanna talk about it or use it?" Sprightly smiled sweetly.

Dennis reached a long arm out of the window and slid the light in place on the car's rooftop. From inside the car, Sprightly activated both the light and a siren just as Dennis hit the gas. The driver of the Vandenberg security vehicle kept pace for a moment, but then thought better of it, and dropped the tail.

Once at a safe distance, she turned off the siren and Dennis retrieved the light from the roof of the car. He phoned Emma, who'd left the coffee shop and relocated to a bench across the street.

"Need you to do a little recon, Honey," he told Emma.

She wasn't used to him calling her 'honey.' Emma wasn't sure how she felt about it. But, she bit her lip. "What is it?"

"Need you to phone Vandenberg HR and tell them there's been an incident."

"Is everything alright?" Emma was concerned.

"Yeah, we're good. Listen, you have to tell them that we were picking up Susan Brown for skipping her parole when she had a health incident."

"Like a miscarriage or something?" Emma offered helpfully.

"Yeah, go with that... a miscarriage. Thanks!" He hung up the phone.

Sprightly's mouth dropped open. "Really? That's the best you could come up with? Skipped parole and then had to be rushed to the hospital because of a miscarriage?"

"You got a better story?" he asked.

"Yeah," she answered. "Like, maybe you just learned my mom was injured in an accident and you were sent to bring me to the hospital! Or, maybe you're my boyfriend and you suddenly had to respond to someone going into labor on the highway, or—"

"Okay, sorry," Dennis apologized. They drove in silence for several minutes. "Now, about that bogus police equipment..."

CHAPTER 27
Discoveries

Florida

"Might wanna keep driving," Sprightly cautioned from the passenger seat as they neared the St. Petersburg house. Emma was in the back seat, after having been retrieved from outside the coffee shop. "Keep your head down, Em," Sprightly warned, crouching low in her seat so that her head fell below the window.

"What are you talking about?" Dennis questioned. It was then that he saw what Sprightly had spotted. Just across the street, a black van was parked. There was nothing remarkable about it, except for one thing... its windshield was decorated with bird poop... just like the van that began following them outside of the factory.

By then, he was already halfway down the block. He considered another blaring getaway, and fumbled with the police siren, now sandwiched in the center console between him and Sprightly.

Just then, a team of Girl Scouts crossed the street. Dennis stopped to let them pass. One of the girls looked at him expectantly as another of the taller, bolder young women went up to the van and rapped on the window. The man in the van angrily rolled down his window as the girl began her cookie speech, motioning for another girl with a clipboard to take his order.

Dennis didn't wait to watch as the man shooed the scouts away, nor did he wait until they could surround his vehicle. He carefully backed slowly down the street and made a three-point turn, rounding the corner with the van unable to follow in time. He took one of the side roads before handing the phone to Sprightly. "Call Detective Ortega," he ordered.

"But I thought he wasn't a detective anymore?" Sprightly answered, missing the point.

"Just call him. Tell him we're heading to his home and we need to either ditch the car or hide it in his garage."

Sprightly nodded, scrolling through the contacts until she found his number.

"Ortega," the voice on the other end answered.

"Hi Detective Ortega," Sprightly answered enthusiastically. "Deputy Nyla Sprightly reporting for duty!"

"Er," Ortega paused. "Where's Dennis?"

"He's busy driving right now. But he said to tell you we're heading your way. I hope you've got space in your garage to hide my beater car."

"Oh," Ortega answered. "I'll put Nancy's car in the drive. How far out are you?"

Sprightly turned to Dennis, "He wants to know how far out we are?"

"Depending on if this crappy ride gets us there in one piece, I'd say about 45 minutes." Dennis answered loudly.

Sprightly held up the cell phone. To Ortega she asked, "You catch that?"

"Got it," Ortega answered. "I don't think I need to remind you to try and avoid being followed? I've already ditched my ride."

"Roger that, Detective," Sprightly answered. She was having a little too much fun playing deputy. "That's why we had to avoid the house." The phone started to crackle as they crossed the Skyway Bridge. "Better hang up now," Sprightly all but yelled into the phone. "Over and out!"

~

Nancy's hair was still wet from taking a shower when they'd arrived at the Ortega residence. She may have enjoyed playing undercover police officer, but somehow she felt the need to rid herself of the 'energy' of that awful jumpsuit they made her wear at the factory. Not to mention the fact that since she had the vial she'd stolen tucked securely between her unmentionables, she may have... leaked a little... trying to smuggle it out. While impressed with her quick thinking, Ortega accepted the bottle from her with a distasteful look on his face.

"What?" Nancy protested. "I rinsed it off."

Ortega let out a sigh and placed it in a sealed plastic bag.

Upon arrival, they quickly hid Sprightly's car in the garage and ushered Dennis, Sprightly, and Emma into their home. Nancy thought to draw the blinds. Meanwhile, Ortega had already scoured their house on the off chance that someone had thought to bug the place. So far, it seemed no one from Vandenberg Nutraceuticals was aware of their involvement. Darwin had promised to send Ortega something new for detecting bugs and all recording devices, telling the older man that it would be a 'game changer.' Only, it hadn't arrived yet. Therefore, he had to do his search the old-fashioned way.

Once he received the 'all-clear' from Ortega, he filled them in on what they encountered at the factory up through their arrival home.

"Yeah, well," Ortega reasoned. "You should consider staying here tonight, just to be on the safe side. This case is getting creepier by the minute."

"Here?" Nancy protested. She caught everyone's confused reaction and countered, "I just mean... is that wise? Perhaps a hotel in Tampa or someplace they wouldn't expect? Wouldn't that be safer for everyone since they don't suspect us yet?"

Emma didn't completely understand Nancy's reservations about having them there, but she wasn't particularly keen on remaining, either. All she knew for damn sure was that Nancy, for whatever reason, didn't want them to stay.

"We'll certainly do that," Emma reassured her.

"Nonsense. You and Dennis can stay in the guest room tonight," Ortega insisted, eyeing Nancy, who merely nodded reluctantly.

To Sprightly, he said, "The couch folds out into a sleeper sofa. You okay with that for the night?"

Emma took Dennis' arm and, once she'd caught his gaze, wiggled her eyebrows suggestively at him. He blushed and averted his gaze.

"Sofa is fine," Sprightly answered. "And I can take turns standing watch if you need me to."

"I don't think that will be necessary," Nancy laughed. "My husband has so many alarms and security cameras on the property, even the raccoons avoid our trash cans at night."

Sprightly nodded. Emma hadn't been in Florida long enough to know what raccoons had to do with anything, so she merely nodded. They had rats raiding the trash bins in Manhattan. *Maybe it was something like that?* She reasoned.

"Well, we've got a few frozen pizzas we can toss in the oven if you're hungry. Why don't I take care of that while you all settle in so we can recap the day?"

With only a counter dividing the space between the kitchen and the dining area, they gathered around the table. Sprightly fought back a grin as Ortega shared that Nancy had managed to smuggle a vial of, what they believed to be, a medical concoction that was about to be infused into nutrition bars. He left out exactly *how* she managed to smuggle it out.

"Any idea where the final product was going to be shipped?" Emma asked.

"No," Nancy called from the freezer. "But Sprightly discovered something interesting. Why don't you share?"

Sprightly saluted Nancy and stood, as if about to deliver a speech. She held out her hand, triumphantly. "They don't seem to like to record anything electronically at the factory, which is super weird, given that they are all about workplace efficiencies."

"What does that have to do with the numbers and letters on your palm?" Ortega asked logically.

Sprightly paused for dramatic effect before continuing. "They had me log inventory of meds coming in from other countries by hand. Only, the log books were missing pages, so I noted which days: March 14, April 8, and September 17."

"Wonder what makes those days so special?" Dennis observed.

"Don't know," Nancy chimed in, having set the oven to preheat and was now bringing a pitcher of sweet tea to set in front of the group. "But it was really odd that when I asked Sprightly to check on missing product, there was no record of it. And, someone had accidentally put the vial in the wrong bin. I'd be willing to bet someone didn't want anyone linking their inventory with traces of anything getting shipped out in those health bars."

"Brilliant thinking, Nan!" Ortega praised.

"Why, thank you, Honey." Nancy smiled gratefully at her husband. He didn't praise her often, so it meant that much more to her when he did.

"Ahem," Sprightly spoke up. "I *do* have an idea about those dates, actually."

"Go on?" Ortega encouraged.

"The first one in March was a log from 1988. The second from 1996, and the third—" She paused for dramatic effect. "This year." She waited while Ortega made the connection.

"Coincidentally, around the two times in history where the church made the news for women dying under suspicious circumstances, followed weeks later by Erasmus Vandenberg."

"Exactly!" Sprightly rocked back and forth on her heels, proud of herself.

"Good work," Ortega praised. "Any chance you got a look at any records of outbound shipments, to go along with Nancy's hypothesis?"

Sprightly's excited eyes dropped. "Sorry, no."

"That's alright," Ortega concluded. "I think we've got enough to approach someone from the sheriff's office and convince them to look into Erasmus Vandenberg's death, not to mention possibly see if we can gain access to the records surrounding the untimely death of the Deaconess and those three girls."

"But you said yourself that you're beginning to think the police are in on it," Nancy reminded him. "Or, at least they were reluctant to get involved because the Vandenberg family and the Church of Infinite Love are so powerful."

"I'm beginning to think that the family and the church aren't two different entities at all," Ortega grumbled. "The Vandenbergs seem to have their fingers in both of the most lucrative rackets in the US... nutritional supplements and religion."

"So, what? How are we going to convince anyone to help us?" Dennis was curious. He really didn't know and was all but banging his head against the wall at this point.

"I've got an idea," Ortega answered. "Are you on the beat tomorrow? Or can you go in late?"

"I am, but it shouldn't be a problem," Dennis replied. "They've got me scheduled part-time while I get settled from the move."

"Good," Ortega said. "Get some rest tonight. I'll let you in on my plan tomorrow."

CHAPTER 28
Contacting the Authorities

Florida

"Can I ask you a question, Jo?" Officer Dennis asked as he and Ortega made their way to the Crime Prevention Unit at the Tampa International Airport on Saturday morning, the day after their undercover work at Vandenberg Nutraceuticals.

"You just did, and—" Ortega stopped abruptly and turned toward Dennis, who all but ran into his former boss. "I know I said you could call me anything other than Detective, but maybe something different from Jo?"

"Sure thing... J..." Dennis caught himself. "But isn't your first name José?"

"It is," Ortega confirmed.

"And the English equivalent is Joe, right?"

"Yes; your point?"

"I just thought it was a fun play on words. J.O. being your initials and Joe being the same name in a different language...So... Jo." Ortega stared at Dennis expressionless. "But clearly you don't like that very much." Dennis put his thumb and forefinger on his chin, thinking. "Do you have a middle name?"

"Yes."

"What is it?" Dennis asked as they resumed walking.

"None of your damn business." Dennis dropped his gaze. He was used to Ortega's gruff manner, but here he was starting to think that they might actually come to see each other as colleagues... friends even. Ortega saw his expression and his heart dropped for the second time in only a few days. First Nancy, now Dennis. He sure seemed to have a knack for disappointing people. "Sorry," Ortega finally answered. "Could we keep it simple and bypass the nicknames? Just call me 'José' or 'Ortega,' either one. Are you okay with that, Officer Dennis?"

"Okay," Dennis agreed. "But only if you agree to call me Dennis when we're not on official police business... like talking to the sheriff, for instance... José." Somehow, even his first name sounded weird coming from Dennis. Ortega couldn't understand it. *Am I still so tied to my old work identity that anything other than Detective Ortega sounds weird to me?* He brushed the thought aside. "Unless," Dennis took the silence as annoyance, "you hate that idea; then we can just skip it."

Ortega came out of his mind wandering. "No, that's fine Off—Dennis," he corrected. "Let's try that for a while."

"Okay, José," Dennis smiled. "Hey, could I ask you a question, man-to-man, José?"

Ortega's deadpan expression returned. "Sure," he answered hesitantly.

"Well, you're a little older than me," Dennis began. "And have more life experience and all—"

"Yes?" Ortega grew impatient. "What is it?"

"It's a personal question."

"You can ask, but I can't guarantee I'll answer."

"Fair enough," Dennis agreed. "But it's more a question on perspective."

"Would you spit it out, man!" Ortega said.

"So, for the longest time, Emma was all distant... sleeping in separate rooms and no funny business and all." The two paused to dart around a woman with a two-seater baby carriage. She also had a third child wearing a protective harness that was wrapped around his chest with a tether that wound around his mother's waist. Dennis almost tripped over the tether as her toddler ran over to a store window and began pressing his sticky fingers on the glass. "Anyway," Dennis continued. "That sort of changed recently."

"Oh, really?" Ortega's eyebrows shot up as he fought back a grin.

"Yeah, so we're sort of... serious now."

"Well, that's a good thing, right?" Ortega encouraged.

"Yeah," Dennis smiled like a cat who ate the canary. "Yeah, it's a really good thing. It's just that—" Dennis paused. "Well, it went from the well being dry to the floodgates opening, if you know what I mean?"

"I'm afraid you've lost me," Ortega confessed.

"I mean," Dennis lowered his voice in a whisper. "It's like now she wants it all the time, at night, in the morning, before dinner. Is that... normal?"

Ortega stopped abruptly once more, leaning toward Dennis in a loud whisper. "Dennis, please tell me you're not asking my advice about your girlfriend wanting to have lots of sex with you?"

"But I mean," Dennis tried again. "Should I do something about that? Honestly, it hasn't even been a week yet, but I'm kinda tired—"

"What am I supposed to do with that?!" Ortega barked. "Stay hydrated and take more vitamins. What the hell do you want from me?!"

Dennis lowered his gaze. "Okay, sorry I asked."

Ortega shuddered to think what was happening in their guest room last night. He put it out of his mind.

By then they had reached the main airport entrance. "After you." Ortega motioned for Dennis to go first. Normally, he would have assumed that privilege, but he wasn't on the beat anymore, was he? Dennis was the one in uniform while he was just a private citizen. The gesture didn't go unnoticed by Dennis, who beamed proudly as he put his hat on and went through the revolving door to the front security desk.

Ortega followed closely behind, thinking about his failing marriage with Nancy. *Hmph,* he thought to himself. *Maybe I should be asking Dennis for relationship advice instead.*

The only other time Officer Dennis had set foot in the Tampa International Airport was when he first arrived with Emma less than two weeks ago. Once inside the main terminal, he stopped so abruptly that Ortega almost walked right into him.

"What, exactly, are we doing here?" Dennis asked, confused.

"We're looking for someone with the Crime Prevention Unit that we can trust." Ortega took the lead, and Dennis picked up the pace to keep up.

"But why not just go directly to the county Sheriff's Office?" Dennis enquired.

"You tried your precinct in New York and in Florida. And Penelope found suspiciously missing evidence in her search in the case of the three dead women at the Church of Infinite Love in upstate Pennsylvania. Nobody is willing to talk about the church nor the Vandenberg family." Ortega surveyed travelers as they struggled with heavy luggage and wove in and out of the crowds. "Makes me wonder just how big this thing really is. Where do we have to go for answers? The factory in Ireland?"

"So, why does that bring us here?" Dennis asked, as they located a sign pointing toward the police station within the airport grounds. "Because Erasmus died in flight?"

"That's part of it." Ortega seemed busy analyzing a large section of the airport with shops and restaurants. His eyes settled on a deli counter. Dennis was wondering how Ortega could possibly be thinking about food at a time like this. "I'm looking for someone... adjacent to this situation, who we can trust to help us."

"What does ordering a corned beef on rye from the man at the deli counter have to do with anything?" Dennis asked sourly as Ortega approached the small restaurant.

"Not him." Ortega pointed to the man behind the counter. "*Him.*" Dennis followed Ortega's line of vision and spotted a man wearing a hunter green sheriff's uniform. He was hunched over a small red table, munching on a bagel.

"Why him?" Dennis was confused.

"Look at his head," Ortega answered. Dennis, dumbfounded, looked. The man was wearing a yarmulke on the crown of his head. His hair was a curly brown with long sideburns on the side of his round face and narrow chin. A lightbulb went off in Dennis's head.

"Not likely to be a member of the Church of Infinite Love is he?"

"Probably not," Ortega agreed. "Not that it means he's not taking a payoff or part of a coverup. But he's also not directly tied to your precinct, so—"

"There's a chance," Dennis finished.

"Exactly."

The two men approached the sheriff, who looked up in surprise. "Can I help you, Officer?" he asked Dennis, before eyeing Ortega, who was wearing a white linen shirt and jeans.

Dennis stammered a little, not sure where to begin. Ortega chimed in.

"Sorry to interrupt your lunch," Ortega apologized. "I'm former Police Detective José Ortega from Manhattan. I have an unusual request. May I?" He motioned toward the seat.

"Of course," the man answered, standing, removing the napkin he had tucked under his chin, and offering his hand. "I'm Deputy Sheriff Shep Stern. What can I do for you?"

The two men joined the deputy sheriff and sat.

"We've got a case that spans two countries, three states, several counties, and three major cities," Ortega began.

"This sounds serious," Shep acknowledged. "Why come to me?" Surprisingly, there was something trusting in Shep's eyes. Unlike Ortega, who assumed that everyone was up to no good, Deputy Sheriff Shep Stern had a gentle way about him, and he was willing to give a man the benefit of the doubt.

"Because it involves the Church of Infinite Love and Vandenberg Nutraceuticals. I'm going to go out on a limb and guess that you're not a member of a Christian organization and don't ingest non-kosher snack bars."

"I see," Shep grinned, pointing to his yarmulke. "Wonder what gave me away... But, why does that matter?"

"Go ahead, son," Ortega motioned to Officer Dennis.

Shep Stern looked curiously at Dennis.

Dennis provided, as quickly and succinctly as he could, what they'd encountered so far, beginning with Erasmus' death and working backward until their convoluted story was told. Then, he waited with bated breath as Shep took it all in.

"So, let me see if I've got this straight?" Shep asked, gathering the remains of his half-eaten bagel and brushing the crumbs from his hands onto a small serving tray. He pushed it to one side, and a deli attendant scooped it up almost immediately. He pointed a finger first at Dennis. "You're a police officer from New York on a temporary exchange program in Florida with a girlfriend who was a suspect in a past murder investigation and is now a millionaire." He turned his meaty finger to Ortega, "And, you're a retired police detective whose wife made you move here. You both enlisted the help of a questionable undercover investigator and a New York forensic scientist who "called in a favor" on your behalf, not to mention several civilians who have no business doing undercover work because you suspect that tycoon Erasmus Vandenberg was murdered. And everyone, including law enforcement in three states, is helping to cover it up?"

Both Dennis and Ortega paused. It sounded ludicrous when put so succinctly like that.

"Pretty much," Ortega clasped his fingers together and rested his elbows on the table. "You're not going to help us, are you?"

After another dramatic pause, Shep began laughing so hard his belly jiggled up and down. "Of course, I'm going to help you... if I can. This is the most insane thing I've heard all day. I love it. I'm in."

And with that, the team of misfits had one more player — Deputy Sheriff Shep Stern.

CHAPTER 29
Moolah

Florida

Ortega had just dropped off Dennis and Emma at their St. Pete residence, but only after Dennis agreed to let Ortega come by later to set up a few cameras. He trusted Dennis' skills as an officer. Although, while he would never admit it to himself, he was beginning to treat Dennis like the son he'd never had. And he was worried about him. Sprightly promised to return home and stash her car out of sight for a few days.

"Not a problem," she agreed. "I use my bike most times anyway."

Now, Ortega's current challenge, after he'd picked up the dry-cleaning, was trying to figure out the best way to lay it in the backseat of his Lincoln Town Car without getting it ruffled. He didn't understand the need for his new overgrown car, but somehow Nancy thought it was a nice show of gratitude for him agreeing to retire early and move to Florida. *A nice gesture would have been bringing me coffee and the Sunday paper in bed,* he thought. This was overkill.

The phone rang as he was settling into the driver's seat. *The car is so fancy, it's even got its own phone.*

"Hello, Honey," he answered. He was expecting Nancy.

"Hi, Doll," a man's voice answered, not without a hint of sarcasm.

"Oh, Moolah," Ortega remembered. "Forgot I gave you this number. You got the van back okay, right?" In the mess of everything that was happening, he forgot to check back in.

"Yeah, I got it. But never mind that. Are you sitting down?" Moolah asked.

"I'm in my car, Moolah," Ortega barked. "What do you think?"

"But you're not driving?" Moolah confirmed.

"Was just about to, why?"

"Got some info about your Lady Love," Moolah sighed. "You're not gonna like it."

"Oh." Ortega's chest sank.

Nancy had assumed that when Moolah dropped off the assets for their factory coup, that it was the first time Ortega had spoken to the man. It wasn't. On an earlier call with Darwin, he had asked him for a favor.

Darwin agreed, and suggested he phone a man named 'Moolah.' "Just tell him 'Finn' sent you, and he'll help you out."

"Where are you now? I can drop some photos your way," Moolah offered hastily.

Ortega looked around. "You know the dry cleaner on 301 near Ellenton? Connected to the laundromat?"

"Yeah," Moolah confirmed. "I know it. I can be there in less than ten minutes."

"Okay, I'll wait. I'm in the metered parking out front. Look for an obnoxious tan Lincoln Town Car."

"Gotcha. Be there in two shakes of a lamb's tail."

"Uh, okay. Bye." Ortega hung up the phone. He didn't get the expression. Nor did he try. He was more concerned about what he'd dug up on Nancy.

As if her ears were buzzing, the car phone rang again.

"Hello," Ortega answered, this time, not certain who was on the other end.

"Is that any way to greet your wife?" Nancy teased.

"Uh, sorry," Ortega fumbled, trying to sound natural. "Still not used to all this new technology."

"Welcome to the 20th Century," she joked. "Hey, listen. Dominic can squeeze me in for a late lesson today. Thought I'd meet some of the girls at the club for cocktails after. Can you manage dinner on your own tonight?"

Ortega thought a moment, just as a beaten up dark green compact car pulled up alongside him. It was a little too worn, even for the likes of this town, so Ortega assumed it must have been Moolah. He was right.

"Yeah, sure," he answered, hitting a few buttons in an attempt to roll down the window. Instead, the car locked and unlocked and his seat shifted. "Damn it!" he cursed, as Moolah, who was now standing just outside the car, waited impatiently, taking furtive glances around him.

"What's wrong?" Nancy asked, concerned.

"Nothing," he sucked in a breath, powering down the window and accepting the manila envelope from Moolah. "Technology and all," he let out a forced laugh. "No, that's fine," he answered, reaching into his pocket to pull out a smaller envelop filled with cash. He handed it to Moolah, who accepted it quickly, gave him a two-finger salute as if tipping a hat to him, and darted off in his green monstrosity. "I can manage."

"Thanks, hon," Nancy cooed. "I'll make it up to you by cooking a nice roast beef dinner tomorrow night. M'wah!" She made a kissing noise into the phone before hanging up.

Ortega hung up the phone. Just then, he spotted a parking meter attendant making the rounds. He looked up and saw that his time had expired. *Ah well,* he thought. *Probably best to look at these when I get home, anyway.*

TEN MINUTES LATER, Ortega was pulling into his subdivision. He waved to his neighbor, Bob, as he pulled into his driveway, but Bob merely wrinkled his upper lip, turned his back toward him, and continued to water his lawn. *Guess he's still sore about the newspaper,* Ortega thought.

Once inside, Ortega set the envelope on the kitchen counter, as if trying to mentally prepare himself. He looked up to see that Nancy had left out a bottle of his favorite bourbon and a small, crystal bourbon tumbler with the letter "J" carved into it. Next to it was a handwritten note: *"Thanks for being so understanding about dinner. There's some left-over chicken in the fridge and green beans. Love you oodles, Nancy."*

Ortega poured himself a hearty serving of bourbon and took a long sip before procuring a butter knife from the drawer and slicing open the envelope. Had Nancy been home, she would have protested his using a food knife to open an envelope. But then, she wasn't here, was she? No, she was having a tennis lesson with Dominic.

After an eternity, he finally pulled the black and white photos from the envelope and fought back a reaction, as if there were other people in the room and he wanted to remain calm. His lower lip quivered. It appeared Nancy was doing more than playing tennis with her instructor. The photos started out innocently enough, pictures of her and Dominic standing next to the court, tennis rackets in hand, sipping water and laughing about some shared joke. But they got progressively worse, showing the couple kissing in the pool... the pool at the Ortega residence. And another featured some indelicate shots of them naked in the water, wrapped together tighter than two river otters on a cold day. There was no mistaking what they were doing, as there were other photos of her leaving what Ortega presumed was Dominic's apartment, hand in hand, and even one outdoors on the grounds of the tennis club... literally, in full display on the grass. Perhaps if Dominic and Nancy hadn't found the potential for getting caught such a turn on, had they been more discreet, maybe Moolah wouldn't have found anything.

Ortega took another long sip of his bourbon. The thing that plagued him the most was not even the infidelity, nor that he had given up everything, his career and his life, to uproot and move to Florida in an effort to save their marriage. It wasn't even the fact that she had lied to him. It was the fact that she thought so little of him as to bring her lover into their home. He forced himself to look at the photos by the pool again, in case he somehow got it wrong. But no, there were the red fire plants and small Areca palms and a money tree that she'd had the landscapers add on one side of the pool. He could even spot the edge of one of their outdoor lounge chairs and the corner of one of their beach towels.

Ortega was not one to cry, but his eyes teared up just a little, his heart aching in a way that it hadn't since —

The phone rang. This time, it was his cell phone. He recognized the number.

"Hi Penelope," Ortega greeted weakly.

"What's wrong?" Penelope immediately asked. "You don't sound right."

Ortega let out a sigh. "Just a long day?" he lied. "Got something for me?"

"Uh, yeah," Penelope finally answered. "I don't know what's happening down there in Florida, but it seems the forensics guy on the case has got his head up his ass."

"Oh?" Ortega's eyebrows shot up.

"Samples of the 'healthy tea' that Erasmus was supposedly drinking the night he died were conveniently absent from the report, along with anything other than the dinner his on-board chef made. And, the coroner attributed the death to natural causes, except—"

"Except what?" Ortega asked.

"Except that he had a mild rash on his forearms, and his lips were swollen, suggesting—"

"An allergic reaction to antibiotics?"

"Possibly, or some other drug," Penelope concluded. "But Erasmus was as healthy as a horse. He didn't take prescription meds for anything."

"So why would the local coroner and forensic expert cover this up?" Ortega asked.

"Must be a lot of money in Vandenberg Nutraceuticals," Penelope suggested.

"I'll say," Ortega finished. "And since Erasmus was conveniently cremated, we'll never know for sure if something was slipped into his food... Come to think of it—" Ortega replayed the news story that Monte shared with him, letting it tumble in his head for a moment. Penelope waited patiently for him to continue. She knew the sign of Ortega about to have an "aha" moment. Finally, he continued.

"Didn't the newspaper say they found valerian root packed in his overnight bag? Could something have conflicted with that... something he ate or drank?"

"There might be something to that," Penelope continued. "And at that high altitude, even being in a pressurized cabin, whatever it was still would have affected him more so than when on land. If he took that on top of what I found... Woo Wee," Penelope huffed into the phone.

"Really? What else have you found?"

"The food samples that your guy Darwin got me each had traces of prescription meds in them. The bar in the red wrapping had traces of ephedrine. The purple one, zolpidem. The green macaroon snacks, opium, and the yellow wafers, sertraline."

"Wow, these guys weren't messing around, a drug for every occasion, energy, sleep, pain relief, depression—"

"And I saved the best for last." Penelope paused dramatically. "The stain on Darwin's shirt had traces of fruit pectin on it."

"Why is that important?" Ortega was confused.

"Think about it, José," Penelope added. "What do drug users do when they want to try fooling a drug test by cleaning out their system?"

"Oh." Ortega's eyes lit up. "So perhaps the church wanted to make sure that no one discovered their 'miracles' by creating a system by which the meds went through someone's bloodstream quickly."

"Or someone serving a healthy tea on a plane heading to Florida," Penelope offered.

"You're a genius. Thank you, Penelope. I can always count on you."

"Sure thing, José." Her voice softened. "José?" she said again.

"Yes, Penelope."

"You know you can always talk to me, right?" She paused for a moment on the other end of the line. Ortega could hear her breathing softly. "About anything... not just work stuff."

"I know, Penelope. I appreciate that," he answered quietly.

"Goodnight, José."

"Goodnight, Penelope."

CHAPTER 30
Mother

Back in Manhattan

Rue paced the floor of the condo nervously, occasionally peering out the window at the near-desolate street below, as if looking for someone or something. Snow mixed with sleet pelted hard on the building, and she watched as it quickly piled up on the sidewalk and the cars below. With the high winds and blizzard outside that struck with little warning, there was nothing to do but pace inside, in a condo that was large by Manhattan standards, but was no match for a woman in distress.

"Shall we talk about it?" Darwin finally asked, offering her a glass of her favorite Willamette Valley wine.

Rue paused, accepted the glass, took a giant swig of it, and handed it back to Darwin. She returned to her pacing.

Oh, this is bad, Darwin thought to himself. In the short time they had been together, Rue had developed quite the refined palate for wine. She didn't guzzle wine, and she rarely drank it unless it was paired with what she deemed were the proper cheese, nuts, and dried fruits or main course.

He set the small dish of dried apricots, gruyere cheese cubes, and hazelnuts aside. Apparently, he had read the room wrong.

"No," Rue finally answered, exasperated. "If there weren't a God-damned blizzard outside, I could at least go for a power walk in Central Park."

That didn't exactly answer Darwin's question. He tried again, this time pacing beside her. "Would it help if I walked beside you and you shared what's on your mind?"

Rue stopped abruptly, agitated. "No, and that's really annoying. I just need a little — space."

Darwin's face dropped. This was the first time since they'd met over a year ago that she'd needed 'space.' He felt helpless.

"Look," Rue huffed, seeing Darwin's crestfallen expression. "This has nothing to do with you—-"

*Oh, crap, h*e thought. He was about to get the *'It's not you; It's me'* speech.

"This is just something I need to work through," she finished.

"Okay." Darwin put his hands in the air and backed away a few paces. "I'm just going to say one more thing, and then I promise I'll leave you alone. I'll disappear into the bedroom for a while until you tell me it's okay to come out... deal?"

"Fine." Rue dropped her arms. "What is it?"

"I realize that everyone grieves in their own way, but you seem to be bottling up an awful lot of emotion lately since you learned of your mother's death."

"It was only a few days ago!" Rue's voice went up an octave.

"I recognize that," he answered. "All I'm saying is that it's okay for you to be however you need to be. You're in mourning, so if you need to cry—"

"That's just it," Rue slammed a hand down on the computer desk. Darwin was startled. This was a side of her he'd never seen before. "I'm not grieving." Darwin winced, unsure how to respond. "If anything, I feel... relieved."

"I see," Darwin answered calmly.

"No, Darwin, you don't see!" She knew she was taking her anger out on him, but she didn't know how else to channel what she was feeling at that moment. "How terrible of a daughter am I that I actually feel *relieved* that my mother is dead?"

"Well, one, I don't think you're a terrible daughter, and—" Rue turned her back on him, wrapping her arms around herself as she started sobbing uncontrollably. Darwin dared not touch her given the icy reception the last time he tried to reach out to her. "Shall I go away for a bit?" Darwin offered helplessly.

Finally, Rue relented, reaching for a tissue on the desk. After blowing her nose and tossing the tissue into a wastepaper basket, she motioned to their couch. He obliged by settling in next to her, noticing that she had backed away to the opposite end. "Sorry," she whimpered. "It just feels as if my skin is all pins and needles, as if every nerve in my body is frayed."

Darwin understood that feeling. That's exactly how he'd felt when he learned his ex-wife had died. And even though he wasn't in love with her, he had still cared deeply about her. He sat back on his side of the couch, stretching his long legs out in front of him, nearly knocking his feet against the base of the coffee table. Rue, by contrast, had managed to fold herself into the tiniest of balls and sat nestled into the couch like a curled-up greyhound.

"It's just that—" Rue tried again. This wasn't easy for her, since she'd never really opened up to anyone before. She simply never trusted anyone enough. The closest she'd found before Darwin was her friend Midge, but that was before — She brought her wandering thoughts back into the room. "It's as if, with her death, I'm closing the door on a part of my life that should have been shut a long time ago."

Darwin bit his tongue. Everything he'd said so far was a miss, so he thought his best option was to nod and just wait for what seemed like an agonizingly long time for her to continue.

"And with the church," she continued hesitantly. "My mom was never actually my mom, really. It was as if we all belonged to the cause. And when I finally escaped that life, she kept tabs on me. I don't know that anyone else would bother, honestly. Hence the —"

"Relief," Darwin finished. Rue nodded. "The door is closed and after years of looking over your shoulder, no one is following you."

"Yes, except—"

"What is it?" He instinctively reached out a hand to her before remembering himself and pulling it back.

"That's not exactly true, is it?"

"What do you mean?"

"We stirred up a hornet's nest by visiting the Church of Infinite Love, Darwin. Don't you realize that? And, in addition to the guilt over not grieving my mother's death, is the added guilt of feeling responsible for her death."

"Responsible, how?"

"You think it was a coincidence that she 'accidentally' fell to her death after she'd helped us by slipping us a few clues that day? Because I don't."

"Nor do I, but that doesn't mean—"

"It kinda does!" Rue insisted. "We're not cops. And while you are an investigator for hire, the guy who hired you isn't even a police detective anymore. So, what the hell were we doing there, Darwin?"

Darwin's face grew flushed. Up until that moment, he was sympathetic toward Rue, assuming that she was grieving the loss of her mother. Now, however, it seemed she was blaming them — both of them — for her mother's death. It was unfair, he reasoned, and hurtful to an ego that was more fragile than he realized. *How dare she suggest that I, as a trained investigator, had no business being there? And that somehow this was our fault!*

Darwin clenched his jaw but said nothing.

CHAPTER 31
The Commitments

A Special Gathering in Pennsylvania

~

The parents of the late Marnie Watson, Jessica Jones, and Linda Parker all sat quietly at the decadent religious ceremony of the Evangelicals. With one exception... Linda Parker's father died of a grief-stricken heart attack not six months after his daughter's death, leaving Linda's mother to mourn both the loss of her husband and her daughter with nothing but the support of the church to guide her.

As long-term members, they had signed non-disclosure agreements following the suspicious deaths of their children... standard procedure, of course.

The church's brainwashing and gaslighting techniques did a fair job of convincing them that their children died because they disobeyed their parents and the laws of God. That's why Marnie Watson had mental health problems. "A demon got in," they reasoned. Meanwhile, Jessica Jones and Linda Parker had been drinking underage and out on the grounds after dark — which was strictly forbidden. Yes, other children had made mistakes in the past without such dire consequences, but more was expected from those young women who grew up in the church from birth, and whose parents were considered among the most well-respected elders.

Still, with Erasmus Vandenberg's recent death, the Evangelicals were concerned the parents of the deceased might be questioning their beliefs. And they wanted to ensure that they were briefed about the right 'message' to tell reporters, detectives, and anyone who might ask. After all, non-believers couldn't possibly understand their larger mission — that of saving humanity from the gates of hell. Sadness and discomfort in this life were minor when compared to the bliss to be enjoyed in the heavenly afterworld.

The ceremony was attended by a dozen Evangelicals, including Edwina Vandenberg, and their Ambassadors. Among the Ambassadors were, as Elsbeth had indicated, servants of the Vandenberg's, Ruth, Ivy, Hugo the security agent, and Vivian the flight attendant. Also in attendance was Reverend Simon from the Pennsylvania church and several of the elders who supported him from nearby church campuses. Had Deaconess Frances not met with an untimely death, she would have been in attendance as well. Ferdinand was *not* in attendance, as he was told to stay behind and look after Elsbeth.

With Erasmus gone, Edwina Vandenberg was next in line to take control of the Church of Infinite Love but was meeting opposition.

"Thank you all for being here on this somber and yet glorious occasion." A short man stood. He was wearing a well-tailored black suit and red tie ... It was Bernie, the pilot on Erasmus' final voyage. "Every pilot needs a co-pilot," he joked. "Thank you, Edwina Vandenberg, for being my co-pilot in light of the very troubling and sad loss of your father, Erasmus."

He stood on a large theater stage, looking freakishly small by comparison. The small crowd seated in the first few rows bowed their head in prayer. Edwina bit the corners of her lip, agitated, so hard that she drew blood that mixed with her deep red lipstick. While the lesser members of the church were told that makeup was vanity, Edwina had no such restriction, nor did she feel the need to explain why she was exempt.

How does Bernie Forger think he can just jump the ranks and take my father's place? Edwina never bought into the idea that women were less capable than men in matters of leadership and business. She just went along with it when it suited her. And, at this moment, it did not suit her.

"Since dear Erasmus had no male children, and women are not called to be in such positions of authority, naturally, the next in line to lead as Governing Evangelist is myself, Bernard Forger. I was anointed by Erasmus to be second in command ten years ago." Bernie paused to take in the somber looks of the family members… Uncle Morris, Aunt Stella… but no Baxter, no Edgar, no Elsbeth… *No matter,* he thought to himself. *Who needs them, anyway?* "Let us pause to recite the seven commitments!"

Like the Ten Commandments, only more streamlined, mercenary, and self-serving, the group droned on in unison, as follows…

We commit to serving God and His supreme will at the expense of our own safety and happiness.

We understand that the Evangelicals must be pure of mind, body, and spirit and act as guardians of their flock, even though it may require sacrifices for the good of all.

We acknowledge the unquestionable authority of the male elders of the church and value the service of the female nurturers.

We vow never to lie, steal, or kill for personal gain, and will engage in warfare only as directed by God for the greater enlightenment and overall salvation of his people.

We promise to set aside personal and professional desires that do not align with the mission of the Church of Infinite Love.

We commit ourselves to spreading love throughout the world, understanding that sometimes love requires punishment for the greater alignment to one's highest purpose.

We vow to serve as beacons of light unto all that we encounter, believers and non-believers, so that they may one day understand the true awesomeness of faith in the Highest.

Amen.

After the 'Amen,' the Ambassadors jumped to attention at the flick of Bernie's wrist and escorted the Evangelicals and the elders into a side room that opened to reveal a long dining table. Mr. and Mrs. Watson, Mr. and Mrs. Jones, and Mrs. Parker were seated along one of the long ends of the table, with the Evangelicals and other elders surrounding them. The Ambassadors began serving food and beverage from an adjacent kitchen.

"How are you getting on, my Dear?" Mrs. Watson asked Mrs. Parker softly. Mrs. Watson had ten years to grieve, and while one never gets over the loss of a child, she empathized with the fact that Mrs. Parker was two years in, after losing both a spouse and a child.

Mrs. Parker sat there, gaunt and pale, trembling slightly. An Ambassador set a bowl of soup in front of the woman. "Thank you," Mrs. Parker answered weakly, before slowly turning her head toward Mrs. Watson, as if it pained her to do so. "I've been better," she confessed. "But I'm trying." Her lip trembled.

"Just remember, my Dear," Edwina—who was sitting at the head of the table — piped up. "Your loss is an opportunity to demonstrate to the world that living an ungodly life leads to misery." Mrs. Parker's face crumbled, as the other parents eyed Edwina with horror. She tried to backpedal. "What I mean is," she softened her voice. "You will be reunited with your husband and daughter again in the afterworld, where God will bless you beyond anything you can imagine. You must remain faithful to the Church, and it will all be okay."

Mrs. Parker nodded, skeptically. But since she had no one to turn to, aside from other members of the Church of Infinite Light, she received no grief support. Therefore, there was no voice of reason to suggest that maybe this life was worth living, instead of what she was currently doing — which was essentially, waiting to die.

A CALL CAME in at 8 p.m., just as Dennis and Emma were going to, for the first time since their arrival, settle in and take the night off. It took a while, but they finally agreed on a rental movie, and Dennis had the cassette in the VCR and was about to hit 'play.'

Just then, a commercial popped up selling a collection of the "Greatest Oldies of All Time," available in CD, cassette, and — for a limited time — in 8-track format. That's when she heard it, Bing Crosby singing, *"Every time it rains, it rains pennies from heaven—"*

"That's it!" Emma squealed.

"What is?" Dennis sat up, alarmed.

"I don't have it all worked out yet," Emma admitted, "But I'll bet any amount of money that there's a connection between that song and this case. He kept singing *Pennies from Heaven* over and over again."

"Who did?"

"Erasmus!" Emma explained.

Dennis opened his mouth to speak, but Emma was already on her cell phone calling the Vandenberg residence in New York. Ferdinand answered the phone.

"You want to talk to Elsbeth?" Ferdinand was surprised. "Now? Seems a little late."

Elsbeth's ears must have been burning, but suddenly there was a click from another line, as Elsbeth picked up the call from a separate phone in the library. "I'll t.. take it, F... Ferdinand."

"Very well," he acknowledged, hanging up the phone.

"What is it?" Elsbeth asked knowingly, whispering into the phone. "I can't talk long. Ivy's asleep, but Mother and Ruth are arriving home from their church travels any minute now."

"I need to know if you still have your grandfather's record collection, the one he wanted to take on the plane with him?"

Elsbeth let out a groan, "No," she lamented. "I would have, but Mother's taken over the entire estate and wanted to get rid of most of grandfather's things, records, art collection, even half the furniture—"

"Get rid of them?" Emma's voice went up in pitch.

"Keep it down," Elsbeth whispered. "Yes, but I phoned Uncle Edgar and let him know of her plans. He put a call in and asked her to ship him everything. She didn't understand why, but he claimed to be sentimental —even offered to pay for it."

"So, all the possessions that Erasmus loved most are—"

"Heading to Ireland," Elsbeth nodded. "If they aren't there already."

"Elsbeth?" Emma asked suddenly. "I need you to do me a favor."

"What is it?" Elsbeth heard the jingle from the front door. "And hurry! They're home."

"I need you to call Edgar, tell him I'm heading to Dublin on the next available flight, and will meet him at the Leitrim estate. Can you do that?"

"Yes," Elsbeth answered, hanging up the phone abruptly.

"Elsbeth?" Edwina eyed her daughter standing in the hallway wearing a nightgown and fuzzy pink slippers. "What are you doing up at this hour?"

Elsbeth thought quickly. Ferdinand knew who was on the other end of the phone line, so she couldn't lie. "It w-w-was Emma," she stuttered. "W-w-wanted to s-s-see how we w-w-ere g-g-getting on after grandfather's death."

"Really?" Edwina was surprised. "Why so late?"

Elsbeth merely shrugged her shoulders and yawned. To herself, she thought, *I need to figure out how to get a message to Edgar without Mother knowing. But how?*

CHAPTER 32
Leitrim

Ireland

Despite Dennis' concern, Emma arrived at the Ireland estate early morning after flying from Tampa to New York and catching the red eye from LaGuardia airport just two days after her call with Elsbeth. Stressed and sleep deprived, Emma dropped her single carry-on bag on the ground and dragged herself up the stone steps leading to Edgar's front door. After several attempts at ringing the bell and even peering through a few of the windows, she realized that Edgar was most likely not at home. *Maybe Elsbeth hadn't gotten the message to him?* Severely jet-lagged, Emma sat on one of the steps, leaning slightly against the thick, cold railing.

With two suspected murders on their hands... one being Rue Brennan's mother and the other being Erasmus Vandenberg, Emma had no intention of staying in the home for longer than what was absolutely necessary. She closed her eyes momentarily to see if she could get rid of the brain fog that had settled in and let out a long yawn. For the briefest of moments, the sun came out, warming her face.

Sprightly had offered to accompany her, but Emma was concerned it would be too dangerous. Unlike the stubborn Emma, Sprightly understood, and promised to stay behind to water the grounds on Emma's new property and make sure that Emma's 'main squeeze,' didn't forget to eat. Emma knew this was a kind gesture. But, one, she never understood that expression, since she only had 'one squeeze' (Dennis), and two, Dennis never forgot to eat... not once. On the plus side, Sprightly was a health nut, so no doubt she'd have a thing or two to say about Dennis' BBQ takeout habits while Emma wasn't home to cook sensibly.

"Ahem," a female voice called out, clearing her throat, just loud enough to jar Emma. It was only then that Emma realized that she was now leaning her cheek against the cool stone railing where she sat, her face pressed so hard against it that it left a mark.

"Oh." She sat upright, rubbing her cheek. She hadn't realized she had dozed off.

Ruth, the housekeeper, stood with a solitary small black suitcase in her hand, wearing an equally black, starched polyester dress, and white Mary Jane shoes with white matching gloves. Elsbeth was next to her, with her severely chopped bangs and bob haircut, button down black blazer and skirt, and a look on her face that suggested she would rather be anywhere but there.

"Are you alright, my Dear?" Ruth asked sympathetically.

"Yes." Emma bolted to her feet. "Just a little jet-lagged is all." She paused to eye them both. "But, what are you doing here?"

"I suppose we could ask you the same thing, my Dear," Ruth answered softly.

Elsbeth shot Emma what could only be described as an unspoken apology. In other words, Elsbeth hadn't intended on being there, and if she had, she hadn't planned on being accompanied.

"Oh." Emma sifted through her mind, trying to sort out her thoughts quickly. "Edgar let me know that Edwina had sent much of Erasmus' things here to be put in storage," she lied, saving involving Elsbeth in all this. "I was hoping to collect a few sentimental pieces to add to my newly acquired Florida home."

"Sentimental," Ruth repeated quietly.

"Yes, that's right," Emma nodded.

"With you being Erasmus' portrait model and all," Ruth pursed her lips. (To be clear, her lips actually did come together like an old coin purse.)

"He was my friend, and I miss him," Emma stammered a little as she tried to defend her position. She wasn't a timid woman, but it was the first time she found herself actually talking about her feelings for Erasmus.

"Enough to fly all this way?" Ruth was unconvinced.

Elsbeth intervened. "I m... miss him too!" She suddenly wailed, running to pull Emma into a tight embrace. Under her breath, she whispered so that only Emma could hear, "I'm sorry. They weren't supposed to come with me."

Ruth was visibly shocked. "Elsbeth," she chastised, her tone ever gentle. "Compose yourself. What would your mother say?" Elsbeth released her hug and backed away slightly, rubbing her eyes until they appeared red.

"What's going on?" Ferdinand's tall frame appeared next to the smaller and wider Ruth.

"The girls are crying over Erasmus' death," Ruth answered softly.

Unlike Ruth, who kept a neutral, serene look on her face at all times, Ferdinand's was very expressive. He dropped into a frown. "I know how you feel, young ladies," Ferdinand acknowledged. "I miss him, too." He shook his head solemnly.

"But the good Lord knows what he's doing," Ruth reminded Ferdinand, who smiled and nodded in a way that suggested he was not so sure anymore. "Well," she turned to Emma. "Get about your business, then." Under her breath she muttered to Elsbeth, "Don't understand how she and Edgar got to be such good friends all of a sudden."

Elsbeth merely shrugged then bolted ahead with the key to the front door, grabbing Emma's arm along the way and pulling her after her. Emma nearly tripped, which would have led to her falling face-first on the stone but managed to catch her footing in time.

Before Ruth and Ferdinand could catch up, Elsbeth whispered to Emma, "I told 'em Uncle was going to meet me at the airport, but they refused to let me travel alone," she explained. "I'll try to distract them as best as I can, though, while you look around."

Emma would have preferred that Elsbeth hadn't interfered and just passed the message on to Edgar as promised, but she'd come to learn that Elsbeth had a stubborn streak, and now that she had Emma as an ally, her courage to stand up to her family was building.

"Where is Edgar?" Emma whispered back.

Elsbeth shrugged. "I couldn't get a hold of him," she confessed. "That's why I'm here." She clammed up when Ruth reached the door.

Ruth crossed the threshold of the household and eyed the room distastefully. She even tsked a little under her breath. At that moment, she wished Ivy were there to help her, but Edwina insisted she needed 'Housekeeper' to stay behind to manage the New York household... even though the household currently contained one very capable woman.

Isaac, the only caretaker of this estate, was currently accompanying Edgar in Dublin for a naturalist convention, but they had no way of knowing that. Ruth made a mental note to give Edwina a full report of her findings when she returned. Although Erasmus' will had made it very clear that the Ireland home now belonged to Edgar, surely Edwina could do... something?

"Ruth," Elsbeth pulled the older woman from her thoughts. "I'm very t-t-tired," she yawned, adopting a childlike voice. "Could y-y-you help me get s-s-settled in one of the rooms upstairs?"

Ruth eyed the girl curiously before shooting Emma a suspicious look. Emma, who was now surveying the room for signs of Erasmus' belongings, pretended not to notice.

"Of course, but—" Ruth answered hesitantly.

"Maybe Ferdinand could g-g-go into t-t-town and get us some groceries... y... you could provide the list." Elsbeth's mood brightened.

"But what about—" She nodded toward Emma, pursing her lips, yet again.

"Emma will have no t-t-trouble finding the s-s-storage unit on the property... It's just by the empty s-s-stables." She paused to fill Emma in. "Let her l-l-look around." Elsbeth was keenly aware of Ruth's apprehension and added, "Grandfather Erasmus s-s-saw fit to t-t-trust her," she reminded Ruth.

"Yes." Ruth eyed Emma head to toe judgmentally. "You certainly have your charms over the men in this household... But how were you planning to get inside, anyway? Edgar isn't home."

"I was... waiting for him," Emma answered. "That's why you found me sitting on the front steps."

"Fine," Ruth eventually relented. Frankly, Ruth liked it better when Elsbeth was younger and needier and didn't have someone like Emma feeding the girl bad ideas. Elsbeth used to be much easier to control. "Let's go." Ruth pointed Elsbeth toward the steps. "Incompetent that man is," Ruth grumbled. "I thought he was supposed to meet us at the airport?"

As Elsbeth and Ruth made their way to one of the spare bedrooms, with Elsbeth doing her best to distract Ruth from the facts, Ferdinand offered, "I can show you where the storage unit is, Emma. I'm heading out, anyway."

The air was crisp when they walked back outside. It seemed as if the sun had immediately vanished and the wind suddenly picked up speed, the icy coolness shocking her face. She hugged herself. Somehow her wool jacket keeping her warm, contrasted by the sudden biting air, refreshed her. She spotted the storage house in the distance.

"I see it, thanks!" she called to Ferdinand. With her newfound second wind, she headed past the stables until she found an old stone building with a rotting wooden door. She tugged at it, and the old door finally gave way and opened, kicking up a mountain of dust that landed in her hair. She coughed a moment, doing her best to brush off the particles with gloved hands. "It's unlocked!" she called again.

No one ventured out to their remote estate, so Edgar was lax about locking the shed. And, even if someone did come by, if they wanted Erasmus' old furniture that badly, they could have it. Edgar had already selected a few pieces from his uncle's collection as keepsakes and had relocated them to the main house. He was more concerned about keeping his collection of reptiles, amphibians, and arachnids behind glass, under lock and key.

Emma watched as Ferdinand climbed into an all-black Citroen he'd rented at the airport, once they realized that Edgar was unreachable. He waved in acknowledgement seeing that she was successful in getting inside.

Whomever was responsible for transporting Erasmus' belongings did a very poor job of it, as old couches, lamps, end tables, several mattresses, framed pictures, and all manner of household appliances appeared to be haphazardly piled on top of one another. Emma sighed as she saw what had become of the very couch she sat on the last time she modeled for Erasmus. Several costumes, including the dress she wore, were strewn on top of it. She made a mental note to tag some of these pieces and ask Edgar to hold them for her so she could have them shipped to her new home in Florida. It didn't exactly go with the decor, but she didn't care.

Suddenly, she saw something scurrying in the corner. Emma let out a scream as a large rat ran across her foot. "Geez!" She grabbed her heart, jumping backward and almost sailing into a very large hallway mirror. "And I thought the subway rats were bad."

Think, Emma, she said to herself. *Where would Erasmus have stored detailed, hard copy records of the underhanded transactions happening at Vandenberg Nutraceuticals?*

It was then that she remembered his vinyl records. And that was what clued her in that he might have been the one who removed the pages from the log books that Sprightly discovered. *But was the song a clue, somehow?* She replayed the lyrics in her mind, over and over again.

She found herself shimmying between pieces of furniture, often getting the hem of her coat stuck on the edge of something as she carefully climbed among the household items. But there was nothing obvious... no old file cabinets, boxes filled with paper, no music... nothing. Perhaps this was a wasted trip.

Hmm, she thought to herself. *Edgar did say he recovered a few sentimental pieces from Erasmus' collection. Maybe there's something in the house?* She did one final, cursory search of the storage unit before climbing, twisting, turning, and all but biting her way out of the room, shutting the old door behind her.

As she made her way to the main house, she saw that Ferdinand's car wasn't back yet. She crept through the front door quietly, tiptoeing past the staircase. Upstairs, she could hear Ruth fussing with Elsbeth about something.

They didn't hear her. She had a little more time.

Emma left the main foyer and headed to the adjacent living room, sparsely filled with two leather couches and a pub chair, surrounding a green Turkish throw rug. Behind one of the couches was a curio cabinet filled with souvenirs from someone's travels... she assumed Erasmus',

Edgar's, or one of several of the family members that stayed there from time to time.

That's when she noticed something. All around the room were remnants of Erasmus' old art studio, several of the paintings that hung on the walls in his New York condo were now hanging here, somewhat out of place with the decor. His tea set sat neatly arranged on one of the end tables, and his easel stood by the window, just the way Erasmus would have placed it to catch the right natural light from outside.

Her heart sank a little, knowing that she'd never get to talk with him again, work together, or share the odd afternoon tea. She brought herself out of her thoughts as she heard a thump from one of the rooms upstairs... she needed to work quickly and made her way through the archway to the small dining area, next to the kitchen. While there, she noticed several more paintings, the odd sculpture, and even Erasmus' old world globe that opened to reveal a secret mini-bar. Just to be sure, she inched up to the globe and carefully lifted the lid... no documents of any kind, just a few aged whiskeys. She closed the lid.

While the estate was sprawling, with several smaller guest houses and servants' quarters, the main house, itself, was rather small. Aside from the kitchen on the ground level, and a small study that was connected to the main bedroom on the second floor, that left only one other possible place to search... the main study. The only thing Emma knew about it was that Erasmus joked that Edgar was converting his research room into a taxidermy shop full of spiders... this made no sense to her, except for this one reference to Edgar's 'collection of death.'

After one more cursory glance to make sure neither Ruth nor Ferdinand were there looking over her shoulder, she scurried down the hallway leading to the study...

CHAPTER 33
Revelations

Manhattan

"Come take a look at these, won't you, Rue?" Darwin asked, popping a 3.5" floppy disc into the computer drive and clicking to open the contents on his desktop.

"Sure." Rue emerged from the kitchen, gnawing on a breadstick that was left over from last night's takeout dinner. She had on red, striped flannel pajamas and matching socks.

Two days had passed since her earlier emotional breakdown. Both found the entire situation unsettling. Beyond the accident surrounding the death of Rue's mother, and the fact that someone tried to injure them by tampering with their rental car, there was something else... What was consuming both of their minds now was that since they had been together, they never really fought. Now they wondered if that was simply because they rarely talked about their respective pasts. And now that they had, and the discussion didn't go well, were there further arguments on the horizon?

Darwin smiled to himself and shook his head. *It'll be okay,* he told himself. They had been living together for months now, but he still wasn't used to Rue being a permanent resident in his condo. Even with the pantyhose hanging over the shower rod to dry, the assortment of cosmetics strewn on the bathroom counter, and the fact that she had so easily claimed one side of the bed and end table as her own, Darwin still felt as if this was all a dream, and he was worried he might wake up at any moment. The truth of the matter was, he liked her being there... a lot.

"What's that goofy expression on your face for?" she smiled back at him, crunching loudly into her breadstick and chewing.

"Nothing," he smiled. "Here, take a look."

Rue looked at the files Darwin had opened. "What am I looking for?" she asked.

"Not sure, really," Darwin admitted. "This is a compilation of everyone even marginally related to this case, along with screenshots of newspaper clippings, and copies of files previously on microfiche. I've gone through it a thousand times. I'm missing something, but I don't know what."

"Don't know if I can help, but I'll try." Rue plopped into the computer chair and set her remaining piece of breadstick on the table, crumbs scattering all around it in a very unhygienic mess. Darwin opened his mouth to say something but decided better of it. He was learning to pick his battles. For example, squabbles over the correct way to load the dishwasher, why you should hang wet towels up instead of leaving them on the floor, and what happens when you run the vacuum cleaner over the carpet without cutting any stray strands with a pair of scissors first, were not that important in the grand scheme of things. He was beginning to learn that 90% of the time none of it was particularly important and, certainly, not worth fighting over.

"Have I lost you?" Rue asked, bringing Darwin back from his daydream.

"Sorry, no," Darwin answered. "These are also a few digital copies of old newspaper stories, three of which link the Church of Infinite Love, and Vandenberg Nutraceuticals to the death of three people. And the last —" Darwin's voice trailed off.

"The last what?"

"The last is a story about... um... the suspicious nature of your mother's death...Look, we can skip that one if—"

"No," Rue was adamant. "It's okay. I can handle it." She motioned toward the file, and Darwin clicked to enlarge it.

The article was published just days after the deaconess' death. Rue's head was spinning. It was surreal. Her mother died just after she and Darwin had visited the church, where her death was deemed a tragic accident. In some strange way, Rue actually thought that maybe some God or the universe had given her the gift of seeing her mother one more time; but now she feared that she may have been partially responsible.

So, now Rue had two things to feel guilty about... being responsible for her mother's death and not grieving properly after it happened. She blinked back a few tears.

"You sure you're okay?" Darwin was concerned.

"Yes," Rue reassured him. "I have to work through this. I have to know what happened." Rue turned and read the headline, "Church Deaconess Dies Following Faith Healing Ritual." The article was deliberate in pointing out how, despite the church's claiming to conduct "thousands of successful healings" each year, one of its highest-ranking members could not be saved, and, in point of fact, may have been the target of God's wrath. This was all said tongue-in-cheek, of course, and had it been someone other than Rue's mother, she might have shared the sentiment.

Her eyes gave a cursory glance over the black and white images that accompanied the article... Reverend Simon holding his hands over a sick woman's head while her mother stood dutifully in the background, a practitioner falling backward in a swoon with a tall man reaching out to catch her, and an outside shot of the Church of Infinite Love building—obviously taken from the parking lot. Nothing stood out as—

"Hang on a minute." Rue sat up, a look of shock on her face.

"What is it?" Darwin asked.

"That woman." Rue pointed to the swooning woman.

"What about her?"

"See the mole on her face?" Rue circled a finger above the image.

"Yes?"

"That was the woman attending to my mother the day we were in her private quarters. Do you remember?"

"Not really," Darwin admitted. "I mean, I remember a woman being there, but she sort of... blended in with the background." Darwin felt bad admitting this. One, because he prided himself on paying attention to the people around him and two, he was an investigator, after all. Of course, unbeknownst to him at the time, they had also given him a special cocktail laced with painkillers, according to Penelope's findings. That had no doubt clouded his judgment and memory of the evening.

"I've seen her before. But where—" Rue grabbed the mouse from Darwin and began clicking through the photos, stopping at the article announcing Erasmus' death. "There!" Rue pointed. She spotted the small woman getting on the plane, following closely behind Erasmus Vandenberg, Elsbeth, and Ferdinand. The caption of the photo identified everyone who was boarding the plane, including Erasmus' in-house chef, and Edwina and Elsbeth's personal attendant, a woman named Ruth Fenstermeier.

"Let's zoom in on her," she muttered, clicking to enlarge the screen. "Look," Rue confirmed. "Same mole, same facial features... it's the same woman."

"So, what was the Vandenberg's personal attendant doing at the Church of Infinite Love, serving your high-ranking mother, not long after Erasmus' death?"

"Was she in attendance at the reading of Erasmus' will?" Rue wanted to know.

"Easy enough to find out," he answered. He pointed to another log. "Click on that one," he instructed. "Should have everyone's name who was at the reading.

"There she is again." Rue pointed. "How can she be both in service to the church *and* a full-time servant in the Vandenberg household?

"Good question," Darwin agreed. "And, where is this woman now?"

He made a quick phone call to Officer Dennis, who relayed Emma's call with Elsbeth.

"So," Darwin confirmed, "Ruth was accompanying Edwina to a church event. Does this happen a lot?" Darwin listened. "I see."

"What is it?" Rue asked after he'd hung up the phone.

"It seems that Ruth travels with Edwina quite often on church business."

"So why wasn't Edwina there when we visited?"

"Maybe she was, and we didn't see her?" Darwin suggested.

"Maybe," Rue thought on this. "But Ruth was also on the plane when Erasmus died. Edwina wasn't."

"Hmmm," Darwin thought a moment.

"What, 'hmmm'?" Rue asked.

"Dennis said that Emma got on a plane to Ireland after Edwina shipped a number of Erasmus' belongings to Edgar Vandenberg."

"Emma thinks there's something in Erasmus' belongings that could provide evidence tying Vandenberg Nutraceuticals directly to the deaths at the church?" Rue was surprised.

"That's what it sounds like," Darwin agreed.

"And no one is there with her?" Rue's voice was shaky.

"She insisted on going alone," Darwin explained. He could see the heat rising in Rue's face as she became flushed.

"Officer Dennis is a dumb ass," Rue spat flatly. "If she suspects something is there, then so will any number of people in the Vandenberg family. You have any leftover connections in the Emerald Isle?" Rue asked pointedly. "Because if you do, you better use them to check in on Emma."

CHAPTER 34
Myrna

Leitrim, Ireland

The study door creaked loudly, as if announcing her arrival. Emma found herself inching it open slowly, cringing the entire time. Finally, she entered the room and looked around with awe.

The three main walls were filled with books, beakers, microscopes, and all manner of scientific equipment—most of which were unrecognizable to Emma. On the center table was the small cage where Myrna the mole lived. Edgar had set up an automatic feeding machine and water dispenser for her while he was away. Unfortunately for Myrna, who had gotten used to a daily diet of earthworms and insects, it was filled with kitten kibble and dried fruits and vegetables—just to tied her over until Edgar returned home.

Finally, the fourth wall, alongside the doorway through which she'd just entered, contained a large, office storage cabinet. She twisted the handle and tugged, in an attempt to open it, eagerly hoping for it to reveal paper files that would prove that Vandenberg Nutraceuticals was not only aware of the Church of Infinite drugging its members in the name of control and 'faith healing,' but that a small sub-division of the factory in Florida was actually dedicated to creating the branded products meant exclusively for the church. Unfortunately, since the church had been growing worldwide for the past decade, there was plenty of time and opportunity to convert lots of new followers, with the church and Vandenberg Nutraceuticals making a killing in profit. And if that amounted to a few hundred deaths over the years? Well, that might be considered 'collateral damage.'

Except that Erasmus didn't see it that way. And when he discovered what was happening, he aimed to put a stop to it. Only someone stopped *him* first.

The cabinet was resistant as Emma tugged at it a second time. The door refused to budge.

"Might want to try these," a male voice called over her shoulder.

The hairs on the back of her neck stood up. She knew that voice. Emma shuddered for a moment.

"I hope I make you nervous for the right reasons, Emma Post."

Emma spun around to see none other than Baxter Baker standing there with a tiny key dangling from his finger, presumably to open the cabinet with which she was currently struggling.

She sucked in her breath. "You just caught me off guard, is all," she barked back, snatching the key from his finger and inserting it in the lock. But the nervousness returned.

"Why *are* you here, Mr. Baker?"

"If you'll remember, Emma, I did tell you that the information I shared with you put me in danger and that I needed to disappear for a while."

"Yeah, but I thought you were going on a trip to the Maldives... or wherever it is that rich people go." Emma opened the cabinet to reveal old stacks of magazines, newspapers, a few VHS tapes, and even several old film reels. She began rifling haphazardly through the stack.

"Uh, no," he answered, pausing with amusement as he watched her trying to focus, even though, it was clear his presence undoubtedly unnerved her. "Media files," he finally said.

"What?" Emma paused, looking up at him.

"Media files," he said again. "This was Erasmus' way of collecting all the press coverage of Vandenberg Nutraceuticals over the years. Not sure how they ended up here but—"

"So, you've already been through all these?"

Baxter leaned a shoulder against the side of the cabinet. "Yes," he answered simply. "Been staying in one of the guesthouses for the past month. Funny, Edgar was so wrapped up in his own work that neither he nor Isaac seemed aware that I was here."

"And you managed to go through the contents of this cabinet? What, exactly, were you looking for, Baxter?"

"The same thing as you, Emma."

"Why?" Emma demanded. "You said yourself that you knowingly allowed the Church of Infinite Love to tamper with the vitamin bars your company was selling, even going as far as to eventually set up a lab in Florida to streamline the process. Wouldn't this incriminate you, among others?"

Baxter took a step toward her. Emma instinctively backed away. "Stop," she demanded, holding out her arm, palm facing him like a stop sign. He held his hands up and backed away.

"Relax, Emma. I'm not here to hurt you."

"Aren't you?" Her thoughts returned to Rue's mother and then to Erasmus. But if Baxter wasn't responsible for their deaths... then who was?

Just then, she saw it. Hanging on the wall, behind glass, were a series of Erasmus' old vinyl records, still in their original cases. Perhaps this was Edgar's last attempt at immortalizing his uncle. Right in the center was Bing Crosby's Greatest Hits.

"Pennies from Heaven," Emma murmured under her breath.

Baxter followed her gaze curiously.

Unlike the cabinet, this case wasn't locked. Of course it wasn't—Edgar put them in there, and he was a trusting soul, except when it came to his 'collection of death' that he kept under glass. Once Emma reached the case, she slid it open with ease. She paused to glance at Baxter once more.

As if reading her thoughts, he answered, "I want to know who killed Uncle Erasmus, too."

Emma furrowed her brows in distrust.

"Fine." He tilted his head from side to side. "And possibly remove any documents or evidence that might tie my name to any connection with the church or the deaths caused by Vandenberg Nutraceuticals."

Emma shook her head, disappointed.

"As I've said before, Emma," he lowered his voice, as if suddenly remembering there were other people in the house. "I'm exactly as you'd expect me to be. I've never tried to hide from you, or anyone, who I really am."

"Except where criminal activity is concerned," she corrected.

He held up his hands again. "I am nothing, if not a practical man," he smiled. "So, what is it you've found?"

"Yes," a woman's voice called from the doorway. There stood Ruth, still in her unpleasant black garb, but this time, wearing crisp white lace gloves. She was also distinctly pointing a Sig Sauer 9mm at Emma's chest. "Show us, Emma, what you've found."

For a moment, both Baxter and Emma froze. Since she already had the case open, there was no getting around it. She began to reach for one of the lesser-known records.

"Not that one," Ruth corrected. "The one in the center. *Pennies from Heaven* — one of Erasmus' favorites, wasn't it? Used to hear you both singing it while you were supposedly modeling for him."

Emma let the 'supposedly' go, but only because she currently had a gun pointed at her. She reached for the album and carefully removed it from the stand Edgar had it hooked to behind the case. Turning to set it on the counter, she carefully reached inside to slide the record out, except that wrapped around the vinyl wasn't a sleeve to hold it, but a handwritten sales log.

"Well, what have we here?" Ruth moved into the room. "Unfold that paper," she commanded. Emma did so. On it were a series of transactions between the Church of Infinite Love and Vandenberg Nutraceuticals. "Pull another record down," Ruth ordered. Emma pulled a second from the display, sliding out more documents that revealed information about payments being made to the Watson, Jones and Parker families as quiet settlements for the loss of their children due to negligence.

"I don't know whether Erasmus was crafty or stupid," Ruth chuckled. "Hiding the records inside actual record sleeves was clever, but paper documents are so easy to destroy."

"You killed him," Emma stated.

"Let's just say, I played my part," Ruth agreed. "And, my dear Miss Post, I'm afraid this is the end of the line for you." Ruth's finger twitched against the trigger as she took aim. Just as she fired, Baxter lunged at Emma, tackling her to the ground. A shot rang out as Baxter landed on top of the woman, who narrowly escaped hitting her head on the concrete floor by instinctively tucking her chin. In the commotion, Myrna's cage was disrupted, sending it toppling over.

Emma scrambled to sit upright, Baxter still laying in a heap across her lap. His shirt was covered in blood.

"Baxter," Ruth was aghast. "What have you done?!"

"What have *I* done?" he choked out, grabbing his belly and wincing at the pain.

Emma was frantic, unsure of which emergency to deal with first, Ruth trying to kill her, or an injured Baxter who, from what she could tell, had been shot near the center of his chest.

Ruth was close enough now that there was no missing her target. She pointed the Sig at Emma's head.

"No!" Elsbeth screamed from the doorway.

Suddenly, Ruth's vengeful face contorted. The older woman hollered in pain as her leg began to buckle. At her feet, Myrna the mole scurried behind the woman, giving her a nasty bite on her Achilles heel. The distraction provided just enough time for Elsbeth to knock her guardian to the ground and grab the gun. She pointed it at Ruth.

"Elsbeth?" Ruth asked. "How are you awake, I gave you a sedative?"

"I didn't eat that stupid nutrition bar!"

"Don't do anything rash, my Dear Child," Ruth implored. "You don't know what you're doing."

"Oh, I'm pretty sure I do!" Elsbeth answered before finally realizing the state Baxter was in, who looked as if he'd coughed up a little blood. Meanwhile, Emma tried in vain to remove her coat and use it to apply pressure to the wound. Baxter let out a groan as he started to lose consciousness.

"What's going on?" Ferdinand burst in the room. "I heard a gunshot —" Then he saw Elsbeth. "Elsbeth, no!" He went to wrap his arms around her.

"That's right," Ruth's eyes widened. "She tried to kill Emma!"

Ferdinand paused in his struggle to contain Elsbeth, who had already wiggled herself free. Unfortunately, she dropped the gun, which Ruth lunged for. "Tried to kill—Emma?" Ferdinand was confused. Something didn't add up.

Just then, a booming voice could be heard from outside. "This is the Garda Síochána; we're coming in!" Several constables burst through the door of the study, immediately grabbing Ruth's arms and roughly dragging her to her feet.

"What are you grabbing me for?" Ruth wailed. "She's the one with the gun! She tried to kill Baxter!"

Moments later, two paramedics arrived, rushing to Baxter's aid. It seemed that Darwin still had a few connections left in Ireland after all.

Before being lifted from Emma's lap, Baxter whispered softly, "I always said that you'd be the death of me, Emma Post."

CHAPTER 35
Hospital

Ireland

"Well, I must say, you're the last person I'd expect to be visiting me in the hospital," Baxter croaked out.

"Yeah, well, Emma is flying back to Florida today under police protection to ensure she, and the missing logs she found, are safe and land in the right hands for a change," Dennis offered.

"But," Baxter's head was throbbing as he thought it through. "Aren't *you* the police?"

"Yes, but I'm here with you," Dennis answered sarcastically. "I just flew in this morning to babysit."

"Lucky me," Baxter answered. Dennis closed the hospital door and pulled a chair bedside and took a seat next to the patient. "Oh, goody. You're staying."

"Cut the crap, Baxter," Dennis whispered as he leaned in. "I'm here to help you, and only because you risked your life to save Emma."

"Did more than risk," Baxter coughed. "I was technically dead for fifteen whole seconds. Saw the light at the end of the tunnel with someone who suspiciously resembled Erasmus at the end." Dennis seemed unconvinced. "Check the medical records," Baxter insisted. "Your woman was nearly the death of me."

"That's right, my woman," Dennis answered possessively. "We'll get back to Emma in a moment, but first—"

"Mind handing me a cup of water," Baxter interrupted. He was still hooked up to an IV and his chest was bandaged. He tried to sit up and let out a groan.

"Here," Dennis relented, hitting the bed's automatic adjustment, and bringing Baxter's torso to a semi-reclined position.

"Oh!" Baxter complained. "Easy man!"

"Sorry," Dennis answered in a way that suggested that he wasn't particularly sorry at all. Though, he did feel a small pang of guilt, so he went behind Baxter and gently helped him prop himself up on pillows. Then, he poured him a small paper cup full of water that was on the nightstand by the bed.

"Thanks." Baxter accepted the water and struggled to get a few sips in. He handed the cup back to Dennis, who set it aside. "How is it that you plan to help me, exactly?"

"Because you know way more than you're letting on about what was happening behind-the-scenes at Vandenberg Nutraceuticals."

"Do I?" Baxter feigned innocence. "As everyone at the company can attest, I wasn't around much these past few years. I was more of a... figurehead."

"Mr. Baker, we now have evidence to connect four out of five deaths...*actual* deaths," Dennis emphasized, "to complications directly resulting from people ingesting health bars laced with varied prescription medications."

"But I had nothing to do with that," Baxter protested.

"But you know people who did. And you kept your mouth shut until it started hitting close to home." For once, Baxter remained quiet. Finally, he asked, "You mentioned *five* deaths? Aside from the three young women in the newspapers years ago, and now Erasmus, who else?"

Dennis surveyed Baxter's face. He was telling the truth. "A deaconess at the Church of Infinite Love was allegedly murdered by the same woman who tried to shoot Emma and got you by mistake."

"Ruth." Baxter shook his head. "Always the quiet ones... But why?"

"The same reason she came after Emma. The deaconess was trying to help a few of our colleagues with the case. Ruth, a devoted member of the church, took it upon herself to take care of things."

"And Elsbeth? Please tell me she wasn't involved in any of this." There was something half-hearted about the question, but Dennis couldn't quite figure out why. "No," Dennis answered, finally. "Most likely not. We're still questioning Edwina, however. While it seems that Ruth acted alone in her attack against Emma, Edwina must have had keen insight into the happenings of the church, being on the high counsel."

"What's going to happen to Elsbeth?" Baxter asked softly.

Dennis was surprised. It seemed that Cousin Baxter really did care about the young woman.

"She'll be just fine," Dennis grinned. "She's not nearly as helpless as you think, you know?"

An odd looked crossed Baxter's face. "I really don't know what to think anymore," Baxter touched a hand to his head. "Any chance we can hold off on questioning until I'm marginally better?"

"Of course," Dennis agreed. "You have to be healthy enough to fly."

"To fly?" Baxter asked. "Where exactly are we flying to, may I ask?"

"We need you back in Florida." It was then that Baxter saw the travel backpack strapped to Officer Dennis, and only then because he slung it forward to retrieve some documents. "Sorry to have to do this to you when you're in such a state, but it's a subpoena to appear in court."

"Ah, I see," Baxter sunk back onto his pillow and slid down the bed slightly, adjusting his torso uncomfortably. "And in the meantime, will I have police protection while I'm stuck in the hospital... and in Florida?"

"What ... here?" Dennis was surprised. "Why would you need a Garda Síochána here?"

"Do you know how damn big the Church of Infinite Love is?" Baxter asked. "I came to the Leitrim estate because I thought no one would think to look for me in this forgotten place. And if Edwina hadn't decided to ship Erasmus' things off to Edgar, and Edgar hadn't been so damn sentimental, I might not be lying in a hospital bed right now."

"But this was one woman with an agenda," Dennis protested.

"Officer Dennis, please tell me you're smarter than that." Dennis curled his lip, insulted. He was about to protest, but Baxter wasn't finished yet. "*Think* how devoted Ruth was despite having no rank in the church but was brainwashed enough to act violently on its behalf, as if she were a mama bear defending her cub. Now, work in Victor Newberry, Mordecai Sanzani, and the other executives at Vandenberg Nutraceuticals, likely to be tied to five deaths, who are not as nice as I am—"

Officer Dennis snorted.

"Trust me, Dennis. I know I'm no prize, but I'm a good deal better than they are."

"Okay," Officer Dennis agreed. "I'll see that you have protection. Let me make a few calls. In the meantime," Dennis pulled a cord next to the bed and, within minutes, a nurse arrived.

"Is something the matter?" she asked, concerned, eyeing Baxter. The nurse seemed flustered, as if in a hurry... given the ratio of patients to nurses, she probably was.

"Yes," Officer Dennis answered. "No rush, but I'm going to need at least one bed, or a stretcher if you don't have a bed, that we can keep in this room."

"May I ask why?" The nurse seemed annoyed.

"Of course," Dennis smiled sweetly. "Because we're going to have a guard on rotation, outside this room, at all times. They'll need somewhere to sleep in between their shifts."

"Oh." The nurse eyed Dennis and Baxter in surprise. "Well, this is unexpected." She thought quickly. "I'll let the doctor on site know and see what I can do." She made a hasty exit.

Dennis began dragging a chair around Baxter's bed and through the front door.

"What are you doing?" Baxter asked, curious.

"Until I can assemble a team, I've got first watch."

"You mean *you're* going to protect me?"

"You got any other options?" Dennis asked, yawning. The effects of the time change were just now beginning to catch up with him.

"No, but how do I know you won't smother me in my sleep for making the moves on your girlfriend?"

"Yeah," Dennis nodded. "About that. I'd appreciate it if you would respect the fact that Emma is with me and not you. Just... keep your distance."

"I'll keep my distance as long as it suits me." Baxter's face grew red. Dennis whipped his head around angrily. "What I'm getting at is," Baxter finished, "you've got a good woman there, Dennis. Don't screw it up. Because if you do, good 'ol Baxter Baker will be there to pick up the pieces."

"Hmph." Dennis accidentally banged the back of the chair against the hospital wall as he set it down with a clatter outside of Baxter's room, raising attention from nurses, other patients, and visitors in the hallway. "I have no intention of screwing it up," he grumbled under his breath. "Quite the opposite. I'm a good boyfriend. Scratch that... a *great* boyfriend. Why else would she take the time to draw up that ridiculous prenup if she didn't l—" Suddenly, it hit Dennis like a ton of bricks. He sat down in front of Baxter's hospital room, crossed his arms, and began grinning from ear to ear. *Emma is nothing if not practical. She wouldn't have drawn up that prenuptial agreement if she didn't love me.* He replayed that notion in his brain several more times. *She loves me!* Thinking about it further, he nodded satisfactorily to himself as a few passersby eyed him curiously. *She may have trust issues, but we can work on that. I'm a very patient man.*

That last part wasn't entirely true. Dennis lacked patience, and he knew it. But Emma was worth the investment. And so, for the next five hours, he sat outside of Baxter Baker's hospital room with a stupid grin on his face until someone from the Guard was able to relieve him.

CHAPTER 36
Good Thing

Back in Florida

~

Ortega was waiting by the front door with two suitcases, three cardboard boxes, and a half-empty bottle of bourbon... the fancy kind that Nancy had given him when he agreed to retire.

He sat on the edge of one of his suitcases and sipped a tumbler of bourbon. He had no idea when Nancy was getting home, as she'd forgotten to call, yet again. But he was in no hurry.

Finally, at half past six, he could hear the jingling of her keys in the lock. She bounded through the door, giggling something into her cell phone. Nancy used it a lot ever since he bought her one at Christmas. They were becoming more popular, but they were still considered a novelty. When she saw her husband's face, and then the suitcases, she spoke quickly into her phone, "Listen... uh... Liz... I'll have to call you back. Okay, bye." She folded her phone and set it on the counter.

Ortega had no idea if she was really talking to a *Liz*. He assumed not. But he didn't care anymore.

Nancy eyed the suitcases and boxes. "What's going on, José?" she asked quietly.

Ortega didn't answer. Instead, he handed her a manila envelope. She slowly unclipped it and glanced, cautiously, inside. She sucked in her breath and held it for a moment before roughly sighing it out.

"You had me followed," she stated quietly.

"I had no choice," Ortega answered softly.

"Of course you had a choice," she whispered back, lacking the energy to even get angry. "You could have talked to me."

"And would talking to you have made a difference?" Ortega was incredulous. "That's all we've been doing is talking…And, I did everything you asked. I quit my job. I retired early. I moved to Florida with you. I've tried everything I could to make you happy."

After an unbearably long time, Nancy answered calmly, "Yes, you did."

"Then, why?" Tears filled his eyes.

"I don't know," Nancy whined. "I thought it was the job. I thought it was because you and my son never got along. Then, I thought it was New York. I never thought it was just —"

"Us," Ortega finished.

"I'm sorry," Nancy sniffed back a few tears as her eyes grew redder. "We just don't work, and I tried—"

"No." Ortega held up a hand. "That," he pointed to the envelope, "is not trying."

"Oh, c'mon now," she challenged.

"What is that supposed to mean?"

"It means that you think I don't know there's a forensic scientist in your life that you just never truly got over?" She gently smiled at him, as if letting him in on the secret she'd known all along.

"You mean, Penelope?" Ortega was surprised. "There's nothing going on with me and Penelope. That was over long ago!"

"I know, José." She held up her hands. "I know. All I'm saying is… maybe there should be."

"Are you honestly trying to justify your affair by suggesting I have one with my ex?"

"José, your bags are packed. You think I don't know what that means?" Ortega hung his head. "Look," Nancy tried again. "We had a good thing once. But maybe we're just too different." She put a hand on his shoulder and watched as he began sobbing uncontrollably. Not a good look for a man who prided himself on keeping his emotions in check at all times. "I'm sorry about—"

"Dominic—" José finished.

"Yes," she whispered. "I know he's only using me for my money. I know I'm a good bit older than him. And I sure as hell know it won't last."

"So, it was worth ruining our marriage over?"

"Our marriage was over a long time ago, José. We just didn't realize it."

"But we were just starting to have fun," he whined. He thought about how keen Nancy was on working on the case with him, giving him renewed hope in their relationship.

"It was fun, wasn't it?" Nancy confirmed. "And for a few moments there, I thought we might have had something salvageable."

"Were you ever planning on telling me?" He lifted his sunken eyes to meet hers.

After a moment, she confessed, "I'm not sure." After a moment more, she added, "Every time, I swore it would be the last. He was just a bandage for my broken ego."

Ortega sighed. He planned on confronting Nancy. He'd even planned on packing. But he hadn't actually thought about the... leaving. And despite everything, he never intended on hurting Nancy any more than she set out to hurt him. He loved her, but it was abundantly clear that he'd done a terrible job at showing it. Ortega blamed himself for Nancy's affair as much, if not more, than he did her.

"Stay here tonight," Nancy offered gently. "I can go visit my sister. In the morning, after you've slept off the bourbon, we can figure out together the best way to end this... as amicably as possible."

Ortega nodded.

Nancy picked up her car keys once again. Before leaving, she turned and said, "I do love you, you know? But I stand behind what I said. I think your heart still belongs to someone else."

CHAPTER 37
Best Friends

Manhattan

Elsbeth Ions knocked on the door of Rue and Darwin's condo at 4:30 p.m. two days after she and Ferdinand returned from Ireland sans Ruth. She waited until Ivy and Edwina were running errands. Ferdinand had the day off.

"Are we expecting anyone? Rue asked cautiously.

"Not that I'm aware of."

The two eyed the door. No one got in without first stopping at the front security desk and being admitted and announced.

"A neighbor?" Rue eyed the keyhole where she spotted a young woman dressed all in black. Having never met Elsbeth, she had no idea who the woman was.

Darwin, while not fond of weapons, pulled a small retractable metal baton from his desk drawer and stood on the opposite side of the door while Rue opened it a tiny crack, peering an eye out.

"Can I help you?" Rue was not typically this paranoid, but when they learned of Emma's nearly getting shot and that she had uncovered evidence that would connect Vandenberg Nutraceuticals with the Church of Infinite Love, just after learning about the death of her mother, both she and Darwin were on edge.

"That's an odd way for a detective agency to answer the door," Elsbeth answered, emotionless.

The lightbulb clicked as Rue realized who the woman was. She had seen a picture of the young girl in one of their briefs, but it must have been taken several years ago. Other than that, she had nothing else to go by.

"Elsbeth Ions?" Rue asked.

"Pretty good super sleuthing, Rue Brennan." Elsbeth's voice remained deadpan. "May I come in or would you prefer to conduct this meeting in the hallway?"

Rue bit back a rebuttal, but only because she was concerned about the woman's safety, knowing that she was an ally of Emma's.

"Come on in." Rue opened the door wider.

Elsbeth stepped inside, spotting Darwin standing beside the front door, shoulder blades pinned against the wall in an effort to minimize himself. Given that Darwin was on the rather tall side, and about as intimidating as a house plant, he looked nothing short of ridiculous.

"Please tell me you're not on the security team?"

Darwin stepped away from the door, crossed the room, and put the baton back from where he had retrieved it. "Hmm," was all he said, grumbling to himself.

Elsbeth eyed the room curiously. Unlike Emma's estimation of the high-end Midtown condo, Elsbeth wasn't impressed. "Cute," she finally offered.

Darwin opened his mouth to speak. Rue, catching the look on his face, smacked the back of her hand lightly into his stomach to silence him.

"Would you care to have a seat, Ms. Ions?" Rue asked politely.

"Sure." Elsbeth sat on the edge of the couch, poised to leave at a moment's notice.

After an unusually long silence, during which each woman waited for the other to speak, Rue finally asked, "Is there something we can help you with, Ms. Ions?"

Elsbeth was surprised. "You tell me. You're the ones who asked me to meet you here."

Rue eyed Darwin. “Uh no,” Rue answered. “We didn’t.”

“Then who the hell sent me this note?” Elsbeth reached into her pocket to retrieve a note that someone had left with the concierge at her place of residence.

“I did,” a female voice answered from the hallway. “Knock, knock!” she continued in a blended New York-mixed-with-Philly accent. “Who’s there?” She spoke deeply, as if imitating a different male voice.

“Midge,” Rue’s words got stuck in her throat as her face went pale.

Darwin regretted having put the baton away so quickly. He thought frantically, grabbing the door in an attempt to slam it before Midge could cross the threshold. She blocked it with the bottom of her foot, kicking it back open violently, almost smacking Darwin in the face in the process.

“Not so fast,” she answered. The last time Rue saw Midge she wore her hair in frizzy, bright red curls, that looked like a Raggedy Ann doll, and colorful clothes about two decades out of style. Today, her hair was shaved on the sides with the top and back spiked in high, dark-green colored locks. She wore a stud leather necklace and a black and white plaid-print dress with oversized brown leather boots. If Rue wasn’t mistaken, they were the same boots that she wore when—

“I come in peace.” She held her hands up. To Rue she said, “I am alone and unarmed. You can search me if you like?” She wriggled her eyes first at Rue and then at Darwin.

“Am I missing something?” Elsbeth eyed the scene, confused.

“Lots of things,” Midge answered, taking a seat on a lounger next to the couch, putting her boots up on their end table and settling back in the chair. “But don’t worry. I’ll catch you up.”

“You have two seconds to leave before I call the cops,” Rue threatened.

“Who? That dough boy Dennis?” she mocked. “Maybe, if he were still in the same state... or country, for that matter, but even then, I doubt that boy could jog to the end of the block without getting winded. Maybe his girlfriend will help whip him into shape.”

“What do you know of it?” Rue demanded.

“Ah, curious now, are ya?” Midge grinned. “Have a seat, Rue, so we can have a chat. It’s been a while.”

Darwin was already dialing 9-1-1.

“Listen, my tall drink of water,” Midge addressed Darwin. “Turn me in and lots of people are gonna get hurt... or worse. Hang up the phone."

Darwin ended the call, just as an emergency representative picked up the phone.

"Elsbeth," Rue said carefully. "You should probably leave."

"No." Midge shook her head. "For her safety, she should probably stay."

Elsbeth didn't share Rue and Darwin's fear. After all, she spent her entire life fearing her family, fearing the cult they belonged to, and fearing what might happen if she spoke up. But this green-haired little woman didn't seem intimidating at all. If anything, Elsbeth found her adorable and fascinating — like discovering that unicorns were real.

Rue framed her words carefully, speaking in a measured tone, "Midge? Friends don't threaten other friends. Besties, remember?"

Midge eyed Rue momentarily before bursting out laughing. "Oh, you are too funny my friend, trying to use my words against me and all." She chuckled uncontrollably for several seconds. "But I'm not threatening you." Her voice turned serious. "I'm trying to protect you."

"Why would you do that?" Rue asked carefully. After all, it was she and Darwin who were instrumental in putting her behind bars.

"Look, I get that we all have a different moral compass—"

"That's one way of describing it," Rue bit the side of her lip.

"Don't get all high and mighty on me, just because your mom is a high-ranking deaconess and all... well... was... Sorry about your mom, by the way."

Rue felt something at the center of her chest. If it had been an image, it would have been a steel trap that wrapped around her heart, not letting any of the hurt in. Midge didn't have empathy, at least not the way most people did. Rue was fairly confident that her former friend had a strange loyalty toward her and cared about her in her own weird and twisted way, but she wouldn't have understood the depth of pain associated with loss, the guilt of feeling responsible, nor the nuanced feelings of trying to forgive and love someone who, for most of your life, convinced you that the world was a dark and scary place.

"Earth to Rue." Midge snapped her fingers. "As I was saying, I'm trying to protect you. *That's* what besties do."

"Okay, I'll bite," Rue answered, finally. "What are you protecting me from?"

"Not just you," Midge clarified. "*All* of you."

"What did you mean by 'for her safety, she should probably stay'?" Elsbeth asked quietly.

"Good question," Midge praised. "I suspect you are very smart. Not as smart as I am, of course, but—" she paused to assess her nails before rubbing them against her chest as if buffing them, "few are." Midge waited for an absurdly long period of time before answering. "Youse guys sure know how to poke the bear and start trouble; that's for sure," she laughed. "Between youse guys visiting the Church of Infinite Love in Pennsylvania and Emma poking her nose around where it didn't belong, it's a wonder I got here in time to save you."

"What the hell are you talking about, Midge?" Rue remained standing a safe distance from Midge.

"You know, you can sit down if you like," Midge offered. "It's not like I bite... at least not often." She chuckled at her own joke.

"You murdered two people and a busload of women. I think I'll stand."

Instead of running for cover, Elsbeth actually leaned in, as if hanging on Midge's every word.

"Correction," Midge replied. "I had nothing to do with the women escaping from prison. That was all Jaks. Had I known he was going to kill 'em, I woulda never gone along with it."

"Really?" Rue crossed her arms. "And given your track record, why should we believe that?"

"Because the women I took out deserved it." Midge waved her hand in the air before Rue could protest. "I'll admit that my initial motivations were, perhaps, somewhat misguided—"

"Misguided?!" Rue's voice shifted a pitch.

"But they were no angels, believe me," Midge reassured her, as if somehow that would make their murders 'acceptable.' "In some ways, I did your new pal Emma Post a favor. I misjudged her, I think. Doesn't happen often, but I'll admit when I'm... er—" Her voice trailed off.

"Wrong?" Rue finished.

"Yeah," Midge confirmed. "That. Or, shall we say, less than right."

"And where is Jaks these days?" Rue was suspicious.

"Damned if I know." Midge looked around the room nervously, as if he would suddenly appear. "That guy is crazy." She eyed Rue and Darwin back and forth, as if waiting for a reaction that didn't come. "Anyhoo," she finally considered. "That's how I found out about your little situation here. Kinda a coincidink, don'tcha think?"

"Why are you here, Midge?" Rue demanded.

"I'm here because youse guys are in way over your head. If Emma had just taken the money and kept quiet, everything woulda been fine. But she had to go all high and mighty on us."

"But we caught the woman who murdered Erasmus, and—" Darwin eyed Rue sympathetically, "the others."

"Who? Ruth?" Midge laughed. "She ain't even the tip of the iceberg. You have no idea."

"So, you're here to—" Darwin egged her on.

"Help you," Midge finished. "Yes."

"Why?" Rue tried again.

"Because Jaks Liebling is batshit cuckoo. When he broke me outta prison and we headed to Florida, he hooked up with someone who worked at Vandenberg Nutraceuticals. Once he realized what they were up to, he devised a scheme to insert himself into their game plan — securing a nice future for us. Except—"

"Except what?" Rue encouraged.

"Different moral compass," Midge sighed. "I, at least have a reason for the stuff I do. Jaks just seems to get off on hurting people. Jaks reacts to killing like most men respond to a sexual conquest. It's weird... even for me."

Rue crinkled her mouth up, as if she'd just discovered moldy bread in the refrigerator or a dead roach under her loofa in the bathroom.

"If I were to read between the lines here," Darwin interjected, "you're helping us because you are afraid of what Jaks Liebling might do to *you*."

"See? I always knew you were more than just a pretty face, you sexy string bean, you." Midge eyed Darwin up and down and winked.

Now it was Elsbeth's turn to crinkle her mouth and wrinkle her nose. She eyed Darwin, then Midge, shrugged her shoulders and assumed there was just no accounting for taste.

"So, you want... protection?" Rue confirmed.

Midge huffed, as if it took too much energy to explain to those who clearly didn't have the mental grasp of reality that she possessed. "What I'm offering is... a compromise. Isn't that what people do in relationships?" She reached a hand toward Rue, cupping her hand over her former friend's.

"We're not in a relationship." Rue drew her hand away. And, as if it needed clarification, she added, "We never were."

Midge sat back and hugged herself. "Disappointing," she sighed, before eyeing Elsbeth, who, unlike Rue, hung onto her every word. Midge winked at the girl, who immediately mirrored Midge, hugging herself and flopping back against the couch, embarrassed. Elsbeth, despite being in her twenties, had no interactions of the romantic or flirtatious nature of any kind, unless you count Baxter. But since he was family and, obviously (to her), an idiot playboy, she didn't take his 'kissing cousins' jokes seriously. They were inappropriate, to be clear, but not enough to cause the level of discomfort she was now feeling as Midge seemed to eye her like one might a prime roast beef.

While Rue may have experienced an arrested development early on, unlike Elsbeth, she'd had more time to work through it. She intervened on Elsbeth's behalf.

"Midge," Rue declared. "You have exactly five minutes to explain what it is you came here to explain."

Midge opened her mouth to say something sarcastic, but her smile suddenly dropped as she eyed Rue's facial expression. She recognized that look from hundreds of times before, from many people... she had gone too far. Only, she never really seemed to 'get' where that 'too far' boundary was located. It was like a moving target.

Midge thought carefully. "Ruth Fenstermeier is now the scapegoat. But make no mistake, while the Vandenberg factory in Florida has been shut down, and the church in the U.S. is under investigation, they will simply rebrand and move elsewhere."

"Rebrand?" Darwin raised an eyebrow.

Midge nodded. "The old Dublin factory is getting a dust off. And if my suspicions are correct, the Church of Infinite Love will come back as the Church of... something else."

"What do you propose we do about it?" Darwin asked simply.

For once, Midge was serious. "My ex-cuckoo-head is likely to be at the center of it. I promise to help you bring the Vandenbergs down... present company excluded." She eyed Elsbeth, who waved a hand as if she'd dismissed her lineage a long time ago. "I can help protect you from retaliation, but—"

"But?" Rue asked.

"But I need you to protect me from Jaks," Midge finished.

"Midge, you're supposed to be in prison for murder," Rue reminded her.

"I know that, silly! And all cuz of you—"

"Don't you even go there," Rue warned. "I had nothing to do with your warped sense of loyalty."

Darwin intervened. "And how are we supposed to do that? Protect you from Jaks?"

"I want a new identity," Midge finished. "I get that I'll end up back in prison. I accept that. But I don't want my death to be because of some lunatic."

Rue blinked a few times, looking at Midge meaningfully. *Lunatic, you say,* Rue thought to herself. But self-reflection was largely lost on Midge.

"I'm just an investigator," Darwin explained. "I have no connection to the police department, the Feds, no one."

"I'm sure you could pull a few strings." She meaningfully rolled her eyes up to meet his. "And if you can't, your pal Ortega can."

There was a knock at the door.

Again, Darwin thought. Rue and Midge braced themselves, as if expecting the worst. Elsbeth was on the edge of her seat, literally, her eyes wide with fascination.

"You all okay in here?" a security guard from the building asked when Darwin finally answered,

"Of course, why wouldn't we be?" Darwin's voice wavered.

"Well, the last guard on duty got a strange call about her home being on fire and left her post. It was a false alarm, and I'm just making sure nothing out of the ordinary happened while she was gone." The guard eyed Darwin questioningly.

Darwin shot a brief glance over his shoulder at Midge before addressing the guard. "No," he finally answered. "Nothing out of the ordinary here," he confirmed. "But thank you for checking."

He closed the door and returned his attention to Midge. "So, what's your plan?"

"So glad you asked," Midge responded, rubbing her palms together. "How do you feel about a vay-cay in Ireland?"

CHAPTER 38

Shep

Florida

Shep sat in small corner of a local library mid-way between Tampa and Parrish. He was careful to pick a spot where they were not likely to be heard, and one where he could finish his coffee and bagel without a librarian telling him he wasn't allowed to eat there.

Moments later, Emma arrived, and then Dennis, and finally, Ortega, a few minutes after that.

They thought it was safest to have Sprightly browse books in the area surrounding their cubby, keeping an eye out for anyone who looked suspicious or could potentially overhear them. Plus, they reasoned, while she was key in turning up evidence, she was not subtle in voice or manner, which worked out perfectly in this instance. Whenever someone got close to them, she would hang over a visitor's shoulder, asking what they were reading with an overabundance of curiosity and little regard for personal space. Since the section closest to the group featured categories of books about sex education, sexual disfunction, and how to save a sexless marriage, her curiosity was not welcome. And, if that didn't deter them, she would scratch her butt and ask if anyone had seen that book about STDs and how to identify them. Sprightly managed to clear the space in record time and keep it that way.

Deputy Sheriff Shep Stern refused to meet at anyone's home, both to avoid suspicion and surveillance, and because he was convinced that their homes were bugged.

But Ortega came prepared. When he arrived, he put a forefinger to his lips and began walking the perimeters of their space, waving his arm curiously. Unlike his usual attire, today he wore a tan Member's Only racer jacket and sporty wristbands that Nancy had bought him last year for Christmas.

"All clear," he whispered.

"What was that all about, Jo?" Dennis asked, falling back to his old naming pattern for his former boss. Ortega let it go for the time being.

Ortega lifted the edge of the terry cloth wristband to reveal a small black wire. He tapped his jacket. "Bug detector," he answered simply. "Not even on the market yet." Darwin Fennec had come through for him again, sending him a TRD-800 recorder-detector that wasn't to be released until later that year. But Darwin had his connections.

"Impressive," Shep said with a mouthful of food as he chewed his bagel.

"Are you ever *not* eating?" Ortega challenged. Shep was by no means a small man, but his size didn't seem to match his appetite.

Shep merely shrugged, crumbling up his napkin and tossing it in a paper bag that he set beside his chair. "We got bigger problems than my eating habits." He licked his fingers and then wiped them on his sleeve. Ortega wrinkled his nose but said nothing.

Shep leaned in and so did the rest of the group. "I nearly got my ass handed to me for asking a few questions at work. Apparently, both the Church of Infinite Love and Vandenberg Nutraceuticals have a history of making very large donations to certain political campaigns, and let's just say their contributions at the Policemen's Charity Ball are exceptionally generous."

"How generous?" Ortega asked.

"In the millions generous."

"Geez." Ortega rubbed his forehead.

"I did a little schmoozing, but any records I could find about Erasmus Vandenberg's death, and anything related to complaints about the church or company, were scrubbed clean. All cases were dismissed and closed."

"I hate to state the obvious," Dennis interjected. "But if Emma gets to keep her house and the money, can't we just lay low for a while? They have their scapegoat in prison. This is too dangerous."

Shep was outraged as he whispered back, little bits of spit coming out of his mouth as he spoke. "Where's your chutzpah? You come to me for help, put my ass on the line, and when we uncover the crime of the century, you just wanna pack it up and go home?"

"Hey pal," Emma spoke up, and then remembering where they were, lowered her voice. "He was just trying to protect me, so lay off."

Shep would never have accused Emma of lacking chutzpah.

Shep held his palms up in surrender and sat back in his chair. He was beginning to question his decision to get involved with this motley crew.

"So, where the hell do we go from here?" Ortega asked.

"Ireland," Shep answered simply.

"What do you mean, Ireland?"

"That dumb schmuck Baxter Baker thought he'd escape the family by hiding out in Leitrim with his Uncle Edgar. Elsbeth was supposed to join him."

"Elsbeth?" Emma sat up. "What does she have to do with any of this?"

"A lot, apparently," Shep answered. "Got an anonymous tip from a gal from New York. At least, that's what her accent sounded like to me. Seems the two were trying to cut all ties with the family. Edgar was the only one they trusted to help them. He was such a hermit that he seemed to fly under the radar of the rest of the family."

Emma was a little hurt. Elsbeth, it appeared, still had secrets.

"But how can you know the source can be trusted?" Dennis asked.

"She said that if I needed confirmation that she was telling the truth, I should reach out to a Rue Brennan directly. I did, and she confirmed that a Midge Pasternack recently visited them. The voice, and information she gave, added up."

The color drained from Emma's face, as she bounced to her feet. "No, no, no, no, no, no!" Emma called out. The group stood, alarmed.

"What did I say?" Shep was concerned. Somehow, in his research, he hadn't yet connected all the dots.

"Emma, let's take this outside," Dennis whispered, wrapping an arm around her shoulder and leading her toward the front of the library, just as a librarian was making her way toward them. "Sorry," he apologized quickly. "She just learned that Betty Davis died. She was a huge, huge fan."

The librarian merely nodded, gesturing her head toward the front door in a polite, unspoken request for them to leave.

Outside, Emma paced angrily back and forth. "The nerve of that... that murderer! Wandering free after what she did!"

Moments later, Shep emerged first, approaching them cautiously. "Look, I'm sorry," he apologized. "I was investigating *this* case. I didn't realize you had been connected to the woman in the past."

Emma sniffed and wiped her eyes with the back of her sleeve.

"But I gotta ask," he continued. "How is it that you seem to be at the center of both of these... eh... situations?"

"Not here." Ortega rushed out to meet them. A loud buzzing could be heard from his sleeve... the bug detector had fired up.

As quickly as they'd come together, the group disbanded. Unfortunately, no one remembered to tell Sprightly, who became immersed in a newly revised book called *The Joy of Sex* and momentarily forgot why she was there. When she finally realized they were gone, a red-faced Sprightly returned the book to the shelf and, after a cursory search of the library, drove to Emma and Dennis's residence, and waited.

"You can't go," Dennis told Emma, once back home and after he and Ortega confirmed there were no listening devices on the premises.

"Why not? I can help," Emma protested. "Besides, I'm the one who got you into this mess."

"He's right," Shep acknowledged, sucking down a bowl of vegetable soup and rye bread that Emma prepared for him. Suddenly, he became self-conscious. "Low blood sugar," he explained as he slurped.

After having been given the run down, Deputy Sheriff Shep Stern requested an immediate leave of absence, citing a family emergency. He was planning to join Ortega in Ireland to continue their investigation into the Church of Infinite Love and look for evidence that they were, in fact, rebranding their church and nutraceutical company into something unrecognizable but equally profitable.

"Em," Dennis reasoned, "you're still a civilian. So is Sprightly. I'm still on the force, so I can hang behind and assist from here if needed."

"But you gotta lay low for a bit." Shep pointed the corner of a piece of toast at him. "Should have thought it through before I chewed you out earlier... sorry 'bout that."

"I know. I know," Dennis nodded. "The point is, Emmam this is the safest and best solution. You think they're not going to notice your sudden interest in the Leitrim estate? Particularly after you uncovered what turned out to be a whole mess of sales receipts and shipping records, both to and from the Florida factory?"

"Yeah, okay," she conceded. "You've got a point. But it still feels weird to have Rue Brennan doing what I think I should be doing." It had only recently been made clear to her that, while *she* was not going to Ireland, it appeared that Rue *was*.

"She knows a lot about the inner workings of the church and can help us."

"But what about Midge? You're not seriously going to be working with *her*, are you?"

"Calm down," Shep answered. Dennis went on high alert, drawing the side of his hand across his neck as if to let Shep know it was curtains if he didn't shut his mouth. Telling Emma to calm down was likely to produce the exact opposite effect. He was right.

"Calm down?" she squealed. "I may not be a huge Rue Brennan fan, but I sure as hell don't want her, or anybody else, dead."

"Midge Pasternak has agreed to remain under surveillance the entire time she's working with us," Shep explained.

"It's a crappy plan, if you ask me," Emma retorted.

"You gotta a better one, Miss High and Mighty?" Shep challenged.

"You know what—" Emma pointed a finger.

"Stop!" Dennis intervened. "It's settled. We stay put and keep a low profile, for now."

"What about Elsbeth?" Emma asked.

"Elsbeth is not in any danger as long as she plays along for a little while longer," Dennis explained.

"You mean, continue to act as if she's mentally challenged in some way? How is *that* a solution?"

Shep sighed. "It's not a solution. But if she bolts now, or comes clean, her mother and the family will know she's involved."

"Well, that's just crap." Emma folded her arms, leaning against the kitchen counter.

"I agree," Shep nodded. "But Rome wasn't built in a day."

"What the hell does Rome have to do with anything?"

Dennis gave up. It was clear that Shep and Emma were not likely to become fast friends. But it didn't matter. Elsbeth was a grown woman capable of deciding for herself what do to, and for the time being, she decided to keep her family in the dark. Darwin made it clear he was staying in New York. So that left Shep, Ortega, and Rue to carry the torch and solve this mystery once and for all.

CHAPTER 39
New Beginnings

Manhattan

~

"I have to go," Rue insisted.

"No, Rue. You don't!" Darwin rarely raised his voice and certainly never to Rue. He ran a hand through his hair as a strange look crossed his face. It was the first time Rue had ever witnessed that expression. Then, she recognized it… fear.

"You could go with me if you want—" Rue offered.

"No, Rue. I can't!" Darwin insisted.

"Well, why not? It's not as if we're swimming in cases at the moment. We could—"

"I can't go back to Ireland," he interrupted.

"Well, why the hell not?" Rue demanded. Darwin turned his back, rapping the edge of his fist on the back of their couch, frustrated. "Why not, Darwin?" Rue tried again, touching his shoulder.

"I can't set foot in Ireland," he repeated, looking over his shoulder at her, as if pleading with her not to ask him anymore questions.

"I see." Rue dropped her hand. "It seems there are still lots of things we don't know about one another," she answered softly.

"But why do you have to go, Rue? You said yourself, you tried for years to get away from your mother and that church, and now you're free."

"But that's just it," she explained. "I might be, but there are a lot of women... just like me, just like Elsbeth... who aren't. Between her and me, we can provide valuable information to take down the entire cult operation... for good."

"And you actually trust Midge to be telling you the truth?" He was incredulous.

"No, but we need her. And she wouldn't hurt me. You know that."

"No, I don't really know that," Darwin answered angrily. "She's a psychopathic killer."

"What choice do I have?"

"You have the choice not to go." Darwin was defiant.

"I have to. In some way, I was responsible for—"

"For what, Rue?" Rue's lip began to quiver. "For your mother's death?" Darwin asked. "Look at the life she brought you up in. What happened to her was a result of her choices."

"I have to go," she answered finally.

"Well, unfortunately, I can't go with you," Darwin replied quietly.

Rue felt a tightening in her chest and her face began to crumble. She began sobbing uncontrollably as she ran into Darwin's arms.

"Despite my sometimes-disagreeable nature, I do love you, you know?" Rue sniffed.

"Yes, I know." Darwin gave a half-hearted smile mixed with sadness. "I love you too."

After a moment, Rue asked, "Is this the end of.. us?"

"No, no, no." Darwin hugged her fiercely and kissed the top of her head. "I'm not going anywhere." He paused, holding her in his arms as if it might be the last time. "But, I don't know, maybe a little time apart might not be a bad thing? Hell, we hardly know each other despite living together."

Rue understood, but that didn't stop the horrible sinking feeling in her belly. Darwin had been her rock for the better part of a year. He was her friend, lover, confidante. She couldn't even explain the driving need she felt within her. She just knew she had to go.

~

"KNOCK, KNOCK," a voice called from the other side of the door. Ortega was busy loading up several suitcases into the back of his car and had left the front door ajar.

"Penelope?" Ortega stood there with a large suitcase in one hand and an oversized duffle bag slung over the opposite shoulder. They were heavy, and the strap felt like it was cutting into his shoulder... He didn't notice. He was still in a state of shock.

"Need some help?" She eyed his luggage.

"Uh, no." He set his bags down and eyed her curiously. She stood there wearing a flowered sun dress with ruffled sleeves. It was as if he hadn't seen her in a lifetime. "You... here... Not New York?" he stammered.

"How about a hug, first," she laughed, opening her arms.

Ortega didn't hesitate. He wrapped his arms around her small frame, hugging her tightly.

"Need... to... breathe," she joked. He lessened his bear hug, but only slightly.

"Why are you here?" he finally asked, releasing her.

"Nice to see you too, José," she teased.

"Of course, I'm happy you're here. Just surprised is all." He paused awkwardly, staring at her, as if memorizing her face and trying to capture this moment in time.

"Well, to answer your question," she leaned an arm on the counter, "I'm going with you."

"With me? What are you talking about?"

"To Ireland," she answered plainly. "I've sorted it all with Shep. You, me, him, and Rue... we're heading to the Vandenberg estate and the old factory in Dublin."

"No," Ortega shook his head. "I don't want you mixed up in all of this. Besides, what about your work?"

"What work? My poking around on your behalf got me fired. So, you have no choice. I'm going with you."

"But—" he protested.

"It'll be just like old times." She smiled up at him and flashed her eyes wide gleefully.

"Well." He thought about it, remembering how he let his work interfere with their relationship. "Hopefully, not just like before. But, hey," he remembered, "what about Garth?"

"Gareth," she corrected. "We broke up." Ortega's eyes lit up like a kid on Christmas before he realized it and lowered his gaze. "You don't have to look so overjoyed," she laughed.

"Can I be a little happy about it? Seeing as, well, I am soon to be unattached as well."

"Don't push it," Penelope joked, grabbing a camera bag he had on the floor. "Let me help you load up." He retrieved his shoulder bag and suitcase, following her as she opened the door wider for him to get through. "Maybe just a little happy," she whispered flirtatiously, as he crossed the threshold.

Ortega glanced behind him at the house and let out a sigh. Sprightly would be along soon to look after things until he and Nancy could decide the best way to divide everything. They agreed to do their best to keep it as amicable as possible.

"Meet you at the airport?" he asked, after his car was loaded up.

Penelope stood with the door of her rental car open. "Yup," she answered. "I'll be right behind you."

Ortega shook his head. He couldn't believe she was there and that they were back on a case together. If you had asked him, 'what's the last thing you think will happen at this moment?' He would have said it was *this very momen*t. And yet, here she was. Ortega hoped he wasn't dreaming.

"What is it?" Penelope asked quizzically.

"I'm getting too old for this shit," he reminisced, a lopsided grin on his face.

"Who are you kidding?" Penelope played along. "You *live* for this shit."

CHAPTER 40
Mr. Lundy

Women's Detention Center, NYC

"How are they treating you, Ruth?" Mr. Lundy was granted access to a private cell where Ruth Fenstermeier, Erasmus Vandenberg's personal chef and Edwina Vandenberg's religious Ambassador, was being held on two counts of alleged murder charges and one count of attempted murder.

"I was Edwina's assistant for years," she smirked sourly. "This is a walk in the park by comparison." Ruth sat on the edge of her prison bed, wearing a hunter green uniform and slippers.

Mr. Lundy nodded, sitting on a small metal bench that was bolted into the floor and setting his briefcase on his lap. Mr. Lundy glanced at the guard standing at the end of the hallway... most likely out of earshot. His briefcase had already been inspected upon arrival. He was let in only after they had confirmed two things: one, that there was nothing in his case but a pencil and legal documents, and two, his status as the family attorney.

"Why don't you sit beside me, Ruth, so I can accurately take your statement?"

Ruth eyed the briefcase nervously, surveying Mr. Lundy's face for any sign of anger or aggression. But no, Mr. Lundy had always been the calm sort, she decided. She stood, shuffling her feet across the prison floor before sitting beside her lawyer.

A guard eyed them from a distance but said nothing.

Mr. Lundy pulled out a pad of paper and pencil. "Now," he announced a little louder than necessary. "Let's start at the beginning—"

Ruth smiled cautiously and nodded. She sighed gratefully. Mr. Lundy would make everything all right. Mr. Lundy *always* made everything all right. After all, he was paid good money to protect the family.

"You screwed up, Ruth," he whispered calmly into the older woman's ear.

Ruth bristled, the hairs on the back of her arms standing up. This was not what she expected from the lawyer at all. Tears began forming in the corners of her eyes. She fought them back defiantly. "I had to do something," she defended quietly. "They were going to ruin everything."

"But who gave you permission to act out on your own?" Mr. Lundy challenged. "You're an Ambassador. You don't make decisions. You take direction," he explained.

She nodded again, "But—"

"But, what?"

"I *was* taking orders."

Mr. Lundy eyed the guard, who was busy talking to another security officer, as if giving instructions.

"From whom?" he asked, surprised.

"Well," Ruth answered. "From God."

"From God?" Mr. Lundy shifted in his seat, biting back his incredulousness. "Since when does God speak through you and not the Evangelicals?"

"I felt it in my bones, I tell you," Ruth tried in vain to explain.

"No, Ruth," Mr. Lundy disagreed. The guard was almost finished talking. He had to work fast.

Before she could react, Mr. Lundy touched the point of the lead pencil to Ruth's arm, pressing on the eraser like a plunger. A small needle poked through the tip of the pencil. The woman's eyes met his, surprised. And then, he held it there momentarily as he met Ruth's fearful gaze.

Mr. Lundy yanked the pencil away and began scribbling something on his notepad just as the guard turned his attention back to them.

"Now," Mr. Lundy whispered calmly. "I'm going to take your statement, in which you will take full responsibility for the murders of Deaconess Frances and Erasmus Vandenberg, as well as the attempted murder of Emma Post." Ruth sucked in her breath but remained silent. "You will wait 24 hours before requesting to make your confession to the police, asking for my presence, where I will confirm that you had made such a confession to me, but I requested you think about your decision fully before coming forward."

"And then what?" Ruth looked at her arm. "What did you do to me?"

"A very concentrated thallium poisoning. You'll get another from me in 24 hours when we talk to the police." He saw her forlorn expression. "It has to be this way, I'm afraid. Remember, you acted alone. No one knew what you had planned. Throw in that God told you to do it, that was a good one."

"But it's the truth," Ruth insisted.

"Of course, it is," Mr. Lundy agreed patronizingly.

"But I can still help you. I know things," Ruth whispered, eyes darting back and forth frantically.

"What sort of things?" Mr. Lundy asked.

"For one thing," Ruth tried, "I know that it was Baxter Baker who stole shipping and receiving logs, along with sales receipts that Erasmus kept hidden. He turned them over to Erasmus on the condition that Erasmus keep Baxter's name out of it when he closed the factory."

"How do you know this?" Mr. Lundy was surprised.

"I'm just the help," she explained. "People let lots of things slip when there's an invisible old woman in the room." Ruth took a moment to run her hands over her legs as if she were smoothing a skirt. "Erasmus was going to shut down our work. His actions would have bankrupted the church and the Vandenberg family. You don't think that would have gotten the attention of the media? He would have ruined everything for all of us."

"Why didn't you tell Edwina?" Mr. Lundy asked.

"Because I—" Ruth stammered.

"Yes?" Mr. Lundy persuaded.

"Because I thought she might look on me favorably if I took swift action. Besides, without the actual evidence, I didn't know if she'd believe me. I didn't know it was right in front of our flippin' eyes the whole time with those stupid records."

"And you murdered him on the plane because?"

"It was supposed to be the night of his birthday party," Ruth explained. "But then Erasmus surprised everyone with his last-minute trip. I knew I had to act fast so—"

"You drugged his food?"

Ruth nodded, smiling at her cleverness. "He had no idea that the experimental cocktail he found record of was the very thing that killed him. I added fruit pectin to the tea, just like we do in church, to make it absorb quickly and go through his system faster. I wasn't 100% sure it would work, but it did the trick."

"Hmm." Mr. Lundy tapped the pencil on the legal pad, before jotting down a few more notes.

"What, 'hmm'?" Ruth asked, trying to peer in vain over his shoulder.

"I wonder if he did know."

"How could he?"

"I don't know. But given his last adaptation to the will, I wonder if he suspected he was a target... or at least knew he would be after shutting the factory down."

"Makes no sense." Ruth hugged herself. "With him dead, the factory would go on as it always has. Why would he willingly sacrifice himself?"

"Maybe he wanted an investigation," Mr. Lundy suggested. "Perhaps *that's* why he went along with it."

"You mean you think he *let* me drug him?" Ruth was filled with a mix of surprise and annoyance. Ruth began rubbing her legs again. She felt itchy all of a sudden.

"Possibly," Mr. Lundy answered, putting his pencil and paper away. He stood.

Ruth eyed him pleadingly. "No chance you'll take pity on an old woman and save me?"

"I'm sorry, Ruth," was all that Mr. Lundy said.

Finally, Ruth asked the dreaded question, "How long have I got?"

"Hard to say," Mr. Lundy answered calmly. "After tomorrow's dosage, maybe a week, a month? Everyone is different."

"And if I *don't* confess tomorrow?"

"Oh, Ruth," Mr. Lundy smiled. "We both know that this is not an option."

Epilogue

A Hospital Room in Ireland, 1998

The phone rang in Baxter Baker's hospital room. Baxter rubbed his eyes groggily as he checked the time on the clock next to his bed... 8 a.m. Wondering who would be phoning him this early in the morning, he lifted the receiver tentatively.

"We've got a problem, Baxter." It was Elsbeth.

Baxter struggled to sit up in his bed. "Elsbeth? Are you okay? It's like, what... 3 a.m. in New York?"

"Yeah," Elsbeth whispered. "Listen, I only have a minute to explain, but in case you weren't aware of it, there's a team heading to the Dublin factory to investigate. No doubt they'll want to case the Leitrim house, too."

Baxter sighed. "I was worried that would happen." He eyed the door where a member of the Garda Síochána was stationed out front.

"So much for me and you hiding out with Edgar for a while," Elsbeth lamented. If only I had the courage to leave with Baxter the night I sent a text to warn him. Maybe if he had texted back, she thought. She didn't know that he was having dinner with Emma at the time.

"Yeah, well," Baxter whispered. "That wasn't likely to happen anyway. The police are going to fly me back to the States in connection with Vandenberg Nutraceuticals and the deaths at the Church of Infinite Love."

"Hmmm," Elsbeth thought a moment. "If only we could think of a way to hide you."

"Who's we?" Baxter asked. "And I don't want you mixed up in this, Elsbeth. I've already got a bullseye on my back because of my involvement. Just lay low for a while longer, El. Really, it's for your safety."

"Fortunately for you, that's not going to happen," Elsbeth answered.

"Why?" Baxter was concerned. "What are you gonna do?"

"Let's just say, I'm heading your way and leave it at that."

"El, no," Baxter protested. The call ended and a loud dial tone buzzed in Baxter's ear. He hung up the phone and collapsed back on the bed. He was healing quickly, but still had bouts of grogginess and pain.

"Knock, knock," a gentle male voice called from the door to Baxter's room. It was a member of the Garda Síochána dressed in a black and yellow uniform. "May I come in?"

"Uh, sure," Baxter answered. How much had he heard? He wondered to himself.

"I couldn't help but notice that you were in a bit of a pickle," the small man continued. His voice was deep and had a slithery quality to it.

"I don't know what you're talking about," Baxter lied.

"Oh, no need to be coy, Mr. Baker. I'm here to help. Allow me to introduce myself." He grinned widely as he stood over Baxter's hospital bed. "My name is Jaks... Jaks Liebling."

To be continued... in Ireland.

It Had to Be You

It has brought me so much joy being able to write the third and final book in the Music Mystery Series. Like with my first trilogy, The Data Collectors, I love all my characters like they are dear friends (even the troublesome ones!). I half expect them to knock on the door one day and come for a visit. (Not really. But how cool would that be?)

I would like to thank my friends, family and fans for taking the time to read, review and share my works with others. Special thanks goes to my friend and colleague, Cindy Readnower of Skinny Leopard Media for her editing and publishing support. Thank you to Graham Mack for co-producing and narrating the audio version of my books with me. Thank you to my 'partner in crime' and the love of my life, John Palli, for his never-ending support.

A trip to Ireland inspired the location of this book, and I'd like to also send a heartfelt thanks to Mike Costello, a guide who regaled us with historical anecdotes about the Emerald Isle (most of which were true!) and left me with these wise words, "Never let the truth get in the way of a good story."

For all the people who have shown up in my life just when I needed them, I am grateful.

Prologue

~

The year is 1999 and almost eleven months after the Troubles ended in Ireland.

Emma Post and her boyfriend, Officer Dennis McCleary, helped solve the murder of wealthy tycoon Erasmus Vandenberg, owner of Vandenberg Nutraceuticals, and were now settling into their new home in Florida.

But they had unearthed a can of worms, Vandenberg nutraceuticals was tied to the Church of Infinite Love, an organization well-regarded as a cult. Somehow, Erasmus Vandenberg had secured supreme control over both the church and the nutraceutical company, working alongside his daughter Edwina and other Elders of the church, selling faith-healing, miracle nutrition bars, and the security of a safe life on one of their many campuses worldwide. The only family members seemingly above suspicion were the socially awkward Elsbeth Ions (Edwina's daughter); hermit Edgar Vandenberg (Elsbeth's uncle); and distant cousin, the ever-charming playboy, Baxter Baker.

Officer Dennis sought the advice of his former boss, Detective Jose Ortega, who gathered a team comprised of his colleague and former love interest, forensic scientist Dr. Penelope Washburn; cybersecurity expert and private investigator, Darwin Fennec; and his partner, Rue Brennan; and finally, an officer with the Tampa sheriff's department, Shep Stern.

The team had managed to shut down the church's operations in Florida, only to learn that the Vandenberg family was returning to their roots...that is, reopening their original factory in Ireland, one that had lain dormant for years. With the reemergence of the factory, the church was likely to resurface as well, rebranded and repackaged...but just as dangerous.

At the behest of Midge Pasternak, a woman Darwin and Rue had sent to prison nearly two years prior, Rue agreed to join Ortega, Penelope and Shep in Dublin. It was Midge whose meddling brought Rue and Darwin together in the first place, after they teamed up in New York to clear their names of a double-murder—one up-and-coming singer and one art model—in order to outsmart Midge's sociopathic partner in crime, Jax Liebling.

In an odd twist, Rue revealed she had been brought up in the Church of Infinite Love and would likely know how they operate. Therefore, her presence on this newest case was essential. Unfortunately, Darwin Fennec's ties with Ireland were not good ones, and he vowed never to set foot on the Emerald Isle ever again.

CHAPTER 1
Edwina

New York

~

Edwina was getting restless. Ever since Vandenberg Nutraceuticals shut down the Florida factory and word got out about the church's questionable practices; they were hounded by the police. And while they found enough evidence to link the company to at least five deaths at church campuses in the Northern United States, family lawyer, Mr. Lundy, and his team had done such a good job of covering their tracks that no one person could be blamed...except of course, one of their Ambassadors who died under suspicious circumstances while in prison. They took the fall for Erasmus's death, and the death of a Deaconess at one of the Pennsylvania church campuses. But the older cases went so far back that it would take many more years and cutting through lots of red tape and corruption to get to the bottom of it all.

Still, the damage had been done. In addition to Vandenberg Nutraceuticals facing bankruptcy, church membership had fallen by nearly 40%. Apparently, the faith-healing business was not what it used to be. Then, of course, there was the fact that Emma Post, a figure model who now controlled the bulk of the company, was planning to sell off both factory properties...one in Florida and the other in Dublin.

And, as if it couldn't get any worse for Edwina Vandenberg, daughter of Erasmus Vandenberg, Erasmus saw to it that Edwina got next to nothing in his will. The New York condo now belonged to her daughter, Elsbeth, and in another few months, Edwina would be tapped out and forced to sell her luxury estate in the Hamptons.

She had already laid off all of the housekeepers at both locations, with the exception of Ferdinand, Erasmus's personal assistant. Despite taking a considerable pay cut, Ferdinand remained a loyal member of the church and to Edwina.

Edwina sat on the couch of the home that now belonged to her daughter, recognizing that she had limited time left as Elsbeth's guardian. She flipped through a tabloid that unearthed a conspiracy theory that everyone on staff at the factory or at the Vandenberg residences were also secret Ambassadors and Elders of an underground cult. Unfortunately, the story was a little too on point.

Edwina let out a huff as she ripped the cover from the tabloid, crumpled it up in a fit of anger and launched it like a baseball into the fireplace. It hit the mantle and dropped, un-singed, in front of the hearth.

"Would you care for a sherry, Madame Edwina?" Ferdinand asked. "It might settle your nerves."

Edwina stiffened her shoulders for a moment before consciously relaxing them away from her ears and tilting her head from side to side to loosen her neck.

"I'm afraid I need more than sherry to settle my nerves tonight, Ferdinand. What I need is...a miracle."

CHAPTER 2

Midge and Jax (Not Jaks)

Dublin

"Okay, I'm here," Midge announced, dropping her carpet bag on the floor with a thud. She struggled to breathe. "Is it me?" she asked, looking around. "Or do you manage to suck the oxygen out of every room you enter?"

"Perhaps, I simply take your breath away," Jax answered, moving toward Midge. "I've missed you."

Midge stepped backward, holding her palms out as a barrier. "That's close enough, mister."

Jax paused, fighting back a smile. "So coy," he admired. "Alright," he agreed, "I'll play your little game."

Midge looked at the handwritten note he had left her. "This is signed Jax with an 'x' versus Jaks with a 'k' and an 's.' Did you forget how to spell your name?"

"I got tired of everyone mispronouncing it. Besides, I thought you'd find it sexy…'Jax.'" He fanned his hand out as if his name were appearing in lights.

"You realize that it's slang for 'toilet' here, right?" Midge slipped the note back into her coat pocket.

Jax frowned.

"And what about 'Liebling?'" she challenged. "Jaks with a 'k' was a problem, but not that unfortunate last name you settled on?"

"'Liebling' means 'darling,'" Jax, now with an 'x', explained.

"So you're a darling toilet?" Midge retorted.

Jax's steely eyes bored into Midge as he fought back anger. "I remember a time when you couldn't get enough of me, baby," he softened his voice. "What happened to us?"

"You know darn well what happened to us, darling!" Midge surveyed Jax from head to toe, along with the surroundings, ensuring that he wasn't armed and that she could make a hasty getaway if needed. She saw two escape routes...one was the door of his flat, through which she'd just entered, the other was a window behind the living room couch that may or may not open, with who knows what beneath it? She stepped backward, closer to the doorway, just in case.

"My goodness, are you planning your escape already?" Jax was surprised. "I thought you knew me better than that." He moved forward.

She jolted.

He stopped.

"Yeah, well, so did I," Midge answered flatly.

"I came home one day and you were gone. Why? What drove you away from me?" Jax appeared almost hurt...almost.

"That would be a series of 'whats', Jax," she answered. "Locking me in the bedroom while you set fire to the living room because you thought I was having an affair—"

"I didn't like the way that barista was looking at you—"

"So, suffocating me was the answer?!"

"I was outside the entire time. I wouldn't have let you die. It was just a—"

"A what, Jax? A warning?" Jax remained silent. "Then there were sex rituals—"

"I thought you liked those," Jax protested.

"Look, I may have my share of kinks, but you took things way too far.

Feather tickling and fuzzy handcuffs are one thing. Almost choking me to death while sticking pins in me is something else."

"They were acupuncture needles," Jax explained. "If anything, they were supposed to help you relax."

"While you were choking me?!"

"So, you didn't like that?" Jax clarified.

"No, Jax!" Midge was astounded. "I didn't like that!" Without thinking, she began pacing the room, nervously. This was a challenge as she was limited to walking from the front door, past the small kitchen on one side, to the living room on the other, to the opposite wall. Behind it, was presumably the bedroom. "It was different when you took your vengeance out on people who deserved it, but not when you turned your violence on me."

"Baby," Jax carefully circled around Midge, his back toward the door. "I would never intentionally hurt you. How could I? I love you."

"I know I'm no expert on love, but I'd be willing to bet what you feel for me isn't love. It's obsession."

"Oh, really?" Jax grinned, taking a cautious step toward Midge, eyeing her from head to toe. Despite her protests and her obvious discomfort, she still craved his attention, and he knew it. "Can't my obsession be out of my overwhelming love and desire for you?" He took another step. "Why do you think I pushed for us to get a marriage license, a destination wedding as it were?"

Midge backed up, only to butt up against a long end table. The side of it pressed into her back. It was then she realized that Jax was now blocking the front door and moving toward her. How could she have let her guard down? She was smarter than that. "Destination wedding, my ass! To you, it's a business opportunity and a chance to get me away from anyone or anyplace familiar to me. You take control by relieving me of mine, by any means possible."

"Maybe I just reel with jealousy at another man...or woman, for that matter...taking your attention away from me. Maybe I just want you all for myself...to possess you. I thought a change of scenery would be good for us."

"What are you talking about?" Midge questioned, uncomfortably.

"What other man? And what other woman? I've never even dated a woman," she protested.

"I'm talking about Rue Brennan," he explained. By now, he had reached his target. Resting his left hand on the table, Jax kept his right arm at his side, leaving just enough room for Midge to slip past him and escape. Only, she didn't budge.

Jax was so close, she could feel his breath on the side of her face and the heat kicking off his body.

"Rue's my bestie, that's all," Midge explained.

"Thanks to your 'bestie,'" Jax whispered, "you ended up in a women's detention center, remember? She's the reason we both almost ended up spending the rest of our days behind bars."

"I thought you liked bars," Midge answered, recalling one of Jax more elaborate cages during a lovemaking session.

"Funny, baby," he smiled. "Last chance—"

"Last chance for what?" Midge choked out as Jax leaned in until his lips were a mere inch away from hers.

"I thought so," he smiled. She knew it too. Unless he planned to chase after her, there was nothing preventing Midge from bolting for the open door, other than perhaps fear or...something else.

Suddenly, Jax grabbed Midge by the hair with his right hand and dragged her lips to his as he kissed her, forcefully. Despite her better judgment, she kissed him back, leaning uncomfortably over the table. She put one hand behind her for support.

She broke her lips free for a moment, only to reaffirm, "Rue is just a friend. I have a friend code and all."

"Do you now?" Jax kissed her again, biting her lower lip, playfully. "Well, I don't like it when your 'friend code' gets in the way of us."

"There is no 'us' anymore, Jax," Midge explained.

"Think so?" he answered simply, as he grabbed her hips and lifted her onto the table until she was seated with her legs dangling off the edge. He separated her knees and moved his hips forward until he was firmly pressed against her belly, and wrapped his arms around her in an embrace, pulling her feverishly toward him. "Then why did you come back?"

"To tell you in person," Midge explained. Even she knew it sounded weak coming out of her mouth. She draped her arms over his shoulders as he nuzzled her neck.

"Tell me what?" Jax asked coyly, kissing her again.

"To stop calling, sending me messages, spying on me, sending me presents. It's over," she whispered as she somehow managed to pull him even closer, so that their bellies and chests were firmly pressed together.

"I can't stand all this space between us," Jax complained, breaking free long enough to unbutton her coat. She struggled to remove it, until it was finally laying behind her on the table with her still sitting on the edge of it. Jax eyed her black dress and matching stockings, noting that the hem only reached mid-thigh. "If I didn't know any better, Midge," Jax confessed, "I'd say you planned this."

"Don't be silly," she whispered, breathlessly, "you and I are finished."

"Are we?" Jax grinned, seductively moving toward her again. Only this time, he slid his hand on the inside of her thighs, moving upward as he used his other hand to press against her chest until she was lying with her back on the table, legs still dangling over the side. "Somehow, I don't think we are."

"The door is open," she reminded him, quietly. "Anyone could come by and see us."

"Well, then I hope they enjoy the show," Jax replied, seductively.

Midge stared at the ceiling momentarily, fighting back a moan. "Maybe once more, for old time's sake?" she offered, gasping at his touch.

Jax smiled, mischievously, before reaching for his belt buckle.

CHAPTER 3

Red Eye to Dublin

~

Dr. Penelope Washburn thumped her carry-on bag behind her as she followed Jose Ortega to their seats in TWA's First Class cabin. Never having traveled so well, she looked sheepishly toward Rue Brennan and Shep Stern as she boarded the plane. They were delegated to Coach. No one knew where Midge Pasternak was. Rue thought that this was probably for the best, at least until they had gotten settled in Dublin.

Penelope paused when she reached her seat, surveying the wide aisles and ample space with childlike wonder. "Wow," was all she could think to say, in her smooth Southern accent.

"Yes, well." Ortega relieved Penelope of her bag, sliding it in a storage unit under her chair. "Say what you will about Nancy, but she certainly knows how to travel in style."

Nancy Ortega was his soon-to-be ex-wife, after he'd discovered, quite recently, that she was having an affair. But she was gracious beyond measure and dipped into her family fortune to finance Jose's (or, Ortega, as he was most often called) tickets to Ireland, even calling to ensure the airline upgraded Penelope at the last minute. Nancy had her connections, and she had no trouble using them, particularly when inspired by guilt.

"I'll say," Penelope answered, uncomfortably, as she sat down and fastened her seatbelt. She was not a diamond and pearls kind of gal. Her definition of luxury was a Sunday afternoon nap on the couch with her cat curled up beside her, purring. And while it had been well over a decade since she and Ortega had been an item, before the breakup and his hasty marriage to Nancy, Penelope felt as if she were somehow stepping into the shoes of a woman of which she could not fill. She wasn't sure why it bothered her so much. It never had before. Yet somehow, she suddenly felt inferior. *Why?* She wondered to herself. She watched as Ortega dutifully procured himself a Jameson whiskey and a glass of Prosecco for her from the flight attendant. *There isn't anything still left between us anymore...is there?*

Penelope eyed Ortega's beverage curiously. She knew him to be more of a Kentucky bourbon sort of guy. Ortega pulled out a Cuban cigar and lit it. After taking a puff, he answered her knowing gaze with a, "Well, 'when in Rome,' as they say."

He sat back and took a sip of his whiskey and another puff of the cigar. Nancy would not approve. And, while the wound was still fresh, somehow he felt an odd feeling. *What was it? Relief?*

Finally, they were en route to Dublin, where the First Class cabin was treated to steak and potatoes delivered on a dining tray with a table cloth and utensils...not a boxed lunch sandwich typically reserved for economy. Penelope's eyes grew wide, but said nothing.

"Excuse me, sir," a flight attendant addressed him, uncomfortably, "but we don't allow cigars on the plane."

"Not even in First Class?" Ortega was surprised. He'd never flown First Class before, but he assumed that the rich could get away with anything. At least, that was his observation from his many years in law enforcement.

"Cigarettes are okay, though," she offered. "May I offer you a cigarette?"

"Oh, no," Ortega cringed. "Nasty stuff."

The flight attendant wasn't sure why the distinction, but smiled politely and extinguished the cigar for him.

Penelope couldn't understand how his palette couldn't be tainted by a cigar before dinner anyway, but she decided not to press the issue. After all, why spoil a good moment?

The attendant announced the in-flight movie, moments before a large screen at the front of the plane lit up. They were screening, *When Harry Met Sally,* one of Penelope's favorites. She plugged her earbuds into the port in the arm of her chair and giggled pleasantly. Ortega glanced her way and smiled, opting to watch the screen in silence with passing interest.

"Aww," she grabbed Ortega's arm, reminiscing, as Harry Connick Jr., launched into *It Had to Be You* from the soundtrack. "They're playing our song," she laughed. She remembered a slow dance one night at a friend's wedding where Ortega had been her *plus one.* The singer was actually a recording by Frank Sinatra, but the song was the same. She removed an ear bud and pressed it into Ortega's left ear. He leaned in, uncomfortably.

"Some others I've seen," Penelope sang quietly to Ortega. "Might never be mean. Might never be cross or try to be boss, but they'd never do —" She smiled up at him. Ortega peered back at her as if he were dreaming and might wake up at any moment. The last 48 hours had been surreal.

"Another drink, sir?" A flight attendant interrupted their revery.

Penelope released Ortega's arm, and slunk back into her seat, the sudden movement pulling the bud from Ortega's ear canal and sailing through the air and landing in her lap. *How embarrassing.* She was behaving like a schoolgirl. She knew it, and she didn't like it.

"No, thank you." Ortega replied, turning to Penelope, motioning to her beverage. "And you?"

"No," Penelope smiled pleasantly at the attendant. "Nothing more for me, thanks."

After dinner, the lights in the cabin were further dimmed and the movie came to an end. Penelope reclined in her chair, slid an eye mask on and turned blindly toward Ortega before putting in ear plugs. "Goodnight, Jose," she whispered quietly.

Ortega, who had decided on another whiskey night cap after all, swirled the ice cubes in his glass and whispered back, "Goodnight, Penelope."

WHILE PENELOPE and Ortega were enjoying dinner and a movie with ample leg space, Rue and Shep were sandwiched in the cheap seats between the smoking and non-smoking sections of the plane. Rue coughed and wrinkled her nose, distastefully. Shep's oversized frame seemed to take up more than his share of space and Rue was certain he was hogging all the extra oxygen too. Despite shrinking into her seat, Shep's elbow seemed to keep digging into her ribs.

Rue was stuck in the middle seat. To her left, at the window, was a small woman who had padded herself up with an oversized pillow and a comforter that she had wrapped around her like bubble wrap. It wasn't long before a gentle snore could be heard from deep within the folds of the blanket.

Rue folded her arms and closed her eyes in a vain attempt to fall asleep, but Shep was having none of it. With case files strewn across his tray table, he sifted through them obsessively, trying to connect the dots.

"Help me make sense of this," his voice boomed in Rue's ear just as she began dosing off. She sat up abruptly, startled. Shep didn't seem to notice.

"Wha?" Rue yawned, rubbing her eyes in an attempt to focus.

"You were a member of the Church of Infinite Love, correct?"

"Yup," Rue answered, groggily. "Born into it. Took far too long to get away."

"And you didn't know anything about Vandenberg Nutraceuticals selling drug-laced products to the church as part of a faith-healing racket... and to control the masses...not even an inkling?" Shep seemed doubtful. "Where did you grow up, under a rock or something?"

"That's one way of describing it," Rue answered flatly. "You've clearly never experienced brainwashing or led a sheltered life. You do what you're told and don't ask a lot of questions."

"What happened if you asked questions," Shep persisted. "You'd think they'd appreciate an inquisitive mind." *For a generally smart man, Shep said a lot of dumb things.*

"More like an obedient one." Rue attempted to roll to one side, turning her back toward Shep. "Could we discuss this in the morning? I'm exhausted."

"Yeah, sure." Shep was visibly disappointed. He took solace in a bag of peanuts offered by the flight attendant. Rue cringed. Somehow, Shep managed to make as much noise as humanly possible trying to open the tiny bag with his thick fingers.

Rue closed her eyes and willed herself to mentally block out the sound of Shep's crunching, which was somehow *not* drowned out by the white noise from the plane.

"But can you just answer one more question?" he tried again, moments later.

Rue flopped on her back in a huff, hunched in her seat as if she would melt into the floor at any moment. "What?" she asked, agitated.

"How'd you get out? I mean, couldn't you just leave?"

Rue wondered that very same thing. It wasn't as if there were armed guards at every campus or even gates that locked at night. So, why did it take her several attempts to get free? And why, once she'd gotten out, had she gone back?

"Well, it's like this, Shep," Rue tried her best, "get a bunch of insecure people down on their luck, like my parents. Tell 'em how special they are, that they're the 'chosen ones' with a reward in heaven. This life doesn't matter, cuz there's a better one, one that will treat 'em like they deserve to be treated."

"So far, that sounds like most religions," Shep offered.

Rue ignored him, she was on a roll. "Feed 'em a nugget of truth that they can bite into so they develop trust. Then, little by little, start manipulating that truth. Do it well enough and no one questions it. Start meeting at out-of-the-way, secret places because non-believers just wouldn't understand and might even try to sabotage the church. Begin cutting off outside influences that might conflict with church doctrine. After all, the Devil hates the chosen ones and the church, and would do anything to destroy them. It's okay if people ridicule you. That's a sign you're doing the right thing in God's eyes. Persecution becomes a badge of honor."

"Wow," Shep replied, "your parents must have been really gullible."

Rue's face felt flushed. "And what about your beliefs, Shep? Last I checked, you have a pretty strict religious code of ethics, to include your wardrobe and your diet...not that anyone could tell, as much as you eat."

"Hey," Shep whined, "I have low blood sugar." After a few minutes of silence, he tried again. "Sorry, didn't mean to strike a chord there—"

"Trigger," Rue corrected.

"What?" Shep asked.

"I think you meant, a 'trigger.'"

"Not sure there's a difference—" Shep stopped mid-sentence at Rue's death glare. "Never mind. But that still doesn't answer the question. Why didn't *you* leave?"

"Why?" Rue bounced the idea around for a moment.

"Stop overthinking and just answer the question," Shep prodded, impatiently.

"Fine," Rue agreed, blurting out, "I didn't leave because I was born into the cult that told me how and what to think from day one. You only got to learn what they thought was important for you to know, and that created a reliance on them for safety and security. They get you believing that the real world is a scary place and that if people don't get you, the Devil will. And if you leave? Well then, now you've pissed off God too." Rue folded her arms, angrily. "Why didn't I leave? Because I had no idea how to take care of myself or think for myself, and the only people I had to ask were telling me that everything would be just fine if I just listened to them and behaved."

"But, somehow you got out," Shep pointed out.

"Yes," she answered. "I did."

"What changed?"

Rue thought a moment. "I was all set to be married off to an Elder in the church." She sifted through the memory in her mind. "Since I was already considered too old by the church's standards, that meant they'd expect me to get pregnant right away. If that happened, then like it as not, I would have been stuck in that life forever. And the thought of that was scarier to me than anything I could expect to experience in the outside world."

"You got out," Shep nodded approvingly. "Against the odds, you got out...good going."

"Yeah, but I didn't know anyone. Midge was the first person I met when I reached Manhattan, and she helped me get settled into my apartment and find a job."

"Your first friend was a psychopath...nice."

"Say what you will about her, but she kinda helped save my life."

"Hmm," Shep answered, nodding his head and grinning. "The Lord works in—"

"Don't!" Rue cut him off.

"Sorry," Shep replied. "Bad joke." He collected his files, folded up his tray table, and stuffed his paperwork in a duffle bag under his seat. "But hey, you said you wanted to get some sleep. We can talk more later." He leaned back and closed his eyes. In a moment, the sound of a small kazoo could be heard as he inhaled and exhaled. Finally, his mouth dropped open and a bit of drool landed on his shirt.

Rue cringed distastefully and turned her back on him for a second time, shifting in her seat, trying in vain to get comfortable. *Great,* she thought, shutting her eyes. *Now, I'm wide awake.*

The blanket-wrapped woman sitting next to her peeked a head out from her cocoon. She touched Rue carefully on the shoulder. Rue opened her eyes to see a cherub-faced woman with bright blue eyes looking at her with deep sympathy.

"I'm sorry, sweetie," she cooed, "I couldn't help overhearing your story. That must have been awful."

"Well," Rue answered, "life is a lot better now." She thought about Darwin and how they'd left things when she'd gotten on a plane to Ireland. "Still got a few things to work out, though."

"Well," the woman answered softly, "if it would help, I can pray for you. Would you like that? Can I pray for you?"

Rue felt her jaw clench, before answering calmly. "Please don't."

THE FOUR ARRIVED at Dublin Airport mid-morning, and by the time they'd reached their short-term rental in Swords, they were dead on their feet. It had been years since Ortega had been to Ireland. The last time was when he was investigating a high-profile case involving one of the longest-running feuds on the Emerald Isle, but Ortega didn't want to revisit that story, even in his mind. Fortunately, some of his old connections were still good, and he was able to line up temporary housing just outside of Dublin. It was a two-bedroom rental with a single bathroom and efficiency kitchen. It wasn't glamorous, but it was functional.

They knew they weren't going to accomplish much that day, so they agreed on a quick trip to the local Tesco for a few groceries to prepare a light meal followed by an early night.

The team had all jumped on a plane to Ireland on short notice and without a plan, a sad reality that only hit them as jet lag set in.

Rue rationalized that she wanted to help make sure the church didn't face a resurrection in Ireland. Yet, in the back of her mind, she wondered if what she really needed was space to process past traumas and work through her relationship with Darwin. Nothing was really wrong, per say, except that she had been pulling away from him and he knew it. Something about the situation, as happy as it was, left her feeling trapped. It's not as if she couldn't leave any time she wanted to, not that she did, but old wounds were surfacing, reminding her of a time where she was stuck in a life she couldn't get away from. And of course, there was the guilt over the death of her mother, a Deaconess who died after trying to help her. And finally, there was that nagging feeling about Midge. Despite all the havoc her friend unleashed in her life, what she told Shep was true. She didn't know anyone when she escaped to New York, and for a long time Midge was the only person she could count on. A small part of her felt like she owed her something, despite everything.

Ortega was itching for a case he could sink his teeth into, and was dying to know why the church had shut its factory down in the first place. Nancy had given him an ultimatum once, and he gave in, retiring from work that he loved in an effort to save their marriage. But now that Nancy was no longer in the picture, there was a part of him that relished an adventure, a complex case spanning two countries.

Shep, as we would come to learn, disliked injustice of any kind, along with puzzles he couldn't solve. If there were other motives, no one really understood what they were. Something about his personality caused him to somehow fall into strange situations, getting wrapped up in everyone else's drama while lacking the ability to say, "No."

Meanwhile, Penelope tried to convince herself that she was doing the right thing by helping the team. And since she was now out of a job, why not take an exciting trip overseas? If she were being honest with herself, she would have admitted that what she was really hoping for was a do-over. What if she and Ortega could go back to the way things were? Minus the fighting and breaking up, of course. They had this electricity between them when they worked together.

While Ortega would have much rather had Penelope stay in his room, he didn't want to make assumptions. And, he was fairly confident that Rue and Shep had no interest in being roommates. So Shep and Ortega took the small room, equipped with bunk beds and a small dresser and chair that sat next to a clothing rack, while Penelope and Rue made do in the slightly larger room with one single bed and a fold-out cot from the closet.

"You want the top bunk?" Shep asked when they had settled into their rooms.

Ortega eyed the oversized man, annoyed. "What do you think?"

"Right," Shep said. "Probably best if I take the top, even though I'm heavier than you, cause your knees probably couldn't handle climbing up and down the ladder."

"Why would you assume that? Just because I'm older? My knees are just fine," Ortega complained.

"So—"

"Go," Ortega motioned. He removed his sweater and pants, draping them across the chair, but left his undershirt and boxers on. He sank into the bottom bunk, uncomfortably. The mattress had little shape left to it, and he could feel the springs beneath it on his spine. *It's like I'm back in college,* he thought. Ortega waiting impatiently as Shep tossed and turned, trying to get comfortable, his mattress sagging so much that Ortega was concerned the bed wouldn't hold his weight. The frame was too short for the tall man, so Shep settled on curling up in a fetal position. It was the best he could do.

Just as Ortega was about to nod off, Shep spoke up. "So, are you an

Dr. Washburn an item?" Shep had a knack for asking inappropriate questions at the worst possible times.

Ortega sighed. "Not for a long time," he answered.

"What went wrong?" Shep asked, inquisitively.

"Goodnight, Shep," Ortega answered, abruptly ending the conversation.

CHAPTER 4

The Plan (According to Midge)

~

"Why did you drag us all the way to Ireland, Midge?" Rue asked, sliding into a chair across from her former friend. Shep, Penelope and Ortega followed suit.

Midge, still a fugitive after having escaped a women's detention center in New York, returned long enough to convince Rue that she needed to help her take down the church, and Jax Liebling, for good. It was she who convinced them to fly to Ireland in a rush, only to promptly disappear and then resurface three days later. A note was left taped to their flat instructing them when and where to meet her later that day—a bar and restaurant not far from where they were staying.

"Correction," Midge eyed Penelope, Shep and Ortega, as the five of them sat gathered around a table in the Old Schoolhouse to talk. "I dragged *you* to Ireland. I wanted your string-bean boyfriend Darwin Fennec along and encouraged your buddy Elsbeth to pay a visit to her dear Uncle Edgar. The rest of youse guys were unexpected."

During the early hours of the day, the restaurant was nearly empty, and the only one planning on eating was Shep who let his stomach override his principles. He ordered the fish and chips even though he was fairly convinced it wasn't kosher. And the only one drinking was Midge who was now on her second Jameson double-shot.

"I swear," she complained, "they water this down."

"You ordered it straight up," Rue reminded her.

"That don't mean they don't fill the bottle with a few parts wuh-ter, if you know what I mean." Midge leaned in and whispered loudly, her Tri-state Philly-New York-Jersey accent becoming thicker the more she drank.

A server shot Midge an annoyed look, but said nothing. As long as they were paying customers, she was going to be polite to the rude American.

"Can I get anything for the rest of you?" the server asked. Penelope, who felt bad about taking up space and not ordering anything, asked for a cup of tea. "Biscuit with that?" the server asked.

After a long pause, Penelope added, "Sure."

Ortega and Rue waved off anything. For once, they were of the same mindset—get what information you needed from Midge, and get out. After all, neither of them trusted Midge, and for good reason. It just so happened that they had no authority to do anything but report her to the New York police department, and they hesitated to do that while she was useful to them. And furthermore, they shouldn't even be here in the first place. Ortega had retired. Penelope was fired. Rue was too close to the case to be objective and Shep was, well, Shep. He was still gainfully employed back home, but if his supervisors got wind of what he was up to, he likely wouldn't be for long.

This plagued the former detective immensely. He had always been on the straight and narrow, but ever since he met Rue Brennan and her cyber forensic investigator boyfriend, Darwin, bending the rules was becoming increasingly easier. He justified it in his mind because it was all in order to bring down the 'bad guy,' but if he sat alone with his thoughts for a little too long, he might have come to the conclusion that one of the 'bad guys' was him. He put it out of his mind.

"I assumed you'd want the help of Ortega and Shep if you had any intention of taking down the church," Rue defended. "And Penelope—"

"Rookie mistake," Midge chastised. "But it's okay. Despite your gross error in judgment, I can work with this."

"What exactly is going on here, Miss Pasternak?" Ortega demanded.

"Calm down, Fuzz," Midge answered. Ortega lurched forward and opened his mouth with a retort but Penelope grabbed his arm before he could answer. Instead, he sucked in his breath "In my revised plan, as of two minutes ago, *you* get to take down the entire Church of Infinite Love operation and the Vandenberg Nutraceuticals empire to boot. Darwin and Rue were supposed to get that honor, but whatevs." She rolled her eyes casually, as if they were discussing what movie to see that weekend, not a murderous cult.

"Kinda thought we already had done that," Ortega answered, feigning ignorance.

"Please," she waved a hand at him. "I know your reputation. You're not *that* dumb."

Ortega balled a fist. Penelope tapped his arm, supportively, glaring at Midge. *She's just trying to bait him,* Penelope thought.

Moments later, the server returned with Shep's meal. She eyed Penelope. "Ah, sorry. Tea will be right up..." The group fell silent until she had scurried off to the kitchen, remembering Penelope's tea.

"You know as well as I do they are rebranding their efforts by selling off the Florida factory and giving the Dublin factory and the church a facelift," Midge explained, leaning forward and watching as the server walked away.

"So, business as usual?" Shep used his fingers to break off a piece of the crispy fish, dipping it into tartar sauce and popping it into his large mouth. He then proceeded to wipe his fingers on a napkin, a touch of the tartar sauce still sticking to his chin.

"Not hardly, Beefcake," she answered, amused. Shep furrowed his brows, taken aback. He wasn't entirely sure how to take that comment. "They may give the illusion of change, getting out of the faith-healing business even, but if Jax Liebling is involved, there's something else going on."

"What?" Shep demanded.

"I don't know yet," Midge answered.

Ortega let out a deflated sigh. He suspected Midge *did* know but she sure as hell wasn't telling.

"Listen, F—" she was about to use her new nickname for Ortega, saw his expression, and thought better of it. Midge wasn't always keenly observant, but Ortega's expressions weren't exactly subtle. "Ortega," she finished. "The one thing I know for certain is that if Jax is involved, it's bad. And he's not one for sharing. He may have put that lemming, Baxter Baker, as the front man at the nutraceutical company, but make no mistake, Jax is the one in charge. And, I know him, give 'em enough time and he'll have both Baxter's job and Bernie's too."

"Who's Bernie?" Ortega questioned.

"You mean you don't know?" Midge was incredulous. To Rue she asked, "Can you believe this guy?"

"Ms. Pasternak—" Ortega tried again.

"Fine, fine fine..." Midge relented. "Following Erasmus Vandenberg's untimely death, the reins of the church fell to his daughter, Edwina Vandenberg. Except, according to church law, a woman can't be in charge, so Bernie stepped in. As I said, Jax doesn't play well with others. Given enough time, he's gonna want both operations."

"And what's it to you?" Penelope chimed in as the server set down her tea and biscuits. Penelope mouthed a 'thank you' and the woman nodded before retreating to the kitchen.

"The church ruined my bestie's life," Midge punched Rue in the arm.

"Ou!" Rue rubbed her arm. "And I wouldn't say 'ruined.'"

"Not to mention what she did to that gal, Elsbeth," she added.

"Why do you care about Elsbeth?" Rue asked. "You barely know her."

"That's not what's important," Midge answered. "What is important is that these gents can go down in history as shutting down the largest global grift of the century, and you can get revenge on the people who screwed up your life."

"Again, I wouldn't go so far as to say—" Rue tried again.

"Fine, revenge on the people who—" Midge began.

"I wouldn't say revenge—" Rue interrupted.

Midge punched the table with a fist, angrily. "Sorry!" She eyed Rue. "You're lucky you're my best friend," she acknowledged, "cuz you sure are a piece of work. Alls I'm sayin' is you can ensure that future generations won't have to go through what you did in your wackadoo upbringing."

Rue caved, "Fine, I can get behind that reason. But the larger question still remains, why would you help us?"

"Like I've told you before, Jax is obsessed with me. The only way to get him off my case is if he's behind bars for a very long time."

"And yet, you came to Ireland seeking him out, not the other way around," Shep pointed out.

Midge smiled and winked at Shep, reaching over the table and dabbing the tartar sauce on his chin with a spare napkin. He blushed, rubbing his chin as if there were still something on his face. "Good observation, Beefcake," she answered. "But Jax has been following me all over the States and parts of Europe for the past year. I even tried escaping to Japan for a bit, but he found me there too. So when I heard what he was up to in Ireland, I knew this was my chance to head him off at the pass."

"Hang on, Midge," Rue interjected. "You told me that after all this was over, you were going to turn yourself in. Why not do that now and return safely behind bars where he can't reach you."

"Where he can't—" Midge shook her head. "Oh you poor, naive little thing. There's no where I can go where Jax couldn't find me. At least if he's under lock and key, I'll know where he is at all times."

"Wait a moment." Penelope asked, "If you're that afraid of him, why are you here in the middle of the day? Does he know you're in Ireland?"

"Of course, he knows it." Midge grabbed the third and final whiskey that the server placed in front of her and stood. She sucked it down and plunked the glass next to the other two. "I'm staying at his flat...ta-ta, my friends. I will be in touch. But don't try to reach me. Jax can't know I'm talking to youse guys."

"What are we supposed to do in the meantime?" Shep whined. "Take in the sights and wait for your call?"

"No, Beefcake," she answered, "you and Fuzz...sorry...Detective Ortega, geez, so sensitive," she eyed Ortega's expression, this time, noticing a few imaginary daggers flying from Penelope's eyes as well. "You can check out the Vandenberg factory and interview Jax and Baxter, maybe do a little snooping. But again, you haven't seen me since Rue visited me at the woman's detention center in New York over a year ago. Capisce?"

"Wait," Rue remembered. "Why is Elsbeth here? Isn't she safer back home?"

"With her nutball mother, Edwina? Not even. As far as I can tell, her uncle Edgar is the only one in her family not mixed up in this business. When you take the family down, she'll be protected."

"Why the sudden interest in Elsbeth, Midge?" Rue wasn't sure what Midge's angle was, but she knew it wasn't empathy.

Midge's eyes bore into Rue's momentarily, the side of her jaw twitching slightly. "As I said," Midge answered, measuring her words carefully, "you and she were innocent victims of the Church of Infinite Love. I don't like seeing the innocent get hurt."

"Then we should probably check on Elsbeth," Shep called out. "Just to make sure she's safe."

Midge had already reached the front door, tugging it open as a gust of wind tore through her hair as it funneled into the room. "You can if you want, Beefcake," she called, "but I think the Westports have already got that covered."

CHAPTER 5

Bernie, Mr. Lundy and Jax

Two Months Ago, Dublin

Bernie Forger wasn't very happy when he arrived by the Oscar Wilde Statue at Merriam Square. If he had his way, he wouldn't be in Dublin at all, but in his high-rise condo in Manhattan. He was just settling into his new role as the ordained leader of the Church of Infinite Love following the death of his predecessor Erasmus Vandenberg when the church came under close scrutiny of the police and the media. He wasn't a bit concerned about the police. Mr. Lundy's team could take care of that. And, he was fairly certain the Vandenbergs had a large number of the police force in their back pocket. The press, on the other hand, were a different story. Even when you did them favors, offered them exclusive interviews and fancy hotel stays, they still found ways to discretely leak information about the church's questionable practices.

They called the Church of Infinite Love a cult. *How dare they?* Bernie thought to himself. Unlike Edwina Vandenberg who very well knew that at the end of the day, it was all just business, Bernie bought into his own hype. He believed himself to the be chosen one to lead his small, elite flock to glory in the afterlife. That's what made Bernie so dangerous. Like Jax, both men had an overwhelming sense of self-importance coupled with a healthy dose of delusion. Perhaps that's why Bernie took an instant dislike to Jax Liebling, who, from his perspective, seemed to appear out of nowhere. He slithered in when no one was looking, and now he was on the verge of taking over Vandenberg Nutraceuticals at the behest of Mr. Lundy.

Jax arrived moments later, gnawing on what appeared to be a piece of freshly-baked soda bread wrapped in white paper. Jax finished chewing as he crumpled the paper and surveyed the area for, presumably, a trash receptacle. Finding none, he tucked the paper discreetly in the ivy vines at the base of the monument, below Oscar's foot—thereby making it someone else's problem.

Bernie eyed Jax, distastefully, but merely nodded a head, acknowledging his presence.

"Gentlemen," Mr. Lundy arrived moments later, briefcase in tow. He never seemed to go anywhere without it. "Thank you for meeting me here. Let's take a walk." He motioned for them to follow. The three men began a slow stroll down the short meandering path around the square.

Jax grinned and silently padded along behind him, while Bernie fell into step beside Lundy. "Lundy, what's going on here?" Bernie whispered. "Do we really need *him* here?" Make no mistake, Bernie wasn't even trying to be subtle.

"I know you don't like me, Mr. Forger," Jax addressed the man from behind. "But you should. I'm about to make life a hell of a lot easier for you."

"How do you figure?" Bernie spat back.

"Ahem," Mr. Lundy cleared his throat. Lundy had the two qualities that Jax and Bernie lacked. First, he never, absolutely never, lost his temper or control over the situation—any situation. Second, his mind wasn't clouded by delusions of grandeur. He was manipulative when it suited his best interests, and he was exceptionally good at it. "You know I'm here only to serve," he said with false humility. "I had the honor of serving Erasmus Vandenberg and his family for nearly two decades, and I know the inner workings of both the church and Vandenberg Nutraceuticals.

Trust me when I tell you that it is refreshing to see both organizations fall into the hands of such worthy men as yourselves."

Jax puffed his chest out a little. Bernie lifted his chin with pride. Both were oblivious that Mr. Lundy was merely stroking their egos. And it worked.

"Bernie, Jax has a plan that can help clear the good name of the Church of Infinite Love and help you turn a profit. That's good business all around. I think you should hear him out."

Bernie bit his lip. The men paused as a few teenagers moseyed past them hooting and laughing loudly at nothing in particular. Finally, he said to Jax, "Well, go on then."

Jax unbuttoned the top collar of his shirt. The tightness around his neck felt suffocating. He sniffed a moment and answered. "I think we should convince the Vandenberg family to name Baxter Baker CEO of Vandenberg Nutraceuticals."

"What?" Bernie was incredulous. "Baxter Baker? Out of everyone in the family, he's not only the least competent man for the task, but he was the one who tried to sell out his family, the business and the church in the first place!"

Jax paused. He knew the strength of a silent pause and used it to frame his thoughts very carefully. Finally, he replied, "And that's exactly why you need to put him in charge and encourage the family to divorce themselves of the company and sell the outstanding shares to me."

"How does this help me and my calling, exactly?"

Jax chewed on his inner cheek to cause enough discomfort that he didn't give anything away in his facial expressions. What Bernie referred to as a 'calling,' Jax would have named it an 'opportunity' or a 'mission.'

"What he means to say," Mr. Lundy intervened, "is that with the rest of the family being out of the nutraceutical business, media attention will turn its attention away from them and the church."

Bernie was struggling to put the pieces together. "But giving up the factory will cut into the church's bottom line," Bernie protested.

"I promise you, it won't," Mr. Lundy encouraged. "My team has been over the contracts with a fine-tooth comb and met with your accountants for countless hours. The only way for the Church of Infinite Love to survive and to keep you out of bankruptcy and out of prison is if you have—"

"A scapegoat," Jax finished, grinning so wide you could see both his upper and lower teeth.

"You mean..." Bernie connected the dots. "Sell out Baxter."

"Your words, not mine," Jax answered in a sing-song voice. "But it would be poetic justice, wouldn't it?"

"That might keep the media and the law off our backs, but I'm in the business of selling miracles. The church has always relied on those health bars to encourage compliance. What will we do without them?"

Mr. Lundy wanted to cringe at the word 'compliance' when talking about members of the church, but he kept his expression neutral.

"What I'm suggesting," Jax finished, "is a rebrand. Let Baxter take the fall, and then I'll step in and help resolve this. By the time I'm done, the church will have seen the light and people will be buying up Vandenberg health snacks like Girl Scout cookies if it means continuing the Word of God."

"So, you'll be in charge," Bernie confirmed. "What happens to the rest of the Vandenberg Elders?"

"Does it matter?" Jax argued. "They'll get a nice chunk of change, and you can encourage them to donate it to the church's mission. They still see you as their new leader. Why not capitalize on that?"

"I don't capitalize, Mr. Liebling." Bernie's face grew red. "My only interest is God's great work," he finished.

"Of course, it is," Jax gloated, condescendingly. Bernie lurched forward and reached for Jax's collar as if to shove him off the path and onto the well-manicured lawn.

Mr. Lundy, being a large man, sandwiched himself between the two. "Would you mind not causing a scene?" he asked calmly. Bernie backed down. To Jax, he said, "You are a real piece of work, you know that?" Lundy shook his head while Jax adjusted his shirt and swept back his hair with his hands.

"Do you really think I should go along with this?" Bernie asked Lundy.

"Yes, Mr. Forger, I do," Lundy nodded. "And I think if you look at this from a clearer perspective you'll realize that no matter the motive, this is in everyone's best interest."

Jax snorted, "Except for Mr. Baker's!"

For once, Bernie couldn't help himself, a deeply-rooted laugh bubbled up from his chest as he joined Jax in uncontrollable laughter at the thought of poor Baxter being the fall guy.

The only one not laughing was Mr. Lundy. He knew better than to let emotions interfere.

CHAPTER 6
Emma's Decision

Florida

"Emma Post, how delightful it is to hear the sound of your voice," Baxter's voice crackled across the phone lines.

Despite her long-standing relationship with Dennis, and her dislike for Baxter's overinflated ego, she had to admit that the sound of his voice gave her the chills...just for the moment. She quickly dismissed them.

"What can I do for you, Mr. Baker?" she asked, flatly.

"Emma, how disappointing," Baxter chastised. "No pleasantries? Cut to the chase? Is that it? After I—"

"After you saved my life," Emma finished. "I am truly grateful for that, Mr. Baker. But it also has not escaped my attention that you bring it up every time you need a favor. What is it this time?"

Behind her, Dennis could be heard rifling through the closet in the hallway of their St. Petersburg home. Once he heard who was on the other end of the line, he made an extra effort to make as much noise as possible, even slamming the closet door closed using much more force than was necessary.

Emma shot him a look. He rolled his eyes, held his hands up in surrender and then retreated to the living room.

"Emma, I'm hurt," Baxter sulked, ignoring the clatter he heard across the line. "By the way, what's all that racket?"

"None of your—" Emma caught herself. Dennis had pointed out to her that sarcasm was her default mode. She was trying to be better. "Nothing for you to worry about, Mr. Baker."

After an awkward pause, Baxter asked tentatively, "I know you already have a sale pending on the Florida factory," he began.

Good news travels fast, Emma thought. But then again, Baxter had been an executive of Vandenberg Nutraceuticals for years. It made sense that he would know about the sale.

"Yes, that's right," she admitted. "I'm sorry, Mr. Baker. I know that must be a financial blow, but I am talking with my accountant and lawyer so that I can offer nice severance packages to all employees of the company, including yourself." Emma couldn't believe what she was saying. *My accountant and lawyer?* This time last year she was barely making ends meet and living in a drab apartment in the lower West side of Manhattan. Now, she and Dennis had waterfront property, premium gym memberships, a property manager and even their own financial and legal team. The thought of it gave her a headache. While life was simpler before, she didn't miss stressing over paying her rent and how to afford the rising price of groceries.

"That's very thoughtful of you, Miss Post, but money is not what I'm concerned about," Baxter answered with false bravado. In truth, he cared quite a lot about money, particularly if he didn't have to work to have it.

"Then, why are you calling?" Emma was confused.

Baxter cleared his throat and sucked in a deep breath. "I want to buy the Dublin factory. Er, I mean, I want to buy you out as primary shareholder."

"You want to buy me out?" Emma was surprised. "With what?" She was under the impression that with the only working factory out of commission, that Baxter's financial resources would have dried up with it.

"Really, Emma. I'm not as bad with money as you seem to think. Besides, I have financial investors."

"Really? Who?" Emma was curious.

"Does it matter?" Baxter become defensive.

"Of course it matters," her voice went up in pitch. "I planned on shutting down Vandenberg Nutraceuticals completely, cutting all ties with the Church of Infinite Love, and selling both properties to ensure this sort of thing never happens again."

Emma was referring to the fact that Vandenberg Nutraceuticals had been owned by her deceased friend, wealthy philanthropist Erasmus Vandenberg, who also headed up a cult that controlled its members through mind-altering products created at the factory. In addition to the psychological harm it caused many members of the church, it also resulted in the death of several women. Emma still hadn't come to terms with the fact that Erasmus turned a blind eye to much of it, convincing herself that he, himself, planned to shut down operations as soon as he found out. His murder cemented this belief. Because anything other than this would mean that a man who was like a kind grandfather to her was a complicit liar.

Baxter tried a different tac. "Okay, okay," he relented. "The truth is, Elsbeth plans to sell the Manhattan condo as soon as Edwina has to legally turn it over to her. She and I will work together to make sure Vandenberg Nutraceuticals returns to what dear old Erasmus wanted...to make the world a healthier place with his nutrition bars."

"Elsbeth?" While Emma had no doubt as to Elsbeth's intellect, she wasn't convinced she had the knowledge to run an operation that large.

Baxter, reading her mind, added, "I also have a silent partner willing to invest. He's apparently pretty well known in certain social circles, so I can't say more than that. But what I can promise you is no more ties to the church and no illegal products."

Emma paused. Baxter knew her weaknesses: Elsbeth and Erasmus. Even knowing that she was being played still didn't completely rule out the possibility of selling her shares, and releasing control of what remained of the company to Baxter. She could be rid of the whole lot of them for good...the Vandenberg family, the church, her old nemesis, Rue Brennan, and that cyber forensic boyfriend of hers, Darwin Fennec...all of them.

She could settle down in their little house in Florida, just she and Dennis, with Detective Ortega as a crotchety neighbor who joined them for dinner once in a while to talk about the good old days when he and Dennis worked together on the force.

"May I ask why the Dublin factory is of such interest to you?" Emma pressed him. "It's been shut down for years. Wouldn't it be easier to re-brand and start fresh in the States?"

"Well, it should come as no surprise to you that I don't exactly fit in with my family there. In fact, I think it's a safer bet for me to remain in Ireland. I know my way around and have my own security team."

"Security team?" Emma was curious.

"Tell you about it some other time. The point is, the factory, while in need of some retrofitting, was set up to specs for product production. It doesn't make sense for me to reinvent the wheel when I have a ready-made location right here, does it?"

Emma had to admit that he had a point. And, truth be told, she did feel guilty about Baxter taking a bullet for her. Not to mention that he was one of the only members of the Vandenberg family who had been honest with her from the beginning.

"Give me a couple of days to mull it over, Mr. Baker," she finally answered.

"Thank you, Miss Post. That's all I ask."

Baxter hung up the phone, sat back in his chair and eyed the weasel-like man who was sitting on a leather sofa across from him in a small office in Dublin.

"What happened?" Jax Liebling's eyes bore into Baxter's skull.

"She said she'd think about it," he answered. Jax's fists balled up as he forced in a breath.

"I see," was all Jax said.

"Why are you so interested in the company, anyway?" Baxter asked. "And why is it so critical to keep your name out of it?" He was growing very suspicious of his new business partner.

"Let's just say, Emma Post and I have a past, and leave it at that."

Baxter eyed Jax, curiously. He doubted it was of the romantic nature, as Jax wasn't much to look at and gave off this weird predator vibe. Truth be told, Baxter didn't much like his company, but thus far, Jax was doing what he promised: he protected Baxter from the police, shielding him from his involvement in Vandenberg Nutraceutical's shady dealings. Jax even convinced the remaining shareholders—family members who, quite possibly, wanted to see Baxter dead, to name him CEO of the company, and now he promised to help him take over the company entirely. And while he was suspicious of Jax Liebling's motives, Baxter was always pretty good at looking the other way when the truth became inconvenient.

Baxter nodded at Jax and quickly changed the subject.

"What was that about?" Dennis asked, struggling to hide his annoyance at learning it was Baxter Baker on the other end of the phone line—the same man who managed to skirt questioning by the police about what he knew about Vandenberg Nutraceuticals selling drug-laced nutrition bars to the Church of Infinite Love as part of their faith-healing scheme. He was also highly aware of Baxter's fondness of Emma. And despite the fact that Baxter was in Ireland, while he and Emma were living together in their home in Florida, Dennis still didn't appreciate Baxter's phone call.

"He wants me to sell him my shares of the company and turn the Dublin factory over to him," Emma answered, surprised.

"After everything that's happened?" Dennis was incredulous. "Rather brazen of him. And does he actually have that kind of cash?"

"Says he has a private investor, not to mention the support of his cousin Elsbeth."

"Hmmm," Dennis thought a moment. "We should probably run this by Jo." Jo was Dennis's nickname for his now-retired boss, Detective Jose Ortega, a name that Ortega hated, but learned to live with.

As if he heard his name from across the pond, Dennis's cell phone rang. "Jo!" Dennis answered cheerfully. "What's up? Aren't you supposed to be in Dublin by now?"

"We are," Ortega answered. "Penelope...er, Dr. Washburn and I arrived a coupla days ago. Still fighting off jet lag. Hey listen, my international cell plan is a joke, so I've got to make it quick."

"No problem, Jo. What do you need?"

"It just so happened that I got wind of some activity at the Vandenberg factory today. It's been dormant for years, and I was curious if you'd heard anything?"

"Actually, it's funny you ask. Emma just took a call from Baxter Baker. Maybe you should talk to her. Hang on."

Emma took the phone and quickly filled Ortega in on her conversation with Baxter, ending with, "What do you think I should do?"

"I think you should take the money and run," Ortega answered, bluntly.

"What?!" Emma was surprised.

"Look, Miss Post. I've seen this sort of thing a million times. Some wealthy family gets caught with their hands in the cookie jar, manages to skirt the law and then rebrand their business in a more wholesome way. They know it's not wise to continue their business dealings in the US, so they've set their sights on Ireland."

"If that's the case, shouldn't I sell off the property to someone else, like I'm doing in Florida?"

"What do you mean, 'like you're doing in Florida?'" Ortega's reaction seemed borderline aggressive. This was news to him.

"Yeah," Emma confirmed. "A nonprofit that sells healthy snacks to raise money to support young women and babies said the set up was perfect for their needs."

"Does this company have a name, by chance?" Ortega was suspicious.

"Honestly, I didn't think to ask," Emma confessed. "My lawyer handled all of it so I didn't have to deal with Mr. Lundy and the Vandenbergs." Mr. Lundy was the Vandenberg's primary attorney, and as such, Emma didn't trust him.

Dennis eyed Emma, questioningly. Emma covered the phone and said, "He's asking if we knew who wants to take over the Florida factory." Dennis motioned for Emma to hand him the phone. She obliged, keeping an ear close as Dennis spoke with Ortega.

"Jo," Dennis began, "want me to see what I can find out?"

"No!" Ortega all but yelled into the phone. "The family is dangerous.

Just connect me with your lawyer so I can ask him some questions, and I'll have Shep do some digging. Outside of that, I want the two of you to stay out of it entirely."

Dennis cringed. He wanted to help, but not only did he have no jurisdiction and wasn't in the position to legally do anything, but he dared not risk putting Emma in harm's way again, particularly given the fact they recently learned she was expecting a baby—their baby.

"So what can we do?" Dennis asked.

"Put Emma back on the phone," Ortega ordered. Then, catching himself, he added, "Please."

Emma took the cell phone.

"Listen Miss Post, my cell phone is about to die, and I just want to be sure to tell you one thing...I think you should take Baxter Baker's offer. It's the only way you'll get out from under that family's influence unscathed. Let me worry what happens after that, okay?"

Emma touched her belly, instinctively. "Okay," she answered. For once, not arguing just for the sake of it. "I'll let Mr. Baker know my decision."

CHAPTER 7
The Westport Grifters

Dublin

The Westport family resented being lumped into the 'Irish mob' category, when, in point of fact, they were neither mafia-related nor Irish. Their family fled to County Mayo sometime during the Russian Revolution, but conveniently, no one can find records of their original surnames. They became the Westports, and managed enough under-the-radar grifts to amass a small fortune. So while they may have been 'mob adjacent' they had a racket all their own. They even set up a side family jewelry business, selling gold-plated watches, manufactured gemstones and the like, careful to not overinflate the value of the items... just enough to turn a profit that would go unnoticed by tax collectors.

But they didn't take kindly to Vandenberg Nutraceuticals setting up a factory in Dublin—not because they were against big business coming to town—but because the Vandenberg's selling drug-laced nutrition bars to members of the Church of Infinite Love under the guise of 'faith healing' was too attention-grabbing a grift. The Westports were successful because they were largely unknown. Therefore, when the Vandenberg factory came to town, they resorted to doing a very mob-like thing...they began demanding money from the late founder and CEO, Erasmus Vandenberg, and his executives for personal and property protection...to the tune of 10% of the executives' annual salaries, along with 10% of the net profits of anything shipped out of the Dublin factory. They called it a 'tithe.' The irony was not lost on the Vandenberg family, though they didn't find it amusing.

Once the Florida factory began thriving, however, the Vandenberg's claimed the Dublin factory was no longer in service and shut it down. So the space sat there, dormant, and the Westports stopped demanding money. After all, if Vandenberg Nutraceuticals and the Church of Infinite Love were no longer drawing unwanted attention to Dublin by the authorities and the global media, then the Westports could safely manage their smaller business ventures without suspicion...until today.

"Mr. Westport," a young man dressed in street clothes and a ball cap cautiously approached the older man who was busy adding butter to the top of a blood pudding muffin before popping the entire pastry into his mouth. His dining habits didn't quite fit the sophisticated image the Westport family was going for, but none dared correct him.

Constantine Westport's throne-like chair had a personal dining table in front of it, both of which were on a raised platform that overlooked the main room of his mansion where he could see all corners of the space clearly. This large sitting area appeared more like one would find when visiting a castle and museum of some indeterminate past. As such, Constantine had all manner of 'historic-like' things, such as a metal suit of armor in one corner, a totem-like pole in the other, and a variety of tribal masks along the central wall. It was a beautiful room that echoed from the high ceilings...but one that really made no aesthetic sense.

"What is it, Scratch?" Constantine Westport asked, licking butter off of his thumb.

"I have some...troubling news." Scratch adjusted his cap, nervously.

"What news?" Constantine's deep blue eyes bore into Scratch's as if trying to read his thoughts. He shifted his large frame in his chair which squeezed beneath his weight as if in pain.

"Well, sir," Scratch continued. He knew that his boss hated small talk and word mincing. He got right to the point. "We have it on good authority that the Vandenberg Nutraceutical factory has resumed their operations as of this week." He paused, waiting for a reaction. He didn't have to wait long.

"What?!" Constantine slammed a meaty fist on the table, sending a cup of tea, along with an open bottle of Jameson sitting next to it, toppling clumsily to the floor, splattering tea and whiskey everywhere. Constantine paused to eye the hot liquid spilling down his hand before shaking it, angrily. Liquid dripped of his hand and onto his pants, the side of the table, and finally, the floor.

Within seconds, the housekeeper was there, mopping his hand off for him with a kitchen towel before she and another servant cleaned up the mess. The Jameson bottle remained unbroken. The same was not true of the shattered tea cup.

"Is Erasmus with them?" he asked.

"No, sir," Scratch answered. "Erasmus Vandenberg is dead."

"Well," Constantine reasoned, "he was pretty old."

"Actually, he was murdered...by one of his own, sir."

Constantine paused for a moment before a hearty laugh bubbled up from his belly. "Hah, well, I can't say as I'm surprised. Nice guy, but didn't understand the rules of the game."

A servant brought the large man a fresh cup of tea, her older hands shaking clumsily.

"Thank you, Iris," he acknowledged, taking the cup before she accidentally spilled it. Iris was getting on in years and could no longer handle many of the household chores she used to tend to, but Constantine valued loyalty above all else, and prided himself on adjusting her work to suit her aging body, making her in charge of hiring and training the younger staff. Iris was also tight-lipped, and that was a good quality to have among your staff when you're a grifter.

Iris nodded, seeming to vanish into the background, silently.

Constantine returned his attention to Scratch who was now busy plucking a bit of leftover breakfast from his teeth with a toothpick and wiping it on his jeans.

"So, who's heading up the operations now? Mordecai? Victor?"

"From what I hear, Baxter Baker, sir."

"Baxter?" Constantine let out a laugh. "That lazy, good-for-nothing playboy? Since when has he taken an interest in the family business?"

"Well, since Erasmus's untimely death, and with the Florida factory being shut down, seems it was in his financial best interest to resume operations here. He's also hired on a consultant."

"A consultant? What consultant?" Constantine demanded.

"Some guy named Jax," Scratch answered.

"Jacks, like a toilet?" Constantine snorted.

"His name is Jax Liebling, and he was involved in the Florida factory, but I don't know in what capacity."

"Who hires a guy who's named after a toilet?" Constantine couldn't let it go. He giggled and shot a glance toward a young servant whose name he hadn't learned yet. She giggled along, supportively, abruptly stopping as soon as her boss did. The room fell silent. "Well, whatever his name is, I'm none too fond of them drawing attention to Dublin again, particularly if, as you say, there were troubles in Florida," Constantine continued, "Are they aware of our rules?"

"Yes, sir," Scratch nodded. "In point of fact, Mr. Baker reached out to me."

"Really?" Constantine was surprised.

"Yeah." The young boy put his hands on his hips and shrugged his shoulders. "It seems Baxter has got a target on his back because he may have been the one who ratted out the family business."

"Why am I not surprised?" Constantine forcefully slapped the table. This time, the young attendant was ready, grabbing the tea cup and Jameson bottle before they could get knocked to the floor a second time.

"He's offering to pay you 15% of all net profits and 20% of his salary."

"Why so much?" Constantine was suspicious. "We were only charging 10% before."

"Because he doesn't just want your blessing to work in your territory," Scratch answered. "He wants your protection against his family. Says he'll cook the books so no one questions the 5% increase on the profit side."

Constantine let out a bellow, grabbing his cup of tea, cradling it in one large palm before taking a sip. After a long pause, he commented, "Cook the books." He laughed. "That's funny." After a long pause he offered, "Tell him we'll accept his deal...but I want 40% of his salary. I won't put my guys at risk for anything less."

CHAPTER 8
The Proposal

~

"You're still frightened of me," Jax stated. It was not a question. He and Midge were reclined on each end of the couch sipping cocktails in the middle of the weekday with their legs intertwined.

"Don't be silly, I'm not—" Midge stammered. She was not easily intimidated, nor flustered. And yet, around Jax, she seemed to be both.

"And you like it." He put his feet on the floor and slid over to her side of the couch, reaching past her to set his drink on the end table. A chill went up Midge's spine. He leaned in to whisper in her ear, "Admit it."

"A little," she confessed, tilting her head sideways as he kissed the side of her neck.

"You came all the way to Ireland to find me." He was so close to her that his torso rubbed against the side of her hip, erotically.

"Correction," Midge sucked in a breath, "you summoned me."

"And you came," he reminded her. "And then, you stayed. Why?"

"I don't know if you've noticed this or not Jax," Midge explained, leaning back to sip her beverage. "But bad things seem to happen to me and the people I know when you don't get your way."

"Whatever do you mean?" he asked, innocently, eyeing her lip as she wiped the bottom of it with her fingertips, holding her cocktail out to avoid spilling it.

"Really?" Midge replied. "I thought we already had this conversation. Remember this?" She pulled the strap of her dress off her shoulder, revealing a scar. "When you burned me with a cigarette because you thought I was hitting on a waitress...who later ended up mysteriously run over by a 'drunk driver' that night?"

Jax leaned in and kissed the scar. "Well, I'm sorry about that. But I had nothing to do with that slut you were flirting with."

"Bullshit." Midge stood, setting her cocktail on the end table by his and taking a step away from Jax, creating some distance between the two of them.

"You don't believe me?" Jax asked, innocently, standing.

Midge softened her voice, somewhat defeated, "I never believe you." She took another step back.

Jax looked pained. "That hurts." He grabbed his chest with one hand as if wounded in the heart. "So when I tell you that I love you and that you're the only woman for me, you don't believe that, either?"

"Not the way you show love, no," Midge answered.

A flicker of something that appeared like anger crossed Jax's eyes quickly and then disappeared, and yet, Midge could have sworn she saw actual flames of fire in them.

"Well," Jax backed away, tapping the fleshy part of his fist on his thigh as if tenderizing a steak. "What would I need to do to prove my love to you? Enough so that you stop running away from me?"

"Marry me," Midge answered.

"What?" Jax was surprised.

"You don't love me enough to marry me?" Midge challenged.

"I do," Jax tilted his head sideways. "I'm just very confused. One minute you're running away from me and telling me you never want to see me again. The next you ask me to marry you, after turning down multiple marriage proposals prior. I'm not sure you even know what you want!"

Midge took a tentative step toward Jax, shyly. "Maybe I'm partly to blame," Midge admitted.

"For what?" Jax grew suspicious. "You've never taken responsibility for anything in your life!" he laughed.

"Hey!" Midge whined, the New York in her accent growing stronger the more agitated she became. "A person can grow, alright?!"

Jax found this amusing and curious. While Midge's actions always seemed reckless to those around her, for him, they were crystal clear...until now. She agreed to marry him once before. They had gone as far as to apply for a license. Then she ran away, and now she was back again. Still, he was confident he would come to understand this supposed 'growth' phase soon enough. *Maybe she is just afraid of her feelings for me,* Jax told himself.

"And what have you discovered, baby," Jax encouraged, "that's causing this recognition that you might be partially to blame?"

Midge bit her tongue for a moment at Jax's all-too-willingness for him to let her cast blame on herself. It was fine when she did it, but she didn't need encouragement.

"I recognize that my friendliness might be construed by some as...encouragement."

"You mean the way you flirted with that waitress," he confirmed.

"Not flirting," Midge wagged a finger at him. "Friendliness."

"I see," Jax chuckled a little.

"But perhaps my friendliness has, in the past, been taken to mean a sexual or personal interest of which I did not intend."

"I hope you're not talking about you and me?" Jax leaned in again and nibbled her ear.

Midge shrank a little at his mouth on her neck. She knew she had a terrible weakness for him, and while she recognized that it made little sense to anyone else, for her, it felt insurmountable. And that was the problem, Jax was her Achilles heel. When she was around him for too long, it not only hurt her, physically, but she made big mistakes, far bigger than ones she'd ever have made on her own.

"Of course not," she whispered, leaning in and stealing a kiss. "I just mean that by marrying you and being a little more conscious of my interactions with other people, perhaps I can prove to you that I'm serious about us. I've had time to think it over and...I'm ready."

"So, no more running away?" Jax set down his drink and relieved her of her empty glass and set them on the coffee table. He took her face in his hands and put his forehead against hers in a mix of hope and disbelief.

"I promise to be loyal, but I need you to stop hurting me." Midge held her breath a moment, not entirely certain how this accusation would land.

"I promise to do my best," he finally agreed. "You know, I never mean to hurt you. I'm just so passionate about you, that when other people get in the way of us, it makes me furious."

"That brings me to another topic," Midge said.

"Really?" Jax moved back, still holding her face in his hands. "Are we almost done talking, so I can have my way with you again?"

"Almost," Midge agreed. "There's just one more thing."

"And what's that?" Jax asked.

"A wedding present."

"A wedding present," Jax repeated. "What exactly did you have in mind?"

"Rue Brennan," Midge answered. Jax tightened the grip on her face angrily digging his thumbs into her cheeks deeply enough to leave marks. "Ow! What did we just talk about?" Midge reminded him.

Jax released his grip and leapt to his feet. Once he'd reached the kitchen counter across the room, he slammed it with the side of his fist. "How am I supposed to keep my wits about me when you rile me up so easily. What about Rue Brennan?" he spat.

"She's in Ireland," Midge answered.

"What? Why? How?" Jax was confused.

"Apparently, she and Detective Ortega, the guy who grilled you after those models died, remember?" Midge paused for confirmation.

"Of course, I remember," Jax's face took on a crimson and purple hue. He couldn't mask how enraged he felt.

"Well, somehow Ortega got tangled up in the Vandenberg case, and since Rue Brennan was a former member of the Church of Infinite Love, she's here to help him shut down the church's operations, for good."

"Does she know you're here?" Jax asked.

"What? No! How could she?" Midge played innocent, leaving out the minor detail that she was the very reason Rue discovered that the church and Vandenberg Nutraceuticals was planning to rebrand and set up shop in Ireland instead of the States, at least until the scandal had blown over and the cops lost interest.

"She followed you," Jax nodded. "Did you lead her to me? Or even worse, did you lead her on?" Jax stood over Midge with an angry expression that she'd come to know all too well. It took every ounce of courage to remain calm.

"No, my husband-to-be," Midge batted her eyes at him. "I have nothing to do with her being here, but I can get rid of her."

"How?" Jax asked. "Are you finally going to shoot her, like we should have done back in her apartment two years ago when we had the chance?"

"Something like that," Midge grinned at him.

"Is she supposed to be my wedding present?" Jax eyed her with sudden interest.

Midge smiled at him seductively. "Now you're catching on." She slid up to his chest and touched a hand lightly just below his collar bone. "While there isn't much I can do when Ortega invariably comes knocking at the factory door looking for you, I can at least provide a distraction. I'm sure Rue's disappearance will rattle his nerves a bit."

"Disappearance?" Jax asked. "Do I get to watch?"

"No, my dear hubby," Midge answered, kissing him on his chin. "If I've learned anything from hanging around with you is that it's much cleaner covering your tracks when there's no body and no weapon to be found."

"Then how will I know when you've done it? A picture?" Jax asked.

"A picture that I'd have to take to a Fotomat to have developed?!" Midge was incredulous. "No, too risky. But don't worry," she assured him, "I have something much better in mind."

CHAPTER 9
Moira Dodd

Dublin

People either liked Baxter Baker or they hated him. There was never any in between. He could usually tell within thirty seconds into which camp a person fell. Baxter didn't care either way. He knew he was, by most people's standards, handsome, charming and quick-witted. It didn't hurt that his family came from money and that he successfully maintained his role as regional manager at Vandenberg Nutraceuticals for nearly a decade. Therefore, if someone didn't like him, they were simply *wrong*. The fact that he was now assuming the role of Chief Executive Officer further solidified his feelings of self-worth, not that they were ever in question.

There were exceptions to this rule, of course. Namely that most of the Vandenberg family got wind that Baxter was likely responsible for procuring incriminating evidence against both Vandenberg Nutraceuticals and the Church of Infinite Love who, as it turned out, were both led by the late great business tycoon Erasmus Vandenberg. Both the Elders of the church and the executives of Vandenberg Nutraceuticals had it in for

Baxter. Were it not for the intervention of opportunist Jax Liebling and Erasmus's personal lawyer and as-needed 'remover of obstacles,' Mr. Lundy, they would have made sure that Baxter Baker disappeared, permanently.

Instead, Jax convinced the family to lay low during police investigations in the States, letting Baxter, and Baxter alone, assume the role as the new CEO and 'face' of the Church of Infinite Love, while the Elders carefully remained in the shadows. Jax was to become a silent partner who served in an 'advisory' capacity to Vandenberg Nutraceuticals. Meanwhile, he also suggested that Vandenberg executives promptly resign from their positions and disavow knowing about any wrong-doing that led to the death of several members of the church over the years—not to mention the long-running faith healing scam that made them millions. Well, everyone but Baxter.

And so, Baxter took over the one remaining factory, located in Dublin, where he now resided. Mr. Lundy saw to it that Baxter was released from police custody and anything tying Baxter to the case surrounding Erasmus Vandenberg was conveniently wiped clean. And after all of Baxter's proclamations of having a change of heart, the money and the title were too good to pass up. What he didn't realize, however, was that he wasn't merely putting up a good front for the family...he was being set up as scapegoat.

And yet, Baxter strolled into the Dublin office at 10:15 a.m. midweek with all the swagger of someone who didn't have multiple people who wanted to kill him, along with his usual clear sense of entitlement, yet no sense of responsibility. He prided himself on being proactive in buying out the remaining shares from Emma Post with the help of Jax Liebling and, eventually, his cousin Elsbeth, of course. And whether warranted or not, he felt confident that being under the wing of the Westports would afford him protection...well, mostly confident.

He brushed a lock of blonde hair away from one eye and winced a little. The gunshot wound he'd received recently still stung on occasion, causing his gate to be a little wider and more awkward when he was walking. Yet somehow, this only served to make him more attractive to women...well, most women.

"Good morning, Mr. Baker," a lilting voice greeted him.

Surprised, he turned to eye the strange woman sitting behind the reception desk. She had a small frame and the desk seemed to all but swallow her whole. She had a round face with even rounder black-rimmed glasses that made her green eyes shine larger than life. Her fiery red hair was tied back in a tight bun.

"I'm sorry, but who are you?" Baxter asked.

"Your associate, Mr. Liebling, hired me as your new assistant," she explained. "I'm Moira Dodd. It's a pleasure to meet you." She stretched a long arm across the desk, but remained seated.

"I see," Baxter answered. (He really didn't.)

Baxter eyed the Moira curiously. She wasn't entirely unpleasant to look at, he decided. Perhaps if she let her hair down? Wore contacts? Perhaps traded in that awful rose-colored blouse that she was wearing for something a little less matronly?

Baxter walked over to the desk, taking her hand and cradling it between his palms. "It's a pleasure to meet you, too, Moira." He held her gaze longer than necessary and flashed a devilish grin. "Perhaps you and I should become more acquainted if we're going to be working together."

"How so?" Moira asked.

"Well, maybe I could take you to dinner at the Mulberry Garden, followed by a stroll through the Temple Bar? A drive to the Cliffs of Moher for a hike, if you're feeling adventurous?"

Moira paused for an inordinately long time before answering. "Not sure I'm up for a stroll nor a hike, Mr. Baker."

Moira's torso moved backward as she wheeled her way around the desk. It was only then that Baxter realized that Moira was sitting in a wheelchair. The corner of her mouth turned up in a grin. And, while she never lost that sparkle in her eyes, one thing was very clear to Baxter. *She did not like him.*

Baxter was quick on his feet. "My apologies, Miss Dodd...or is it Mrs. Dodd?" He glanced down at her left hand, but she had inconveniently covered it by laying her right palm across it and resting them in her lap.

"You might have thought to ask that before you began hitting on me," she replied curtly.

Baxter was confused. Her voice was songlike, but he couldn't quite place her accent...Irish...Scottish...Welsh? Perhaps it would have been easier had he spent more time in Ireland prior to his recent relocation. But that wasn't the confusing part. What had him stumped was that although her words dripped of sarcasm, her voice was ever sweet, as was the expression on her face.

"I beg your pardon," Baxter defended, lifting his nose as if offended. "I most certainly was not hitting on you. I was merely being cordial. If we are to work together, we should get to know one another." This was uncharacteristic of Baxter who prided himself on being true to his nature and making no apologies for it.

"With all due respect, Mr. Baker, that's a load of crap and we both know it," Moira said, as gentle as ever, peering up at him. "Now, if you're any sort of a gentleman, you'll take a seat, so I don't have to get a neck cramp staring up at you and so that you don't appear so domineering."

Baxter opened his mouth to speak, but closed it again. He'd never had anyone, particularly not an employee, talk back to him. The closest he'd come to that was Emma Post, the woman who inherited the bulk of Erasmus's fortune, and one of the few he'd actually started developing feelings for. But whereas Emma was brazen, fiery and fierce, Moira's wit was like a well-sharpened blade, the kind that took a moment before you'd even realized you'd been cut.

Baxter merely smiled, and rolled his office chair from behind his desk, and stationed it in front of Moira, where he took a seat in front of her so they could meet eye-to-eye.

"That's better," Moira nodded. "Now before you go talking about getting to know one another...which, you'll agree, would be highly inappropriate, anyway, seeing as how I'm working for you, and that automatically puts you in a position of authority—" Baxter opened his mouth to speak, but Moira held up a delicate hand to silence him. "Don't you think we should talk about my responsibilities here?"

For the second time, Baxter was confused. Never having taken much responsibility at his work prior, he wasn't entirely certain what to expect from Moira. People who worked for him previously just sort of...knew what they were supposed to do without being asked.

"Didn't Mr. Liebling explain the role, seeing as he hired you?" Baxter asked.

Moira let out a songlike chuckle. "The only thing he explained to me,

Mr. Baker, is that he point-blank hired me because I was just pretty and professional enough to make a good impression with the media and potential investors, but not so attractive that you'd be distracted by me."

"How on earth could I not be distracted by you?" Baxter questioned softly with a genuineness that surprised even himself.

"Em," Moira rolled back and forth in her chair. "Not exactly your type, am I? I mean, Mr. Liebling seems to think you only have eyes for saucy athletic girls and skinny, long legged supermodel types. And, as you can see, Mr. Baker, I'm am neither of those."

"Well, Moira," Baxter said calmly. "It seems to me that Mr. Liebling doesn't know me very well at all."

CHAPTER 10
Shooting Lesson

Edgar's Leitrim Estate

Shots rang out in the air as Elsbeth downed a clay pigeon. It shattered mercilessly, landing in pieces on the ground.

"Great going!" Isaac yelled. Isaac was her Uncle Edgar's personal assistant. He smiled at Elsbeth, and then, realizing that she couldn't possibly hear him with her protective headgear, gave her a thumbs up. She smiled back, momentarily lowering her semi-automatic target shotgun before he quickly pointed to the ground.

Isaac then unleashed a clay rabbit, nearly catching the girl off guard. She hoisted her gun back up and quickly took aim. It took her several rounds, but she finally hit it, its head flying off in a large chunk.

The clay rabbits, Elsbeth decided, were not as fun as flying clay pigeons. For one thing, they were slightly easier for her to hit and they didn't splinter into a thousand pieces in midair and spray every which way, which is how Elsbeth preferred it.

Uncle Edgar signaled for her to lower her weapon, which she did. He followed suit, setting his gun on a long table from which the two were safely stationed behind, away from the field. He removed his safety goggles and earmuffs and motioned for her to do the same.

"Well done, my dear," he praised. "Just give me a moment, won't you?" Edgar unloaded his shotgun before doing the same with Elsbeth's. When he was confident all safety precautions were taken, he called out to Isaac, "All clear!" He waved his arms in the air. Isaac waved back, his sign that it was safe to clear the field, which really meant nothing more than for Isaac to gather the non-used targets and gently rake the field to spread the clay remains around evenly. Since they were biodegradable, he only wanted to encourage them to decompose faster by ensuring there were no unnecessary piles in one particular area of the field.

Edgar turned to Elsbeth. "I must say, you're far better at this than Baxter. I wouldn't have expected it from—"

"A girl?" Elsbeth finished, saltily.

"I was going to say, for someone who hasn't been shooting for very long." Edgar winked at his niece. "Your mother, Edwina, was pretty good at it, but too impatient to really develop the skills. And then," he sighed, "she got so wrapped up in the church that she stopped visiting altogether...pity."

Elsbeth nodded, "W-w-w-ell," she stammered. "E-enough about her." Elsbeth furrowed her eyes, confused. She had faked the stutter for so long out of fear, that the mere mention of her mother actually set her off again.

"Let's talk about something else," Edgar answered, gently, wrapping an arm around her.

Moments later, Isaac joined them as they walked back toward the house.

"Did you show her your venomous snake room yet?" Baxter called from the house as he made his way toward them.

"Back again?" Edgar was surprised. "Aren't you supposed to be under cover or something?"

"Protection," Baxter answered, after catching up with the trio. "The Westport goons are surveying the property as we speak."

One such 'goon' overheard Baxter, tilting his head and muttering, "What an arse," before promptly returning to his routine.

"Sorry," Baxter cringed. "I was just kidding, of course."

"Feck off," the guard answered, flicking Baxter the finger.

"You make friends everywhere you go, it seems," Edgar laughed. "But how did we not notice them. Isaac?" he questioned.

Isaac shrugged. "Not used to anyone caring too much about the likes of us," he replied. "I barely remember ta lock the house at night, half ta time."

"Hmmm," Edgar thought, rubbing a tired eye. "We should probably make it a point to start doing that."

"Aye," Isaac nodded. "Particularly with this mug around." He shot a glance at Baxter who merely smiled as if he had just been given a compliment.

Baxter sidled up next to Elsbeth and asked, "When did you get here?"

"A couple days ago," she answered.

"Does your mother know you're here?" he wondered.

"What do you think?" She frowned. "I can't even go to the bathroom without her asking about my bowel movements."

Baxter snorted. "Well then, I should probably be sure to head out soon. If I have a target on my back, I don't want to put you in danger."

"What makes you think mother wants to hurt you?" Elsbeth was surprised.

"After the evidence I supplied to the cops about Vandenberg Nutraceuticals and the church?" His voice rose in pitch. "Let's just say, I'm glad it was you on the field today and not Edwina."

Elsbeth thought back to why she was there. It had been Rue Brennan's friend, Midge, who convinced her that she'd be safer in Ireland with Uncle Edgar while the dust settled on the home front. She'd only met Midge once in Rue and Darwin's condo, and yet, the woman's energy made an impression on her, somehow.

"Will ya be wantin' dinner, Baxter?" Isaac finally asked as the four made their way indoors. "Gonna begin preppin' shortly."

"No, thank you, Isaac," Baxter answered, touched that he even had an invitation. Although, he typically just showed up while an angry Isaac plopped food on his plate and complained about not making enough. Therefore, Baxter reasoned, perhaps Edgar's personal servant was just being proactive.

Issac nodded and peeled away from the group, heading toward the kitchen.

"I'm heading this way," Baxter pointed toward the study. "Won't you join me, Elsbeth?"

"Can't," Elsbeth answered. "Edgar is showing me his body collection."

"I'm sorry...what?" Baxter was certain he'd misheard his cousin.

"The bodies," she repeated, a little louder this time.

"She's exaggerating just a little bit," Edgar answered, uncomfortably. "I happened to have attended an exhibit on the ancient Jivaro of Ecuador and was able to procure a few historic remains for my collection. Different from my usual, I know, but just as fascinating."

"You mean like shrunken heads, and such?" Baxter asked, surprised.

"Heads, teeth, some clothing and weapon samples, basic stuff, really," Edgar explained, leaning in as if sharing a secret. "Except for a couple of fairly well-preserved corpses...mums the word," he whispered.

"But I thought you only collected reptiles and poisonous bugs and things?"

"Well," Edgar explained, chuckling, "this is a bit of a departure from my usual, but curiosity got the better of me."

Baxter swallowed with some difficulty. With the threat of violence looming over his head, he found Edgar's recent collection to be somewhat unsettling. Baxter couldn't understand it. Edgar was so against killing anything that he insisted on clay pigeons and rabbits instead of hunting and made it a habit of saying a Native American prayer over dinner anytime Isaac prepared meat. Yet, he was fascinated by deadly plants, animals and insects that killed other things...now, add humans to that list.

"Would you like to join us?" Edgar asked.

"Pass," Baxter held up a hand. "But you two go ahead." He touched Elsbeth on the shoulder. "Er, but stop in for a chat once you're done, won't you?" he asked.

"Sure, Baxter," Elsbeth nodded before heading off to view Edgar's newest additions to his collection.

Baxter shuddered, wondering how exactly he ended up with such a strange family.

CHAPTER 11

Not What He Seemed

Edgar's Leitrim Estate

~

"You shouldn't be here, Elsbeth," Baxter chastised his younger cousin after they found a moment to themselves.

"Nice to see you too, Baxter," Elsbeth answered flatly, walking over to the whiskey decanter sitting atop the mini bar in the corner of Edgar's study. She picked up a tumbler and splashed a hearty pour into it.

"Since when do you drink?" Baxter was surprised, glancing down at his own pint of Guinness and wishing he could chase it down with a shot of Jameson, but he dared not. He had to keep his wits about him these days.

"Since the moment I realized how nutty our family was," she plopped down on a leather chair across from her cousin and crossed her legs, one bouncing nervously as she sat.

"So...age three?" Baxter joked.

Elsbeth smiled. There was a glimmer of the care-free Baxter she used to know and sometimes even liked.

Ever since Baxter agreed to help Elsbeth's grandfather Erasmus gather evidence against the church and the family, he had become slightly more serious, more...*what was the word?* Elsbeth thought to herself. *Hesitant. That was it.* Frankly, she missed the more annoying, cavalier Baxter. It was a fun departure from the household her mother Edwina ran.

Elsbeth, herself, not wanting to grow up in the family business and being too afraid to stand up to them, feigned a learning disability and incurable stutter. An embarrassment to the church, Edwina did her best to keep Elsbeth out of the public eye as having an 'abnormal' daughter flew in the face of the church's claims to faith healing.

Elsbeth took a sip of her whiskey, trying not to sneeze as the aroma tickled her nose. Baxter stifled a laugh.

"I miss Grandfather Erasmus," Elsbeth lamented. "He was a good deal better than the lot of 'em." Baxter let out a snort. "What's so funny?" she demanded.

"Dear old Erasmus may have developed a conscience in his old age, maybe even bought into his own hype and had the fear of God and eternal damnation on the brain, but he wasn't at all the man you thought he was." Baxter stretched an arm out over one side of the couch and thumped his fingers on the back of it.

"How dare you say that!" Elsbeth's face turned beet red. "He was the only one who was kind to me, even when everyone else treated me as if there was something wrong with me! He loved me."

"While that may be true, though I take slight offense that you don't think I care about you, did it never occur to you that perhaps he felt guilty that his healthy snack bars may have permanently damaged you?" Baxter pointed out.

"Are you implying that my grandfather Erasmus was only nice to me because he felt sorry for me?" Elsbeth blinked, fighting back tears that were stinging her eyes. It was true that at a young age, Edwina filled her up on those 'healthy' church-branded bars as a way to control her. This caused abnormal side effects that she only discovered after innocently swapping lunch snacks with a young girl in grade school. The girl had a seizure. Elsbeth got better. From then on, Elsbeth only pretended to eat her snacks and kept the illusion of having a disorder out of concern over what might happen if her mother learned the truth.

"I'm merely pointing out that you are lionizing a man who wasn't as nice as you seem to think he was."

Elsbeth all but dropped her glass on the end table with a thud and crossed her arms like an angry child. "Well, he was a good deal better than you," she pouted.

Baxter sighed. He had bigger things to worry about than placating his cousin. "I'm sure he was," he conceded. "But I've never pretended to be anything other than exactly who I am."

Elsbeth slunk back and sank into the couch. "A jerk," she blurted out.

Baxter took another sip of Guinness and nodded in agreement. "Can't argue with that."

That broke Elsbeth, who covered her mouth so he couldn't see her stifling a laugh. Her shoulders and belly quivered a little. It was contagious, and moments later, Baxter let out a boisterous laugh, and for the next several minutes, he couldn't stop. It had been quite some time since he'd laughed and he needed it.

Finally, Elsbeth asked, "Okay, I'll bite. What do you know about our late Erasmus that I don't know?"

At that moment, Baxter heard the sound of a motor car and jumped uneasily. He glanced out the window and breathed a sigh of relief as he watched a black Mini Cooper purposefully meandering up the driveway.

"What's that all about?" Elsbeth asked.

"Protection," Baxter explained. "They'll be popping in to check on me in just a moment, so let me make this brief."

"I'm listening," Elsbeth answered.

"You weren't even born when most of this was happening," Baxter began, draining his beverage and placing it on the coffee table without a coaster. As if the sound of a water ring staining the furniture could be heard like an emergency siren, Isaac appeared out of nowhere, grabbed the glass and wiped the table off with a white towel. He paused to grimace at Baxter before leaving the room as soundlessly as he'd entered.

Baxter continued, "Didn't you ever find it odd how Erasmus Vandenberg, business mogul and multimillionaire, could suddenly take charge of the Church of Infinite Love *and* ensure that our family ran both companies simultaneously?"

"You just said it, yourself, Erasmus was a business mogul."

"Three decades ago, Vandenberg Nutraceuticals was on the verge of bankruptcy." Elsbeth sat up, surprised, but said nothing. "Dear Erasmus was approached by then church Elder, Herman Armory, a longtime resident of the Emerald Isle. The church was having trouble selling faith healing and Armory had an idea."

"The birth of the 'healing' nutrition bars," Elsbeth answered, putting 'healing' in air quotes.

"Exactly, snacks to treat everything from pain, anxiety, fatigue, depression and insomnia all specially branded for the church to be used in its healing ceremonies. Suddenly, Vandenberg Nutraceuticals is back in business and the church is raking in a fortune off of those who are desperate enough to try anything to ease their suffering." Baxter saw Elsbeth's expression change. "I know what you're thinking."

"Do you?" Elsbeth asked.

"You're wondering what happened to Armory."

"That's right," Elsbeth admitted. She may have thought Baxter was a louse sometimes, but he was a good deal smarter than most gave him credit for.

"He died under mysterious circumstances, along with several others among the Elders of the church, all within a one-year period."

"And no one became suspicious?" Elsbeth was dumbfounded.

"Of course people became suspicious...particularly when Vandenberg Nutraceuticals set up a second location in Dublin." Baxter lowered his voice to a whisper. "The Westports weren't too keen on having Erasmus encroach on their territory."

"The Westports?" Elsbeth asked. "You mean the grift—"

"Ahem," Baxter cleared his throat as a young security officer, dressed all in black, stepped soundlessly into the room. Baxter looked up at the man, shooting Elsbeth a sideways glance.

"The perimeter is secure, Mr. Baker," the man announced. "But we should get you back to Clontarf before dark."

"Of course, Scratch. Give me ten minutes?"

"Aye," Scratch answered, eyeing Elsbeth with considerable interest.

"My cousin, Elsbeth," Baxter explained, before adding quickly, "she's under the Westport protection as well. Constantine is sending Dough to look after her." The corner of Scratch's mouth turned up in a sly grin. "So, don't get any funny ideas!"

"Hmph," Scratch scowled. "What d'ya take me fer, anyhow?"

"Ten minutes," Baxter repeated.

Scratch nodded. "I'll jest be in the cahr then, yeah?" The young man retreated.

"What the hell was that all about?" Elsbeth asked.

"The long and short of it?" Baxter finished. "Rumor has it that dear old Erasmus teamed up with Lundy, your mother, Bernie, Mordecai, Victor, and the rest of the Elders to take the original leaders out, one at a time."

"You mean murder?!" Elsbeth's eyes grew wide. "Not dear Erasmus! I don't believe it!" Elsbeth stood, folded her arms and stamped her foot like a small child.

Baxter looked up at her. "And they tried to pin the murders on the Westports."

"I assume you have proof of all this?" Elsbeth was incredulous. And yet, deep down, she knew Baxter was telling the truth. At least, he was telling the truth as far as he saw it. Perhaps her fear of telling Erasmus and Edwina her secret 'miracle' return to health was because a part of her knew that it was the safest option.

"Not really," Baxter answered. "I was working on it before all at the shit hit the fan when Erasmus died and left his money to Emma Post."

"But how come that goon—" Elsbeth motioned toward the driveway, "is looking after you? Isn't he a Westport henchman?"

"He is," Baxter nodded. "But the Westports aren't typically in the murder game. They didn't like being framed any more than they liked Vandenberg Nutraceuticals and the Church of Infinite Love encroaching on their territory—and being obvious about it in the process."

"So, what did they do?" Elsbeth asked.

"They demanded money for 'renting' space in their territory."

"How were they planning to enforce that if they aren't in the murder business?" Elsbeth wanted to know.

"I didn't say they *wouldn't* resort to murder, just that they might try other painful and persuasive methods first."

"Hmmm," Elsbeth thought a moment. "Is that why Erasmus eventually closed the Dublin factory and moved to Florida?"

"Bingo," Baxter confirmed. "He used to joke that in Florida, you could get away with just about anything...and get people to pay you to do it!"

The lights on the Mini flickered through the window.

"Listen, I gotta go." Baxter stood.

"Where are you going? Clontarf, did he say?"

"Better if you don't know, exactly. I'll contact you again when I can, or you can come by the factory during business hours. It's a public place and I don't think anyone would risk harming me there."

"Hmmm, not so sure about that." Elsbeth was uncertain.

"Let's hope you're wrong," Baxter answered, his voice cracking a little. "In the meantime, Dough should be arriving soon. He's a tall, overweight leprechaun with a curly ginger beard and mustache. I've already let Edgar and Isaac know."

"What is this Dough supposed to do for me, exactly?"

"Protect you," Baxter answered. "After all, you were responsible for helping the police uncover the truth about the Vandenberg family the moment you stepped into the Florida factory." Elsbeth cringed. *How'd he know about that?* In the recent past, Elsbeth aided Emma Post in sneaking into the factory to investigate. The family may not have known that at the time, but by now, they may have figured it out.

Chills went up Elsbeth's spine. Desperate to get away from Edwina, she was hoping that Midge was right, and that hiding out at Uncle Edgar's estate in Leitrim for a while would be safety enough. She was wrong.

CHAPTER 12

Gaslighting

Dublin

Bernie Forger met with a small ensemble of church Elders in a reserved conference room at the Alexander Hotel in Dublin. Notably absent were members from the Vandenberg lineage, and a few Ambassadors unable or unwilling to make the trip to the Emerald Isle. There were, of course, a handful of Elders whose whereabouts were a mystery, but Bernie dismissed any concern about them.

No matter, Bernie thought. He was just being tested by God. He knew it.

He stood at a podium wearing a blue suit and matching tie. His crisp white shirt had been starched so severely that you could hear it crackle as he moved.

"How long before we go live?" he asked, wiping beads of sweat from his brow with a handkerchief.

"Five minutes," Mr. Lundy answered, sitting beside Jax Liebling at a long conference table. Meanwhile, one of the church Ambassadors dotted

Bernie's face with powder until he grew frustrated and shooed the man away. "I'm certain it's fine," he muttered.

A hired videographer and IT specialist announced, "Places!" His sound technician nodded, making minor adjustments to a large soundboard sitting on the table in front of him. Meanwhile, a backup cameraman stood at the ready, there to capture the side angles of Bernie as he spoke, and to prepare for scene changes when they transitioned in and out of commercial breaks.

Finally, the moment arrived, and Bernie's Ambassador, a make-up artist who doubled as a show runner, announced with mounting excitement, "We are live in 5-4-3-2-1..." He gave Bernie the thumbs up.

"Ladies and gentlemen," Bernie addressed the camera, squinting at the bright lights that were stationed in front of him and flanked him on each side. He did his best to ignore them and focus on the message.

Just then, the sound of a wailing child could be heard outside the conference room door, followed by a mother shushing the child as they hurried past the room. A flash of anger crossed Bernie's face before he regained composure, joking to the camera, "Blessed are the children, for they shall lead the way."

An amen erupted from a non-existent crowd, manufactured by the audio engineer.

Bernie scanned the room, as if addressing thousands. In truth, he may have been, as this live broadcast was being aired at the Church of Infinite Love locations throughout parts of Europe and the United States. However, he couldn't see the crowds that had gathered. In point of fact, he couldn't even be sure that many crowds *were* gathered. The media attention had not been good for the church and membership had been suffering. And while he tried to give the illusion that he was addressing many, there were fewer than a dozen people in the room during his speech, himself included.

"It is written that the closer we become to the Almighty, the more the Devil will try and smite us down. The recent persecution of the church by the media and those who claim to be of 'the law' is a clear indication that the End Times are near." He paused for dramatic effect. "Now," he continued, "you, the faithful, bear witness to this pivotal moment in history when nearly half of the flock has fallen away. This is not due to the failings of the church. This is not even due to the false claims that the church was responsible for the deaths of a few members who turned their backs on God." Bernie paused again, scanning the fake audience before looking directly into the camera. "No, this is because our God continually sets the bar higher and higher, and only the chosen ones, his most righteous, will ever join him as great leaders in the Kingdom of Heaven."

"Amen," Jax, the make-up artist, and Mr. Lundy said from the audience. The sound technician strategically added a few shuffles and ambient noise from the fake audience, along with a few 'amens' and 'yes's' from the audio mixer.

"For that reason," Bernie continued, "we have to be diligent in our understanding of Him." He looked toward the heavens. "We need to be spending less time watching television and reading newspapers and more time studying and understanding his word."

Jax bristled a little. *This isn't part of the script. What is Bernie up to?* He eyed Lundy who sat there, expressionless. They had gone over the speech just that morning.

Bernie held up a small book. "The Church of Infinite Love is proud to announce that it is starting its very own publishing house. Beginning in the new year, we will be selling—at a nominal fee to members, of course—a series of educational materials meant to simplify the Bible and distill the wisdom of God into a message that is digestible to all ages, particularly our youth."

The cameraman held up his hand, indicating that Bernie had less than thirty seconds to finish his message before they had to switch to a commercial.

"That's not all," Bernie announced, a gleam in his eyes. "As we know, the children are our future. Therefore, I'm also excited to share that the church is breaking ground on a new facility in Belfast that will serve as an educational school for our youth. Tell you more about it after the break."

The cameraman indicated that Bernie was off air, and quickly switched to footage to some generic instrumental music and a backdrop of what appeared to be a large audience. The stock footage was meant to convince viewers that this, in fact, was the crowd in which Bernie had been speaking. It was a delicate balance, the messaging they were going for. The crowds had to appear just large enough to feel as if the message were worthwhile and important, but not so many that people no longer felt special and unique.

"You've got about five minutes, Mr. Forger," the show runner announced before pouncing to add more powder to Bernie's brow as a few beads of perspiration were forming across his forehead.

"A towel might be better, don't you think?" Bernie complained. "These lights are hotter than Hades!"

"Interesting choice of words," Jax sneered at him. "And by the way, where *did* those words come from?" he challenged. "You were supposed to discuss the rebranding of Vandenberg Nutraceuticals and how support of the company's new direction will directly impact the work of the church."

"And that's exactly what I'm doing," Bernie defended. "After the break, I fully intend to share how the sale of our refined snack bars will help feed the kids in Kenya and poorer populations, etc. etc., and how a portion of the proceeds will also go toward educational materials and the new publishing house."

"What publishing house?" Jax challenged. "What new school? This is all news to me!" Jax didn't like being kept in the dark about such things where money and power were concerned.

"We're back in thirty seconds," the show runner alerted.

Bernie took his place at the podium and said, "You're in charge of overseeing the factory, and that's all! You have no say whatsoever in the direction of the church."

Jax's face turned an odd shade of red mixed with a little purple as a vein stood out on the side of his temple. He moved toward the podium, arm raised, when Mr. Lundy intercepted. Lundy, being a large man, had no trouble body-blocking Jax. "Let's step outside," he whispered, just as the camera's started rolling again.

Once they were a safe distance from the room, Lundy offered, "Join me for a drink." He motioned toward the hotel bar and restaurant, empty at this time of morning, save for a few jet-lagged travelers having coffee and pastries in one corner of the room. To the bartender he asked, "Can I get a drink for my associate?" To Jax, he asked, "What'll you have?"

"Midleton," Jax spat out. "If you have it."

The bartender eyed Lundy for confirmation. "We have it, but er—"

"It's fine," Lundy replied, reaching into his suit pocket and pulling out a large wad of bills and laying several on the counter.

"Make it a double," Jax sneered, knowing full well how expensive a pour was, given that the distillery had been closed for more than two decades, making what was left a rare find. "Neat."

"Is there any other way?" the bartender nodded, smiling. "What about you?" he asked Lundy. "The same?"

"Oh no," Lundy answered. "Never touch the stuff. Just a club soda with lime, thanks."

The bartender set two coasters down and placed their drinks on them. Jax took a moment to swirl the glass in his palm, sniffing the whiskey's aroma appreciatively before taking a sip. His mood lifted slightly.

"Better?" Lundy asked.

"Only a little," Jax answered, still fuming. "Why the hell wasn't I let in on these new developments? I thought I was part of this operation?"

"You are," Lundy confirmed, "but there's a reason you were kept in the dark."

"What reason might that be?" Jax questioned, taking another sip.

"Bernie's a hot head," Lundy reasoned. "Not rational like you and I."

The irony was lost on Jax, who merely nodded.

"The point is, I had to make it look like he had a leg up on you, so he could feel more in control. And I needed you to be convincingly surprised. Which, you were. Well done."

"What are you up to?" Jax asked, suspiciously.

"Bernie's a loose cannon," Lundy answered. "If he had his way, he'd take his whole 'armor of God' speech and start his own army—literally. No, you're the one I see running the school as president. That is, if you want it. After all, you are an educator."

Jax thought back to his days as an in-house artist and instructor at the Atelier in New York. He'd never gotten the recognition he deserved back then, but maybe now?

"Bernie will never go for that," Jax complained. "How are you going to convince him?"

"I like to think of it more as a 'we,'" Lundy pointed at the space between he and Jax. "I've got an idea. Meet me back here after Bernie and his crew have wrapped up for the day. For now—" Lundy took a sip of his previously untouched club soda before plunking the glass back on the bar. "We should get back in there. Bernie will wonder where we've gone."

~

LUNDY SLIPPED OUT of the taping a few minutes early and had a double-shot of whiskey awaiting Jax's arrival. Given that Jax's favorite was no longer in production, it cost a pretty penny. Even the bartender was befuddled, but Lundy tipped well, so he didn't ask any questions.

"Do you have a menu?" Lundy asked quietly. He was surprisingly meek for such a looming man with an imposing presence.

"Certainly," the bartender reached behind the counter and drew a small, laminated page filled with bar bites and handed it to Lundy. There was nothing on there that would suit Jax's expensive taste, so Lundy improvised. "What can you get me from the main dining room that will look like a modest bar menu item but will satisfy someone who likes to think he has a refined pallet?" The bartender chortled, until he saw that Lundy wasn't laughing. "I'll make it worth your while," Lundy promised. "I just don't have time to waste on a four-course dinner."

"Hmm," the bartender thought a moment. "I might be able to rustle up a few lamb chops a la carte."

"Excellent," Lundy nodded. "Any foie gras or pâté?"

"I've got a chicken liver pâté."

"Can you smear it on a small burger and set it on a bed of lettuce and call it a foie gras and sirloin small plate?" Lundy slipped him a few bills.

The bartender nodded. "For that price, I'll call it anything you like. I'll even throw in a jig if you want." He danced a moment from side to side, bending his arms in the process.

"That won't be necessary," he answered, just as Jax made his appearance. Jax had an odd expression on his face, and his lips twitched as if he were having a conversation with someone who wasn't there. His mood lifted when he saw the beverage. *Finally, someone treating him the way he deserved to be treated.*

"Hope you don't mind," Lundy explained. "But I've put in an order for few small plates while we chat."

Jax nodded and reached for his beverage. Meanwhile, Lundy sat with his usual club soda and lime.

"How did the rest of the taping go?" Lundy asked. "Sorry I had to miss it, but I had other family matters to attend to."

"It was Bernie being Bernie," Jax lamented. "He all but incited his audience to violence in defense of maintaining the 'old ways.'"

"Well, the man is steadfast in his beliefs, I'll give him that," Lundy acknowledged.

"He's got a God complex, if you ask me," Jax complained, sucking down his whiskey and motioning for another.

"I'm afraid you've polished off our only bottle of Midleton," the bartender explained. Before Jax could express his discontent, the server offered, "I've got a small batch, 25-year-old Teeling though?"

"Fine," Jax blurted out, as if he shouldn't have to use his energy to answer questions from a mere bartender.

Several other hotel guests began to wander into the bar area. Lundy stared at them intently, making them just uncomfortable enough to choose seats at tables on the opposite side of the bar from where they sat.

The server returned a few minutes later with the Teeling, setting it before Jax and quickly removing his hand as if Jax were a dog and he was afraid he might suddenly get bitten. He retreated, silently.

"So, what's your great idea?" Jax asked. It sounded more like an accusation than a question.

Lundy paused, weighing and measuring his words carefully. "Bernie may be a great spokesman for the church, but he lacks your business acumen," Lundy complimented. "I would rather have him stick to what he does best and have you focus on what it is *you* do best."

The bartender returned with a small plate in hand, a white linen towel draping his arm, ceremoniously. "Petite lamb chops with a raspberry reduction sauce and mint glaze with a hint of our signature seasonings."

Lundy looked at the bartender, surprised. The man winked at him, as if in on a joke, and set down two small plates in front of each of the men.

Jax pinched one of the chops between his fingers and nibbled at it like a mouse nibbling on a piece of cheese. He nodded, approvingly.

"So, what is it that I do best?" Jax asked, between bites.

"Well, you have been a successful businessman and investor in many industries. I heard your scholarship program alone drew hundreds of students to the Atelier school in New York, not to mention that you yourself are a skilled artist and teacher."

"Flattery will get you everywhere," Jax grinned.

"But it's true," Lundy paused to take a bite of his own lamb. Somehow, he was such a pristine eater that his face and hands remained immaculate, even while eating with his fingers. "I would like to see you more involved in the Church of Infinite Love's budding publishing house, COIL Publishing, for short, and be a key investor and partner in the COIL Young Ambassador's School."

"Bernie will never go for that," Jax lamented.

"You let me deal with Bernie," Lundy answered. "What I need to know from you is your level of interest. I can share the financials and business plans for each, but I'd hate to waste your time, or mine, if you've got your hands full with your rebrand of the factory...or should I say, factories, plural?" Lundy eyed Jax for confirmation.

"Oh, you figured that out, did you?" Jax smiled.

"I'm a pretty smart guy," Lundy smiled back. Lundy didn't smile often, but when he did, it appeared mostly genuine.

"Yes, I managed to convince Erasmus's little benefactor, Emma Post, to sell the Florida factory to me, but did my best to keep my name out of it."

"I suspected who the silent partner might be. But that subtle switch from Jaks with a 'K' to Jax with an 'X' might have been a brilliant legal maneuver. It's amazing how a letter change can screw up title and other searches."

"But you still figured it out," Jax sipped his whiskey before polishing off his remaining lamb chop.

"Of course, I did," Lundy answered. "My associate, Mr. Adani, may have handled most of the arrangements on my behalf, but I'm still the one who has to oversee everything in the end."

The bartender returned again. He stood silently with two more small plates in his hand. "I have another small plate of morsels for you," he announced. If Lundy didn't know any better, he could have sworn the man's voice went from a heavy Irish brogue to British, as if he were trying to sound posh. Lundy was not easily amused, and yet he had to chuckle momentarily to himself as the bartender set the plates on their table. "A petite filet of beef topped with a duck pâté on a freshly baked brioche bun," he finished, quickly clearing the soiled plates. As he leaned over Lundy's shoulder, the lawyer slipped yet another bill into the server's pocket. The server nodded, gratefully. Without asking, he returned moments later with a fresh whiskey for Jax, and while he didn't request it, a glass of water.

As Jax bit into his petite burger, Lundy continued. "A small-print production of 'never seen by the public before' church doctrine and 'mystery knowledge' is already underway, but in order for the academy and the publishing house to reach its potential, we would need a sizable investment."

"And there it is," Jax sat back, wiping his mouth with a napkin. "I knew there had to be a reason you were schmoozing me with expensive food and liquor. You want money."

"You're not wrong," Lundy confessed. "But even more than that, I need people at the helm who, shall we say, are not emotionally invested in the teachings of the church."

"You mean a practical man, like me," Jax answered. "Someone who is interested in the bottom line and not dogma."

"Exactly," Lundy nodded. "Let's be honest, Mr. Liebling. I have lots of connections thanks to my long-standing ties with the Vandenberg family. But you can see how Erasmus Vandenberg's conscious got him killed and nearly wiped out the Vandenberg family fortune in the process."

"Good thing I don't have a conscious," Jax observed. "But I'd have some say over how the academy and the publishing house were run, yes? Bernie as much as told me to keep my nose out of church affairs and focus on healthy snacks and the factory side of things."

Lundy knew his opportunity had arrived. He leaned in as if sharing a secret. Jax did the same. "Between you and I, Bernie is not likely to be at the helm for long. I've already got his replacement in mind."

"Really? Who?" Jax demanded.

"All in good time," Lundy answered. "But I need more of a commitment from you before I divulge too much."

"Okay, you show me your plans, minus this mystery leader, and I'll consider making an investment. How much are we talking, anyhow?" Jax waved his fingers as if money were no object.

"An even million should get us through the door," Lundy threw out the number, casually.

Jax's face dropped for a microsecond before recovering. "What makes you so sure I have that kind of money?"

"Oh, I know all about your accounts in the Caymans, Mr. Liebling. As I said, I'm a pretty smart guy. And what you don't have, I know you have creative ways of procuring."

"You just show me the plans and I'll decide then," Jax answered.

"Of course, and I'm happy to discuss it with your lawyers as well," Lundy offered.

Jax sneered. "Lawyers? Don't need 'em and don't trust 'em," he answered blatantly. "Present company excluded, of course."

"Of course," Lundy answered. Lundy took a dramatic pause, as if once again making mental calculations in his head.

"What is it?" Jax asked. "I can see the wheels in your head turning so fast there's smoke coming out of your ears."

Lundy forced a practiced chuckle. "Once again, you are not wrong, Jax. Forgive my impertinence, but if we are going to do business together, I have to ask...you're an independent guy, right? From what I've heard, you have no wife and kids, and no family to speak of."

Jax smiled as his gaze floated away for just a moment. He was thinking about Midge, and her recent proposal. Still, it was too soon to count those proverbial chickens and all. "I am currently unmarried," he answered. "And you are correct that I am a lone wolf, so to speak."

Lundy sighed. "Well, that puts an added stress on this arrangement."

"What stress?" Jax asked. "I haven't even agreed to anything yet."

"I've been in this business a long time," Lundy shook his head, mournfully. "Years go by, and a board member or key company figure dies with no will to speak of, and their estate becomes escheated."

"Ah," Jax nodded, knowingly. Lundy could tell from Jax's blank expression that he was bluffing. Lundy played along.

"And you know what happens from there." Lundy nodded and gestured as if Jax were following along. "The state takes over if there is no heir, and those of us who were counting on investment funds lose our shirts. We have no access to the money promised, unless...well, unless the investor creates a will and leaves his money to a charitable cause—"

"Like a church or nonprofit academy," Jax finished for him.

"Exactly," Lundy answered. "I know it's an uncomfortable topic, and I look forward to many years of working together, but if I'm going to get buy-in from the Elders of the church who are still very much involved in the church behind the scenes, they need to feel confident."

Jax drained his glass, his water still untouched. "I'll tell you what, Mr. Lundy." He stood. "You get me your proposal and I'll consider my options."

CHAPTER 13

Lundy and Bernie

~

"Where did you run off to today, anyway?" Bernie Forger asked Mr. Lundy, when they met for breakfast the morning following his first televised broadcast since Erasmus Vandenberg's death.

"I had to soothe someone's nerves," Lundy answered calmly, taking a sip of his decaffeinated tea. Meanwhile, Bernie downed his second cup of coffee that morning and flagged down the waitress for a refill.

"Lemmee guess, Jax Liebling?" Bernie answered as the server refilled his cup. "Bless you," he said to her and smiled. She flashed a smile back, baring a set of yellowing teeth that were not nearly as pristinely polished as Bernie's manufactured pearly whites.

"The same." Lundy nodded.

"I think bringing him in was a mistake," Bernie answered. "He's got a screw loose, somewhere."

"Yeah, but he's a screwball with a lot of money," Lundy answered.

"Is he that good of a businessman?" Bernie seemed surprised. "How does that little scamp of a man have that kind of money? He's not good looking. He's not well-connected, and he doesn't seem all that bright."

"He's smarter than he looks," Lundy admitted. "But not by much. From what I can tell he gained his fortune flying under the radar and swindling unsuspecting billionaires out of their money. Then, he did the genius thing of dumping his money into publicity and managed to make a name for himself as an up-and-coming artist back in the late 70s, selling his works to some of the same people he swindled."

"Heck of a guy," Bernie answered. "Are you sure the church should be involved with him? If he's that shady? Aren't we trying to repair our reputation?"

"Of the church, yes. Vandenberg Nutraceuticals, not so much," Lundy replied.

"I don't follow," Bernie answered. "The Vandenberg name IS the church."

"Not anymore," Lundy replied. "The more we can separate ourselves from the nutraceutical business and funnel our efforts into the academy and the publishing house, the greater our chances of rebuilding our reputation and our wealth."

"For the good of the church, of course," Bernie answered.

"Obviously," Lundy agreed. "But you know as well as I do that the Lord works in mysterious ways. If he brought us Jax Liebling to launch us into a new era, then why not let him use his dirty money for good?"

"But he's expecting the church to retain partnerships with Vandenberg Nutraceuticals. Heck, many of the Elders are still heavily invested."

"About that," Lundy said.

"What about that?"

"I think that once we've secured Jax Liebling's seed money for the academy and COIL Publishing House, I think we should convince the Vandenberg family to re-invest elsewhere and get out of the nutraceutical business altogether."

"But Jax purchased with the idea that we'd be a partnership. A large portion of the factory's money came from church members who wanted healing from their ailments, or from non-believers who were out of options and willing to try anything."

"After we get what we need, I say we abandon a sinking ship," Lundy suggested. "Let he and Mr. Baxter Baker go down, while we walk away."

Bernie smiled. "All for God's work," he reaffirmed. "It's just too bad that the Vandenberg name is still attached to the factory.

A lightbulb went off in Lundy's head. "Good thinking," he replied. "Perhaps I should put it Jax's head to rename the company as part of the rebrand."

Bernie's hand began trembling as a result of too much caffeine. He set his coffee cup down and wiped his brow with a napkin. "But won't Jax retaliate after we've ripped the rug out from under his feet?"

"You just keep doing what you do best and lead the church," Lundy answered. "Let me worry about Jax Liebling."

Bernie nodded. "I trust you, Lundy. We couldn't have gotten this far without you."

CHAPTER 14

The Vandenberg Factory

"Detective Ortega, how nice to see you again," Jax oozed friendliness when Ortega dropped by the Dublin factory, seemingly out of the blue. Friendliness was out of character for him; therefore, it merely came across as slithery and condescending.

"You don't seem surprised to see me, Mr. Liebling," Ortega observed. "I'm going to assume you got an inkling that I might be popping by?"

"A small inkling." Jax set the book he was leafing through onto his desk, remembering Midge's warning about his potential visit. "But perhaps you can let me in on what brings you all the way from New York to Dublin? Or should I say, Florida? I heard a rumor that you retired."

"Well, you have me at a disadvantage, Mr. Liebling," Ortega confessed. "As I am having trouble connecting the dots between our last conversation, where you got away with murder and now seem to be running a million-dollar nutraceutical factory."

"We prefer to think of it as healthy lifestyle products these days," Jax corrected. "And if you'll recall, I was never convicted of anything."

"Oh, that's right," Ortega answered. "You managed to pin the blame on your girlfriend, Midge Pasternak, and then leave her in jail to rot."

Jax's expression dropped. Ortega remained silent and waited for his response.

"The actions of my ex-girlfriend have nothing to do with me," Jax answered simply.

"Don't suppose you've been in touch with Ms. Pasternak lately, have you?"

"What? In prison?" Jax feigned ignorance of her escape, the one that he initiated. "Needless to say, I was disappointed to learn that my former love interest would do such horrible things and ended things immediately."

"I see," Ortega played along, tugging at his ear, thoughtfully. "I do find it a little strange that your name crossed my path once again, though, Mr. Liebling."

"Likewise," Jax answered. "I'll share if you will."

"Well, that's just fine," Ortega agreed. "I'll go first if you don't mind." Jax turned a palm up and motioned for Ortega to continue. "You see, while in Florida...you were right, by the way, I am semi-retired...but again, while in Florida, my services were enlisted to research the untimely death of Erasmus Vandenberg, which led me, as I'm sure you know, down a deep rabbit hole that ultimately led me here...to you, Mr. Liebling." Ortega paused for Jax's reaction.

Jax stared directly into Ortega's eyes for an uncomfortable few moments in which neither man blinked. "Yes," Jax finally spoke. "Nasty business. Mr. Baker, our new CEO, enlisted my help after the police unveiled a crude faith-healing and drug-using scheme that left people dead. Tragic really."

"You seem really broken up about it," Ortega noticed.

"We've been down this road before, Detective," Jax reminded him. "Just because I don't buy into the media hype and get all emotional over people who mean nothing to me, doesn't make me a criminal."

"Don't suppose you'd mind sharing with me how it is that you and Mr. Baker found one another?" Ortega asked.

"If you must know, I have many business dealings in Florida. I'm a wealthy man, Detective Ortega. I got that way by diversifying, and coming in to save sinking ships like the Vandenberg empire. It happens to be what I'm good at."

"I see," Ortega answered. "So, the rumor that you're simply going to pick up where the late Erasmus Vandenberg left off is just that—a rumor? No more weird cult practices and bogus faith healings?"

"I don't like to speak ill of the dead, Detective," Jax replied. "But with my influence, the products of this factory will all be legal and in compliance with all food and drug safety rules. In fact, you're welcome to take a tour of the facility if you like. We're rolling out a new natural food bar line with all organic ingredients. I recommend you try the Calm bar for stress reduction...made with valerian root and chamomile leaves. See? Nothing secret about any of the ingredients."

"Well, thank you for the recommendation," Ortega agreed. "I am feeling a little stressed, and might just take you up on that."

Jax smiled, feeling self-satisfied as if he'd won the argument.

"And, two of my people are already touring the factory downstairs, thanks to Mr. Baxter Baker...very helpful, cooperative young man," Ortega finished.

Jax's face dropped for a microsecond before his practiced smile returned. "Of course, I'm glad to hear it. According to what I've read, it was Mr. Baker who led the police to learn about dear old Erasmus's underhanded dealings to begin with."

"Yes, he's been most helpful," Ortega concurred. "Think I will join them and see what Mr. Baker and my team are up to if you don't mind. Thank you for your time." Ortega tipped a hat to Jax.

"That's it?" Jax called after him.

Ortega spun on his heals. "What else would there be?"

"It's just that," Jax answered. "I really shouldn't be saying anything seeing as how I'm invested in the company and all...but you might have a longer conversation with Mr. Baker to find out what more he's not telling you about the factory operations back in Florida."

"Oh really?"

"Yes," Jax lowered his voice. "But you didn't hear it from me. If it's all just horrid rumors, then so be it. But if he was in some way responsible for the scheme that led to many premature deaths, then I'd rather know before I get in too deep...business-wise."

"Seems like that might have been something to consider before investing?" Ortega pointed out.

"Indeed," Jax grit his teeth. "It's just that I recently learned some news that had me grow suspicious of the young man and the church."

"Thought the church was dead?" Ortega asked, doing a fair job of feigning surprise.

"No, you didn't," Jax shook his head, unconvinced. "But what you may not know is that Bernie Forger, the man who took Erasmus's place as head of the Church of Infinite Love, plans to open up an academy to 'spread the word,'" Jax used air quotes. "There's also talk of a small publishing house."

"So, you're not convinced that the church is turning a new leaf?" Ortega confirmed.

"I am not," Jax answered. "Don't get me wrong, I'll happily sell them products from our healthy food line, but I'd rather not be involved with people who have questionable practices."

"Hmmm," Ortega smiled insincerely. "Seems to be the exact people you like to be involved with."

Jax sat on the edge of his desk and picked up his book, pretending to leaf through it. "Just be sure to have a talk with Mr. Baker. And when you're done, you might want to look up Bernie Forger."

While Ortega was busy in his talks with Jax Liebling, Shep and Penelope were busy touring the factory with Baxter Baker and his assistant, Moira Dodd. Unlike past interactions with Vandenberg Nutraceuticals, where the only way to get into designated areas was undercover, Baxter seemed as welcoming as a tour guide at a history museum. If one didn't know any better, they might assume that Baxter had pretended to be in charge for so long, that now, he was actually happy to be *doing* something.

"Nice of you to take time out of your schedule to show us around Mr. Baker," Shep commented. Shep, being a bit taller and heavier than Baxter, slunk with his shoulders hunched, like an oversized monster from a B-movie. Meanwhile, Baxter kept his pace slow and measured with Moira rolling in her wheelchair at his side. He seemed to intentionally ensure that he didn't step in front of her. Meanwhile, Moira buzzed along in a hybrid electric chair with manual options. Every once in a while, she underestimated the space between two workstations and got stuck on the edge of a bench and had to manually reverse and move forward by grabbing the wheels. When that happened, Baxter always tried to intervene. And every time, Moira slapped his hands away in defiance.

This interaction did not go unnoticed by Dr. Penelope Washburn who smiled to herself, but said nothing.

"Of course," Baxter answered. "We're always happy to show members of the US police force around. I know we've had our...differences...in the past. But I can assure you that under my direction, Vandenberg Nutraceuticals is fully transparent, an open book, if you will." Baxter smiled and raised his arms wide, like Willy Wonka giving a grand tour of the chocolate factory. It was, admittedly, a little over the top.

On the inside, Baxter was a bundle of nerves. It was no secret who tipped the police off as to Erasmus Vandenberg and the family's underhanded dealings with the church. And he was well aware that he didn't have many friends left, but he decided it was better for both him and the reputation of the company if he were as compliant as possible with the authorities—even ones who, technically, had no jurisdiction in Ireland.

"Correct me if I'm wrong," Shep began, "but in the Florida factory, you had the main production area and one for research and development. Is that still the case?"

Baxter didn't know the answer to this. He looked to Moira for support.

"Ah, you did your homework, lad," Moira chimed in, pausing as she spoke. She had trouble rolling and talking at the same time...another thing that Penelope couldn't help but notice. "Aye, we do have an R&D department, but we're so new that it's more, as you would say, a work in progress. We're happy to show it to ya, though," she offered.

"That would be great," Shep responded. "I guess I'm curious how your products have changed, given—" Shep scratched his chin, not really sure how to be delicate about it.

"That the last ones were laced with illegal drugs?" Moira finished.

Baxter was surprised by Moira's candor, but relieved that she took the initiative all the same. While most bosses might have taken offense to their assistant speaking out of turn, Baxter found it refreshing. Not only did it take the pressure off him, but Moira had this uncanny knack for knowing what to say and what not to, something he had never mastered.

"Well…yes," Shep admitted.

"The health bars general ingredients are the same with ones for energy, sleep and mood-boosting, only our new line uses all natural ingredients: cocoa, valerian, lemon balm and the like. And all are clearly labeled on the package to account for allergies."

"So, no funny business," Penelope offered.

"No funny business," Moira confirmed.

The factory was much smaller than the old one in Florida with fewer workers on the floor. Shep also noticed that in Florida, women and young boys made up the workforce, but here in Ireland, it seemed quite a mix of men and women of all ages.

"I don't mean to be rude," Penelope began, embarrassed, "but I don't suppose you'd be okay with us taking a few samples of your product line? It's just that it would go a long way to proving to the authorities that Vandenberg Nutraceuticals has turned a new leaf."

"By all means," Baxter smiled. "Moira? Could you see to it that they have an ample collection of all our products? Enough for lab testing and a few extra should they get snacky later in the day?"

"Of course, Mr. Baker," Moira smiled. To Shep and Penelope she said, "If you would accompany Mr. Baker back to his office, I can see to it that supplies are sent up over the next few minutes."

"Thank you," Penelope replied.

Moira lagged behind as Baxter, Shep, and Penelope made their way to the elevator leading to the executive suite. Once inside, Baxter suddenly hit the emergency stop button on the lift. Shep eyed him, confused.

"Okay," Baxter whispered. "This may be the only chance I've got to speak in confidence, so listen up." Shep nodded, but said nothing. "It's true that the factory appears on the up and up, and my family won't come near this company with a ten-foot pole with its reputation, but I wouldn't trust any of 'em as far as I could throw 'em. If you have further questions, I suggest you contact me through Moira. Above all, I'd appreciate if you'd conduct as much of your business as possible off property, understand?

One visit is quite enough. Any more than that, and Jax Liebling and my family will be breathing down my neck."

Before Shep could respond, Baxter hit the button and the lift resumed its route to the main offices. The doors of the lift opened, where Baxter nearly collided with Ortega, just having finished his talk with Jax. Ortega put his arm out, planting a hand on Baxter's shoulder to steady himself and avoid running into one another.

"Er, sorry," Ortega said, awkwardly.

"No problem," Baxter sidestepped, giving Ortega room to pass and Shep and Penelope to get out of the lift.

"Actually," Penelope intervened. "I don't believe you've met Detective Ortega in person, have you, Mr. Baker?"

Baxter looked up in surprise. "No, we haven't." He offered a hand to Ortega. "But your reputation precedes you."

Ortega shook Baxter's hand...decent grip, not wishy-washy. Ortega felt you could tell a lot about a person from their handshake. "Not sure what that reputation might be," he admitted. "But you're just the man I want to see. Mind if we chat for a moment?"

"Not at all," Baxter agreed. "Your colleagues are welcome to join us as well. As I've been telling them, I have no secrets."

As Ortega followed Baxter into the main office, he asked. "So, where is it that you're staying while in Ireland?"

"Okay," Baxter laughed nervously. "Maybe one secret. Given the sensitive state in which I left Florida, I do have to be careful who knows my whereabouts."

"Fair enough," Ortega nodded as the four of them piled into the office.

As expected, within minutes of their arrival, Moira resurfaced with a collection of healthy snacks boxed up and sitting in her lap.

"There ya go." She pushed the box across her knees. Shep took the cue and lifted the box from her lap. "Service with a smile," Moira laughed.

Jax, who hadn't yet left the office, had no intention of sticking around for any more questions. "Moira," he asked abruptly. "Call downstairs for my driver. I'll be dining out for lunch."

Moira bit her lip. Jax never requested anything; he just barked orders.

"Of course, Mr. Liebling," she agreed, rolling over to her desk and picking up the phone.

"It's a shame I can't stay," Jax answered with all the emotion of an android.

"No problem, Jax," Baxter smiled uneasily. "I can see to our guests from here."

CHAPTER 15

Just "Derry"

Last Night

"Really, Midge," Rue slid into a booth at Beckett's Bar on a weekday evening when not much was happening. She dropped her small backpack beside her and pulled back the hood of her sweatshirt, letting her tousled hair fall down around her shoulders. "You had me rent a car and drive two-and-a-half hours to Londonderry to meet...on the wrong side of the road, I might add. You couldn't have picked a place near Dublin? Hell, even Belfast would have been quicker."

Midge took a long sip from a tiny straw that dipped into a nearly-finished Bramble cocktail. After a long slurping sound, she used the straw to stab a loose blackberry huddling at the bottom of the glass as if hiding behind several blocks of melting ice.

"Derry," she corrected. "I believe it's just 'Derry' now."

"Whatever, the point is—" Rue huffed.

"The point is, I'm trying to save your life," Midge finished. "Isn't that what best friends do? Look after one another?"

"What are you talking about?" Rue asked loudly, before Midge put a finger to her lips, reminding her to keep her voice down. Rue lowered her voice to a whisper. "You were the one who brought me to Ireland in the first place!"

Just then, a server stopped by their booth. "Any 'ting I can get for ya?" the server asked.

"Yeah," Midge answered, "Another Bramble for me and a—" Midge motioned to Rue.

"Uh, the same... I guess?" Rue finished. The server nodded and quickly moved on. "What exactly did I just order?" Rue questioned.

"Gin and blackberry... you'll like it, trust me. Now, about me saving your life—" Midge continued. Rue crossed her arms and rolled her eyes. "Would you look at you?" Midge sat back in the booth, exasperated. "No gratitude!"

"Explain!" Rue commanded, simply.

"Okay, fine." Midge leaned in. "You've been walking with a target on your back since you left New York, see?" She twirled her curly green hair anxiously, looked down at her beverage and swirled the remaining ice as if there were some small sips of gin left in the glass...there wasn't. "I brought you here to help bring down the Vandenberg family business at its core, only—" Midge paused uncomfortably.

"Only...what?" Rue asked.

"I didn't realize that the turbulence spanned this wide and far," Midge finished.

"Meaning, what, exactly? That you made a mistake?"

"What?" Midge stumbled. "A mistake? Bite your tongue. Midge Pasternak does not make mistakes." She continued the back and forth routine of twirling the ice in her glass with the small sip stirrer, and twirling an unruly piece of her hair, impatiently. Rue could almost count the rhythm...twirl, twirl...five twirls of the ice followed by seven twirls of her hair. One could write a haiku to the rhythm.

The server returned a few minutes later with two beverages. Midge breathed a sigh of relief as she retrieved hers and she relinquished her near-empty glass. She pushed Rue's beverage across the table toward her, encouraging her to drink.

Rue eyed the beverage, cautiously, looking at it and then Midge, and back again, as if Midge's touching it could have led to something sinister. It was a subtle reminder that this wouldn't have been the first time that Midge had poisoned someone.

"Are you kidding me!?" Midge all but yelled before collecting herself and lowering her voice. A few bar goers glanced in their direction with a mix of annoyance and amusement. "After everything we've been through together?"

"You don't exactly have the greatest of track records," Rue reminded her, before conceding to take a small sip of her beverage. "I'd hate to wake up tomorrow dead on account of you poisoning me," Rue finished, smiling.

"Em," Midge laughed. "You know that what you said is impossible, right?"

"My attempt at a joke," Rue added.

"Oh," Midge thought on this a moment before nodding. "Funny!" She nodded, supportively.

"Okay, so why am I a target all of a sudden?" Rue asked. "They caught the person responsible for my mother's death, and the death of Erasmus Vandenberg."

"My sweet, naive, Rue," Midge reached her hand across the table and rested it overtop of Rue's. Rue quickly withdrew her hand. Midge sat back, nonplussed. Rue's mother, a Deaconess in the Church of Infinite Love, and Erasmus Vandenberg, wealthy businessman turned artist in retirement, were murdered by a member of the church. It was regarded as a religiously-motivated killing and that they had been working alone.

After a long sip of her drink, Midge continued, "Their Ambassador was just a convenient scapegoat who happened to go unhinged at the perfect time. It's a shame that more people don't know how to control their anger and emotions, like me."

Rue framed her words carefully, before continuing, "You do remember that you killed two innocent women, not to mention a busload of convicts from a women's detention center in New York, not to mention—"

"That was Jax!" Midge protested. "The first gal, I never meant to kill. The second one had it coming, and I had nothing to do with any of those gals from prison! I'm telling you, that man is crazy!" Midge crossed her arms and looked around the bar nervously, as if by saying his name would cause him to appear. Rue thought Midge to be unflappable and was surprised by what appeared to be an unusual emotion for Midge...fear. "What?" Midge finally asked after a long moment of silence where Rue eyed her friend, curiously.

"You really are afraid of him, aren't you?"

"Who, Jax?" Midge waved a hand nonchalantly, but refused to make eye contact. "Please. I just said that to Fuzz and Beefcake so they would help me. Do I want Jax to leave me alone, absolutely. Am I riddled with fear—"

"Let's try this again," Rue folded her hands and placed them purposefully on the table. "If you were worried Jax was after me, why bring me here and put me in the line of fire?"

"Because I thought you were in greater danger back home. At least here, I can keep an eye on you."

"So, *you're* going to protect me?" Rue shook her head. "I don't buy it."

"Well, it's true," Midge insisted before rolling her eyes to the ceiling.

"You're lying to me, Midge," Rue accused her former friend. "I've learned how to tell when you're lying."

After what seemed like an eternity, Midge let out a sigh and chuckled a little. "You got me," she threw her hands up in the air. "While I do intend to protect you, I need you for another purpose," Midge confessed.

"What purpose?" Rue narrowed her eyes.

After another long pause, Midge answered simply, "Bait...I need you as bait."

"Bait," Rue confirmed. "And what makes you think I'll go along with whatever crazy scheme you're cooking up?"

"Because it's a win-win for everybody, and I mean *everybody*." Midge sucked down the rest of her beverage and motioned for another. "Can I get something salty over here? Maybe some peanuts or crackers or something?"

The server was attentive, plunking down a menu. "Fraid we're fresh outa nuts," the young woman eyed the menu. "But the stew and boxties are pretty good."

"A boxty," Midge smiled. "That sounds fun, like me." She winked at the waitress who merely smiled back and nodded politely as she walked away.

"You were saying," Rue reminded her. "How is this a win-win for everybody?"

"Easy, Ortega and Shep get to bust up the biggest con of the century, I get Jax off my case and yours, and—"

"And?"

"I can help resolve the bad blood between that tall drink of wat-uh boyfriend of yours and Constantine Westport."

"Darwin?" Rue sat up. "What does Darwin have to do with any of this?" She knew he said he couldn't set foot in Ireland again, but she refused to believe that after all this time, Constantine Westport would still blame Darwin Fennec and his sidekick Bristol for his own daughter's choice in lifestyle and accidental drug overdose.

Midge read her thoughts. "It sometimes takes people an awful long time to forget," she said. "Not only did Westport lose a daughter, but his son and your precious Mr. Fennec tried to con the conner. That don't typically go over too big according to the Westport code."

The color started to drain from Rue's face. "Please tell me you're not planning to hand me over to Constantine Westport to appease his need for revenge?"

"Of course not," Midge defended. "I would never put you in harm's way like that. That's just irresponsible!"

Rue cleared her throat and shot a wide-eyed look. "Really? It sure seems like that's exactly what you're doing, putting me on the radar of both Jax Liebling and Constantine Westport. And what's all this bait shit, anyway?"

The waitress dropped off a small plate of cheesy potato pancakes with an extra plate and two forks. "In case ye wanna share, yeah?" she offered, winking at Midge before walking away.

"Eat up," Midge encouraged. "You're too skinny as it is, and who knows when your next meal will be."

"Well, that's encouraging," Rue retorted, but relented and took a small bite of the boxty. She was hungrier than she realized.

Midge leaned in and whispered. "I'm gonna let you in on a little secret, but just one." She paused while Rue leaned over the table. "Jax thinks he's clever enough to move into the Westport territory and not have to pay Westport's, shall we say, 'residence fee.' Once Constantine realizes that you and your team are here to move the Vandenberg operation out, it will go a long way to clearing the bad blood between Constantine and Darwin."

"Does Constantine even know who I am?" Rue asked.

"Between you and Darwin's entanglement in SpencerTech and B.A. Ellis Industry face-off, and your help in uncovering the church's and the Vandenberg's shady dealings, I'm pretty sure he knows all about the crime-stopping dynamic duo."

Rue cringed at the reference to SpencerTech. Its founder, Spencer Hargrove, had been her first boyfriend in New York and it was his under-handed dealings that brought she and Darwin Fennec together in the first place.

"Won't Constantine be worried that we'll turn the attention of the authorities onto the Westport empire?"

"You sure ask a heap-load of questions, Bestie." Midge took a bite of food, decided it needed salt, and sprinkled a hearty dose on the entire dish, including Rue's portion. "Not after we convince him that you're on his side...code of ethics, honor among thieves and all—"

"And how are we going to do that?" Rue asked, suspiciously.

"Ah, that's the million-dollar question, my friend. But that's for me to know, and you to find out."

RUE WAS A MIX OF HORRIFIED, fascinated, skeptical and fearful of Midge's plan...what little of it she knew. She was ready to tell Midge 'thanks, but no thanks' and hightail it back to the safe house where Ortega, Shep and Penelope were holing up, were it not for one problem.

All of a sudden her eyes began to feel a little sore. She gazed at Midge who now appeared as a hazy blob.

Midge smiled, "That's enough for you, my friend," she joked loudly. "Waiter. Check please!"

"No," Rue protested. "I'm not okay with this. I need to get back home. Darwin was right, I should have never come here."

Midge wrapped Rue's arm around her and helped her to her feet. A few bystanders at the bar stood to offer assistance.

"Be a doll, and help me get my friend into my car," Midge said to a middle-aged man who wiped the beer mustache from his lips and set down his pint.

"Happy to oblige," he answered.

"No, I'm fine," Rue protested. "My rental's just outside."

"Don't think it's safe for you to be drivin' anywhere, lass. Yer friend is right."

It was only after Midge and Rue were safely in Midge's compact Opel Astra heading to who knows where, that their main server stepped outside to see what the fuss was about. A few gathered at the doorway, laughing.

"A young maiden jest couldn't hold her liquor is all…Americans!"

"The green-haired one?" the server nodded. "Aye, she downed at least four Brambles in under an hour."

"Nah," one of the bar goers answered. "Nah her. De other normal-lookin' one wit the brown hair. Could barely stand, that one!"

The group laughed.

"That one?" The server shook her head. "Barely touched her drink, she did." She watched as the car faded into the distance.

The bartender rested a hand on her shoulder. "Don't be getten' yer funny conspiracy ideas, Lil," he cautioned.

Lil nodded, but paused to eye the only rental car parked on the street outside. "Hmm, I wonder," she said, and went back to work.

From the passenger's side, Rue whined in an uncharacteristically infantile manner. "What did you give me?" Rue asked, leaning her cheek against the side of the window. It felt pleasantly cool while the rest of her skin felt as if it were somehow on fire.

"Don't worry about it," Midge answered. "You'll sleep it off in about eight hours." Then, after noticing how affected Rue seemed to be, she added, "Maybe twelve hours."

"If I'm going to die, can I at least call Darwin and say goodbye?"

"You're not gonna—" Suddenly, Midge got an idea. "Sure, call Darwin. But *don't* tell him where you are, understood?"

"No," Rue shook her head fervently, like a small child. "I wouldn't want him to get hurt."

"That's right," Midge answered. "Tell you what. You just dial and let him know you're fine. Okay?"

Rue nodded. It took her three attempts to focus enough to hit the correct numbers on the keypad.

"Rue?" Darwin picked up the phone on the first ring. "I've been so worried about you. I know I shouldn't be, but I haven't heard from you all day so—"

Rue breathed heavily into the phone.

"Rue?" Darwin was concerned. "What is it? Are you hurt?"

"No, I'm okay," Rue struggled to form her words. "I just called to tell you something."

"Yes, of course," he answered. "What it is, darling?"

"I want you to know that I love you."

Midge pulled the phone from Rue's grasp and hit the red button to end the call. She then rolled down the driver's side window and tossed the cell phone into traffic, glancing in the rear view mirror as it went skipping along the road, smashing to pieces before several cars ran over it. Midge then grabbed Rue's backpack with one hand, pulling it roughly from Rue's shoulders with her other hand still on the wheel. At the next red light, Midge quickly unzipped it and rifled through the contents.

Rue drifted off to sleep, only to awaken some time later. It was dark out, and the temperature had dropped considerably. Rue shivered, having suddenly gone from feeling very hot to very, very cold.

Midge pulled off the main road into a wooded area. On her lap, she couldn't help but notice a small, compact Swiss army knife...one that Rue carried with her when she traveled. She tried to move toward it, but Midge put a hand out and shoved Rue back into her seat with a little more force than was necessary for someone who had been drugged.

"Ow," Rue winced as the side of her head hit the window.

"Serves you right," Midge chastised. "Don't be so grabby."

"Where are we?" Rue asked, rubbing her head, fear mounting as she watched her friend, suspiciously. Chills danced up and down her spine. When Midge didn't answer, she added, "So it comes down to this, does it?" Rue slurred her words. "Is this the moment where you finally decide I'm no longer your 'bestie' and kill me?"

Midge winced, an annoyed twitch on her lips. She finally answered, "Just making a little pitstop."

CHAPTER 16
Disappearing Act

Leaving the Factory

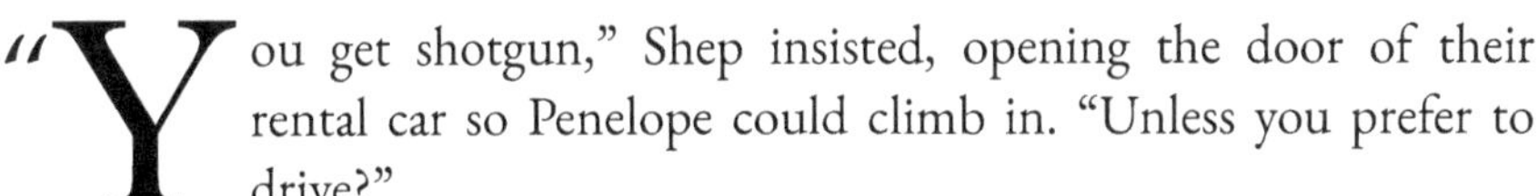

"You get shotgun," Shep insisted, opening the door of their rental car so Penelope could climb in. "Unless you prefer to drive?"

"No, thanks," Penelope answered. "I don't even drive in Manhattan. Probably best to leave it to Jose...I mean, Detective Ortega."

Shep nodded and closed the door. Ortega waited while the Tampa Sheriff stuffed himself in the back seat, folding his knees into his chest. Penelope tried her best to pull her seat all the way forward to give him more room, but it was a tight fit any way you looked at it. Beside him, they had placed the 'evidence' collected from their factory visit. While they were fairly convinced Baxter wouldn't freely give them health bars to test if he didn't believe they were clean, they still wanted to check in with Ortega's connections at the local Guard to ensure everything was on the up and up. For whatever reason, Ortega's spidey sense didn't get triggered by Baxter. But Jax Liebling, on the other hand, was another story.

Ortega and Penelope chatted pleasantly from the front seat, replaying their meeting with Baxter Baker and Moira Dodd. It was quite a bit different from Ortega's previous visit to a Vandenberg Nutraceuticals factory. The last time was in Florida, and it was more an undercover stakeout with his soon-to-be ex-wife, Nancy; former crime suspect turned amateur detective, Emma Post; and her overly-enthusiastic assistant, Sprightly. Not to mention that Erasmus Vandenberg's own granddaughter, Elsbeth Ions, was on the scene helping the ragtag group gain access.

Today, however, was different. They were greeted with open arms after boldly walking through the front doors.

"What are you thinking?" Penelope asked when Ortega fell silent.

"Oh, I'm just wondering if they are playing nice for the time being, but plan on returning to their old tricks in a few months when the spotlight is off of them."

"Baxter Baker seemed on the up and up," Penelope answered.

"Baxter Baker has to be," Ortega offered. "He barely skirted getting arrested himself on manslaughter and racketeering thanks to a combination of him feeding info to the police and the Vandenberg lawyer, Mr. Lundy, working whatever underhanded deals he needed to cover up the boy's tracks."

"Not sure why," Penelope reasoned. "Why try to clear Baxter Baker's name, and then put him front and center here?"

"So, you think his comeuppance is more a 'not now' versus a 'not ever?'" Ortega offered.

"Exactly!" Penelope confirmed. "I guess we'll know more when we follow your lead to talk with the new head of the church, Bernie Forger."

"Right," Ortega confirmed. "For now, we settle in for a meal of whatever it is Ms. Brennan scrounged up for us and head to Belfast in the morning."

"Guys!" Shep groaned, grabbing his side. "I don't mean to put a damper on your plans, but I think maybe you should get me to a hospital first."

Penelope twisted in her seat, witnessing several health bar wrappers on the seat next to Shep, crumbs sprinkled down his shirt and a pained look on his face.

"What did you do?!" Penelope cried out. "Not only is that evidence, but we have no idea what's in those things!"

"Well," Shep defended, clenching his teeth. "You said yourself that they were likely clean. And I was hungry...low blood sugar and all."

"Right," Ortega wrenched the steering wheel and redirected them to the nearest hospital. "St. James is just a few minutes from here." He swerved in and out of traffic, taking turns that were a little harder than necessary, and not particularly safe.

"What's hurting?" Penelope asked, trying to get the run-down from Shep on the symptoms.

"A stabbing pain in my side," Shep groaned, holding his belly. "Not to mention some really unpleasant digestive issues...and nausea...are we there yet?"

"Almost," Penelope answered, not really sure. She did her best to keep him calm.

Ortega pulled into the emergency entrance as a triage nurse ran out to attend to them.

"My friend is not doing well," Ortega told her, flustered. "We think he may have been poisoned, but we can't be certain."

Within moments, Shep was whisked away on a stretcher while Ortega and Penelope were left in the ER waiting room. Ortega paced back and forth while Penelope just sat in one place with her knee bouncing nervously up and down.

"I tried phoning Rue," Ortega informed Penelope. "But she's not picking up at the house."

"Maybe she's out shopping?" Penelope offered.

Ortega looked at his watch. "Maybe," he concurred. "But my spidey sense is telling me something is wrong."

"You wanna take the car home and check on her while I wait here for news on Shep?"

"That might not be a bad idea," Ortega agreed. "Thank you, Penelope."

"Just be careful, Jose!" she called after him.

He smiled, despite the situation. It wasn't often she called him by his first name, given their sometimes-professional relationship, but he liked when she did. Ortega reached the parking area, climbed into their rental, and headed back to Swords.

"Ms. Brennan!" Ortega called out, cautiously, when he'd reached the small apartment they were renting. "Are you home?"

There was no answer. Ortega wasn't fond of carrying a weapon, but secretly wished he had his gun at this moment. Unfortunately, it was back in the States. He looked around for a suitable weapon, settling on a small Ogham stone statuette sitting on the end table by the front door. He held the weighted piece in his hand as he cautiously walked from room to room—which didn't take long, considering how small the place was. Windows were locked, and nothing appeared out of the ordinary.

Just then, the phone rang.

"Rue, is that you?" Ortega asked, concerned.

"Aww, so sweet that you care...but no!" A mouthy voice with a New York and Jersey hybrid accent replied.

"Miss Pasternak," Ortega caught his breath, agitated. "Mind telling me where Ms. Brennan is? I'm assuming if you're calling, you've got something to do with it."

"Gee," Midge was offended. "Thanks for asking how I am. Not that you care."

"I don't," Ortega answered, gruffly. "Why are you calling? Where's Rue?"

"She's safe, let's start there," Midge answered, calmly. "Look Fuzz, I only got a minute, so stop yapping and listen."

"Go on."

"All you need to know is that she has willfully chosen to help me. She's safe for now, but in order to stay that way, you have to do exactly what I tell you."

Midge's orders were pretty straightforward. Ortega was supposed to wait twenty-four hours and file a missing person's report, and nothing else. "No snooping, no investigating, no checking in with your buddies at the Guard. And above all, don't tell Darwin Fennec nothin'."

"What am I supposed to do if he calls?" Ortega protested.

"Ignore his calls. He can't know anything."

"I don't think that's gonna fly. He loves—"

"I don't care what you think!" Midge yelled into the receiver. "Missing person's report, and that's all! Forget she even came with you to Ireland until further notice."

"How am I supposed to trust you?"

"You don't have a choice," Midge threatened. "If you don't follow my instructions, she dies." With that, Midge slammed the phone down.

Ortega stared numbly at the receiver, now buzzing a dial tone. Just then, his mobile phone rang. He set the house phone back in its cradle and pulled his cell phone from his pocket.

"Penelope," he answered.

"Good news," Penelope answered. "Well, sorta."

"What is it?" Ortega asked. He was due for some good news…ish.

"Shep wasn't poisoned," Penelope paused and added quietly, "too bad they didn't figure that out before they had his stomach pumped."

"Ooh," Ortega asked. "Is he okay?"

"He will be. Turns out he had a ruptured appendix. By the time you make it back here, he should be out of surgery. After he's assigned a room, we should be able to see him," Penelope said.

"Sucky timing," Ortega admitted. "But I'm glad he's okay. Sit tight and I'll be there to pick you up as soon as I can."

"Is Rue with you?" Penelope asked.

"That's another story," Ortega answered. "Can't say more by phone. Talk to you in a bit. Just do me a favor?"

"Of course," Penelope answered.

"Don't leave the hospital and just stay where people can see you, okay?"

"Uh, okay," she said.

Ortega had just finished his call with Penelope when his cell phone rang once again…it was Darwin. Ortega sighed and let it go to voicemail.

It was nearly midnight when they finally returned from the hospital with Shep left to sleep and recover from surgery. Darwin had called two more times, one with a voicemail message, "Ortega, what's going on over there? I got a cryptic call from Rue. She sounded as if something was wrong, told me she loved me, and hung up. Call me back, man!"

Ortega fumbled with the cell phone for several minutes. Penelope eyed him, but said nothing. She knew what he was thinking. He didn't trust Midge, but he also didn't want to do anything that might put Rue's life in danger. And he certainly didn't like this feeling of helplessness, not one bit.

She put a hand on his shoulder. Ortega glanced over at her before hanging his head in shame. "I let my ego get the better of me, Penelope... once again."

"And once again, you're being too hard on yourself," Penelope tried to console him.

"Not this time," he began pacing the floor which was difficult to do in the hovel that they had been sharing with two other people.

Knowingly, Penelope reached under the kitchen counter and pulled out a bottle of Jameson whiskey and fumbled through the cabinets until she'd found a small juice glass. She poured a healthy shot before reaching into the icebox for a cube. She swirled the cube as well as possible in the tiny glass and offered it to him just as he'd spun around and circled back.

"Thanks," he accepted it, surprised. "But where did this come from?"

"A gal has to have some secrets," she batted her eyes at him, her Southern drawl a little affected for emphasis. "I figured it might come in handy on a day when you needed...reinforcements."

Ortega smiled and took a sip.

"Alright, I'll bite," Penelope asked. "How is your ego to blame?"

"I was so set on bringing down the Vandenberg family, their cult, their shady company, and their empire that I put several civilians in harm's way by dragging you to Ireland."

"Hang on," Penelope corrected him. "Shep and I are far from 'civilians' and Rue Brennan is now an honest-to-goodness private investigator. We all knew what we were getting into. Or, at the very least, what we didn't know, we accepted and assumed the risks."

"But now I've got a mentally ill escaped con out there with Rue, and who the hell knows what her plan is? All I know is that it somehow involves that murderer Jax Liebling, and whatever it is, it isn't good!" Ortega raised his voice before downing his drink. "Sorry," he slammed the juice glass on the kitchen table. "I didn't mean to yell...or slam the glass down just then." He rubbed his forehead and resumed pacing.

Penelope fell in step behind him, expertly pivoting as he did, so that she followed, but never got in his way.

"Well, let's think about this a minute," Penelope reasoned. "Why did Midge kill in the first place?"

"What? Why—" Ortega thought a moment. "Because she thought she was helping Rue."

"By creating a dramatic scene to push Darwin and Rue together," Penelope held her palms up, "And—"

"And when someone threatened to try to pin it on Rue—"

"Midge stepped in."

"Yes," Ortega answered. "But why put her in danger again now?"

"So Midge could rescue her?" Penelope offered. "She does seem awfully concerned about what her 'bestie' is up to."

"Hmmm, maybe," Ortega answered. "You don't think she'd actually harm Rue, do you?"

"No, not intentionally," Penelope offered. "She might be putting her in danger, but there's more we're just not seeing."

"Damn, this is frustrating. Being outsmarted by a young hooligan."

"Hooligan?" Penelope laughed. "Listen to you." She abruptly stopped in front of him as he turned. Ortega bumped into her before catching himself.

"Sorry," he said, as he stood, his body only an inch from hers. He didn't back up.

"Neither one of us have had a decent night's sleep in days; we're in the wrong time zone, and it's late," Penelope reasoned, touching his arm.

"But if we don't report it—"

"We could report it and get her killed," Penelope said.

"We could not report it and get her killed," Ortega reasoned.

"And what will the police do with what little we have to go on?"

Ortega glanced off into space for a minute. "Rue said she was going to get us groceries," he peered into the distance.

"Yes? What of it?" Penelope asked.

"We had our rental car. There's nothing within walking distance."

"Maybe she called a cab?"

"Maybe. Or—"

"Or what?" Penelope asked.

"Maybe she called Midge?" Ortega suggested.

"Why would she do that without telling us?"

"Because they were friends from a long time ago," Ortega answered. "And you said it yourself, Rue is a bona fide investigator."

"I don't think we're going to make any wise decisions tonight," Penelope yawned. "I'm exhausted and so are you. For just this once, what if we sleep on it and file a missing person report in the morning, just as Midge said."

After a dramatic pause, Ortega put his hands on Penelope's waist. She glanced down at them in surprise and then lifted her chin to meet his gaze. "You're right about one thing, Penelope."

"What's that?" she whispered. There was apprehension in her eyes, and something else. Ortega hadn't seen that look from her in a long time.

"I don't think we're going to make any wise decisions tonight," he whispered back.

Ortega pulled Penelope in close and kissed her, the way someone kisses the one they love when they haven't seen them in a very long time. And it did go on...for a very long time. Finally, Ortega led her back to his room.

"Just one question?" Penelope gasped, breaking free from his lips.

"What's that?" He nuzzled her ear.

"Top bunk or bottom?" she snorted.

Ortega laughed, and then pulled her to the floor alongside him, rolling over her and pinning her arms over her head.

"Just like old times," she giggled. "Such a gentleman."

"Gentleman, my ass." He held her arms down and kissed her fervently on her lips. She lifted her hips slightly and moaned. "Are you trying to get away?" he joked.

Penelope shook her head. "No, never," she kissed him back. He released her arms and she circled them around his neck, hugging him to her with her back on the floor. He put the weight of his body on top of her, bracing himself with his hands, worried he might be too heavy for her small frame. She didn't seem to mind. She wrapped her legs around his legs, as if trapping him on top of her. "Never again."

CHAPTER 17
The Temple Bar

~

"It's just up here," Baxter pushed Moira's wheelchair along the cobblestone street with some difficulty. "Sorry," he apologized as the chair made jerky movements from side to side and back and forth, leaving Moira to hang onto the arm rests and brace herself.

"Where is it we're going again?" Moira asked.

"I'm told there's a little speak-easy-type pub up this way. It's supposed to be fun...very hush-hush and not too many people know about it."

"Really?" Moira was interested. "What's so special about it?"

"Don't know," Baxter confessed. "Just that it's so little known?" he suggested.

Against her better judgment, she finally agreed to a date with Baxter Baker on the condition that he knew there would be 'no funny business.' He agreed, wholeheartedly. After weeks of asking, she finally said, 'yes,' and he was not going to mess this up. She knew it was a bad idea, given that he was her boss and all, but she reminded herself that she was actually the one doing Baxter's job. So, that made it okay, didn't it?

Moira wore a bright red dress that evening, one with large ruffled sleeves that fanned out as if she were flamenco dancer. On her feet were small red ballet-type flats. An odd choice from a woman who was bound to a wheelchair and couldn't dance. Still, she wore one side of her hair down, letting it fall gracefully around her shoulder, the other side pinned back with a flower clip. Her lips, Baxter notice, had just a hint of a pink gloss. He tried not to look at them for too long because he found them distracting. Finally, he turned down an alley in the Temple Bar district.

"Should be around here somewhere," Baxter ran his hand through his hair, flustered. He was never flustered, always self-assured. And yet, for reasons which he could not explain, he felt the need to impress Moira. He wondered, *was it because she was one of the few women who seemed immune to his charms?* He found Emma Post alluring, too, and she couldn't be bothered with him. Did he only crave women who played hard-to-get? *No,* he thought to himself, *that can't be it. What was it?* While Baxter pondered to himself, Moira waited patiently for as long as she could before suggesting, "Em, could that be it?" She pointed to a black door that somehow blended nicely with the brick buildings that seemed to swallow it. It sat a few inches back from the building itself, making it easy to pass without seeing it.

"No, I don't think so," Baxter shook his head. "Should be up this way, I think."

Moira hung her head and pinched her lips together as if stifling a laugh. "I really think you might give it a knock and see," Moira suggested. "I mean, seeing as we're here already and all. What have we got to lose?"

Baxter relented and rapped on the door with two knuckles on the back of his fist. No one answered.

"See?" Baxter walked toward Moira, arms spread wide.

Just then, a small window in the door opened. It wasn't much larger than an index card. Eyes could be seen on the other side of the door, but they said nothing, merely staring. "That you, Moira?" a muffled voice finally asked.

"It is, Skinny," Moira answered. "Fancy meeting you here."

The door flung open and a very rotund man with a bald head and a graying beard greeted her. "As I live and breathe!" He smiled. "Moira Dodd, I haven't seen you in ages! Best come inside. Can't have the door open too long." He eyed Baxter up and down suspiciously. "This bloke with you?"

"I'm afraid so," Moira laughed.

"You've been here before?" Baxter was surprised.

"Eh, no." Moira winked at Skinny. "Skinny and I just go way back." Skinny tipped his head in return. He made his way over to the street where Moira sat.

"Didja injure yourself, then, Moira?" Skinny stood beside Moira, peering down at her in the chair. She grabbed the wheels and took a hard rotation to the left, leaving Skinny just at her right. While Baxter was momentarily distracted by the noise coming from the inside of the venue, Moira grabbed the moment. She elbowed Skinny in the side of his gut. He sucked in his breath.

"Well, get on in," Skinny urged, lowering his voice and wincing. "We're almost at capacity tonight."

Baxter took the handles on the back of Moira's wheelchair and rolled her through the door, only to be greeted by a narrow set of stairs. At the top, music and the loud voices of people laughing and carousing could be heard. Baxter's face dropped.

"Hmmm," Moira answered. "Sorry, Mr. Baker. But it looks like this might not work out as we'd hoped."

"Nonsense," Baxter answered. "I can carry you."

"Up those stairs!" Moira laughed. "You'll break your back, and likely drop me on my arse! No, thanks."

Baxter took Skinny aside and slipped him a few bills. "Anything we can do?" he whispered. Moira pretended not to notice.

"Not to worry," Skinny was confident. "Give me a tick and I'll be right back." Skinny bounded the steps two at a time. Moira eyed the stairs, reluctantly. Minutes later, Skinny returned with three other men. Before she could protest, they grabbed her chair, with her still in it, two in the front and two in the back and bounded up the steps. Moira's single hair clip came loose and bounced down the steps while her red locks flew haphazardly down her back. She struggled to keep her head and neck upright at the angle at which she ascended. She gripped the arm rest, half exhilarated, and half terrified at the threat of them accidentally dropping her, sending them all crashing onto the concrete below.

Baxter followed behind, occasionally putting his hand out as if there were any way he could protect her if she *did* take a spill. He spotted the flower clip and grabbed it on its descent, stuffing it in his jacket pocket.

At the landing, Moira breathed a sigh of relief as the men set her down. "Thank you, boys," she laughed. "But you lads are nutty! You might have dropped me!"

"You, Moira?" One of the men answered. "Never!"

Baxter turned to Skinny. "Thanks, but I coulda helped carry her, you know?"

Skinny looked Baxter up and down. "Couldn't risk it," he finally answered. "You have the smoothest hands I've ever seen fer a man. Not sure heavy lifting is yer strong suit."

Baxter's face became flushed. He was about to retort when he realized Skinny wasn't being purposefully unkind. He was just unabashedly honest.

"Hey, Moira," one of the men tried again. "What happened to ya?" Before he could say anything more, it was Skinny's turn to jab an elbow into someone's ribs. The man fell silent, confused.

"Thank you, again, gentlemen," Moira praised. To Baxter, she said, "Shall we go and see what the fuss is all about?"

"Excellent idea, Miss Dodd," Baxter agreed, once again regaining control of the handles behind the chair and guiding his date toward what he assumed was the main area. "Oh," he paused, "your hair clip." He pulled the clip out of his pocket and attempted to fluff the flower back into its original shape.

"Nah," Moira shook her head. "You keep it. Probably look better on you," she teased.

Baxter grinned, mischievously, as he clipped the small red flower to the side of his blonde locks. Moira lifted a hand to her mouth to stifle a laugh, but it was no use. "I was...right!" Tears of laughter streamed down her face. "Better on...you," she breathed heavily.

"I doubt that," Baxter laughed. "But now I've committed to it, there's no turning back."

They crossed the threshold, hesitantly. Inside, it was a struggle to squeeze through the crowd without the footrests of Moira's chair nearly clipping people's ankles at every turn. But eventually, they found a spot catty-corner to the stage. The place was packed to the gills with every chair or booth filled. Baxter didn't mind, he leaned against a pole and rested his hands on Moira's shoulders as they gazed with anticipation at the stage. It was a bold move, he realized, but Moira didn't seem to mind.

Moments later, without introductions, the band launched into their rendition of 'Whiskey in the Jar.' Applause erupted.

"Is that—" Baxter began, stunned.

"The same," Moira answered confidently.

"But they're famous!" Baxter protested. "What are they doing in a dive bar in a small corner of Dublin playing for a handful of people and making crap money in the process?"

"You think too much, Mr. Baker," Moira chastised, peering at him from over her shoulder. "Here, look." She pointed as solo singer-songwriters and members from at least one other world-traveled band joined the first. No one bothered to warm up, as each performer was ready with his or her instruments, they just joined in...keyboard, guitar, bass, drums, fiddles, vocals.

Baxter listened with appreciation and awe as the music soon morphed into a version of 'Dreams.' The music grew louder, drowning out the voices of the crowd. Baxter could feel his heartbeat pulsing in his head, seemingly to the rhythm of the music, and despite the body heat and limited elbow room, this was the most exciting time he could remember... and he had experienced a lot.

Moments later, Skinny pushed his way through the crowd, sloshing two pints of Guinness along the way. "Here ya go, lass," he handed one to Moira and offered the second to Baxter. "On the house, just promise not to stay away so long next time, okay, Moira?" He winked and disappeared into the crowd.

"Never been here before, you say?" Baxter leaned close to her ear. His breath on her neck gave her the chills.

"Well," she answered mischievously, "never with you. That's fer sure." She sipped her Guinness.

How odd, Baxter thought to himself. *And she's obviously never been here while in a wheelchair before. Her friends all seemed surprised to see her that way, and she was visibly shaken when they carried her up the steps.* The best that he could tell was that whatever happened to her, happened somewhat recently, but she didn't want to talk about it.

At that moment, Moira did the most surprising thing, she bent her Guinness-free arm and rested her left hand over his, clasping it over her shoulder.

Baxter's luck was turning around. He could feel it.

~

BAXTER AND MOIRA waited until most of the club had cleared out before they attempted the staircase a second time. Fortunately, with an assist from Skinny's men, the descent was easier. Except this time, Baxter insisted on helping, and so it was Skinny's turn to stand guard, always keeping two steps ahead, treading carefully backward while holding the rail, just in case Moira took a topple.

At last, they reached the bottom, and they welcomed a cold blast of fresh air after the stuffiness of what had become a smoke-filled room. It was so heavy; they could still smell the cigarette smoke on their clothes. Baxter's eyes were a little red and his nose stuffy, but he didn't care.

"Good seeing ya, Moira," Skinny offered.

"Don't stay away so long next time," another friend added, glancing at her chair, but saying nothing.

"Will do," she nodded. "Gotta make sure you lads aren't getting up to no good!"

"You're a fine one to talk, lass," he wagged a finger, good-naturedly.

To Baxter, Skinny warned, "You be good to her, ya hear me? Otherwise, you'll have to deal with Skinny." He pointed a thumb at himself as if it needed clarification.

"I plan on it," Baxter answered, attempting to run his fingers through his hair in what he hoped would be a suave moment. Only, he connected with the flower he'd forgotten about. His sleeve got stuck on it, and for a moment, his wrist was trapped to his head lest he accidentally pull his hair out.

The men laughed, shutting the door behind them. The sound of several locks being latched could be heard from the outside.

"Would you look at you?" Moira teased. "Here, lean over."

Baxter obeyed as Moira reached up and untangled his sleeve from his hair. She retrieved her hair clip and stuck it lopsidedly on her head. She didn't care and neither did Baxter. He grinned sheepishly.

"You hungry?" he asked. While the bar was great on drinks and peanuts, it was sadly lacking food.

"Yeah," she answered. "And I gotta find a loo," she confessed. "It was too crowded to move in that place."

"Know of any place open at this hour?" he asked.

"Not at this hour," she confessed. "We could always—" But she stopped herself. *Go back to her place? Nah,* she thought. *Too risky.*

"Yes?" he answered, hopefully.

"Go back to the office," she suggested. "I always keep a couple of extra frozen dinners in the break room in case I get stuck working late or can't make it out to lunch."

Baxter took the handles on the back of her chair and aimed them toward the office. "We need to talk to that arse boss of yours about your hours," he joked. Really, he had no idea she put in that kind of time. But how could he? He was always late to arrive and early to leave.

Moira chuckled. "Quite."

"So why do you suppose famous people hang out in little dive bars like that one?" Baxter was perplexed. "There's no money in it."

"Did it ever occur to you that it's not all about the money," Moira suggested. "Maybe they want to practice their craft among friends, to feel normal again by stepping out of the public eye. To play music just for the music's sake."

"Why, Moira," Baxter commented, "I had no idea you were such a poet." He pushed her chair carefully across the cobblestones. "I suppose you are right."

CHAPTER 18
Betrothed

"What's this?" Jax found Midge draped across his couch wearing nothing but a silk robe opened at the front, yet strategically covering all the intimate places of her body. Her hair was washed from a fresh shower and wrapped in a cotton towel.

"I have a present for you," she smirked.

"I can see that," Jax made his way over to her.

"Not me," she stuck her bare foot out and pressed it into his chest, stopping him. The robe slipped away, revealing the bottom half of her torso. He paused to admire her, grinning back at her, seductively. "Over there," she gestured toward the coffee table. On it, sat a little white box wrapped in a red ribbon.

"What do we have here?" Jax asked, curiously, venturing over to the table. He held the box up to his ear, playfully. "It's not ticking, so it's not a watch or a bomb," he joked. "Shall I shake it, or is it fragile?"

"Not anymore, it's not," Midge retorted. "But it used to be when it was alive."

"You don't mean?" Jax was taken aback.

"Proof of my commitment to you," Midge explained, an uncustomary tear forming in the corner of her eye.

"Are you crying?" Jax asked, more surprised than concerned.

"Let's just say, it wasn't easy murdering my bestie," Midge answered. "So open it, you lug. Then maybe you'll be convinced that I fully intend to marry you...tomorrow, if you like."

Jax picked up the box and pulled at the ribbon until it unraveled. Lifting the lid, he peered inside. There, he found a tuft of hair and what appeared to be the tip of a human finger, both carefully sealed in tiny clear bags, the kind someone uses when they don't want their silver jewelry to tarnish. He lifted the finger out, hesitantly. "You don't mean—"

"Extracted from Rue's corpse after I killed her," Midge explained.

"How did you do it?" Jax was intrigued.

"My, you are morbid," Midge answered. "Single gunshot wound to the head. I removed the tip of her finger and cut a lock of her hair, then rolled her body off the cliff."

"Which finger? What cliff?" Jax asked, suspiciously.

"What difference does it make? Don't you believe me?" Midge asked, indignantly. "Fine." She rolled her eyes. "Pinky finger and a remote area of the Causeway at night. Are you happy now?"

"Not much blood." He turned the bag with the finger over. "Other than a little smeared bit on the bag here," he noticed.

"It was making a mess everywhere, so I cauterized it and cleaned it up," Midge explained.

Jax moved on to the hair. "I thought hers was more a mousy brown. This appears darker with a bit of gray in it."

"Maybe you misremembered." Midge became agitated. "And even I have a few early gray strands. I just dye mine. Listen, I didn't have to do that. I did it to prove my love and devotion for you, but if that's not enough—"

"Take it easy, my pet." Jax put the box on the table, concerned. "Of course I believe you. I guess I was just surprised, given how much I know Rue Brennan meant to you." Even now, he had trouble saying Rue's name. It dripped off his tongue with jealous disdain.

Midge sniffed back a few more tears. "I did it for you...us." She slipped the robe off her shoulders, revealing her breasts. She lifted her chest to give Jax a better view.

Jax lunged at her, dragging her to her feet and pulling her close to him.

As he kissed her neck, she asked, "You did say we were cleared to marry, didn't you?"

"I applied for the license months ago. We're in the clear, but we should do it soon before anyone finds out that I'm marrying an escaped convict."

"Do you think anyone in Ireland would care what I did in America?" Midge unbuttoned the top of Jax's shirt with her fingers. "Correction... what *we* did?"

"I'd just as soon not take any chances," Jax answered. "I've got big plans for us," he boasted. "Let's head to the local registry in the morning."

Jax was unusually cheerful when he arrived at the factory early Monday morning.

"Good morning, Mr. Liebling," Moira greeted Jax as he made his way past her desk and to his private office.

Most times, Jax grunted at her or waved a hand by way of acknowledgment. But today, to her surprise, he stopped to smile at her. She flinched a little. It was as if the Devil himself were baring his teeth. "Good morning, Ms. Dodd," he greeted. "Did you have a nice weekend?"

Moira thought back to the Temple Bar and the evenings that followed, all with Baxter Baker...all innocent, of course. She refused to let him lift her out of her chair, even when he asked, claiming that she wasn't ready for him to see 'down there' just yet. She was referring to her legs, but his mind went elsewhere. The most they'd shared were a few kisses at the end of each date. In a way, Moira thought it was better this way. She had to be sure.

"Yes," Moira smiled dreamily, "a very nice weekend, indeed." It was an extended weekend, actually, as Baxter convinced her to call in sick before the week was out. As an afterthought, she added, "And you? Good weekend?"

"Yes," Jax answered, tucking the Irish Times Moira had left out for him under one arm. "As a matter of fact, I got married."

"Oh," Moira was surprised. "Well, congratulations, Mr. Liebling."

"Thanks," he unlocked his office door before gazing around the room. "No Mr. Baker?"

"Not yet," she sighed. In her head, all those 'rational' thoughts began flooding in. *If he can't even be bothered to run his own company, how can I trust that he'll be responsible in other areas of his life? Can I even count on him to be there for me if I need him to?* She flushed those thoughts from her mind. After all, it was just the beginning. Nothing said she had to commit to anything, just yet. Still, she was beginning to regret following his suggestion to call in sick Friday so that they could spend a little more time together. It was careless of her.

"Well, when he does, can you have him pull the quarterly sales numbers for me?" Jax brought her out of her thoughts.

"Of course...but, er, I can do that for you now, if you like?"

"You?" Frankly, Jax hadn't really thought of Moira as anything more than a convenient pretty face. "Well, that would be fine...thank you." He closed the door of his office behind him.

Had Moira not have been clenching her teeth so forcefully, her jaw might have dropped. While it boggled the mind at who might want to marry Jax Liebling, she was most astounded that he asked how her weekend was and even said, 'thank you.' *Perhaps marriage agrees with him,* she thought.

She clicked on the keypad of the Apple Powerbook Baxter had purchased for her, amazed at how small and portable it was compared to the large and clunky desktop PC she was accustomed to. After entering her password, she navigated to the financial folders and printed out the reports she knew Jax would want to see, balance sheets, income statements, and the like. She retrieved them from the office printer, but before dropping them into a manilla folder to deliver to Jax, she snuck a peek at the numbers.

Aside from the fact that she felt Baxter's pay, which far exceeded her own, should be swapped for her salary, given that she was doing the work for the both of them, something else caught her eye...two 'something else-s' in fact. First, Jax Liebling appeared to take no salary at all. *How can that be?* Second, the company appeared to have taken a substantial hit this last quarter. She flipped through the pages of the profit and loss statement.

From what she could tell, almost none of the Church of Infinite Love campuses bought any of their health bars in the last quarter. Most sales were to smaller grocery chains, herbal shops and organic food stores.

She heard a shuffling in Jax's office and quickly closed the folder, papers inside, just as he threw the door open. "Ah," she spun her wheelchair around, handing him the folder. "I was just about to bring this to you."

He took the folder from her. "You didn't happen to look through any of this, did you?" Jax eyed her suspiciously.

"No," Moira lied. "Of course not. I wouldn't know what I was reading even if I did...which I didn't, of course."

After a long pause, Jax nodded, mumbling under his breath as he turned his back on Moira, "Who's pulling the strings now, Jersey Girl?" He retreated back into his office and closed the door, just as Baxter finally arrived for work.

"Hello, gorgeous," Baxter stroked the side of Moira's hair and leaned in to kiss her on the cheek.

"Not here," she whispered back, gesturing her head toward Jax's office. "Let's keep it professional, shall we?"

"Right," Baxter agreed, sitting on the edge of her desk with one leg on the floor and the other dangling in midair. "Anything interesting happening today?"

Just then, Jax's door flew open. His face was hot with anger as he blew past Moira and Baxter without so much as a word. He was so livid, he went right for the stairwell instead of the elevator, using the descent to flush out some of his pent-up energy.

"What was that all about?" Baxter asked.

"He asked to see the quarterly reports," Moira answered.

"I take that to mean they weren't good?"

"No, they weren't," she confirmed. "But you didn't hear it from me. I'm just the secretary, got it?" She winked.

Baxter caught on and winked back. He wasn't worried. He certainly took little time to bother about the numbers, so he was grateful to have someone working for him who did.

Just then, there was a knock at the open door as an older woman wearing a gray uniform peered around the corner. It was the floor manager, Orla.

"Are ye feeling any bett-ah?" Orla asked.

"Am I—" Moira seemed confused until Baxter nudged her chair with his foot. "Oh, right," she smiled, remembering. "Yes, much better. Thank you for asking. Hope everything went okay while I was gone."

"Oh, fine," Orla answered. "I run a tight ship."

"Well, good," Moira seemed relieved.

"I've jest got a question about a box of bar wrappers we received," Orla crinkled her forehead, confused.

"What about them?" Moira asked.

"Well...here." She reached into her pocket and pulled out the pink wrapper cover and handed it to Moira.

Baxter peered over Moira's shoulder as they took a closer look. Instead of the standard Vandenberg Nutraceutical logo, it had been replaced with a cartoon-like image of Jax himself, the side of his face prominent like a Victorian cameo.

"Did you know anything about this?" Moira asked Baxter.

Baxter's eyes grew wide as he tilted his head as if to say, *not in front of the help.*

She fell silent.

"Well, of course I did!" Baxter stood, speaking with much more bravado than he felt. "A little rebranding we're doing."

"Oh," Orla nodded, uncertainly. "Will you be wantin' us to use these new ones from now on then?"

"Er," Baxter thought a moment, eyeing Moira for help.

"How many of the old wrappers do you have for the, er...*Love*, bar?"

"Not many," Orla laughed. "They are the first to sell out because everyone hopes the ingredients will help add spice to the bedroom, if you know what I mean." Orla blushed at Baxter.

"Not with that man's face on it, they won't," Moira mumbled under her breath.

Orla and Moira shared a chuckle while Baxter tried to find a way to bide some time.

"Hmm," Baxter thought a moment. "Why don't you use the old stock first, and I'll be sure to check in with our marketing team to see when the official rollout is."

"Yes, Mr. Baker," Orla blushed, feeling a little guilty about laughing at Moira's joke.

"Thank you, Orla," Baxter smiled, escorting Orla out of the office and closing the door behind her.

Turning to Moira, he asked, "Did you know anything about this?"

"No," Moira answered. "I'm as surprised as you are."

"There's something fishy going on here," Baxter said.

"Several somethings, if you ask me," Moira confessed.

"What do you mean?" Baxter was confused.

Moira reached into her desk and pulled out a second copy of the Irish Times. "Turn to page three," she instructed.

Baxter unfolded the newspaper and turned the pages. There was his picture, a closeup of him on a Vandenberg company yacht standing next to, none other than Erasmus Vandenberg, with the headline, 'Getting Away with Murder.' Baxter's face dropped. In it, an 'unnamed source' accused Baxter of being the real mastermind behind Erasmus Vandenberg's death, and how he'd planned all along to take over as their new CEO.

Baxter bunched up the paper, angrily, and tossed it on the floor.

"It's just tabloid gossip," Moira reasoned. "I wouldn't take it too seriously."

"No, the *Irish Mirror* is celebrity gossip, this is a legit newspaper," Baxter complained. "I think someone in my own family has been after my head since the skeletons in the Vandenberg closet have surfaced."

Moira treaded carefully. "Wanna talk about it?" she asked gently.

Baxter held her gaze for a moment, trying not to get distracted by the flecks of gold in her bright green eyes. *Well, if I can't trust Moira, who can I trust?*

CHAPTER 19
Fuming

~

Jax Liebling was quiet, calculated, and seemingly calm as a cucumber as he entered the old poorhouse in Belfast, the same one that Bernie Forger was repurposing into COIL's new Young Ambassador Academy. He'd had time to get ahold of his anger before it got away with him on his journey from Dublin.

Bernie was busy going through plans with one of the contractors hired to help renovate the thirty-five rooms on the premises, into dormitories with boys on one side and girls on the other. On each end, were sleeping quarters for several of the soon-to-be headmasters and lead instructors. At the center, were plans for a dining hall and main classrooms.

"Will you be wantin' a quote on the flooring and paint as well?" the contractor asked, making large squiggly marks on a legal-sized clipboard with notepad. He used the edge of the pen to slide under his hard hat and give the itchy side of his head a scratch.

"Not necessary," Bernie answered. "The students will take care of that."

The contractor appeared confused for a moment, but decided it was best not to ask.

It was then that Bernie noticed Jax Liebling standing there, fists balled. "Mr. Liebling," Bernie turned toward the smaller man in surprise, clearing his throat awkwardly. *Slithery fellow,* he thought to himself, *I didn't even hear him come in.* "I had no idea you had an interest in our school. What brings you to Belfast?"

"You know very well why I'm here," Jax's bottom lip quivered as he struggled to remain calm.

The contractor eyed the scene, uncomfortably. They had already been working late and certainly didn't want any more delays. "Eh, me men are going to knock off now, but will crack on again first thing in the mornin."

"Er, right," Bernie acknowledged as the contractor rounded up the few men still at work, even though it was past dinner time. "Appreciate the extra time!" he called after them.

To Jax, he said, "I'm afraid you've lost me." Bernie shrugged his shoulders.

"At least 39% of the revenue generated at Vandenberg Nutraceuticals... soon to be known as the Jax Corporation...came from the Church of Infinite Love."

"Is that so?" Bernie feigned ignorance. "I had no idea."

"You had every idea," Jax accused. "With church membership dwindling, I took a risk in buying you out, but I was promised my partnership with the church would continue, and even grow during the rebranding period."

"So, what's the problem?" Bernie asked. "We're still partners."

"Purchases from the church have come to a startling halt, even though we've been fully operational for several months now. Mind telling me why?"

"You'll have to speak to Mr. Lundy about that, I—"

"I'm asking you!" Jax sucked in a deep breath and forced himself to exhale slowly through his mouth. He regained his composure.

"Look," Bernie explained. "We have limited funding at the moment, and I've been putting everything into getting this school underway. Plus, I've always said the factory should be relocated somewhere out of the Westport family's turf." The corner of Bernie's lips turned up in a smirk. "On the plus side, you can't pay a tithe if there's no money, can you?"

"So what was your plan?" Jax demanded, ignoring the comment. "To put me out of business and then set up a new nutraceutical factory in Belfast? Or, just leave Baxter Baker and I hanging out to dry?"

Bernie paused dramatically, staring into space. *I wish Lundy were here,* he thought. *He's much better at these confrontations.*

"I assure you that I have no intention of harming Vandenberg…Er… Jax Corporation. It's just that the timing is off."

"But I'm investing everything—" Jax caught himself. "I am investing a very large sum of money in your school to support the church. Lundy just had me sign an agreement. Had I known you were going to stop promoting our products in favor of selling members books and school admission, I might have done things differently."

"Don't you understand?" Bernie questioned, solemnly. "The faith-healing business isn't what it used to be, and there's more money to be had in selling parents on prestigious, religious-based education. They'll drop a year's tuition and room and board if it means their son, *or daughter,* we allow girls in our school too, can climb the ranks to Ambassadors, Deacons and Deaconesses, Ministers and Elders of the church. And, what better way to recruit prospective members than by sending our young army out with meaningful pamphlets and pocket-books that explain our faith in simple terms?"

"Well, why not just print a few quotes from the Bible on the inside of our health bars? I would argue people would be more inclined to enjoy a tasty snack than to actually take the time and read," Jax argued.

"Not a bad idea," Bernie answered. "You should run with it."

"You and Lundy are screwing me over," Jax argued. "Keep it up and I may have to rethink my investments in your academy."

"Well, then you'd be making a huge mistake," Bernie replied. "Besides, you just said yourself, you've already signed the agreement." Bernie may have been arrogant and shortsighted, but brave he was not. He saw the color rise on Jax's face. Jax looked like a tea kettle ready to boil over. "Look," he tried again. "We all stand to get rich off this school…not that it's about the money, of course." His eyes shot upward toward heaven.

"How do you figure?" Jax eyed the walls of the old building, noting that the air felt clammy and damp. "This place could only hold a small number of students, at best."

"Well, that's the brilliant thing," Bernie's eyes lit up. "Walk with me, Jax. And, I'll show you around."

Against his better judgment, Jax fell into step beside Bernie who took two steps to Jax's one given their height disparity. Upon noticing that, Bernie walked faster. He seemed to be enjoying Jax's struggle to keep up.

"If we put in bunk beds and have the benches in the dining hall also serve as a study area, why, we can stuff about four students in each room." Bernie led the way down the corridor, stopping at one of the rooms in question. There was one tiny square window to the outside world. It had bars on it, but no window panes. A cold draft could be felt as it blew through the room. Jax shuddered a little. The room resembled an ancient prison cell, and he couldn't imagine four young kids fitting in there comfortably. He didn't particularly care, either way. It was just an observation.

Bernie led the way to a more spacious room, a good three times the one they were just in. This room already had a desk and chair, a modest bookshelf, and a very large window with a view overlooking the grounds. In the corner was a full-sized bed. This room even came equipped with a small fireplace.

"The headmaster's suite," Bernie explained. "I imagine I shall live here in the interim, until we can find a suitable replacement."

Given Jax's recent conversation with Lundy, he could easily see himself there. But that wasn't to be shared with Bernie...at least, not yet. Jax eyed a half-eaten muffin on a plate, and a soiled coffee cup beside it on the desk. If he didn't know better, he'd have guessed Bernie had already taken up residence.

"But there's more," Bernie added, "much more. This way, please."

Bernie led Jax down another very long and dark hallway that had a damp, musty aroma mixed with bleach. Jax choked a little on the repugnant mix of smells. The walls, he noticed, were stone whereas the front of the school was a mix of brick, wood and concrete.

Bernie read his mind. "You can see where we've already made some additions. And this building is at the forefront of fifty acres of property, seventy-five if we're able to buy out the modest widget factory next door." He motioned toward the wall as if pointing to the neighboring factory on the opposite end of the property line. "The poor ingrate has yet to figure out that wooden toys and plastic dollies are dying products that no one wants anymore. Lundy made him a nice offer...more than what anyone else would ever offer."

"With my money," Jax retorted. "So, your plan is expansion, then?" His eyes suddenly grew wide as they reached the end of the hall where an open-air window revealed a vast landscape that overlooked what appeared to be a very large concrete pit, at least the length of tennis court. On the horizon, a soft orange hue signified the setting sun. It would be dark soon. "What is that supposed to be?"

Bernie cleared his throat uncomfortably. "While we have every intention of building out more dormitories that will allow us to house more students and offer degree programs in sought-after topics other than religious studies, degrees like business administration, retail management, marketing and such, we have to first address the elephant in the room, so to speak.

"And what elephant would that be?" Jax asked.

Bernie clasped his hands behind his back in a professorial manner, shaking his head, solemnly.

"The reason the Church of Infinite Love came under so much scrutiny was not because of our healing practices or the ingredients in our food products," Bernie explained.

"It wasn't?" Jax played along, but not without a hint of sarcasm in his voice. "Then pray tell, what was it?"

"The problem was a few bad seeds ruining the church's otherwise stellar reputation," Bernie explained.

Jax's eyes lit up in recognition. "Oh, I see," he nodded, "you mean the incidents that hit the newsstands claiming the church was responsible for the death of several young women."

"Wretched girls, if you ask me." Bernie pursed his lips as if he just tasted something sour.

"I suppose it didn't help that one of your Ambassadors saw fit to take out Erasmus Vandenberg and anyone else who stood in the church's way?" Jax reminded Bernie. "Isn't that what really blew the lid on everything, causing you to have to rebrand in the first place?"

Bernie was stuck on a thought that he couldn't seem to let go of.

Instead, he answered, "If the children were taught to behave properly from the get go, none of this would have happened."

Jax found Bernie's blinders to the truth somewhat fascinating. "But then, dear old Erasmus would still be alive and you wouldn't be in charge, now would you?"

A hint of a smile crossed Bernie's lips as he glanced in Jax's direction. He could tell that Jax was beginning to understand his perspective... finally. The smaller man's face had returned to a normal shade and he appeared decidedly less aggravated.

"True," Bernie answered. "But I attribute that to God stepping in and showing everyone who's boss."

"Do you really believe that God would kill a man to continue the church's work? Why not just use his powers to change people's minds?"

"God gave us free will, so he neither killed Erasmus nor did he prevent him from being killed. Rather, through his teachings, I was led to recognize that he was calling me to take my divine place as the leader of this flock."

The shear narcissism, Jax thought, vehemently. *Where does this idiot get off thinking himself the likes of Jesus, the Pope, Gandhi, or even...me, for example.* Jax may not have been religious, but he definitely saw himself as vastly smarter, more accomplished and more worthy than Bernie, and yet God hadn't bothered to reach out to *him.* This reaffirmed Jax's belief that there was no God, and if there ever *had* been a God, he was now dead.

"So, about the pit?" Jax reminded him.

"We're establishing a building here where the more troublesome students will reside. These will be the ones sent here not just for religious education, but for behavioral reform."

"I see," Jax nodded. "But what's the purpose of such a large concave hole? The base of it looks like solid concrete." His face twitched a little, gleefully almost.

"There will be a basement with several secluded rooms where the unrepentant can be left alone to pray and learn the error of their ways."

"Solitary confinement?" Jax was aghast. "Prison cells?" It's not that Jax cared one way or another, he was just surprised that a 'man of God' would go to such extreme measures.

"We like to think of them as private prayer rooms," Bernie answered simply. After a long pause, he turned to Jax. "Well, it's getting dark. I suppose we should be locking up for the evening. But I hope I've eased your mind about a few things. I know things with the factory are a bit tricky right now, but once the school gets up and running, we'll be expanding our programs, and...I almost forgot," Bernie's eyes lit up, "as I mentioned, we want to procure the property next door. Instead of outsourcing for our printed materials, we can do them all in house and have the students run it...sort of like a work-study program."

Even Jax had to admit this was a pretty good idea. As Bernie motioned for Jax to follow him back through the hallway to the main entrance, Jax felt something growing in the center of his chest. It gnawed at his insides like an angry scavenger bird eating its prey. *What was this feeling?* he asked himself. Then he realized it...*envy, disgust, and anger.*

Jax took a deep breath and commented pleasantly, "I see where you and Mr. Lundy are going with this, but I will have a talk with him about the financial aspects, to see what else we might do to keep the factory afloat in the meantime."

"That's the spirit!" Bernie encouraged. "And who knows? After we've filled these halls with lots of hungry students, maybe your snack bars will be part of the dining program here."

Jax nodded, thoughtfully, before asking, "But do me a favor, would you?"

"What's that?" Bernie hesitated.

"Before it gets much darker, could we walk a bit of the grounds, just so I can see more of your...vision?"

Bernie tugged at the collar of his shirt, uncomfortably. "Perhaps the morning would be better—"

"I'm busy in the morning," Jax interrupted. "It's the start of a long week at Jax Corporation. Just another ten minutes or so." He felt Bernie's reluctance. "That way, I can feel more confident in our joint venture and speak more competently with Lundy. If I had been a smarter man, I would have asked to see the grounds before signing anything. But, I realize I can be a little...impulsive." Jax smiled, eyes boring into Bernie as if willing the taller man to change his mind.

It worked.

"I suppose a few extra minutes won't hurt. I'll just grab a flashlight from the headmaster's room, just in case." Bernie paused to snatch a small light and hung its chord around his wrist. He also pulled out the desk drawer and retrieved a set of keys. Jax noted that Bernie seemed to know where all the supplies were in a place that he supposedly had yet to occupy.

Finally, they had reached the main hall. As they stepped out into the night air, a cold chill passed through them. The temperature had dropped considerably since Jax's arrival a short while earlier. The contractors were gone and save for the sound of an owl in the distance, it was silent.

"Are we the only ones here?" Jax asked, surprised.

"For now," Bernie answered, leading the way down a dirt path that passed the pit that would become the 'private prayer rooms.' "The workers should be back at first light though, but until school is in session, nights are like a graveyard around here." Bernie circled around the pit. "Watch your step," he warned Jax. "The edges are unstable and the ground can give way. Wouldn't want either of us to fall in," he laughed nervously. "Once we pass that circle of trees up ahead, you'll see where we've cleared some of the wooded area to create space for additional dormitories and classrooms. It's—"

Bernie felt something on the back of his heel, as if his shoe got caught and started to slip off, causing him to feel unsteady. His eyes grew wide as he lifted his arms out to the side to regain balance. Bernie's jerky movements caused him to drop the keys into the pit. As they tumbled in the dirt, rolling toward the concrete block at the bottom, Bernie reached out in vain to attempt to grab them, leaning his body forward, bending his knees slightly to remain upright. Just then, Bernie felt a swift thrust as Jax's boot connected with Bernie's bottom, sending him topping headfirst into the pit. The drop was at least two stories.

Bernie screamed, not entirely certain what bumped him and caused his fall. And yet, the man had just enough of his wits about him to spin his body mid-air in an attempt to land on his feet, bending at the knees. When his body impacted the concrete, he let out a yell in agony. For a moment, it was silent save for the wind in the trees. The bottom of the pit was dark, Bernie's body barely visible in the shadows. Eventually, the sound of heavy breathing could be heard from the floor of the pit, followed by a mild whimpering.

In the commotion, Bernie also managed to drop the flashlight, now lying in the dirt at Jax's feet. Jax picked it up and shined it into Bernie's eyes. Bernie's leg was contorted to one side and there was a large red blood splatter around his head.

"My leg is broken!" Bernie whined as the reality of what caused his fall finally sank in. "And, you nearly killed me!"

"Oh, don't be so melodramatic," Jax answered. "As you said, the crew will be here in the morning and can fish you out."

"The morning?!" Bernie's eyes grew wide. "You're nuts! It's freezing out and my head is bleeding. I could die out here if left alone! Call for help!"

"I think a little time in the private prayer pit will do you a world of good, don't you? Here," Jax rolled a bottle of water down the side of the hill that eventually landed at Bernie's broken leg. He followed it with a wrapped snack. "Have some water and a Jax Corporation nutrition bar. That ought to keep you until morning."

Jax turned to walk away.

"You can't leave me here!" Bernie screamed. "Jax! Come back here! You and Lundy can't run this place without me! If I die, it's all over!"

Jax grinned to himself. *What a self-absorbed prick,* he thought. At that moment, he had no idea whether or not Bernie could survive the night or not. He probably could, he reasoned. Might even be able to climb out, even with a broken leg. *Oh well,* he thought to himself. *Guess we'll find out come morning.*

"The Peelers are here, boss." A young contractor tapped on the superintendent's shoulder at the site where Bernie had taken his fall. Now a shade of blue, the body still lay untouched at the bottom of the prayer pit. Even from a great height, a decent pair of binoculars could tell you that the leader of the Church of Infinite Love was dead.

The superintendent nodded as members of the Royal Ulster Constabulary arrived on the scene. One of the officers twitched nervously. "What have we got here?" he asked. It was too soon after the Troubles and any suspected foul play was met with tension.

"That down there is Bernie Forger," the superintendent explained. "He's the one who hired us fer work on the property. He was plenty alive when we last saw him yesterday. But today he's...well, see fer yerself."

"Can your men help us safely get down there?" the officer asked.

"Uh, yeah, sure," the superintendent looked around. "Bobby, get the men to bring round the aerial ladder and harnesses, would ya?" The contractor nodded and ran off. In a matter of minutes, the ladder was stationed near the pit which in the light of day, looked more like a giant sinkhole.

It took little time for the RUCs to make their assessment to the chief constable. Bernie Forger could have died from head and internal injuries as a result of his fall, hypothermia, or at the notice of one of Vandenberg's half-eaten old nutraceutical bars near Bernie's corpse, poison or allergies. There were a few odd boot and shoe prints on the grounds, but they could have belonged to any of the contractors traipsing through there. Bernie's own shoes had slipped off in the fall, and while they could determine the location where he fell by the displaced soil and grass, it was unclear whether he jumped, was pushed or slipped due to dislodged soil. Since he obviously had a bit of the munchies, it was assumed that he likely fell, and given his physical state, was unable to climb out. By the time the contractors discovered his body the next morning, he'd been dead for about seven hours. One contractor noted seeing a man arrive at the academy just as they were leaving late the evening prior, but couldn't be sure they'd recognize him if they saw him again.

"Found this too," an officer handed a bagged item to the constable.

"What's this?" he asked.

"It's a cufflink, sir," the officer answered. "Gold plated with a Waterford crystal piece in the center. Me missus got me the same kind for Christmas last year from Westport Jewelers."

"You mean the same Westports suspected of small to medium-sized grifts in County Dublin?"

"The same, sir."

"Christ," the Chief Constable stood over the body, befuddled. "It could take weeks for a full autopsy report to figure out if it was foul play, and if it was, who the suspects are...the Westports...the Vandenbergs... someone else?"

"Poor fella," one of the officers commented, sympathetically. "If he had time to eat a bite, it meant that he couldn't have died on impact. Musta been rough at the end."

"Yeah, well at least his troubles are over," the constable answered, brashly. "Ours are just beginning."

CHAPTER 20
Affairs of the Heartless

"How are you holding up, Edwina?" Lundy asked, sympathetically, over the crackle of the static from a long-distance call over an outdated landline.

"As well as you might expect from a woman whose father left his family in ruins after sinking his own corporate battleship and leaving his money to harlots with no breeding," Edwina spat, bitterly.

"Not well, it sounds," Lundy answered quietly. "Well, perhaps I can cheer you up?"

"Really?" Edwina sat up. "Tell me you have good news."

"I have *potentially* good news," he replied. "I convinced Jax Liebling to invest in the academy."

"After everything he's already spent on the factories?" Edwina as surprised. "Where did he get the money? The Vandenberg family has been well connected to the who's who in the industry for nearly a century...the Rockefellers, Carnegies, you name it. But I've never heard of him."

"I couldn't say, exactly," Lundy answered. "However, I don't care where his money comes from as long as it gets us where we want to go."

"And so, he's investing. What good does this do me, exactly?" Edwina was not about to mince words.

"It will do you plenty good when you become the headmistress of the academy."

"You can't be serious!" Edwina answered.

"What?" Lundy questioned. "Are you opposed to acting as headmistress to a school in Ireland purpose-built to forward the work of the Church of Infinite Love?"

"Not at all," Edwina answered. "I would relish it, but according to church law, I'm as high in the ranks as a woman is allowed."

"But the man who made the rules is dead," Lundy answered, curtly. Erasmus Vandenberg, Edwina Vandenberg's late father, had lots of rules around the 'dos and don'ts' of the sexes. Most times, the 'dos' applied to the men and the 'don'ts' to the women.

"Bernie will never agree to that," Edwina clucked.

"Why don't you let me worry about Bernie."

"Well, what am I supposed to do in the meantime?"

"Be patient, my love," Lundy answered, affectionately. "I told you before, I'm playing the long game."

"Is it the long game that resulted in me getting cut out of my father's will?" Edwina sulked.

"Now, pet," Lundy replied, sympathetically, "you know I did my best to talk Erasmus out of that, but if I pushed too hard, he'd would have been on to us. And I might have lost my job. Then where would we be today?"

"Hmm," Edwina remained unconvinced. "Not sure I like where *we* ended up."

"Give me some time, Edwina," Lundy pleaded in a show of emotion that was uncharacteristic of him. "Once Vandenberg Nutraceuticals goes under with Jax and Baxter at the helm, we can swoop in and buy it back for a song."

"If he's as rich as you say, why on Earth do you think it might go under?" Edwina asked, reasonably. "Seems good with money."

"Perhaps so," Lundy agreed. "But I appealed to his ego, of which he has in plenty. If he's tying up resources in the academy and future publishing house, what recourse will he have once he realizes the church has stopped buying products from him?"

"What?" Edwina was surprised. "Stop buying? When did this happen? Why did the church stop purchasing from Vandenberg Nutraceuticals?"

"The new branding of the church," Lundy reminded her. "No more faith healing for a while. It draws too much attention. The money is now in education."

"So, without the church's partnership, he'll suffer?" Edwina asked. She had a little twinge in her heart, the last remnant of a conscience. She sucked in a deep breath and brushed the feeling aside.

"Yes, and Bernie will get the…err…credit."

"He'll murder him," Edwina was convinced. "Liebling has a questionable past. If Bernie takes the fall for screwing him over, I pity what Jax will do to him."

"But with Bernie out of the way, guess who gets to be the new head mistress…and head of the church?" Lundy dangled that carrot, confidence seeping into his voice.

"And what makes you think the church will allow it, given that I am a mere woman?" Edwina's voice dripped of disdain.

"Ah," Lundy replied, "what if the Church of Infinite Love finally stepped into the 20th century? We can make that happen, you and I."

"You and I?" Edwina gave it some thought. She knew Lundy cared for her, as much as any lawyer could care for anybody, but she never thought of him as a potential life partner, let alone a life partner *and* a business partner."

"Yes," Lundy affirmed. "What do you think?"

"I think my father must be turning in his grave." she answered, curtly.

"Probably," Lundy agreed. "He only liked me slightly better than you, and probably only because I protected his money." There was an agonizingly long pause across the phone line. "Edwina," he coaxed, "you still haven't answered my question."

"I think you're a crazy bastard," Edwina laughed. "But you're my kind of crazy."

"I'll take that as a 'yes,'" Lundy smiled. Not much brought Lundy joy, but somehow, the thought of running an empire with he and

Edwina reigning supreme was enough to send a pleasant chill up his spine. He hung up the phone moments later, whistling to himself as he sorted the last of the contracts he'd drafted for Jax Liebling...the most important of which was the one where Jax confirmed that should anything happen to him, everything he'd invested in the Church became theirs to use the money as they see fit because Jax agreed to escheat his accounts. Lundy clicked his briefcase, closed and snapped the small desk lamp that hovered over the tiny table in his hotel room, and the room went dark.

~

THE NEXT EVENING Lundy's room phone rang just as he was stepping out of the shower, a good hour before Edwina usually rang him up.

"Miss me already?" he asked Edwina, sweetly. It sounded strange coming from Lundy.

"Looks like I was right," Edwina barked. "Turn on the news."

"What happened?" Lundy snapped on the small television in his room and twisted the squeaky knob until it tuned into the Raidió Teilifís Éireann nightly news. "What am I looking for?"

He didn't have long to wait. The news ticker at the bottom of the telly read, "Leader of the Church of Infinite Love found dead in Belfast." In the scene, the area behind the academy where the prayer pit was located, was blocked off with yellow tape and a swarm of RUCS were on scene.

"Bernie's dead," Edwina answered sourly. "I told you Jax was a loose cannon, didn't I?"

"Relax, my love," Lundy reassured her. "We don't know that. And, even if he did it, as I told you last night, we move on without him."

"I don't feel good about this, Lundy."

Lundy could feel her sour expression across the phone line. "Don't tell me you're suddenly developing a conscience, my love," he answered, playfully.

"I'm not sure how to take that, Lunds."

Lundy raised an eyebrow. Edwina always resorted to calling him 'Lunds' as a pet name when she was about to do something manipulative. "I just mean that we can't take responsibility for what one man chooses to do to another, can we? Might as well make the best of it," Lundy reminded her.

Just then, there was a loud banging at the door. "Hang on, pet." Lundy put the phone down and eyed the keyhole at the front door...Jax. Lundy left the chain on the door as he opened it just slightly, peering an eye out. Jax stood there, beside himself.

"How did you get up here?" Lundy demanded. "No one but guests are permitted past the lobby. And you, most certainly, are not a guest."

"Never mind that," Jax whispered. "We've got more important things to discuss. I know you murdered Bernie!"

"Me?" Lundy was confused. "I did nothing of the sort."

"Have you seen the news?" Jax tried again.

"Just now," Lundy answered. "Give me ten minutes and I'll meet you in the lobby downstairs. We'll find an empty conference room or someplace quiet to chat."

Jax ran a hand through his hair and nodded, anxiously. "Good plan. I don't much care to be alone with a killer," he whispered. "It's best to be in a more public space."

Lundy closed the door and picked up the receiver. "That was Jax, coming here to accuse me of killing Bernie."

"He's accusing you?!" Edwina was flabbergasted. "But that's preposterous!"

"I know, but I'm meeting him downstairs. I've got to know what he's up to."

"Be careful, Lunds," Edwina pouted. "I couldn't bear it if anything happened to you."

"I will, my darling. I promise to phone you as soon as I'm back upstairs."

Lundy hung up the phone, and within minutes, found Jax in the hotel bar gulping down a scotch.

"I told them to charge it to your room," Jax told Lundy when he arrived.

"That's fine," Lundy sucked in a breath. He considered himself a patient man, but he was beginning to unravel the longer he had to deal with Jax Liebling. "But what's all this about..." he paused to make sure no one else was in earshot, "well, you know."

"I know it was you who took out Bernie," Jax leaned in and whispered.

"What are you talking about?" Lundy whispered back. "I only just heard the news moments before you arrived. And from the looks of it, it was an accident...no foul play."

"Right, well, between the church's lack of support for the factory and this, I'm afraid I'm rethinking my business investments. I've changed my mind about the school."

Lundy coughed. "You're upset, I can see that. Why don't you have another scotch and let me put this whole thing to rest, alright?"

Jax nodded and motioned the bartender for a refill. While his voice was shaky, Lundy couldn't help but notice that his hands were steady...odd.

After Jax's fresh drink arrived, Lundy continued, "I'm just as shocked to learn about Bernie's death as you, and what's this you say about a 'lack of support for the factory?'"

"Sales are down 39% since the church stopped buying product from us, something of which I have only just learned, by the way. Between that and the bad press, I'm barely getting by as it is."

"Well now, I didn't know that, else I would have had a talk with Bernie." Lundy feigned a look of pain, touching his fist to his lips in a moment of grief. He recovered in the blink of an eye.

"You're his lawyer and closely associated with his accountants," Jax spat. "How could you not know?"

"Look, Jax, I promise I'll talk to my associate, Mr. Adani. I'm sure there's been a misunderstanding."

Jax said nothing, his lip twitching as he stared blankly at the bar.

"But since Bernie isn't here anymore," Lundy offered, "perhaps you might consider taking his place?"

"Of the church, you mean?" Jax's eyes widened, turning his head to face the lawyer.

"Well, yes," Lundy answered. "We already talked about your role at the school. And if you assume a leadership role, then you and I can figure out the budget, together. How does that sound?"

Jax stared at Lundy for several seconds as if at the end of a tight chess match. Finally, he answered, "The investigation into Bernie's death might shut down construction of the academy for months. So for now, why don't we focus on Jax Corporation and how to make it work for us?"

Lundy was beginning to put the pieces together, though he didn't like to think he might be outmatched by this irritating little man with a very large ego. "It's been a long day for the both of us, and I'm still torn up over Bernie's death," Lundy lied. He wasn't the slightest bit concerned, but he put on a good front. "Why don't we chat in the next day or two and see what we can come up with?"

Jax slid off the stool and grabbed the jacket he had strewn on the pub chair beside him. "Certainly," he turned to leave before remembering, "oh, and about that clause we spoke about in the event anything happened to me?"

"Yes," Lundy answered, biting the inside of his lip, nervously. "What about it?"

"Turns out, I just got married the other day. There's a new beneficiary to my money. So, don't think about murdering me, as well, as it will hurt your cause, not help it."

Jax bounded out of the lobby as if late to catch a train, leaving Lundy speechless and with yet another expensive bar tab.

When he phoned Edwina back later that evening, he said, "Jax Liebling is turning out to be a bigger problem than I thought."

CHAPTER 21
Phone Call

~

Against his better judgment, Ortega followed Midge's orders and reported Rue missing the morning after their call. The Guard asked uncomfortable questions that Ortega did his best to answer. *What was your relationship to Rue Brennan? What was she wearing when you saw her last? Do you have a recent photo of her? When and where did you see her last?*

He couldn't let on that they were here on an investigation that he really had no business investigating, with a woman he once suspected of murder. He had no photos of Rue, and the last time he saw her was before he, Shep and Penelope left for the factory, leaving Rue with grocery duty. He thought he was protecting her by having her stay behind. In hindsight, perhaps the only reason she agreed to it was because she already had plans to meet up with Midge. Or maybe Midge kidnapped her? He really couldn't be certain.

The only thing he had going for him at this moment was his keen observation skills. "She is about five-foot-three or four with brown hair and hazel eyes, thin and generally travels with a small denim backpack instead of a purse. The last time I saw her, she wore a red hoodie sweatshirt with blue jeans and black sneakers."

"Any distinguishing features?" an officer asked. The name tag on his uniform read, 'Doherty.'

"Other than a few freckles on her nose and a round face with chubby cheeks, not much."

"You seem to remember quite a bit about her, Mr. Ortega. How did you say you know her, again?" Doherty asked, suspiciously.

"I'm a retired detective," Ortega explained, tiredly. "She and her boyfriend run their own private investigation company. We crossed paths at work."

"Hmmm." Doherty asked, "And how is it that you 'crossed paths' again in County Dublin?" He rested his arms on his desk, one on top of the other, and leaned in with interest.

"It was a social trip," Ortega lied. "Me and my fiancé...Penelope...were planning a destination wedding. The girls are friends, you see."

"I see," the officer nodded. "And why isn't Penelope here with you as well?"

"Because she's busy picking up our other friend from the hospital... burst appendix."

"And if we contact the hospital, they can confirm this?" Doherty squinted his eyes at Ortega.

"Of course—" Ortega began before catching himself. "I'm sorry, but is there any reason why you are acting as if I'm a suspect in the missing person I'm reporting?"

"Just doing my job," Doherty explained. "I'll see what I can find out. Just leave your contact info with the desk clerk on your way out." Doherty reached into his desk and pulled out a carbon copy form with two duplicate yellow and pink layers under the white top sheet. He then popped the cap off a stick pen and pressed hard into the form, lowering his head in a way that suggested to Ortega that the conversation was over.

Ortega was about to offer some passive-aggressive quip, but then thought better of it. After all, that was in no way going to help Rue's case. And second, as he peered at Doherty hunched over his desk with burnt out aggression, he saw something...himself.

"Oh, and just one more thing," Doherty remembered, looking up.

"Don't even think about investigating this yourself, detective...enjoy your retirement."

Outside the Garda's offices, Ortega reached into his pocket to phone Penelope with an update, and to see how she was getting on with Shep who was just released from the hospital.

Nothing.

He rifled through his pockets, then looked around him in vain, as if he'd dropped it. No...in his frazzled state, he'd left his cell phone behind.

~

Back at their rental, Shep lumbered slowly through the front door with Penelope standing guard, just in case he toppled.

"I'm okay," he reassured her, wincing a little as he walked. "Just gonna rest in this chair for a minute." He settled into a small kitchen chair that creaked beneath his weight.

"Can I get you anything?" Penelope offered. "Something to eat, perhaps?"

"You know what?" Shep eyed her with amusement.

"What?" she asked, concerned.

"I'm not hungry!" he bellowed and then winced again, grabbing his side. Shep did his best to stifle a laugh as a few tears formed in his eyes. Finally, he said, "Maybe I should lie down for a bit."

Penelope rushed to his side, putting his arm around her shoulders and bending her knees to help him stand. He did his best not to put too much pressure on her, while she remembered to exhale on the lift like she was lifting weights at the gym. Still, he was a bit heavy for her slight frame.

The two staggered to the bedroom he and Ortega shared. "Tell Ortega I'm sorry, but I'm gonna have to take the bottom bunk tonight."

Penelope bit her lip. She wasn't sure Jose was going to be in that room at all, but they'd figure that out this evening.

After depositing a recovering Shep to his room, Penelope closed the door.

Just then, a cell phone rang...Ortega's cell phone. She hadn't even realized it was sitting on a side table by the front door. It seemed to get even more insistent with each ring. She glanced down at the number...Darwin.

Her heart sank. Maybe Ortega could ignore his calls, but she couldn't.

"Hello, Mr. Fennec," Penelope answered quietly. A frantic Darwin rambled incessantly, asking where Rue was, but not waiting for the answer. He went in circles ranting about how Ortega hadn't called him back. What was happening over there? Was everyone okay? Finally, he ran out of steam. After a moment of silence, Penelope replied. "For Rue's safety, we were told not to ask any questions and not to look for her."

"What?!" Darwin could be heard yelling into the phone above the sound of airplanes taking off and descending, followed by loud announcements over an intercom with the bustle of hundreds of people chattering in the distance. "What do you mean, you—"

"Mr. Fennec? Are you at the airport?" Penelope demanded. He ignored her, cycling back to his combination of ranting while demanding information. Penelope couldn't stay on the line. She knew it wasn't safe... not for Rue and not for them. "Goodbye, Darwin. Please be careful." She hung up the phone and broke into a sob. She could feel Darwin's desperation. She knew it all too well in her own life, but there was nothing she could do for him, save for her failed attempt to at least let him know that Rue was alright...probably.

THE CALL CAME in from Officer Doherty not twenty-four hours later. He got a lead from the County Londonderry police after a pub owner called in a couple of suspicious women who climbed into one woman's dark hatchback while leaving the other's rental behind. The rental car was in Rue Brennan's name, and they were calling to have it brought in for evidence. Not far from the scene, another report came in of a body discovered by a bicyclist the next morning during one of his early-morning rides. The body was thought to be that of a woman.

"The corpse had been charred so badly that it could take weeks to make a positive identification," Doherty explained to Ortega over the phone. "There were a few traces of blood at the scene. We're having it analyzed now."

Ortega coughed, fighting off the queasiness in his stomach. His face went pale, and the room began to swirl.

"Did you hear what I said, Mr. Ortega?" Doherty spoke a little louder into the phone.

"I did," Ortega sucked in a deep breath. "Just...processing."

After a long pause, Doherty continued, "Consider this a courtesy call...I looked you up, detective. Seems you had an excellent reputation while you were on the beat...even solved a number of high-profile cases that were deemed unsolvable."

If ever a time when Ortega found enlightenment, this would have been the equivalent of Newton's apple landing on his head, or what some spiritualists would call an 'awakening.' He'd spent his life solving the unsolvable cases, but where did it get him? He neglected his friends, his family, his health, and his sanity, and for what? The pursuit of social justice? No, he decided. It was all ego. What began as a noble effort in making the world a safer place spiraled into an obsession. But no matter how many of the bad guys he put away, a fresh breed always seemed to crop up. Even worse were the rich crime families like the Vandenbergs and the Westports, the cults like the Church of Infinite Love, and the oligarchs who didn't care who they murdered if someone got in the way of their best interests.

"You still there?" Doherty finally asked.

"Yes, sorry." Ortega rubbed his forehead. "What can I do to help?"

"Nothing!" Doherty snapped into the phone, before catching himself. "Under normal circumstances, I'd be bringing you and your lady friend in for questioning...I still might have to. But given your reputation, I'll just ask politely that you don't leave the country any time soon. You get me?"

Ortega smirked and shook his head. *He sounds just like I did two decades ago, the poor sap.* "Don't worry," he reassured him, "I have no intention of going anywhere. Not until I find out what happened to Ms. Brennan. Thank you, officer."

"Was that about Rue?" Penelope asked, concerned, once he'd ended the call. Then she saw the look on Ortega's face. "What happened?" her voice trembled.

Ortega gently took Penelope's arm. "I think you had better sit down."

CHAPTER 22
Rescue

~

Baxter arrived at the factory at his usual time...a good hour and fifteen minutes past the time he promised to be there. He could hear a loud beeping from the parking lot, and as he neared the entrance, he saw it.

There, along the side of the building a large yellow crane was hoisting what appeared to be a golden-lettered sign and aligning it against the building. On the ground, were pieces of the company's old sign as if it had been ripped down like old wallpaper. Baxter could make out a "V", an "EN", and a "TI." That was what was left of the Vandenberg Nutraceuticals signage. As he watched with mounting anger, the new name became clear...JAX.

Baxter spotted Jax near one of the crew members installing the sign, wearing a hardhat, his arms crossed like some sort of a god. Jax nodded with approval.

"What the hell is this?" Baxter demanded.

"This," Jax answered simply, "is the dawn of a new day."

"You're one crazy fella. You know that? Completely—"

Baxter's rant was cut short suddenly, as a potato sack was slung over his head, plunging him into darkness and making it difficult to breathe. Someone bound his arms while another grabbed his feet. He could hear the sound of heavy boots on the ground and the squeal of tires screeching to a halt. A heavy door slid open, and the next thing that Baxter knew, he was being thrown onto a hard metal floor, his head banging against the edge of what he assumed was the opposite wall of a van. He heard muffled sounds outside, followed by a "let's go!"

The van slammed shut with Baxter and his assailants inside.

Jax smiled, approvingly, and returned to witness his new name being plastered on the side of the factory wall. Somehow, the contractors missed the kidnapping. Or, it's possible that they simply didn't care.

Inside the van, several men could be heard congratulating one another on a job well done. One of the men leaned over and shouted in Baxter's ear, "How do you feel about swimming with the fishes in the Irish Sea, my boy?!"

He jolted at the noise erupting in his ear. Then, something occurred to Baxter. The man spoke with an American accent, a Northern one.

"That'll teach him to bring the Devil into a house of God," another chimed in. Baxter couldn't be sure, but from the shuffling, he suspecting there were at least three men in the van with him, maybe more.

They traveled across bumpy roads for what seemed like an eternity, some loud with heavy traffic, and others with jagged hills and twists and turns that sent Baxter sliding uncomfortably across the floor. At one point, the van jolted so hard he was certain that his head was going to smash into the side again, but at the last minute, something intervened...a hand.

"Still alive in there?" a lilting voice asked.

"Moira?" Baxter muffled.

"Shhh," Moira whispered, smiling devilishly at the three men in the van with her. Unlike the others who sat on bench seats, Moira had a fixed place in her wheelchair, clumsily strapped in with a large belt that ran shoulder to hip. Across her lap was a wool blanket. It was fairly warm that day, but she complained about always feeling a bit cold. She blamed it on mild anemia.

The three men laughed, two had large builds and bellies that suggested a fixed diet of beer and lots of all-you-can-eat dinners. The other, by contrast, was a bit taller and leaner, but lacked any muscle definition. His shirt had 'Leo' embroidered on it, a clear indication that he had no idea how a secret kidnapping was supposed to work. And yet, all three acted as though they were part of some covert military operation.

The van made one final drive down a steep incline before stopping abruptly on a flat section of asphalt. The largest of the men stepped over Baxter's feet and slid the side door open until it clunked into place. "Out with ya!" He grabbed Baxter's legs and began sliding him out of the van, his head and shoulders about to smack the ground when Moira intervened.

"Hang on, boys," she said. "Do the lass a favor and get me out into the fresh sea air so I can have a chin wag with him first, yeah?"

The man stopped and smiled, elbowing his other large friend in the ribs. He blushed slightly.

"Anything for you, sweetheart," he agreed. "Milton, go help the lovely lady out."

"Thank you, Tom," she winked at him. "Just sit the heathen upright so I can look him in the eyes."

Tom relented, grabbing Baxter by his arms and hoisting him to a standing position just long enough for the men to lower the wheelchair lift and help Moira out.

"Thank you, gentlemen." She positioned her chair several feet from Baxter. "Now, if you don't mind, sit him up and pull that sack off his head."

"You sure that's a good idea? I mean, our orders were to—" the thinner man intervened.

"Feed him to the fishes, I know, Leo," Moira nodded. "But I'll have you know this bastard put the moves on me. Me, a lame woman. Let me at least say my peace, won't you, loves?"

"Alright, Moira. I suppose that would be okay."

"What's all the racket back there?" the driver called from the front seat. Until now, nobody had given any thought to him.

"Give us a minute," the large man called.

The driver merely tapped his fingers on the side of the open window, impatiently, but said no more. He took a moment to adjust his rearview mirror to see what was happening behind him.

The man tugged the sack off of Baxter's head, purposefully grabbing a tuft of hair along the way.

"Ow!" Baxter yelled. A small patch of blood could be seen on the side of his head where it had made contact with the van wall. Baxter sucked in the sea air, finally able to breathe fully. His eyes darted around his location. Behind him was a small, deserted stretch of beach with the cliffs surrounding them on both sides. He could only catch a glimpse of the water from his periphery view. In front of him, a steep paved access road led to the spot where they currently sat. While not a public spot, it wasn't likely for any strangers to stumble upon them anytime soon, but he hoped for the best, nonetheless.

"Can someone please explain what this is all about?" Baxter caught how frantic his high-pitched voice sounded and took in another breath to calm his nerves. He returned with a different voice, a soft-spoken, charming one. "Gentlemen," he began, "there must be some misunderstanding."

"Oh, there's no misunderstanding, son," the man spat, leaning his face just a few inches from Baxter's nose. "We know who's responsible for the death of all those innocent girls, not to mention some of our church leadership. It was you and your Satanic ways all along!"

"Satanic—" Baxter was confused. It took a moment, but suddenly all the links came together. They were blaming him for every death related to the Church of Infinite Love and Vandenberg Nutraceuticals, no matter how unlikely. Up until now, he thought his own family was responsible for this. Suddenly, it became clear...he was the scapegoat, and Jax had set him up. He looked at Moira, betrayed. "But you?" His heart sank.

Moira paused long enough to survey the scene, as if making calculations. Satisfied, she grinned mischievously, and then in one swift moment she yanked the blanket from her legs, revealing a sawed-off shotgun. She cocked it and took aim at the large man. "Back away from the van," she commanded.

"What?" The man was confused. Then he smiled down at her, taking a step toward her chair. "Listen, little lady. I know you probably got what they call...Stockholm...whatever. But you're safe now from this bastard's advances."

Moira took a warning shot at his feet. He squealed and shifted back and forth, lifting his feet as if standing on hot coals.

"Over by your friend," she pointed the barrel at him, motioning toward the other large man, who was now hiding around the back of the van. "But come out so I can see you both. Hands up and behind your heads!"

In a show of braveness, the thinner man charged her from the side, lunging for Moira's shotgun.

"Not so fast," the young driver appeared in a flash, grabbing the back of Leo's shirt, pulling him backward and holding a small knife to his neck. Leo winced, making a feeble attempt to grab the driver's arm, but the driver was quick, shoving him forward.

Moira stuck out a leg and tripped him. He fell, face first onto the asphalt, managing to break his fall with his hands. "Ow," he wailed. "My wrist!" He rolled on the ground nursing his wrist, his one foot still hooked to the footrest on the wheelchair. Moira kicked his foot out of her way, taking a moment to lean over and lift the footrest up so her legs were clear. With shotgun still in one arm, she stood, tossing her blanket on the chair behind her.

"Over by the other two," she commanded. To the driver, she said, "Thanks, Scratch."

Scratch merely nodded, standing dutifully beside her.

Leo clambered to his feet and stood by Tom and Milton, all with hands behind their heads.

"My arms are getting tired," Milton complained to Tom.

"Shut it!" Moira threatened, taking a moment to shake out each leg from the long journey she spent sitting. After shifting from side to side, she finally settled with both feet firmly planted on the ground.

"What in the hell is going on, Moira?" Tom demanded. "I thought you were on our side?"

She glanced at a stunned Baxter who merely whispered, "You can walk?"

"Course I can, Sweet Face," she laughed. "And dance and hike the Cliffs of Moher."

"Scratch, wanna free the handsome bloke so he can help you tie these boys up?"

"I don't—" Tom's face grew red.

"No, you don't," Moira finished for him. "Shut it, or it's you who will be swimming with fishes. But don't worry, I'm sure there's a heavenly afterlife waiting just for you."

The waves from the sea started rolling in faster now. Moira looked for a place to tie her hostages, but couldn't find a suitable source.

"Guess we coulda planned this out a bit better, huh, Scratch?"

"We could ditch the van and have Quid pick us up?" Scratch cut the ties binding Baxter's arms.

"Thanks," Baxter rubbed his wrists, gratefully. He winced a little where the ropes had dug into his flesh. His wrists now had raw, red and deeply imprinted marks on them.

"Looks like that's our best option," Moira agreed. "Get the ropes out."

"Run!" Tom yelled, and the three men darted, two to the left and one to the right.

Moira took aim and shot Tom in the leg. He screamed as he fell onto the sand. Then, she recalibrated her sights on Milton and Leo. She fired a shot in the sand beside Leo's foot.

"Stop," she ordered. They did. "I'm doing my best not to shoot you dumb arses, but you don't seem to be gettin' the message."

"You shot me in the leg, Moira!" Tom yelled.

"Nothing but a flesh wound," Moira countered. "You'll live."

Moira stood guard while Scratch, with the help of Baxter, secured the men to the seats in the van. Not wanting to chance a dead man on her hands, they took a few moments to tie a makeshift tourniquet on Tom's injury from a piece of the potato sack that had once covered Baxter's head.

"Here's how this is gonna go down, boys," Moira addressed them. "The three of us are going to get a safe distance. Now, you can yell for help all you want. That's fine. But when the good detective gets here, you're going to let him in on exactly what it was you had planned for poor Baxter here. And if you don't—" she paused.

"If we don't," Tom spat, angrily. He wasn't sure what was worse, the fact that they failed in their mission, or that he was outsmarted by a woman.

"Well then, the Westport family won't be as kind to you as I have been just now. You'll be safer if you just confess."

Scratch slammed the door of the van shut before Tom could respond.

"It's gonna be a warm day," Moira noticed. "Crack a window on the passenger side before you lock up, would ya?" Scratch nodded.

Baxter, now standing beside Moira for the first time, turned to look her in the eyes. Even standing, she was still a good five or six inches shorter than he was. "I—" he fought to find the right words as they shared a moment.

"Oh," she seemed to remember something, "one second." Moira pulled a knife from underneath her skirt and systematically dug it into the two front tires of the vehicle. "Just in case." To Scratch, she asked, "Got the keys?"

"Yup," he answered, as the three trudged up the concrete ramp.

"What about your chair?" Baxter asked.

"Think my covers blown now, don't you?" she laughed.

"Aren't you worried they'll tell 'em you were involved? How are we going to explain them being tied up?"

"Good thinking, Sweet Face," she agreed, "help me out."

Baxter followed Moira back to the beach, where they procured her chair. Baxter folded it up and dragged it behind them as the three headed back to the road.

"Not gonna get much of a signal out here, I'm afraid," Scratch said.

"Not to worry," Moira answered. "There's a little coffee shop about a mile away that most people don't know about. We can use their pay phone to call for Quid to come pick us up."

"A mile?" Baxter cringed, touching the side of his head which he just realized was hurting and was matted with a dried-out blood stain."

"Yeah," she smirked, "looks like we're taking that hike after all."

CHAPTER 23
Moira and Constantine

Flashback: Two Weeks Ago

Moira found her uncle playing bocce ball in a designated court on the grounds behind his mansion. Too large a man to bend and pick up the balls, he'd spent years having one of his servants retrieve the weighted balls for him and line them up on a cart so that all he had to do was merely throw them when the time came. Whomever he was playing also knew better than to beat him. Well, everyone except Moira.

"Hello, Uncle." She arrived wearing jeans and a green blouse.

"Moira!" Constantine greeted his niece, gleefully. With both Moira's parents gone, and having lost his own daughter, Molly, at such a young age, Moira had become like a daughter to him. "What brings you here today?"

"Do I need a reason to visit my favorite uncle?" she answered.

Constantine knew her too well. "Cut the bull crap, Moira. You and I are cut from the same mold, and you know it."

"Fair enough," she answered, planting a kiss on his cheek. "I have found myself in a predicament and I need your help."

"What kind of a...predicament?" he eyed her belly, instinctively.

"Not *that* kind!" she chastised. "I need to ask you, what do you know about a man name Jax Liebling?

"The toilet guy?"

Moira scrunched her nose. "What? Never mind," she continued, picking up a bocce ball. The attendant who had been playing politely bowed out, but not before gathering and re-stocking the balls on the cart. "I'm talking about the man who is the silent partner attempting to help Baxter Baker buy out the Vandenberg factories."

"And how is it that you know Baxter Baker?" Constantine asked, once again eyeing her belly.

"Again, it's not about that!" she whined, putting her hand on her belly, protectively. "I know Baxter Baker...and not in the Biblical sense, I might add...because when I was looking for a job, Jax Liebling hired me."

"Why would you be looking for a job when you are working for me?"

"No offense, Uncle, but I'm old enough to make my own way in the world. No more handouts."

"Handouts? You're the best associate I've got."

"I applied to become a receptionist two months ago," Moira explained.

"Receptionist?" Constantine was incredulous. "I didn't spend years training you to perform the most intricate grifts in the country to resort to some low-paying job that—"

"It's a respectable job, and I stand to be promoted to executive assistant if I do well over the next three months."

Constantine pursed his lips. "My statement stands."

"I can't go on doing petty jobs conning tourists to purchase funny traveler's checks or pay me cash settlements for fender benders anymore. And sometimes, during those slip and falls," Moira's voice went up in pitch, "I actually fall...and hurt myself!"

"You're as bad as your mother," Constantine complained. "She had a conscience and look where it got her."

"You'll kindly leave my mum out of it." Moira's nose grew red, the only feature on her face that let on that she was becoming angry. "She died honorably."

"Honorably," Constantine agreed, "but penniless. Why she ran off with that musician fellow, I'll never know."

"It's called love, Uncle. You should look it up."

Constantine shook his head. He missed his sister. Following a messy divorce, she ran off with a man who played the local music circuit. For years, the man dreamed of going on tour and traveling the world. Finally, his chance arrived. They got as far as Iceland before the plane went down in a freak accident. Moira was only ten years old at the time.

"The point is," Moira took the ball Constantine was holding and tossed it on the field, drawing him out of his daydream, "it started off like a normal interview and then got weird."

"What do you mean, weird? Did Baxter—"

"No!"

"Did Jax—"

"No, would you listen?"

"Sorry," Constantine apologized, "continue."

"At the end of the interview, Mr. Liebling said that the job was mine on one condition."

"Why, that little—"

"No!" Moira patted his arm. "He asked me to promise to come to work in a wheelchair. He'd rent one for me."

"A wheelchair? Why?" Constantine took a ball from the cart and flung it. It landed next to Moira's, tapping her ball slightly.

"He said that Baxter has a thing for the ladies, and wanted to ensure he wouldn't make a pass at me."

"And he thought a chair would do it?" Constantine was surprised. "Not only is he an idiot, but he must be blind. Has he even looked at you?"

"I wish him being shallow were the worst of it," she explained.

"What do you mean?"

"I mean, I don't think Jax Liebling is on the up and up."

"Men in high places rarely are."

"No, worse than that," Moira shook her head. "I did a little digging. You remember the blowup in the news that uncovered the fraudulent faith healing that led to deaths at the Church of Infinite Love...the ones traced back to the Vandenberg family?

"Of course, I do." Constantine furrowed his brows. "Why do you think I've been hired to protect that dolt playboy, Baxter Baker, in the first place? He was the one who sold his family out. I should have tossed him out on his ear. He's the reason the Dublin factory is up and running again."

"No, he isn't," Moira explained, "this was all Jax Liebling's idea."

"What are you getting at, Moira?"

"What I'm getting at is that I think Jax knows very well who my famous uncle is. I think it's a trap...a well-laid plan so that Jax can make Baxter the fall guy for all the bad that happened in the family. And, I think he plans to take out Baxter and pin the blame on the Westports."

"He wouldn't dare!" Constantine's face turned to rage.

"Jax Liebling *would* dare. He's a sociopath with an overinflated ego who will take out anyone who gets in his way."

"Well, then you've gotta get out of there."

"I've got a better idea," Moira offered. "One that will protect Baxter... er, Mr. Baker, and keep the family name out of it."

"I don't want you in any danger." Constantine shook his head.

"It's too late for that, Uncle," she replied. "I've been brought into the fold, so to speak."

"What does that mean, exactly?"

"I've convinced Jax that I'm on board with the church's new direction and that Baxter is clearly the anti-Christ and needs to be stopped."

Constantine's face dropped. "Are you being serious right now? You mean that boy really *is* in danger?"

"Yes," Moira's lip quivered a little. "They're going to kill him if we don't stop it."

"Correction," Constantine replied, leaning a hand on the cart for support, "*you* have nothing to do with this. Leave it to me to protect him. After all, it's *me* he's paying for security."

"Uncle Constantine," Moira was serious, "I can lead you right to the men who are going to try and take him out."

"No."

"You have to let me help," Moira pleaded.

"Why?" Constantine looked at her belly again.

"For the thousandth time, I'm not pregnant. I haven't even kissed the man!" she nearly yelled. "But I'll gladly pretend I am, if it will mean you'll help me!" A few tears were forming in the corners of her eyes.

Constantine put out a meaty thumb and wiped one away. "You really like that boy, don't you?"

Moira nodded.

"Why him?" he was confused.

"I dunno," Moira shrugged, "I just do."

"Okay, Moira. Okay," Constantine promised. "Let's come up with a plan, together."

MOIRA LEFT her uncle's house nearly three hours later, after they'd devised a plan to prevent the untimely demise of Baxter Baker. She climbed into one of Constantine's limos so that Dough could drive her back to her small flat in Dublin. Dough tried to open the door for her, out of habit, but she waved him away. She was having none of it. All this pretend chivalry was starting to get to her. As she slammed the door shut on the front passenger's side, Dough climbed in beside her on the driver's side. He looked at her, questioningly, as the Westport family usually rode in the back seat, not side-by-side with the 'help.' But Dough thought better than to say anything.

"Wouldja like ta hear some music?" he offered, reaching toward the radio and snapping it on. U2's "The Sweetest Thing" came through the speakers, gravelley at first, but then clearer as Dough adjusted the dial for better reception.

Moira didn't answer. Instead, she leaned on one hand, peering out the window, a weighted feeling of regret in her belly, mixed with an odd sense of relief. On the one hand, she was glad that Baxter was going to be safe. On the other, she didn't feel right about her current grift. She had convinced herself that her deal with Jax was the last one she'd be a part of, and now, she was falling in the footsteps of her cousin Bristol and his friend Darwin Fennec. They had to flee to the States to avoid Constantine's wrath. What made her think this one would be different? She was about to pull one final grift...on Uncle Constantine.

~

"Can I get you anything else, sir?" Iris asked Constantine gently after Moira had gone.

Constantine had since relocated to his favorite chair where he and Moira had hatched a plan to prevent bad things from happening to Baxter Baker. There was something about the whole situation that didn't sit right with him. For example, if Moira was so concerned about Baxter's safety, why not warn him before they kidnapped him? Why even let it get that far? Furthermore, if Jax Liebling was set on pinning this on the Westport family, why on Earth would he bring a member of the family into his plan? No, he thought to himself. Something didn't add up.

Iris stood patiently, waiting on Constantine's answer.

"Uh, no, thank you, Iris." Iris turned to leave before he stopped her for a moment. "Just one more thing, Iris," he added. "How is our unexpected house guest doing?"

"Oh, fine, sir. As a matter of fact—" Iris began before Constantine held up a hand to stop her. "That's alright, Iris. The less said, the better."

"Of course, sir," Iris nodded.

Moira's surprise visit almost revealed that Constantine had a secret of his own. Hidden away in a lesser-traveled area of his mansion, an American was being kept out of the public eye. He still hadn't put all the pieces together yet, but he knew one thing for certain, Jax Liebling was becoming a royal thorn in his side.

CHAPTER 24
Convergence

Present Day

Quid was a bit shorter and rounder than Scratch, but had a friendly round face that somehow inspired trust. He picked up Moira, Scratch and Baxter at the small, out-of-the-way coffee shop that, for whatever reason, was closed that day. And so the three stood out front, with little but a thin awning to protect them from the rain. Thanks to the wind, it didn't work and the three were a soggy mess by the time he arrived.

"Want me to turn the heat on?" he offered when they had settled into a white Ford transit van. It had two black racing stripes down the hood, but outside of that, it was pretty unremarkable.

But perfect for flying under the radar, Baxter thought.

"Nah," Scratch answered. "We can dry off proper when we get to Constantine's."

"Constantine?" Baxter sat up, surprised. "You mean, it's Constantine Westport I have to thank for saving me?"

"No, Sweet Face," Moira answered. "You may have paid my uncle for protection, but were it not for me, he'd have had no idea this was going down."

"Your...uncle?" Baxter instinctively touched his head again before sitting back in the seat, his head still throbbing.

Moira took Baxter's hand supportively, weaving her fingers with his and whispering, "We'll get that bruise on your noggin' fixed up in no time," she promised.

He looked down at their intertwined hands, more confused than ever.

Some time passed, but eventually, they arrived. Once at the main Westport mansion, they pulled into what appeared to be a series of horse stalls, except once past the initial entrance, it turned into a private parking garage. One side was lined with utility and transportation vehicles, such as the one they were in, and on the other were stretch limos and black sedans and smaller compact cars.

"You should see Uncle's personal sporty collection." She flashed her green eyes at him as they exited the vehicle.

Baxter merely nodded, following Moira and Scratch through a secret tunnel that led from the garage to the main house.

Once inside the main room, Constantine Westport's primary housekeeper, Iris, quickly attended to them. "I'm sure you'll be wanting to dry off," she said, sympathetically. "Give me a few moments to tend to the jacks, and you can go freshen up there."

A boisterous laugh erupted from the corner of the room, as Constantine Westport lumbered his way to his favorite leather chair situated at the helm of the main sitting area. As soon as he sat, an attendant handed him a whiskey, neat.

"Thank you, Siobhan," he acknowledged.

For the first time in his life, Baxter was speechless.

Moira interrupted the silence by running and giving her uncle a soggy hug to him in his chair.

"What are you doing, silly lass? You're getting rainwater all over me and my good chair!" But he laughed in a way that very few got to hear.

Moira was a force to be reckoned with. She stood back and shook her head from side to side flinging droplets of rainwater from her soaking-wet fiery red hair all over him and his precious chair.

Constantine bellowed louder, "Cheeky. You've got the same attitude as my Molly had." He laughed so hard he had to fight back a tear.

Moira touched his shoulder, sympathetically. "Aye," she answered. "But even she would have had better sense than to get mixed up with the likes of him, now wouldn't she?" Moira motioned to Baxter who felt suddenly conspicuous, and for once, humble. He was used to controlling the room. This new dynamic left him feeling extraordinarily uncomfortable.

"Where is he?!" A voice erupted from the hallway.

"Who the hell is that?" Constantine demanded.

The doors flung open, and a crazed Darwin Fennec rushed into the room, red-eyed as if he hadn't slept in a week. He probably hadn't.

"Finn?" Constantine lurched forward in surprise.

"Why did you do it, Constantine?" he yelled as Scratch and Quid grabbed him and pulled him backward. He was fit to be tied.

"Do what?" Constantine was confused.

"You murdered Rue! You did it to get back at me for Molly!"

Baxter had never formally met Darwin Fennec nor Rue Brennan, but he'd learned about them after Emma Post had begun investigating the death of his uncle, Erasmus Vandenberg. They were the ones who helped solve the murders of two of Emma's close friends and blown the cover of the Vandenberg's criminal dealings. *But why was he here, now?*

"Just hold your tongue, Finn." Constantine waved a hand at him. "Just listen."

"I'm not going to—" Darwin fought against the arms that held him back.

"Darwin," a female voice called.

There, from the shadows, stood Rue Brennan, wearing a flowing red summer dress with ruffles at the ends that flared just around her knees.

Darwin stopped struggling. Moira eyed the scene, confused. *What the heck is going on, and who is this strange woman?*

Constantine motioned for the two men to release him. Darwin sailed toward Rue and hugged her so hard that the two of them buckled to their knees.

"Darwin," Rue huffed. "Loosen up so I can breathe," she smiled, tears pouring down her face. She hugged him close, wrapping the back of his head with her hand and pulled him toward her shoulder, where they sat on their heels, crumpled together on the floor in a tight embrace.

If there were other people in the room, Darwin and Rue were not aware of them.

"But I thought you were—" Darwin began.

Rue shook her head. "No," she explained, "Midge set it up to protect me from Jax Liebling."

Baxter's eyes widened at Jax's name. He couldn't yet connect the dots between Rue, Darwin and Jax since he wasn't around during that particular drama, but it occurred to him rather late that Jax was likely the instigator behind his kidnapping. Perhaps he had gotten Bernie to convince a few members to get involved. He couldn't be sure...

"Well," Rue continued, "first I was bait, and then—never mind. I'll tell you more later. What's important is that Mr. Westport has been letting me stay here to keep me safe."

Darwin eyed Constantine, questioningly. Constantine merely shrugged his shoulders.

"But I thought you wanted me dead after what happened to Molly." Darwin was confused. Molly had been Constantine's daughter and Darwin's first love. She got into both drugs and the wrong gang, leading to her early demise. Constantine threatened to kill both his son, Molly's brother Bristol, along with his best friend, Darwin. Or as Constantine had always known him, *Finn.*

"For a long time, I did," Constantine confessed. "But then I realized that I was misplacing my anger."

Darwin stood, helping Rue to her feet and wrapping an arm around her, unwilling to let her go again.

Constantine took a sip of his whiskey. "See, I was really angry with myself and how I led my daughter into a life of addiction and crime, but I channeled that grief and anger and directed it at you, Finn. But I know now that you were only trying to help my daughter." After a long sigh, he added, "I'm sorry."

Darwin eyed Constantine with disbelief, waiting for the punchline or the other shoe to drop...a shoe that involved him being dragged away and his dead body dumped in a river somewhere. Confused, he asked, "You're...sorry?"

"Yes," Constantine answered.

Channeled grief and anger? Darwin thought. *An apology?* None of that sounded a bit like the hard man Darwin knew as a young lad.

"And you don't want to kill me...or Rue?" Darwin asked for confirmation.

"I do not." A long silence ensued before Constantine added, "I can see you're confused. But after years of therapy, I have learned a healthier way to process my emotions and not cast blame on others. I'm taking responsibility for my life," Constantine finished, proudly.

Moira gave her uncle a supportive pat on the shoulder. Darwin stood, jaw dropped in disbelief. Moira was finally starting to put the pieces together of who these two new visitors were and why they were here.

"Tell me, Finn," Constantine asked, "how is Bristol?"

"Bristol?" Darwin answered, scratching his head nervously. "Uh, fine. He's fine."

"And his wife and kids? How are they?" Constantine leaned forward, eyes blazing directly into Darwin's eyes.

"They are, uh, fine," he stammered. Suddenly, it was as if he were a teenager again, meeting Constantine after he'd gotten caught in a grift gone wrong. "How did you—"

"I got friends everywhere," Constantine explained. For a man angry at his son, it was clear that in his heart, he wanted nothing but the best for Bristol and his family.

"Darwin," Rue suddenly realized. "How did you find me? Midge stole my phone and threw it into traffic and—" Suddenly, a lightbulb went off in her head. "You tracked me through my phone, didn't you?" She wrinkled her nose at him. Then, she remembered. "But how? There's no way the signal would reach—"

"No," Darwin explained. "I couldn't track you in the US, and since Ortega and Penelope weren't giving me any answers, I hopped on the first available flight from New York. Once here, I traced your phone as far as Derry."

"I'm surprised there was anything left to track," Rue remembered Midge wrestling the phone from her and watching with anger as her friend sent it bouncing on the road.

"Well, I guess I got lucky," Darwin explained. "Once I was in the area, it was just a question of figuring out where you'd be. If Midge were involved, I reasoned, a pub."

"Good guess," Rue snorted.

"I hit the only one with a rental car abandoned out front. Turns out, the woman who owned the bar is a sleuth herself. She remembered two women leaving the bar, one seemingly very drunk—"

"Or very drugged—" Rue pursed her lips, annoyed.

"Indeed," Darwin paused to shake his head. "But she also remembered the license plate, make and model of the car that Midge was driving."

"Wow, maybe we should hire her." Rue was impressed.

"She then went on to complain that the rental company she called was taking forever to pick up their 'feckin car,' claiming it wasn't theirs. She was aggravated that it was taking up space in her 'feckin parkin lot.' She finally called the Garda out of aggravation."

Darwin smiled before turning to Constantine. "They eventually tracked the rental to Rue Brennan, but the other car, the one Midge and Rue drove off in, was unregistered. However, it was easy enough to tie the vehicle to you, Mr. Westport. It was one of the many brands you've always used, even back in the day...manufactured by Opel."

"If only everyone had the same brand loyalty as I do," Constantine chortled. "Impressive, Finn."

Iris, who had been waiting in the wings, finally felt it safe to return to the room.

"If you would care to freshen up, Mr. Baker, you can follow me this way, please."

Both Darwin and Rue looked over their shoulder in surprise.

"Baker?" Rue said. "As in Baxter Baker?"

"The same," he cringed, "sorry to meet under such extreme circumstances."

Darwin offered a hand. "No, not the best circumstances, I'll agree. But if I understand it, you helped Emma uncover a cult scheme that had previously led to the death of several people, and nearly took a bullet in the process."

"Er, not nearly," Baxter pulled up his wet shirt to reveal a scar where he was shot trying to protect Emma Post.

There was a slight gasp from Iris and several attendants. Moira's eyes perked up, not at the fact that Baxter's torso was undeniably toned, but that he had been brave enough to actually risk his life for someone. His stock just rose in her book.

"I'm starting to feel like I'm running a sanctuary," Constantine complained. "First her," he pointed to Rue, "and now him," he motioned to Baxter.

Moira kissed the top of Constantine's balding head. "You did good, Uncle," she said. "Alright," Moira announced, noticing her uncle's fatigue and taking charge. "Iris, can you help see to it that our guests are looked after? Everyone, get some rest and we can all discuss this further over dinner."

"But what about—" Baxter sidled up to her and whispered.

"I'll put in an anonymous call to Detective Ortega. He was working with Emma, no?"

"That's right," Baxter agreed. "So they'll check in on our friends by the sea?" He was, of course, referring to the men who had tried to kidnap him and drown him in the ocean not hours earlier.

"What friends?" Moira asked, winking.

"Emma who?" Baxter played along.

"That's better," she smiled. "And you, Sweet Face, are coming with me."

With that, Moira led a willing Baxter out of the room. From the hallway, he could be heard whispering, "How is it that you stumbled on Detective Ortega's number, exactly?"

"Shhh," Moira whispered. "You ask far too many questions, Sweet Face." She guided Baxter to the end of the hall, making a left toward yet another long hallway.

"C'mon," Rue took Darwin by the arm. "You need some rest after the shock you've had."

"I'm afraid if I let myself go to sleep, I'll awake and discover this was all a dream, and that you're really gone," he lamented. Darwin was still convinced he must be hallucinating.

Rue stood on her toes and planted a soft kiss on Darwin's lips.

"I'm not gone," she promised. "And I swear, I'll never leave you again."

Moira had a private guest room at Constantine's house. It was her home away from home. Compared to the rest of the estate, her room was simple. From the doorway to his right, Baxter noticed a queen-sized white canopy bed with a ruffled top. On the left side of the bed, there was a small end table with a lamp and a white rotary phone and what appeared to be a bathroom door. On the bed's right, stood a tall ash armoire. Directly across from him, bright sunlight beamed through a double-paneled window with French shutters that were currently open. Under the window sat a small writing table and chair. And against the wall opposite the bed was a matching ash dresser and a tall rocking chair in the corner, facing the window.

"What?" Moira questioned Baxter's expression.

"Nothing," he answered. "This room feels like you only...softer." He smiled.

"Hmmph," she answered. "Sit."

He sat at the writing table while Moira disappeared into the bathroom. She appeared moments later with cotton balls and hydrogen peroxide.

"Thank you, Nurse Moira," he joked. He lifted his chin and grinned, closing his eyes as he waited for her to apply the antiseptic to his bruised head. He braced himself for the pain and was determined to put on a brave face.

"Here," she clunked the bottle on the table and dropped the bag of cotton balls. "I've got that call to make, remember?"

She spun on her heels and headed to the phone where she dialed Ortega's cell phone number, apparently from memory.

Disappointed, Baxter soaked a cotton ball. Oddly enough, there was no mirror in the room. He noticed a long, silver letter opener on the desk, squinting to see his reflection in it as he applied the antiseptic to his head. He couldn't really see the injury well at that angle, but the stinging let him know he had reached the right area. He winced, then quickly darted a glance in Moira's direction to make sure she hadn't noticed. She had her back to him.

Moira was busy dialing in a code to block her number to outgoing calls. She wasn't taking any chances on being traced. Baxter also noticed she screwed something over the mouthpiece...*to disguise her voice?*

"That's right, detective," she said, moments later. "Probably best to get there soon before the tide comes in." Detective Ortega could be heard asking a question, but Baxter couldn't hear exactly what. Moira hung up while he was still talking. She returned, eyed Baxter sitting there, a soggy, bloody cotton ball in his hand.

"You are hopeless, Sweet Face. You know that?" She smiled at him, holding up a wastepaper basket just next to the desk. He hadn't noticed it before now. He tossed the cotton away. "Aww," she wrinkled her lips. "You missed a spot." Moira grabbed a fresh cotton ball, tipped the bottle of hydrogen peroxide just enough to soak it, and then reapplied it liberally over the wound.

"Ouch!" he complained.

She smiled, wickedly.

"You're enjoying this, aren't you?" Baxter complained.

"A bit," she confessed. "If I hadn't seen that bullet wound with my own eyes, I woulda thought you'd never gotten your pretty little head bruised or your hands calloused."

"What's that supposed to mean?" Baxter was indignant.

"It means that you're a wee bit more genteel than what I'm used to."

"Well," Baxter grimaced at her, "You're rough and tumble enough for the both of us."

"You've got that right," Moira smiled seductively as she walked backward toward the bedroom door, bending her knee and kicking it closed with her boot, locking the two of them inside.

CHAPTER 25
No Witnesses

~

Penelope, Ortega and Shep approached the van cautiously. It was exactly where the anonymous caller said it would be, except that now, it was turned on its side with tidewaters flowing in and out around it. It was still shallow this time of day, but suspiciously quiet.

Ortega thought he recognized the caller's speech patterns as someone he had met, but the voice was distorted, and there was such a sense of urgency that he wasted no time in getting to the scene once they had hung up.

Meanwhile, Shep, having been newly released from the hospital, still winced every three steps. The doctor had ordered bed rest, but Shep was on a mission and simply wouldn't listen.

Suddenly, Shep grabbed Ortega's arm as he stepped onto a dry part of the beach, a mere four feet from the van. Penelope paused behind them. Much smaller than the large man, she struggled to peer around him. Shep pointed a silent finger that traced a line marking the van...a line of machine gun holes.

Ortega nodded, carefully motioning for Shep to go one way while he went the other, circling the van. Ortega paused long enough to roll his pants up, but his socks and shoes were soon to be sloshing on mucky sand with sea water lapping around his heels. In the States, both men would be armed, but here, they only had batons as weapons.

Shep eyed the driver's seat through the only available window. The glass was smashed in with fragments scattered over the steering wheel and seat, most of it settling on top of the passenger window, now steeped in the sand but largely intact. At first glance, there was no evidence to suggest the driver side door had been tampered with, nor any blood stains to indicate that someone up front had been shot.

Penelope sucked in a nervous breath as Ortega struggled to climb over the side of the van and tug at the side door. Finally, the heavy door slid open and clambered to a stop.

"Holy shit," Shep muttered as he and Ortega witnessed what was inside. Ortega gagged a little as he turned his head. Penelope took a step toward him but he waved an arm and shook his head.

Inside, the three men who attempted to kidnap and kill Baxter Baker were not only still tied up from when he, Scratch and Moira left them, but each had multiple gunshot wounds to the chest. Whomever shot them wasn't taking any chances because, in addition to the peppered shots to the van, they must have opened it long enough to distribute single gunshot wounds to each of their heads: Tom, Milton and Leo. The bodies lay in a heap at the bottom of the overturned vehicle.

It's not as if Ortega hadn't witnessed gruesome scenes before. But most times, he was expecting it. After some time off in retirement, coupled with a call from a woman that clearly indicated there were three men, all of whom were alive and waiting for him...he didn't expect this.

Penelope, however, recognized the look on Ortega's face. It's the one he got when he was both overwhelmed and somehow blaming himself for an invisible failure of which only he was aware of.

"Jose," Penelope said calmly, "whatever it is, I can help."

She was, after all, a forensic scientist by profession. Although, thanks to her involvement in her former boss's cases, she was now and ex-one. But she had been the best in the business and despite her kind heart, when it came to gruesome scenes, she had nerves of steel and a stomach to match.

Ortega composed himself, climbing down as there wasn't much space alongside the open van for two people. "Okay," he relented as he and Shep backed away from the scene. "Just brace yourself. Looks like there are three men inside, as promised, but all have been shot to death." Ortega put out a hand to help Penelope up onto the side of the van. She handed her camera bag and forensic accessory duffle bag to Shep who dutifully held them until she was safely up.

She sat on the edge of the open door, her legs dangling inside the cargo space. "Hand me the hazard gear first...shoe covers, gloves, jacket." She announced. "Thanks," she replied as Shep handed them up to her, piece by piece. "Camera next." She ordered. Shep handed her the camera bag and waited as she unzipped it and procured her Nikon. After several minutes she said, "Hang on. I'm goin' in."

Ortega and Shep awaited further instruction, until Penelope finally declared in a muffled voice from within, "Need my flashlight!"

Shep scrambled to comply, hanging a long arm over the edge.

"Thanks" she accepted it.

"How'd she know she'd need her equipment?" Shep asked.

"Dr. Washburn always plans on a crime scene," Ortega explained. "Even if the men had been alive, we would have wanted to collect photos of the scene for evidence, anyway."

Shep nodded. "That makes sense."

Just then, the team heard sirens in the distance...An Garda Síochána.

"How did they—" Shep began to ask.

"Don't know," Ortega answered, "but it's not great for us to be caught here uninvited."

"Hey there!" A gruff voice called as a larger older man clambered down the steep slope, struggling in what appeared to be a bullet proof vest. Just then, Penelope popped her head out from the van. The man's eyes shot them a glare. "Inspector Clover, don't move!"

Ortega's eyes lit up. His look of dread turned to one of relief. Maybe this wasn't such a bad thing at all...

When the Inspector reached the sand, he squinted at Ortega, "What in the feckin' hell are yew grinnin' at?" Then, his eyes grew wide. "Detective Jose Ortega?"

"The same," Ortega grinned. "Nice to see you again, Ian."

"Well, as I live and breathe," Inspector Clover laughed. "I heard you retired."

"I did," Ortega nodded. "Or, so I thought."

Penelope and Shep shot each other questioning looks before Shep interceded, "I hate to be the one to state the obvious here, but we've got a triple homicide on our hands."

Clover eyed Shep up and down before darting a look from Penelope, who was still in the van, and Ortega on the ground. He smirked. "Still together, I see," he whispered, jabbing Ortega in the ribs.

By then, two of Clover's officers were on hand, awaiting Inspector Clover's instructions.

"Dr. Washburn," Inspector Clover addressed Penelope. "Nice to see yew again. But wouldja mind tellin' me what yer doin' messin' with the evidence of a crime scene in a country where yew have no place messin'?"

Penelope eyed Ortega who knowingly nodded.

"Oh, I wasn't messin'," she began. "Er, messing." The two guards helped her climb out of the van, but not before she'd handed Shep her camera case and a few evidence bags. Once on the ground, Penelope looked mournfully at her rain boots, now covered in mud. She could feel the cold water soaking her socks. Somehow, she hadn't thought to bring waterproof rain boots in her haste to pack. She adjusted the camera, now hanging from a strap around her neck. "We received an anonymous call that there were three people of interest tied up and waiting for us here, ones that could shed light on the Vandenberg case."

"I'm afraid yew've lost me, lass." Clover lifted his cap and scratched his head, before leaning back and speaking quietly to Ortega, "Care to catch me up on what in the feckin' hell is goin' on?"

"Inspector," one of the guards called. "You really need to see this."

Inspector Clover pushed past Penelope and Ortega and looked down into the van.

"I can assure you, the three of us had nothing to do with this," Shep explained.

"Oh, can yew now?" Clover tilted a head up at the excessively tall and large Shep. What Clover lacked in height, not that he was small by any means, he made up for in girth and attitude.

"It has to do with a case we were on in Florida involving the Vandenberg family and the Church of Infinite Love," Ortega explained. "We expect they are trying to cover their tracks in the States and re-open operations in Ireland."

Clover eyed the dead men in the van distastefully. "Any idea who these men are?"

"Not yet," Ortega answered. "We only arrived moments before you did, expecting to find three very alive men."

"Well, we got wind when several calls came in about civilians hearing what sounded like machine gun fire, but, for obvious reasons, no one wanted to get close to it to see what was going on," Clover explained. "I haven't even had time to call anyone else in yet." He turned to Penelope. "Seeing as you're already here, what have you got fer me?"

"Well," Penelope explained. "I can't tell for certain without access to a lab, but the bodies are still relatively fresh. And given you just got the call, I'd say that adds up."

"What else?" Clover waved his hand.

"One of the men had his passport on him," Penelope motioned for Shep to bring over the evidence bags. He obliged, handing it over to the Guards. "He's American, and given their shoes and clothing, I suspect they all are."

"Three persons of interest gunned down during daylight hours with a machine gun?" Clover clarified.

"AR-15," Penelope confirmed. "So, they either smuggled them in themselves and were shot with their own weapons or—"

"Mob hit?" Clover finished.

"Maybe," Penelope shrugged.

"Feckin' hell," Clover removed his hat and scratched his head again. A flaky red bald patch at the top of his scalp seemed to glow angrily at the abuse.

"There's one more odd bit," Shep offered. "Look," he pointed at some of the track marks just at the edge of the dry part of the beach where the sand met the ramp that led to higher ground. "Most of it is washed away, but they appear to have come from a wheelchair."

Penelope's eyes lit up as she turned to Inspective Clover, hopefully. "If you can give me just a little more time to scour the van. I can see if there are tread marks inside and any other pieces of evidence."

"How am I going to explain this to my superintendent?" Clover asked Ortega. "You're not even supposed to be here. And, you're retired!"

"I'm not," Shep explained. "I'm currently active with the Sheriff's department in Tampa, Special Investigations. We regularly work with contractors in situations like this one. And since these men are likely American and tied to a case I was already investigating—"

Shep paused to let Inspector Clover connect the dots any way he saw fit, leaving out the part about the fact that he wasn't, technically, assigned to this case, either. He merely took a temporary leave of absence citing health issues. But he didn't feel the need to tell Clover that.

"Inspector!" one of the Guards called. "Look at this!" The officer reached a gloved hand down and pulled out a small broach that was wedged between one of the victim's feet and the edge of the floor.

"What is it?" Clover asked.

"A ladies pin of some sort."

"Lemme see that," Penelope ordered, before eyeing Ortega and Clover and adding, "please." She put her plastic gloves back on and eyed the broach, tumbling it over in her hand. It was gold with a cleanly polished Connemara stone at the center. She sighed, loudly.

"What is it, Penelope?" Ortega asked.

"If I didn't know any better, I'd say this custom ditty is a creation from Westport Jewelers," Penelope said. "My mother was mad about this stuff back in the day."

"The Westport Grifters are in on this?" Inspector Clover replied. "Feckin' hell!" He motioned toward his guards. "Men, we're going ta have ta pay a visit to Constantine Westport's home."

"Wait," Ortega intervened. "Ian, how's it gonna look with the Guard barging in there without all the evidence? Let Dr. Washburn finish scouring the scene for clues, and we'll report anything we find."

"He's right," Shep added. "They know you, but not us. They see you anywhere near the property and who knows how the family will react? Why not let us have a talk with them first?"

Inspector Clover thought a moment, before letting out a forced cough. "Come to think of it," he coughed again. "I think I'm…Tá mé tinn. Think I'll take the rest of the day off to recover." He leaned in and whispered quietly to Ortega and Shep, "I'll have my men block off the crime scene. You leave Dr. Washburn here to finish up her report while you pay the Westports a visit. I can stall until tomorrow morning, but then I need to send my men in to start investigating. Understood?"

"Understood," Ortega nodded. "Thank you, Ian."

Inspector Clover shook his head as he walked over to the two Guards assisting him, muttering under his breath, "Feckin' hell."

Ortega's phone buzzed just moments after he'd left Penelope and Shep at the crime scene commandeering their rental vehicle for investigative purposes. Penelope was tasked with finishing up on collecting evidence and Shep on documenting what they found. It hadn't escaped Penelope's attention that she only knew of one person, potentially, involved in this case who used a wheelchair...Moira Dodd. *But how is she involved in this? If she is involved?*

Inspector Clover left one officer behind to oversee the crime scene, ensuring that evidence didn't disappear and to see to it that the two returned safely to their temporary residence. It wasn't so much that Clover suspected them of anything, but he still had to cover his ass with his superiors.

Ortega eyed his phone...an encrypted message. That could only be from one person—Darwin Fennec. *But how did the signal reach him overseas? Hell, he couldn't even get good reception a block from his house.* A sudden flash of heat crossed his face. *Darwin must be in Ireland.* He feared what his occasional colleague and sometimes friend would do, as he was convinced that it was Constantine Westport who was responsible for Rue Brennan's death. *I hope he doesn't do anything stupid,* Ortega thought.

Then he decoded the message. It read: *Rue is alive. Westport is innocent.*

That was it. *Guess he's not in a place where he can share more,* Ortega reasoned. But given this new information, all signs still pointed to Constantine Westport's involvement in this. He just wasn't entirely sure what it was.

Time to find out, Ortega muttered to himself.

CHAPTER 26
The Visit

"He can talk to me first or he can talk to Inspector Clover," Ortega's voice could be heard in the hall. "Mr. Westport stands a better chance with me because I actually wanna believe he's innocent."

Dough, Mr. Westport's front-line security guard blocked Ortega from entering the premises. With a name like Dough, one might have expected the guard to be on the softer, lumpier side and more than a little overweight. Instead, he was a small, thin man with lean muscles and a spring in his step that suggested years in the boxing rink. There was something in his eyes that Ortega used to recognize in himself in his younger years —fearlessness.

Dough signaled Scratch to remain with Ortega as he went to see Constantine. A few minutes later, Dough returned and Ortega was ushered into a small library, just off to the side of the main living room where people usually gathered. Scratch remained guarding the front door while Dough, after Ortega was seated across from Constantine at his desk, slid the panel of the library door closed. He stood at the door, directly behind the retired detective, watching his every move. Meanwhile, Constantine sat stuffed behind the desk, his large frame struggling to fit in the space provided. His chair squeaked painfully under his weight.

Ortega and Constantine eyed each other in silence for what seemed like an eternity before Constantine finally asked, "Do I know you?"

Ortega opened his mouth and let out a puff of air, as if he were a balloon that had suddenly been popped. "No, Mr. Westport, you have no reason to know me. However, I believe Moira does," Ortega treaded carefully.

"My niece?" Constantine was surprised. "What does Moira have to do with anything?"

"I got a call from someone on my private cell phone not two hours ago. The voice was disguised, but we have reason to believe it was her." He thought back to the factory visit and wheelchair track marks in the sand at the crime scene. It was a long shot, but his spidey sense, along with Penelope's findings, left him confident that he was on the right track. "Don't know how she got my number, but that's not what's important."

"What *is i*mportant, Detective Ortega?" Constantine tried to lean in, formidably, but his belly got in the way. *Gotta go on a diet,* he thought to himself and sat back.

"She alerted me to the fact that three men who'd botched a kidnapping were tied up with a neat little bow and waiting for me to pick them up, and to get there before high tide so they didn't drown."

"Is that so?" Constantine feigned ignorance. "What's that gotta do with me?"

"Do you know where your niece is at the moment, Mr. Westport? She is your niece, isn't she?" Ortega confirmed.

"Wait a minute," Constantine wagged a finger at Ortega. "I thought you were here to question *me* for something. Every time anything interesting happens in this town, officers are banging down my door, assuming I was involved in some way."

"We'll get to you in a minute," Ortega tried again. "But first, where's Moira Dodd?"

Constantine thought carefully before answering simply, "Dunno. Haven't seen her," he lied.

Ortega considered his options. He could drag this out and see if

Constantine slipped, giving him information about the crime that he shouldn't have known, or be direct. He decided on the latter.

"Mr. Westport, we did find three men exactly where Miss Dodd said they'd be."

"Well, there you go," Constantine bellowed.

"They were dead," Ortega finished. Constantine's face dropped in surprise. "Shot to death. I'd like to know why and by whom."

"As I said, I haven't seen Moira in days. And I know nothing about these men you found."

"They found a broach at the crime scene with the family logo on it, one from the Westport jewelry line," Ortega added.

"So?" Constantine mocked. "That don't mean nothin'."

Ortega twitched uncomfortably. He could fish for the next few minutes, or do what generally worked in these situations. He picked the latter...and lied. "They also found a few red hairs at the scene, belonging to a woman, and DNA samples that will no doubt be traced back to Moira Dodd." In truth, Ortega couldn't confirm that any human hair was found at the scene that didn't belong to the deceased, nor would DNA test results be available that quickly. He was taking a gamble. "Since Moira is a known member of the Westport family, how long do you think it'll be before Inspector Clover comes banging down your door asking about your involvement?"

"I'm not saying nothin' else without my lawyer present—"

Just then, there was a knock at the door. "Uncle, let me in!" It was Moira.

"Oh, geez," Constantine rubbed his forehead with a meaty hand. "You gotta be kidding me."

Dough backed away as Moira bolted through the door.

Moira seemed frazzled, having only just now realized that Ortega was on the property. "Are you Detective Ortega?" she asked.

"I am," he answered.

"And did you receive an anonymous call about three men tied up on the beach?"

"I did," he replied.

"And did they confess to trying to kidnap and murder Baxter Baker, CEO of Vandenberg Nutraceuticals?"

"Confess," Ortega scratched his head. "No, they didn't confess."

"How is that possible?" Moira was incredulous, eyeing Ortega and Constantine back and forth.

"Because they're dead, Moira," Constantine finished.

"What?!" Moira's face dropped. "That's not possible. When I left —er—"

"Not another word," Constantine cut her off. "Keep your mouth shut until we talk to the lawyers."

"Mr. Westport—" Ortega began.

"Out!" Constantine stood, pressing his palms into the desk for support. "I want you out!" Dough grabbed Ortega by the arm. Instinctively, Ortega tried to shrug him off, but Dough had the grip of a pitbull.

"I'm here in an unofficial capacity," Ortega raised his voice. "But tomorrow, you can expect a swarm of Guards at your door who won't be as understanding as I am. Let me help you."

"Let him go, Dough," Moira commanded. To her uncle, she said, "Let Mr. Baker and I talk to him. We can sort this out."

"Baxter Baker...is here?" Ortega was surprised.

"He's not the only one," a voice at the door called. Ortega turned to see Darwin standing there, Rue at his side.

"Oh sure," Constantine complained. "Let's let everyone in here, shall we?" To Dough he said, "There's not enough therapy in the world for this shit!"

Ortega's eyes fell to Rue. At one time, he didn't think much of Ms. Brennan. In fact, when she was a suspect in a case, he wasn't very nice to her at all. But she'd come to earn his respect over time, and his opinion of her softened. He felt a little lurch in his heart. His lip quivered. Rue caught his expression for just a moment, surprised that it was filled with such sentiment. She hadn't known him to be compassionate.

"It's nice to see you again, Ms. Brennan," he greeted her cordially, fighting back a few tears and a lump in his throat. "I'm glad you're not...dead."

Rue grinned, "Oh, stop. You old softie," she teased.

Ortega cleared his throat as his eyes darted from Rue, to Darwin, to Moira, Constantine and Dough. "Someone wanna fill me in on what's going on here?"

"I was hoping to speak with you in private," Moira confessed. "I mean, Mr. Baker and me."

"Actually, Moira," Baxter crept into the doorway when no one was looking, peering around Darwin. "Since Mr. Fennec and Ms. Brennan are here too, I think we should have a larger conversation to include them. We're all connected in ways of which I'm not even sure yet."

A look of fear crossed her face as Moira eyed her uncle, and Constantine caught it. "What have you been up to, lass?" he questioned.

Moira replied, hesitantly, "Uncle, remember the conversation we had a couple of weeks ago about Mr. Baker?"

"Where you thought he was in danger. Of course. Isn't that what today was about?"

"Yes, but there's more." She turned to Ortega. "Perhaps I should start there and fill you in..."

CHAPTER 27
Secrets

Moira finished telling Ortega about her conversation with Constantine surrounding Baxter Baker's safety and her concerns about Jax Liebling.

"So, you did like me all this time!" Baxter declared, triumphantly, missing the point entirely.

Moira punched him in the arm. "Now's not the time for that," she whispered.

At Constantine's suggestion, Baxter, Moira, Darwin and Rue joined him in the living room where he could sit comfortably in the chair that was quickly becoming his throne, with each couple sitting on either side of him. Ortega opted to stand. This time, Dough and Scratch stood at each end of the room, like two Fu Dogs guarding their master.

"So," Ortega offered, "you knew Jax Liebling was up to something and went to your uncle for help. And so, it was you who intercepted today's unfortunate kidnapping with Mr. Baker."

"Yes," Moira admitted, shooting an apologetic glance toward her uncle.

"And you, Mr. Westport," Ortega addressed Constantine, "were less than honest when you said you knew nothing about the men we found on the beach under the cliffs today. Is that correct?"

Constantine shrugged before adding, "But I had nothing to do with their deaths. Alls I did was provide transportation to rescue pretty boy over there because Moira was so concerned about him. Had no reason to suspect anything might happen to them."

"But," Baxter thought a moment, ignoring the 'pretty boy' reference altogether. "Moira," he turned to her, "if you suspected that I was in danger, why did you let it get this far? Why didn't you warn me?"

"Well," Moira thought quickly. "I didn't want to worry you—" Even as she said it, she knew how unconvincing that sounded.

"Moira," Baxter adopted a sullen voice. "I may be a cad and am not everyone's cup of tea, but I never pretend to be something I'm not. And more importantly, I've always been honest with you about...everything." He took her hand. Constantine's eyes shot up. Baxter released her hand and let out a cough.

"What's going on?" Constantine demanded?

Moira's eyes darted from Baxter to Constantine, uncomfortably. Darwin and Rue watched the scene with fascination, not entirely sure how all of this pieced together.

"Uncle," she confessed, fighting back tears. "I messed up."

Iris, who stood silently in the corner of the room, rushed to Moira's side with a tissue.

"Thank you," Moira accepted it. Iris merely nodded and went back to her corner. To the group, she said, "Jax Liebling called me into his office one day—"

"Why that—" Constantine's face became flushed.

"That's not it!" Moira squealed. "He had been putting feelers out there for weeks seeing my whole opinion of the Church of Infinite Love, and Mr. Baker, and my work at the factory as an assistant, and even you, Uncle Constantine. It was like he was testing the waters."

"For what?" Ortega asked.

"For my loyalties, I think," she confessed. "Once he realized that I wasn't interested in religion any more than I was interested in the family business, he offered me a way out."

"What kind of way out?" Ortega coaxed.

"Well," Moira looked apologetically at Constantine and Baxter. "He said he had a plan that would give me the freedom to forge my own path, and one that would get him the money he needed to buy out the Vandenberg family and run the factories his own way."

"Factories?" Ortega questioned. "As in — plural?"

Moira nodded. "I'll bet if you dig a little deeper into who really purchased the Florida factory, you'll find that Jax Liebling was involved."

"But what does this have to do with my kidnapping—" Suddenly, Baxter was hit with clarity. "Oh, I was to be ransom."

Moira nodded.

"Wait, though," Baxter added. "They were planning to kill me! Did you know about that?!"

"No!" Moira cried. "I most certainly didn't know about that! That's just what I told Uncle Constantine to get him on board with the plan."

"What? You lied to me...and you used me?" Constantine was wounded. He darted an angry glance at Darwin, as if this were somehow his fault. Darwin held his hands up and shook his head. He had no idea what this was about.

"What was the plan, Moira?" Ortega redirected the conversation.

"The plan was to have some of Bernie Forger's uber-devoted followers kidnap Baxter out of some religious commitment."

"Bernie Forger," Rue confirmed. "The new Elder of the church following Erasmus Vandenberg's murder?"

"Yes, exactly," Moira confirmed. "I was to intercept and redirect Baxter safely here, where he'd hole up thinking it was unsafe to return to work."

"And then Jax would send a ransom note to the Vandenberg family... and the matriarch, Edwina Vandenberg, would get her lawyer, Mr. Lundy, to give them what they asked." Ortega put the pieces together. "And you and he would split the profits."

Moira nodded.

"You used me?" Baxter's betrayal could be heard in his voice. "But I...I really liked you. And furthermore, my family is furious with me. Why would they pay the ransom instead of saying, 'good riddance'?"

"Because they needed you to be the scapegoat for both the church's and Vandenberg Nutraceutical's bad deeds. Let you take the blame, and after some time passes, it's business as usual," Ortega realized.

"For the record," Moira tried to explain. "I do like you, an awful lot." Baxter shook his head, disgusted. "The plan was for me to take my share of the ransom and get you to run away with me," Moira confessed.

"What?" Baxter uncrossed his arms and recrossed them.

"Well, your family hates you—"

"I wouldn't say hate," Baxter defended.

"They were trying to put the blame on you," Moira answered fervently. "And if the Vandenberg and Church of Infinite Love collective empire fell, or even if it didn't, I wanted you to be free from all that."

"You did?" Baxter's voice softened. When she put it like that, it was rather touching. He took her hands in his, staring into her bright green eyes.

"But then I realized those men were going to kill ya," she finished.

And the romantic bubble was burst.

"How did you know that, Moira?" Ortega asked.

"The way they were talking," she confessed. "They kept saying how proud Bernie would be to see them carry out justice, and the favor God would have on them...amour of God and all that."

"Not to mention them telling me I was going to swim with the fishes," Baxter added.

"At first, I thought they were just a little overly enthusiastic," Moira offered, brushing a wisp of red hair behind her ear. "But the closer we got to the destination, the more convinced I was that they were serious. Scratch heard it too."

At the mention of his name, Scratch (one of the Fu dogs), nodded. "Aye," he agreed. "They sounded pretty serious ta me."

"So, how did they end up dead?" Ortega asked.

"I dunno," Moira answered. "When I phoned you, we had just gotten here after Quid picked us up. I told 'em to confess, fully expecting them to try to pin some of the blame on me. What I didn't expect was someone to kill 'em."

Ortega turned his attention to Constantine. "As of right now, the Guard assumes Moira and the Westport family are involved. So, if there's anything in this story that's missing, I suggest you fill it in for me now."

"I had nothing to do with any of this," Constantine complained. "I mean, other than providing transportation when Moira needed it...and now you know why I hate that the Vandenberg family business returned to Ireland. They leave a wake wherever they go and give the respectable work of grifting a bad name." Constantine shook his head.

"Honor among thieves, is that it?" Ortega asked.

"Something like that," Constantine nodded. "An art form, at the very least."

"Jax is trying to frame me and the family," Moira was convinced.

"How can you be sure?" Ortega asked.

"I heard you telling Uncle about that broach."

"And?"

"And, I make it a point to never wear jewelry, nail polish, makeup, nothing that can obviously be traced back to me if accidentally left behind. If they found something that belonged to me, it was planted."

"By?"

"The same man who tried to murder me," Rue chimed in. "Jax Liebling. He's had it in for me ever since I helped put his girlfriend away for murder."

"Speaking of his girlfriend," Ortega added. "Have we heard from Ms. Pasternak recently? Because where she goes, death seems to follow."

"Does this Ms. Pasternak have a pretty thick New Jersey or New York accent, by chance?" Moira asked. "I'm not great with American accents, but that's what it sounded like to me."

"Yes, why?" Ortega raised an eyebrow.

"Because I received an anonymous call from a private number the night before the kidnapping," Moira answered. "The woman was trying to put on a passable Irish accent, but it was *really* bad." Moira chuckled.

"And what did she say?" Ortega asked.

"She said, 'if things go south tomorrow, call Detective Ortega.' Then she added, 'I'm only gonna say this once, so you'd better commit this to memory.' She rattled off your number and hung up."

"Good memory," Baxter commented.

"It's part of the job description," Moira answered. "But that's what caused me to get my guard up. In either plan, Baxter ended up here, under my protection—"

Constantine loudly cleared his throat.

"Under Uncle's protection," she corrected. "I just decided it might be best to plan for the worst, just in case."

"Why would you trust an anonymous voice on the phone, anyway?" Baxter was curious.

"Because I remembered something peculiar that Mr. Liebling said under his breath one day at work," Moira's eyes darted away as if triggering a memory. "He said, 'who's pulling the strings now, Jersey Girl?'"

~

"MIDGE SAID I WAS BAIT," Rue told Ortega, after she and Darwin had requested a private meeting with the retired inspector. "I thought I was supposed to help unravel the workings of the church and help you take them down for good, but I suspect she had other plans."

"Do you think she's working for Jax?" Ortega asked. "Maybe that it's all a ruse but they're actually working together?"

"I don't think so," Rue answered, thoughtfully. "I know that's a naive thing to say, but I really suspect that she's afraid of him. And she has this strange 'friend code.' Do I think she used me for her purposes? Yes. Do I think she put me recklessly in danger? Absolutely. Do I think she cares about me and doesn't want to see me dead? Yes...in her own twisted way."

"So, she helped you fake your murder," Ortega confirmed.

"Yes," Rue nodded. "She let Jax think he'd won."

"But, how did she get Constantine to offer to keep you in hiding?"

Suddenly, a disembodied voice chimed in. "She dropped Rue off on the lawn near my front doorstep. Told my guys that Jax Liebling was trying to pin the blame of her death on the Westports in a turf war," Constantine's voice may have been muffled, but it was definitely him. "And that Finn was sweet on her. My boys were so confused to find a girl, nearly dead, lying on the lawn. Or, at least one that appeared drunk or strung out on drugs, possibly an overdose, that they didn't notice that the bearer of such news had vanished...with one of our vehicles, I might add! Do you know how hard it is to spot a woman with dark green hair wearing all black in the middle of the night? It wasn't until they noticed the headlights in the distance that they caught on that she was getting away."

Darwin searched under the desk in the library where they spoke and in the fake plant on top, smiling at his discovery of both a tiny termite bug and a speaker. He glanced around the room before waving at a porcelain bust that sat on one of the shelves. He had discovered the hidden camera as well.

"Since we're clearly not getting any privacy, would you care to join us?" Ortega invited.

"No, you carry on. Forget I'm even here," Constantine bellowed before the sound dropped off with a bout of noisy static.

"None of this explains why she insisted you come to Ireland, Rue," Ortega commented.

"Maybe it was my super sleuthing on the last case we worked on?" Rue suggested, hopefully.

Darwin and Ortega sent her a questioning look.

"No," she relented. "You're right. While I understand a good bit about how a Church of Infinite Love campus operates, I'm a little out of my element here. Come to think of it, there's the factory. But are there even any church campuses out here?"

"Don't know," Ortega confessed. "We got distracted by you and the murders; we haven't had a chance to look. All that's come to light recently is the school that Bernie Forger recently broke ground on."

"But either way, you anger Jax," Darwin cut in, deep in thought.

"What?" Rue asked.

"He was angry enough to try and kill you. And what is bait after all, but a distraction?" Darwin added.

"So, what was Midge trying to distract Jax from?"

"And what makes him so angry?"

"Well, you did help put Midge behind bars," Darwin suggested. "Not to mention having a big role in uncovering the church's and the Vandenberg family's shady dealings."

"That's not it," Rue was convinced. "If anything, that would lead Jax to convince the Vandenberg family how much they really needed his help."

"No, I agree." Darwin all but read her mind, nodding.

"What am I missing?" Ortega's glance darted back and forth between the two of them.

"He's jealous of me," Rue answered.

"How so?" Ortega asked.

"I'm Midge's 'bestie'—her words. The only thing he can't control is how she feels about me. And that angers him to no end."

"What would dangling you out as bait do for Midge? What's her end game?" Darwin asked.

"I'm really not sure," Rue answered. "Midge wouldn't tell me, other than she was trying to clear up tensions between you and Constantine Westport, and help take down the church, but I find it hard to believe her intentions are honorable."

"Well," Ortega interjected. "Here's what I *do* know...both of you are on the next flight out of here back to the States, even if we have to use Darwin's resources to get you a fake I.D."

"Already taken care of," Darwin tapped the side of his pocket. To Ortega he added, "Don't ask."

"But wait," Rue complained. "I still wanna help."

"The best way you can help, honey, is to be safe." Darwin took her shoulders. "I can't lose you again." Rue nodded, wrapping her arms around his waist for a prolonged hug—just long enough to make Ortega, who was standing right in front of them, feel a little uncomfortable.

"That's right," Ortega confirmed, "I want you both out of this investigation. Do you understand?"

The two nodded, somewhat reluctantly.

"I think we're done here for now," Ortega spoke directly into the planted bug. In the distance, they could hear Constantine's deep breathing, but he still pretended not to be there.

As they were leaving, Darwin turned to Ortega. "Oh," he whispered, handing him a tiny flash drive. "Something I thought you could use."

"What is it?" Ortega whispered back, palming the small device.

"Thumb drive," Darwin explained. "Not on the market yet, but will be soon. You'll find some beta data mining tools on there."

"Data mining?" Ortega asked.

"Yeah," Darwin nodded. "I can fill you in when Rue and I are safely back in the States. Essentially, it'll help you cross-examine the data from different crime scenes, including the people involved, and formulate the relationships between them."

"So, essentially what I do," Ortega smiled. "I'll be out of a job soon."

"Hardly," Darwin answered. "But it can help you work faster and more efficiently."

"At my age," Ortega reasoned. "I'll take all the help I can get."

Darwin laughed. "Don't sell yourself short, Ortega. You've got a lot of fight left in you."

Ortega slapped Darwin on the back. "Thanks, Mr. Fennec. As always, you are just full of surprises."

DARWIN GENTLY KNOCKED on Constantine's bedroom door in the early hours of the morning. It was Quid's turn at overnight duty. He opened it hesitantly.

"We're heading to the airport," Darwin whispered. "You'll let Constantine know?"

"You can tell him yerself," Quid answered, opening the door wide. "He's been waiting for you for the last hour."

"Come in, me boy," Constantine's tired voice could be heard from the bed. "Pardon my indiscretion, but you are leaving rather early." Across Constantine's lap was a custom-built breakfast tray large enough to fit over his frame. On it were eggs, bacon, blood pudding, baked beans, tomatoes, toast and...yogurt. Darwin eyed the yogurt, amused. "What?" Constantine defended. "I'm trying to eat healthier."

Darwin smirked. "I can see that."

"Ah, screw you, Finn," Constantine laughed. It turned abruptly into a phlegmy cough. "See what happens when I eat dairy?" he complained. "That's the yogurt."

Darwin bit his lip. "Just wanted to let you know that we're off...and I wanted to thank you for looking after Rue."

"Of course," Constantine answered. "Despite what you might think, I still consider you family."

"Well, I appreciate that," Darwin answered, uncomfortably. He was still trying to shake the notion he'd had that Constantine was out to get him for all these years. He still wasn't completely convinced.

"Thank you, Mr. Westport," Rue added. "I am very grateful for your protection."

"And that goes on even after you've gotten back to the States," Constantine added. "I've got my connections. You're under the protection of Constantine Westport now."

Rue wasn't entirely sure what to make of that, as the last people who tried to 'protect her' were her cult family. She simply nodded, appreciatively. Wasn't worth causing a fuss that close to their departure.

"Well," Darwin added. "We'll be off then."

Just as they'd reached the door, Constantine stopped him. "Tell my son that I welcome a phone call."

"I will let him know," Darwin answered, simply, before closing the door behind them.

BAXTER BAKER and Moira Dodd were on the next available flight out of Shannon airport. They'd slipped out shortly after their conversation with Ortega. At best, Moira would have been accused of attempted kidnapping. At worst, she could be facing murder or attempted murder charges.

"I can't believe I ended up doing to Uncle Constantine what Finn did all those years ago," Moira's face contorted, miserably. To add insult to injury, the two had 'borrowed' a service vehicle from Constantine's garage.

"Well, look on the bright side," Baxter explained. "You see how he forgave Darwin, right?"

"Yeah, after Bristol and Finn ran to the states over a decade ago!" Moira whined.

"Yeah, but this time no one he cared about got killed...I'm still here."

"I guess," Moira shrugged, sinking into her airplane seat. "Not sure how much Uncle Constantine cares about you, though...if I'm being honest. And I'm sure he's not thrilled about being tied to a triple homicide."

"Well, no matter...at least, I forgive you," Baxter added with a hint of a whine. "You did try to kidnap me for ransom and almost got me killed."

"Trust me, Sweet Face," Moira smirked, "given your gunshot wound, I'd say there are lots of people who've got it in for ya."

"Hey now," Baxter's whine increased in volume. "You know as well as I do that that bullet wasn't meant for me."

"Hmm, all I know is you must have a guardian angel to have escaped death twice now."

Baxter took her hand in his and kissed it. "Angel is right."

"Oh, cut that out," Moira blushed. "Your charms don't work on me."

"And yet, here we are on a lovely adventure together."

"Yeah, if you had your way, we would have taken a flight out of Dublin to Manhattan and been picked up as soon as we landed," Moira mocked. "Guardian Angel is right. Just leave the planning to me."

"Alright, my dear," Baxter leaned back in his chair and let out a happy sigh. While he had some money in reserve, he didn't have a lot of it. So, things might be tight for a bit. For the first time, he didn't care. He felt this odd sense of relief sitting next to his green-eyed beauty. It was as if he was home for the first time in his life. "I'll leave it to you." Moments later, he added, "Although, I hear Cambodia is rather nice this time of year."

CHAPTER 28
Penelope's Revelation

~

Ortega returned to the flat just in time to see Shep wheeling a piece of luggage into their small living room, the same one he'd had at the start of their trip. He was dressed in black traveling slacks and a sweater with a wool coat draped over his arm, looking enormous next to his tiny bag.

Penelope stood beside him, tiredly, wearing a bulky bathrobe, her hair wet, and no makeup.

Ortega was enamored, but tried not to show it. *She looks even more beautiful without makeup, having her hair done or wearing fancy clothes,* he thought. *How is that possible? In fact, how is it possible that she becomes even more beautiful every time I see her?*

"What's going on?" Ortega finally asked, bringing himself back to the situation at hand. "Is everything okay?"

"Yeah," Shep nodded. "For the most part. My wife called at the tail-end of our investigation today. Just found out my littlest has to have his tonsils out. I need to be there to support the missus...four kids is a lot for one woman to handle on a good day, let alone when one has to go in for surgery."

"Married?" Ortega echoed. "Four kids?"

"You're looking at me with as much shock as she did," Shep motioned toward Penelope. "Why is it so hard to believe that someone chose to marry and procreate with me?" Shep seemed almost hurt. Though, he could have been joking. With Shep, it was difficult to tell.

"Not hard to believe at all," Ortega tugged at his shirt collar, awkwardly. "It's just that you never mentioned them, is all."

"For security reasons," Shep explained. "Given my line of work, I think it's best that people don't know everything about me."

Ortega nodded, trying to understand. After all, up until their recent case, the one they'd dragged him into, he wasn't certain that Shep's work was all that dangerous. But, what did he know? Maybe he was wrong.

"Do you need a lift to the airport?" Ortega offered. In truth, he was dead on his feet, and he wanted nothing more than to take a hot shower and climb into bed, preferably with Penelope...in both places, the shower and the bed.

A car horn could be heard honking outside.

"Nah," Shep answered. "That's my taxi. Thanks, though. Oh, Dr. Washburn can fill you in," he motioned to Penelope. "But while I was stuck in the hospital, they kept replaying this broadcast about Bernie Forger and his new plans for the church, before he was found dead—"

"Bernie's dead?" Ortega was surprised. This was news to him.

The car horn honked again.

Penelope touched Ortega's arm while saying to Shep, "You get home safe. I'll fill the good detective in."

Shep nodded, eyeing the two of them quizzically—as if he'd only now just figured something out—and made his way to the cab outside.

After Shep's cab had driven away, Ortega closed the door and eyed Penelope. "It's very hard to concentrate with you in that robe," he commented, flatly.

"Would you rather I took it off?" Penelope grinned, seductively.

"You know I would, but—"

"But you wanna know about Bernie's broadcast?" Penelope pinched her lips together, fighting back a smile.

"Curiosity has gotten the better of me," Ortega admitted.

"First things first," Penelope answered. "Rue is—"

"Rue's fine. So is Darwin."

"He's here too?" Penelope remembered the sounds she heard on her last call with Darwin, ones that sounded suspiciously like an airport.

"Not for long," Ortega answered. "I sent them packing on the first plane out this coming morning."

"About Mr. Fennec—" Penelope began, biting her lip, awkwardly.

"I know about the phone call," he finished for her.

"You did? But how?" Penelope had been riddled with guilt since answering Ortega's phone just a few nights ago without him realizing. Only, apparently, he *had* realized.

"It registered in my cell phone call log," Ortega said. "Unless you specifically delete it, I can see that a call came in, and was answered, and lasted about a minute and a half."

"I'm sorry," Penelope sulked. "But it was killing me to see Mr. Fennec suffering like that!"

Ortega took her shoulders and gave her a kiss on the forehead. "You're a compassionate soul. I would have expected nothing less from you. I understand."

Penelope was surprised. *No criticism? No, 'Well, you should have...'* She was growing fond of this new and improved, and emotionally intelligent Ortega. She just wished they'd both gotten to this point a hell of a lot sooner.

"So, what's this about Bernie Forger?"

"While we were focused on Baxter Baker and Jax Liebling, Bernie was busy announcing a new direction for the church, one that includes a new training academy and publishing house near Belfast."

"They don't waste any time, do they?" Ortega grumbled, angry that he hadn't caught on to this sooner.

"It was all hush-hush until that broadcast," Penelope explained. "But now, Bernie's dead, and they haven't ruled out homicide yet."

"I'm starting to think we should bow out of this whole mess while we still can. Rue and Darwin are safe. Baxter is safe—"

"What happened to Baxter?" Penelope asked.

"Let's just say, he's created his own witness protection program with Moira."

"I see." Penelope wiggled her eyebrows and rolled a shoulder, suggestively.

"The point is," Ortega finished. "Why not let the Garda do their job and we go back to minding our own business, like we should have done from the beginning?"

"That doesn't sound like you," Penelope pointed out.

"Well, maybe I've had a change of heart," Ortega answered, unconvincingly.

Penelope was quiet as if wrestling with some bit of news that she dreaded sharing.

"I know that look," Ortega accused.

"What look?" Penelope asked, innocently.

"That look that suggests you're afraid to tell me something...either because you think it will make me angry or you think it will send me like a rabid dog after the next big lead."

Penelope bit her lip. "Probably the latter."

"Penelope," Ortega took her shoulders and peered into her eyes. "If you don't tell me, you'll be riddled with guilt and regret it. Transparency is always the best policy...learned that the hard way with Nancy and her affair."

Penelope sighed, "It seems that a press release went out announcing Edwina Vandenberg as the new head of the Church of Infinite Love," Penelope relented.

"I assumed it would have been Jax Liebling." Ortega was shocked, releasing her shoulders. He began making small circles around the room as he thought.

"I'm pretty sure he did too," Penelope sighed. "Nothing but a bunch of terrible people doing terrible things to one another in the name of religion."

Ortega slumped his shoulders. "Not everyone," he answered.

"What do you mean?" Penelope asked, quizzically.

"I seem to remember Elsbeth Ions being innocent in all of this. I mean, she pretended to have a developmental disorder to protect herself from getting involved with the family, but I look at that as self-preservation," Ortega reasoned.

"And, Emma Post seemed quite fond of the girl, taking her under her wing and all."

"I tell you what," Ortega decided. "What if I pay a visit to Elsbeth at her Uncle Edgar's estate, just to fill her in and make sure she's okay. Maybe ask a few questions about her mother, Edwina, and pass on whatever we discover to my buddy Inspector Clover. Then, we can leave with a clear conscience."

"What makes you think she'll talk to us?" Penelope asked.

"Hmm," Ortega thought a moment. "I'll contact Ms. Post in the morning. See if she can't put a call in to Elsbeth and see if she'd be willing to chat with us."

"Good thinking, Jose." Penelope touched the side of his face, lovingly. "But for now, we should get some rest."

Ortega yawned, nodding in agreement. He knew he should be phoning Doherty to let him in on Rue's re-appearance, but there was a part of him that needed to know she was safely back in the States first. Though, in the back of his mind, he knew he was lying to himself. *Let sleeping dogs lie,* he thought. *Why not let the trail end and give Darwin and Rue the chance to go back to their lives as usual, without having to answer uncomfortable questions from the Irish police?*

"Jose?" Penelope brought him out of his thoughts. "You're drifting again. Come back to me." She took his hand and led him into the bedroom.

CHAPTER 29
Elsbeth

~

Elsbeth's Uncle Edgar, Edwina Vandenberg's brother, greeted Ortega and Penelope at the door of his estate.

Not having met him before, Ortega assumed he must be one of the servants. "We're here to see Edgar Vandenberg," Ortega announced. "Jose Ortega and Dr. Penelope Washburn. He's expecting us."

Edgar paused for a moment before letting out a chuckle. "I dare say he is. Please come in." Ortega and Penelope entered the main hall and couldn't help but admire the high ceilings and grandeur of Edgar's home.

Edgar closed the door behind them. "May I take your coats?" he asked, eyeing Ortega's windbreaker and Penelope's light rain jacket.

"That won't be necessary," Ortega answered. "We won't be staying long."

"Tea, perhaps? Biscuits?" Edgar offered.

"Er, no, if you could just tell—"

"Uncle Edgar, you're not funny," Elsbeth appeared suddenly at the bottom of a grand staircase. She was so swift and silent that no one heard her enter the room.

Edgar stuck his tongue out at Elsbeth, like a small child. She did the same, in return, before the two started laughing at their inside joke.

"I beg your pardon," Edgar explained. "My companion, Isaac, is running errands today for Elsbeth's last supper before returning home... my, that sounded ominous as soon as I said it, didn't it?" He eyed Elsbeth, amused.

"So, you're Edgar Vandenberg?" Ortega confirmed.

"You're a quick study," Elsbeth retorted.

Ortega eyed her, questioningly. According to Emma's description, Elsbeth was a timid girl who stumbled over her words and kept to the shadows. While this young woman, on the other hand, was—in Ortega's mind—mouthy.

"Now, Elsbeth," Edgar chastised, "don't be cheeky." To Ortega, he said, "I apologize for my little ruse there. There's so little fun to be had for this old man, that I like to have my little gaffs now and again. I'm Edgar, nice to meet you." He offered a hand to Ortega. Ortega shook it, somewhat puzzled. After all, while Edgar gave the appearance of being much older than he was, Ortega was fairly convinced that they were both about the same age.

"Nice to meet you," Ortega offered.

"And you, my dear," Edgar cupped Penelope's hand with both of his own. "Aren't you lovely? I'm allowed to say that, aren't I?" Edgar asked. "I mean, at my age."

"Uncle Edgar, don't be gross," Elsbeth wrinkled her nose. "Besides, she's not much younger than you, anyhow."

Penelope stiffened, the smile on her face dropping momentarily before she recovered. Elsbeth caught that micro expression across Dr. Washburn's face, and smiled to herself.

"Cheeky is right," Penelope whispered to Ortega.

Edgar released Penelope's hand. "I don't suppose either of you would care to see my collection, would you?" Edgar offered.

"I think they're here to see me, Uncle," Elsbeth answered, somewhat impatiently. Edgar caught Elsbeth's eye for a moment, before she turned her gaze to the floor. It was the briefest of exchanges, where, for the first time, Edgar saw something in Elsbeth's manner that he didn't like...

Edwina. Elsbeth shuddered, as if she could read his mind. "But we could talk *and* see your collection at the same time?" she suggested, brightly.

"Collection?" Ortega asked.

"Yes," Edgar explained. "An eccentric habit, I'll admit. But I have one collection of rare reptiles, amphibians and insects, all dead now and well-preserved under glass, but all *deadly* when they were alive."

"I don't think—" Ortega began.

"I would love to see it," Penelope gushed. Ortega was surprised. "What? I'm a forensic scientist. What's not to love about a deadly collection?"

Ortega furrowed his brows at her, confused.

"I also have an ancient bodies collection too." Edgar winked. "Isn't *that* exciting? I've even got a few shrunken heads."

"Well, now you're just sweet talkin' me," Penelope said, accenting her Southern drawl.

What is she doing? Ortega wondered.

Edgar took Penelope's arm. "Allow me," he said as he escorted her to his lab with Elsbeth and Ortega following awkwardly behind.

"Emma said you wanted to talk to me," Elsbeth said to Ortega, quietly.

"Yes," Ortega answered. "She's worried about you...so are we."

"Why?" Elsbeth asked.

"Because we got wind of Bernie Forger's death. Do you know who he is?"

"No, should I?" Elsbeth's eye twitched, just a little. Ortega had spent far too long on the force to not know what that twitch meant...Elsbeth was lying.

"Not necessarily," he played along. "He took over when your grandfather...er...passed."

"You can say 'died,'" Elsbeth retorted. "Saying 'passed' doesn't really make it any gentler now, does it?"

"No," Ortega shook his head. "I suppose it doesn't."

By now, they had reached the lab. Edgar had cleared out a small corner that once housed a plethora of insects, redistributing them under a glass counter by adding a few more shelves to accommodate them. Now, the exhibit featured a decayed body with strands of long hair behind a glass case. Adjacent to the body, were, as promised, what looked like a few shrunken heads, an assortment of teeth, some miscellaneous bones and hair samples, and even a few cloth remnants of ancient clothing and some pottery.

"I've got two more bodies that I haven't figured out how to display yet." Edgar's eyes gleamed. "Would you like to see one of them?" he asked Penelope.

"What do you think?" She grinned.

Ortega just shook his head.

"Excuse me," Edgar reached past Ortega, unlocked a long drawer and slid it out from under the exhibit. On it lay a body, probably belonging to a man, rather small-boned and frail.

Penelope squealed with delight. "How did you procure such a find?" she gushed.

"Last visit to Ecuador," Edgar explained. "If you have the financial resources for such a purchase, people rarely ask questions."

"You devil," Penelope teased.

"For you, I could be," Edgar flirted.

This was a side of Penelope that Ortega had never seen, and he wasn't quite sure what to make of it.

"Could I take a picture?" Penelope asked. "With my cell phone, I mean."

"Phones can take pictures now?" Edgar was surprised. "When did this happen?" Edgar asked.

"While you were hanging out with dead bodies," Elsbeth retorted.

To Penelope, Edgar said, "By all means...but," he added, "this is just for your personal use, yes? No publicizing this, okay?"

"I wouldn't dream of it," Penelope answered, while snapping some of the body along with the other body and items on display. "I just find all of this completely fascinating."

"Well, you must return more often," Edgar grinned, putting an arm around her waist.

"Isaac will be home soon," Elsbeth reminded him.

"What does Isaac have to—" He caught Elsbeth's expression. "Oh, right—"

Ortega wasn't clear on Edgar's relationships with Isaac, his companion, but apparently it didn't include Penelope in the mix.

"Wanna see the other one?" Edgar reached for the next drawer over, and fumbled with the lock as he tugged at the drawer's handle. "Must be stuck," he frowned as he fought with it.

"Listen," Ortega said to Elsbeth. "Before I head back to the States, I made a promise to Emma that I'd keep you safe." This time, Ortega's eyes twitched a little, but Elsbeth didn't catch it. While he did speak with Emma the night before, he had made no such promise. "We learned that your mother is about to take Bernie's place, just as he had taken your grandfather's place."

"What does any of this have to do with me?" Elsbeth asked. "I came here to get away from all that," she explained.

"Well, if Edwina...sorry, your mother...accepts the position, then she will likely also move to Ireland and assume the role of headmaster of the church's new school."

"New school?" Elsbeth feigned surprised. *There was that twitch again.*

"So, you didn't know anything about it?" Ortega pressed her.

"Of course not. My mother doesn't share anything with me. Not even the fact that she's been boinking her lawyer, Lundy, for years now without anybody knowing. Anytime he was over at the house, Mother kept referring to him as 'Uncle Lundy.' What a joke."

Ortega's eyes widened. Elsbeth realized she had inadvertently given the detective information that he didn't already have.

"May I ask you one more question, Elsbeth?"

"I guess," she answered, reluctantly.

"In your heart of hearts, do you think your mother, Edwina, is capable of murder?"

Elsbeth gave this a moment's thought before answering, "I believe my m-m-mother is capable of anything." Elsbeth was frustrated, and Ortega knew it...the stutter was real.

"Are you going to be okay?" Ortega asked Elsbeth, as they turned their attention back to Edgar, Penelope and his odd collection. Edgar was making apologies about being unable to show her the other body. She reassured him that it was fine. She had seen more than enough, anyway. He insisted they move on to his snake collection.

"Of course," Elsbeth answered. "I'm leaving here tomorrow. With any luck, the New York estate will soon be turned over to me, and my mother can do whatever she likes."

"Won't the family bother you or try to recruit you into the church?"

"I'm an embarrassment to my family," Elsbeth answered. "They would just as soon forget me as I them."

With that, Edgar looked up from a viper he was showing Penelope. In his eyes, he appeared hurt.

"Present company excluded," Elsbeth reassured him. To Ortega, she said, "Aside from Uncle Edgar and Cousin Baxter, the lot of them can go to hell."

"Excuse me, sir," Isaac appeared in the doorway. Edgar jumped, stepping a few inches away from Penelope, as if he had been doing something untoward.

"Yes, Isaac," Edgar answered, "what is it?"

"Would you like me to clear the field for clay shooting this afternoon?"

Edgar eyed Elsbeth who merely shook her head. "No, thank you, Isaac," he answered. Then, turning to Penelope, "Unless you would fancy a shooting lesson?"

"Perhaps some other time," Penelope declined.

"I'm a sporting man," Ortega answered. "Mind showing me the field?"

"Not at all," Edgar answered. "This way."

"SATISFIED?" Penelope asked as she and Ortega returned to their flat.

"Almost," he answered, reaching into his pocket to retrieve the thumb drive Darwin had given him. "You brought your laptop with you, right?"

"Yes," Penelope giggled. "One of us has to be up on the times. Why?" She eyed the small plastic drive Ortega had pinched between his fingers.

"A present from Darwin before he left. Some kind of 'data mining' tool," he explained. "What say we have a look at it?"

Penelope brought out her laptop and opened it on the kitchen table.

After restarting her computer, Ortega intuitively plugged the drive into the side of it.

Nothing happened. Ortega and Penelope gazed at the screen.

"Do we need to tell it to do something?" Penelope suggested.

"Good thinking!" Ortega explained. He sifted through the Rolodex in his mind to something Darwin had shown him a while back and used a Finder to track down the location of the drive's content and open it.

Within moments, the tool was launched, but most of the navigation was foreign to Ortega. "Here," Penelope offered. "Mind if I poke around a bit?"

"Poke away," he agreed.

It took about fifteen minutes of 'What does this button do?' before she figured it out. "Oh, I get it," she explained. "We have to feed it info and tell it to sort it out. Here—" She pulled out her phone. "If I can send my phone images to my computer and upload it here...voila!" The images of Edgar's odd collection popped up on the screen.

"Not sure I follow," Ortega confessed.

"I think you just have to tell it what you know of the case so far, and let it sift through the data and draw its own conclusions."

"Hmmm, worth a try," Ortega conceded. "You may have to help me, though."

Penelope grinned at him. "You know, you're pretty sexy when you're helpless."

"Well, then," Ortega leaned over and planted a kiss on her lips, "you must find me sexy all the time because I am helpless around you."

Penelope paused. "Not as much when you're being corny." Ortega pinched her bottom. "Hey, now!" She jumped.

The two were suddenly distracted by a strange whirring sound. The fan on the computer powered on as if it were working very hard.

"Think it's okay?" Penelope asked.

"Not sure," Ortega confessed. "Why don't we let it sit overnight. Assuming the laptop doesn't blow up, we'll check it again in the morning."

"Sounds like a plan." Penelope wriggled her eyes at him. "I need a shower. Wash my back?"

"Your back, your front...in between," he joked.

"Corny!" she said again.

"You love it," Ortega laughed, following her into the shower.

~

THE NEXT MORNING, Penelope was fixing herself a cup of tea when she saw it.

"Jose!" she called. "I think you better come out here!"

"What is it?" he asked, groggily.

She pointed to the laptop. A collection of images and text flashed across the screen. The program had come to some conclusions.

"Shit! Shit! Shit!" Ortega exclaimed, "How could I have been so blind? I've gotta call Clover."

CHAPTER 30
New Bestie

~

"Want to tell me what's going on here?" Jax eyed Midge lining up her suitcases outside the front door of Jax's apartment, Elsbeth beside her wearing a wool coat, cap and gloves.

"I'm afraid there has been a change of plans," Midge explained.

Jax eyed the two of them, suspiciously. "What are you up to?"

"I'm leaving you, Jax," Midge answered. "For good this time."

"Is that so?" he answered. His voice was calm, but his balled fists suggested he was doing his best to keep his temper under control. "May I ask why, after you and I just married? We were going to rule the new Jax nutraceutical empire together, not to mention my stock in the new Church of Infinite Love college and publishing house. Are you opposed to being rich?"

"No," Midge sighed. "But I am opposed to you."

Jax tilted his head and tucked his chin, uncomfortably. "What changed?" His eyes rose to meet Elsbeth's, who despite her rigid disposition, lowered her eyes, uncomfortably.

"It has nothing to do with her," Midge explained. "And you know, for the briefest of moments, I thought it might work. But—"

"But?" Jax encouraged.

Midge hugged herself and let out a laugh. "For the longest time, I thought you were the smartest of them all, but it turns out that you're not."

"I'm not?" Jax raised an eyebrow.

"No," Midge shook her head. "Granted it took me a while to put all the pieces together before I could start moving them. Would you like a quick summary?"

"Please," Jax answered. "Would you care to come back inside and sit down?"

Just then, a man wearing a wool jacket with the lapel pulled up, hands in pockets, reached the top of the stairwell that was situated down the hall.

"Just for a moment," Midge agreed. "I promise, this won't take long."

To Elsbeth, she asked, "I hate to leave the heavy lifting to you, but could you be a dear and get our driver to load up our bags?" Elsbeth nodded, summoning the large man to assist her.

"Heavy lifting, indeed," Elsbeth grinned as she did little more than point to the bags.

He grabbed them, wordlessly, pausing to give a sideways glance at Jax, who merely glared back at him.

"Shall we?" Midge pointed to the door. Jax obliged, pushing it open and following behind her inside. She shuddered a moment as he closed the door behind them.

"How can you leave, when I can still give you the chills, even after all this time?" he grinned, hopefully.

"That's fear, Jax," Midge answered honestly. "And I'm tired of being afraid. Please open the door."

"But you're the only person I've ever loved," Jax protested. "You have nothing to fear from me."

Midge eyed the door, and so Jax relented and opened it just wide enough that the outside hallway was visible from where they stood.

"I know you *think* you love me," Midge answered. "But I've come to understand with time and wisdom that what you feel for me is obsession.

And the day you stop being obsessed with me, is the day it's all over for me."

Jax paused to frame his words carefully. "You were going to tell me what pieces you have put together?" he reminded her.

"Oh, of course," Midge remembered. She swiftly and succinctly explained everything she had discovered, beginning with how Jax planned on taking control of everything, the newly rebranded nutraceutical company (conveniently now in his name), the Church of Infinite Love, and even the soon-to-be established church academy and publishing house. He was even presumptuous enough to think he could oust the Westport grift family from Dublin and assume the territory, establishing a new order with his own people in place.

It was Jax who convinced Bernie to rile up several of his followers to kidnap Baxter, with no intention of letting Baxter live. It would be far easier to make Baxter a scapegoat for the church's and Vandenberg Nutraceutical's past wrong doings if he wasn't around to explain himself in the long-term.

Jax wanted Moira Dodd involved so that he could point to the Westports as the ones to blame for Baxter's death, only his plans went awry when he arrived at the scene and discovered that the three kidnappers had been murdered. He quickly left the broach and other evidence intended to frame the Westports and vanished, later pretending he knew nothing about it.

Meanwhile, Bernie wanted to cut all ties from Jax's nutraceutical company, believing that the new college and published works would bring in money more quickly. He wanted to re-establish the old ways, and if there was to be a new faith-healing practice, it would be in Belfast, not Dublin, and out from under the Westports's watchful eyes and 'insurance policies.'

Once Lundy let Jax in on Bernie's plans for the school, suggesting that Jax would be a better fit at running it and convincing Jax to make a sizable investment to secure his place with the budding nonprofit, it was Lundy who put the idea in Jax's head that Bernie was too much of a hothead to properly run the church and the school. This was reinforced by the discovery of the three dead men, who Lundy likely blamed on Bernie (even though he didn't entirely believe he was responsible). Jax took it upon himself to stage Bernie's unfortunate accident, though Lundy might have inadvertently put the suggestion in his head...or at the very least, incited violence. Once again, Jax took the opportunity to try to pin it on Constantine Westport, and his not receiving a tithe for Bernie's practices on his turf. Despite the fact that the school was setting up shop in Belfast, Bernie was still broadcasting to his members all over Ireland, including the Westport turf. And Constantine Westport had no way of knowing that Bernie was beginning to sever ties from Vandenberg Nutraceuticals.

"What you didn't realize, my sweet," Midge finished, "was that Lundy had no intention of putting you in charge of everything. It was just your ego getting in the way, once again."

Jax stood upright, lifting his chin, defiantly. "What are you talking about? What do you know?" he demanded.

"He wanted your money, that was all," Midge confided. "Once you purchased the remaining shares of the former Vandenberg Nutraceutical company and helped fund the school, he was done with you. Lundy only needed your backing to cover the trail of old crimes in the States and put a new head in place of the rebranded Church of Infinite Love, or COIL, as they like to call it now."

"A new leader? What are you talking about?" Jax's face began twitching, agitatedly. "You don't mean...you?!"

Midge snorted. "No, dummy. Not me! Though, they could do worse. I'm talking about Edwina Vandenberg."

"Edwina? What does she have to do with anything?" Jax was incredulous.

"Lundy and Edwina have been playing bouncy-bouncy for quite some time now. Edwina was denied the right to take her father's place at the helm because she was a woman, but under the new code, one that she and Lundy were busy cooking up, there would be no such rule in place."

"Then how did they plan on getting rid of me?" Jax's brow broke out in a sweat. "Were they going to murder me like they did the men who kidnapped Baxter?"

"Oh, Jax. My poor, stupid husband." Midge shook her head. Jax lunged at Midge who revealed her trusty .32 Beretta and he jumped back. She pointed it at his chest. "Don't make me shoot you. It's bad enough you convinced me to murder all those girls back in New York." Jax backed away and Midge lowered her gun. "But that's your MO, isn't it? Getting other people to do your dirty work? They, nor a member of the church, weren't the ones who shot those men."

"Then who?" Jax asked.

"Me," Elsbeth answered timidly from the doorway. Jax's energy unnerved her.

"You?" Jax was astounded.

"They were going to kill Cousin Baxter. Aside from Uncle Edgar, he's the only family member I actually give a rat's ass about," Elsbeth explained.

"Final question," Jax asked Midge. "Why did you marry me if you had no intention of staying?" If Midge didn't know any better, she'd say that Jax's voice cracked, just a little, in sorrow.

"Because I wanted my name tied to your bank account should anything happen to you. But more importantly, I wanted you to know that you can't control me anymore."

A lightbulb went off in Jax's head. "You little minx," he smiled. "That's not it at all." He pointed a finger at her. "You just wanted to prove you were smarter than me."

"It wasn't hard," Midge grinned.

"Are you the one planning to kill me so Lundy and Edwina can have me out of the way?" Jax asked. "Did you have some arrangement with them?"

"Are you kidding me?" Midge squinted at him, annoyed. "To this day, they don't know anything about me."

"Then exactly how do you plan to get rid of me and take my money?" Jax asked. "And might I remind you, you're a fugitive. How do you plan to cash in?"

"I'm going to give you an out clause, Jax," Midge offered. "This is your one chance to keep your cash, and your head, before Elsbeth and I head to the Netherlands. Not sure you're aware of this, but they are the first country expected to approve same-sex marriage...very progressive, don't you think?"

Jax looked back and forth between Midge and Elsbeth. "You mean?" He connected the dots in his head.

"Between her inheritance and mine, we stand to have quite a little nest egg. But again, it doesn't have to be like that. I don't want to take your money. You can pull up shocks and disappear, and we never have to see one another again."

Jax took a step toward her. "Is that what you really want?"

"Yes, Jax," Midge answered. "It's what I really want. I told you; I'm leaving you, forever."

She and Elsbeth turned to leave, hand in hand.

"I'll come after you," Jax promised. "I'll never let you go."

Midge sighed. "I was afraid you'd say that...goodbye, Jax."

As Midge walked out of Jax's life for the last time with Elsbeth at her heels, the man who was presumably their driver walked in. The two women quickly found their vehicle waiting for them outside. Midge slid behind the wheel and started the engine. "Unless you prefer to drive?" she asked Elsbeth.

"Who are you kidding?" Elsbeth teased. "I've never driven a car in my life."

"Spoiled brat," Midge joked.

Elsbeth merely laughed, sinking back into her seat, feeling a sense of relief for the first time in her life, soon to be rid of her family for good. She was sad that she'd likely never see Baxter or Edgar again. That was unfortunate. She rested a hand on Midge's knee. But the tradeoff was worth it, she decided.

Meanwhile, inside Jax's apartment, the man in the wool coat closed the door behind him and stared directly into Jax's deep-set eyes as if studying him.

"Did Lundy send you?" Jax asked. "I know my Midge talks a big game, but she wouldn't have the heart to hurt me. I know she loves me, in her own way."

"Don't know any-ting 'bout what yer woman would or wouldn't do, mate," he answered.

"Whatever Lundy offered you, I can double it," Jax offered.

"Who the feck is Lundy?" The large man eyed Jax, tilting his head like a confused puppy.

"If Mr. Lundy didn't send you to kill me, then who did?" Jax was more confused than scared. He still had unwarranted faith in his powers of persuasion.

"It seems that Constantine Westport is tired of getting blamed for crimes he didn't commit. Thanks to you, the inspector keeps poking his nose around, asking questions about Bernie Forger's death and his three henchman who tried to take out Baxter Baker. To add insult to injury, ya never paid yer tithe, neither."

"So, you've come to collect, have you?" Jax smiled.

"In a manner of speaking," the man retrieved a large wire with leather loops at each end. "He jest feels that if he's gonna git blamed for some-ting, he might as well have it be for some-ting he was actually responsible fahr."

Jax's eyes grew wide as he realized that negotiations were useless. Midge tried to give him one last out, but he didn't take it. And now, it was too late.

In less than a minute, Jax Liebling was dead.

CHAPTER 31
Giant's Causeway

~

Penelope Washburn stood on the basalt rocks overlooking Giant's Causeway, letting out a shiver as the wind picked up. Jose Ortega wrapped his arms around her. She clung to his arms in front of her belly and leaned into his chest. In the past, Ortega would have been a little uncomfortable with the fact that Penelope was a bit taller than he, and that he was caught showing a public display of affection. But these days, none of that seemed very important. What *was* important, was that the two of them were together.

"It's been a pretty wild turn of events, hasn't it?" she sniffed, trying not to let emotions get the better of her.

"I'll say," Ortega agreed, hugging her more tightly.

They watched as the waves crashed against the coastline, blinking occasionally as wind and sea spray stung their faces...they didn't care.

The two thought back to what Darwin's beta program spit out. There, clear as day, was one image of Elsbeth Ions along with all the data points connecting her to the death of the three Americans. It also predicted with 93% certainty that Midge was somehow involved, and that there was reasonable probability that Rue Brennan's kidnapping was a distraction...though, the beta mining tool was better about sorting and predicting data than it was about understanding human thought patterns.

"What will happen to Elsbeth and Midge?" Penelope asked.

"Don't know," Ortega answered. "If I know Clover and this Doherty fellow, I suspect they'll join forces and swarm all roads leading to all airports in the vicinity, large and small."

"Too bad the program didn't predict where they'd go next," Penelope offered. "Any chance they'll hide somewhere in Ireland?"

"Doubtful," Ortega answered. "It's too risky for them, not only because they are both wanted for murder but they racked up quite a few enemies in the short time they were here."

The two began walking the Causeway's paved path, hand in hand, while a crowded tourist bus drove past. A few hikers steamrolled past them, but neither Ortega nor Penelope were in any hurry.

Penelope took a deep breath of fresh air and smiled, blissfully. "Under normal circumstances...paradise."

"Would you live here?" Ortega asked, curiously.

"What? In Ireland?" Penelope asked, thinking a moment. "I suppose I might. Hard to say, I've been a New Yorker for so long. Though, I don't really have a job to go back to now, do I?"

"I'm sorry about that," Ortega grimaced, knowing he was at least partially responsible for her dismissal, given that she'd pulled one too many favors to support Ortega on crimes neither one of them had any business investigating.

"It's alright," she answered. "Probably time for a change, anyway."

"What kind of change did you have in mind?" Ortega asked.

"I don't know," Penelope replied, thoughtfully. "Work that's rewarding but doesn't involve crimes of passion and dead bodies."

Ortega nodded as they rounded the bend. The wind picked up a little while the clouds rolled in, threatening rain.

"What about you?" Penelope asked. "We still don't know who killed Bernie Forger and Jax Liebling. Was it Midge, members of the church, the Vandenbergs, or the Westports? Someone else?"

"You know what, Penelope," he squeezed her hand, "I really don't care."

"You? Not care? How is that possible?" Penelope's mouth dropped.

"I almost lost the woman of my dreams thanks to this damn job. I've risked my life and those I've cared about, and I'm done. Leave it the young Dohertys of the world to pick up where I left off. I'm through sacrificing my life for criminals that keep cropping up and festering like termites and roaches."

"You mean, you're going to stay retired?" Penelope was doubtful.

"No," Ortega confessed. "But maybe something along the lines of what Darwin Fennec does...a little consulting, but nothing involving the Vandenbergs and Westports in a turf war...more like, finding someone's missing cat...or something."

"Not sure there's a career in that," Penelope teased. "But I support whatever you decide." She stopped, turned toward him, and leaned in for a kiss.

Ortega kissed her back, before his mind wandered, blissfully. He stared out over the ocean, lost in thought.

"What is it?" Penelope asked.

"Time for a complete change of scenery. Somewhere where I don't have to get caught up in the day-to-day drama."

"Like where?" Penelope asked.

"I dunno," he answered. "Where would you consider moving to with me? Unless, of course, you're opposed to that idea."

Penelope beamed, looping her arm through his as they stared off into the distance. "You couldn't keep me away if you tried."

"So, where do two reunited lovers go for a fresh start?"

Penelope thought on this. "Portugal," she finally announced.

Ortega was surprised at her definitive answer. "Okay," he agreed, "Portugal it is."

About the Author

Danielle Palli is a multi-genre author, Board Certified Positive Psychology & Mindfulness coach, and a multimedia content creator & book coach. She lives in Florida with her husband and a plethora of pets. She finds joy in nature, travel, music, theater and the arts, and is known for singing and dancing around the living room at any hour of the day or night. As a free-spirited outlier enamored with life, she finds that life is more exciting when you color outside the lines. Learn more: www.DaniellePalli.com.

www.ingramcontent.com/pod-product-compliance
Lightning Source LLC
Chambersburg PA
CBHW060527310726
48982CB00002B/452

* 9 7 8 1 7 3 6 7 9 8 2 7 0 *